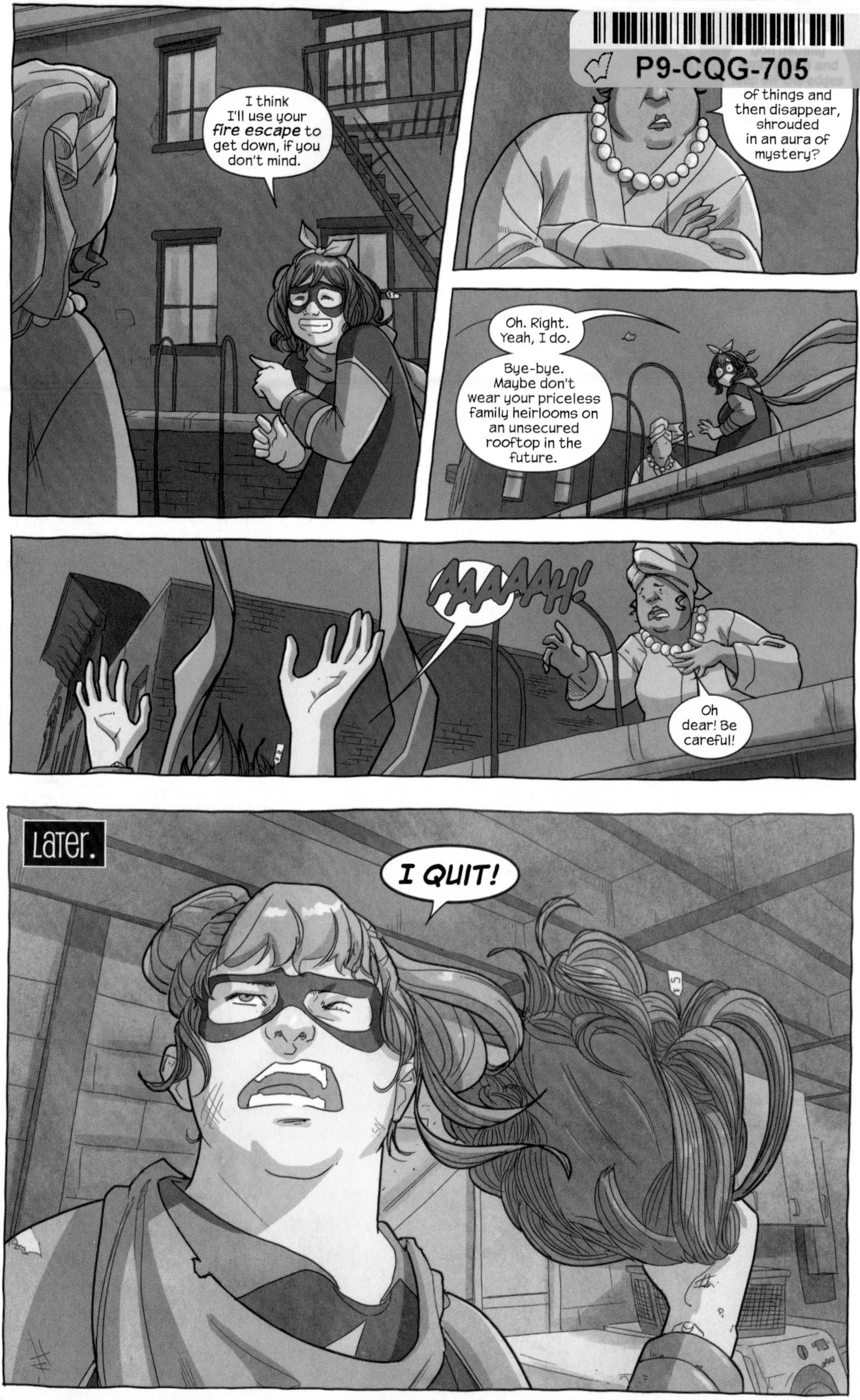

I think I'll use your *fire escape* to get down, if you don't mind.
of things and then disappear, shrouded in an aura of mystery?
Oh. Right. Yeah, I do.
Bye-bye. Maybe don't wear your priceless family heirlooms on an unsecured rooftop in the future.
AAAAAH!
Oh dear! Be careful!
Later.
I QUIT!

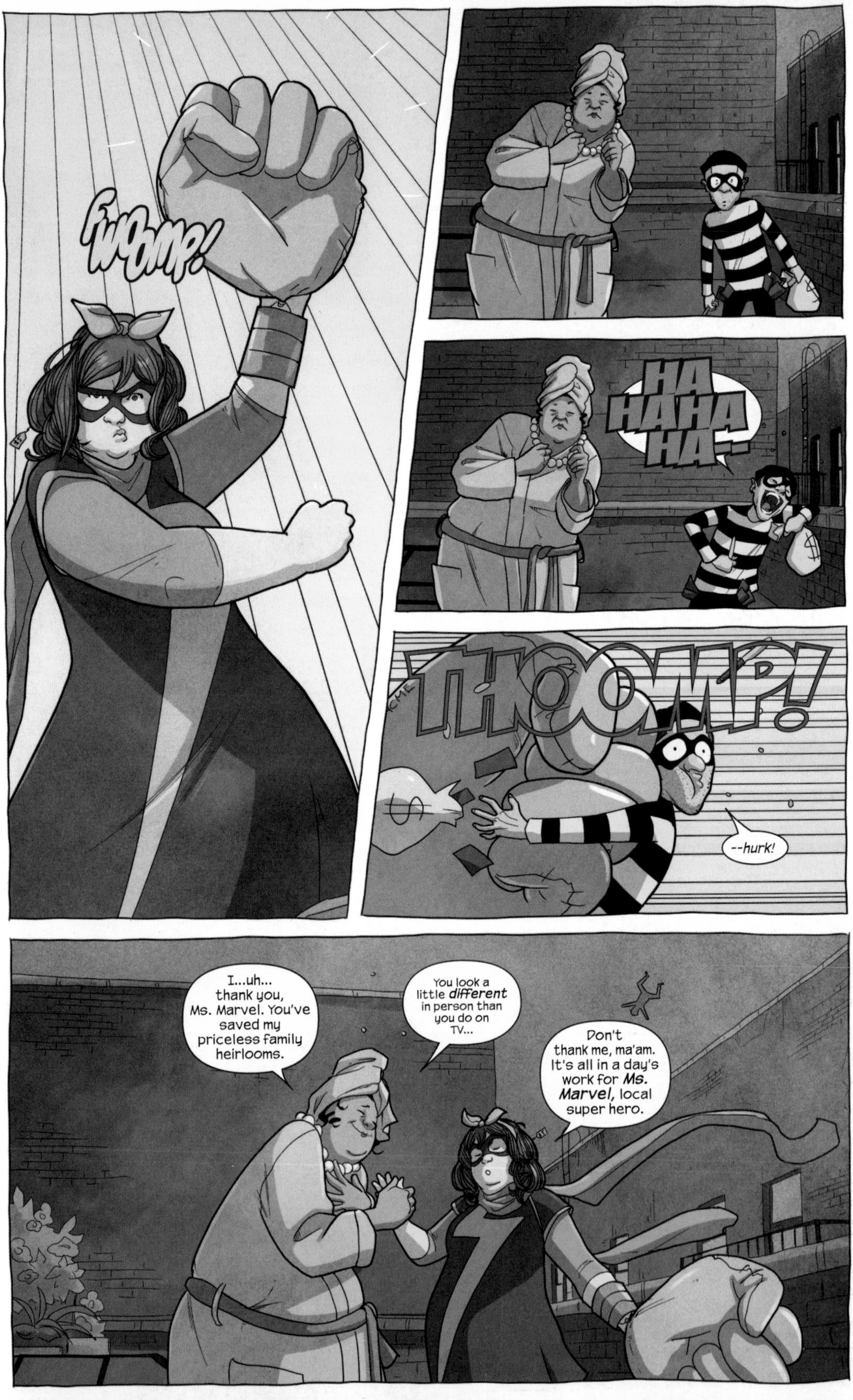

FWOOMP!
HA HA HA HA-
THOOMP!
--hurk!
I...uh... thank you, Ms. Marvel. You've saved my priceless family heirlooms.
You look a little *different* in person than you do on TV...
Don't thank me, ma'am. It's all in a day's work for ***Ms. Marvel,*** local super hero.

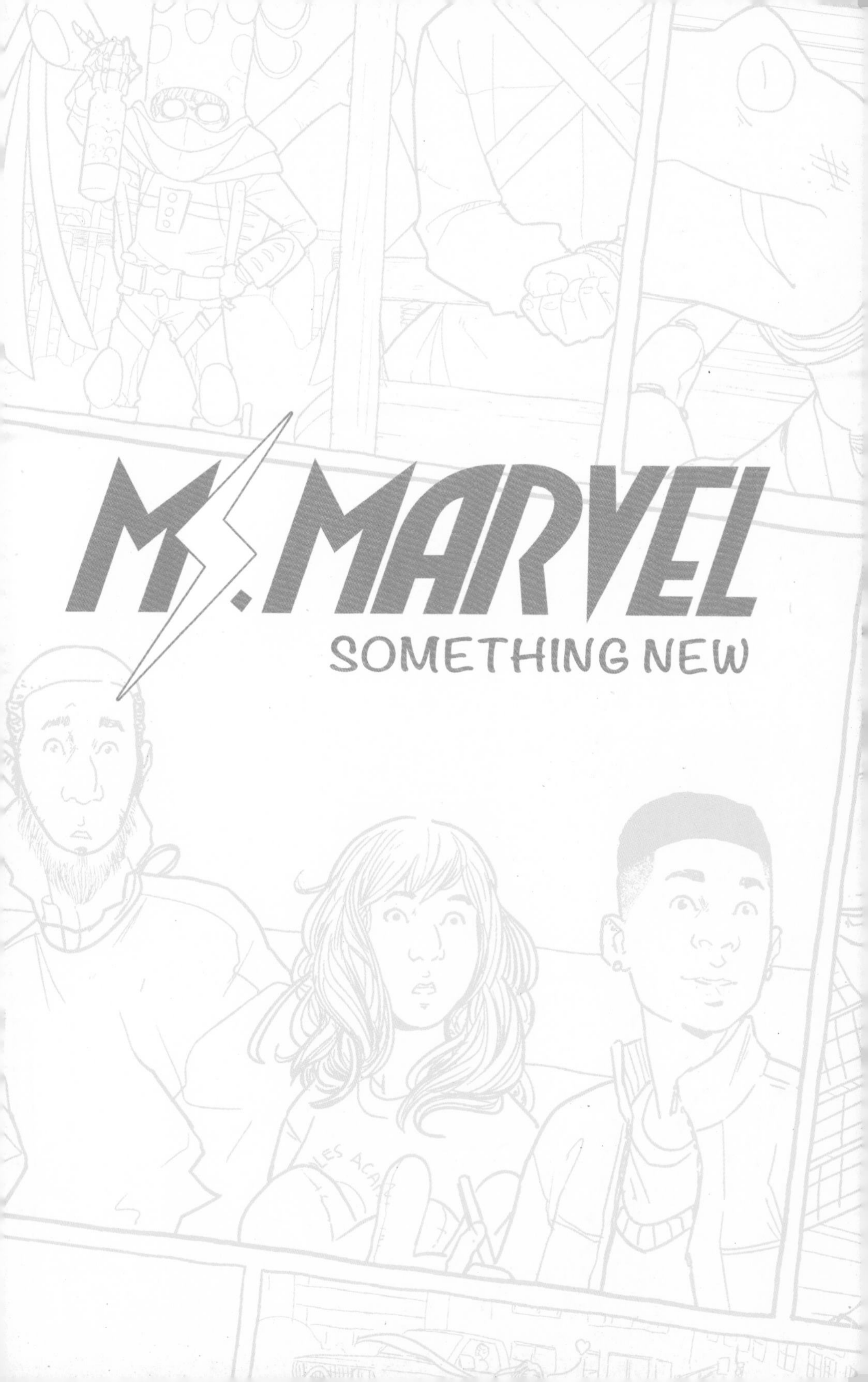

MS. MARVEL

SOMETHING NEW

PREVIOUSLY

Things haven't been going so well for Kamala. Her best friend Bruno moved to Wakanda. She's fallen out with her super hero colleagues and mentors like Carol Danvers and Tony Stark. A new hero from Pakistan, the Red Dagger, has relocated to Jersey City, and after all he's been able to do in the short time he's been there, it's only added to a nagging thought in her mind: Is Ms. Marvel no longer needed?

collection editor JENNIFER GRÜNWALD
assistant editor DANIEL KIRCHHOFFER
assistant managing editor MAIA LOY
assistant managing editor LISA MONTALBANO
vp production & special projects JEFF YOUNGQUIST
svp print, sales & marketing DAVID GABRIEL
vp licensed publishing SVEN LARSEN
editor in chief C.B. CEBULSKI

MS. MARVEL: SOMETHING NEW GN-TPB. Contains material originally published in magazine form as MS. MARVEL (2015) #25-35. First printing 2021. ISBN 978-1-302-93167-4. Published by MARVEL WORLDWIDE, INC., a subsidiary of MARVEL ENTERTAINMENT, LLC. OFFICE OF PUBLICATION: 1290 Avenue of the Americas, New York, NY 10104. © 2021 MARVEL No similarity between any of the names, characters, persons, and/or institutions in this magazine with those of any living or dead person or institution is intended, and any such similarity which may exist is purely coincidental. **Printed in Canada.** KEVIN FEIGE, Chief Creative Officer; DAN BUCKLEY, President, Marvel Entertainment; JOE QUESADA, EVP & Creative Director; DAVID BOGART, Associate Publisher & SVP of Talent Affairs; TOM BREVOORT, VP, Executive Editor; NICK LOWE, Executive Editor, VP of Content, Digital Publishing; DAVID GABRIEL, VP of Print & Digital Publishing; JEFF YOUNGQUIST, VP of Production & Special Projects; ALEX MORALES, Director of Publishing Operations; DAN EDINGTON, Managing Editor; RICKEY PURDIN, Director of Talent Relations; JENNIFER GRÜNWALD, Senior Editor, Special Projects; SUSAN CRESPI, Production Manager; STAN LEE, Chairman Emeritus. For information regarding advertising in Marvel Comics or on Marvel.com, please contact Vit DeBellis, Custom Solutions & Integrated Advertising Manager, at vdebellis@marvel.com. For Marvel subscription inquiries, please call 888-511-5480. **Manufactured between 8/6/2021 and 9/7/2021 by SOLISCO PRINTERS, SCOTT, QC, CANADA.**

10 9 8 7 6 5 4 3 2 1

MS. MARVEL

SOMETHING NEW

Ms. Marvel #25-30, #32-35
writer
G. WILLOW WILSON
artist
NICO LEON
color artist
IAN HERRING

Ms. Marvel #31
writers
G. WILLOW WILSON (pp. 1-5, 11-12, 19-20, 26-30),
SALADIN AHMED (pp. 6-10), **RAINBOW ROWELL** (pp. 13-18)
& HASAN MINHAJ (pp. 21-25)
artists
NICO LEON (pp. 1-5, 11-12, 19-20, 26-30),
GUSTAVO DUARTE (pp. 6-10), **BOB QUINN** (pp. 13-18)
& ELMO BONDOC (pp. 21-25)
color artist
IAN HERRING

letterer
VC's JOE CARAMAGNA
cover art
VALERIO SCHITI & **RACHELLE ROSENBERG**
editors
SANA AMANAT & **MARK BASSO**

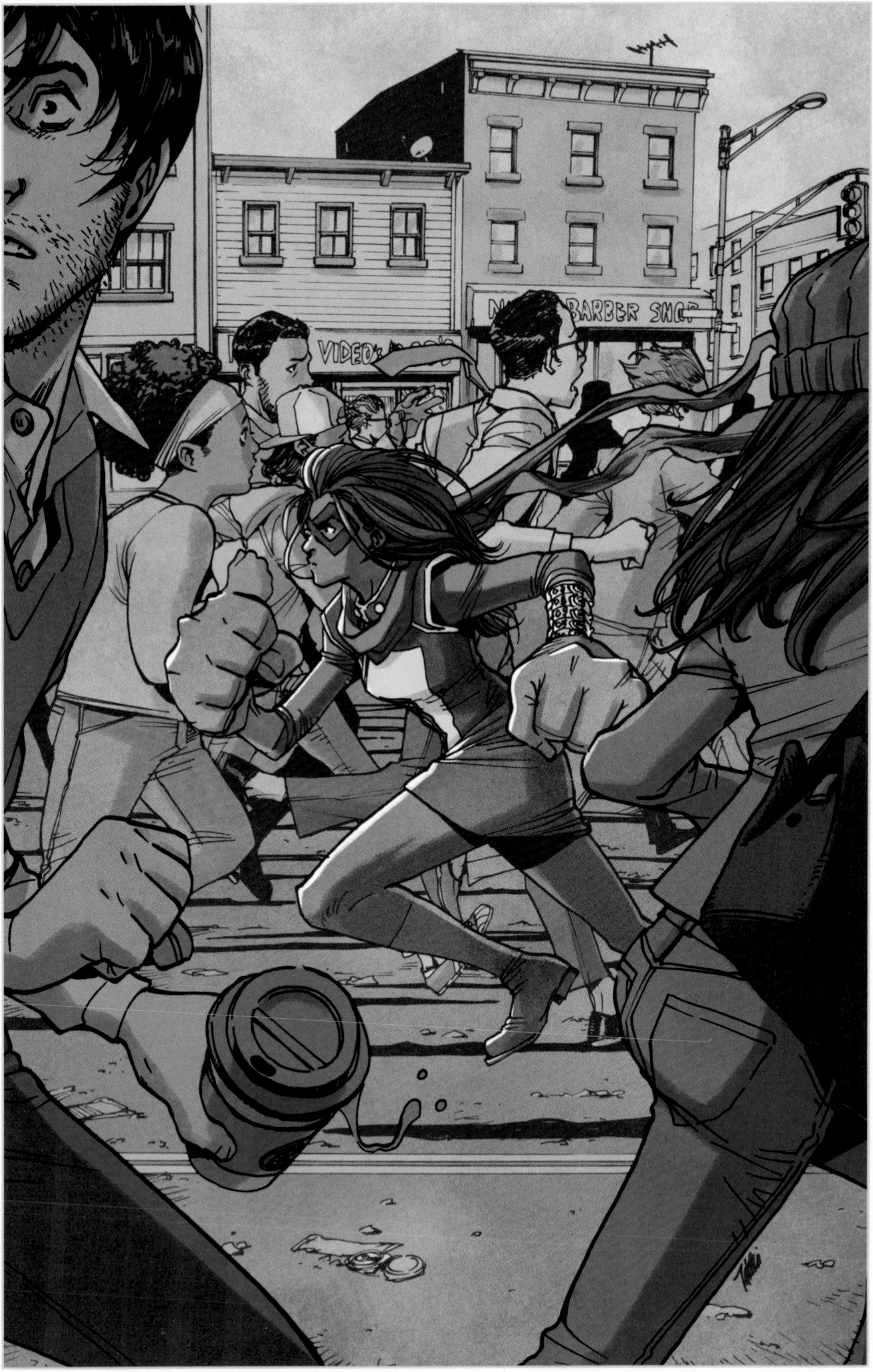
VIDEO's
BARBER

MS. MARVEL #25 VARIANT
BY TAKESHI MIYAZAWA & IAN HERRING

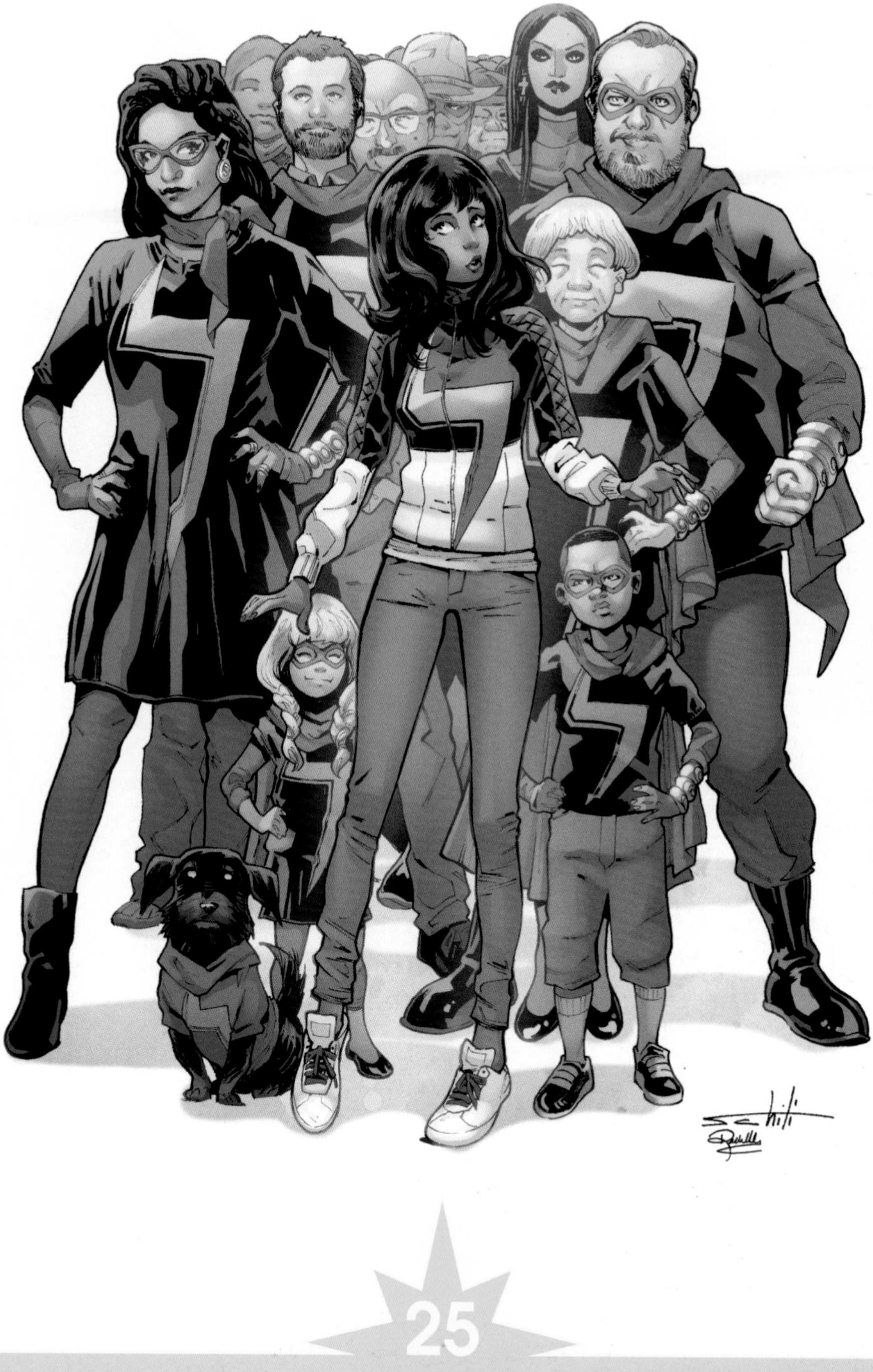
25

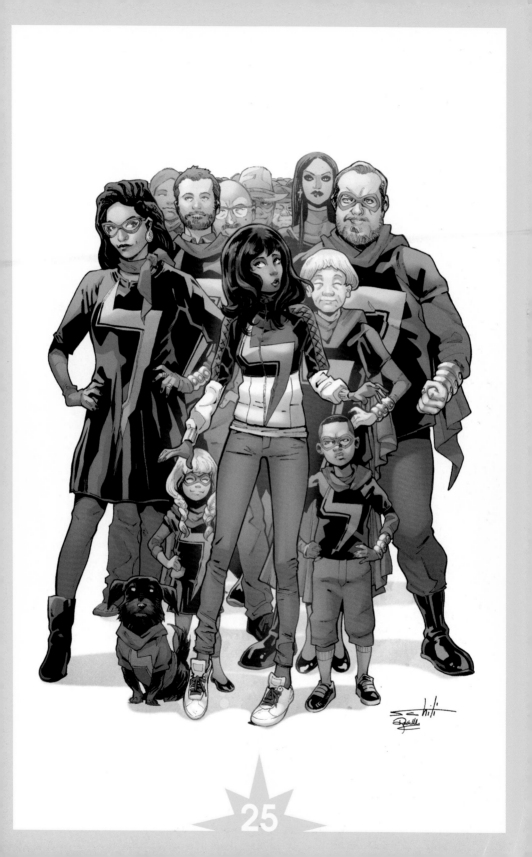

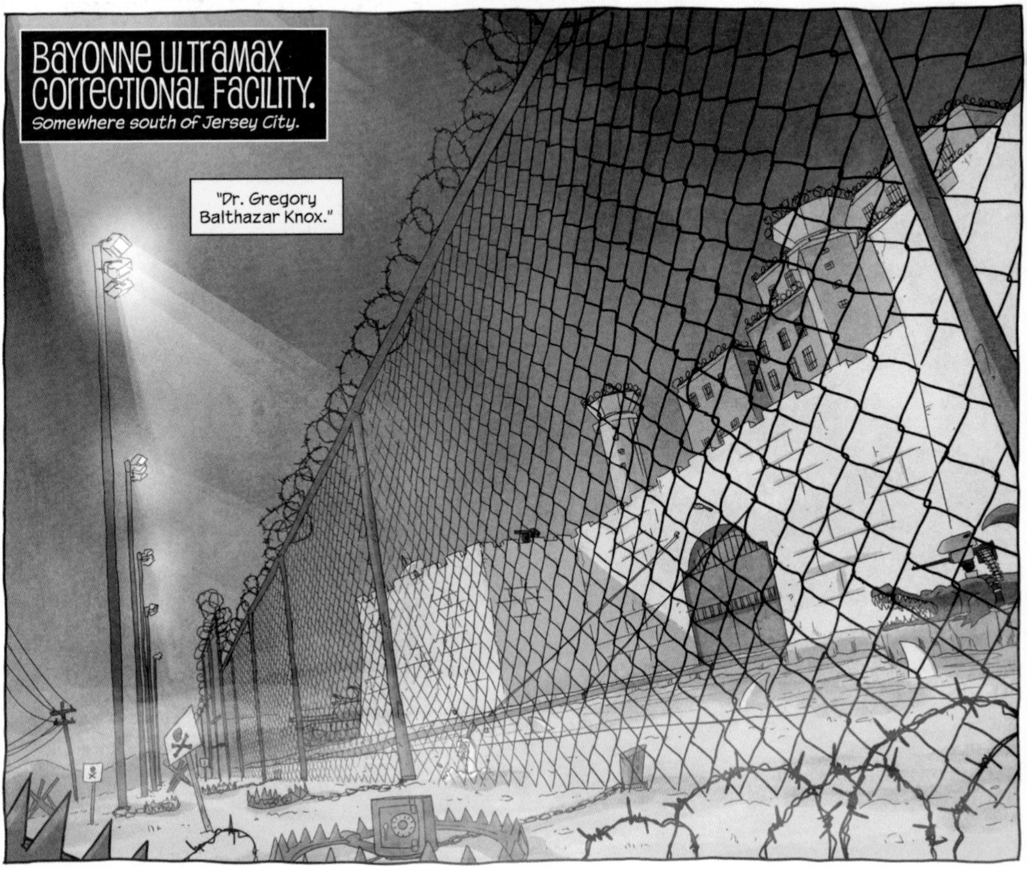
BAYONNE ULTRAMAX CORRECTIONAL FACILITY.
Somewhere south of Jersey City.
"Dr. Gregory Balthazar Knox."

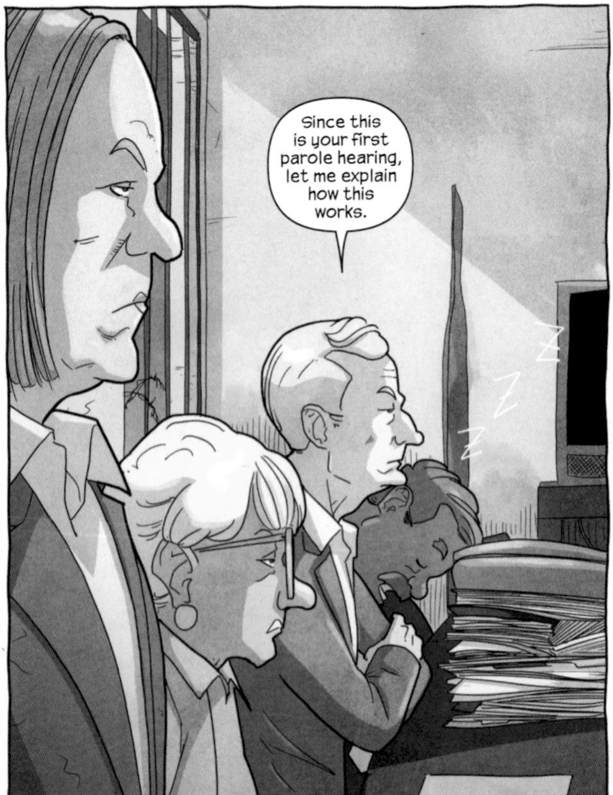
Since this is your first parole hearing, let me explain how this works.
Z Z Z

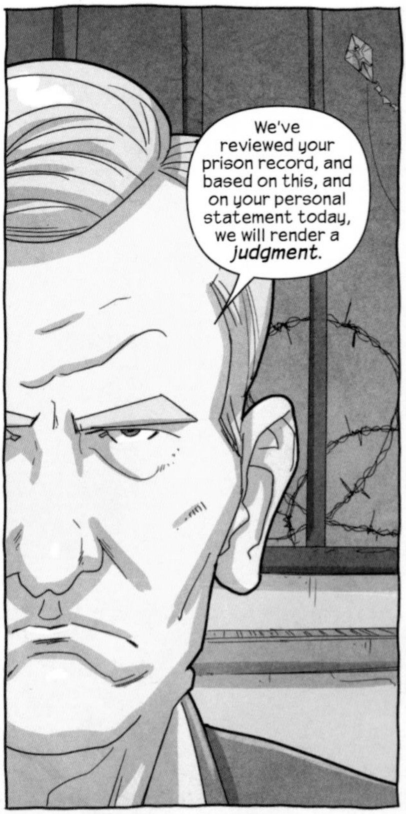
We've reviewed your prison record, and based on this, and on your personal statement today, we will render a *judgment*.

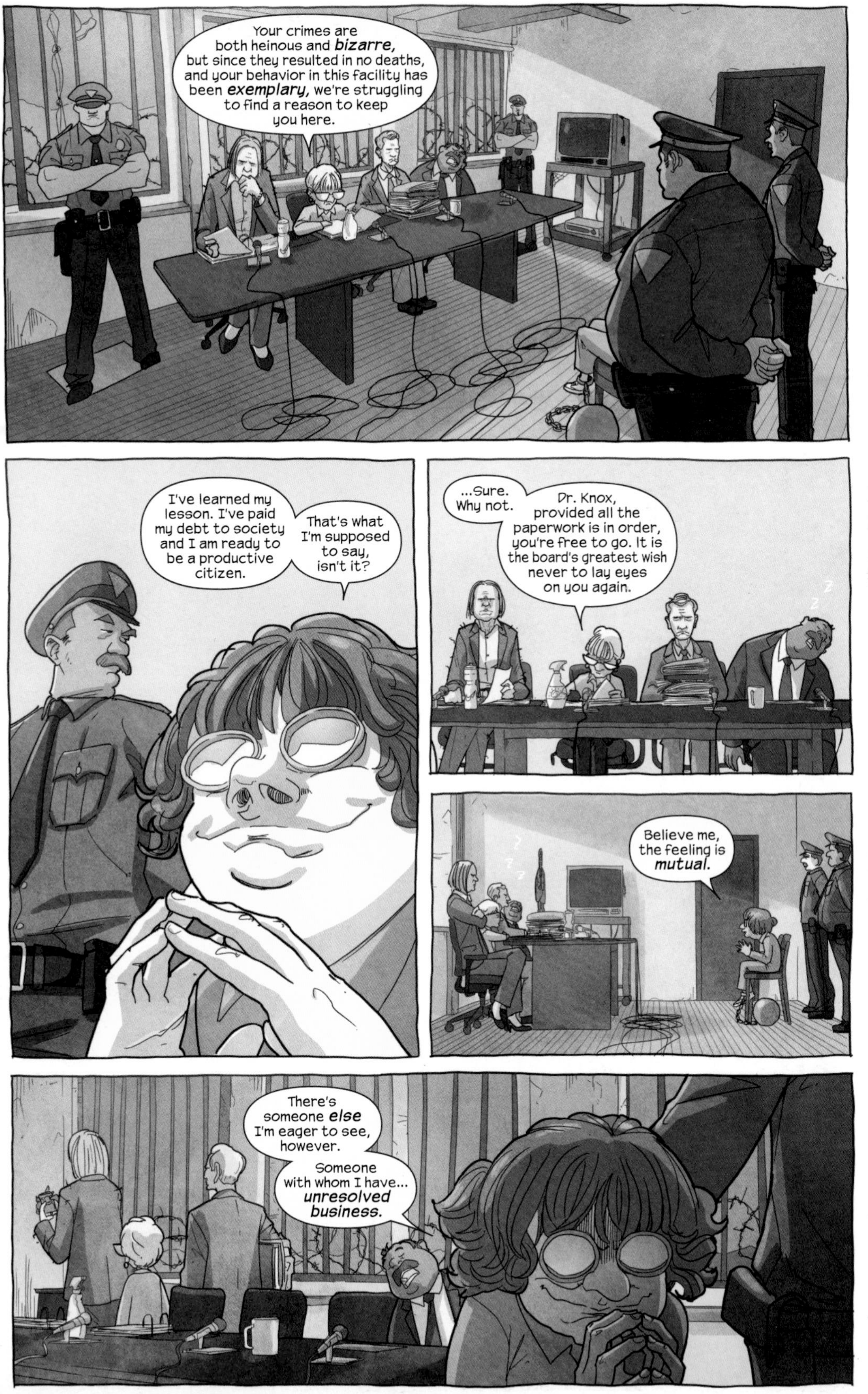
Your crimes are both heinous and bizarre, but since they resulted in no deaths, and your behavior in this facility has been exemplary, we're struggling to find a reason to keep you here.
I've learned my lesson. I've paid my debt to society and I am ready to be a productive citizen.
That's what I'm supposed to say, isn't it?
...Sure. Why not.
Dr. Knox, provided all the paperwork is in order, you're free to go. It is the board's greatest wish never to lay eyes on you again.
Believe me, the feeling is mutual.
There's someone else I'm eager to see, however.
Someone with whom I have... unresolved business.

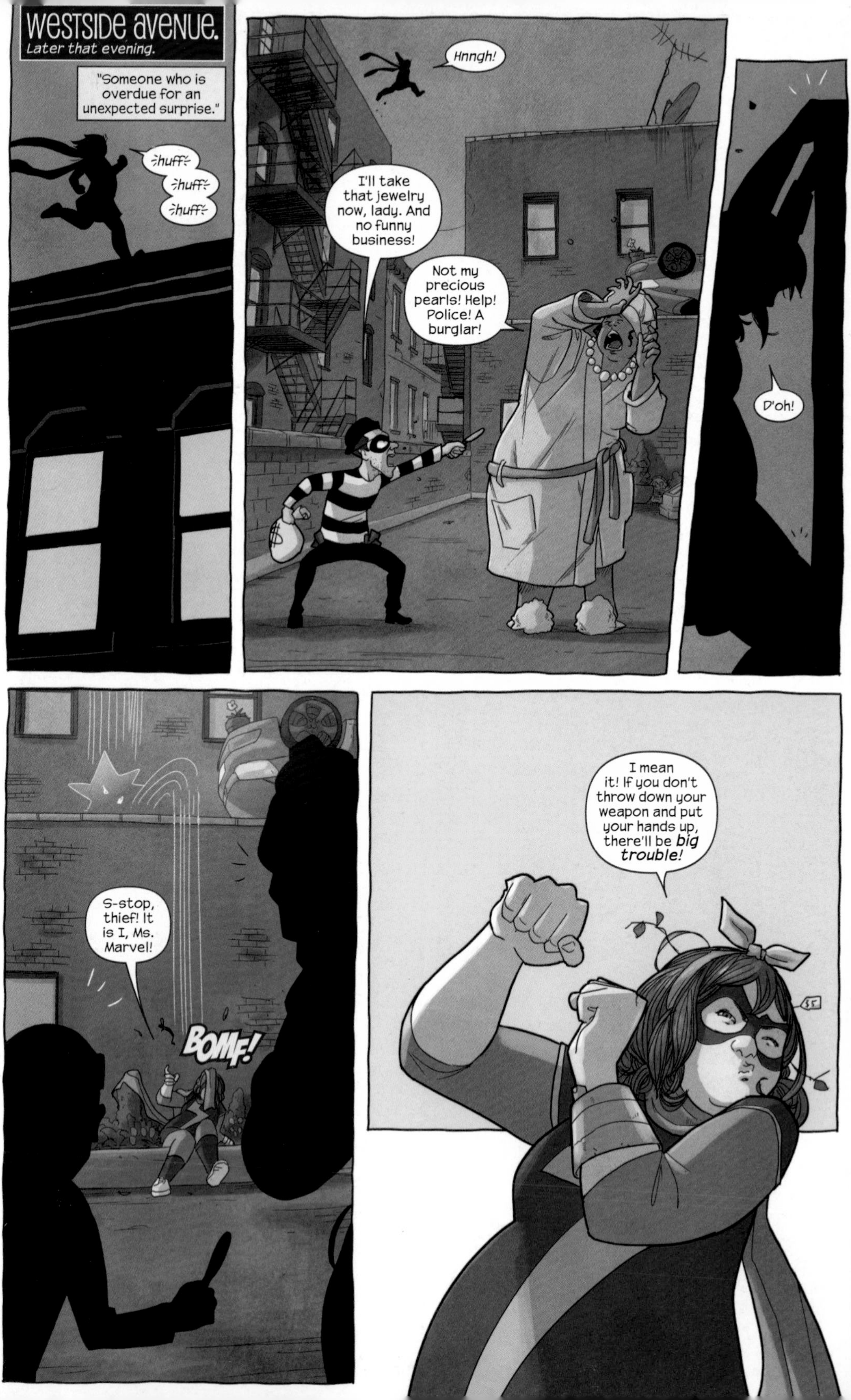
WESTSIDE AVENUE.
Later that evening.
"Someone who is overdue for an unexpected surprise."
huff
huff
huff
Hnngh!
I'll take that jewelry now, lady. And no funny business!
Not my precious pearls! Help! Police! A burglar!
D'oh!
S-stop, thief! It is I, Ms. Marvel!
BOMF!
I mean it! If you don't throw down your weapon and put your hands up, there'll be *big trouble!*

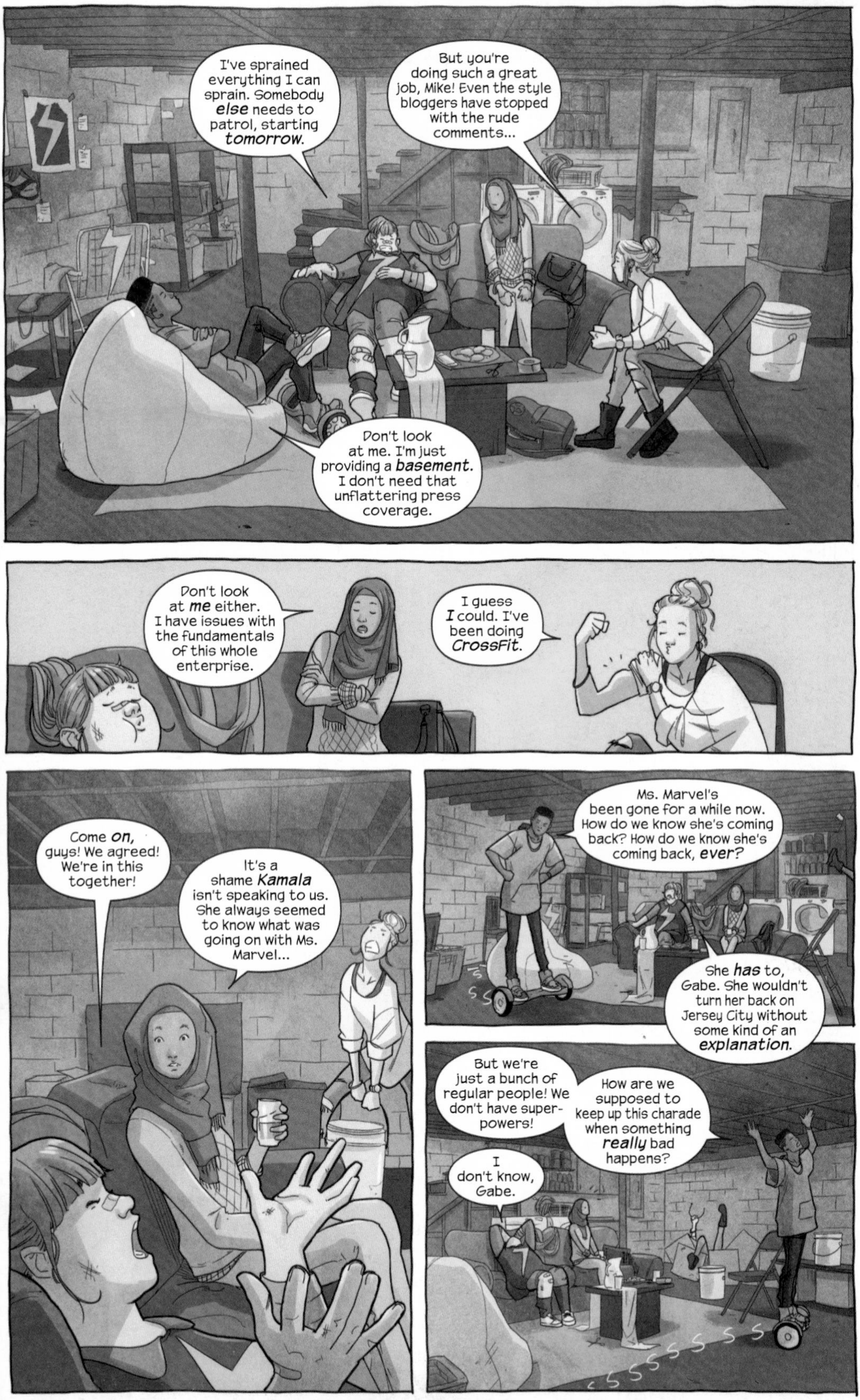
I've sprained everything I can sprain. Somebody else needs to patrol, starting tomorrow.
But you're doing such a great job, Mike! Even the style bloggers have stopped with the rude comments...
Don't look at me. I'm just providing a basement. I don't need that unflattering press coverage.
Don't look at me either. I have issues with the fundamentals of this whole enterprise.
I guess I could. I've been doing CrossFit.
Come on, guys! We agreed! We're in this together!
It's a shame Kamala isn't speaking to us. She always seemed to know what was going on with Ms. Marvel...
Ms. Marvel's been gone for a while now. How do we know she's coming back? How do we know she's coming back, ever?
She has to, Gabe. She wouldn't turn her back on Jersey City without some kind of an explanation.
But we're just a bunch of regular people! We don't have super-powers!
How are we supposed to keep up this charade when something really bad happens?
I don't know, Gabe.

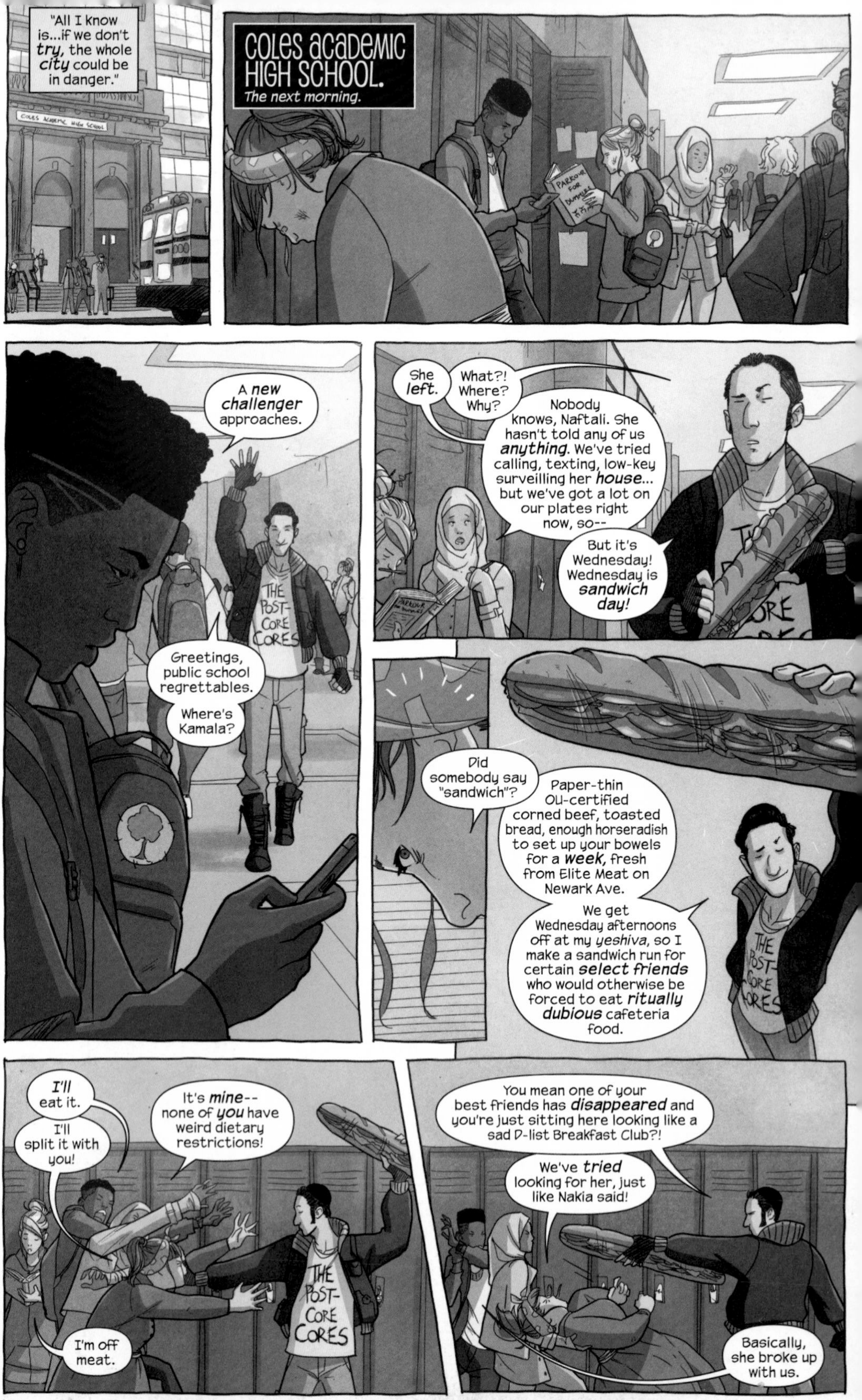
"All I know is...if we don't *try,* the whole *city* could be in danger."
COLES ACADEMIC HIGH SCHOOL
COLES ACADEMIC HIGH SCHOOL.
The next morning.
PARKOUR FOR DUMMIES
A *new challenger* approaches.
Greetings, public school regrettables.
Where's Kamala?
THE POST-CORE CORES
She *left.*
What?! Where? Why?
Nobody knows, Naftali. She hasn't told any of us *anything.* We've tried calling, texting, low-key surveilling her *house*... but we've got a lot on our plates right now, so--
But it's Wednesday! Wednesday is *sandwich day!*
Did somebody say "sandwich"?
Paper-thin OU-certified corned beef, toasted bread, enough horseradish to set up your bowels for a *week,* fresh from Elite Meat on Newark Ave.
We get Wednesday afternoons off at my *yeshiva,* so I make a sandwich run for certain *select friends* who would otherwise be forced to eat *ritually dubious* cafeteria food.
I'll eat it.
I'll split it with you!
It's *mine*-- none of *you* have weird dietary restrictions!
I'm off meat.
THE POST-CORE CORES
You mean one of your best friends has *disappeared* and you're just sitting here looking like a sad D-list Breakfast Club?!
We've *tried* looking for her, just like Nakia said!
Basically, she broke up with us.

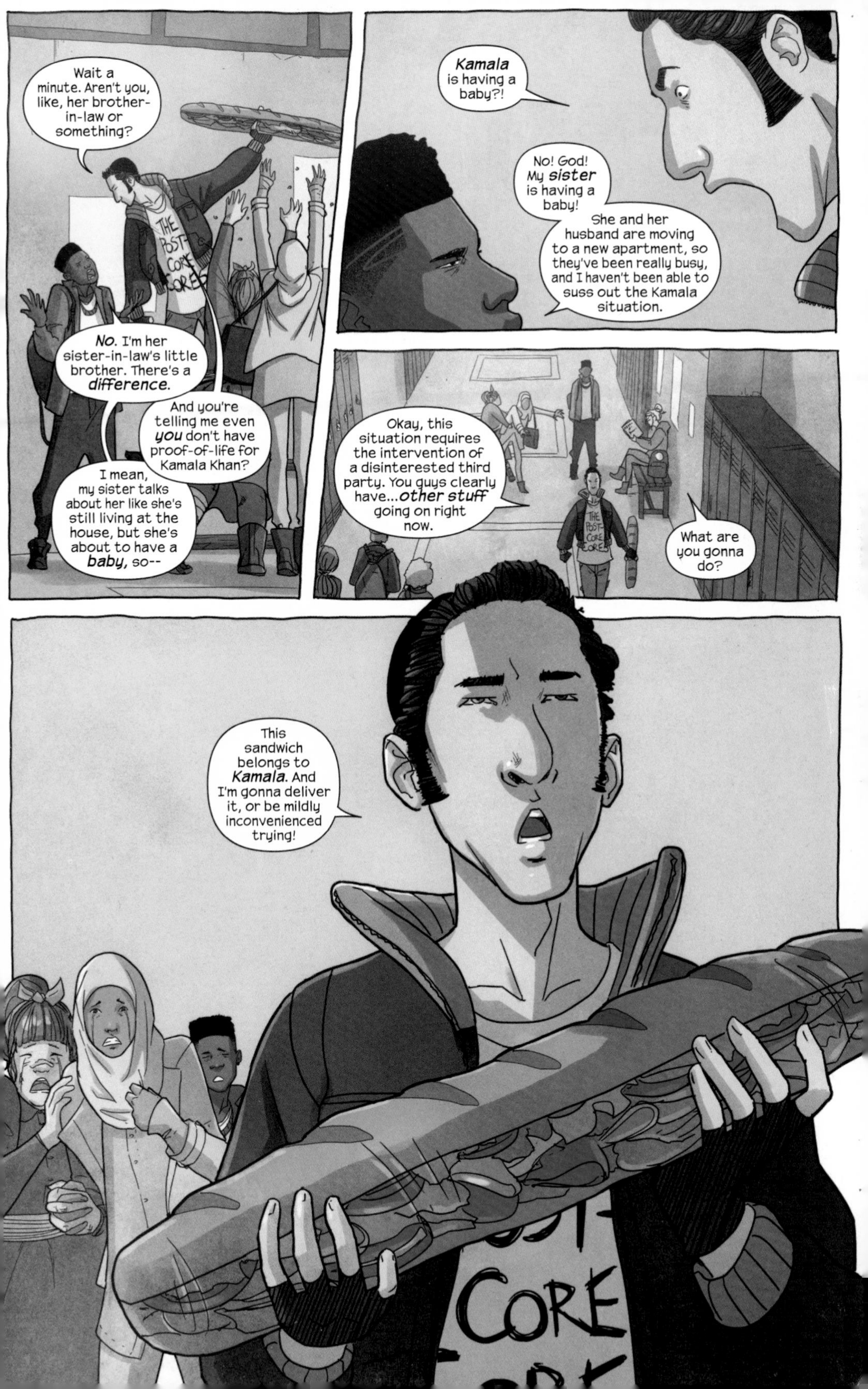
Wait a minute. Aren't you, like, her brother-in-law or something?
No. I'm her sister-in-law's little brother. There's a difference.
And you're telling me even you don't have proof-of-life for Kamala Khan?
I mean, my sister talks about her like she's still living at the house, but she's about to have a baby, so--
THE POST-CORE CORES
Kamala is having a baby?!
No! God! My sister is having a baby!
She and her husband are moving to a new apartment, so they've been really busy, and I haven't been able to suss out the Kamala situation.
Okay, this situation requires the intervention of a disinterested third party. You guys clearly have...other stuff going on right now.
What are you gonna do?
This sandwich belongs to Kamala. And I'm gonna deliver it, or be mildly inconvenienced trying!
CORE

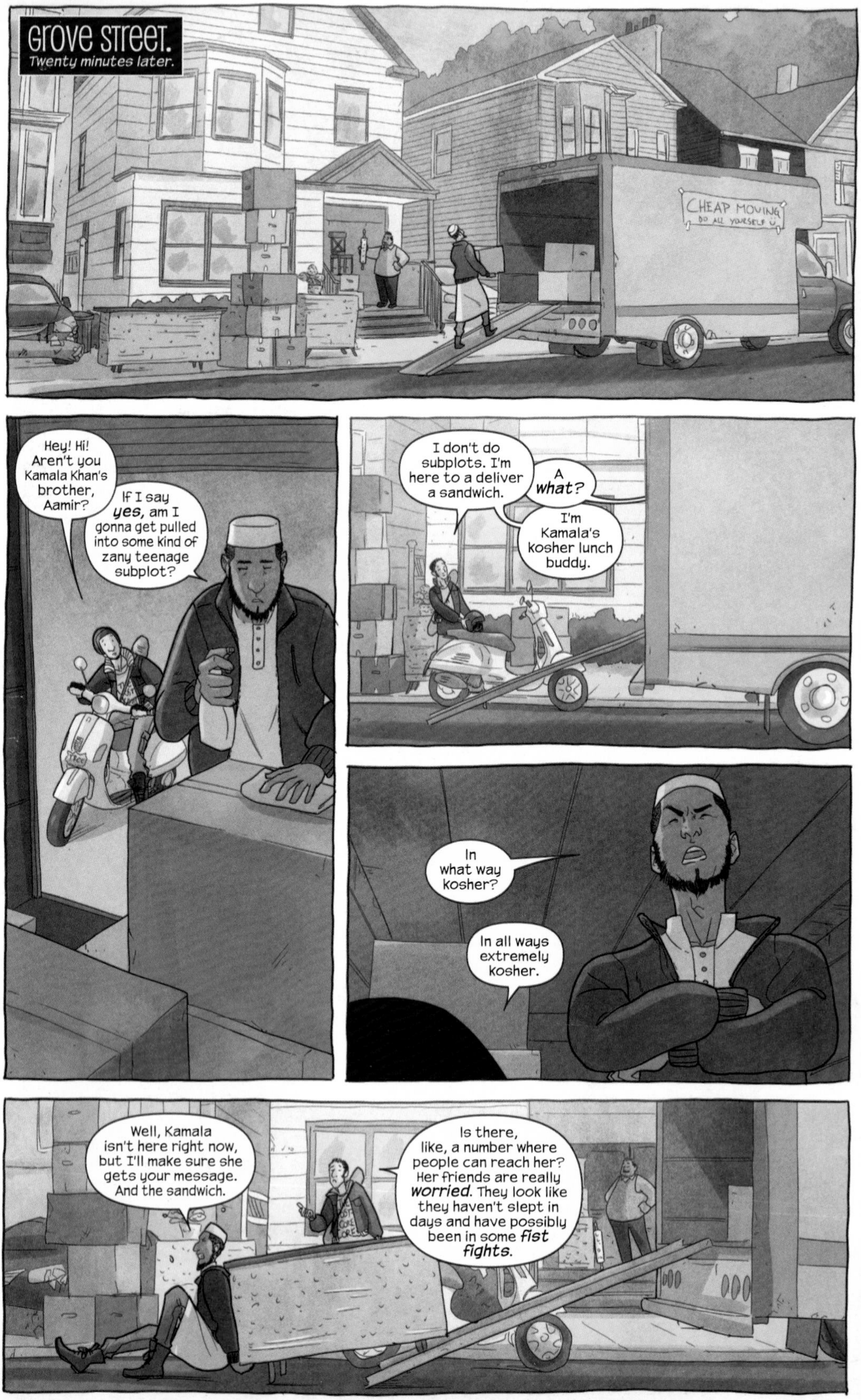
GROVE STREET.
Twenty minutes later.
CHEAP MOVING DO ALL YOURSELF
Hey! Hi! Aren't you Kamala Khan's brother, Aamir?
If I say *yes,* am I gonna get pulled into some kind of zany teenage subplot?
I don't do subplots. I'm here to a deliver a sandwich.
A *what?*
I'm Kamala's kosher lunch buddy.
In what way kosher?
In all ways extremely kosher.
Well, Kamala isn't here right now, but I'll make sure she gets your message. And the sandwich.
Is there, like, a number where people can reach her? Her friends are really *worried*. They look like they haven't slept in days and have possibly been in some *fist fights*.

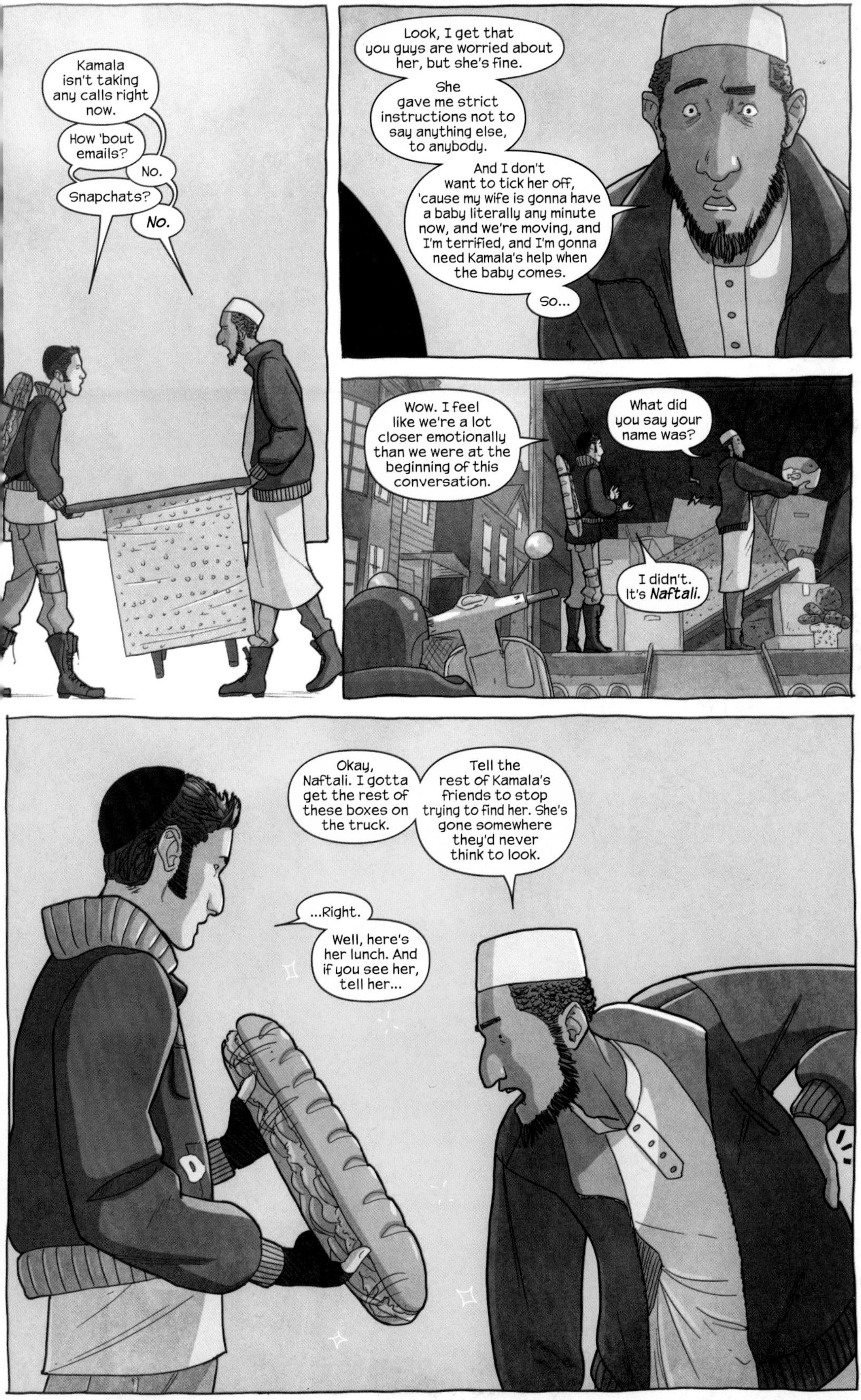
Kamala isn't taking any calls right now.
How 'bout emails?
No.
Snapchats?
No.
Look, I get that you guys are worried about her, but she's fine.
She gave me strict instructions not to say anything else, to anybody.
And I don't want to tick her off, 'cause my wife is gonna have a baby literally any minute now, and we're moving, and I'm terrified, and I'm gonna need Kamala's help when the baby comes.
So...
Wow. I feel like we're a lot closer emotionally than we were at the beginning of this conversation.
What did you say your name was?
I didn't. It's *Naftali.*
Okay, Naftali. I gotta get the rest of these boxes on the truck.
Tell the rest of Kamala's friends to stop trying to find her. She's gone somewhere they'd never think to look.
...Right.
Well, here's her lunch. And if you see her, tell her...

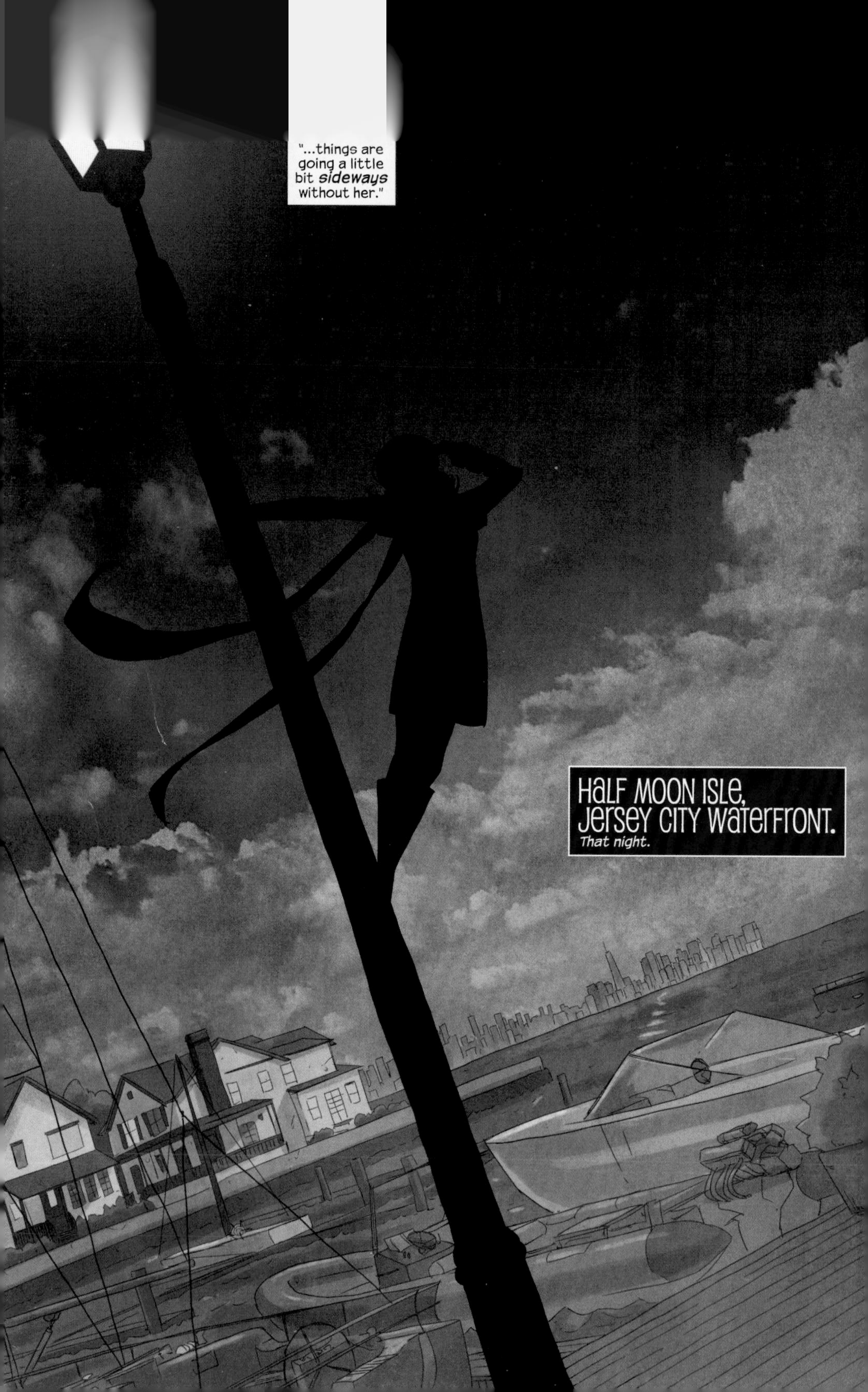
"...things are going a little bit *sideways* without her."
HALF MOON ISLE, JERSEY CITY WATERFRONT.
That night.

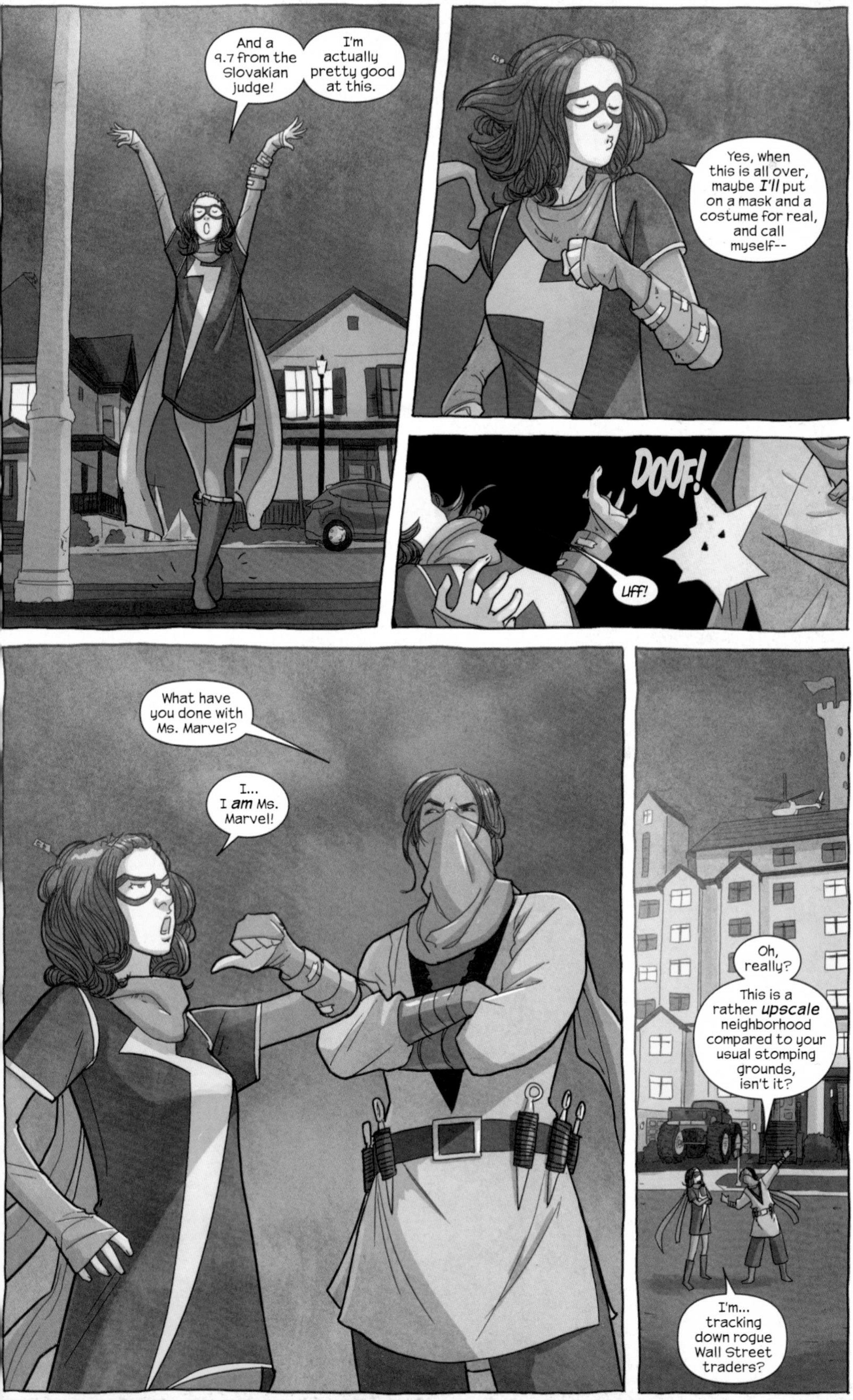
And a 9.7 from the Slovakian judge!
I'm actually pretty good at this.
Yes, when this is all over, maybe I'll put on a mask and a costume for real, and call myself--
DOOF!
UFF!
What have you done with Ms. Marvel?
I... I am Ms. Marvel!
Oh, really?
This is a rather upscale neighborhood compared to your usual stomping grounds, isn't it?
I'm... tracking down rogue Wall Street traders?

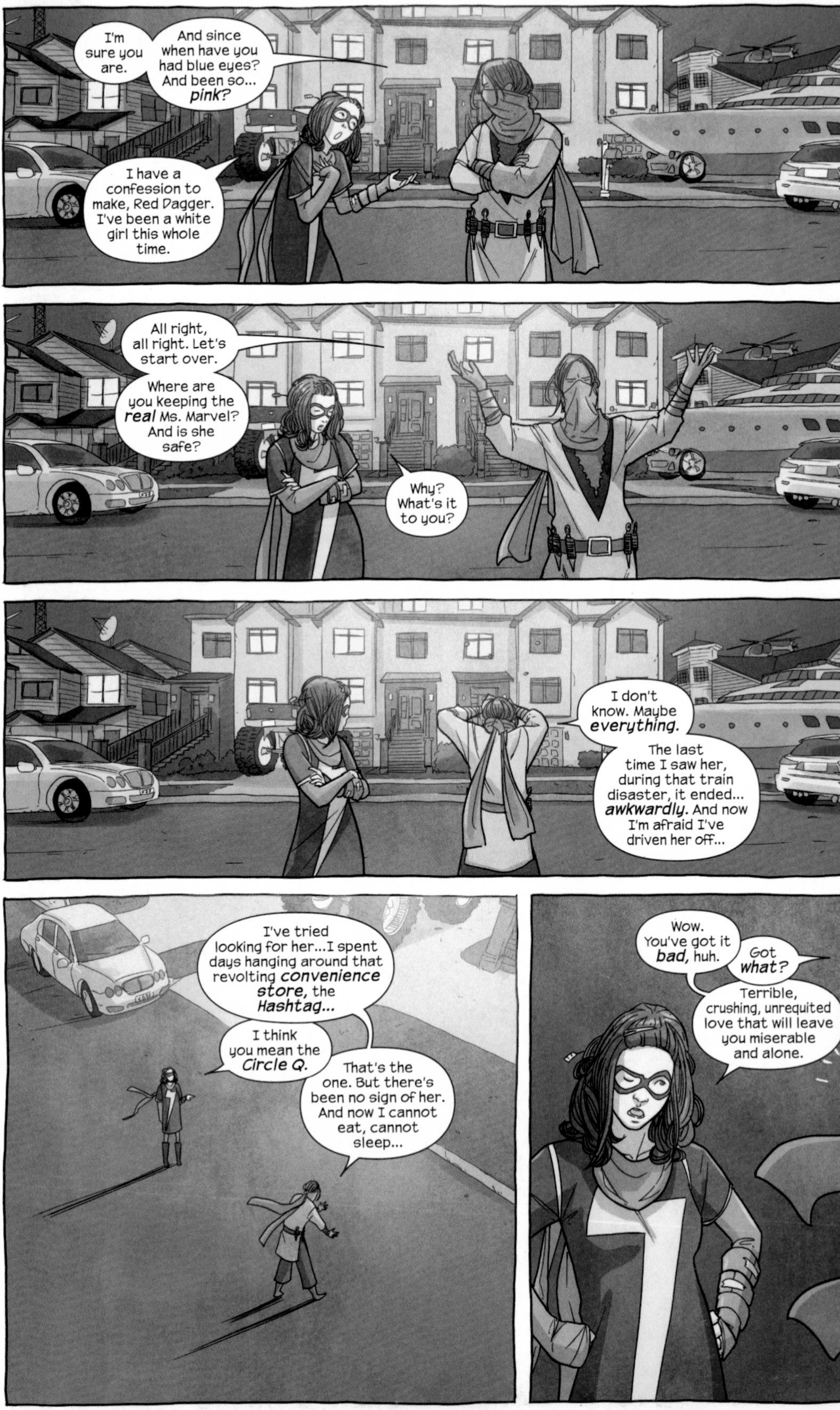
I'm sure you are.
And since when have you had blue eyes? And been so... pink?
I have a confession to make, Red Dagger. I've been a white girl this whole time.
All right, all right. Let's start over.
Where are you keeping the real Ms. Marvel? And is she safe?
Why? What's it to you?
I don't know. Maybe everything.
The last time I saw her, during that train disaster, it ended... awkwardly. And now I'm afraid I've driven her off...
I've tried looking for her...I spent days hanging around that revolting convenience store, the Hashtag...
I think you mean the Circle Q.
That's the one. But there's been no sign of her. And now I cannot eat, cannot sleep...
Wow. You've got it bad, huh.
Got what?
Terrible, crushing, unrequited love that will leave you miserable and alone.

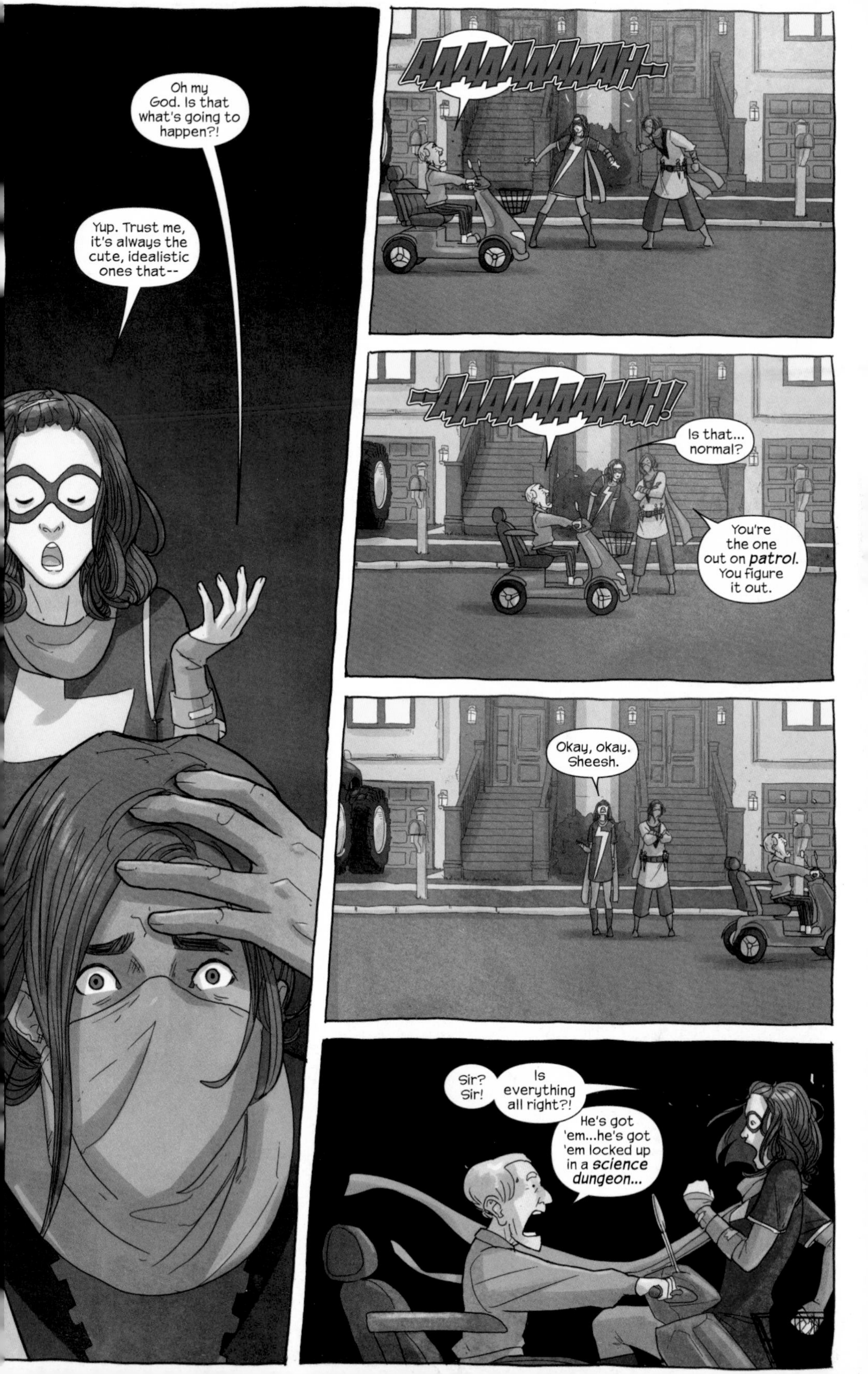
Oh my God. Is that what's going to happen?!
Yup. Trust me, it's always the cute, idealistic ones that--
AAAAAAAAAH--
-AAAAAAAAAH!
Is that... normal?
You're the one out on *patrol*. You figure it out.
Okay, okay. Sheesh.
Sir? Sir!
Is everything all right?!
He's got 'em...he's got 'em locked up in a *science dungeon*...

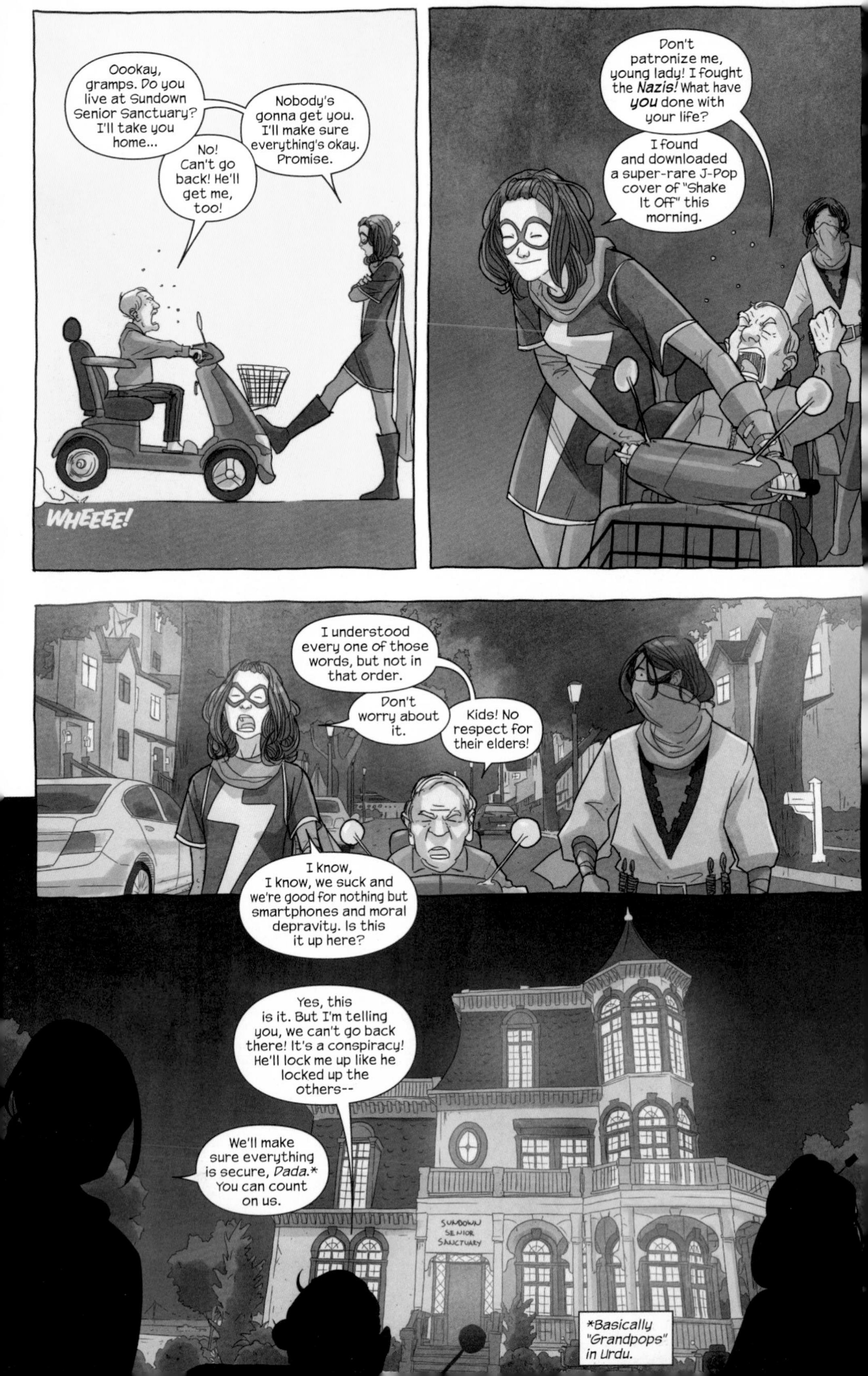

Oookay, gramps. Do you live at Sundown Senior Sanctuary? I'll take you home...
No! Can't go back! He'll get me, too!
Nobody's gonna get you. I'll make sure everything's okay. Promise.
WHEEEEE!
Don't patronize me, young lady! I fought the *Nazis!* What have **you** done with your life?
I found and downloaded a super-rare J-Pop cover of "Shake It Off" this morning.
I understood every one of those words, but not in that order.
Don't worry about it.
Kids! No respect for their elders!
I know, I know, we suck and we're good for nothing but smartphones and moral depravity. Is this it up here?
Yes, this is it. But I'm telling you, we can't go back there! It's a conspiracy! He'll lock me up like he locked up the others--
We'll make sure everything is secure, *Dada.** You can count on us.
SUNDOWN SENIOR SANCTUARY
*Basically "Grandpops" in Urdu.

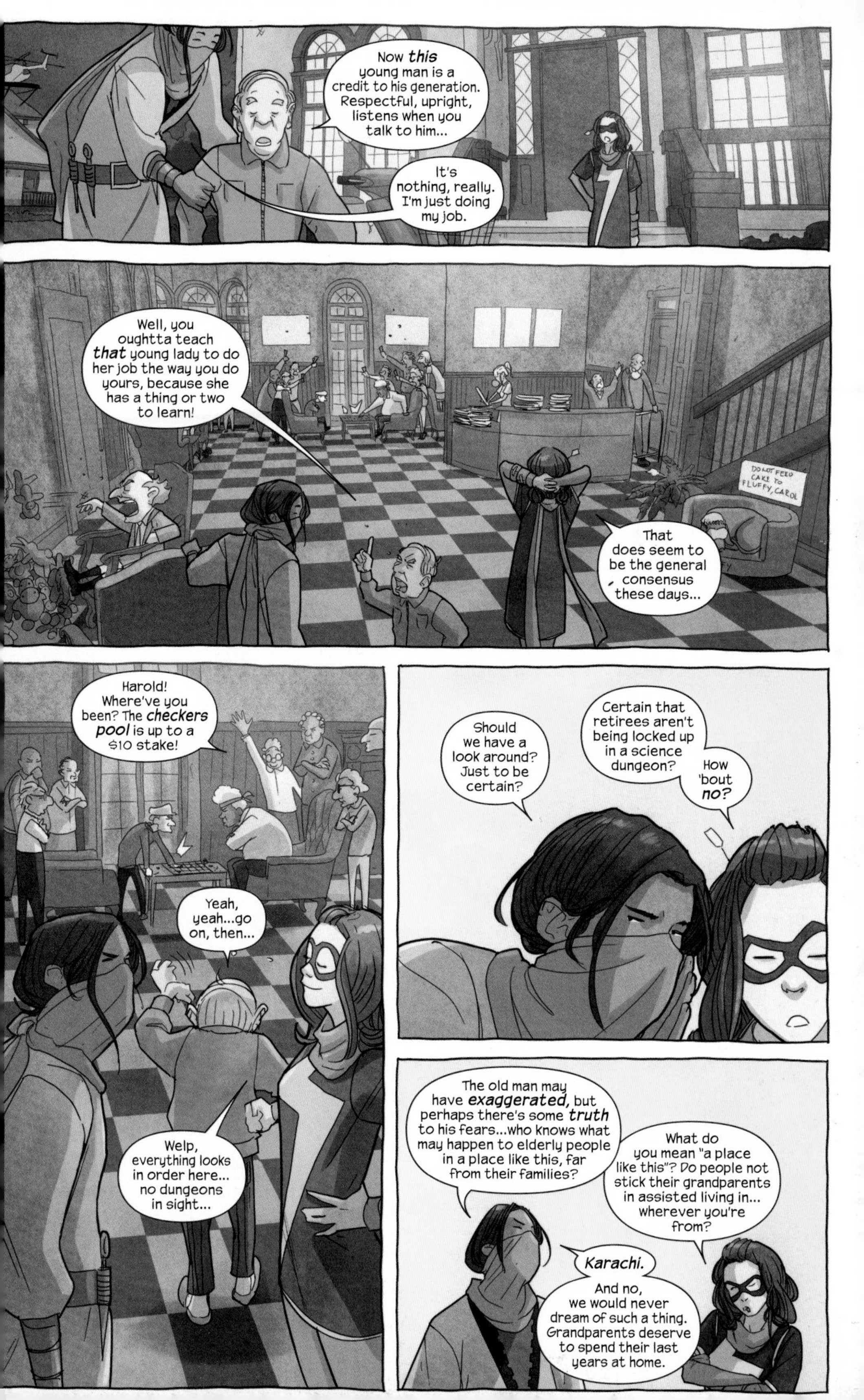
Now this young man is a credit to his generation. Respectful, upright, listens when you talk to him...
It's nothing, really. I'm just doing my job.
Well, you oughtta teach that young lady to do her job the way you do yours, because she has a thing or two to learn!
That does seem to be the general consensus these days...
DO NOT FEED CAKE TO FLUFFY, CAROL
Harold! Where've you been? The checkers pool is up to a $10 stake!
Yeah, yeah...go on, then...
Welp, everything looks in order here... no dungeons in sight...
Should we have a look around? Just to be certain?
Certain that retirees aren't being locked up in a science dungeon?
How 'bout no?
The old man may have exaggerated, but perhaps there's some truth to his fears...who knows what may happen to elderly people in a place like this, far from their families?
What do you mean "a place like this"? Do people not stick their grandparents in assisted living in... wherever you're from?
Karachi.
And no, we would never dream of such a thing. Grandparents deserve to spend their last years at home.

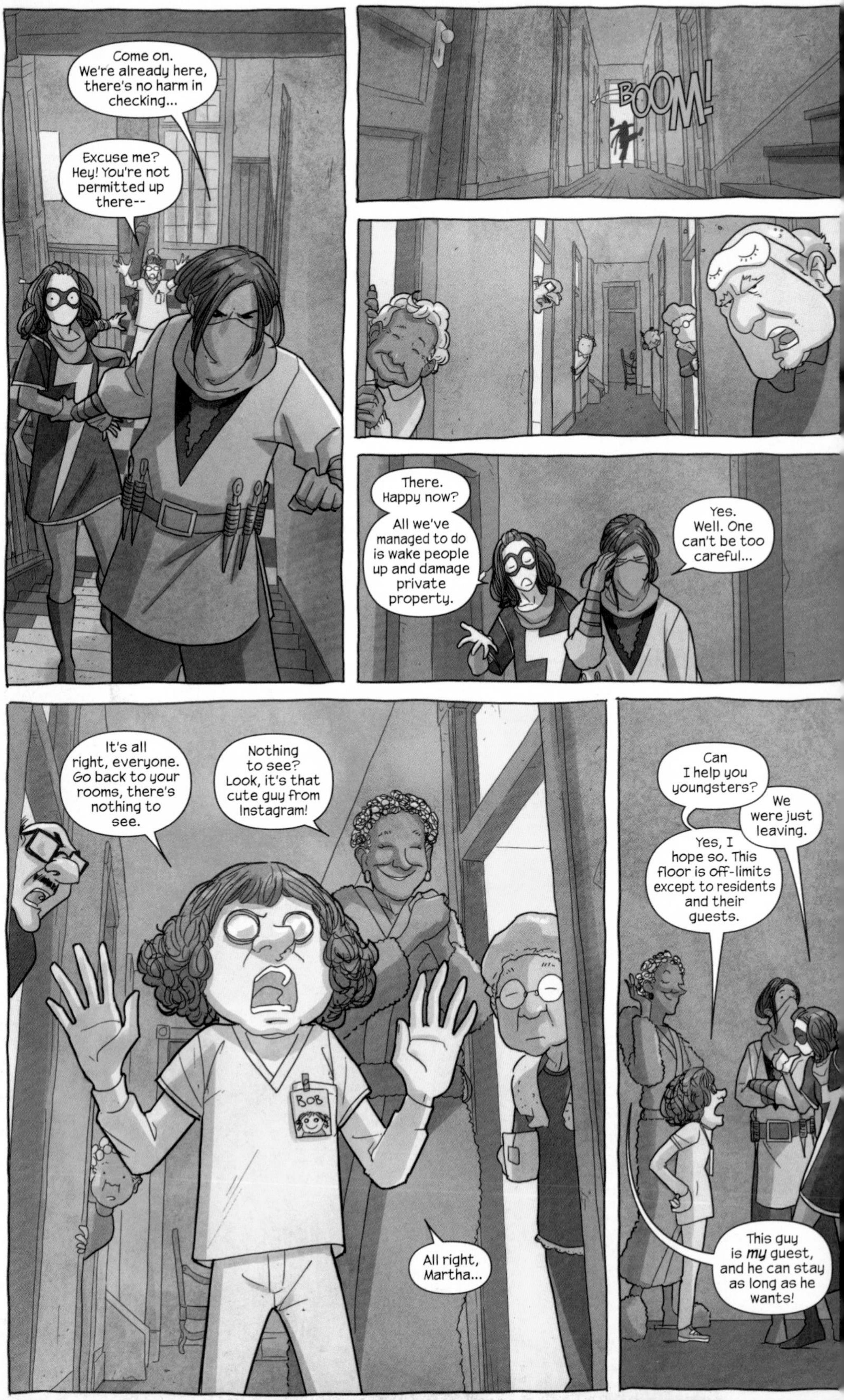
Come on. We're already here, there's no harm in checking...
Excuse me? Hey! You're not permitted up there--
BOOM!
There. Happy now?
All we've managed to do is wake people up and damage private property.
Yes. Well. One can't be too careful...
It's all right, everyone. Go back to your rooms, there's nothing to see.
Nothing to see? Look, it's that cute guy from Instagram!
All right, Martha...
BOB
Can I help you youngsters?
We were just leaving.
Yes, I hope so. This floor is off-limits except to residents and their guests.
This guy is *my* guest, and he can stay as long as he wants!

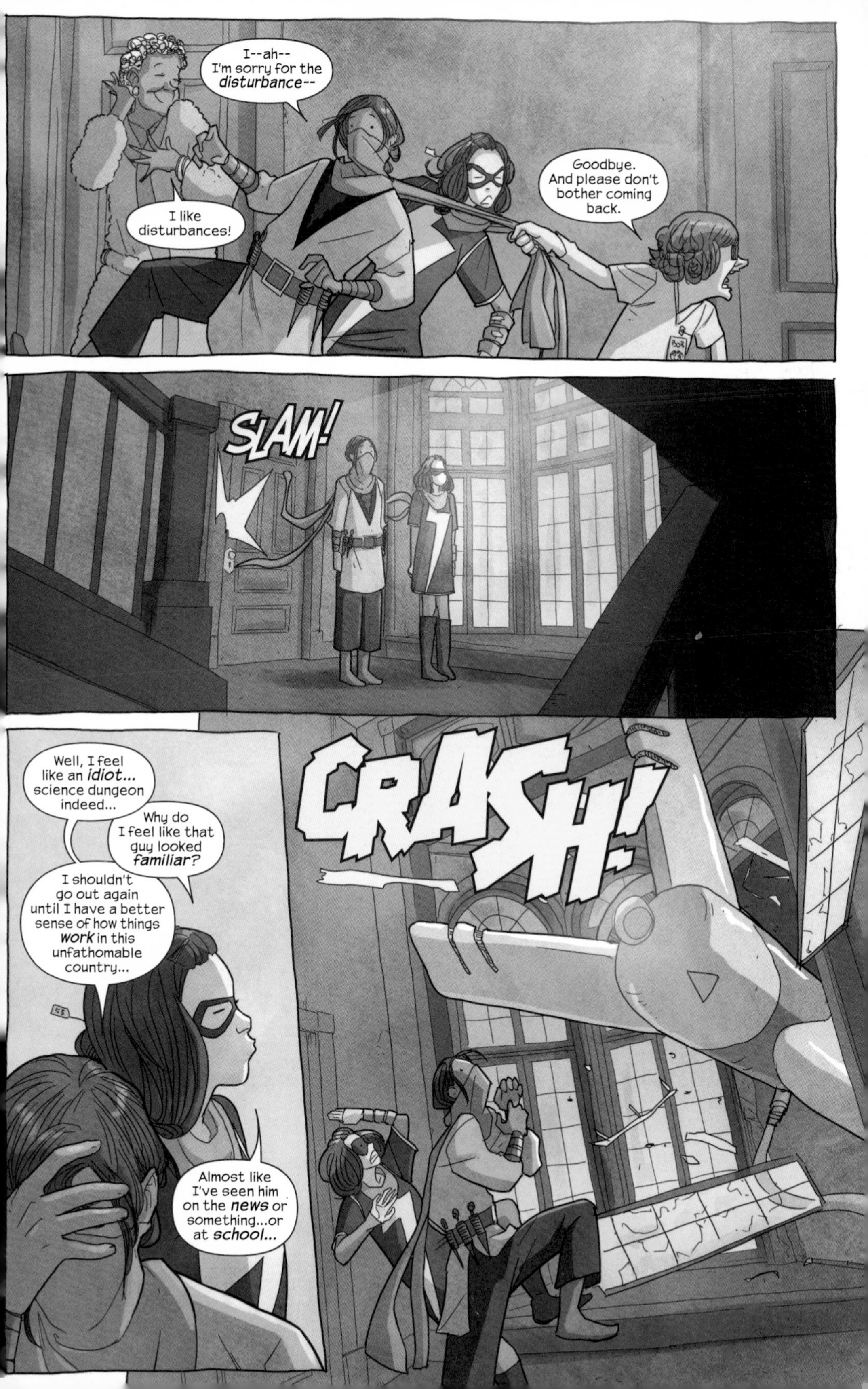
I--ah-- I'm sorry for the disturbance--
I like disturbances!
Goodbye. And please don't bother coming back.
SLAM!
CRASH!
Well, I feel like an idiot... science dungeon indeed...
Why do I feel like that guy looked familiar?
I shouldn't go out again until I have a better sense of how things work in this unfathomable country...
Almost like I've seen him on the news or something...or at school...

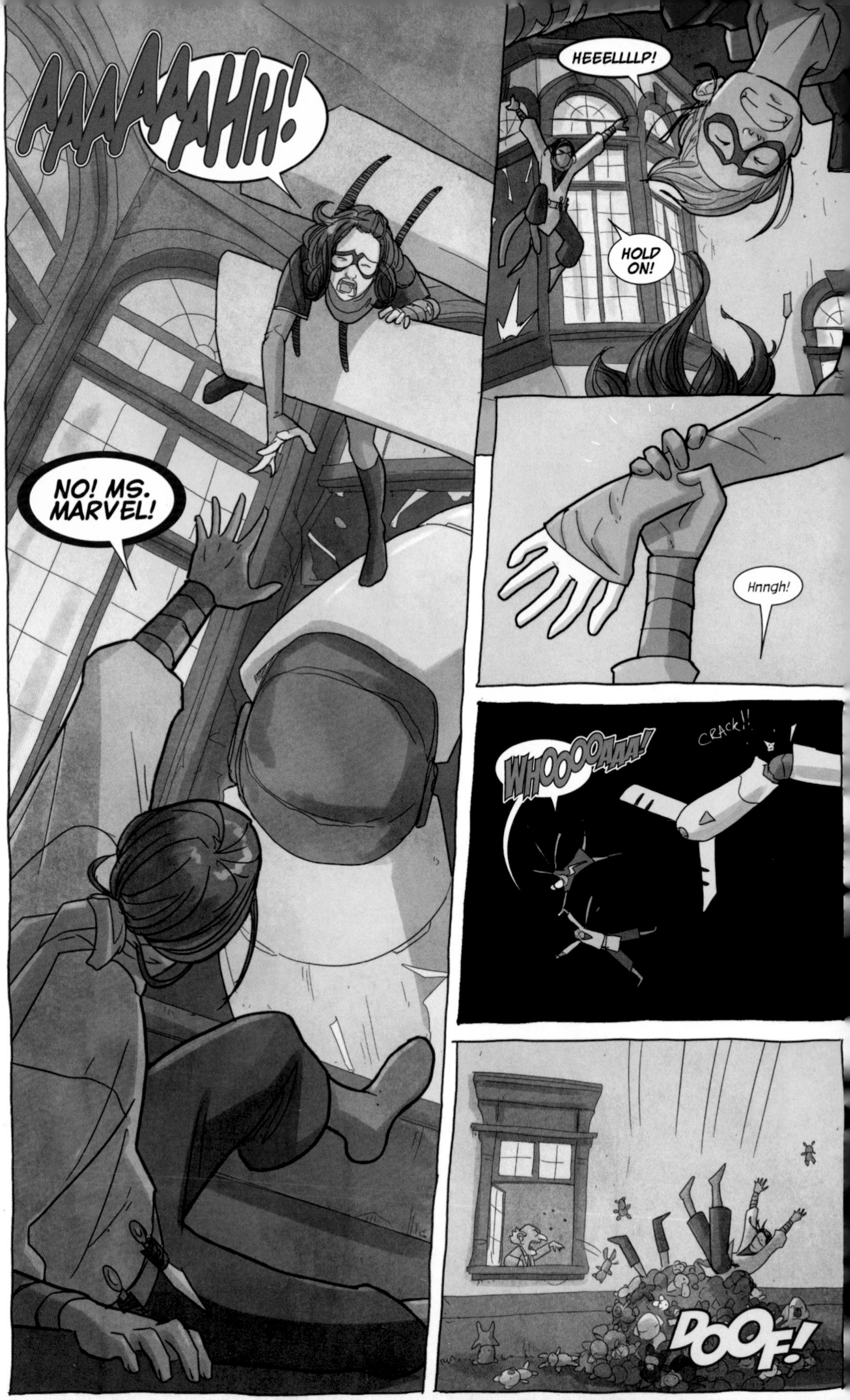
AAAAAAHH!
NO! MS. MARVEL!
HEEELLLLP!
HOLD ON!
Hnngh!
WHOOOOAAA!
CRACK!!
DOOF!

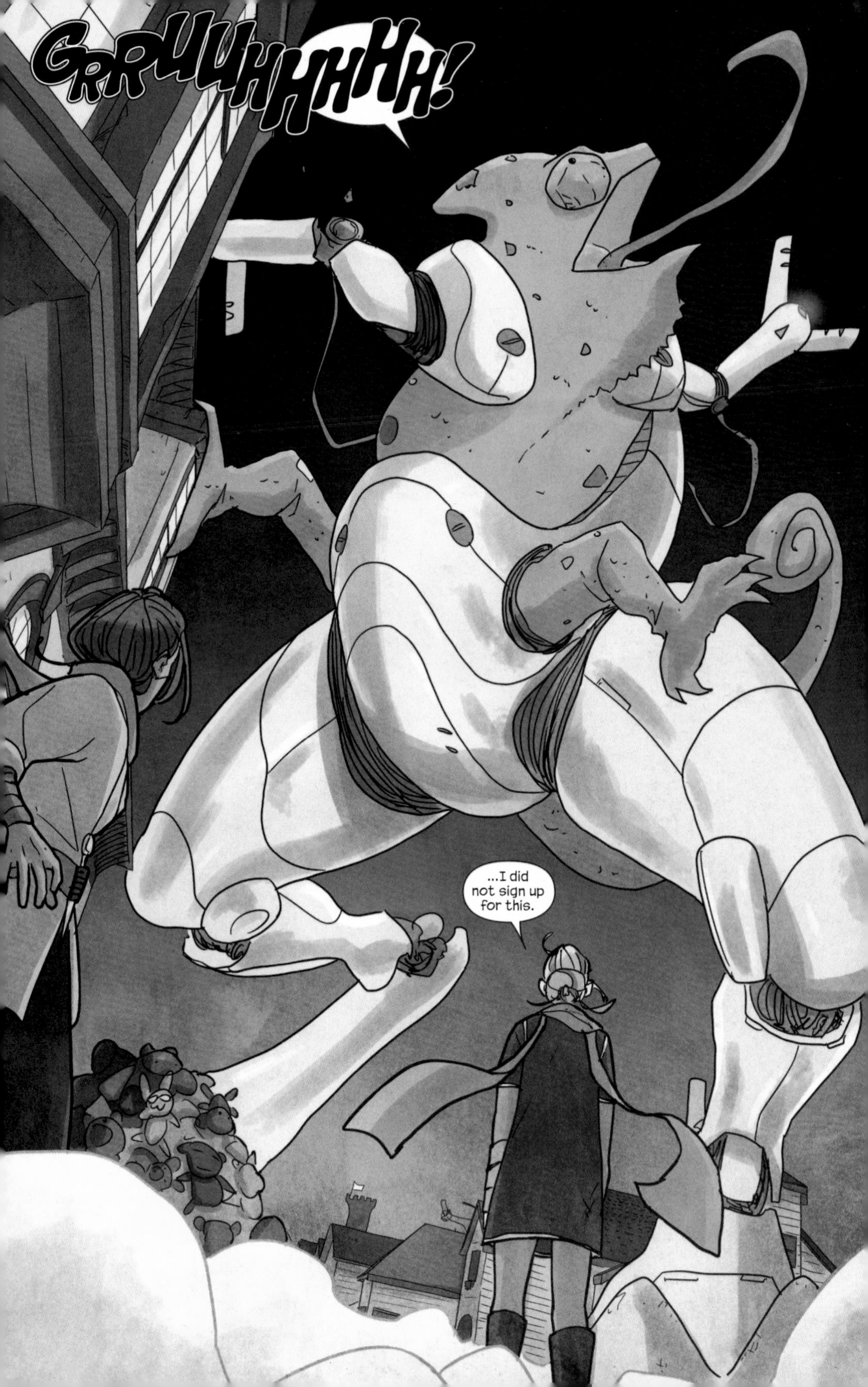
GRRUUUHHHHHH!
...I did not sign up for this.

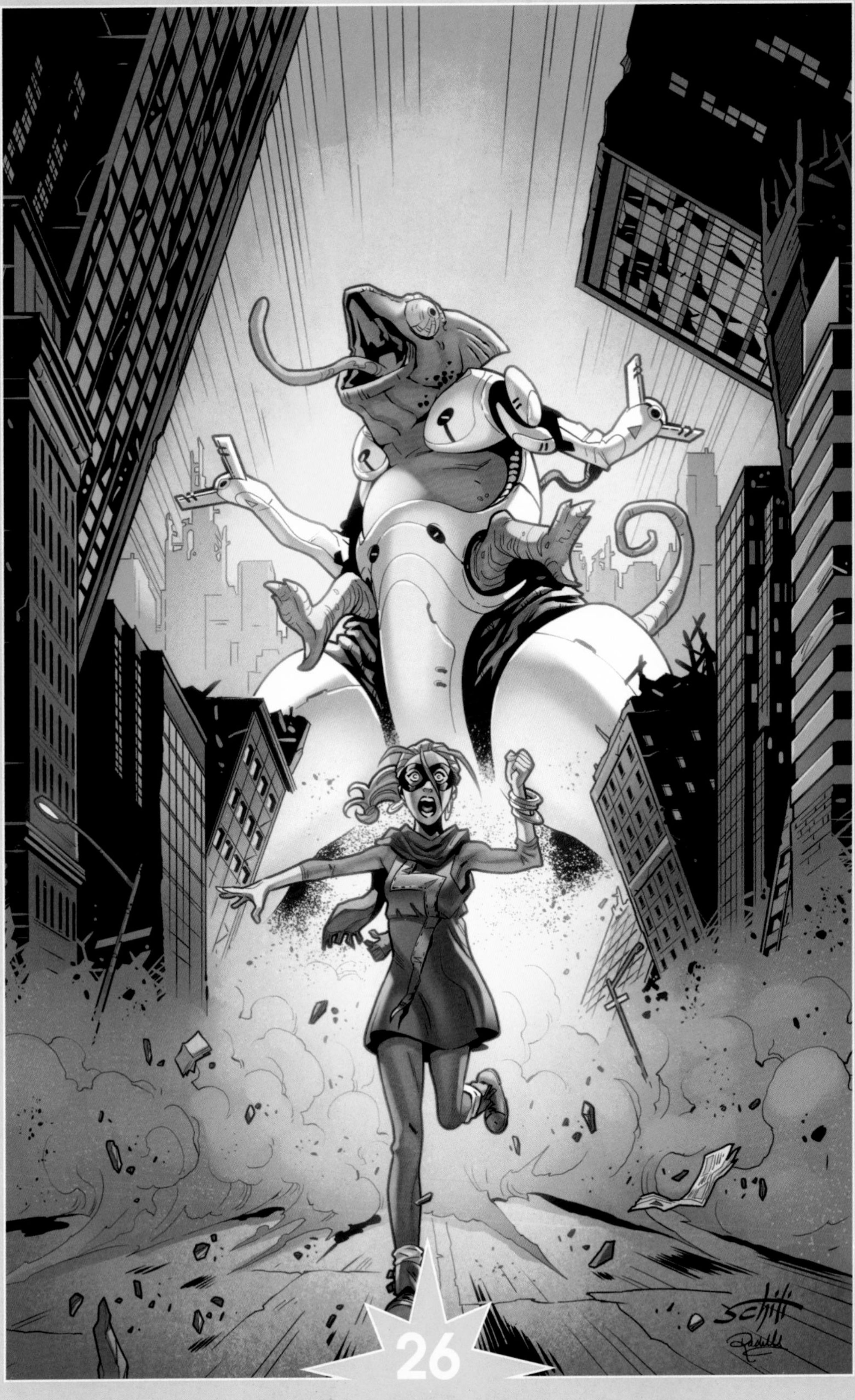

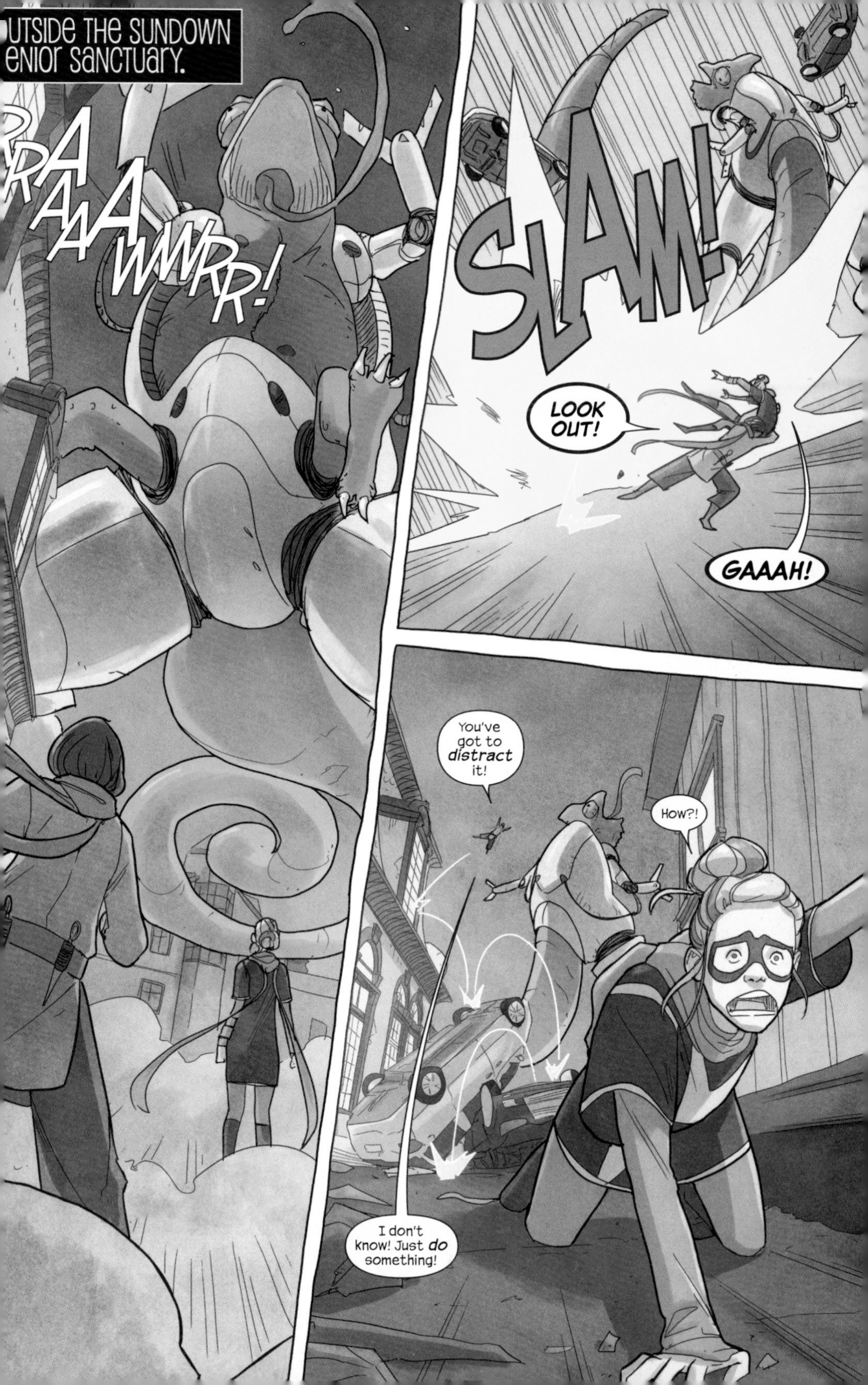
UTSIDE THE SUNDOWN
ENIOR SANCTUARY.
RRAAAAWWRRR!
SLAM!
LOOK OUT!
GAAAH!
You've got to *distract* it!
How?!
I don't know! Just *do* something!

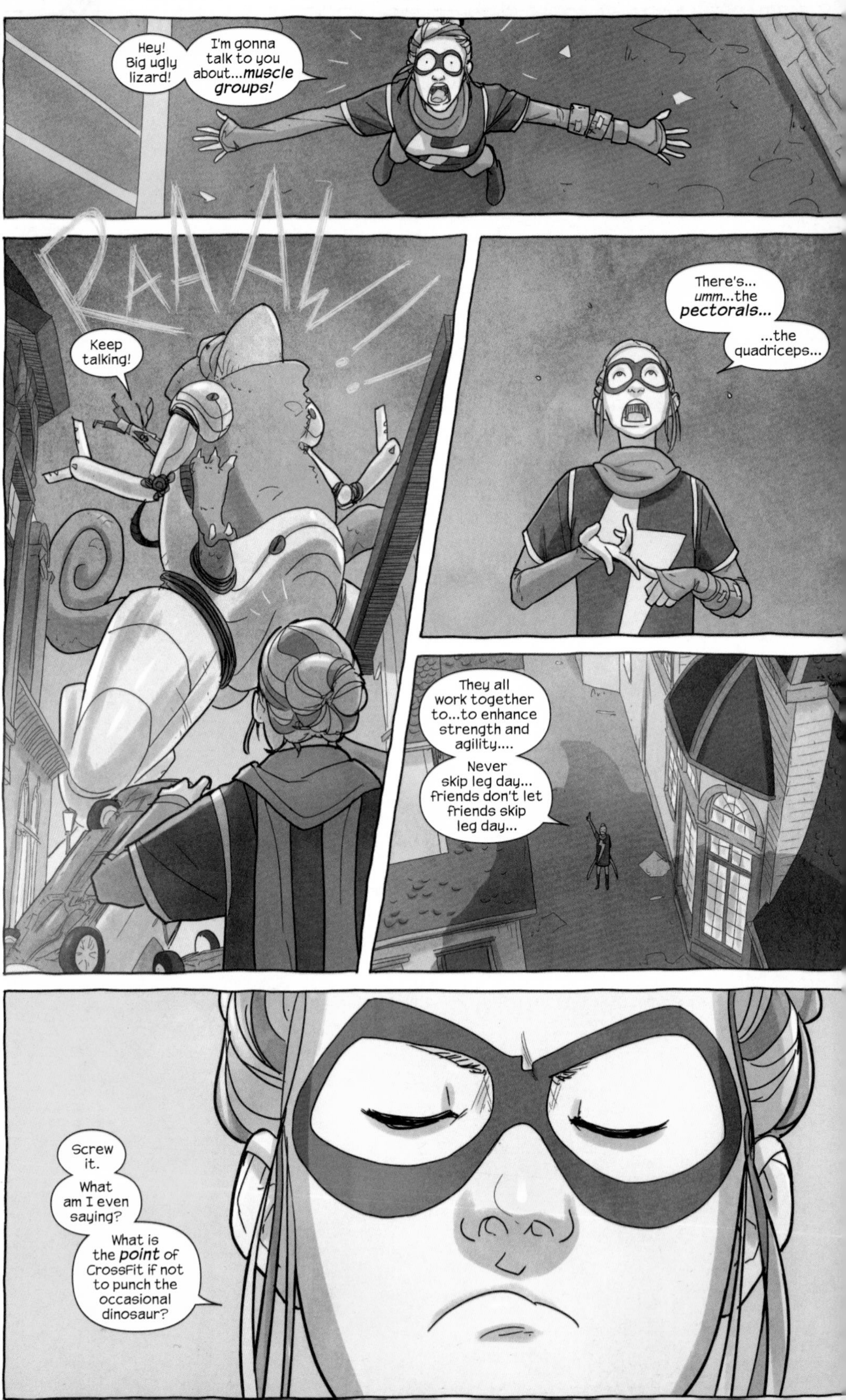

Hey! Big ugly lizard!
I'm gonna talk to you about...*muscle groups!*
RAAAW
Keep talking!
There's... *umm*...the *pectorals...*
...the quadriceps...
They all work together to...to enhance strength and agility....
Never skip leg day... friends don't let friends skip leg day...
Screw it.
What am I even saying?
What is the *point* of CrossFit if not to punch the occasional dinosaur?

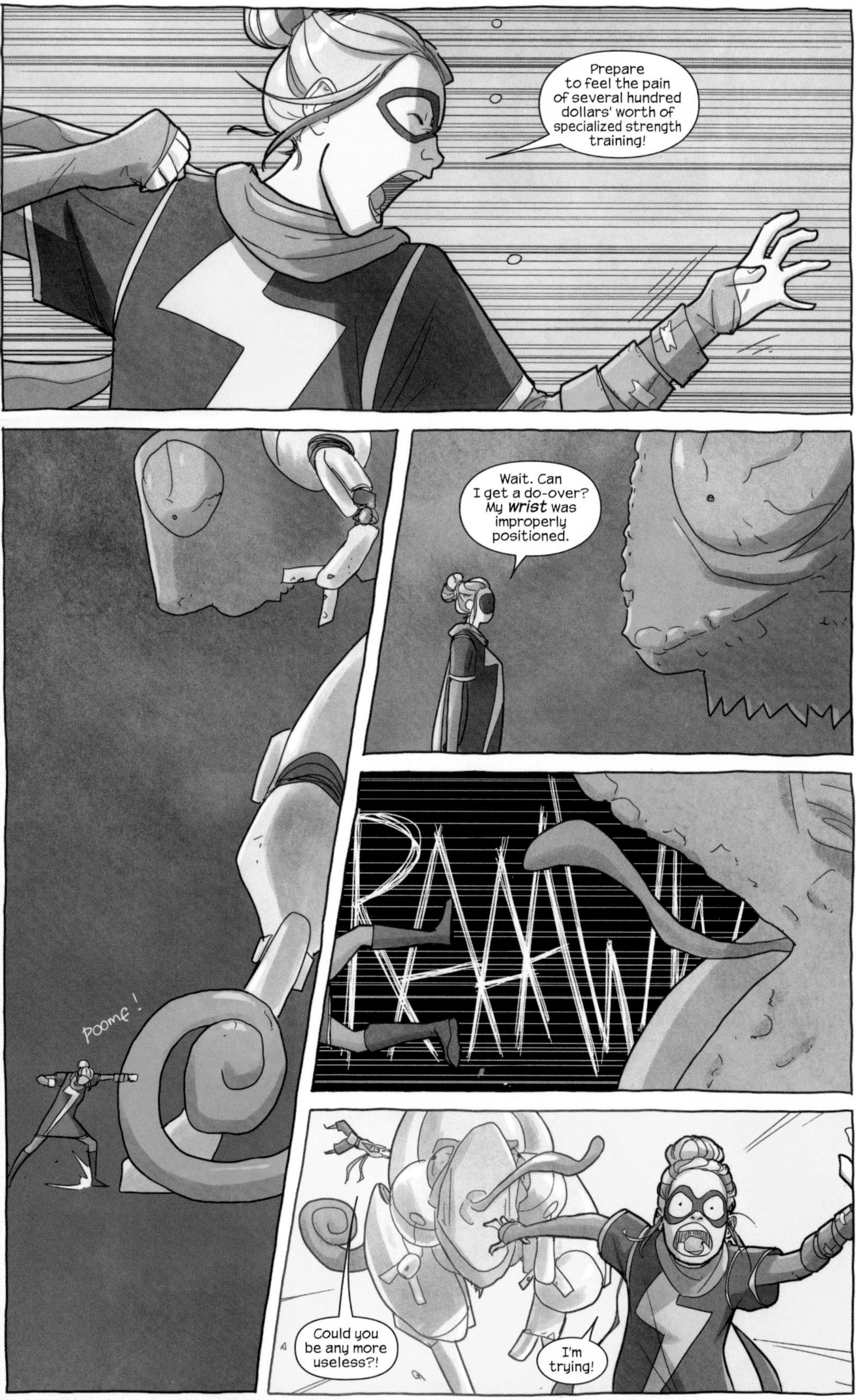
Prepare to feel the pain of several hundred dollars' worth of specialized strength training!
Wait. Can I get a do-over? My **wrist** was improperly positioned.
POOMF!
RAWWW
Could you be any more useless?!
I'm trying!

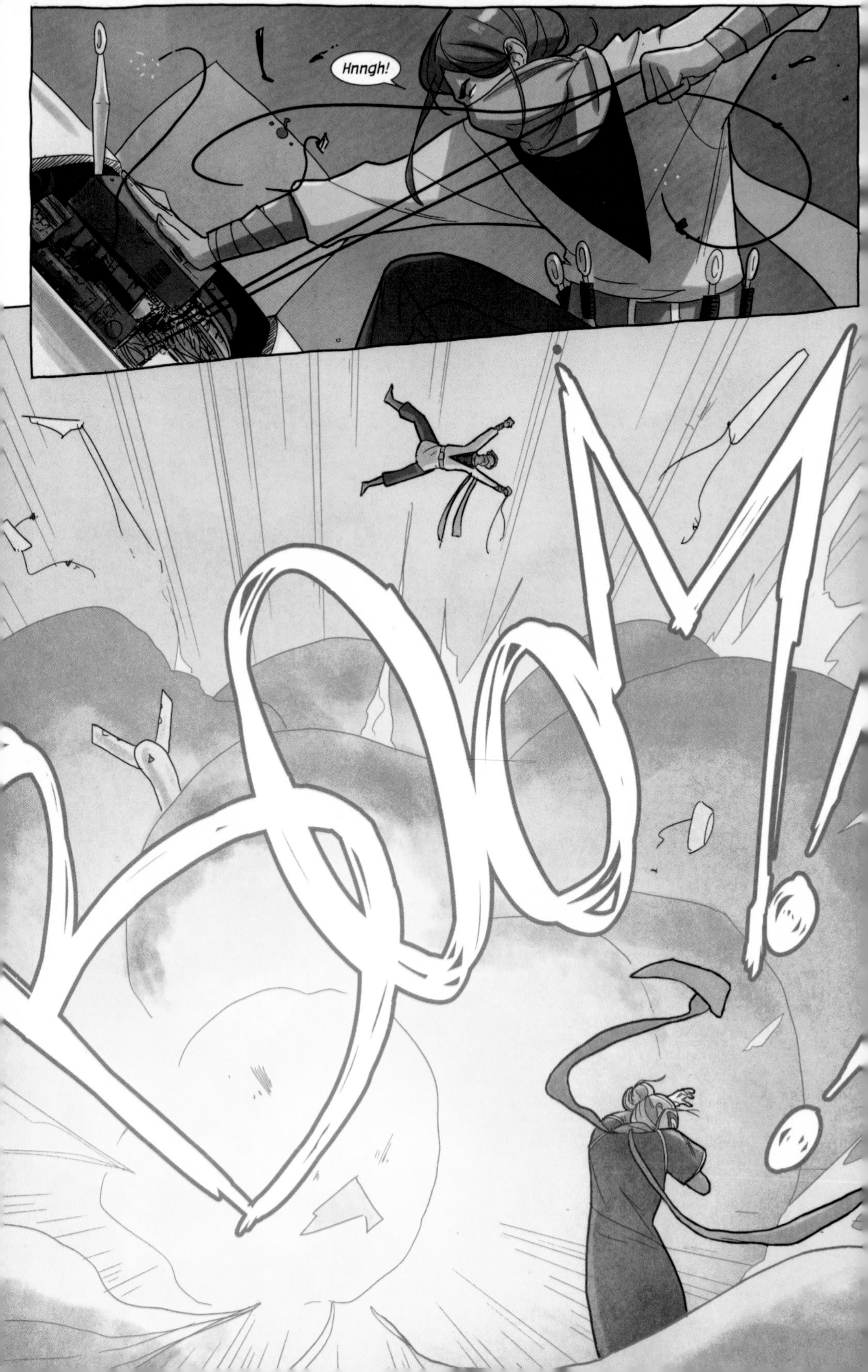
Hnngh!
BOOOM!!

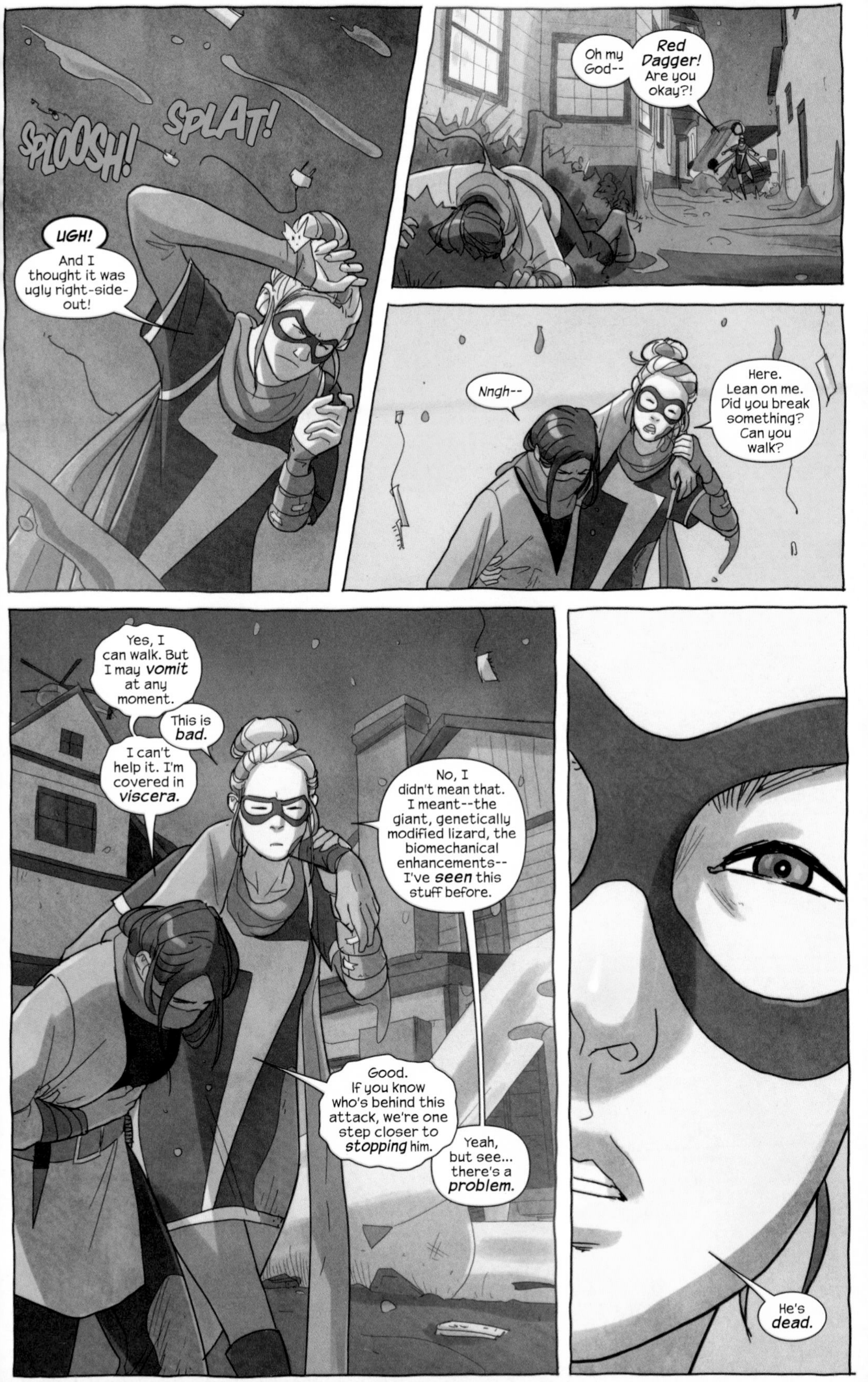
SPLOOSH!
SPLAT!
UGH! And I thought it was ugly right-side-out!
Oh my God--
Red Dagger! Are you okay?!
Nngh--
Here. Lean on me. Did you break something? Can you walk?
Yes, I can walk. But I may vomit at any moment.
This is bad.
I can't help it. I'm covered in viscera.
No, I didn't mean that. I meant--the giant, genetically modified lizard, the biomechanical enhancements-- I've seen this stuff before.
Good. If you know who's behind this attack, we're one step closer to stopping him.
Yeah, but see... there's a problem.
He's dead.

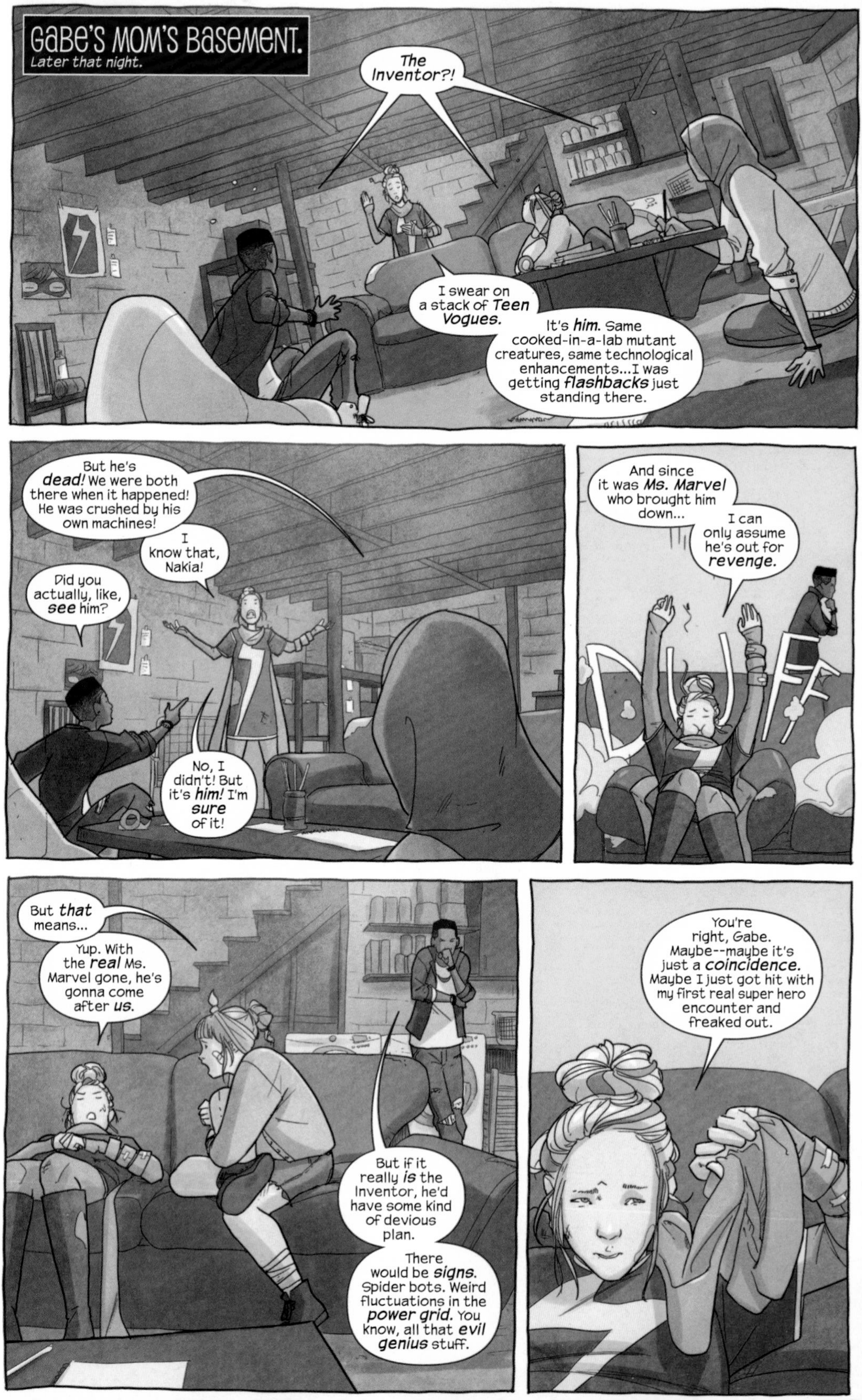

GABE'S MOM'S BASEMENT.
Later that night.
The Inventor?!
I swear on a stack of Teen Vogues.
It's him. Same cooked-in-a-lab mutant creatures, same technological enhancements...I was getting flashbacks just standing there.
But he's dead! We were both there when it happened! He was crushed by his own machines!
I know that, Nakia!
Did you actually, like, see him?
No, I didn't! But it's him! I'm sure of it!
And since it was Ms. Marvel who brought him down...
I can only assume he's out for revenge.
DUFF
But that means...
Yup. With the real Ms. Marvel gone, he's gonna come after us.
But if it really is the Inventor, he'd have some kind of devious plan.
There would be signs. Spider bots. Weird fluctuations in the power grid. You know, all that evil genius stuff.
You're right, Gabe. Maybe--maybe it's just a coincidence. Maybe I just got hit with my first real super hero encounter and freaked out.

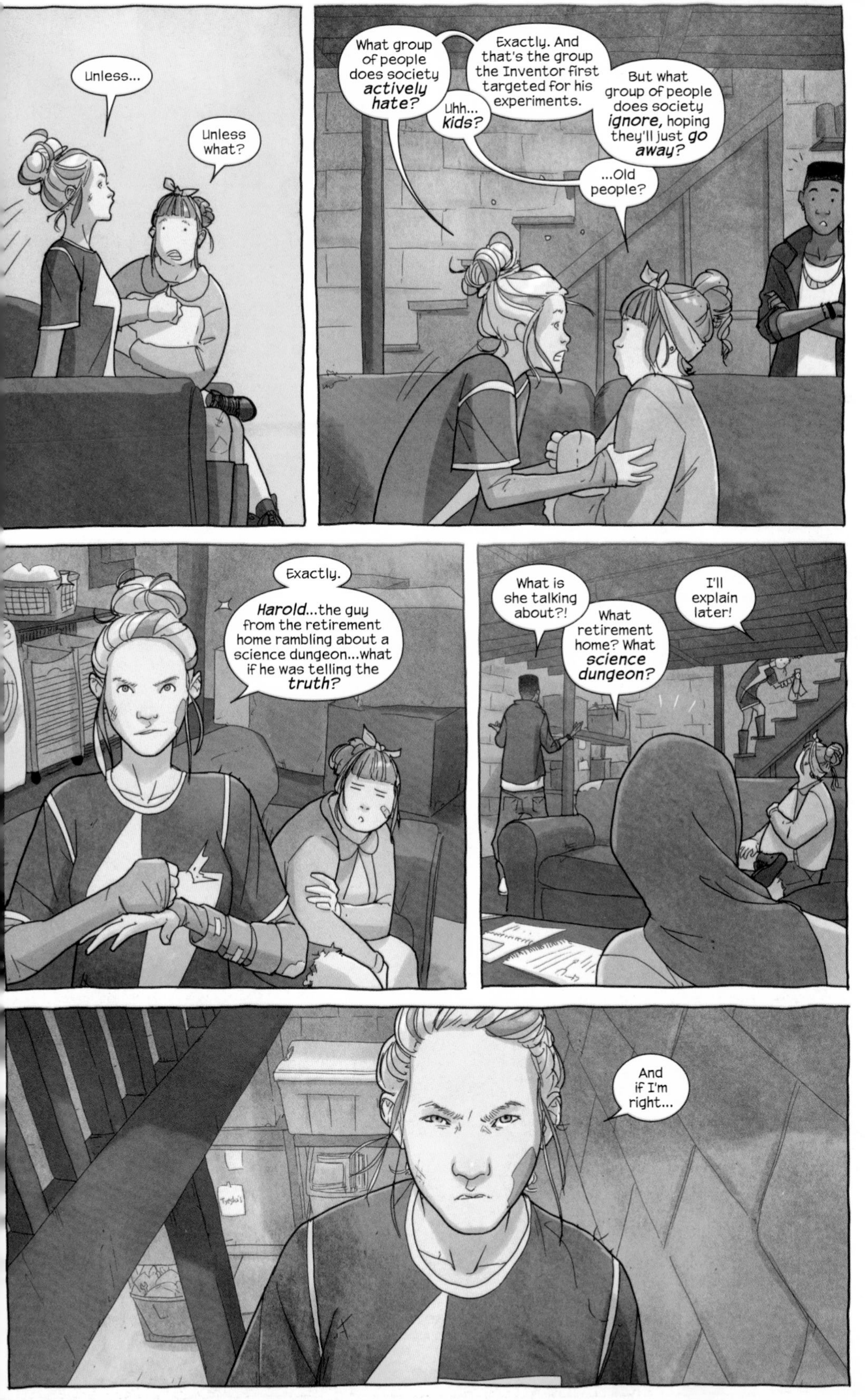
Unless...
Unless what?
What group of people does society actively hate?
Uhh... kids?
Exactly. And that's the group the Inventor first targeted for his experiments.
But what group of people does society ignore, hoping they'll just go away?
...Old people?
Exactly.
Harold...the guy from the retirement home rambling about a science dungeon...what if he was telling the truth?
What is she talking about?!
What retirement home? What science dungeon?
I'll explain later!
And if I'm right...

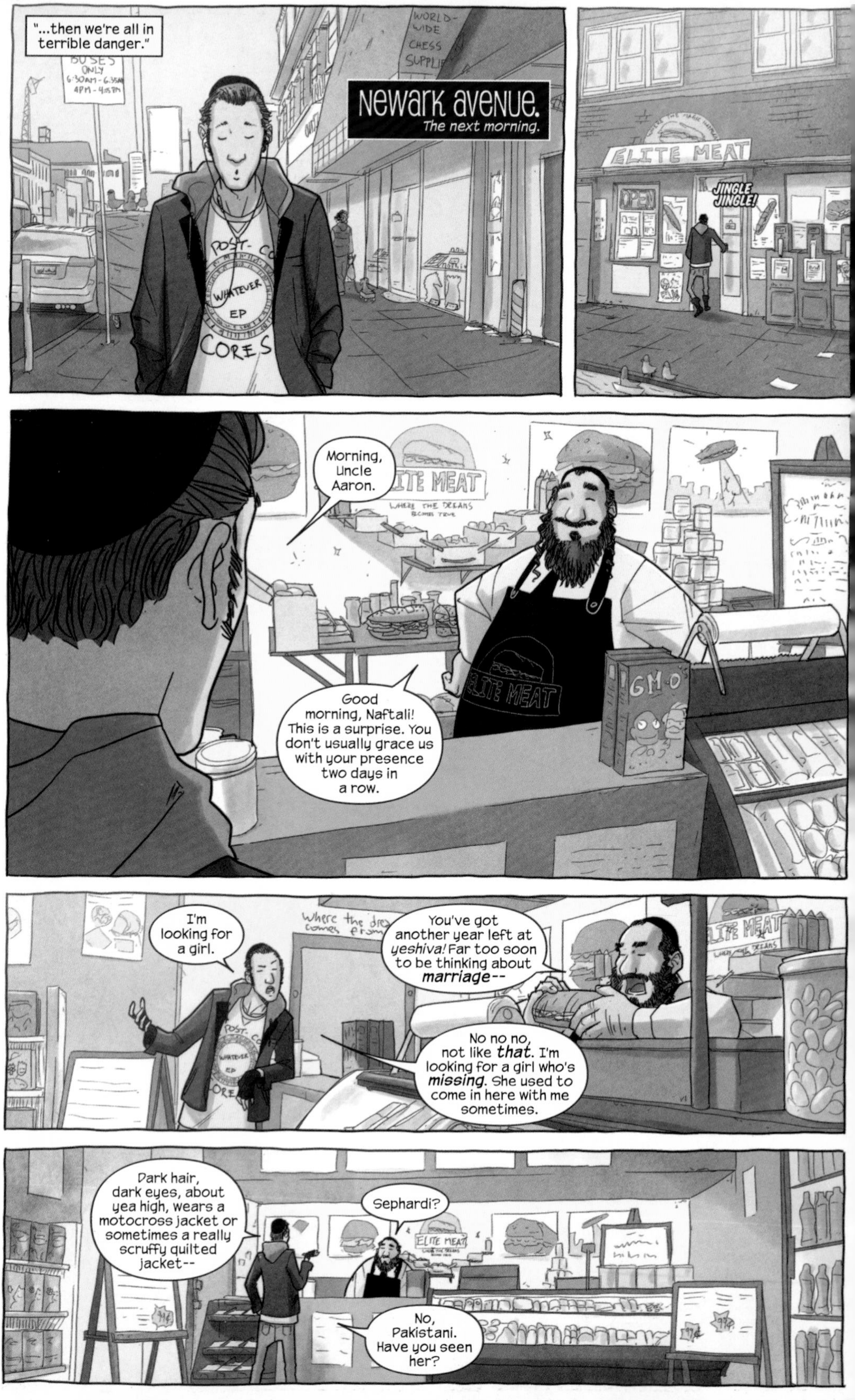
"...then we're all in terrible danger."
BUSES ONLY 6:30AM-6:35AM 4PM-4:15PM
WORLD-WIDE CHESS SUPPLIES
Newark avenue.
The next morning.
POST-CO WHATEVER EP CORES
ELITE MEAT
OPEN
JINGLE JINGLE!
Morning, Uncle Aaron.
ELITE MEAT
WHERE THE DREAMS COMES TRUE
Good morning, Naftali! This is a surprise. You don't usually grace us with your presence two days in a row.
GMO'S
I'm looking for a girl.
You've got another year left at *yeshiva!* Far too soon to be thinking about ***marriage***--
No no no, not like ***that***. I'm looking for a girl who's ***missing***. She used to come in here with me sometimes.
Dark hair, dark eyes, about yea high, wears a motocross jacket or sometimes a really scruffy quilted jacket--
Sephardi?
No, Pakistani. Have you seen her?

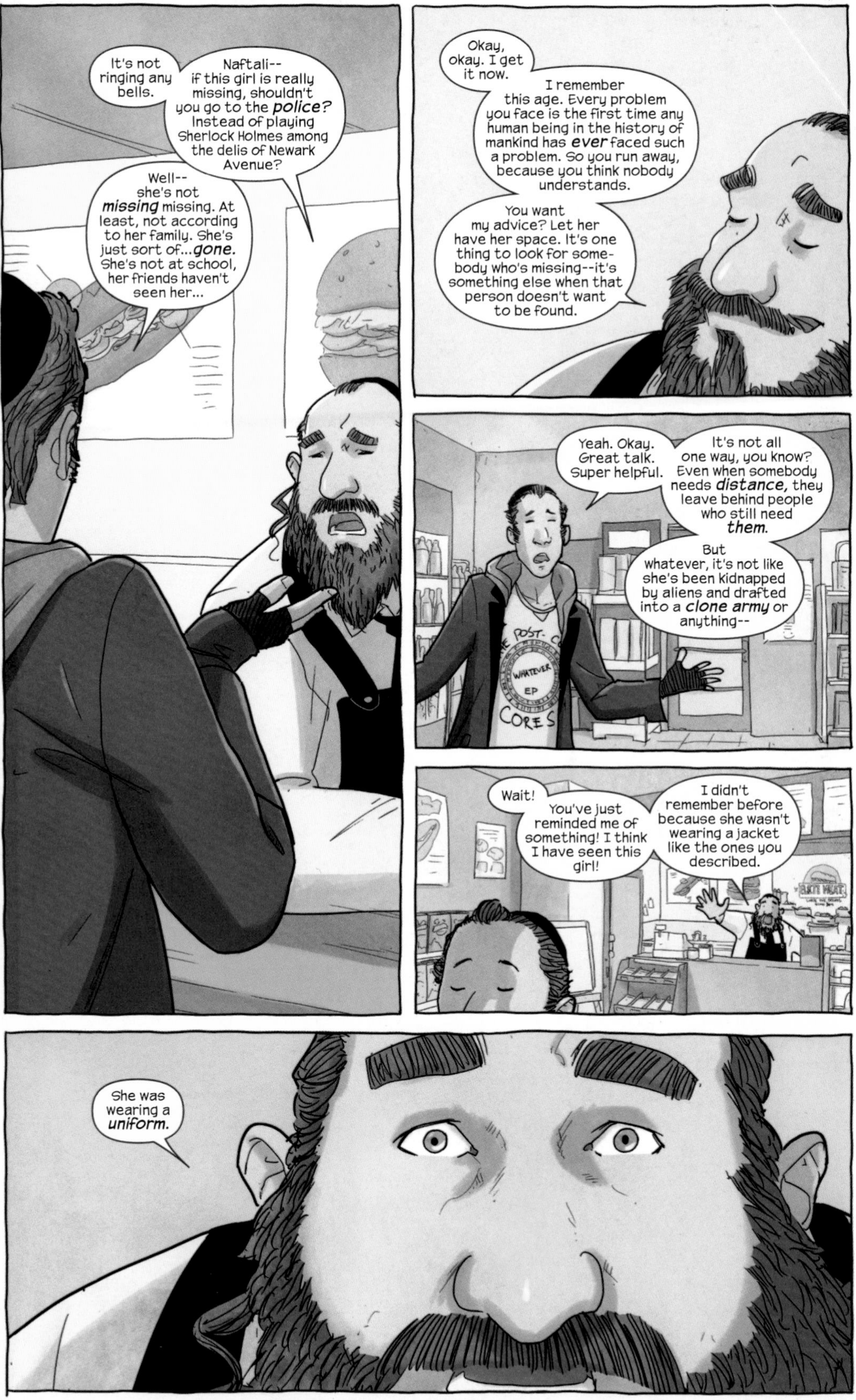
It's not ringing any bells.
Naftali-- if this girl is really missing, shouldn't you go to the police? Instead of playing Sherlock Holmes among the delis of Newark Avenue?
Well-- she's not missing missing. At least, not according to her family. She's just sort of...gone. She's not at school, her friends haven't seen her...
Okay, okay. I get it now.
I remember this age. Every problem you face is the first time any human being in the history of mankind has ever faced such a problem. So you run away, because you think nobody understands.
You want my advice? Let her have her space. It's one thing to look for somebody who's missing--it's something else when that person doesn't want to be found.
Yeah. Okay. Great talk. Super helpful.
It's not all one way, you know? Even when somebody needs distance, they leave behind people who still need them.
But whatever, it's not like she's been kidnapped by aliens and drafted into a clone army or anything--
THE POST-
WHATEVER
EP
CORES
Wait!
You've just reminded me of something! I think I have seen this girl!
I didn't remember before because she wasn't wearing a jacket like the ones you described.
She was wearing a uniform.

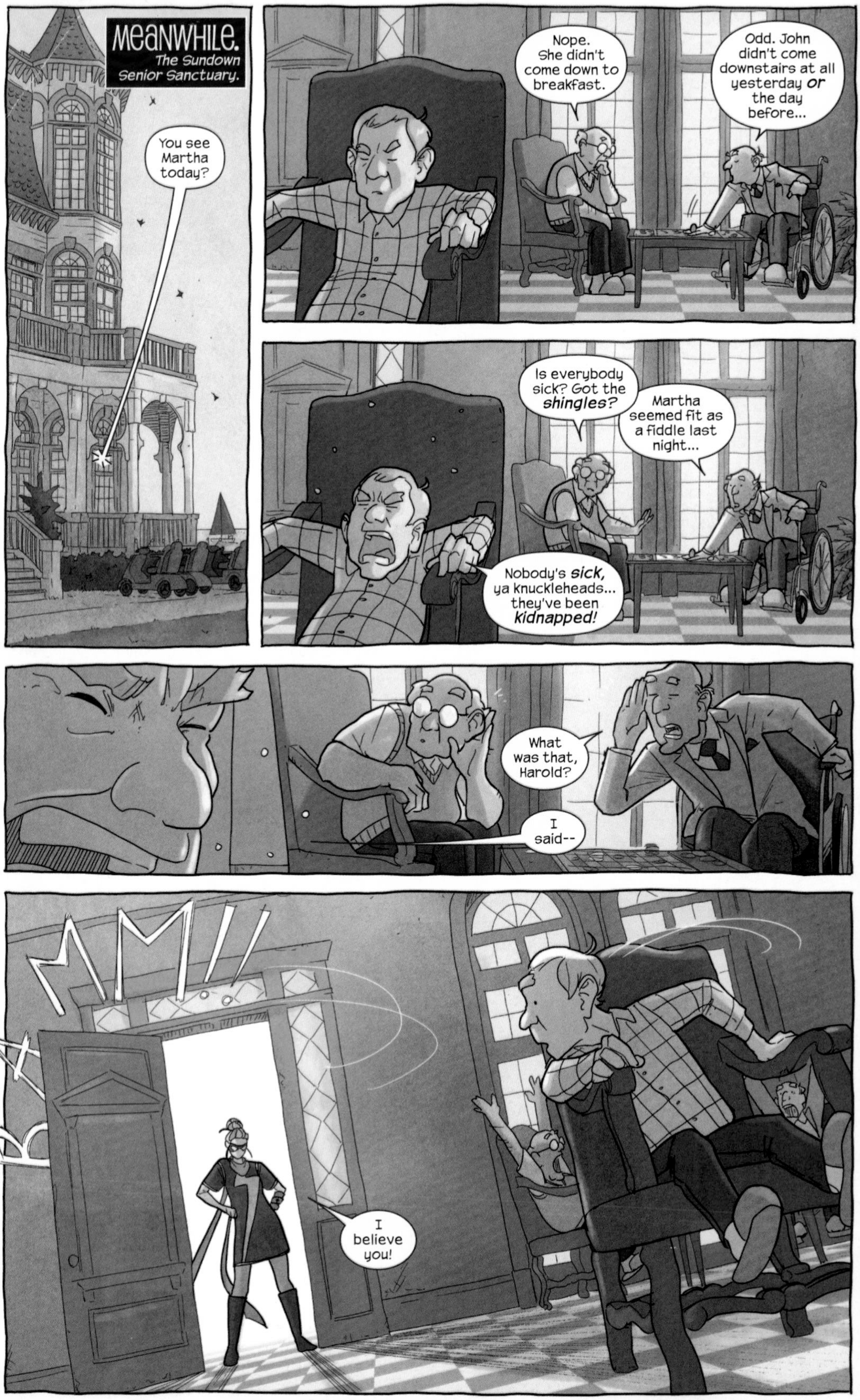

MEANWHILE.
The Sundown Senior Sanctuary.
You see Martha today?
Nope. She didn't come down to breakfast.
Odd. John didn't come downstairs at all yesterday *or* the day before...
Is everybody sick? Got the ***shingles?***
Martha seemed fit as a fiddle last night...
Nobody's ***sick,*** ya knuckleheads... they've been ***kidnapped!***
What was that, Harold?
I said--
BAMM!!
I believe you!

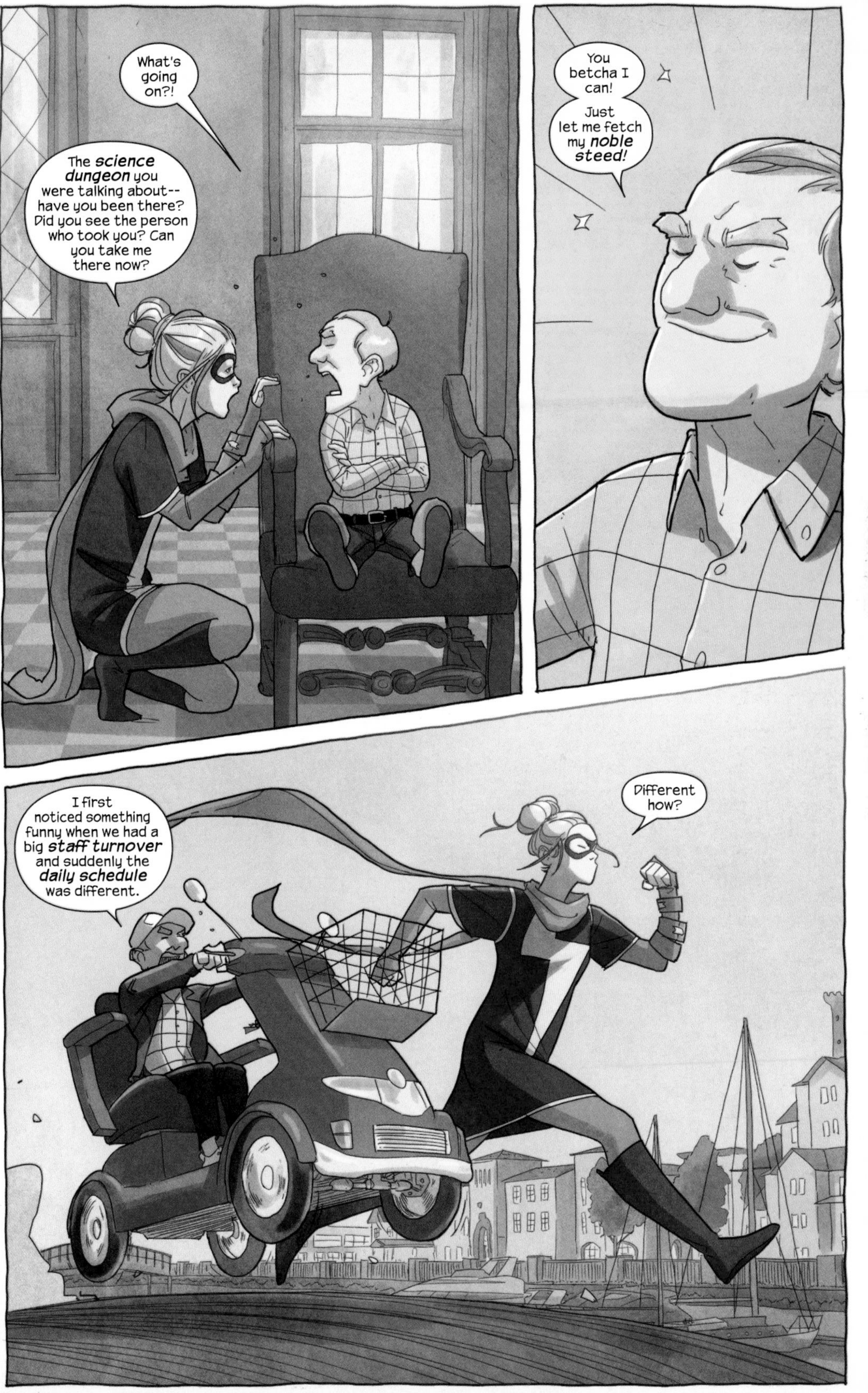

What's going on?!
The science dungeon you were talking about--have you been there? Did you see the person who took you? Can you take me there now?
You betcha I can!
Just let me fetch my noble steed!
I first noticed something funny when we had a big staff turnover and suddenly the daily schedule was different.
Different how?

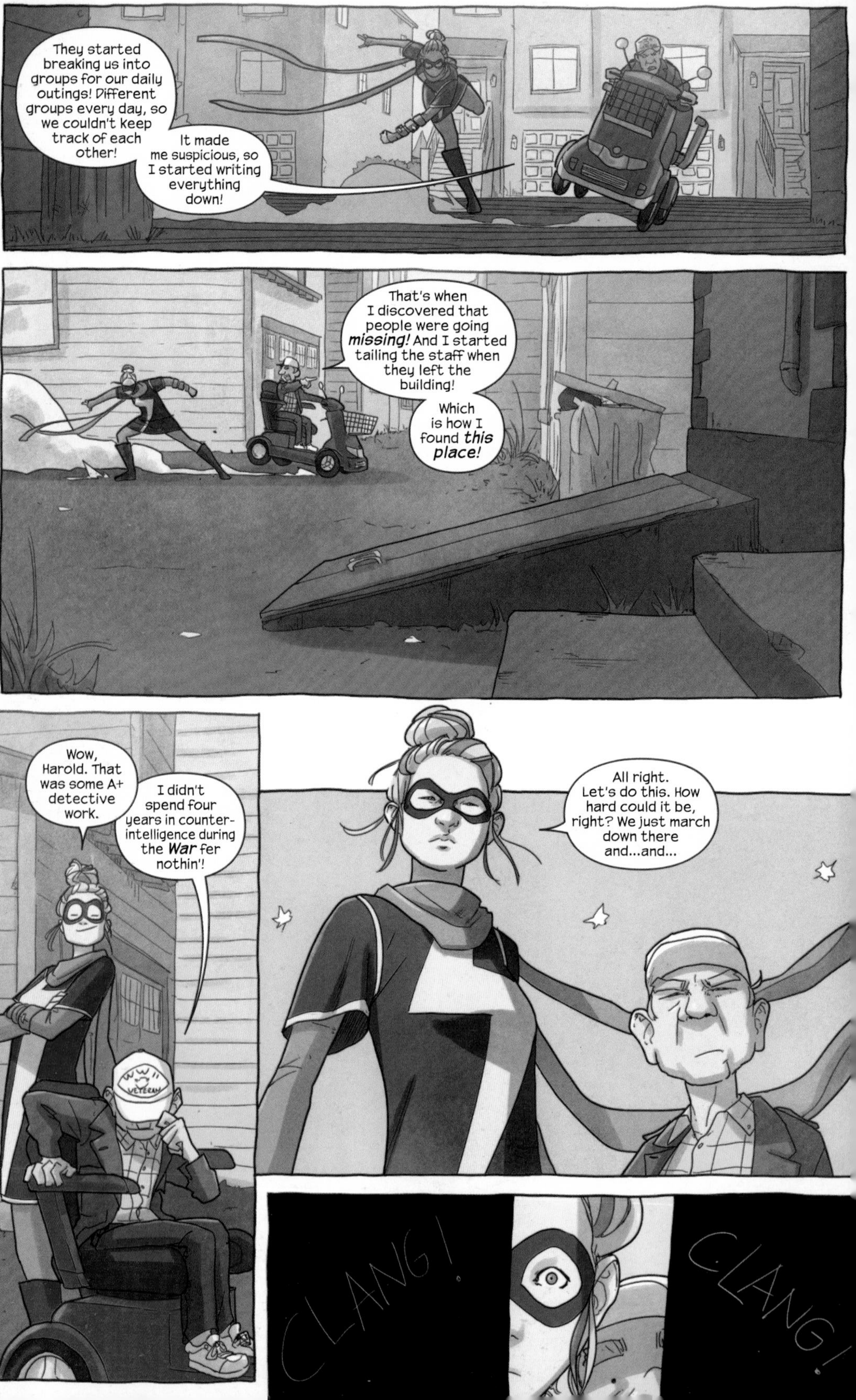
They started breaking us into groups for our daily outings! Different groups every day, so we couldn't keep track of each other!
It made me suspicious, so I started writing everything down!
That's when I discovered that people were going *missing!* And I started tailing the staff when they left the building!
Which is how I found *this place!*
Wow, Harold. That was some A+ detective work.
I didn't spend four years in counter-intelligence during the *War* fer nothin'!
All right. Let's do this. How hard could it be, right? We just march down there and...and...
CLANG!
CLANG!

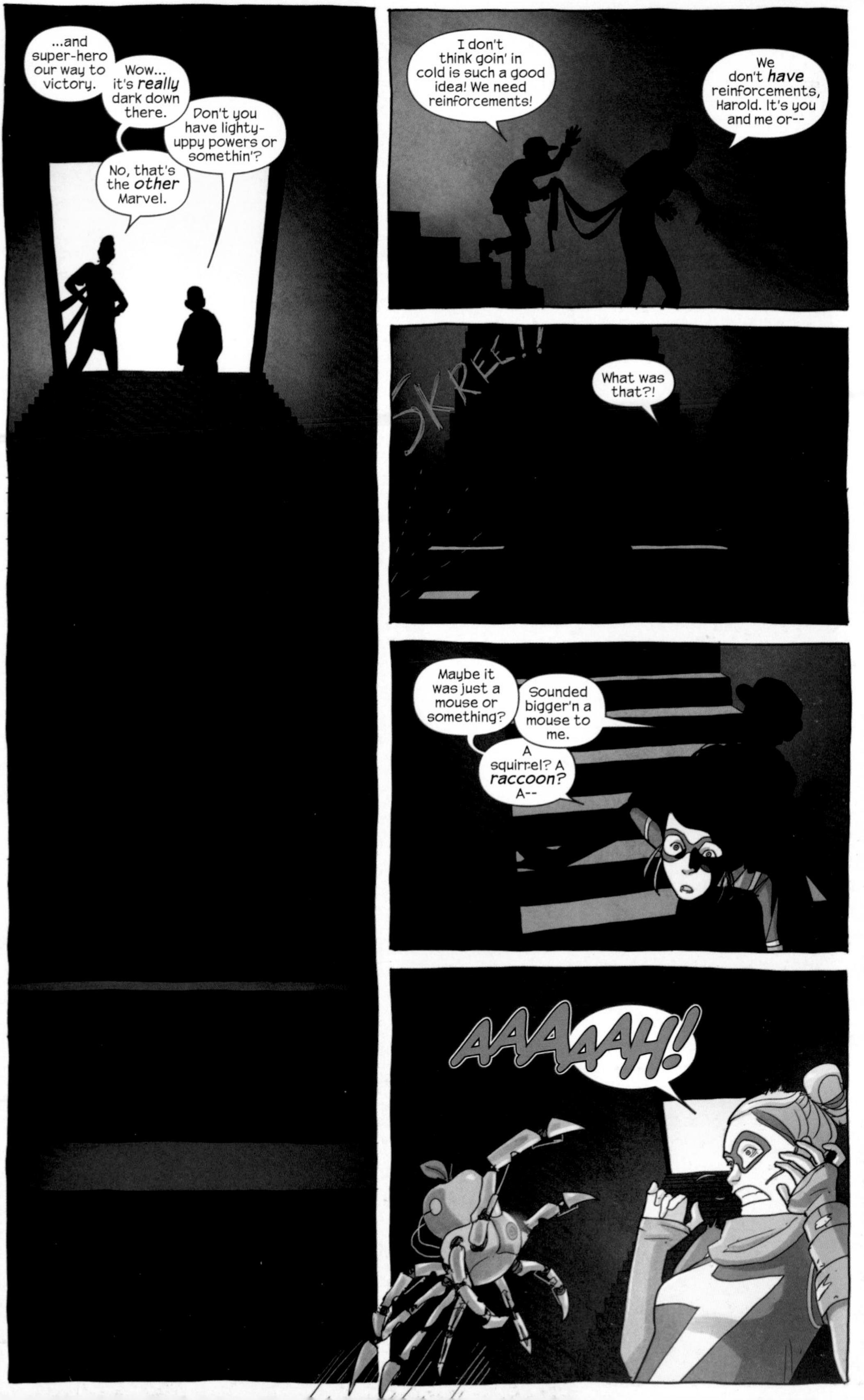

...and super-hero our way to victory.
Wow... it's *really* dark down there.
No, that's the *other* Marvel.
Don't you have lighty-uppy powers or somethin'?
I don't think goin' in cold is such a good idea! We need reinforcements!
We don't ***have*** reinforcements, Harold. It's you and me or--
SKREE!!
What was that?!
Maybe it was just a mouse or something?
A squirrel? A ***raccoon?*** A--
Sounded bigger'n a mouse to me.
AAAAAH!

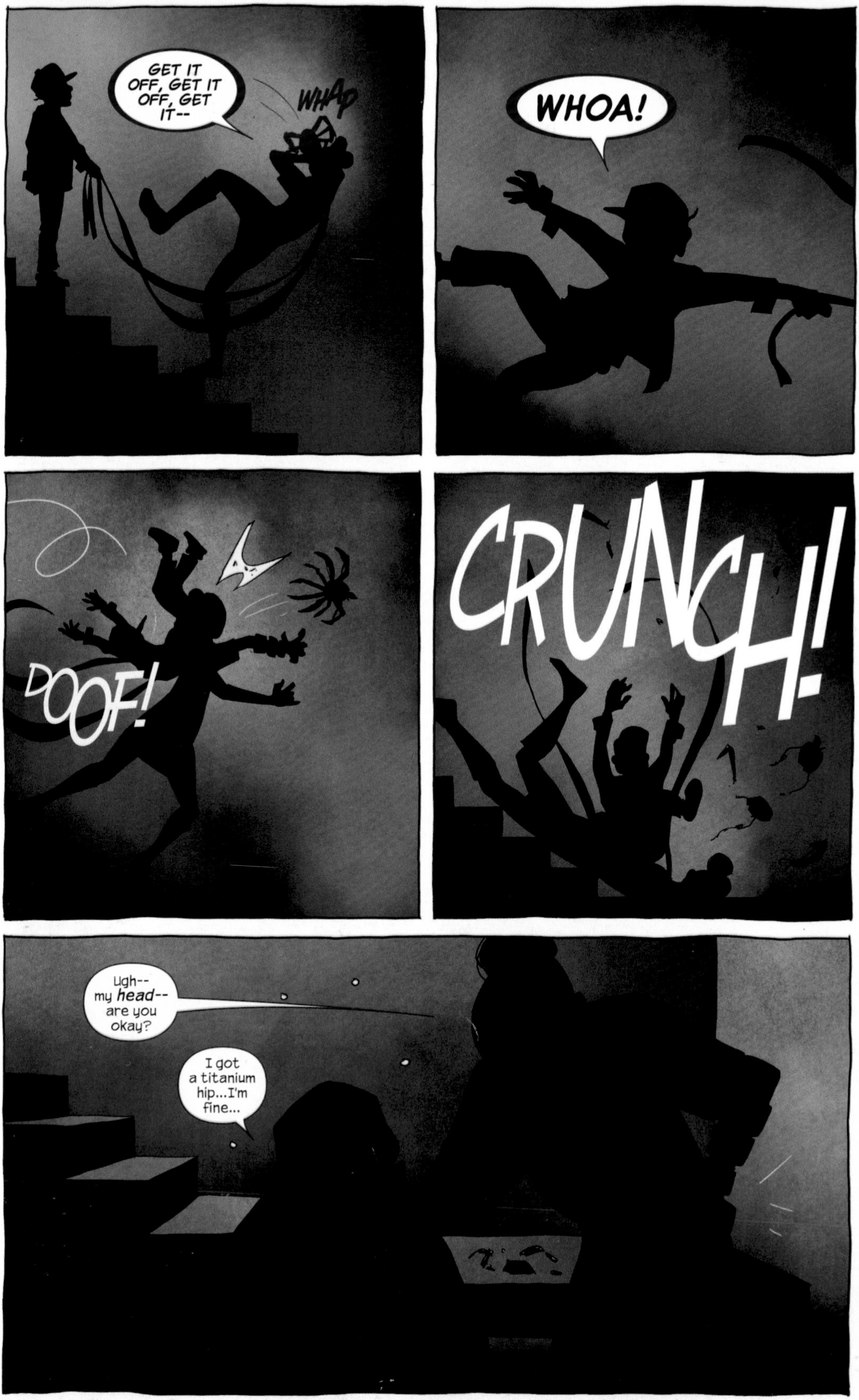
GET IT OFF, GET IT OFF, GET IT--
WHAP
WHOA!
DOOF!
CRUNCH!
Ugh-- my *head*-- are you okay?
I got a titanium hip...I'm fine...

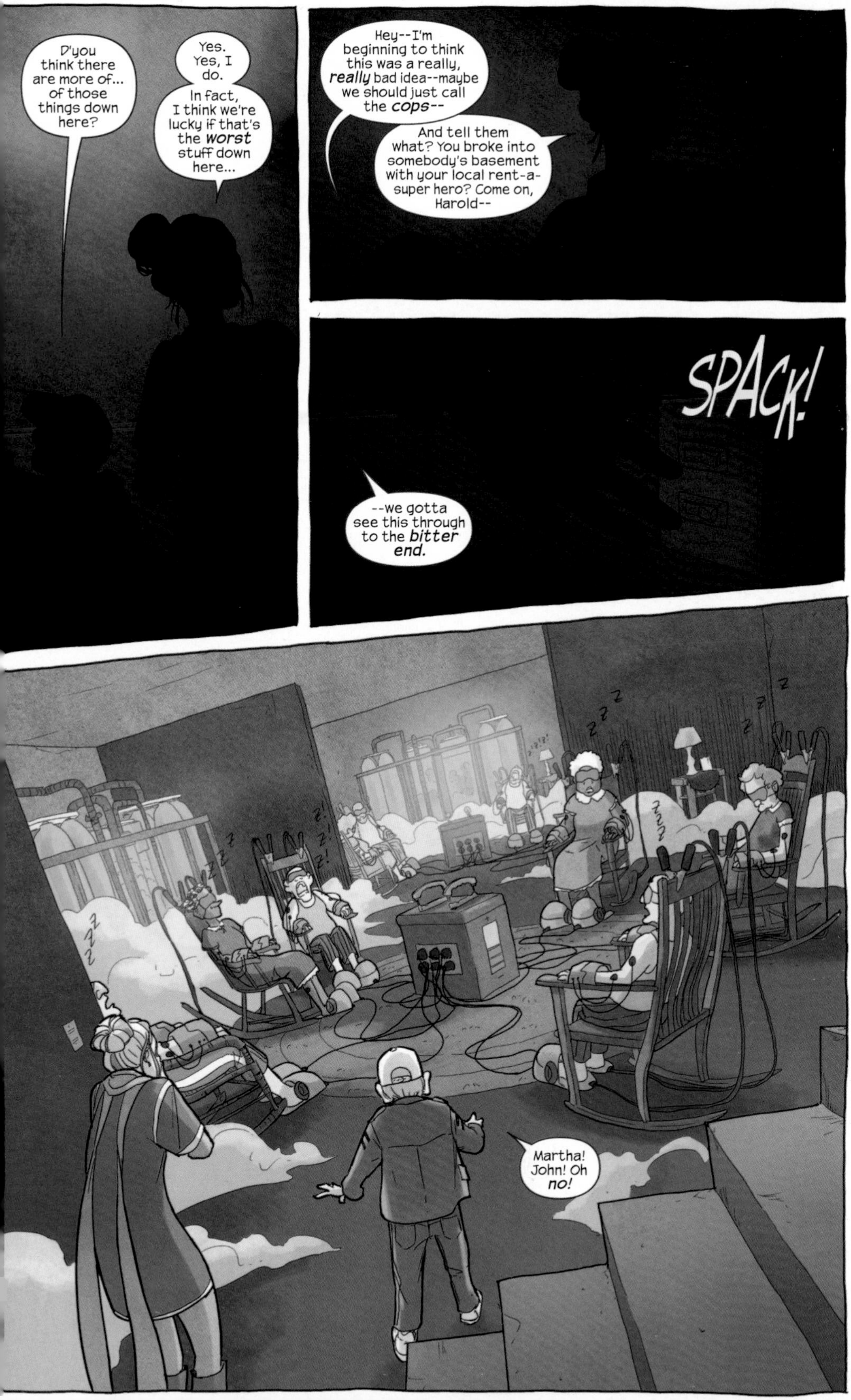
D'you think there are more of... of those things down here?
Yes. Yes, I do.
In fact, I think we're lucky if that's the worst stuff down here...
Hey--I'm beginning to think this was a really, really bad idea--maybe we should just call the cops--
And tell them what? You broke into somebody's basement with your local rent-a-super hero? Come on, Harold--
SPACK!
--we gotta see this through to the bitter end.
Martha! John! Oh no!

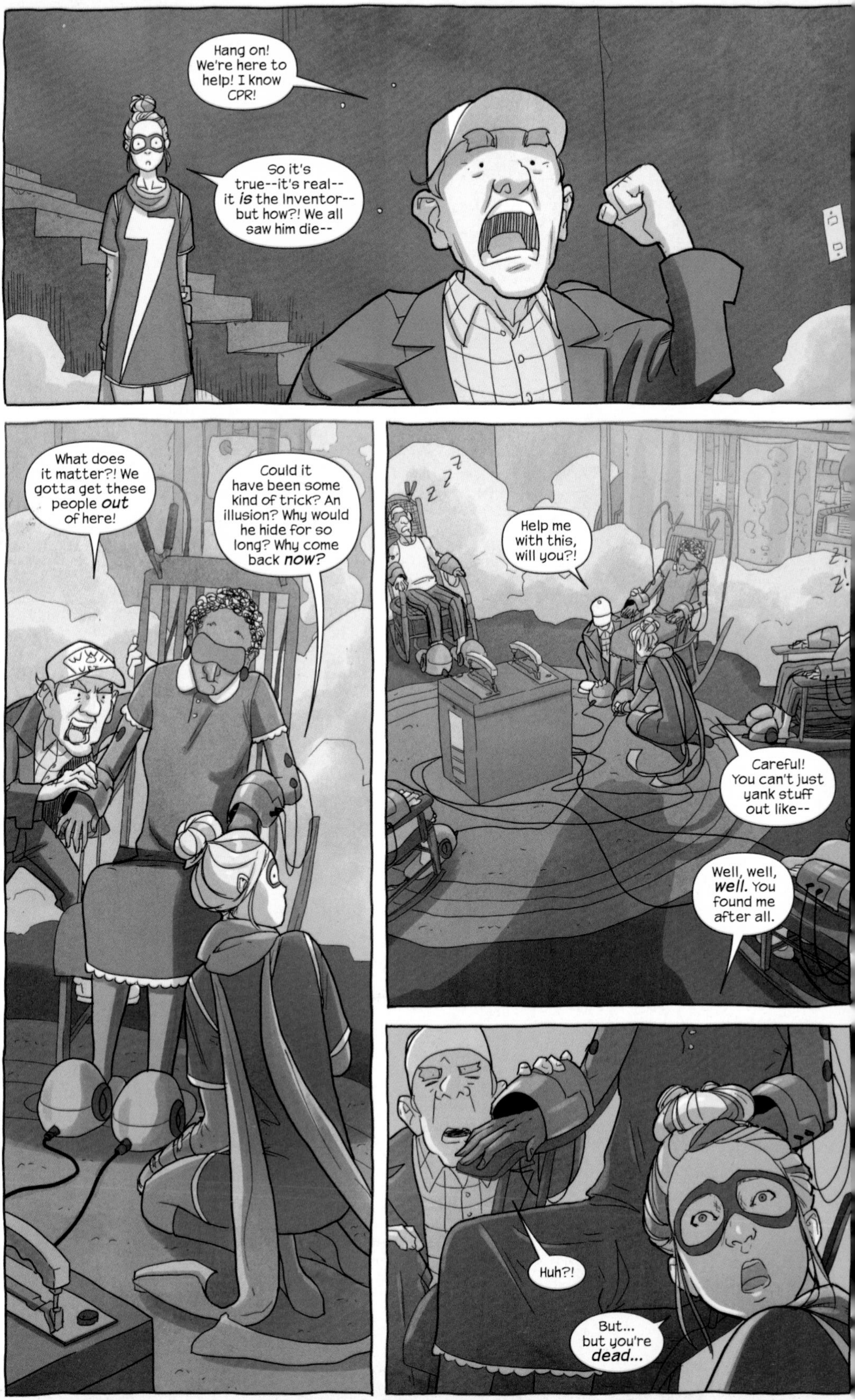
Hang on! We're here to help! I know CPR!
So it's true--it's real--it *is* the Inventor--but how?! We all saw him die--
What does it matter?! We gotta get these people **out** of here!
Could it have been some kind of trick? An illusion? Why would he hide for so long? Why come back **now?**
Help me with this, will you?!
Careful! You can't just yank stuff out like--
Well, well, **well.** You found me after all.
Huh?!
But... but you're ***dead...***

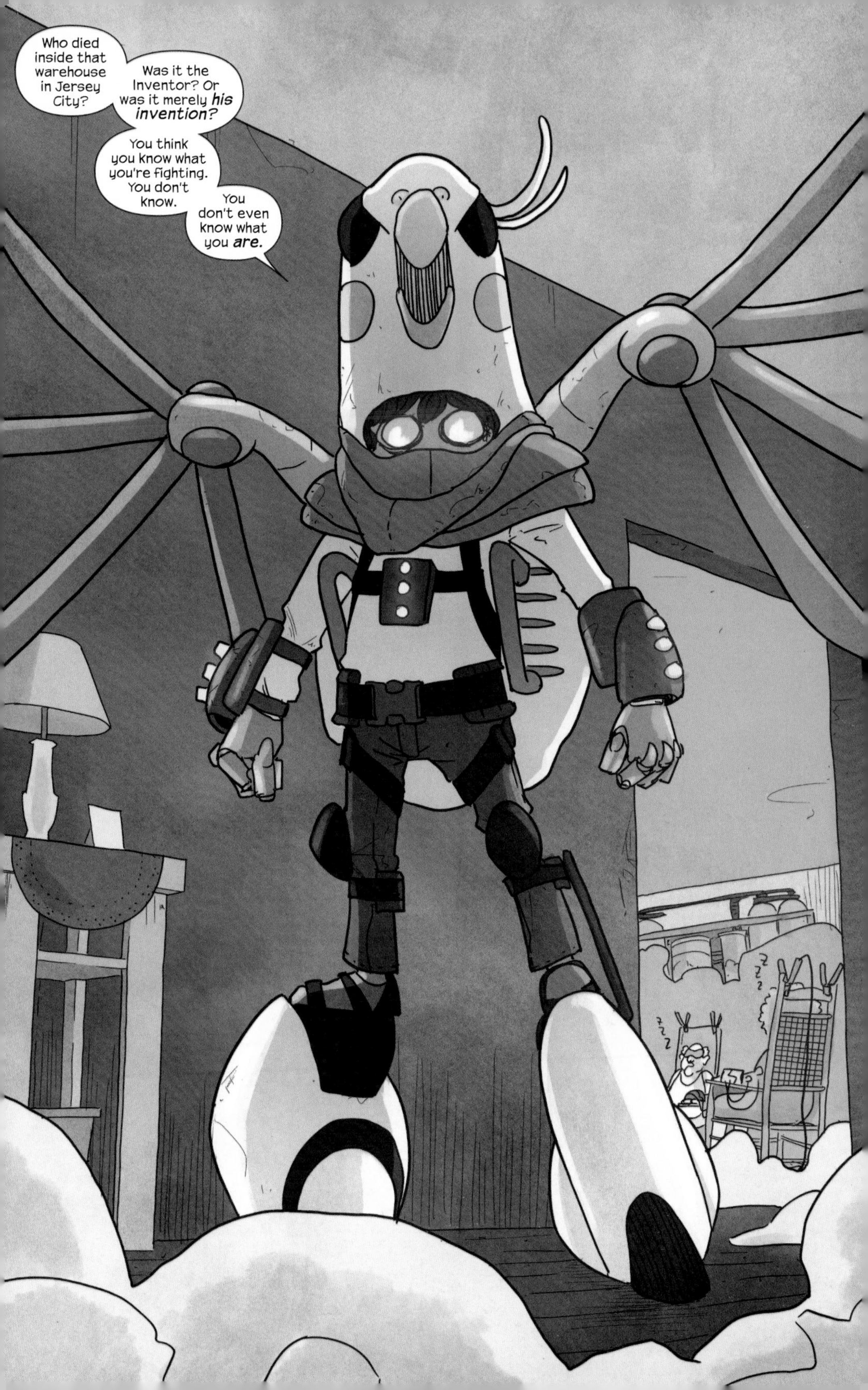
Who died inside that warehouse in Jersey City?
Was it the Inventor? Or was it merely *his invention?*
You think you know what you're fighting. You don't know.
You don't even know what you *are.*

Why isn't she answering her phone?!

You mean Kamala?

No! *Zoe!* She was absent from school, she didn't show up at the Circle Q for coffee like she always does, and now her phone goes straight to *voicemail.*

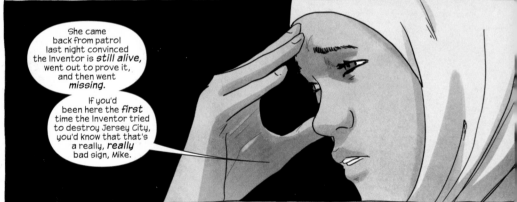

She came back from patrol last night convinced the Inventor is *still alive,* went out to prove it, and then went *missing.*

If you'd been here the *first* time the Inventor tried to destroy Jersey City, you'd know that that's a really, *really* bad sign, Mike.

We don't *know* she's been captured. She could be totally fine! Maybe after all the excitement last night, she decided to take a *mental health day*--

Then why isn't she answering her phone?!

She would *never* ghost me like that.

Something is *wrong.*

Okay, assuming that's *true,* what are the three of us supposed to do about it? We can't fight somebody like the Inventor alone!

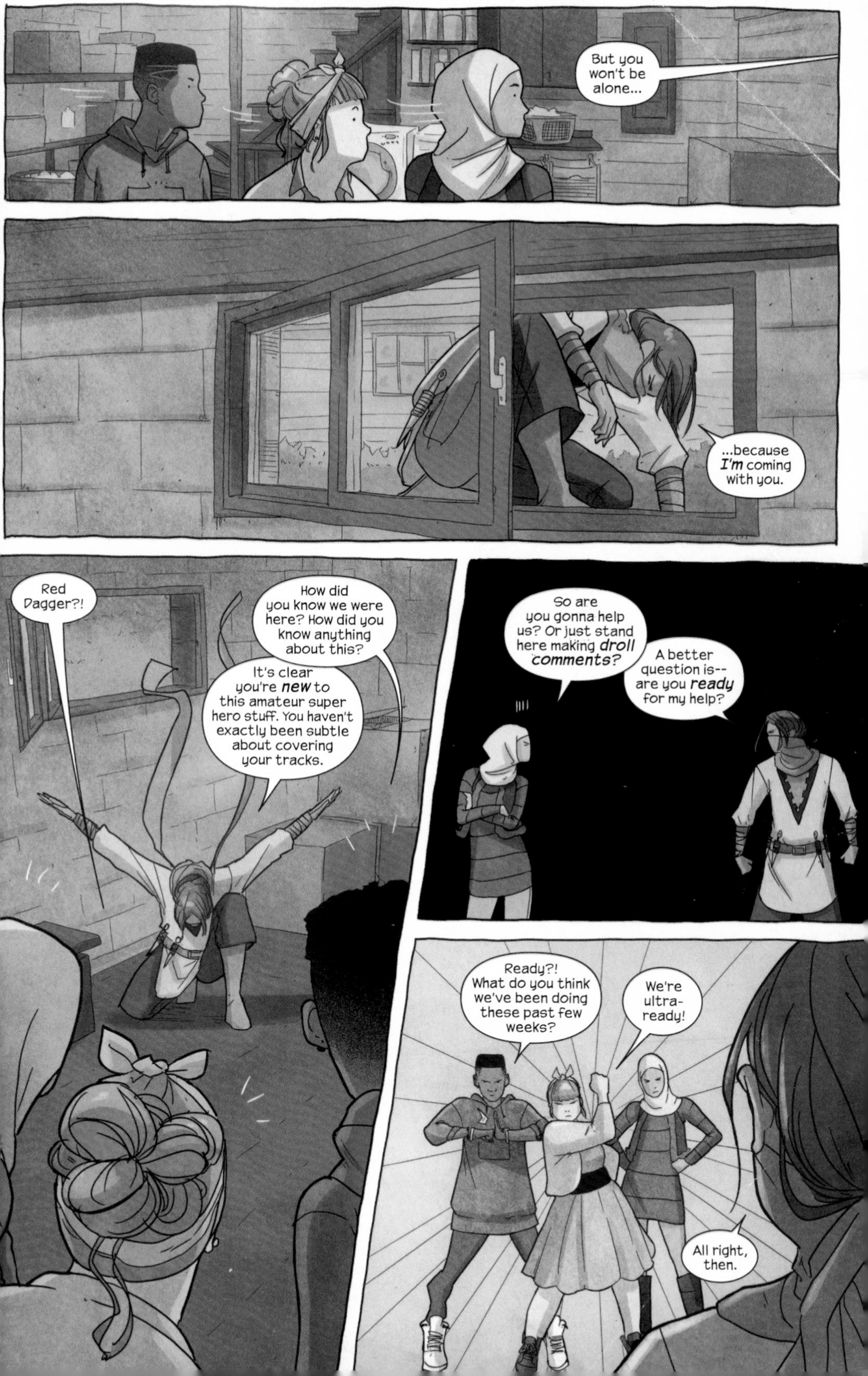
But you won't be alone...
...because *I'm* coming with you.
Red Dagger?!
How did you know we were here? How did you know anything about this?
It's clear you're *new* to this amateur super hero stuff. You haven't exactly been subtle about covering your tracks.
So are you gonna help us? Or just stand here making *droll comments?*
A better question is-- are you *ready* for my help?
Ready?! What do you think we've been doing these past few weeks?
We're ultra-ready!
All right, then.

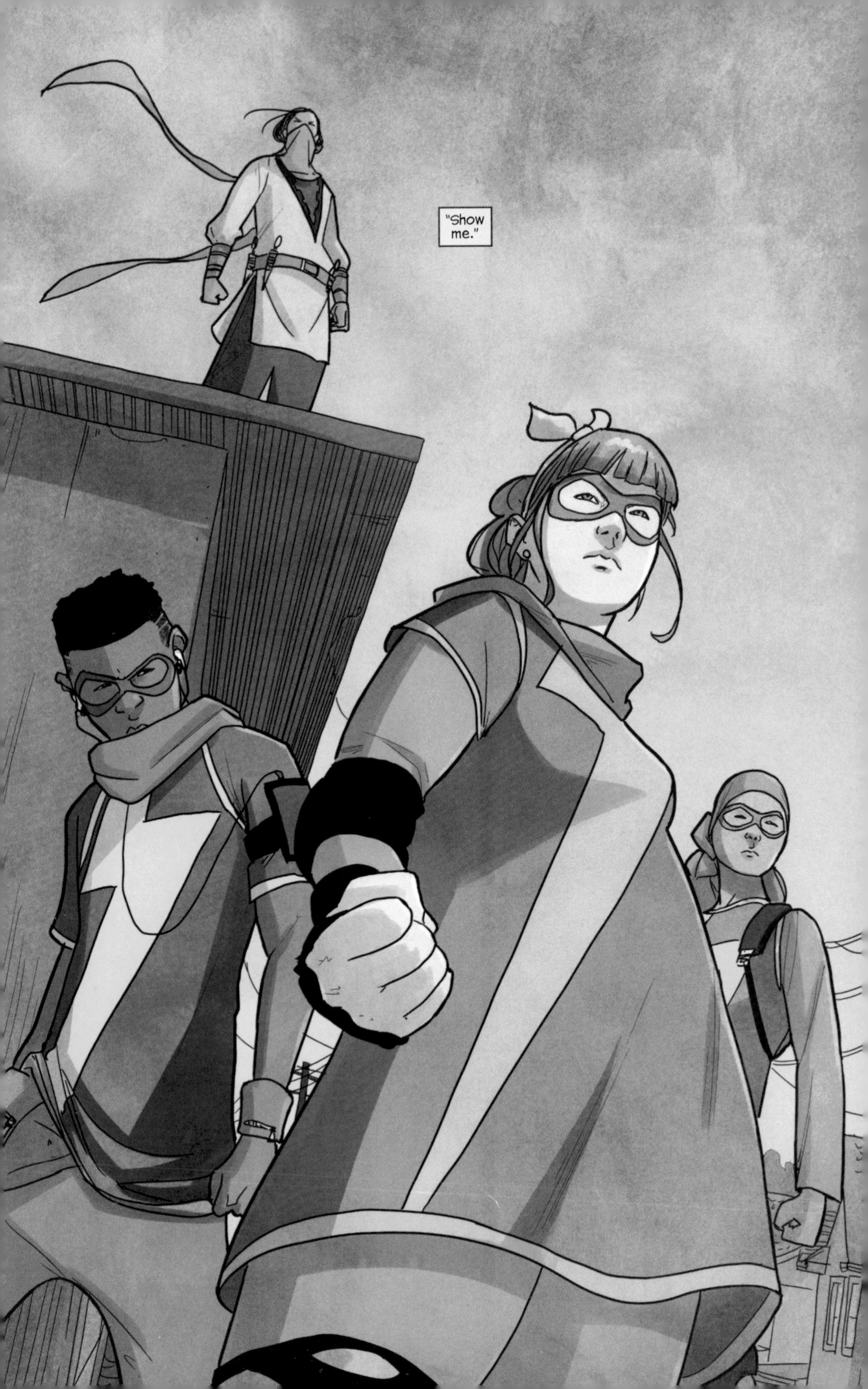
"Show me."

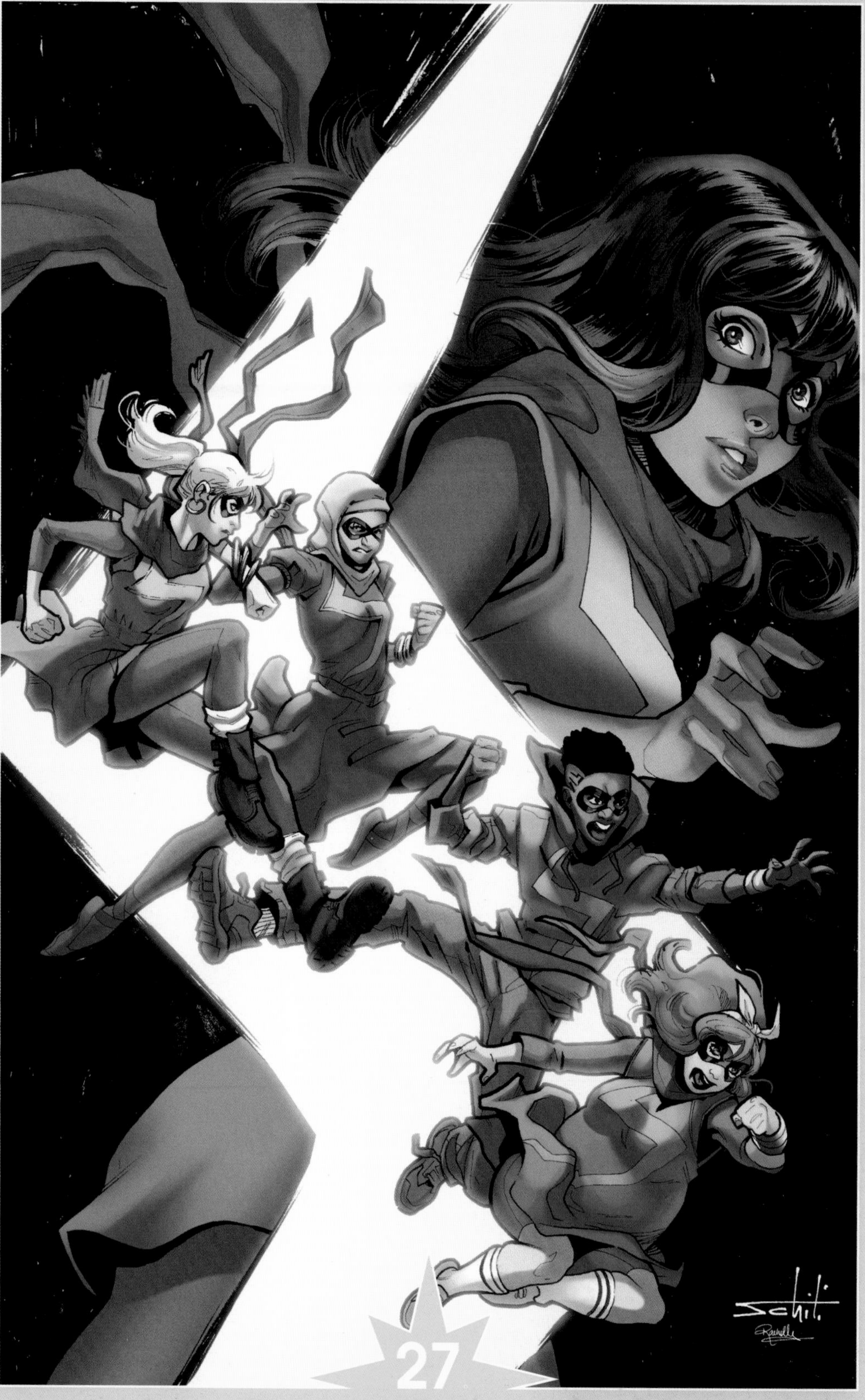
27

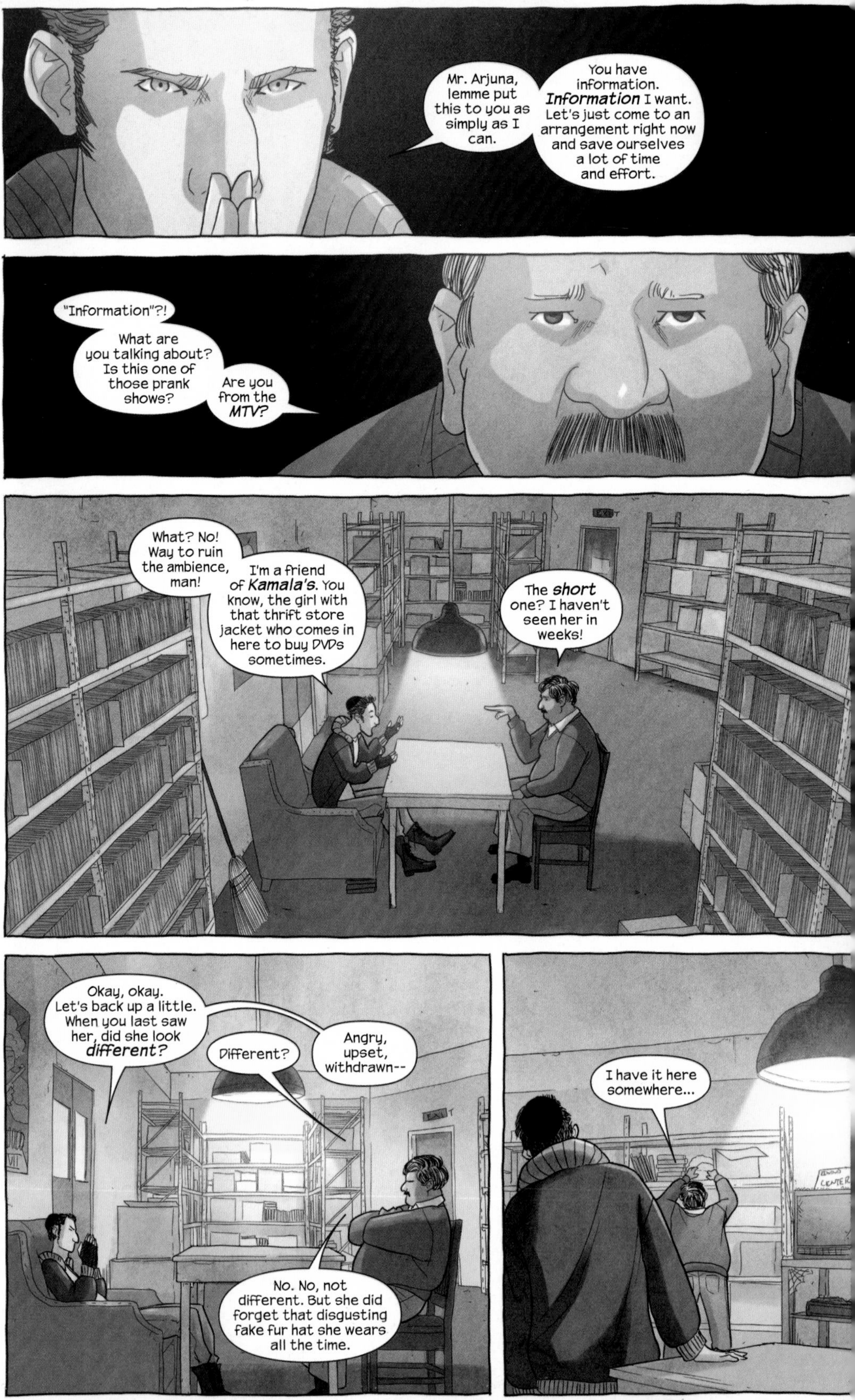
Mr. Arjuna, lemme put this to you as simply as I can.
You have information. *Information* I want. Let's just come to an arrangement right now and save ourselves a lot of time and effort.
"Information"?!
What are you talking about? Is this one of those prank shows?
Are you from the *MTV?*
What? No! Way to ruin the ambience, man!
I'm a friend of *Kamala's*. You know, the girl with that thrift store jacket who comes in here to buy DVDs sometimes.
The *short* one? I haven't seen her in weeks!
Okay, okay. Let's back up a little. When you last saw her, did she look *different?*
Different?
Angry, upset, withdrawn--
No. No, not different. But she did forget that disgusting fake fur hat she wears all the time.
I have it here somewhere...

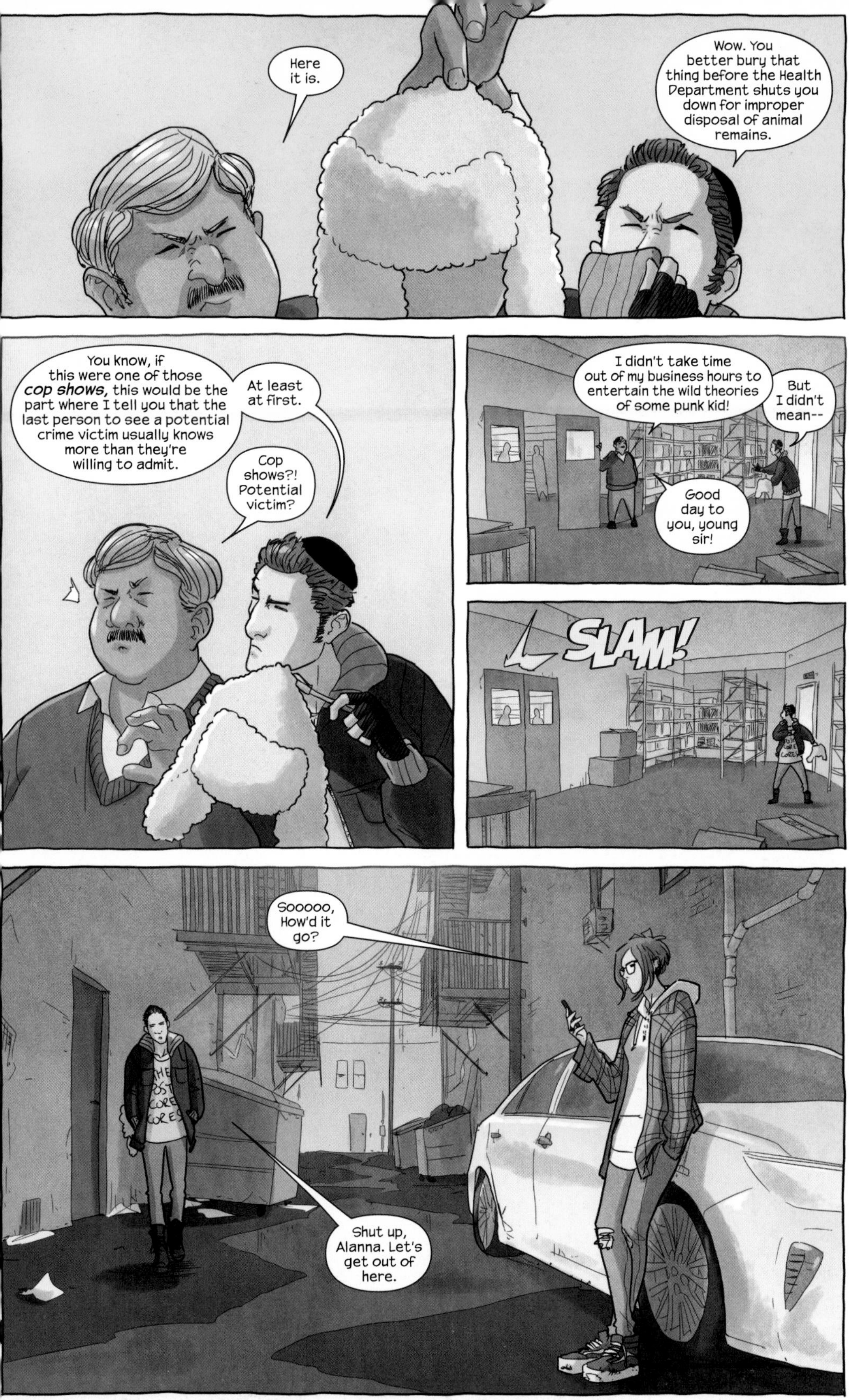
Here it is.
Wow. You better bury that thing before the Health Department shuts you down for improper disposal of animal remains.
You know, if this were one of those *cop shows,* this would be the part where I tell you that the last person to see a potential crime victim usually knows more than they're willing to admit.
At least at first.
Cop shows?! Potential victim?
I didn't take time out of my business hours to entertain the wild theories of some punk kid!
But I didn't mean--
Good day to you, young sir!
SLAM!
Sooooo, How'd it go?
Shut up, Alanna. Let's get out of here.

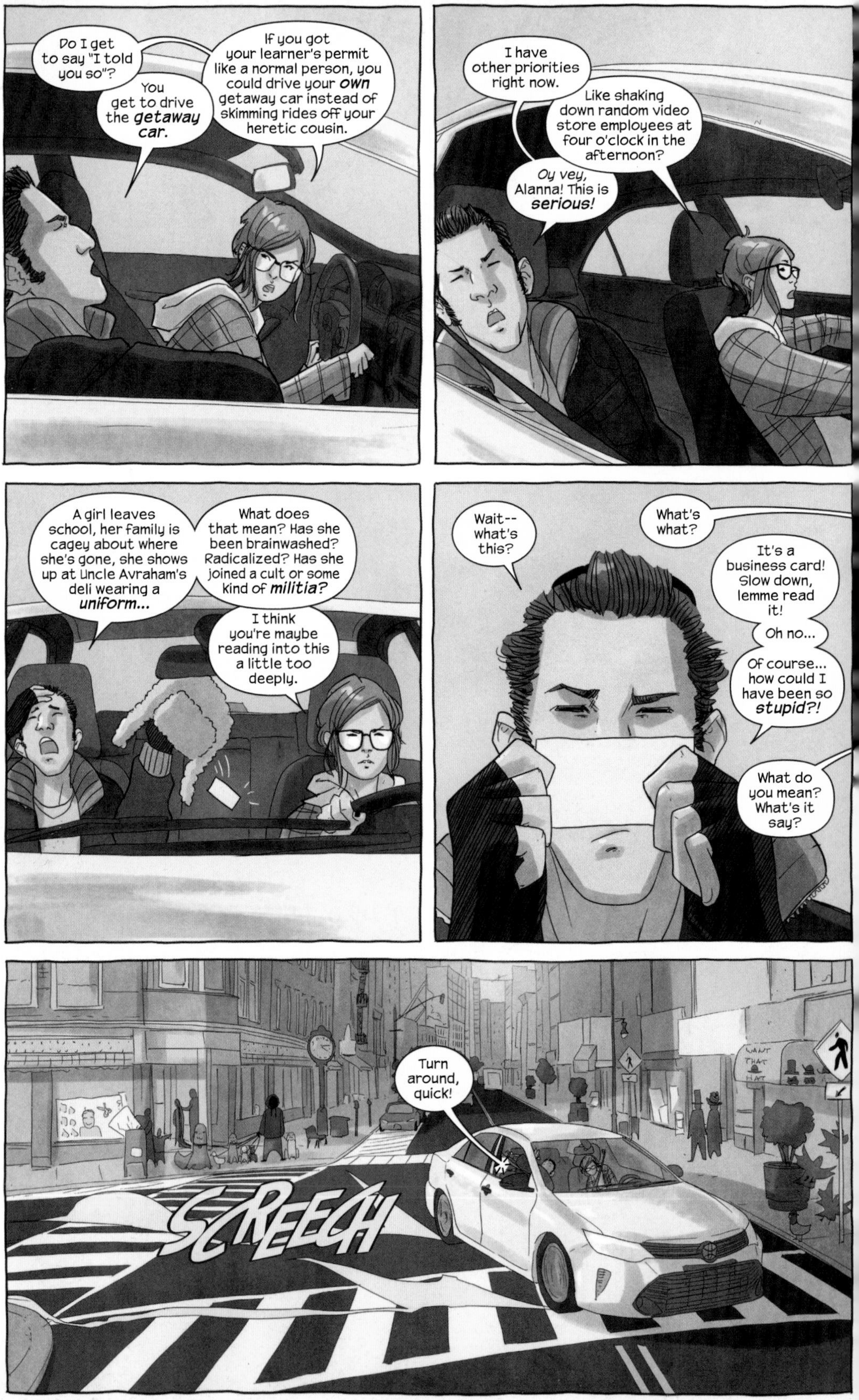
Do I get to say "I told you so"?
You get to drive the *getaway car.*
If you got your learner's permit like a normal person, you could drive your *own* getaway car instead of skimming rides off your heretic cousin.
I have other priorities right now.
Like shaking down random video store employees at four o'clock in the afternoon?
Oy vey, Alanna! This is *serious!*
A girl leaves school, her family is cagey about where she's gone, she shows up at Uncle Avraham's deli wearing a *uniform...*
What does that mean? Has she been brainwashed? Radicalized? Has she joined a cult or some kind of *militia?*
I think you're maybe reading into this a little too deeply.
Wait--what's this?
What's what?
It's a business card! Slow down, lemme read it!
Oh no...
Of course... how could I have been so *stupid?!*
What do you mean? What's it say?
Turn around, quick!
SCREECH

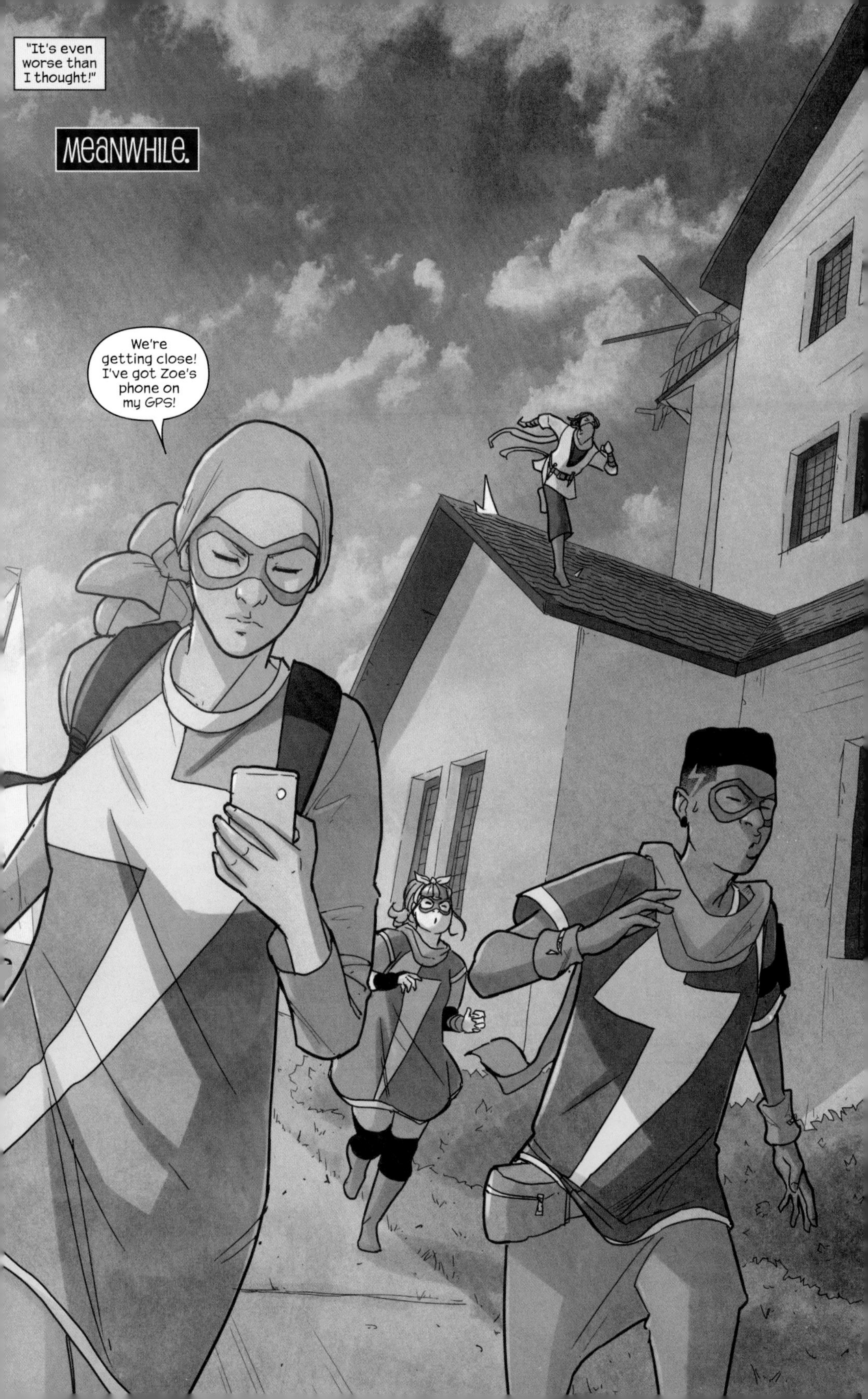
"It's even worse than I thought!"
MEANWHILE.
We're getting close! I've got Zoe's phone on my GPS!

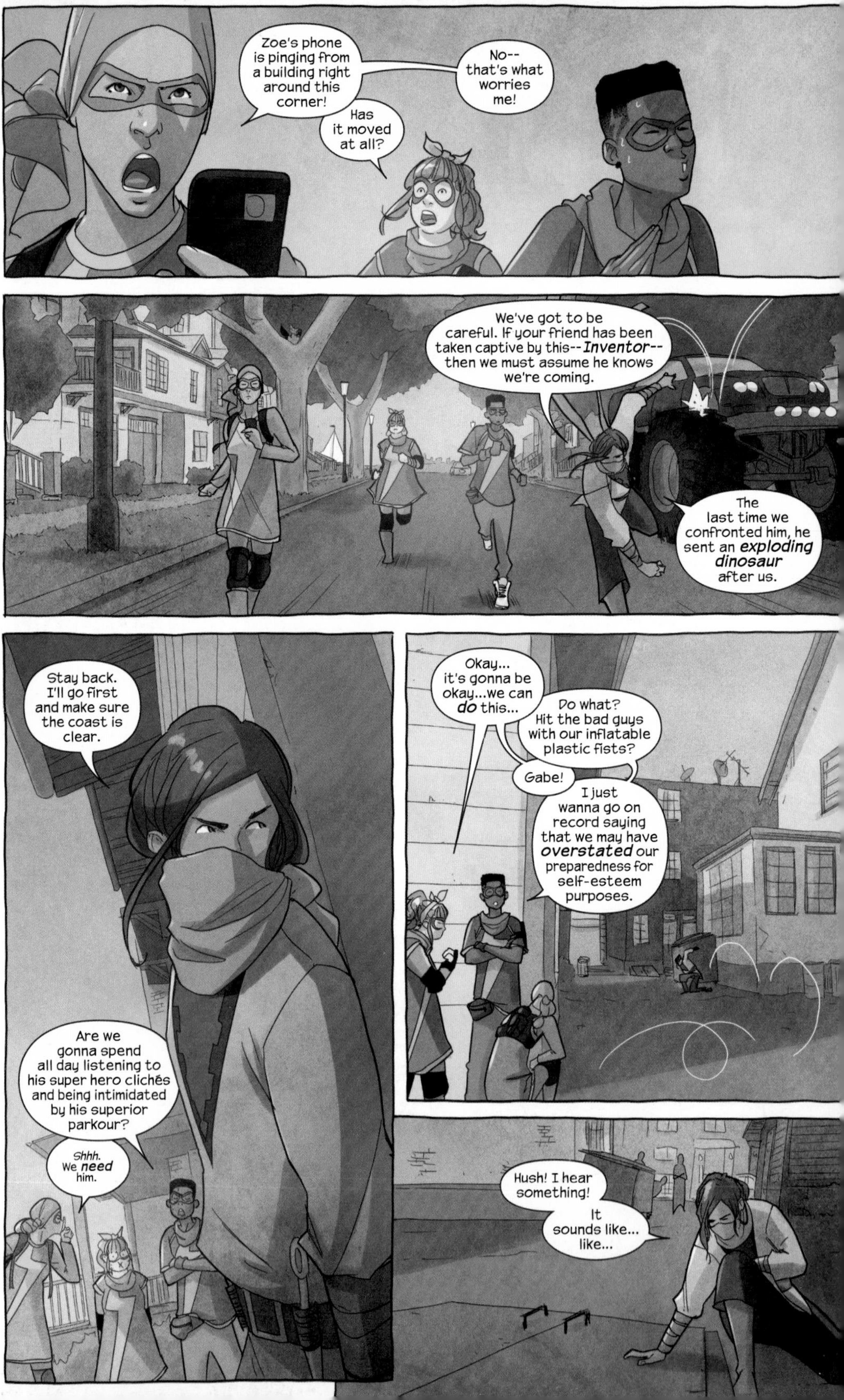
Zoe's phone is pinging from a building right around this corner!
Has it moved at all?
No-- that's what worries me!
We've got to be careful. If your friend has been taken captive by this--Inventor-- then we must assume he knows we're coming.
The last time we confronted him, he sent an exploding dinosaur after us.
Stay back. I'll go first and make sure the coast is clear.
Are we gonna spend all day listening to his super hero clichés and being intimidated by his superior parkour?
Shhh. We need him.
Okay... it's gonna be okay...we can do this...
Do what? Hit the bad guys with our inflatable plastic fists?
Gabe!
I just wanna go on record saying that we may have overstated our preparedness for self-esteem purposes.
Hush! I hear something!
It sounds like... like...

WHMMMMMMMMMM

Harold... I have a *confession* to make.

Eh?

I'm *not* the real Ms. Marvel. I'm a *fraud.* A poser. And I don't think I can get us out of here in one piece.

I'm *sorry.*

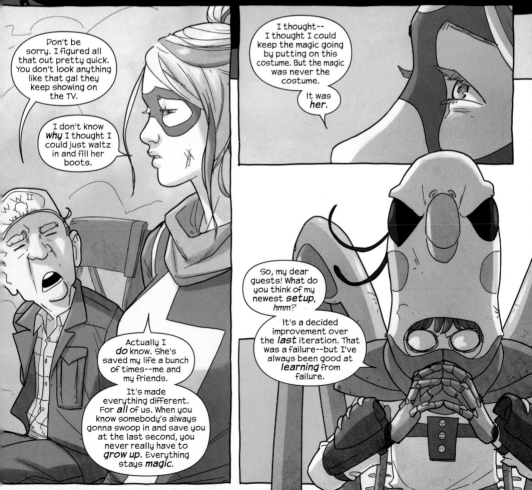

Don't be sorry. I figured all that out pretty quick. You don't look anything like that gal they keep showing on the TV.

I don't know *why* I thought I could just waltz in and fill her boots.

I thought-- I thought I could keep the magic going by putting on this costume. But the magic was never the costume.

It was *her.*

Actually I *do* know. She's saved my life a bunch of times--me and my friends.

It's made everything different. For *all* of us. When you know somebody's always gonna swoop in and save you at the last second, you never really have to *grow up.* Everything stays *magic.*

So, my dear guests! What do you think of my newest *setup,* hmm?

It's a decided improvement over the *last* iteration. That was a failure--but I've always been good at *learning* from failure.

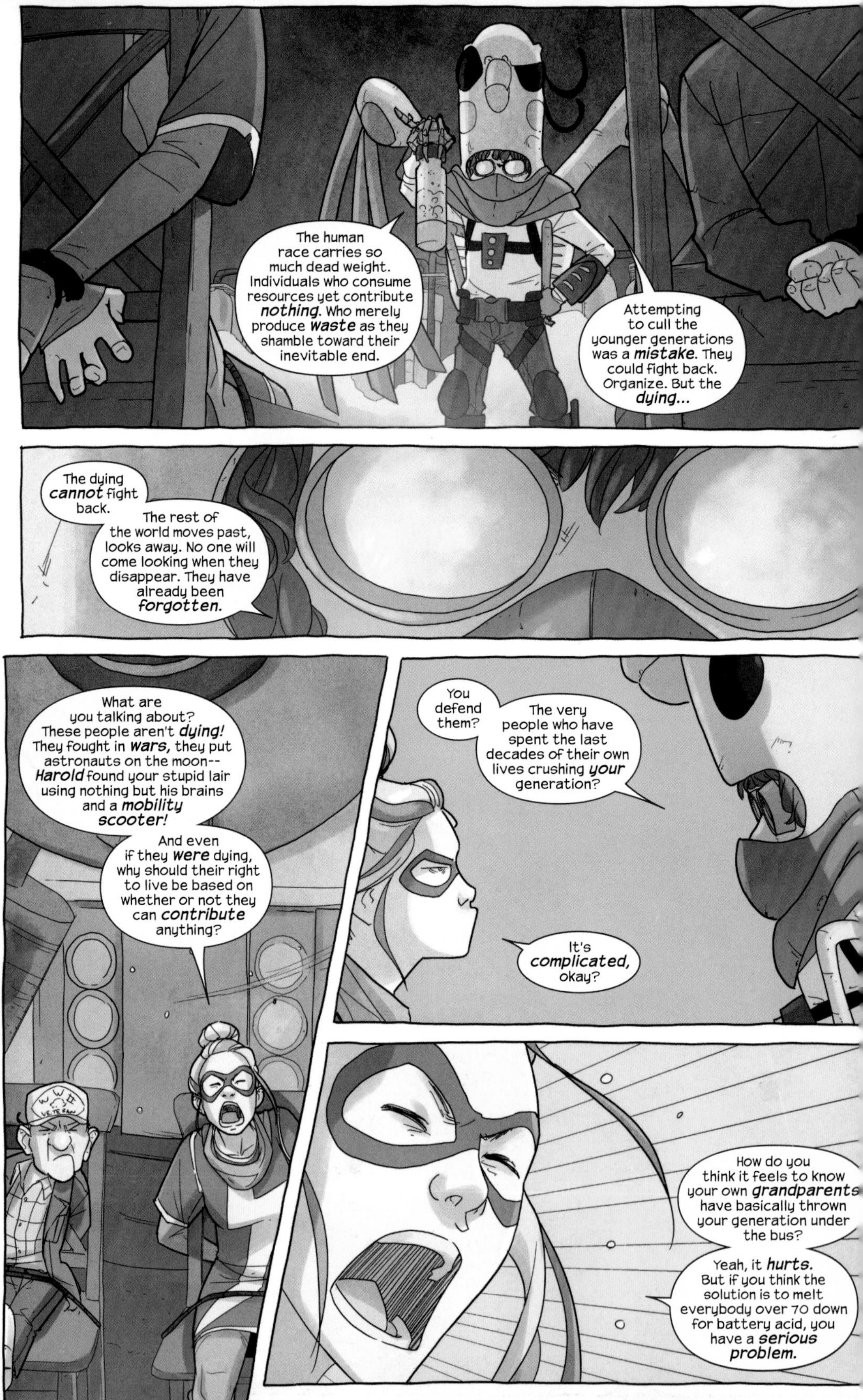
The human race carries so much dead weight. Individuals who consume resources yet contribute nothing. Who merely produce waste as they shamble toward their inevitable end.
Attempting to cull the younger generations was a mistake. They could fight back. Organize. But the dying...
The dying cannot fight back.
The rest of the world moves past, looks away. No one will come looking when they disappear. They have already been forgotten.
What are you talking about? These people aren't dying! They fought in wars, they put astronauts on the moon-- Harold found your stupid lair using nothing but his brains and a mobility scooter!
And even if they were dying, why should their right to live be based on whether or not they can contribute anything?
You defend them?
The very people who have spent the last decades of their own lives crushing your generation?
It's complicated, okay?
How do you think it feels to know your own grandparents have basically thrown your generation under the bus?
Yeah, it hurts. But if you think the solution is to melt everybody over 70 down for battery acid, you have a serious problem.

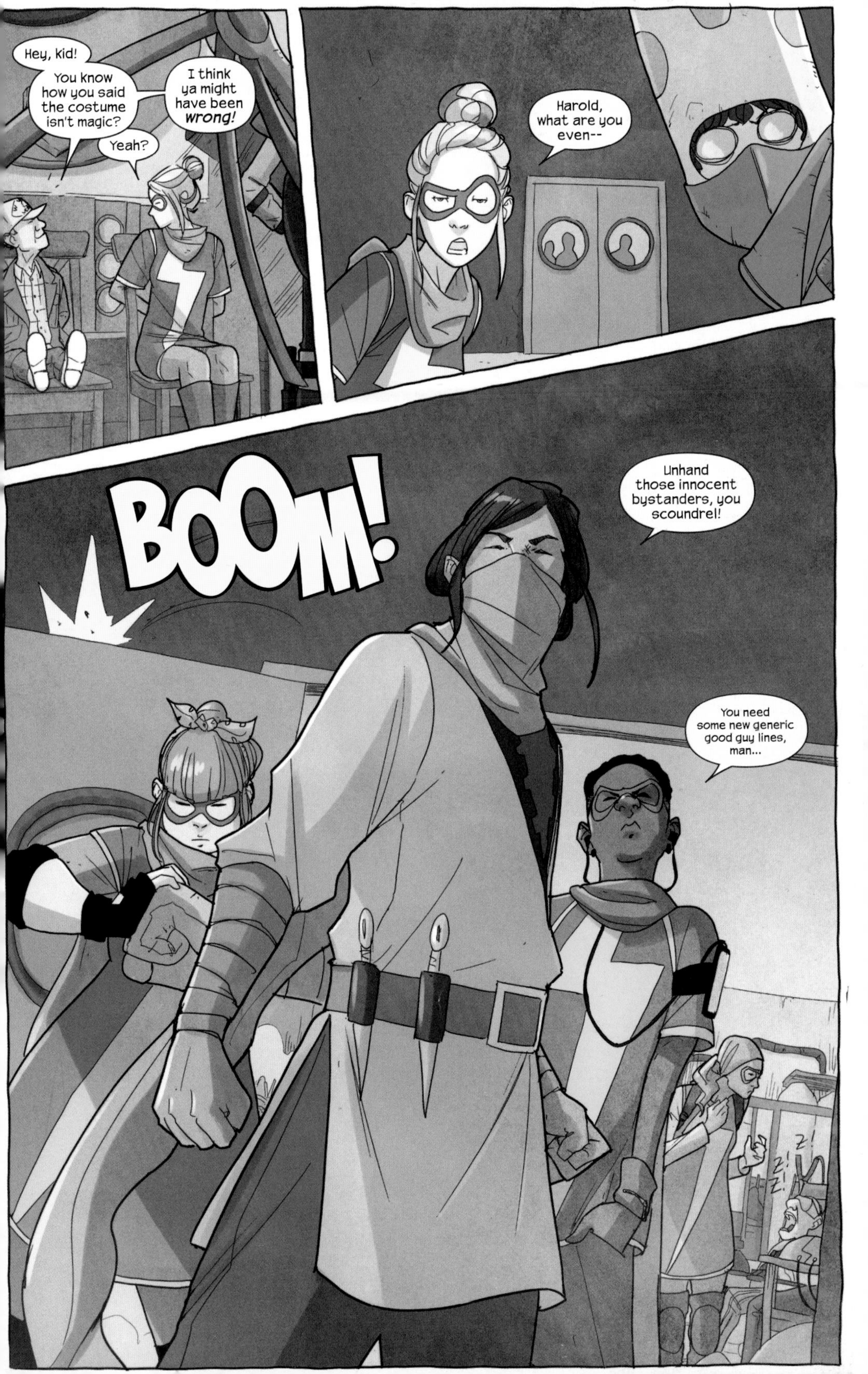
Hey, kid!
You know how you said the costume isn't magic?
Yeah?
I think ya might have been *wrong!*
Harold, what are you even--
BOOM!
Unhand those innocent bystanders, you scoundrel!
You need some new generic good guy lines, man...

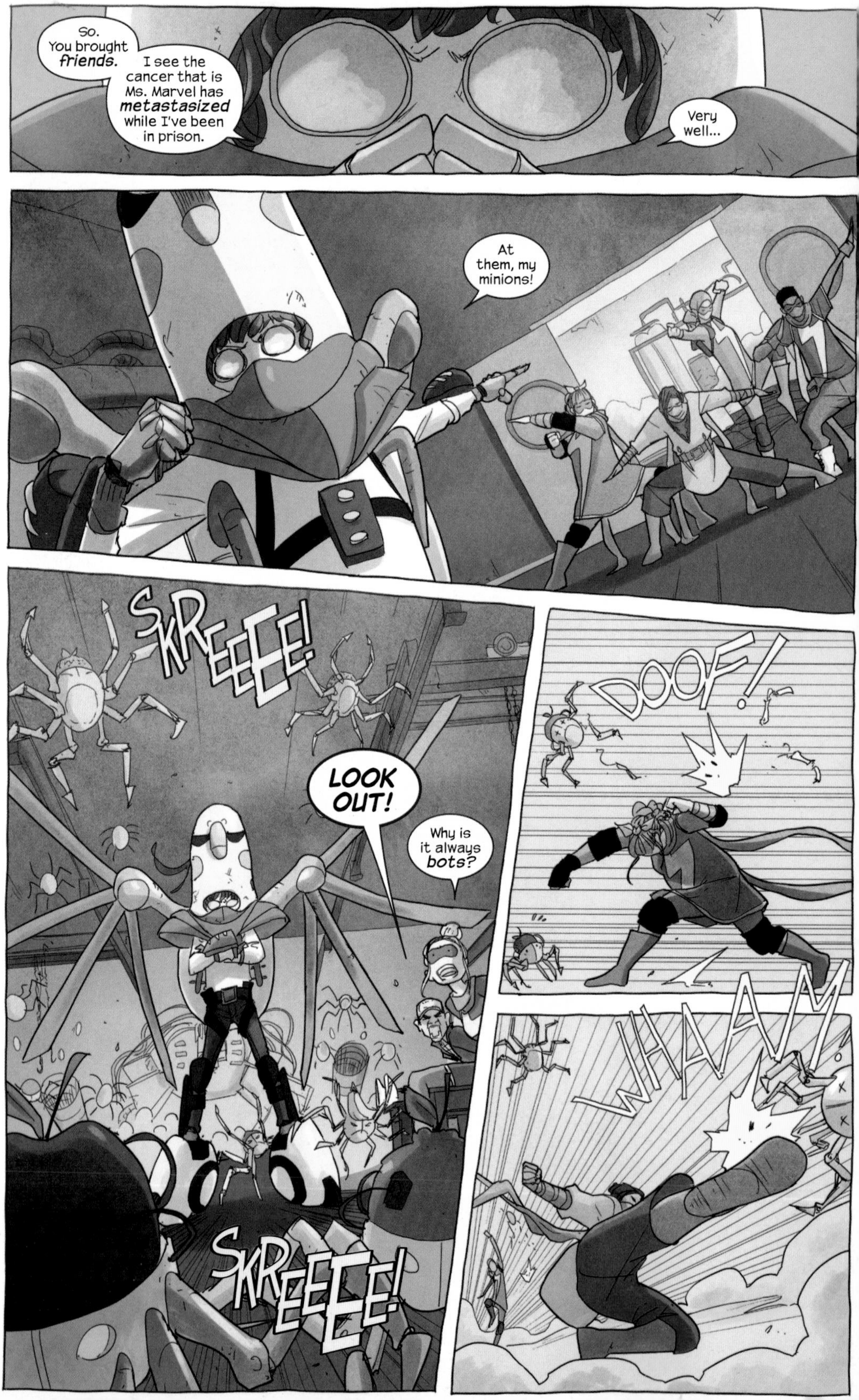
So. You brought *friends.*
I see the cancer that is Ms. Marvel has ***metastasized*** while I've been in prison.
Very well...
At them, my minions!
SKREEEEE!
LOOK OUT!
Why is it always *bots?*
DOOF!
WHAAAM!
SKREEEEE!

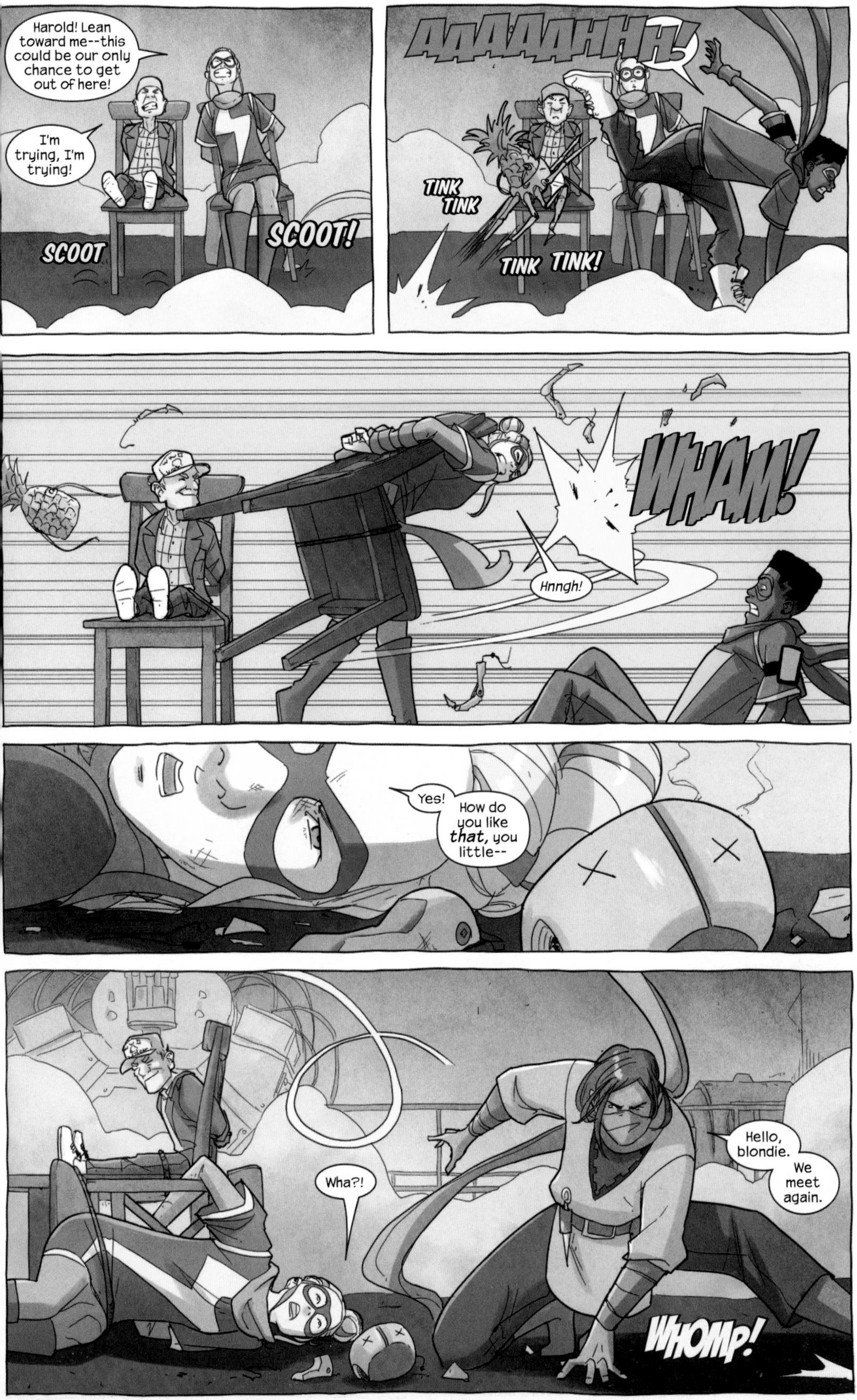
Harold! Lean toward me--this could be our only chance to get out of here!
I'm trying, I'm trying!
SCOOT
SCOOT!
AAAAAHHH!
TINK TINK
TINK TINK!
WHAM!
Hnngh!
Yes!
How do you like *that,* you little--
Wha?!
Hello, blondie.
We meet again.
WHOMP!

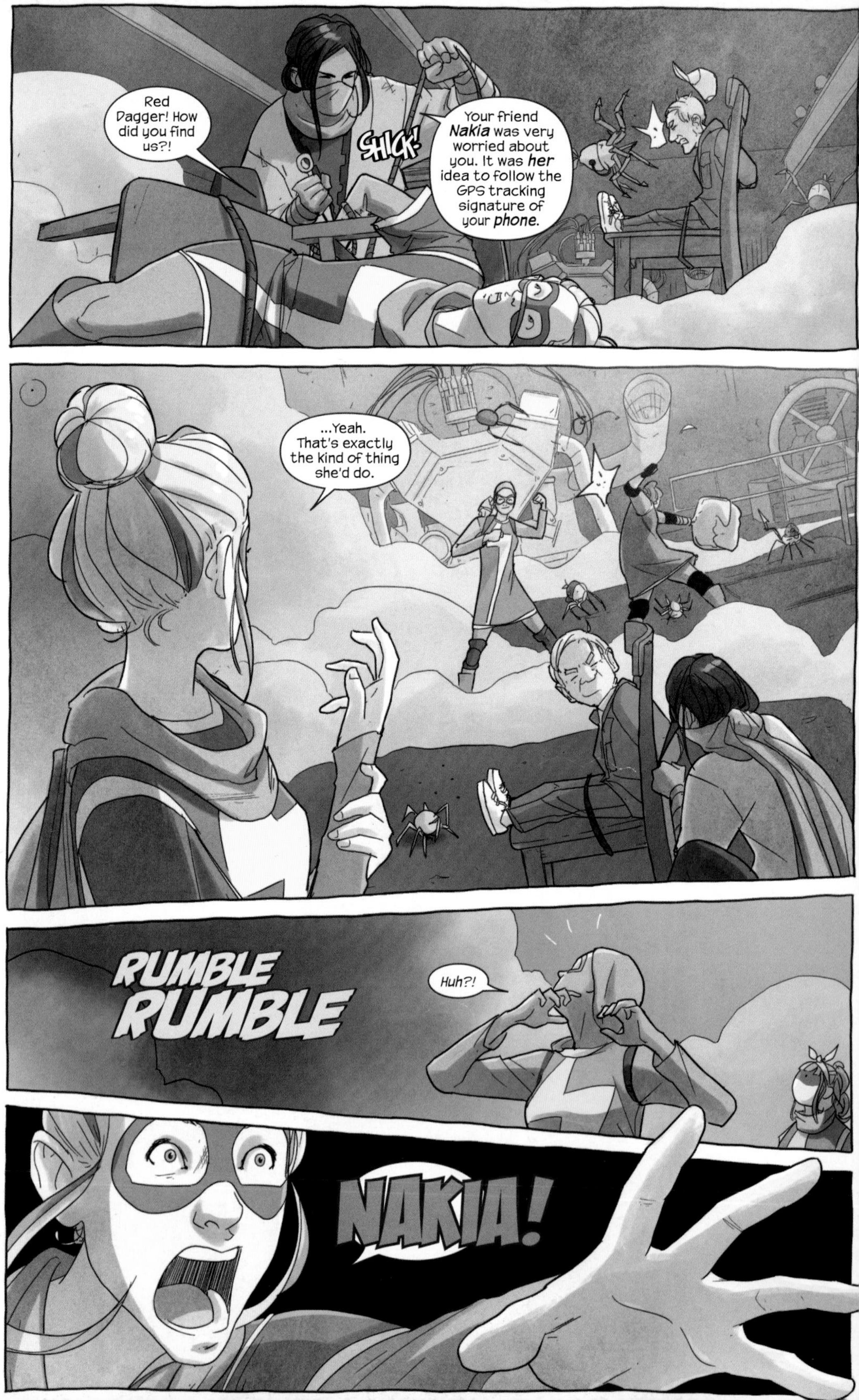

Red Dagger! How did you find us?!
SHICK!
Your friend Nakia was very worried about you. It was her idea to follow the GPS tracking signature of your phone.
...Yeah. That's exactly the kind of thing she'd do.
RUMBLE RUMBLE
Huh?!
NAKIA!

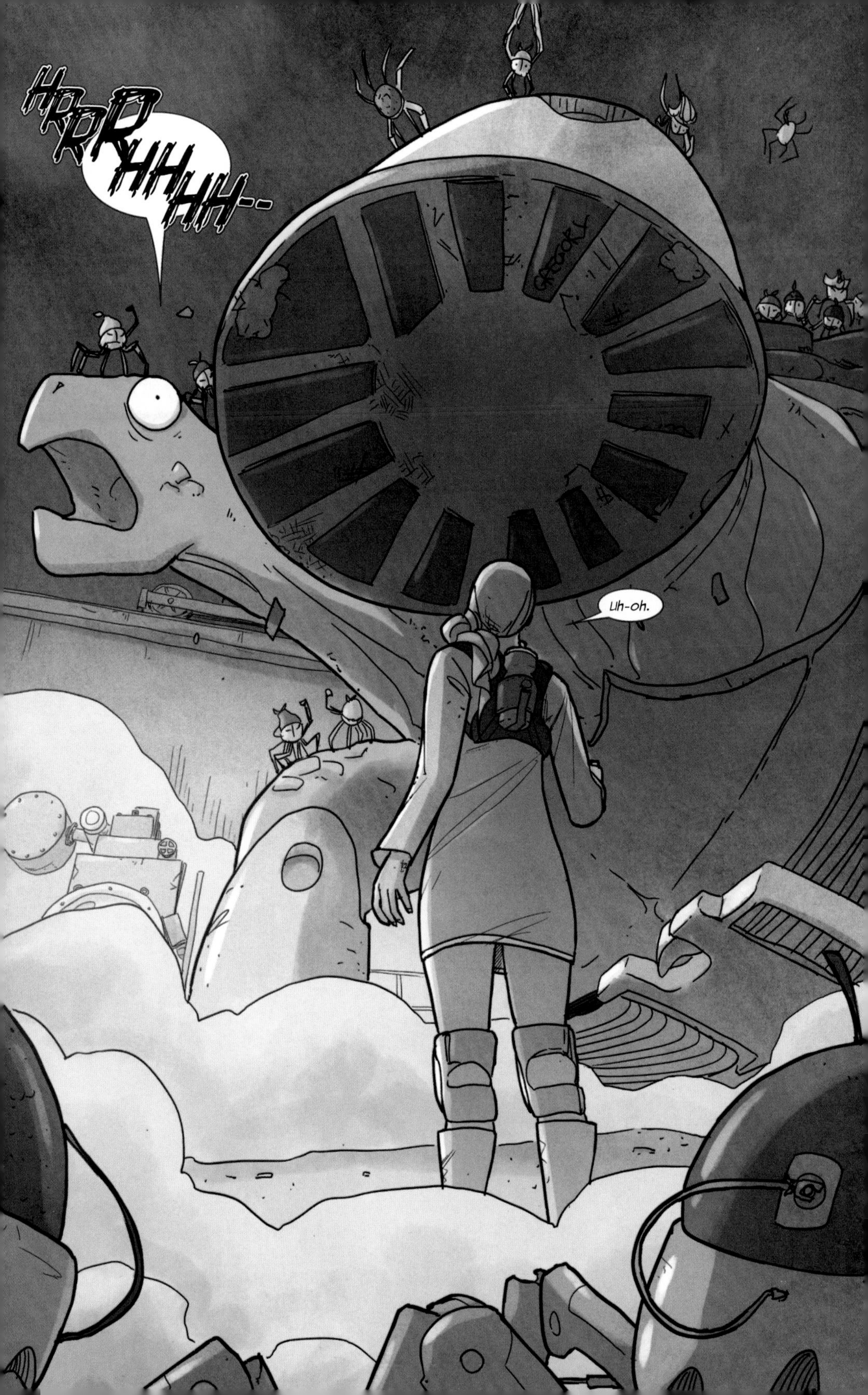
HRRRRHHHHH--
GREGORY
Uh-oh.

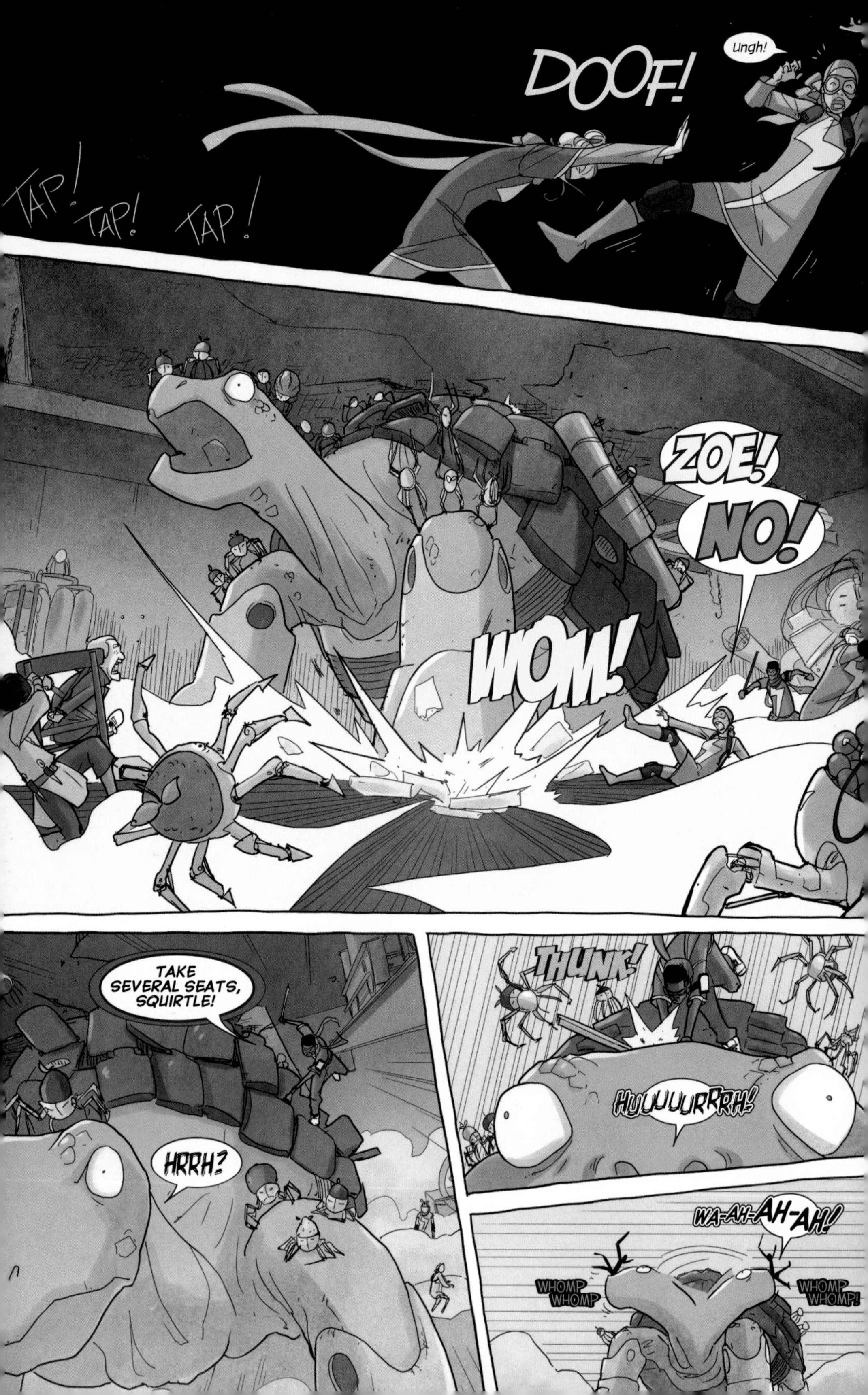
DOOF!
Ungh!
TAP! TAP! TAP!
ZOE! NO!
WOM!
TAKE SEVERAL SEATS, SQUIRTLE!
HRRH?
THUNK!
HUUUUURRRH!
WA-AH-AH-AH!
WHOMP WHOMP
WHOMP WHOMP!

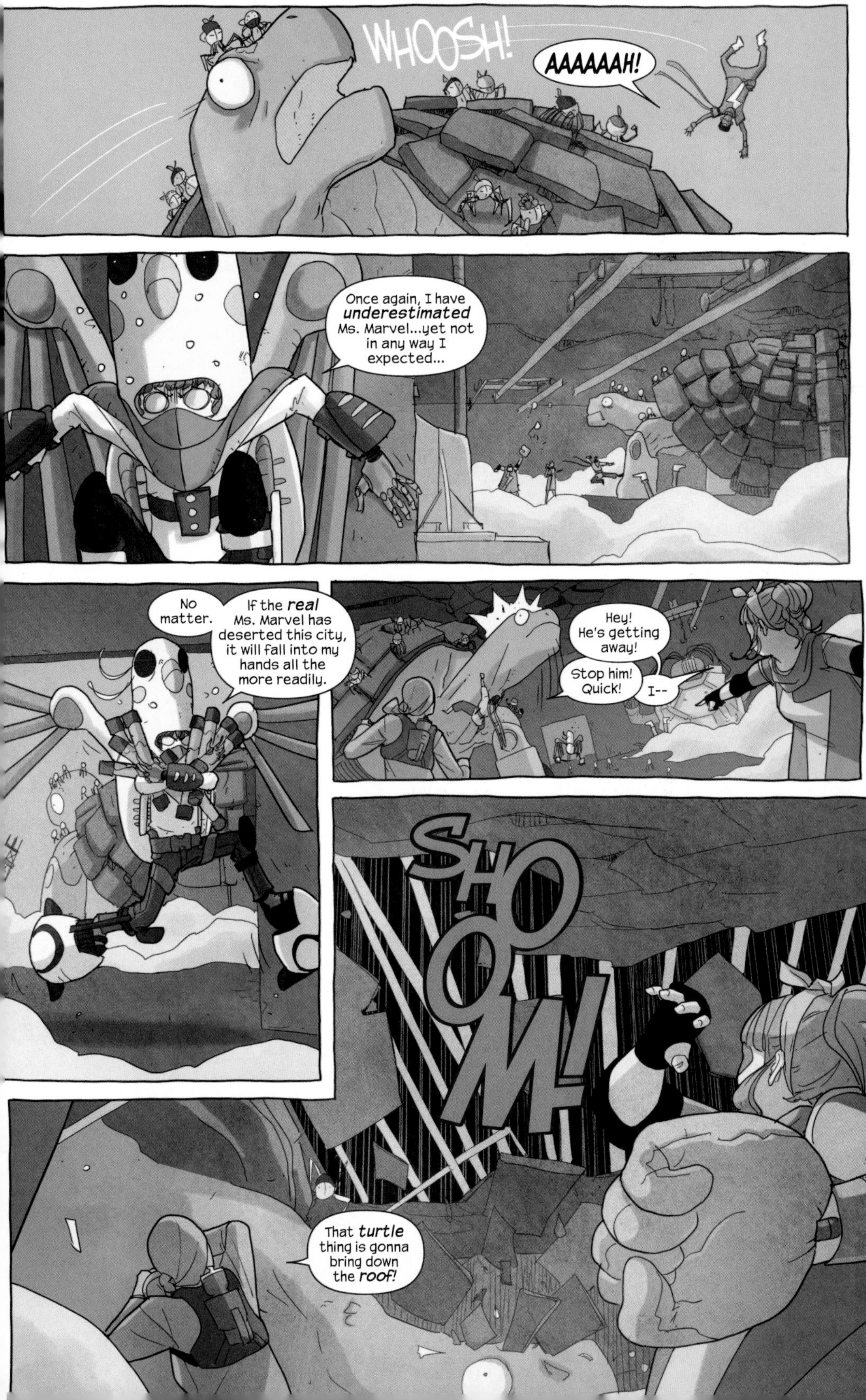
WHOOSH!
AAAAAAH!
Once again, I have *underestimated* Ms. Marvel...yet not in any way I expected...
No matter.
If the *real* Ms. Marvel has deserted this city, it will fall into my hands all the more readily.
Hey! He's getting away!
Stop him! Quick!
I--
SHOOOM!
That *turtle* thing is gonna bring down the *roof!*

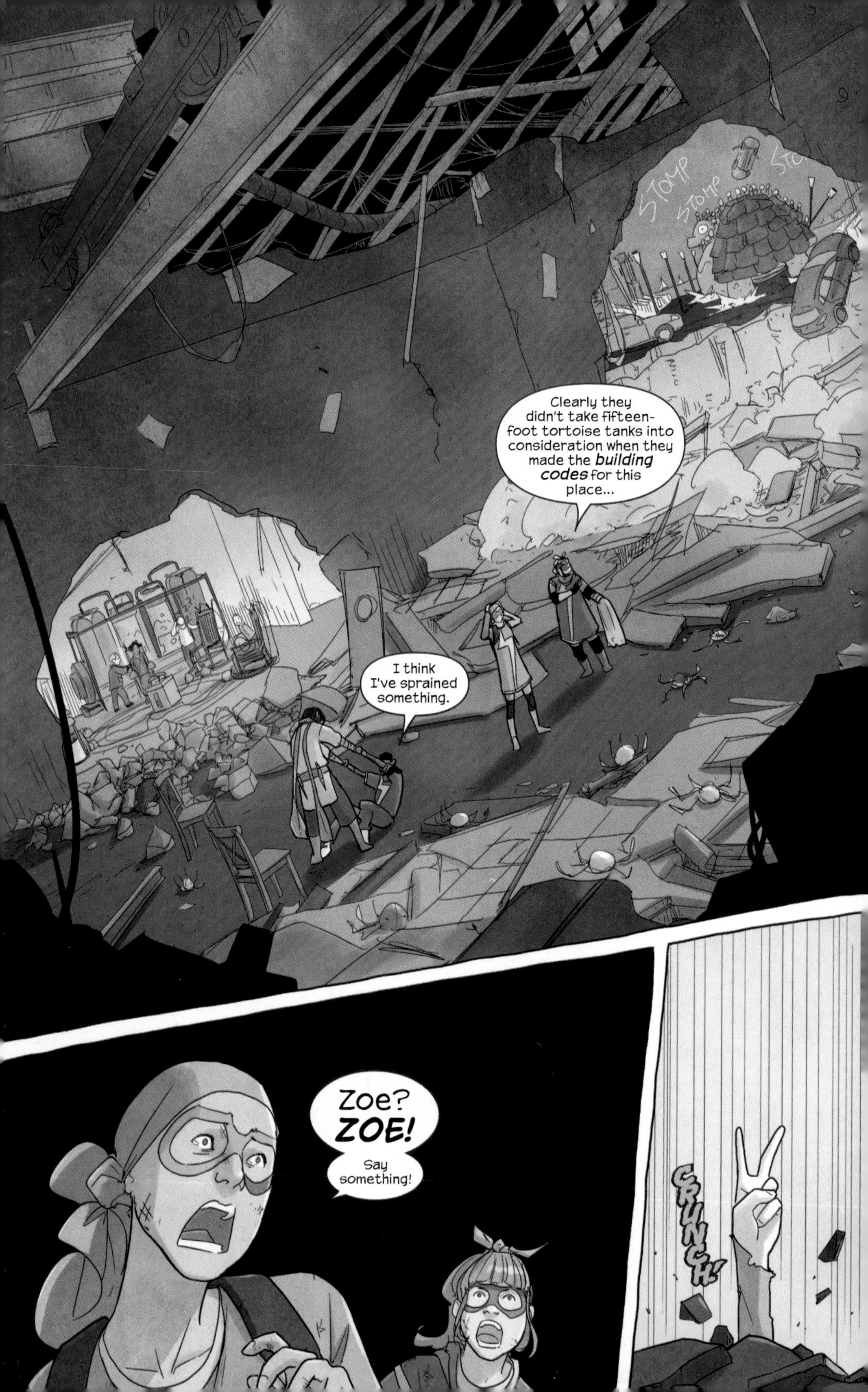
STOMP STOMP STO
Clearly they didn't take fifteen-foot tortoise tanks into consideration when they made the *building codes* for this place...
I think I've sprained something.
Zoe? **ZOE!**
Say something!
CRUNCH!

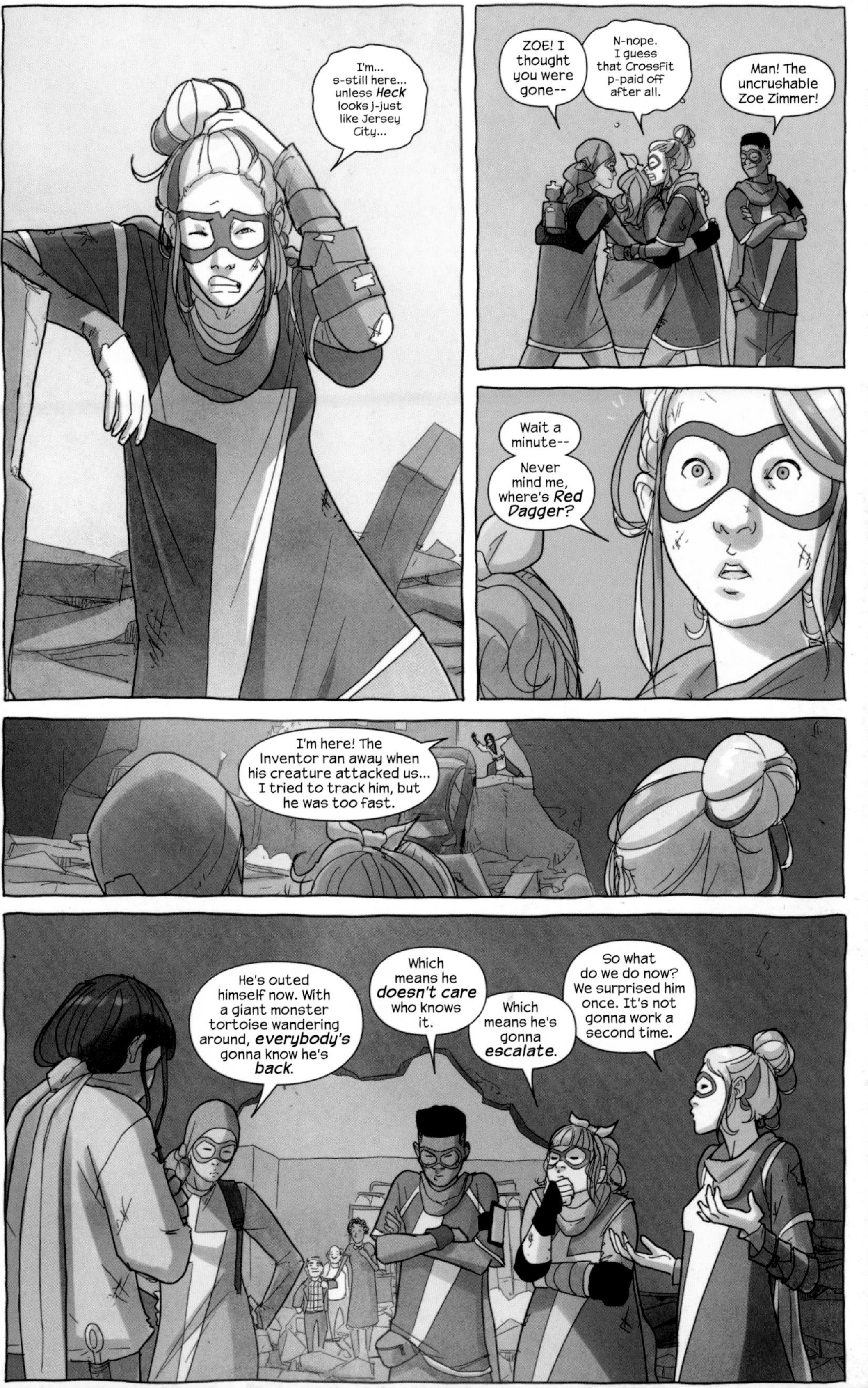
I'm... s-still here... unless *Heck* looks j-just like Jersey City...
ZOE! I thought you were gone--
N-nope. I guess that CrossFit p-paid off after all.
Man! The uncrushable Zoe Zimmer!
Wait a minute--
Never mind me, where's *Red Dagger*?
I'm here! The Inventor ran away when his creature attacked us... I tried to track him, but he was too fast.
He's outed himself now. With a giant monster tortoise wandering around, ***everybody's*** gonna know he's ***back***.
Which means he ***doesn't care*** who knows it.
Which means he's gonna ***escalate***.
So what do we do now? We surprised him once. It's not gonna work a second time.

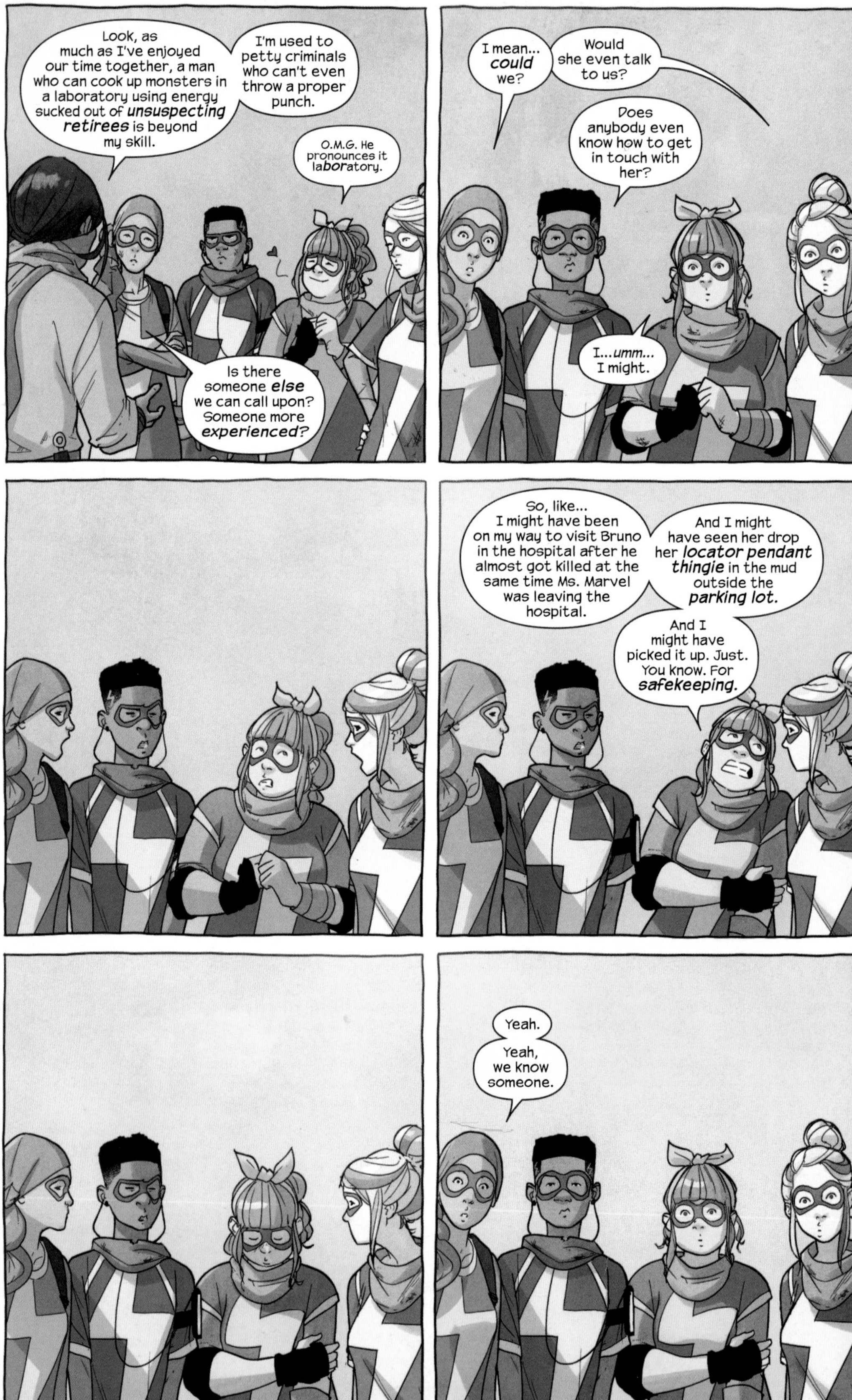

Look, as much as I've enjoyed our time together, a man who can cook up monsters in a laboratory using energy sucked out of *unsuspecting retirees* is beyond my skill.
I'm used to petty criminals who can't even throw a proper punch.
O.M.G. He pronounces it la*bor*atory.
Is there someone *else* we can call upon? Someone more *experienced*?
I mean... *could* we?
Would she even talk to us?
Does anybody even know how to get in touch with her?
I...*umm*... I might.
So, like... I might have been on my way to visit Bruno in the hospital after he almost got killed at the same time Ms. Marvel was leaving the hospital.
And I might have seen her drop her *locator pendant thingie* in the mud outside the *parking lot.*
And I might have picked it up. Just. You know. For *safekeeping.*
Yeah.
Yeah, we know someone.

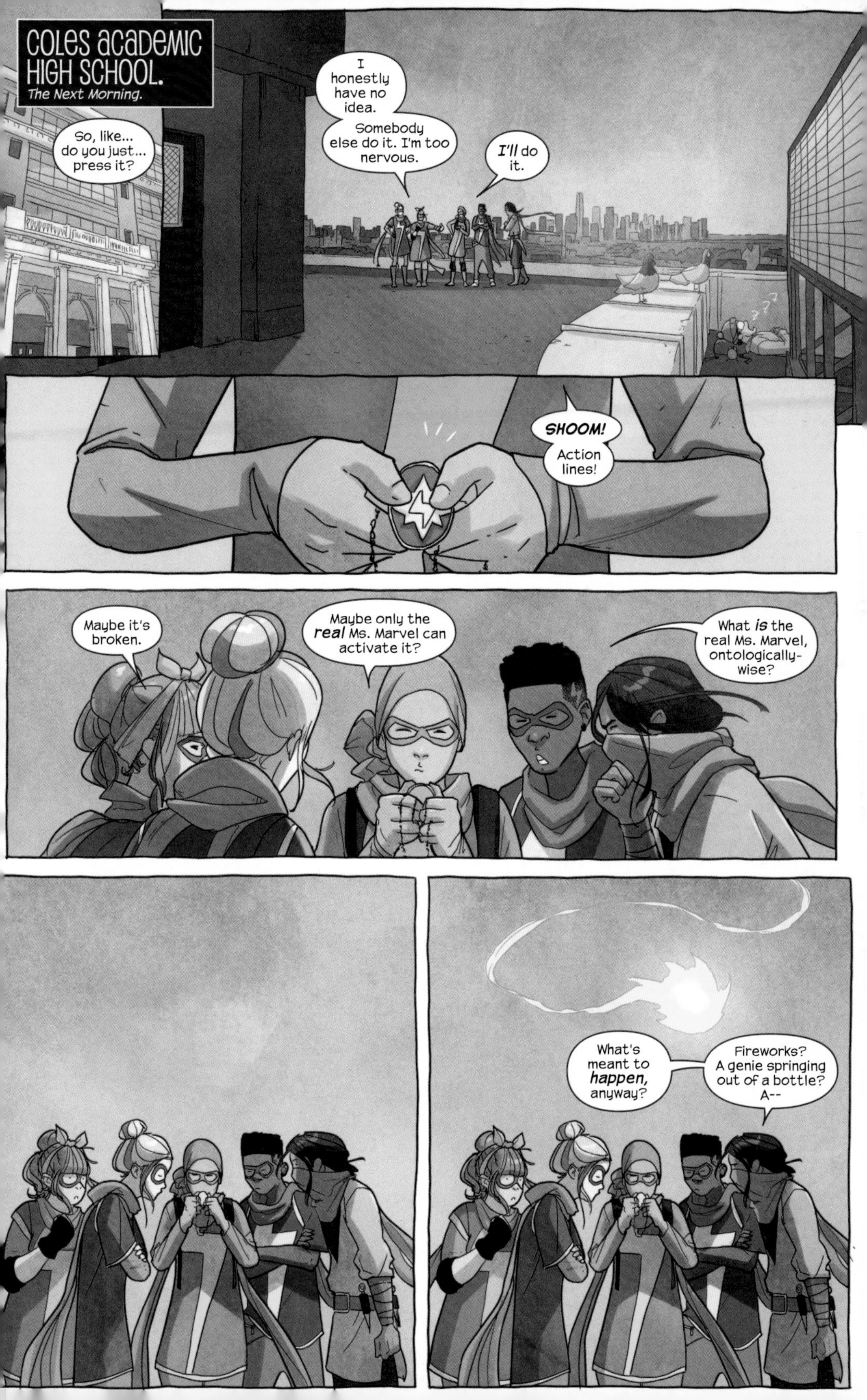

COLES ACADEMIC HIGH SCHOOL.
The Next Morning.
So, like... do you just... press it?
I honestly have no idea.
Somebody else do it. I'm too nervous.
I'll do it.
SHOOM! Action lines!
Maybe it's broken.
Maybe only the real Ms. Marvel can activate it?
What is the real Ms. Marvel, ontologically-wise?
What's meant to happen, anyway?
Fireworks? A genie springing out of a bottle? A--

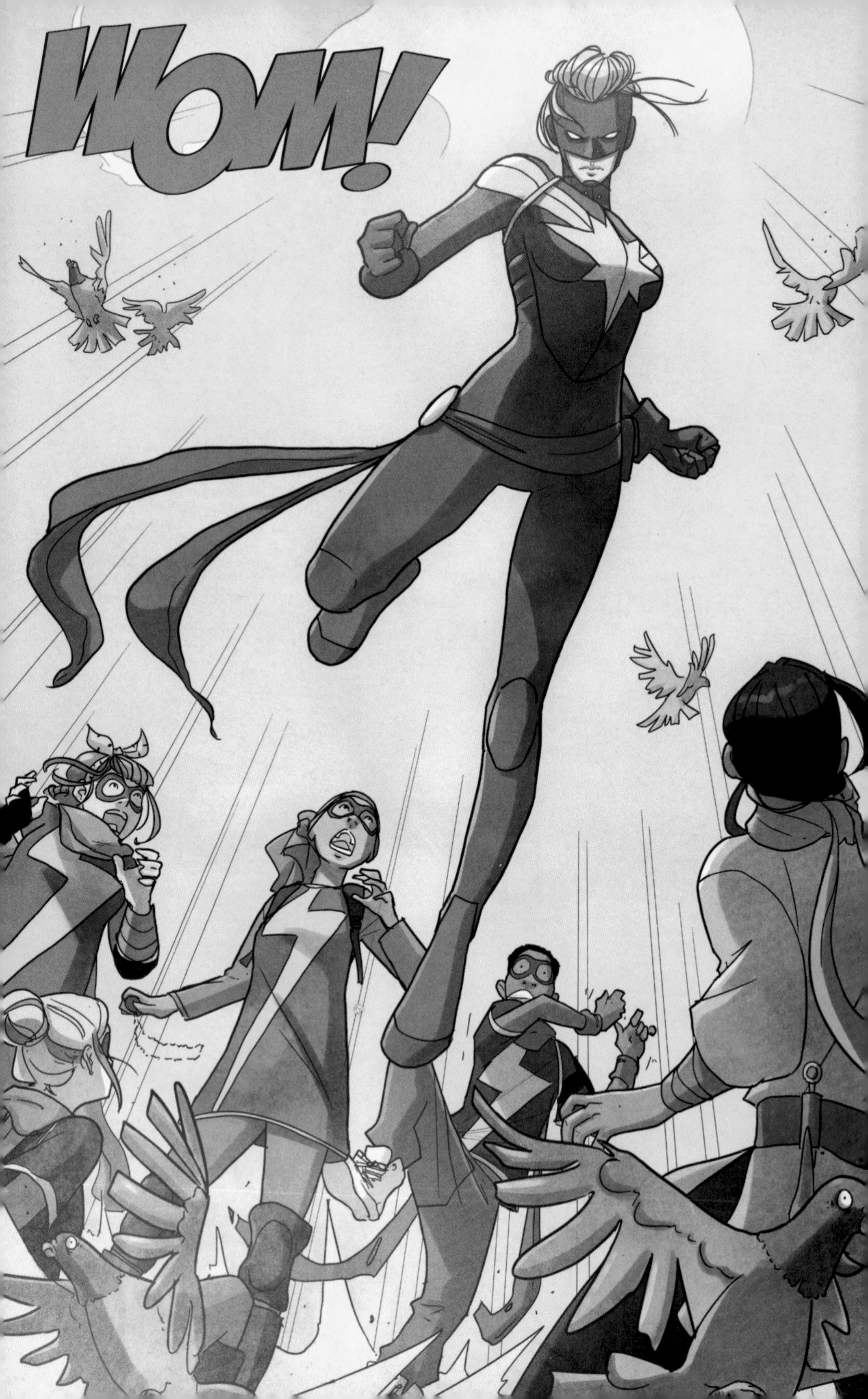
WOM!

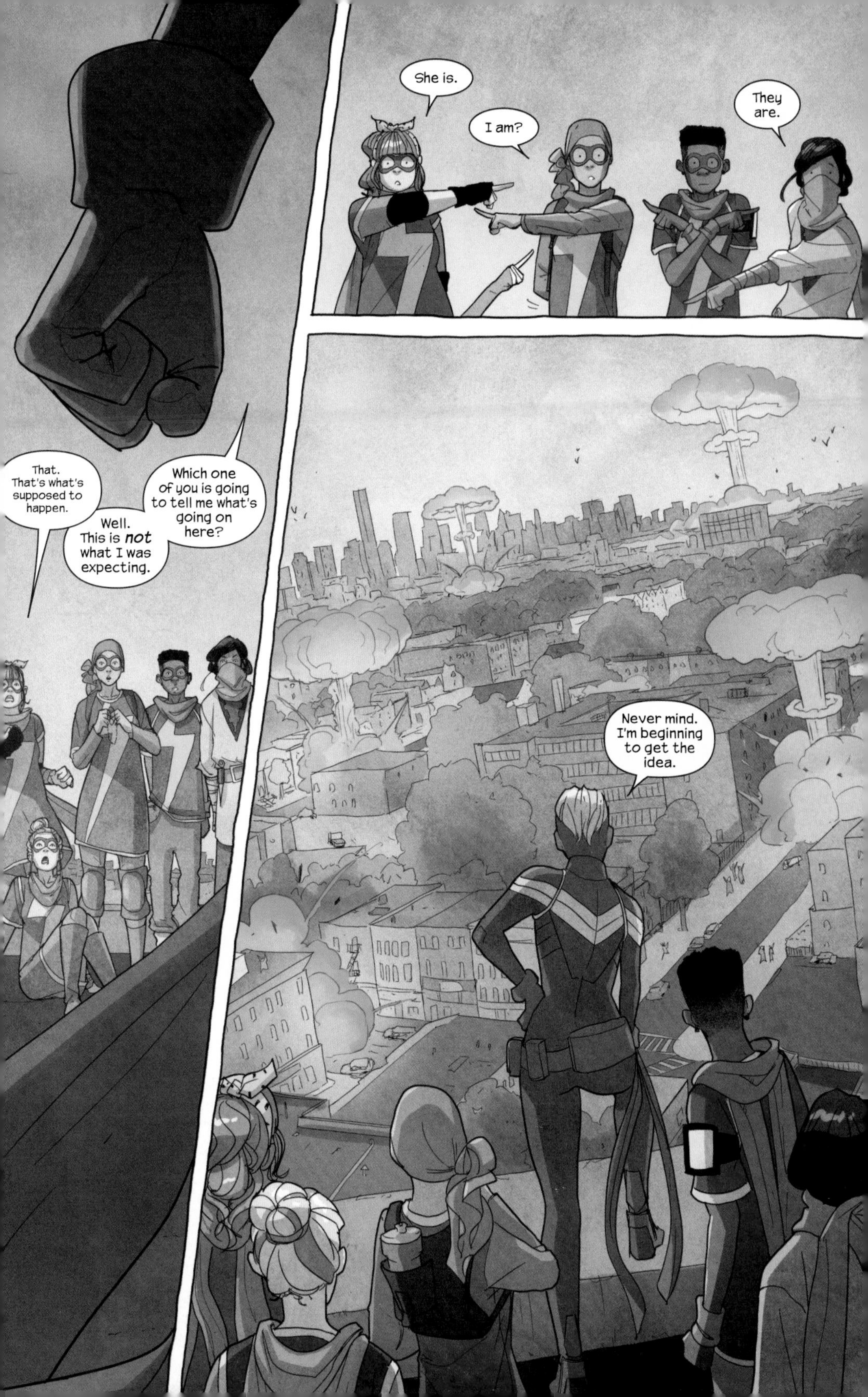

That. That's what's supposed to happen.
Well. This is *not* what I was expecting.
Which one of you is going to tell me what's going on here?
She is.
I am?
They are.
Never mind. I'm beginning to get the idea.

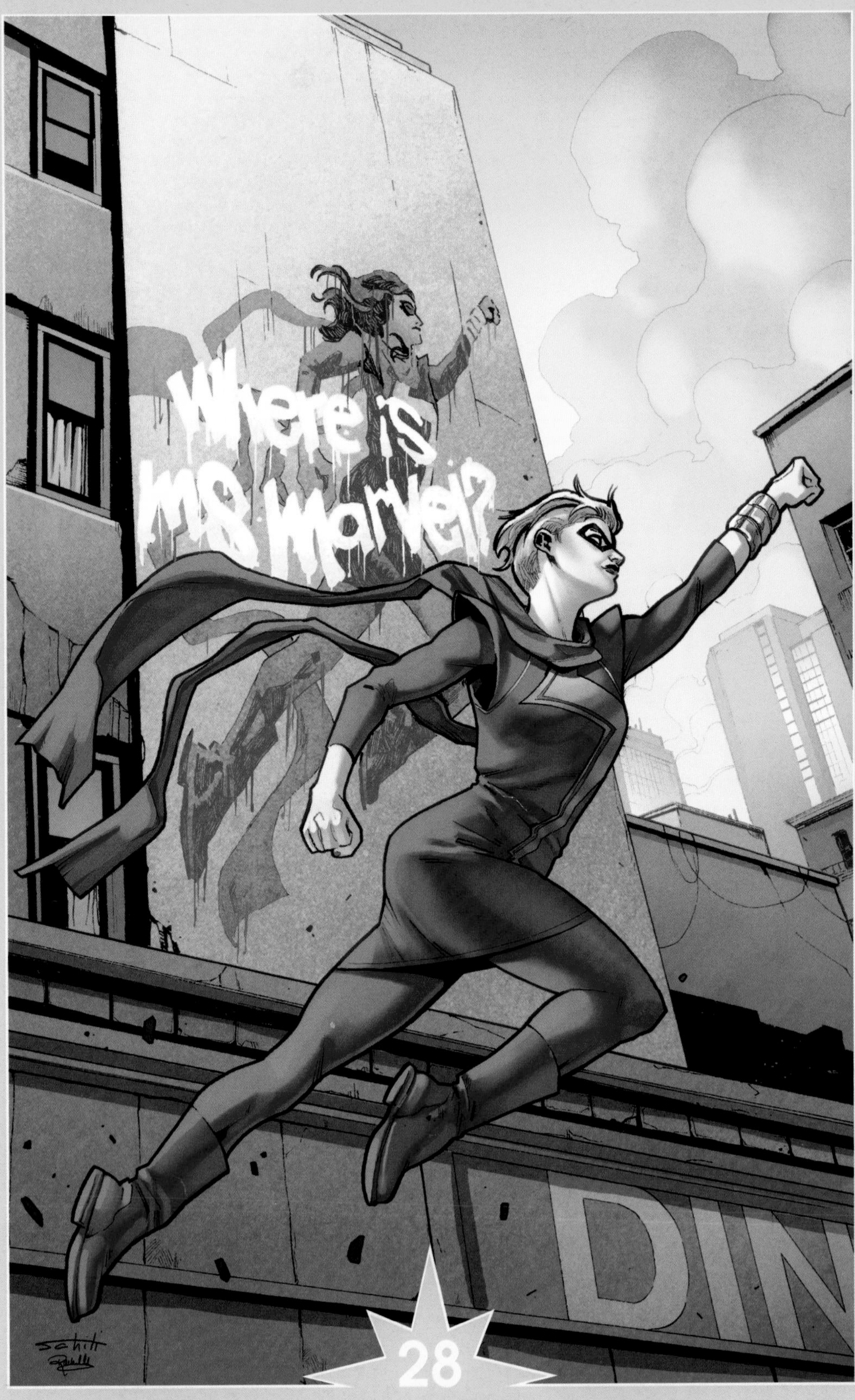
Where is Ms Marvel?
DIN
28

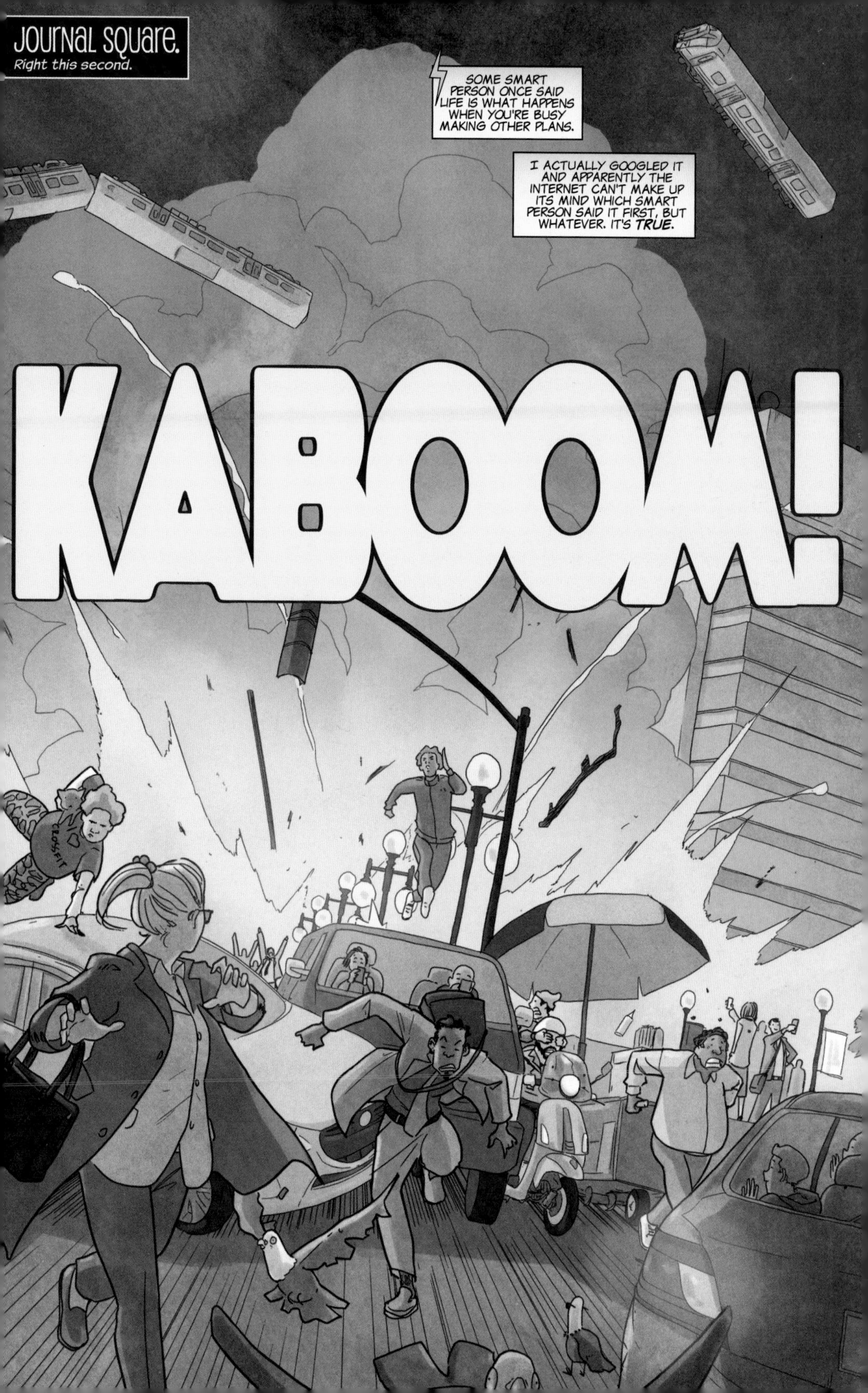
JOURNAL SQUARE.
Right this second.
SOME SMART PERSON ONCE SAID LIFE IS WHAT HAPPENS WHEN YOU'RE BUSY MAKING OTHER PLANS.
I ACTUALLY GOOGLED IT AND APPARENTLY THE INTERNET CAN'T MAKE UP ITS MIND WHICH SMART PERSON SAID IT FIRST, BUT WHATEVER. IT'S TRUE.
KABOOM!
CROSSFIT

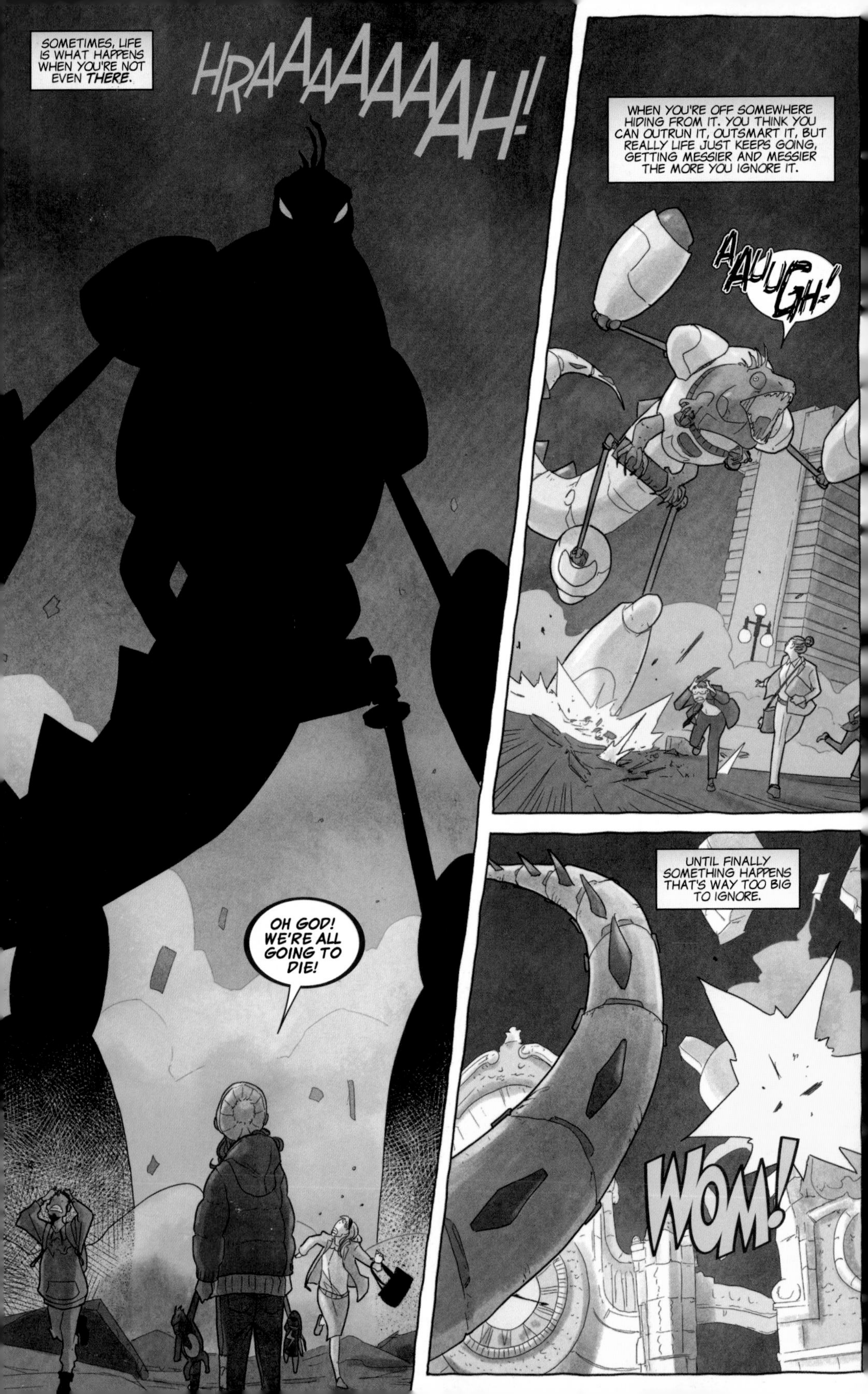
SOMETIMES, LIFE IS WHAT HAPPENS WHEN YOU'RE NOT EVEN THERE.
HRAAAAAAAAH!
OH GOD! WE'RE ALL GOING TO DIE!
WHEN YOU'RE OFF SOMEWHERE HIDING FROM IT. YOU THINK YOU CAN OUTRUN IT, OUTSMART IT, BUT REALLY LIFE JUST KEEPS GOING, GETTING MESSIER AND MESSIER THE MORE YOU IGNORE IT.
AAUUGH!
UNTIL FINALLY SOMETHING HAPPENS THAT'S WAY TOO BIG TO IGNORE.
WOM!

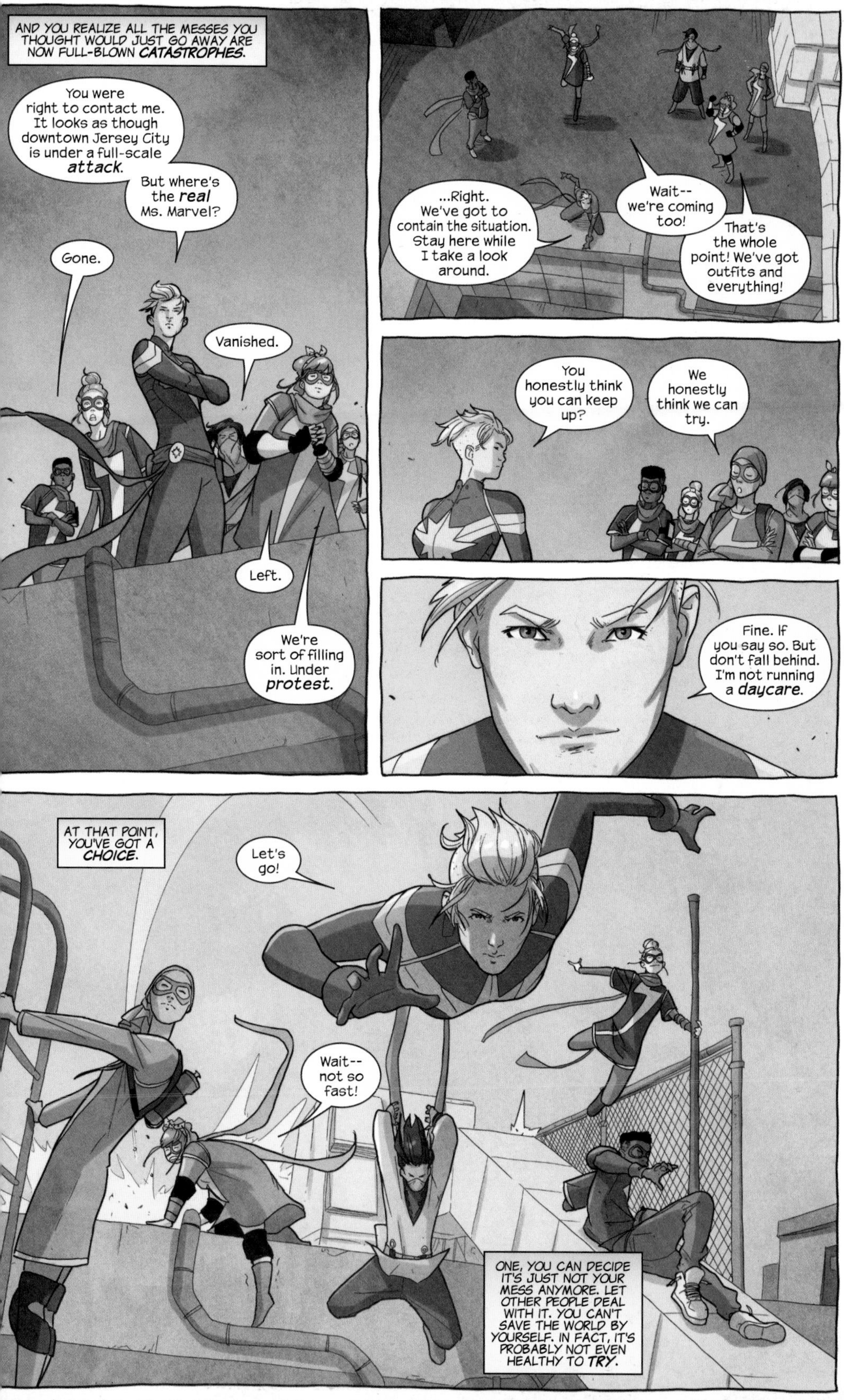
AND YOU REALIZE ALL THE MESSES YOU THOUGHT WOULD JUST GO AWAY ARE NOW FULL-BLOWN CATASTROPHES.
You were right to contact me. It looks as though downtown Jersey City is under a full-scale attack.
But where's the real Ms. Marvel?
Gone.
Vanished.
Left.
We're sort of filling in. Under protest.
...Right. We've got to contain the situation. Stay here while I take a look around.
Wait-- we're coming too!
That's the whole point! We've got outfits and everything!
You honestly think you can keep up?
We honestly think we can try.
Fine. If you say so. But don't fall behind. I'm not running a daycare.
AT THAT POINT, YOU'VE GOT A CHOICE.
Let's go!
Wait-- not so fast!
ONE, YOU CAN DECIDE IT'S JUST NOT YOUR MESS ANYMORE. LET OTHER PEOPLE DEAL WITH IT. YOU CAN'T SAVE THE WORLD BY YOURSELF. IN FACT, IT'S PROBABLY NOT EVEN HEALTHY TO TRY.

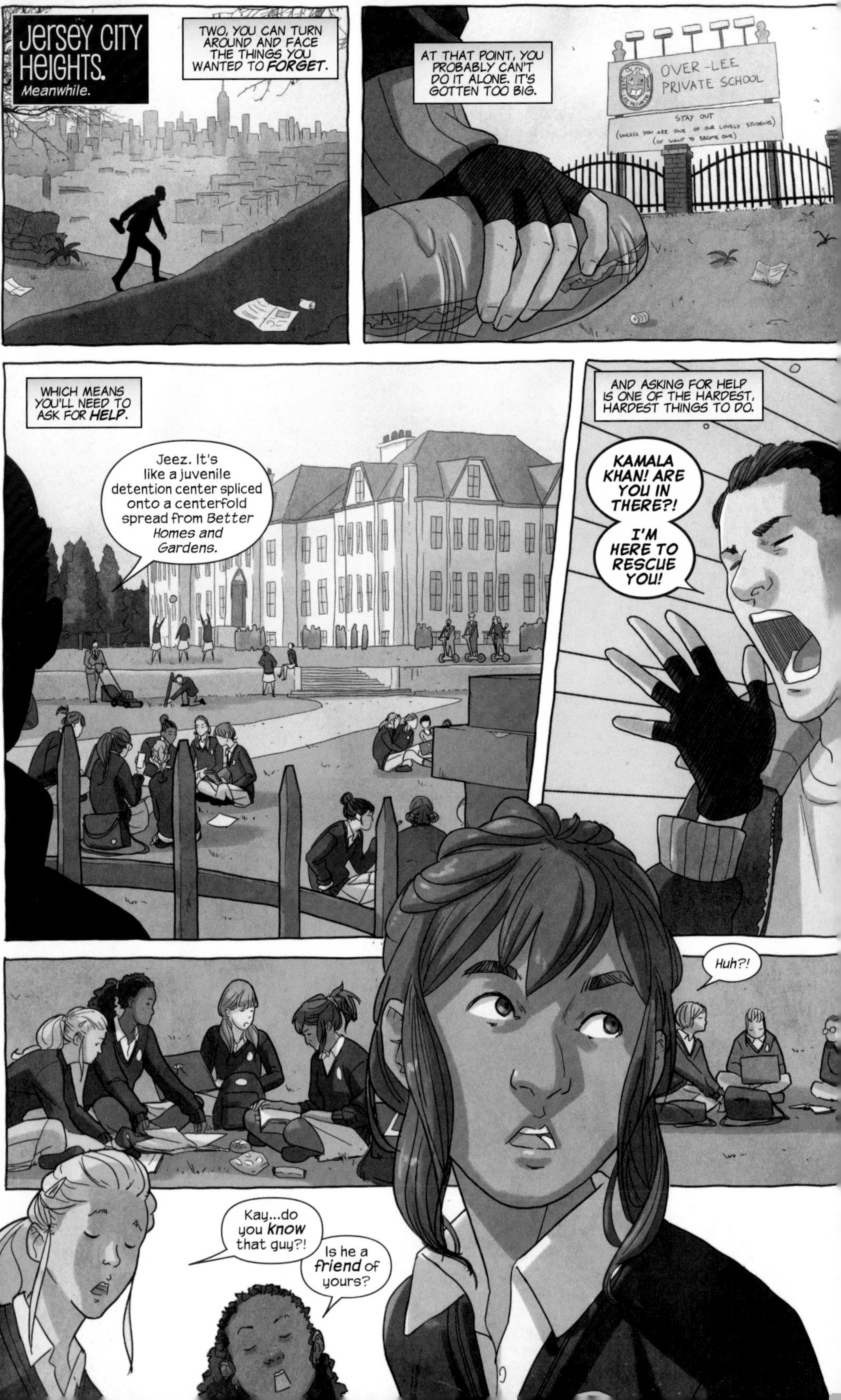
Jersey City Heights.
Meanwhile.
TWO, YOU CAN TURN AROUND AND FACE THE THINGS YOU WANTED TO FORGET.
AT THAT POINT, YOU PROBABLY CAN'T DO IT ALONE. IT'S GOTTEN TOO BIG.
OVER-LEE PRIVATE SCHOOL
STAY OUT
(UNLESS YOU ARE ONE OF OUR LOVELY STUDENTS)
(OR WANT TO BECOME ONE)
WHICH MEANS YOU'LL NEED TO ASK FOR HELP.
Jeez. It's like a juvenile detention center spliced onto a centerfold spread from Better Homes and Gardens.
AND ASKING FOR HELP IS ONE OF THE HARDEST, HARDEST THINGS TO DO.
KAMALA KHAN! ARE YOU IN THERE?!
I'M HERE TO RESCUE YOU!
Huh?!
Kay...do you know that guy?!
Is he a friend of yours?

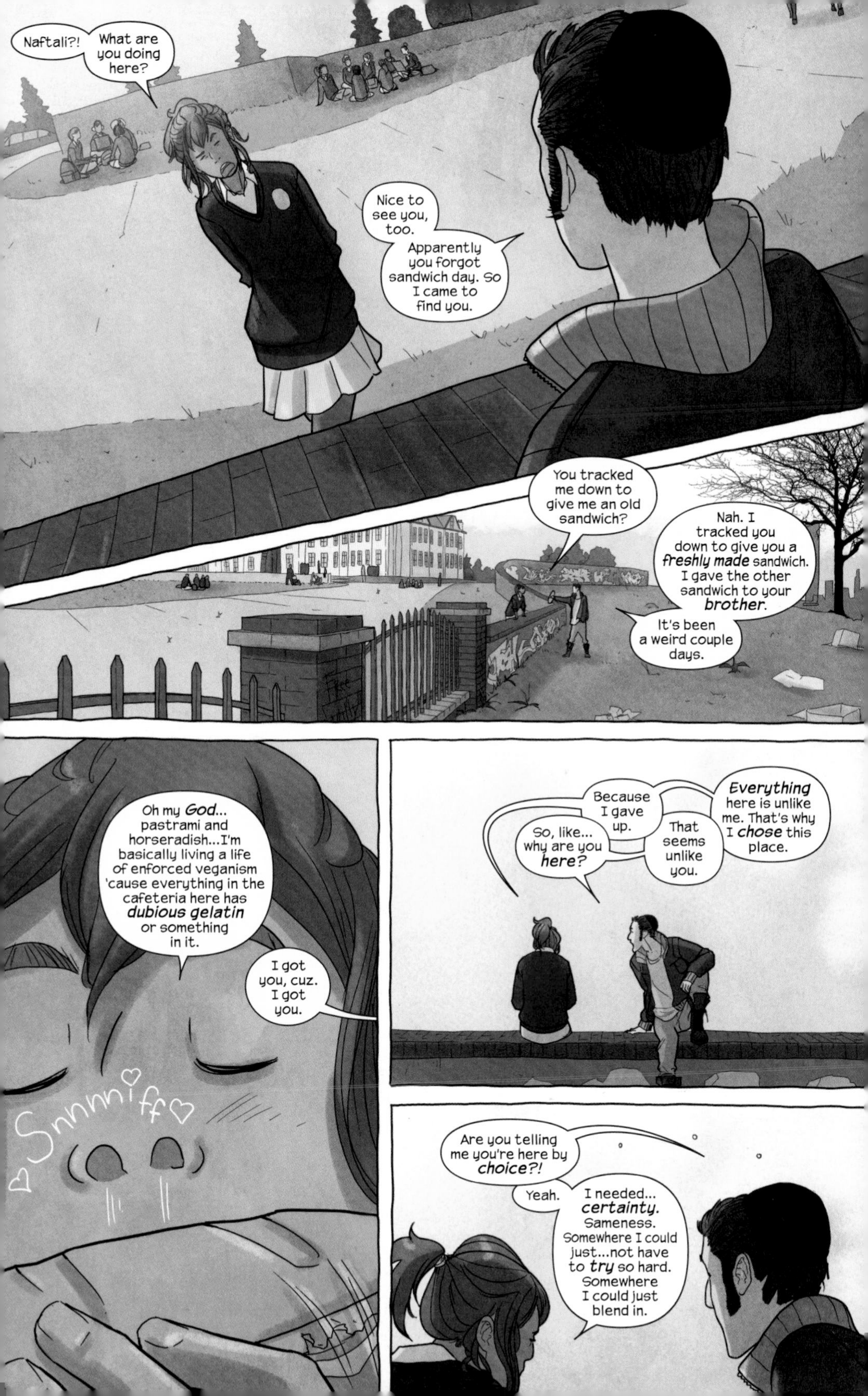
Naftali?!
What are you doing here?
Nice to see you, too.
Apparently you forgot sandwich day. So I came to find you.
You tracked me down to give me an old sandwich?
Nah. I tracked you down to give you a freshly made sandwich. I gave the other sandwich to your brother.
It's been a weird couple days.
Oh my God... pastrami and horseradish...I'm basically living a life of enforced veganism 'cause everything in the cafeteria here has dubious gelatin or something in it.
I got you, cuz. I got you.
Snnniff
So, like... why are you here?
Because I gave up.
That seems unlike you.
Everything here is unlike me. That's why I chose this place.
Are you telling me you're here by choice?!
Yeah.
I needed... certainty. Sameness. Somewhere I could just...not have to try so hard. Somewhere I could just blend in.

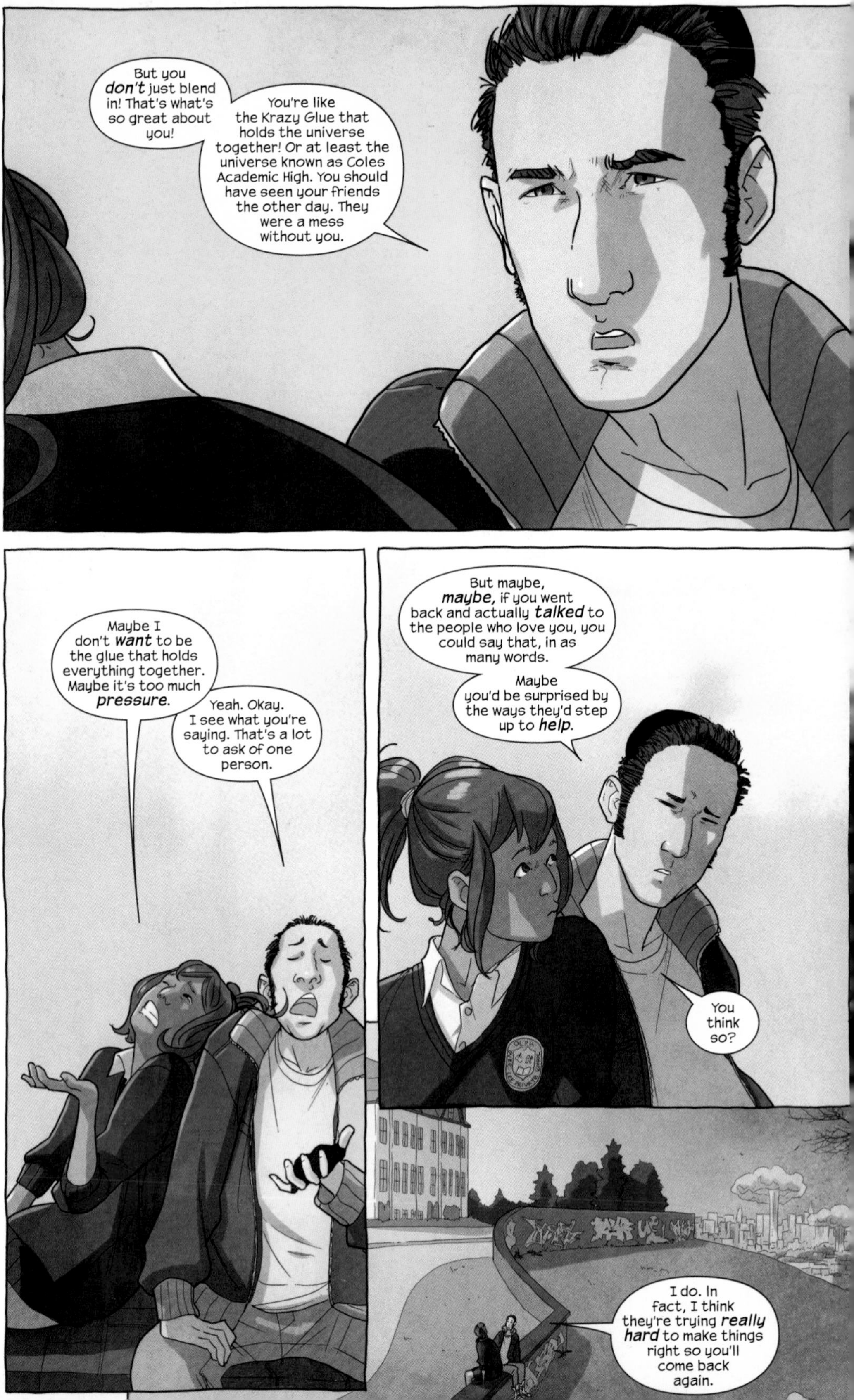

But you don't just blend in! That's what's so great about you!
You're like the Krazy Glue that holds the universe together! Or at least the universe known as Coles Academic High. You should have seen your friends the other day. They were a mess without you.
Maybe I don't want to be the glue that holds everything together. Maybe it's too much pressure.
Yeah. Okay. I see what you're saying. That's a lot to ask of one person.
But maybe, maybe, if you went back and actually talked to the people who love you, you could say that, in as many words.
Maybe you'd be surprised by the ways they'd step up to help.
You think so?
I do. In fact, I think they're trying really hard to make things right so you'll come back again.

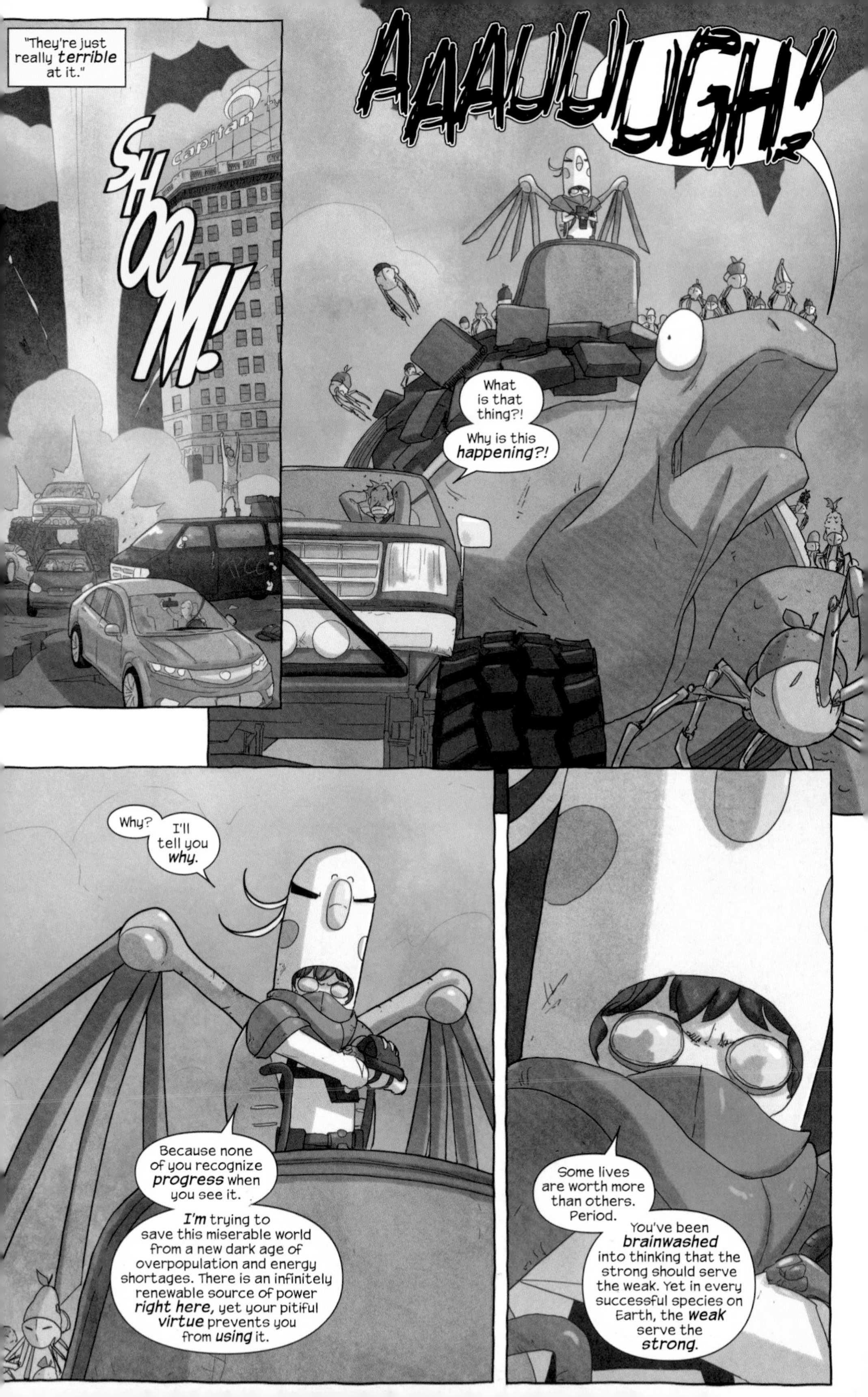
"They're just really terrible at it."
SHOOM!
AAAUUUGH!
What is that thing?!
Why is this happening?!
Why?
I'll tell you why.
Because none of you recognize progress when you see it.
I'm trying to save this miserable world from a new dark age of overpopulation and energy shortages. There is an infinitely renewable source of power right here, yet your pitiful virtue prevents you from using it.
Some lives are worth more than others. Period.
You've been brainwashed into thinking that the strong should serve the weak. Yet in every successful species on Earth, the weak serve the strong.

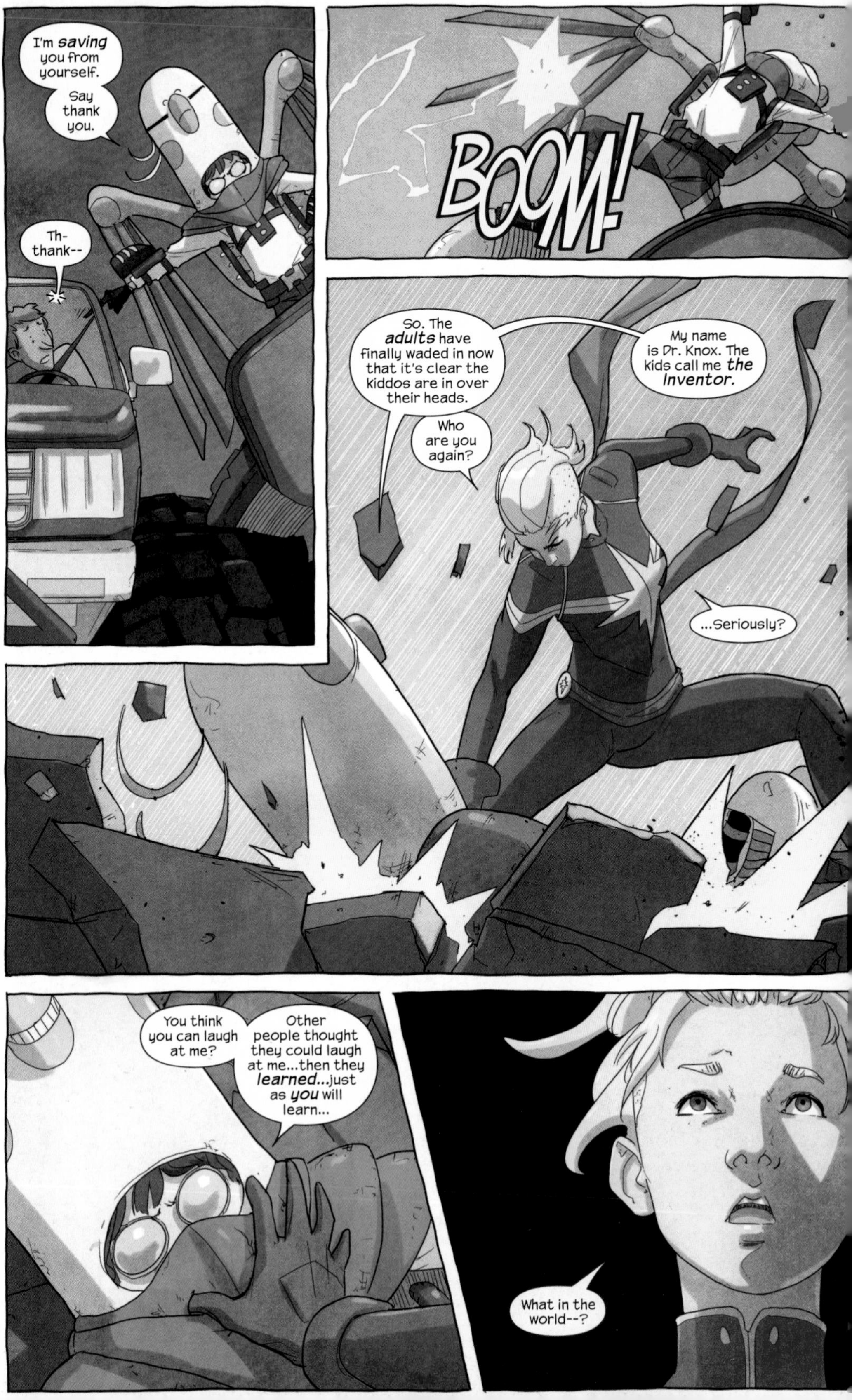

I'm saving you from yourself.
Say thank you.
Th- thank--
BOOM!
So. The adults have finally waded in now that it's clear the kiddos are in over their heads.
Who are you again?
My name is Dr. Knox. The kids call me the Inventor.
...Seriously?
You think you can laugh at me?
Other people thought they could laugh at me...then they learned...just as you will learn...
What in the world--?

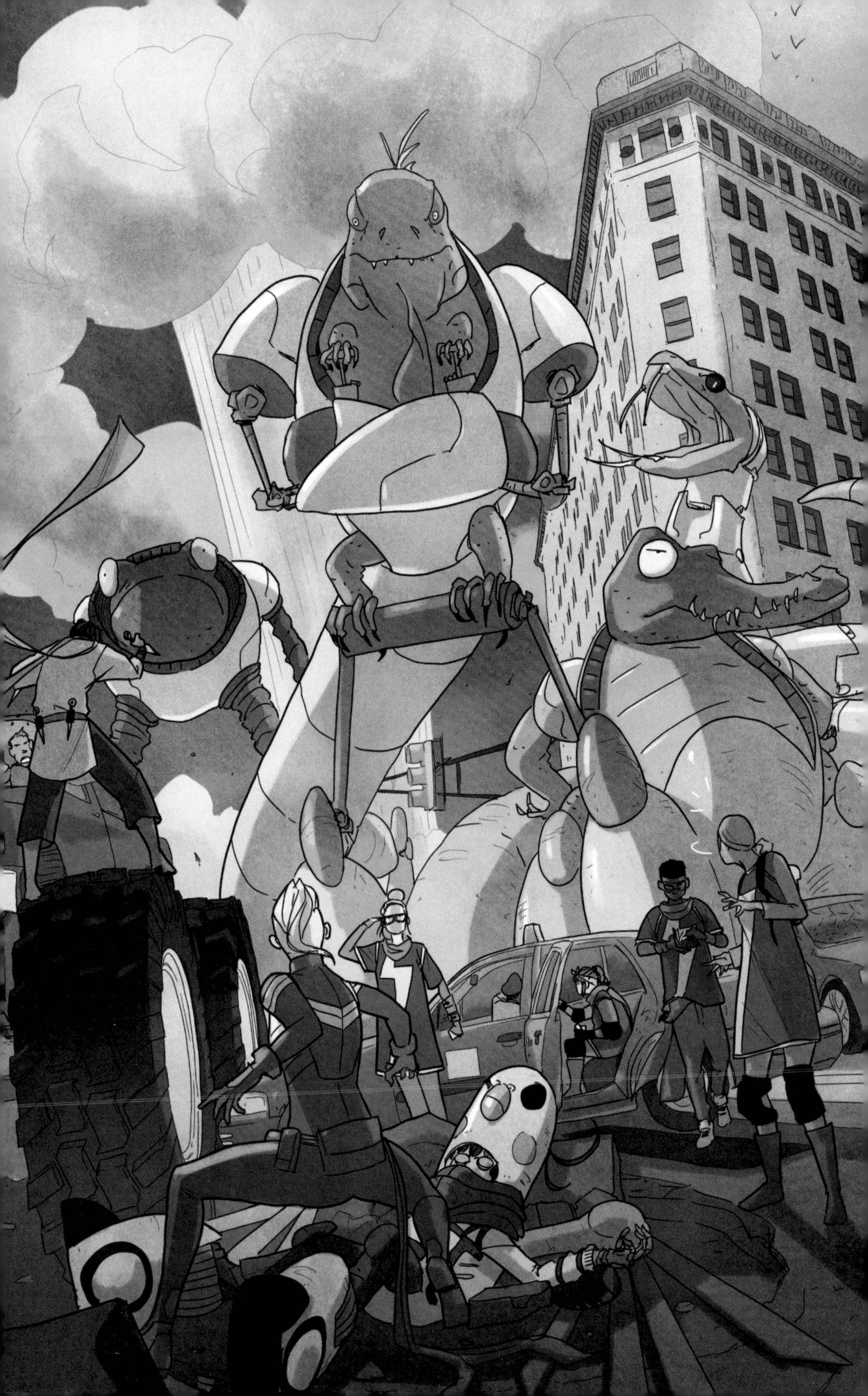

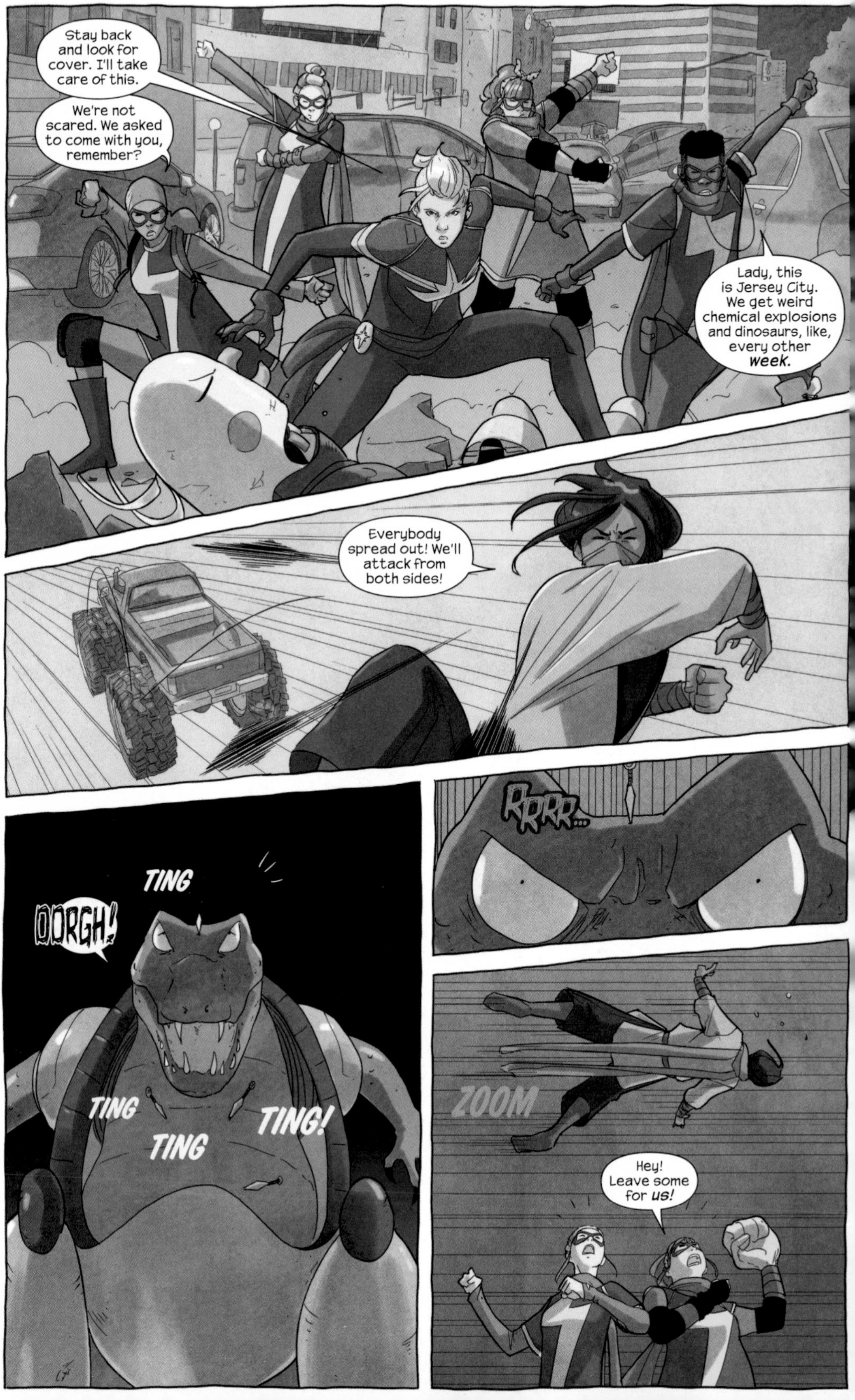
Stay back and look for cover. I'll take care of this.
We're not scared. We asked to come with you, remember?
Lady, this is Jersey City. We get weird chemical explosions and dinosaurs, like, every other *week.*
Everybody spread out! We'll attack from both sides!
RRRR...
TING
OORGH!
TING
TING
TING!
ZOOM
Hey! Leave some for *us!*

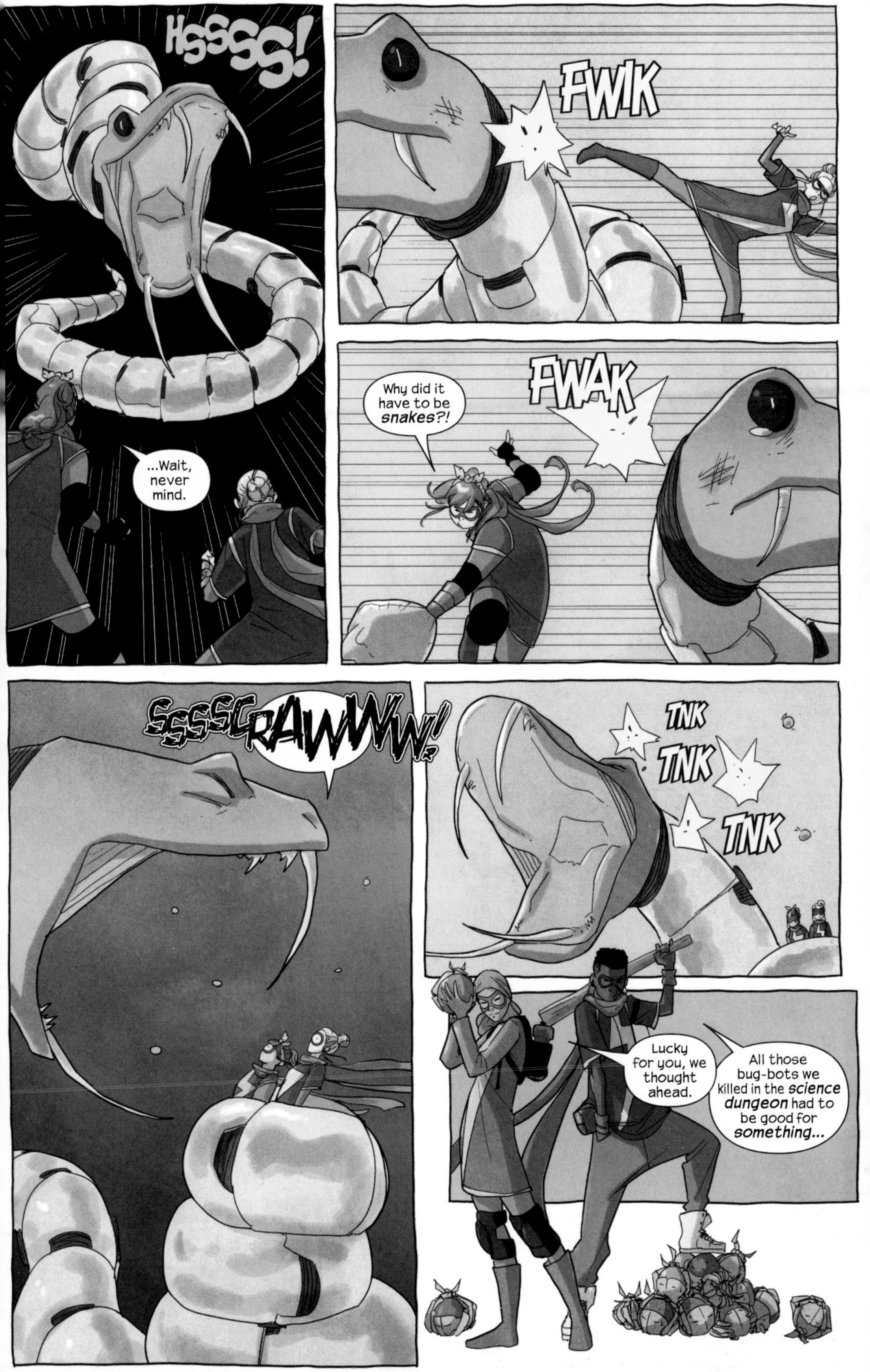
HSSSS!
...Wait, never mind.
FWIK
FWAK
Why did it have to be *snakes*?!
SSSSCRAWWW!
TNK
TNK
TNK
Lucky for you, we thought ahead.
All those bug-bots we killed in the *science dungeon* had to be good for *something...*

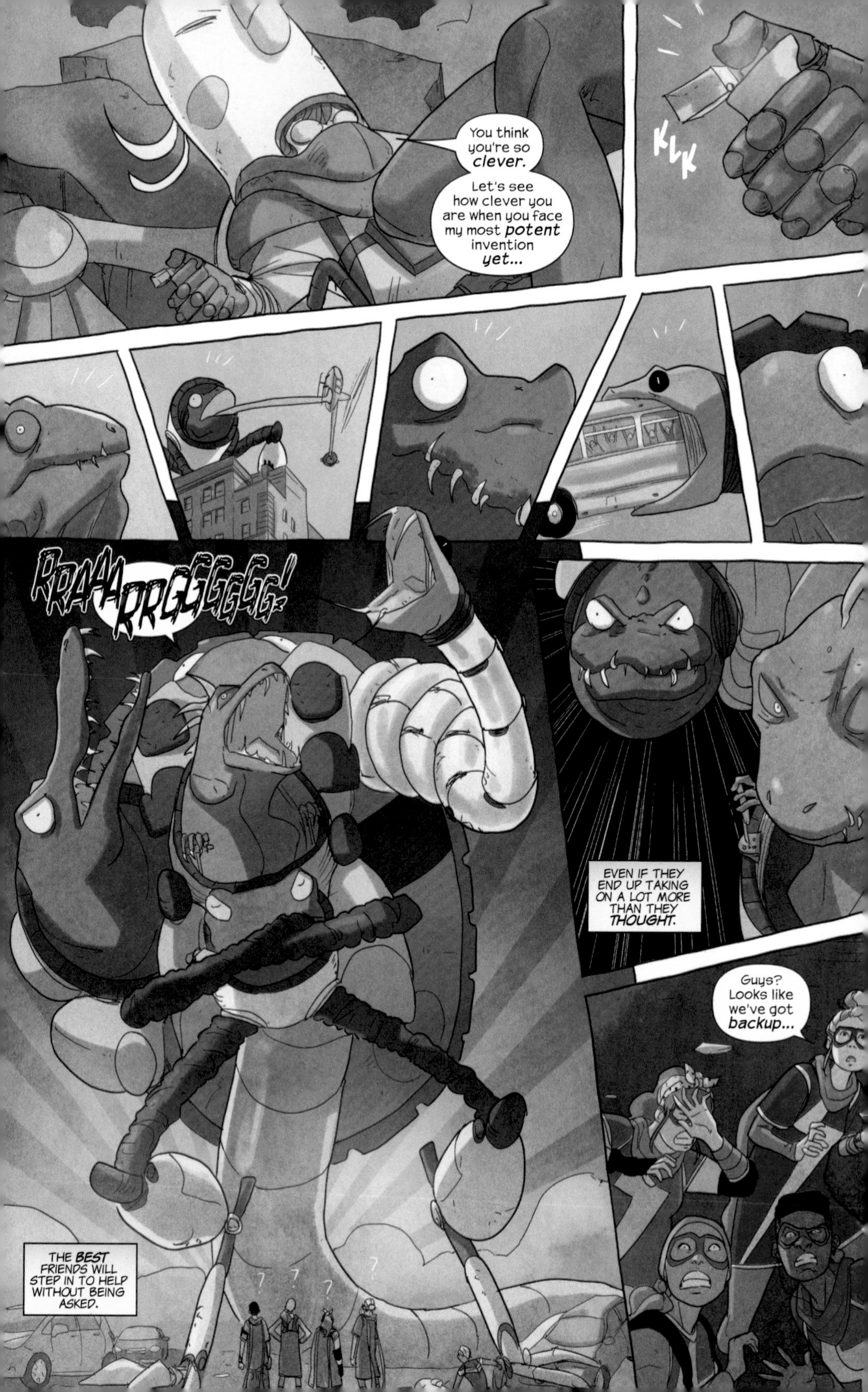
You think you're so clever.
Let's see how clever you are when you face my most potent invention yet...
KLIK
RRAAARRGGGGGG!
EVEN IF THEY END UP TAKING ON A LOT MORE THAN THEY THOUGHT.
Guys? Looks like we've got backup...
THE BEST FRIENDS WILL STEP IN TO HELP WITHOUT BEING ASKED.

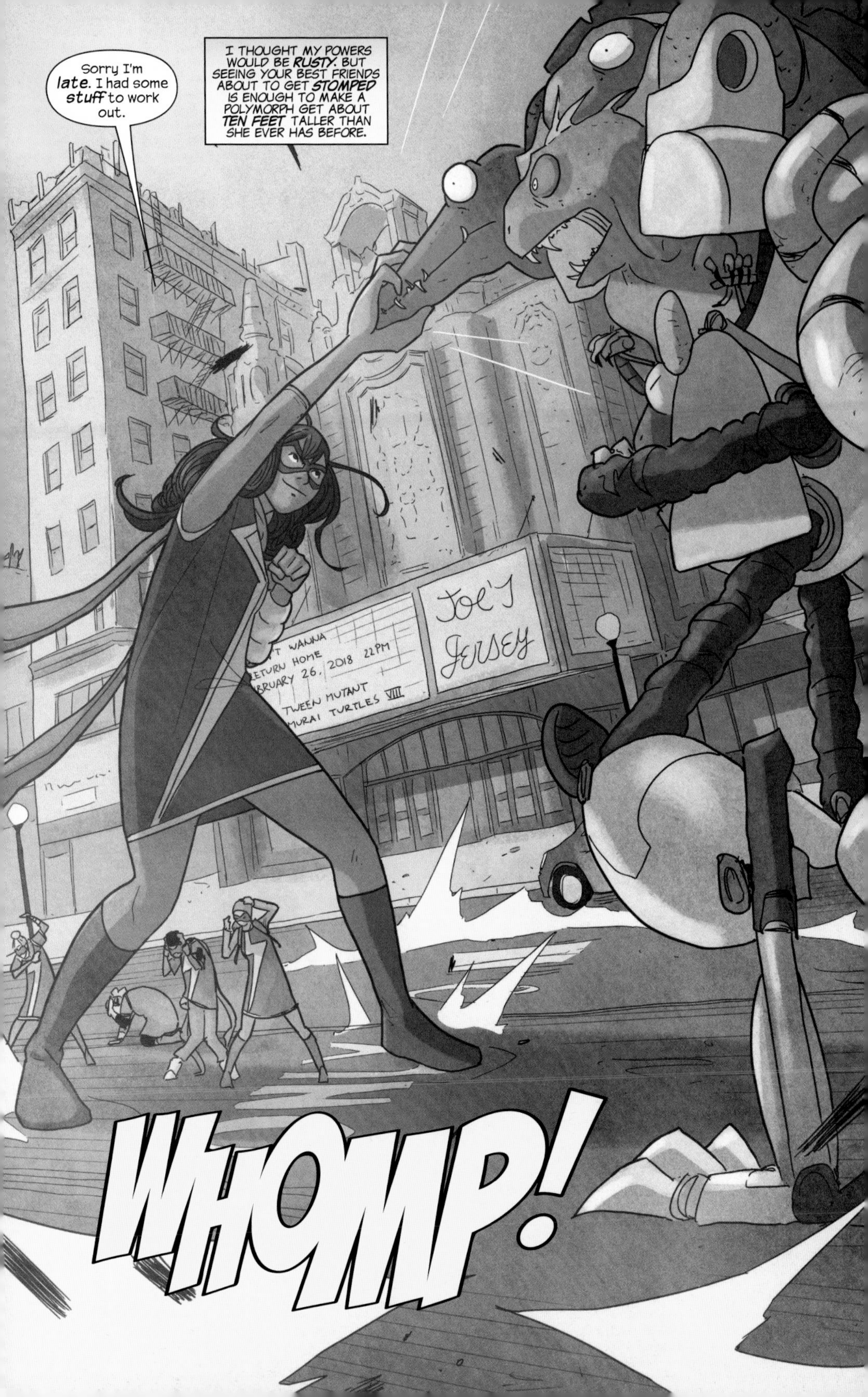

Sorry I'm *late*. I had some *stuff* to work out.
I THOUGHT MY POWERS WOULD BE ***RUSTY***. BUT SEEING YOUR BEST FRIENDS ABOUT TO GET ***STOMPED*** IS ENOUGH TO MAKE A POLYMORPH GET ABOUT ***TEN FEET*** TALLER THAN SHE EVER HAS BEFORE.
Joe'J Jersey
T WANNA
ETURN HOME
BRUARY 26, 2018 22PM
TWEEN MUTANT
MURAI TURTLES VIII
WHOMP!

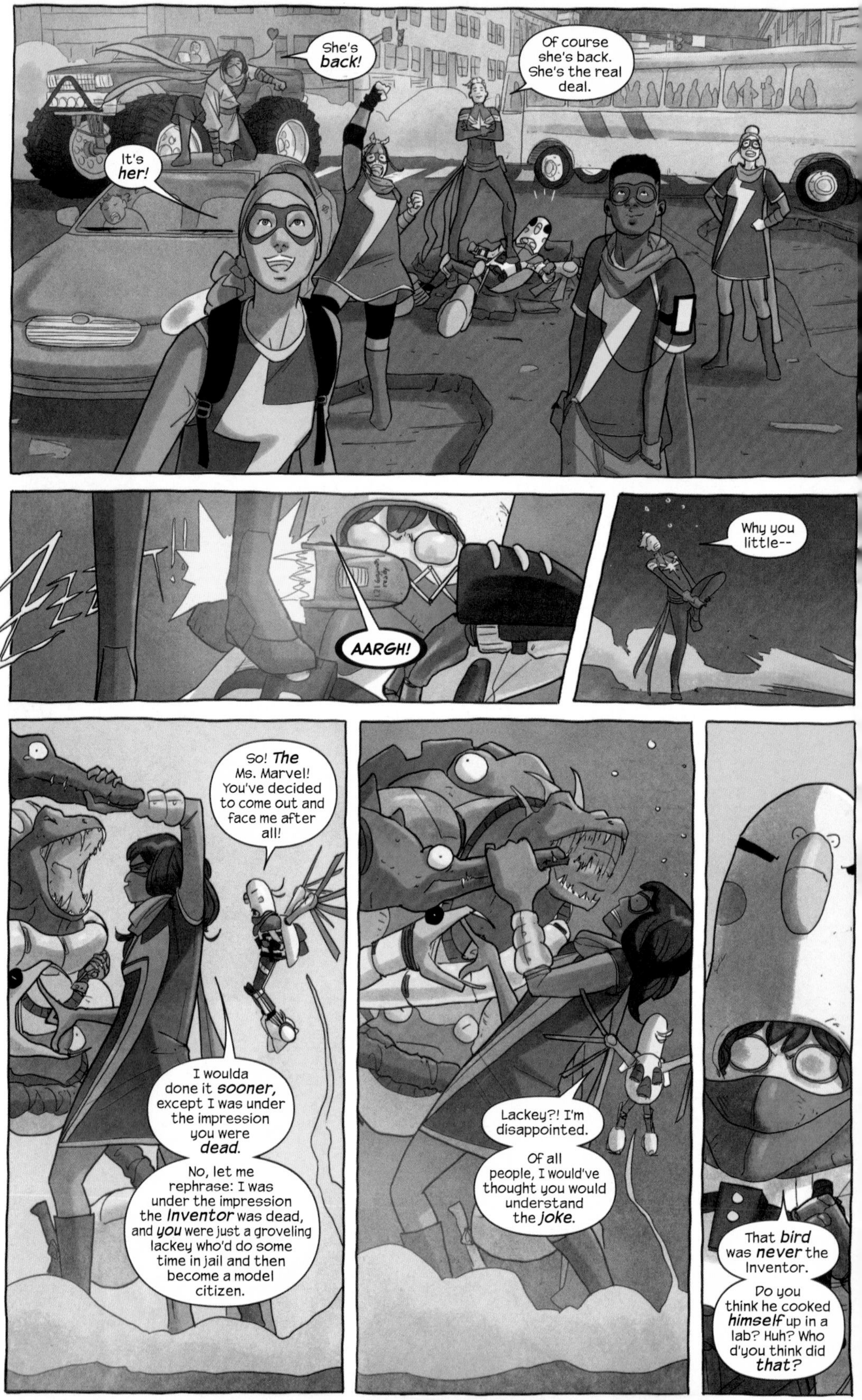
She's back!
Of course she's back. She's the real deal.
It's her!
AARGH!
Why you little--
So! The Ms. Marvel! You've decided to come out and face me after all!
I woulda done it sooner, except I was under the impression you were dead.
No, let me rephrase: I was under the impression the Inventor was dead, and you were just a groveling lackey who'd do some time in jail and then become a model citizen.
Lackey?! I'm disappointed.
Of all people, I would've thought you would understand the joke.
That bird was never the Inventor.
Do you think he cooked himself up in a lab? Huh? Who d'you think did that?

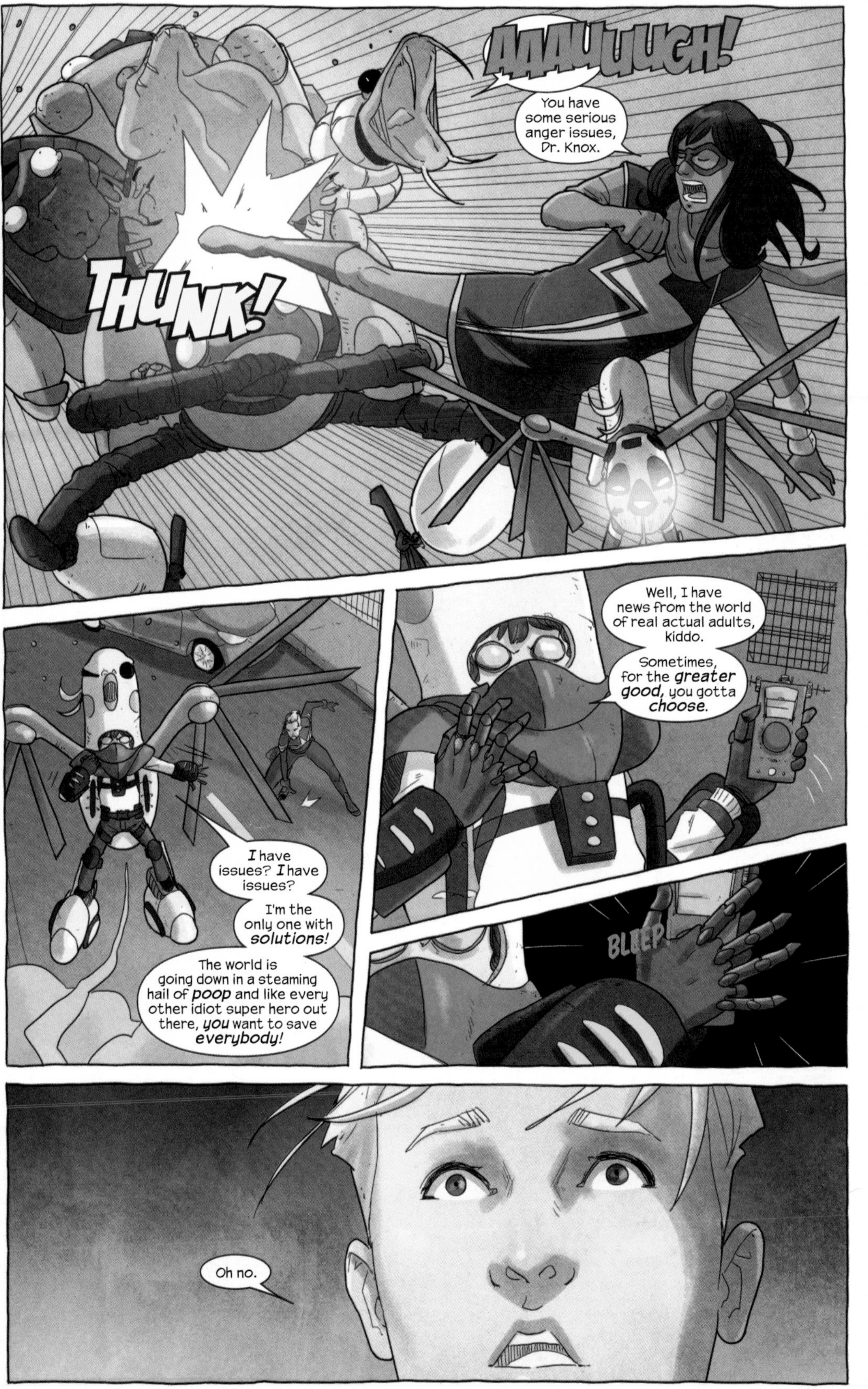
AAAUUUGH!
You have some serious anger issues, Dr. Knox.
THUNK!
I have issues? I have issues?
I'm the only one with solutions!
The world is going down in a steaming hail of poop and like every other idiot super hero out there, you want to save everybody!
Well, I have news from the world of real actual adults, kiddo.
Sometimes, for the greater good, you gotta choose.
BLEEP!
Oh no.

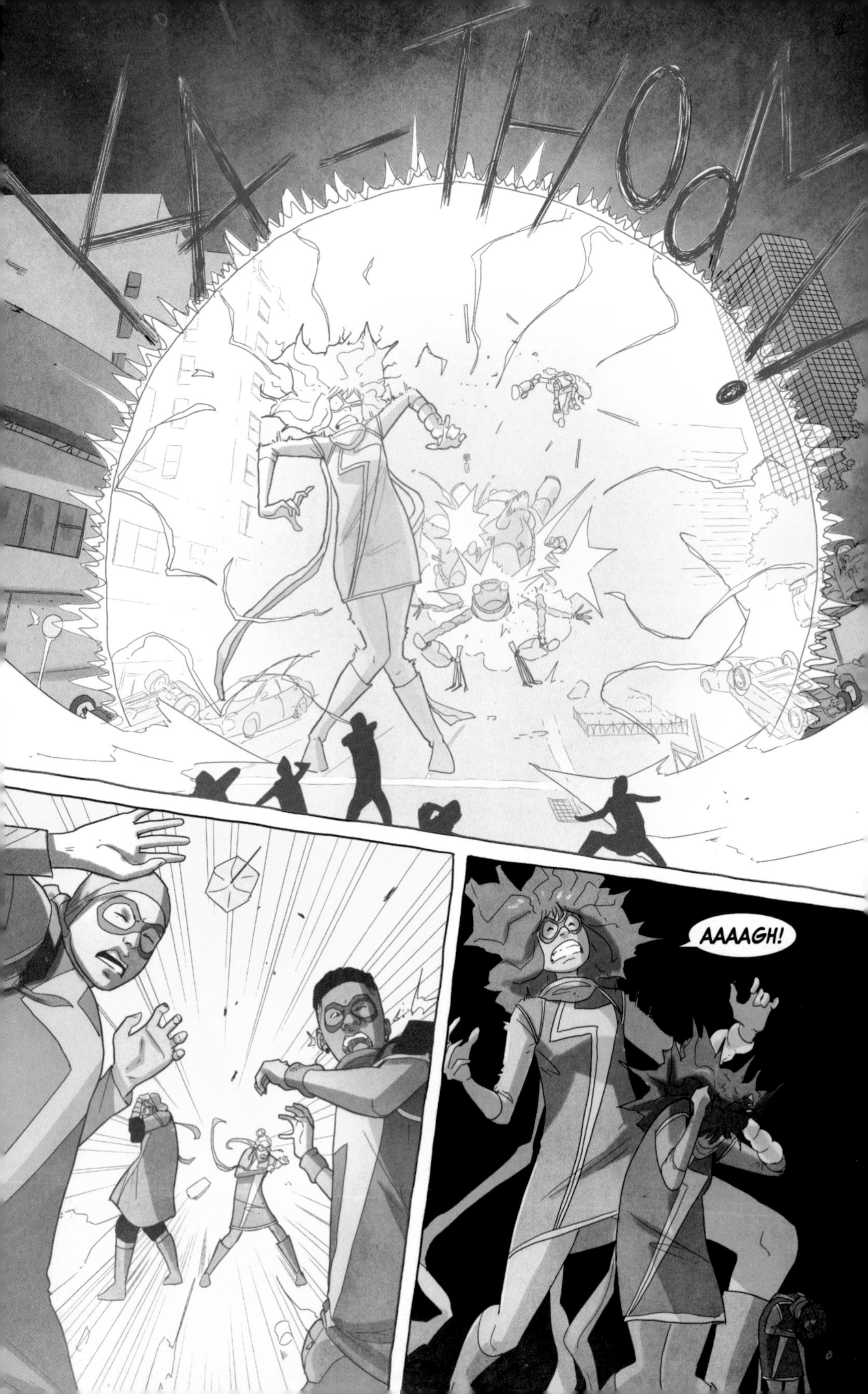
KA-THOOM!
AAAAGH!

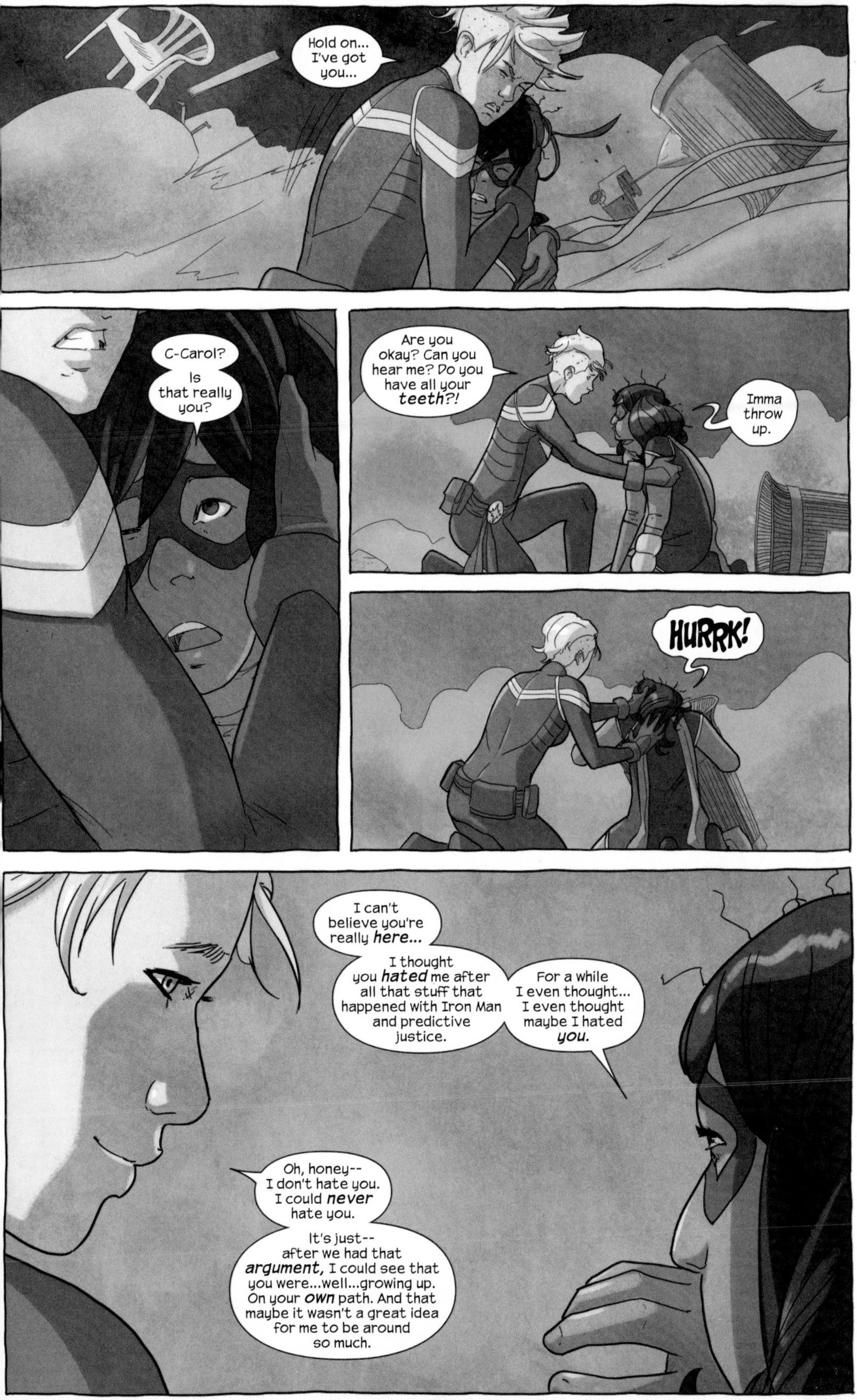
Hold on... I've got you...
C-Carol? Is that really you?
Are you okay? Can you hear me? Do you have all your *teeth*?!
Imma throw up.
HURRK!
I can't believe you're really *here...*
I thought you *hated* me after all that stuff that happened with Iron Man and predictive justice.
For a while I even thought... I even thought maybe I hated *you.*
Oh, honey-- I don't hate you. I could *never* hate you.
It's just-- after we had that *argument,* I could see that you were...well...growing up. On your *own* path. And that maybe it wasn't a great idea for me to be around so much.

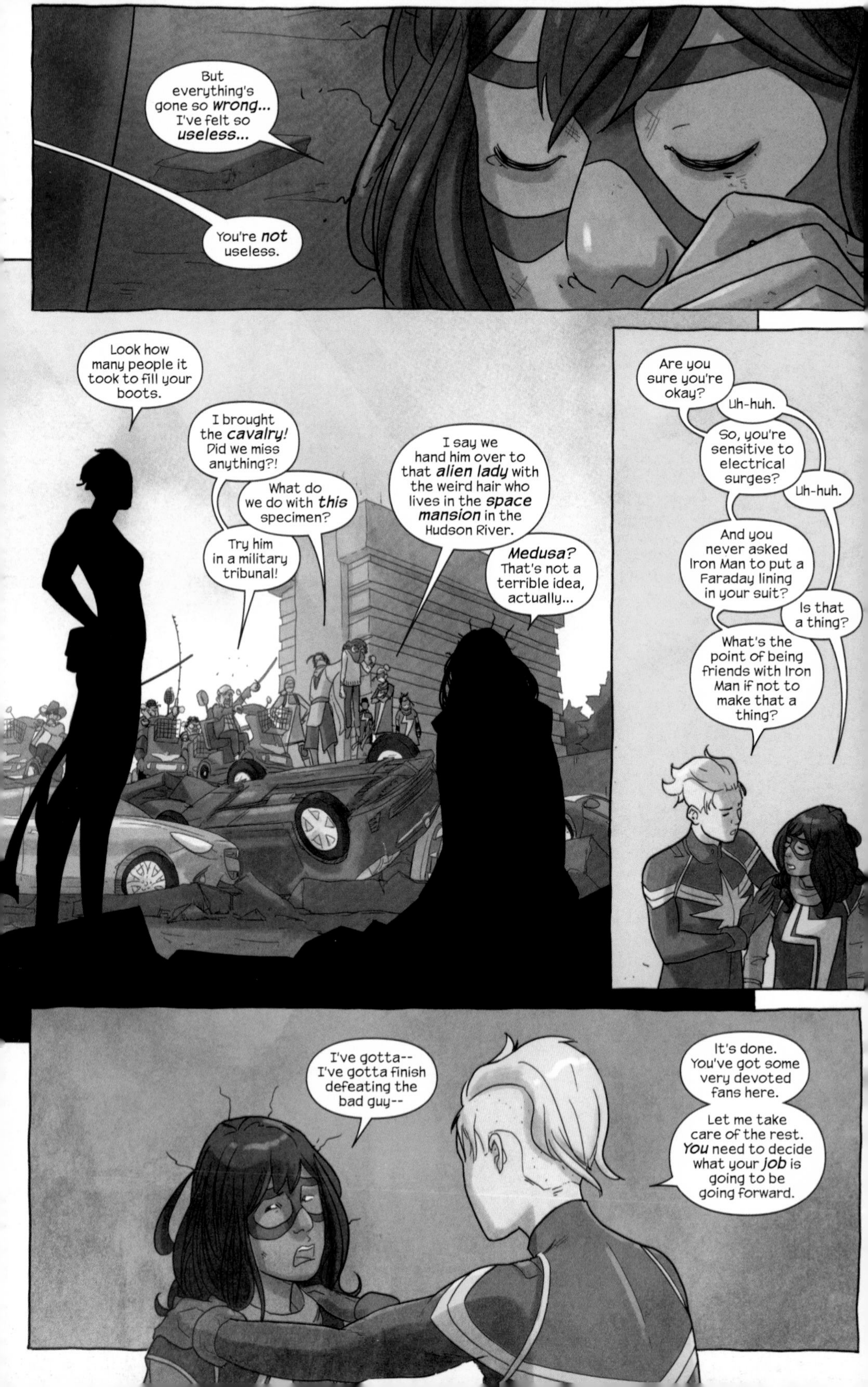

But everything's gone so *wrong*... I've felt so *useless*...
You're *not* useless.
Look how many people it took to fill your boots.
I brought the *cavalry!* Did we miss anything?!
What do we do with *this* specimen?
Try him in a military tribunal!
I say we hand him over to that *alien lady* with the weird hair who lives in the *space mansion* in the Hudson River.
Medusa? That's not a terrible idea, actually...
Are you sure you're okay?
Uh-huh.
So, you're sensitive to electrical surges?
Uh-huh.
And you never asked Iron Man to put a Faraday lining in your suit?
Is that a thing?
What's the point of being friends with Iron Man if not to make that a thing?
I've gotta-- I've gotta finish defeating the bad guy--
It's done. You've got some very devoted fans here.
Let me take care of the rest. *You* need to decide what your *job* is going to be going forward.

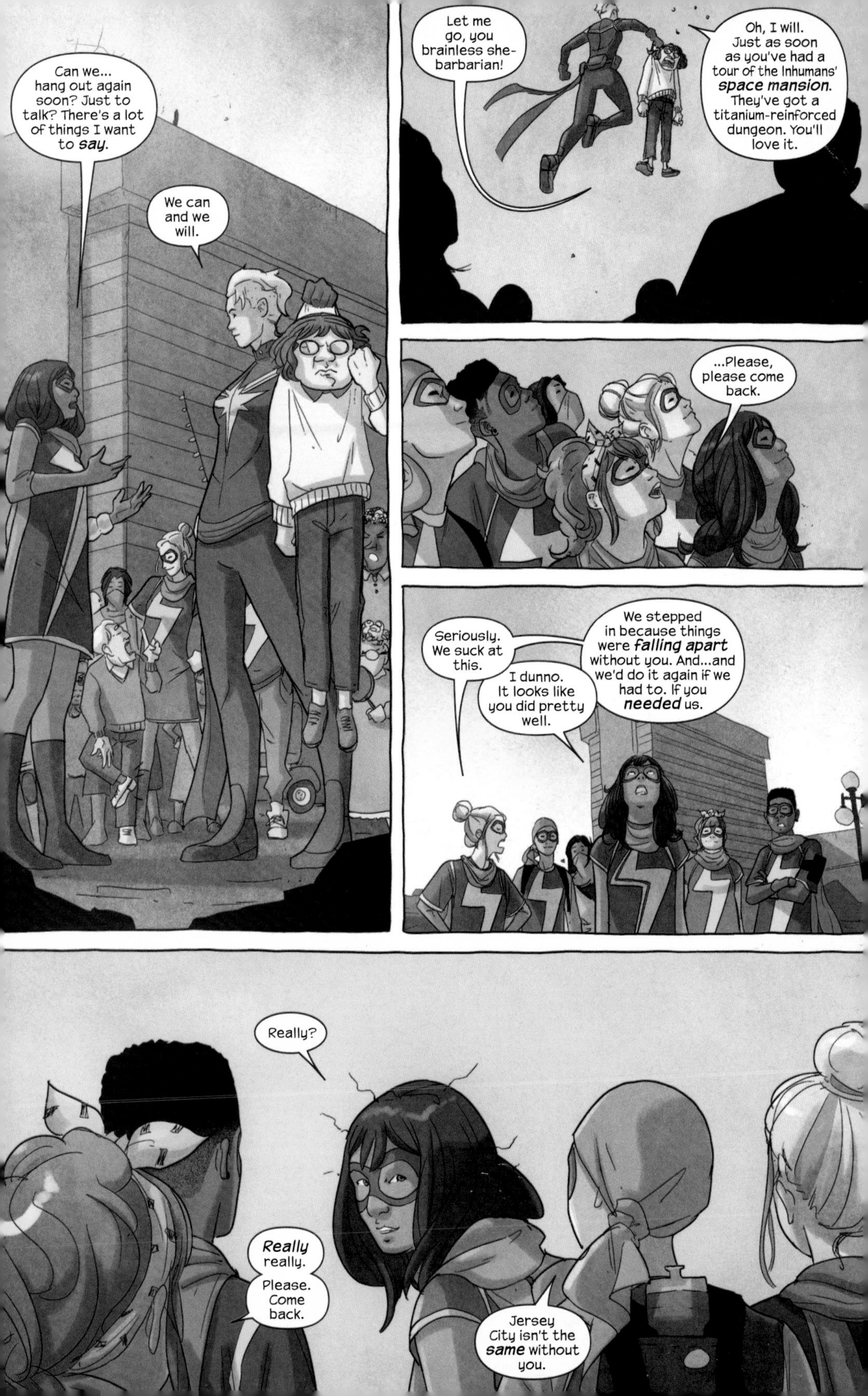
Can we... hang out again soon? Just to talk? There's a lot of things I want to *say*.
We can and we will.
Let me go, you brainless she-barbarian!
Oh, I will. Just as soon as you've had a tour of the Inhumans' ***space mansion***. They've got a titanium-reinforced dungeon. You'll love it.
...Please, please come back.
Seriously. We suck at this.
We stepped in because things were ***falling apart*** without you. And...and we'd do it again if we had to. If you ***needed*** us.
I dunno. It looks like you did pretty well.
Really?
Really really.
Please. Come back.
Jersey City isn't the ***same*** without you.

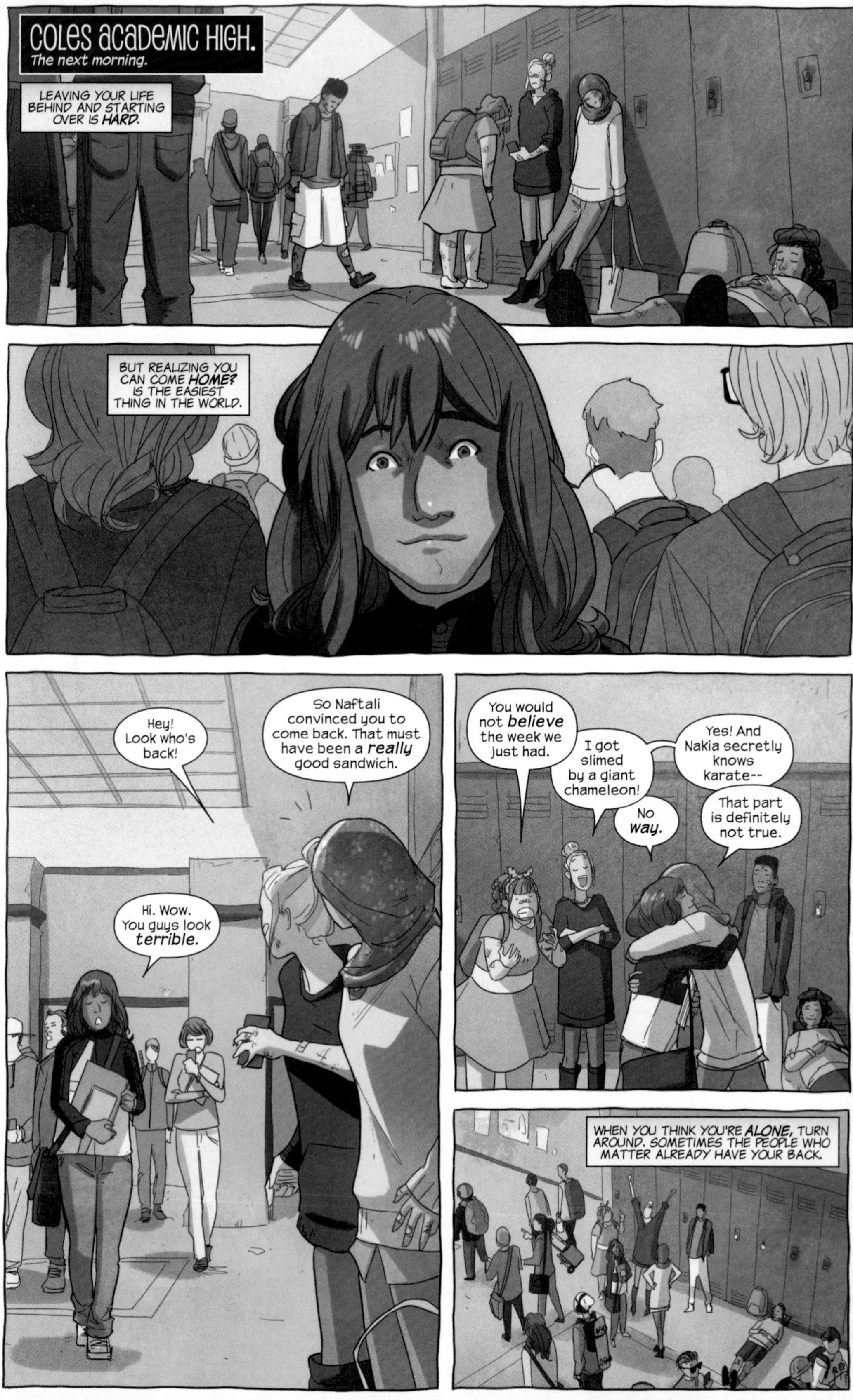
COLES ACADEMIC HIGH.
The next morning.
LEAVING YOUR LIFE BEHIND AND STARTING OVER IS HARD.
BUT REALIZING YOU CAN COME HOME? IS THE EASIEST THING IN THE WORLD.
Hey! Look who's back!
So Naftali convinced you to come back. That must have been a really good sandwich.
Hi. Wow. You guys look terrible.
You would not believe the week we just had.
I got slimed by a giant chameleon!
Yes! And Nakia secretly knows karate--
No way.
That part is definitely not true.
WHEN YOU THINK YOU'RE ALONE, TURN AROUND. SOMETIMES THE PEOPLE WHO MATTER ALREADY HAVE YOUR BACK.

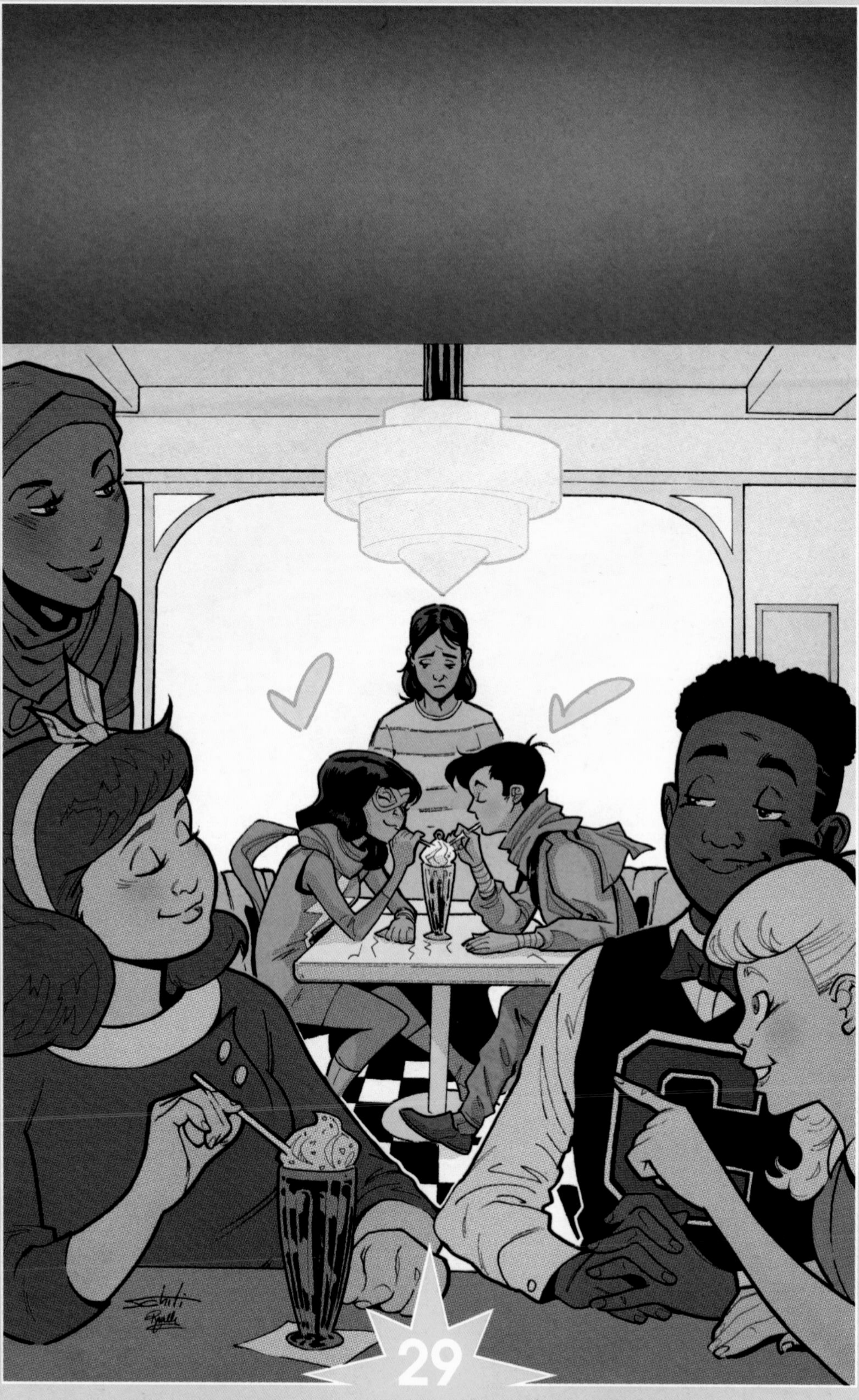
29

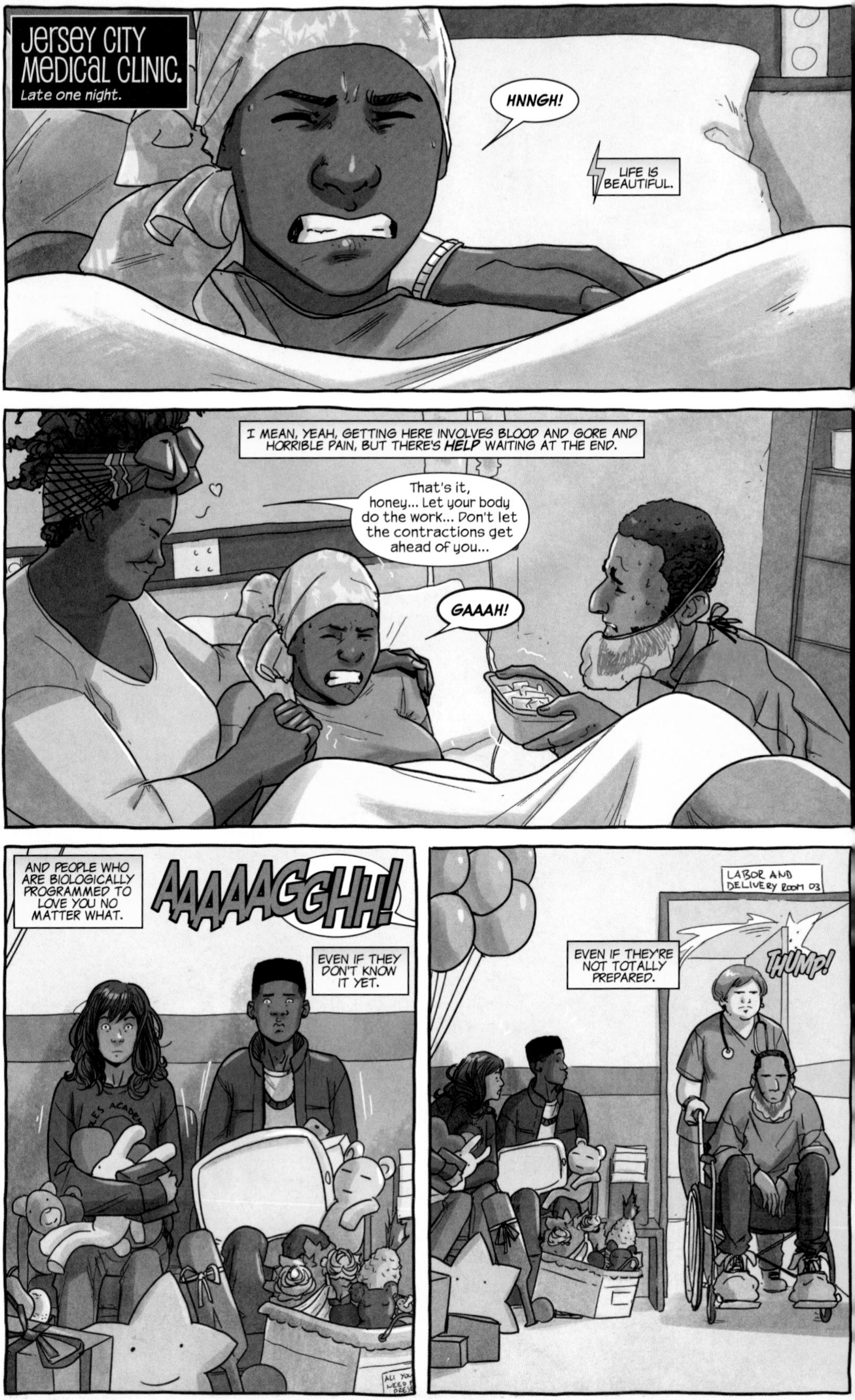

JERSEY CITY MEDICAL CLINIC.
Late one night.
HNNGH!
LIFE IS BEAUTIFUL.
I MEAN, YEAH, GETTING HERE INVOLVES BLOOD AND GORE AND HORRIBLE PAIN, BUT THERE'S HELP WAITING AT THE END.
That's it, honey... Let your body do the work... Don't let the contractions get ahead of you...
GAAAH!
AND PEOPLE WHO ARE BIOLOGICALLY PROGRAMMED TO LOVE YOU NO MATTER WHAT.
AAAAAGGHH!
EVEN IF THEY DON'T KNOW IT YET.
LABOR AND DELIVERY ROOM 03
EVEN IF THEY'RE NOT TOTALLY PREPARED.
THUMP!

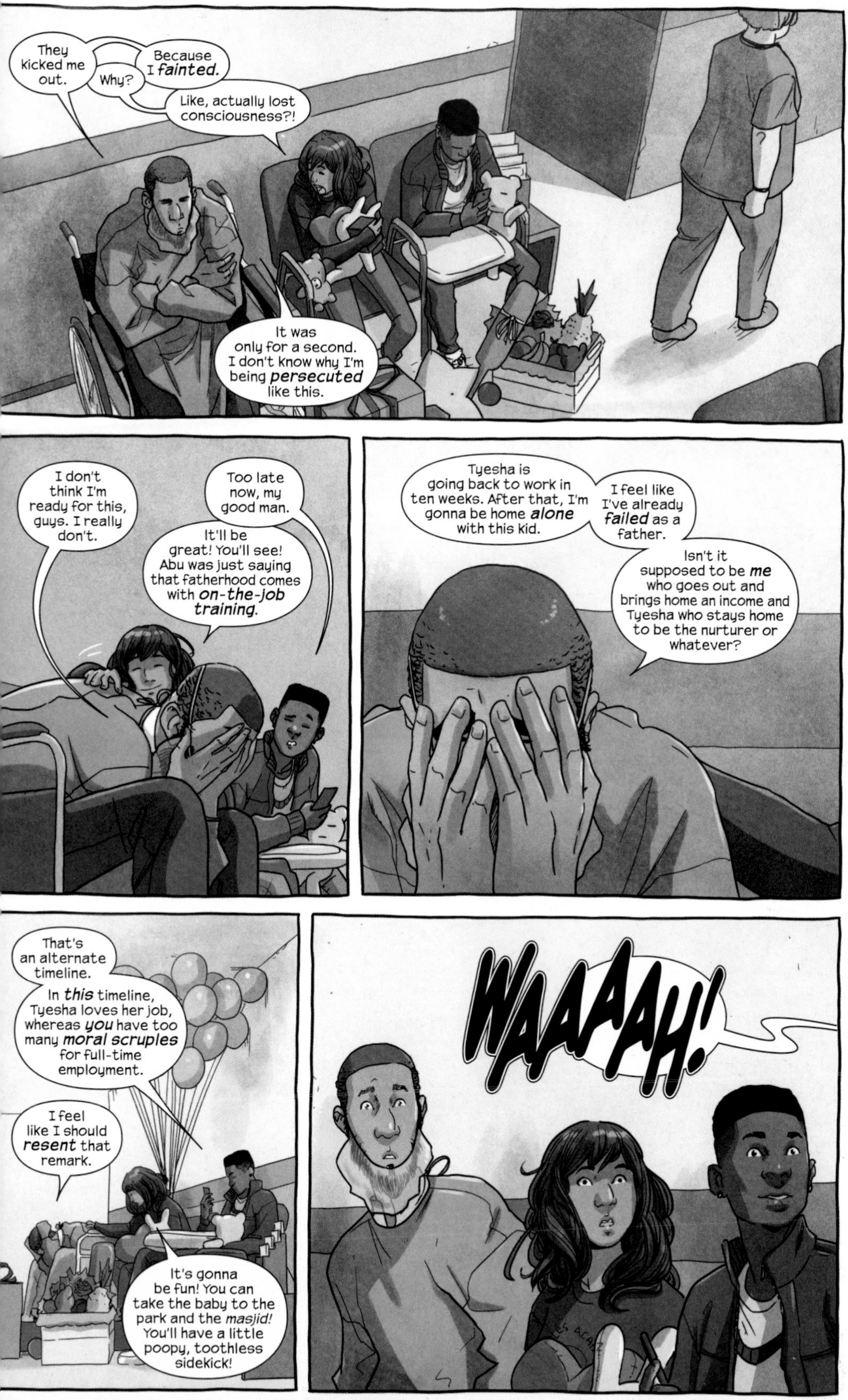
They kicked me out.
Why?
Because I *fainted.*
Like, actually lost consciousness?!
It was only for a second. I don't know why I'm being ***persecuted*** like this.
I don't think I'm ready for this, guys. I really don't.
Too late now, my good man.
It'll be great! You'll see! Abu was just saying that fatherhood comes with ***on-the-job training***.
Tyesha is going back to work in ten weeks. After that, I'm gonna be home ***alone*** with this kid.
I feel like I've already ***failed*** as a father.
Isn't it supposed to be ***me*** who goes out and brings home an income and Tyesha who stays home to be the nurturer or whatever?
That's an alternate timeline.
In ***this*** timeline, Tyesha loves her job, whereas ***you*** have too many ***moral scruples*** for full-time employment.
I feel like I should ***resent*** that remark.
It's gonna be fun! You can take the baby to the park and the *masjid!* You'll have a little poopy, toothless sidekick!
WAAAAH!

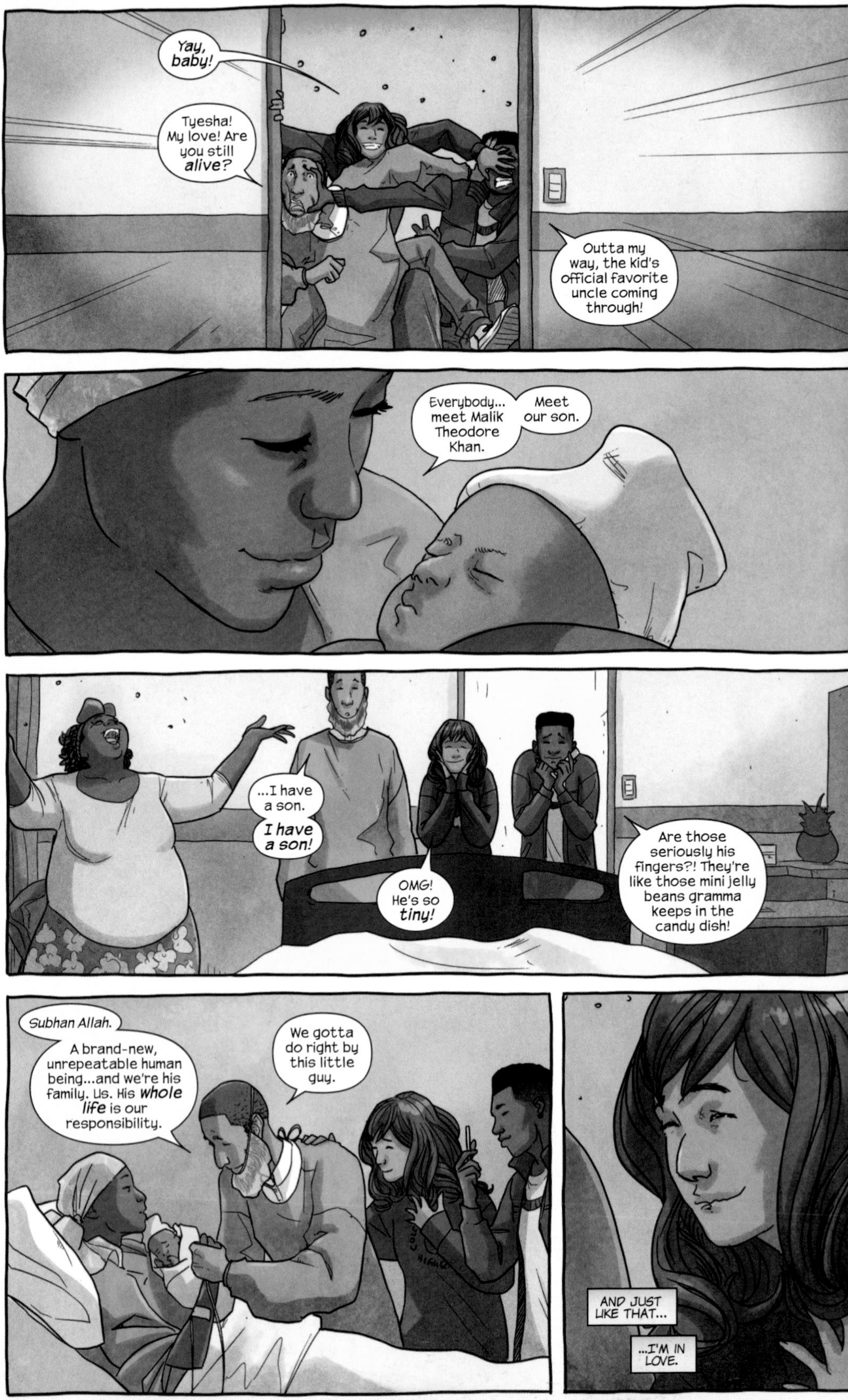
Yay, baby!
Tyesha! My love! Are you still alive?
Outta my way, the kid's official favorite uncle coming through!
Everybody... meet Malik Theodore Khan.
Meet our son.
...I have a son.
I have a son!
OMG! He's so tiny!
Are those seriously his fingers?! They're like those mini jelly beans gramma keeps in the candy dish!
Subhan Allah.
A brand-new, unrepeatable human being...and we're his family. Us. His whole life is our responsibility.
We gotta do right by this little guy.
AND JUST LIKE THAT...
...I'M IN LOVE.

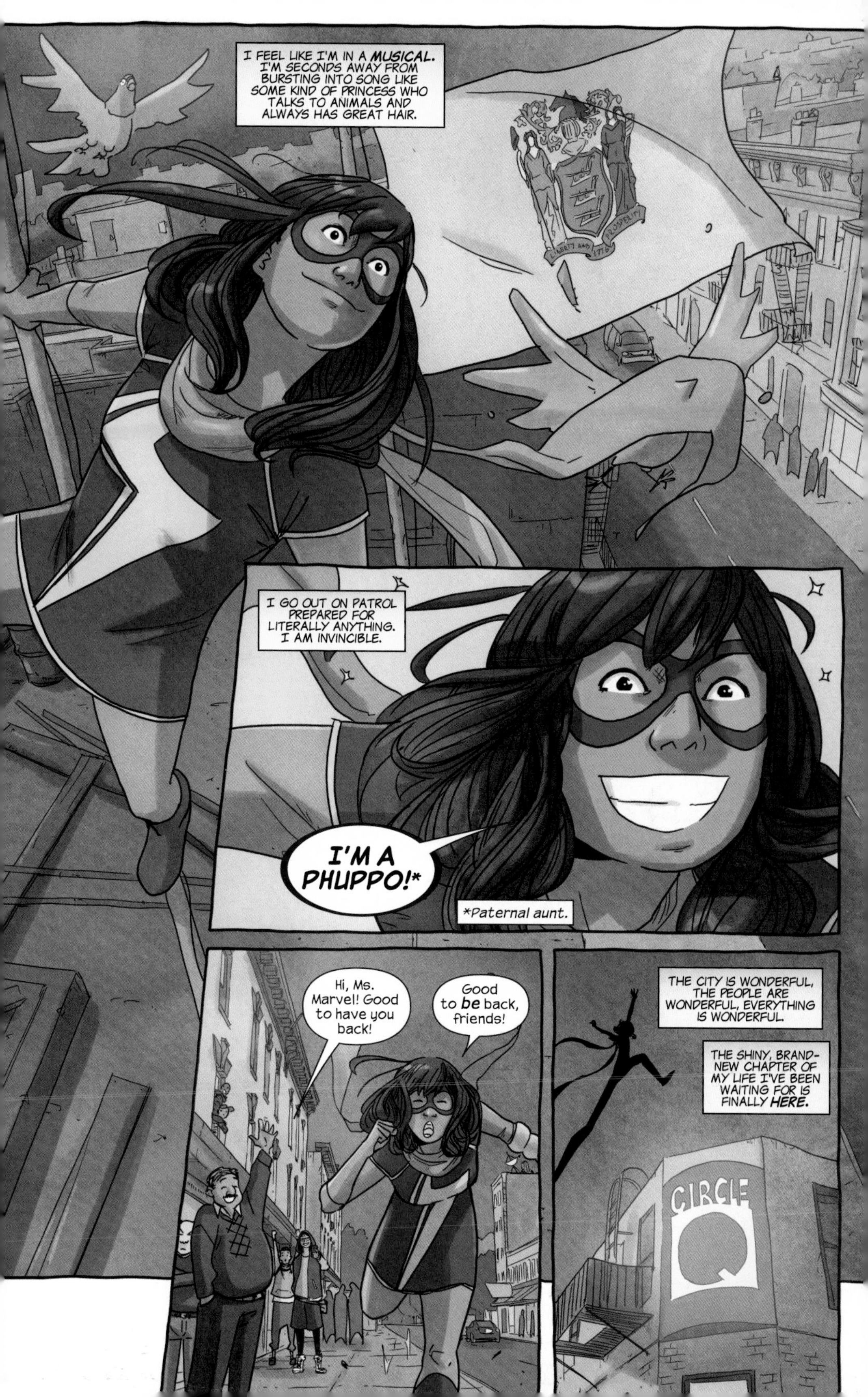
I FEEL LIKE I'M IN A MUSICAL. I'M SECONDS AWAY FROM BURSTING INTO SONG LIKE SOME KIND OF PRINCESS WHO TALKS TO ANIMALS AND ALWAYS HAS GREAT HAIR.
LIBERTY AND PROSPERITY 1776
I GO OUT ON PATROL PREPARED FOR LITERALLY ANYTHING. I AM INVINCIBLE.
I'M A PHUPPO!*
*Paternal aunt.
Hi, Ms. Marvel! Good to have you back!
Good to be back, friends!
THE CITY IS WONDERFUL, THE PEOPLE ARE WONDERFUL, EVERYTHING IS WONDERFUL.
THE SHINY, BRAND-NEW CHAPTER OF MY LIFE I'VE BEEN WAITING FOR IS FINALLY HERE.
CIRCLE Q

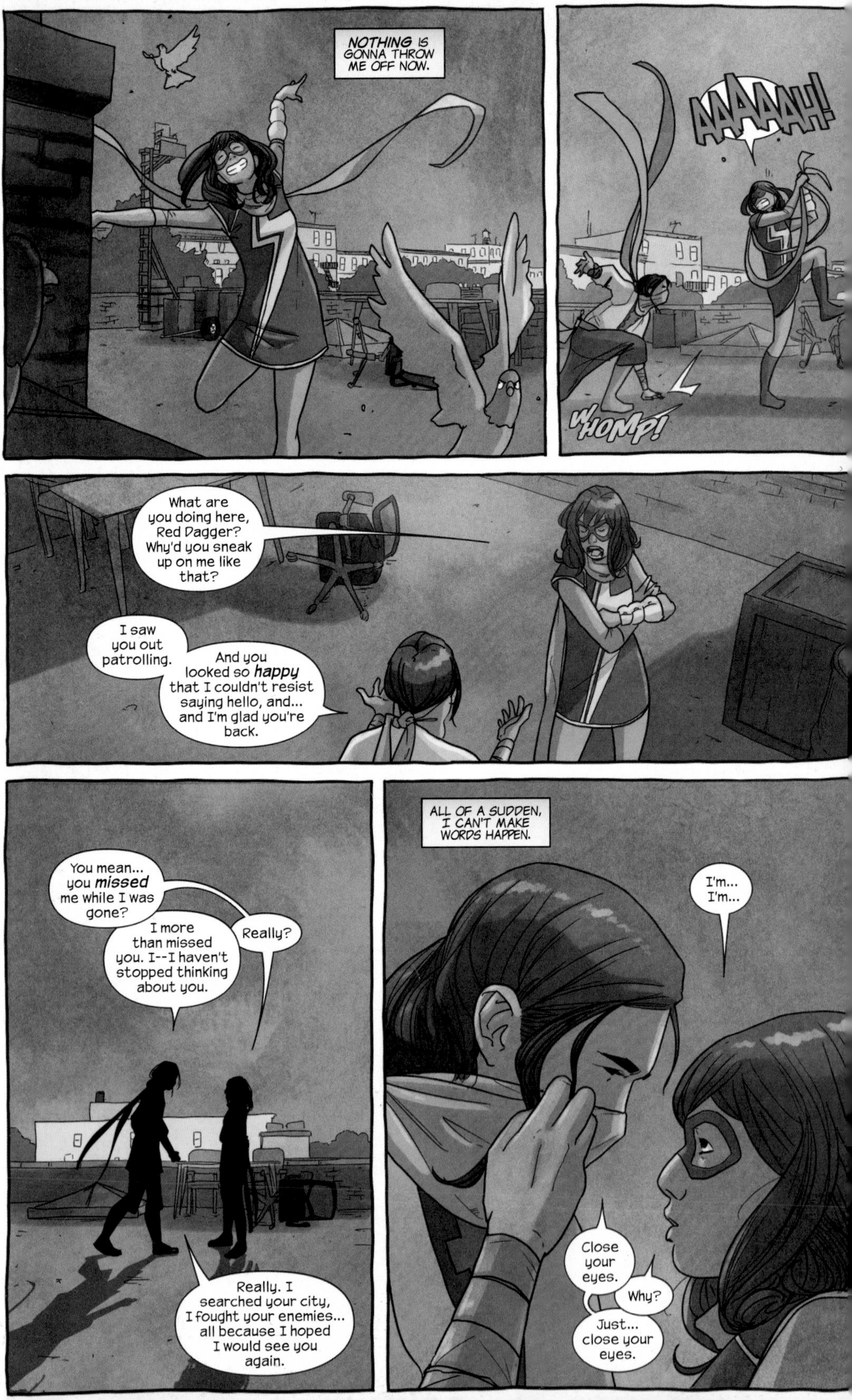

NOTHING IS GONNA THROW ME OFF NOW.
AAAAAH!
WHOMP!
What are you doing here, Red Dagger? Why'd you sneak up on me like that?
I saw you out patrolling.
And you looked so happy that I couldn't resist saying hello, and... and I'm glad you're back.
You mean... you missed me while I was gone?
Really?
I more than missed you. I--I haven't stopped thinking about you.
Really. I searched your city, I fought your enemies... all because I hoped I would see you again.
ALL OF A SUDDEN, I CAN'T MAKE WORDS HAPPEN.
I'm... I'm...
Close your eyes.
Why?
Just... close your eyes.

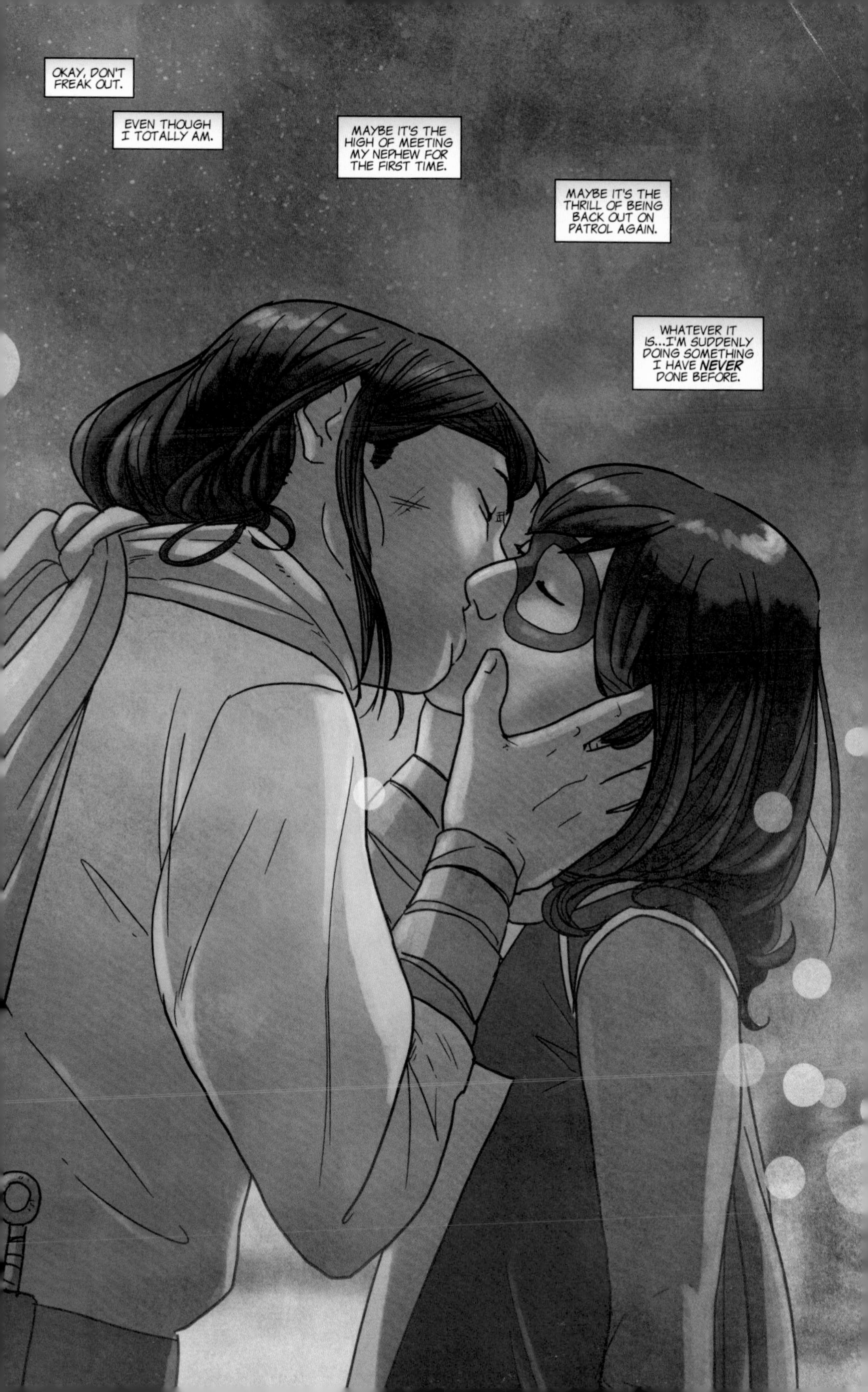
OKAY, DON'T FREAK OUT.
EVEN THOUGH I TOTALLY AM.
MAYBE IT'S THE HIGH OF MEETING MY NEPHEW FOR THE FIRST TIME.
MAYBE IT'S THE THRILL OF BEING BACK OUT ON PATROL AGAIN.
WHATEVER IT IS...I'M SUDDENLY DOING SOMETHING I HAVE ***NEVER*** DONE BEFORE.

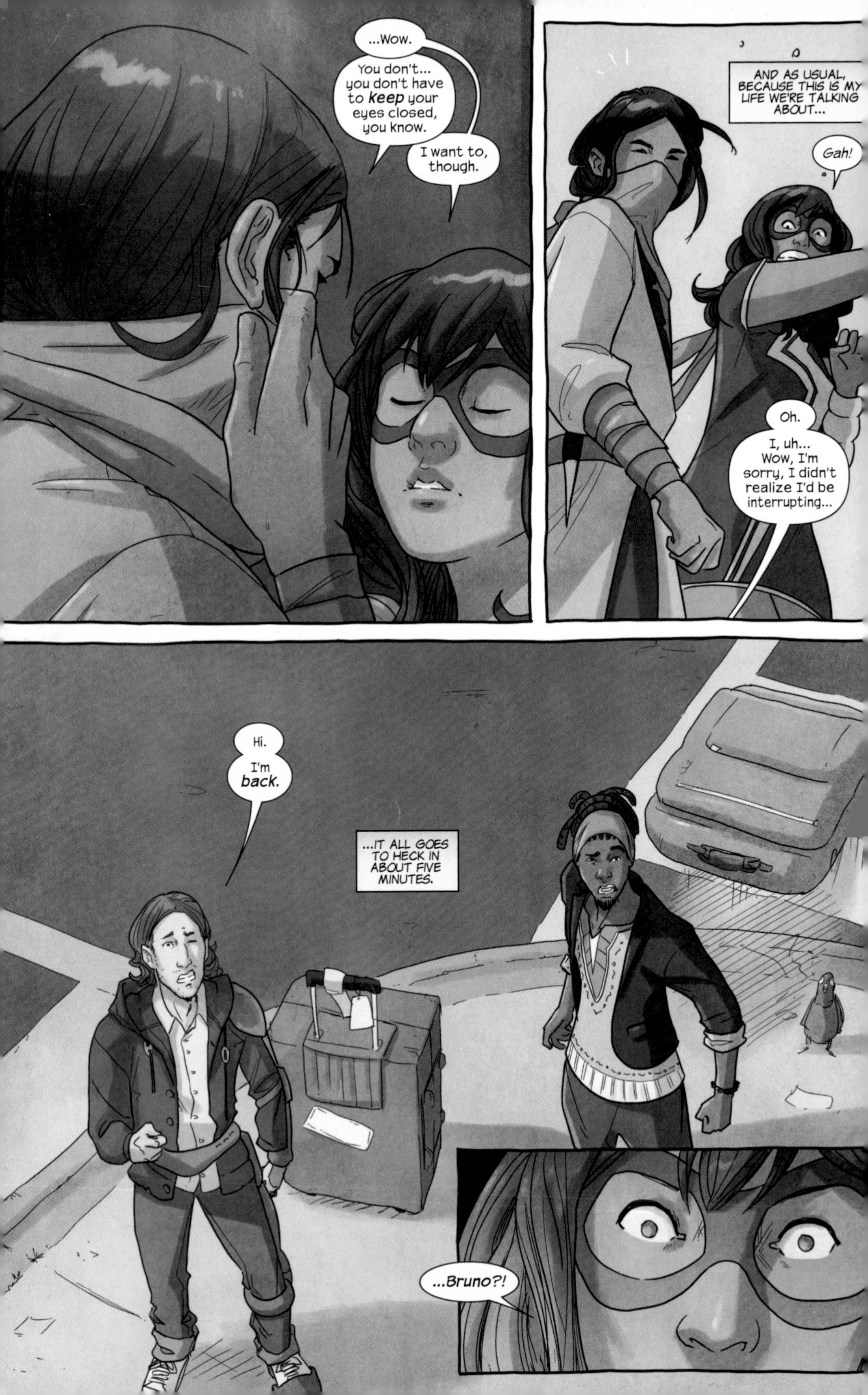
...Wow.
You don't... you don't have to *keep* your eyes closed, you know.
I want to, though.
AND AS USUAL, BECAUSE THIS IS MY LIFE WE'RE TALKING ABOUT...
Gah!
Oh.
I, uh... Wow, I'm sorry, I didn't realize I'd be interrupting...
Hi.
I'm *back.*
...IT ALL GOES TO HECK IN ABOUT FIVE MINUTES.
...Bruno?!

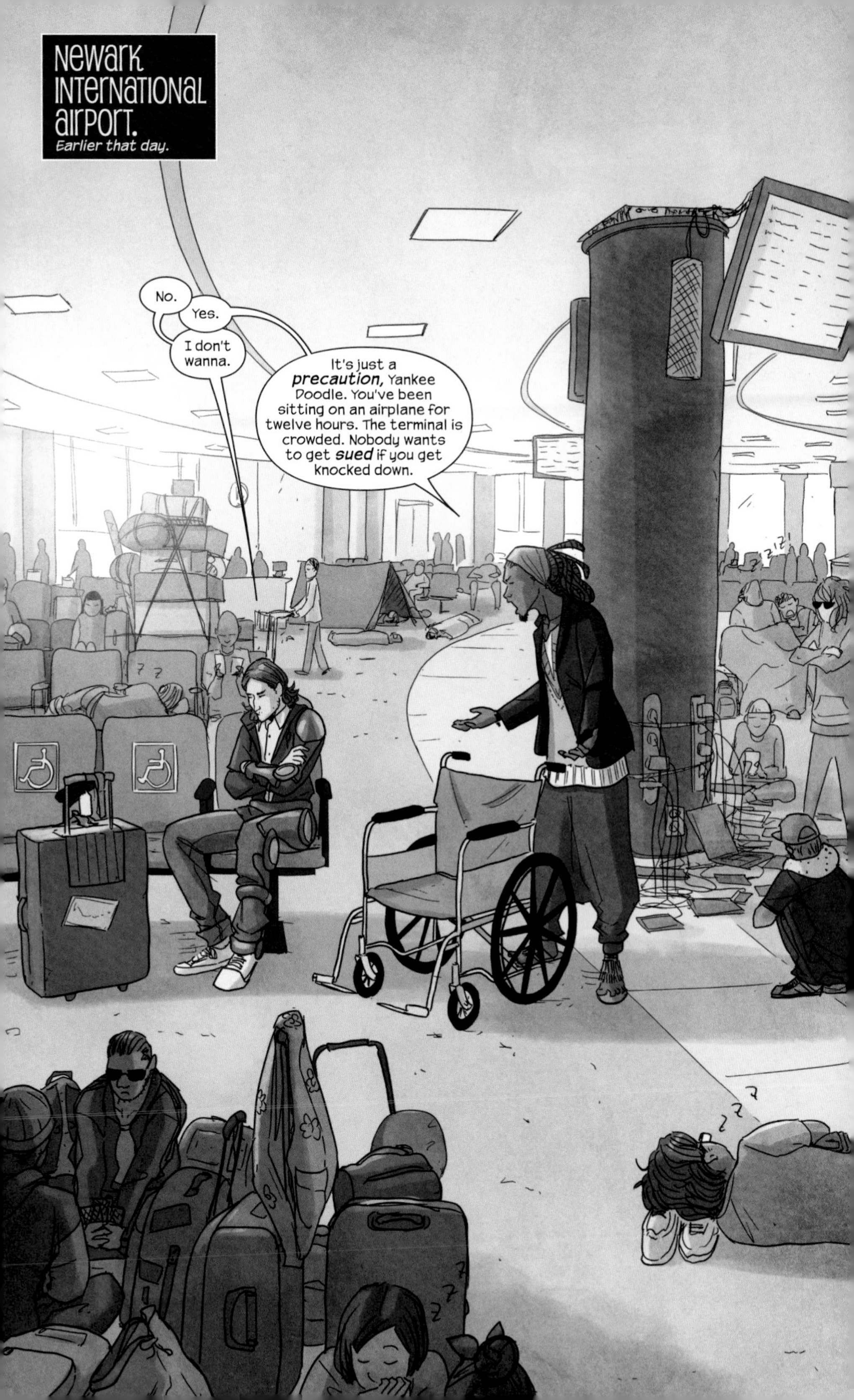
Newark International airport.
Earlier that day.
No.
Yes.
I don't wanna.
It's just a precaution, Yankee Doodle. You've been sitting on an airplane for twelve hours. The terminal is crowded. Nobody wants to get sued if you get knocked down.

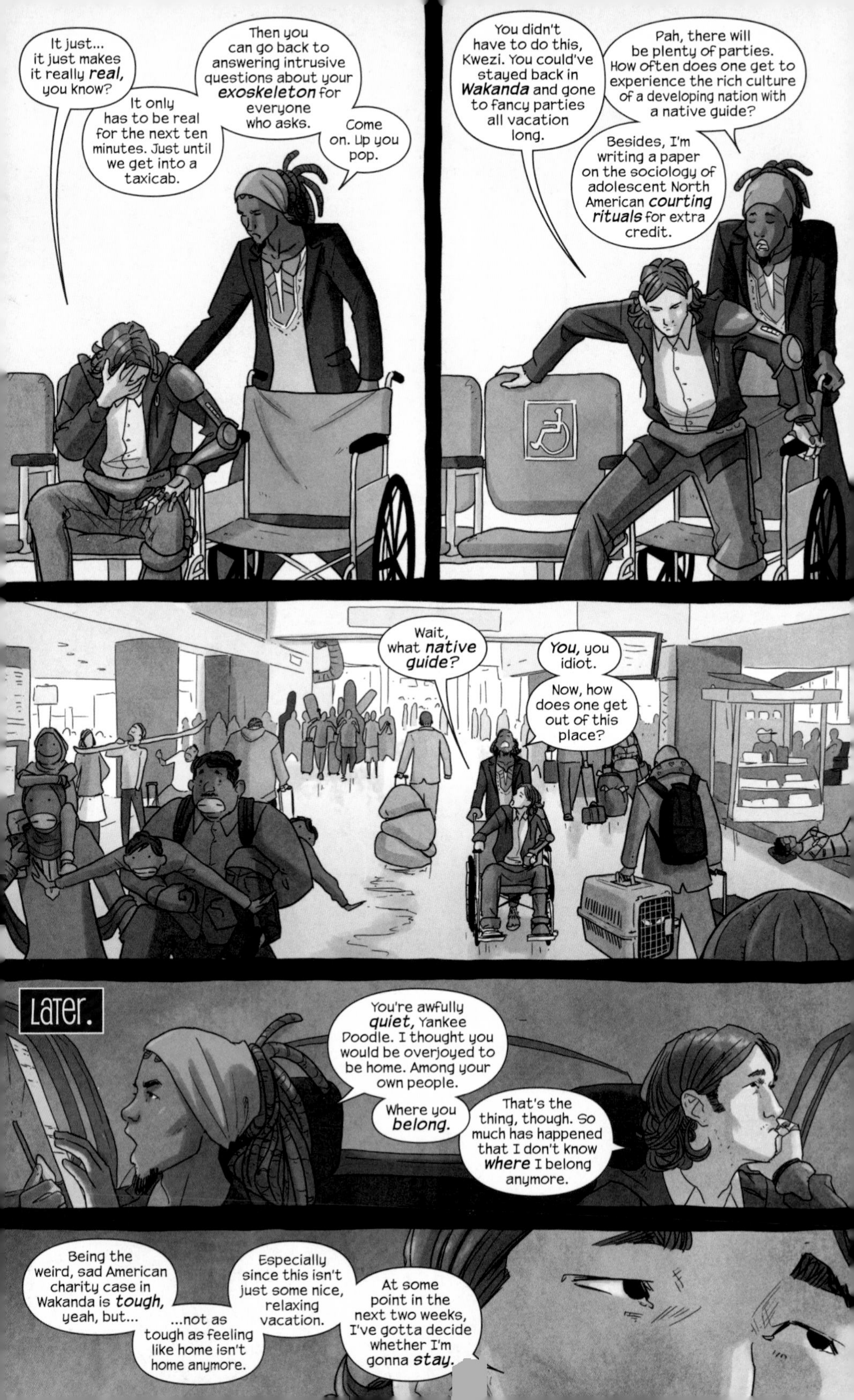
It just... it just makes it really real, you know?
Then you can go back to answering intrusive questions about your exoskeleton for everyone who asks.
It only has to be real for the next ten minutes. Just until we get into a taxicab.
Come on. Up you pop.
You didn't have to do this, Kwezi. You could've stayed back in Wakanda and gone to fancy parties all vacation long.
Pah, there will be plenty of parties. How often does one get to experience the rich culture of a developing nation with a native guide?
Besides, I'm writing a paper on the sociology of adolescent North American courting rituals for extra credit.
Wait, what native guide?
You, you idiot.
Now, how does one get out of this place?
LATER.
You're awfully quiet, Yankee Doodle. I thought you would be overjoyed to be home. Among your own people.
Where you belong.
That's the thing, though. So much has happened that I don't know where I belong anymore.
Being the weird, sad American charity case in Wakanda is tough, yeah, but...
...not as tough as feeling like home isn't home anymore.
Especially since this isn't just some nice, relaxing vacation.
At some point in the next two weeks, I've gotta decide whether I'm gonna stay.

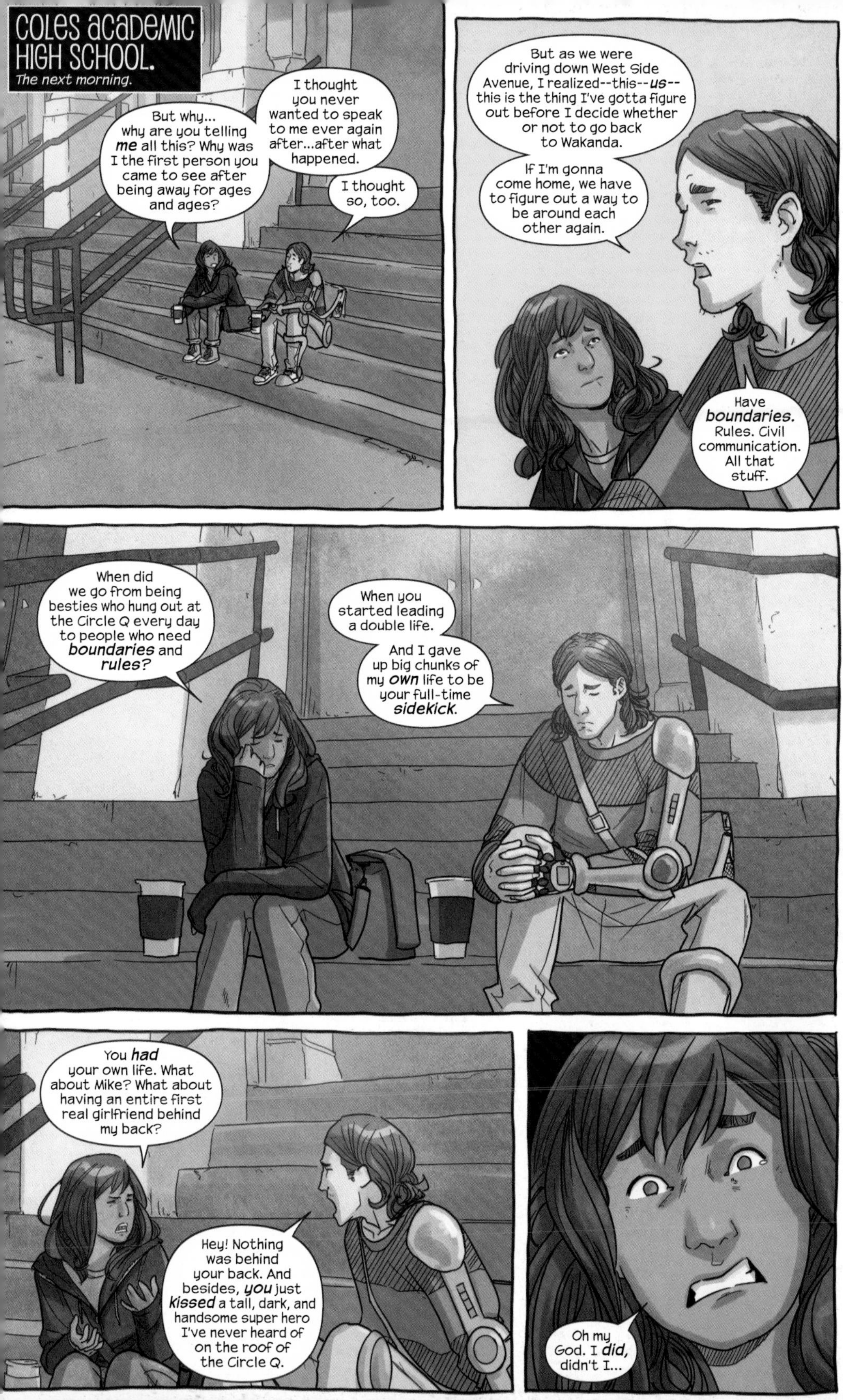
COLES ACADEMIC HIGH SCHOOL.
The next morning.
But why... why are you telling me all this? Why was I the first person you came to see after being away for ages and ages?
I thought you never wanted to speak to me ever again after...after what happened.
I thought so, too.
But as we were driving down West Side Avenue, I realized--this--us--this is the thing I've gotta figure out before I decide whether or not to go back to Wakanda.
If I'm gonna come home, we have to figure out a way to be around each other again.
Have boundaries. Rules. Civil communication. All that stuff.
When did we go from being besties who hung out at the Circle Q every day to people who need boundaries and rules?
When you started leading a double life.
And I gave up big chunks of my own life to be your full-time sidekick.
You had your own life. What about Mike? What about having an entire first real girlfriend behind my back?
Hey! Nothing was behind your back. And besides, you just kissed a tall, dark, and handsome super hero I've never heard of on the roof of the Circle Q.
Oh my God. I did, didn't I...

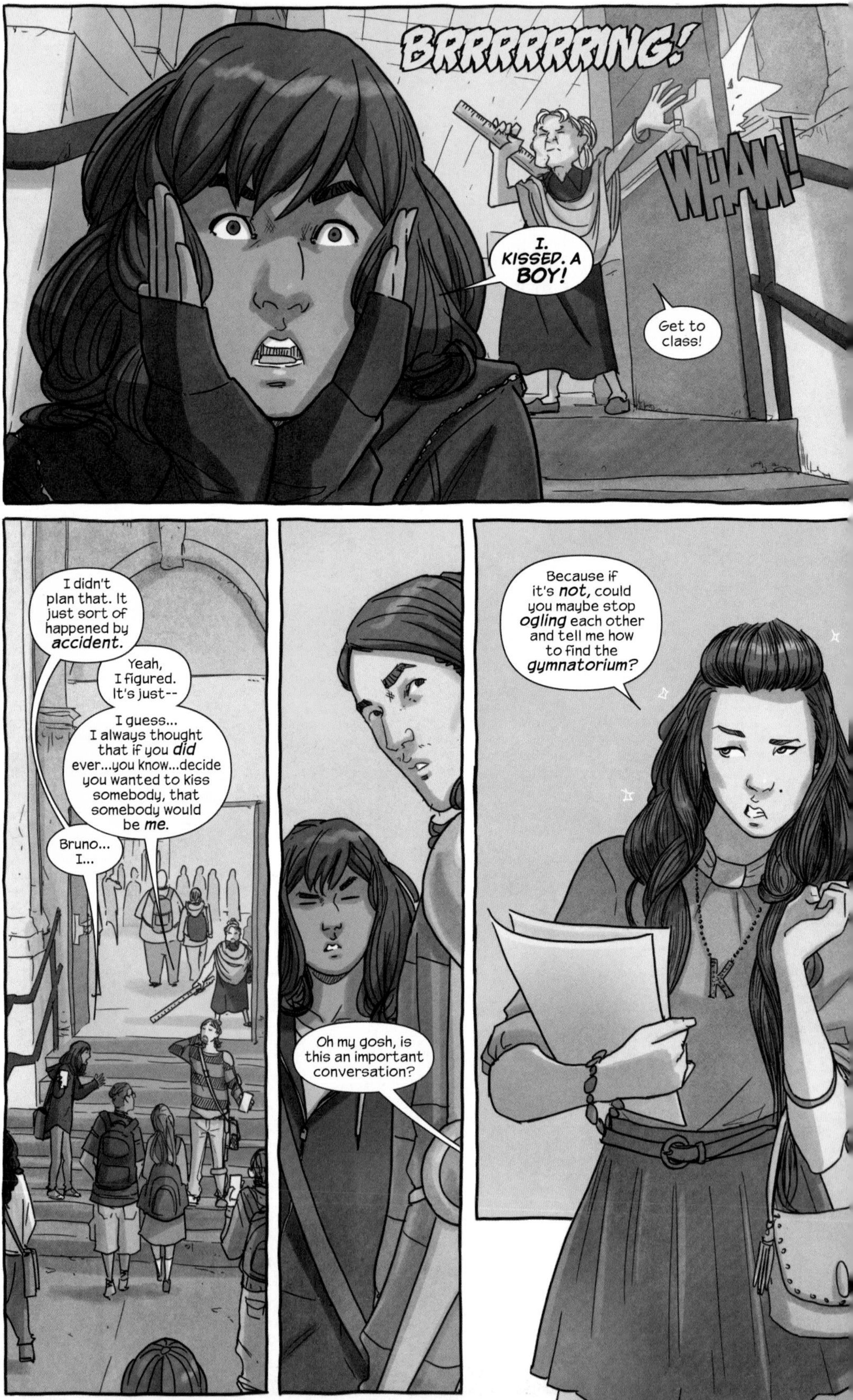
BRRRRRRRING!
WHAM!
I. KISSED. A BOY!
Get to class!
I didn't plan that. It just sort of happened by accident.
Yeah, I figured. It's just--
I guess... I always thought that if you did ever...you know...decide you wanted to kiss somebody, that somebody would be me.
Bruno... I...
Oh my gosh, is this an important conversation?
Because if it's not, could you maybe stop ogling each other and tell me how to find the gymnatorium?

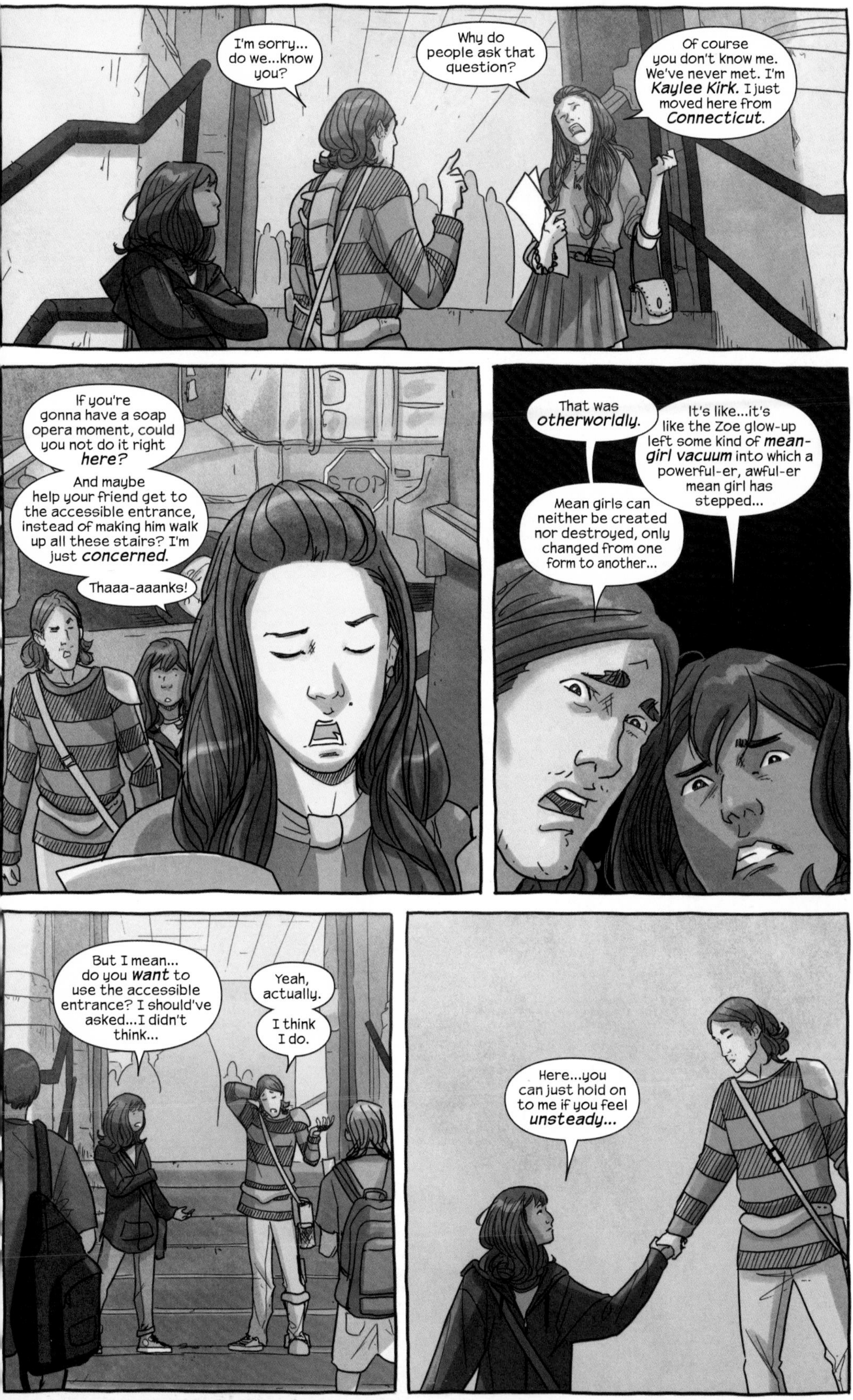
I'm sorry... do we...know you?
Why do people ask that question?
Of course you don't know me. We've never met. I'm *Kaylee Kirk.* I just moved here from *Connecticut*.
If you're gonna have a soap opera moment, could you not do it right *here?*
And maybe help your friend get to the accessible entrance, instead of making him walk up all these stairs? I'm just *concerned*.
Thaaa-aaanks!
STOP
That was *otherworldly*.
It's like...it's like the Zoe glow-up left some kind of *mean-girl vacuum* into which a powerful-er, awful-er mean girl has stepped...
Mean girls can neither be created nor destroyed, only changed from one form to another...
But I mean... do you *want* to use the accessible entrance? I should've asked...I didn't think...
Yeah, actually.
I think I do.
Here...you can just hold on to me if you feel *unsteady...*

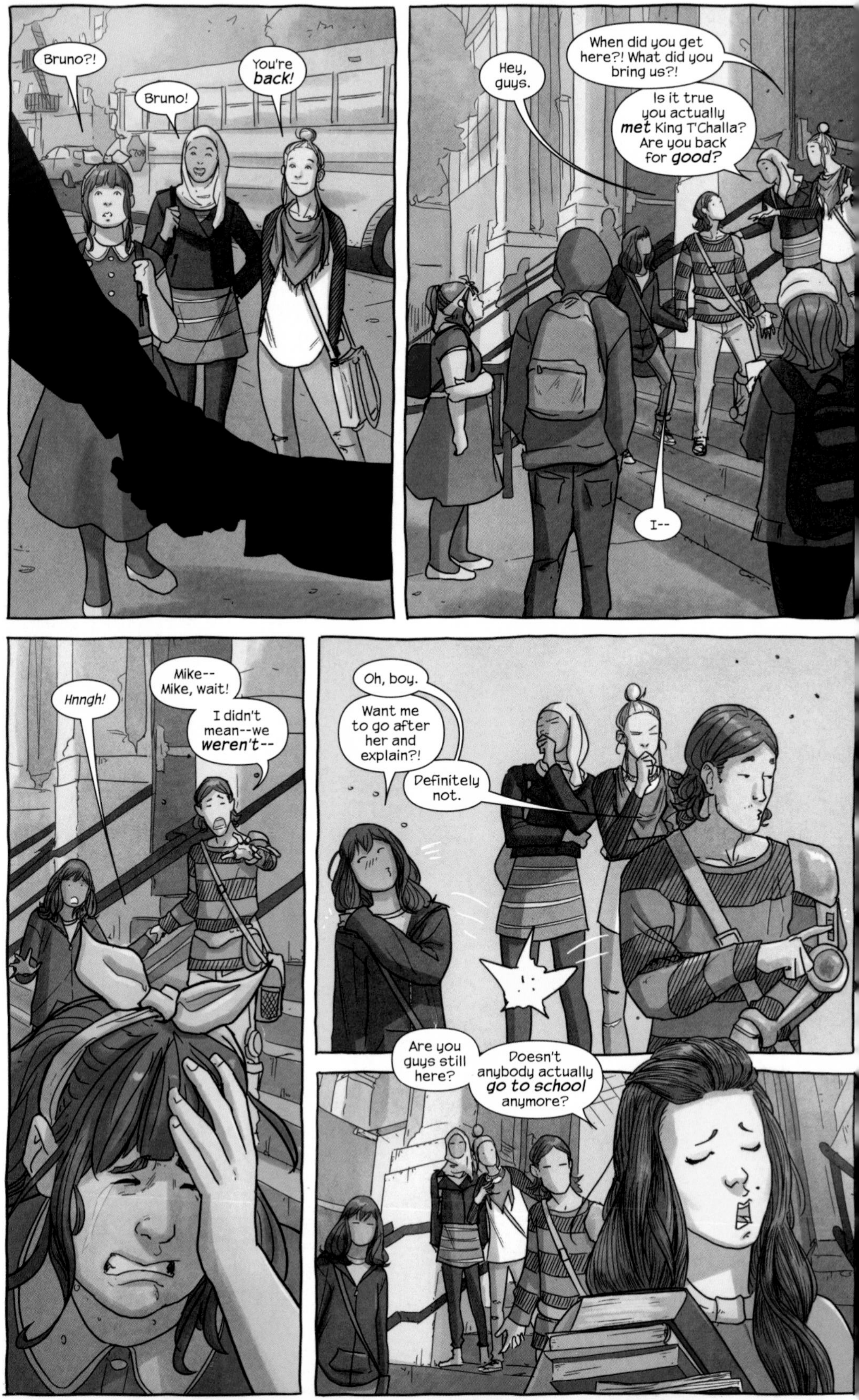
Bruno?!
Bruno!
You're back!
Hey, guys.
When did you get here?! What did you bring us?!
Is it true you actually met King T'Challa? Are you back for good?
I--
Hnngh!
Mike-- Mike, wait!
I didn't mean--we weren't--
Oh, boy.
Want me to go after her and explain?!
Definitely not.
Are you guys still here?
Doesn't anybody actually go to school anymore?

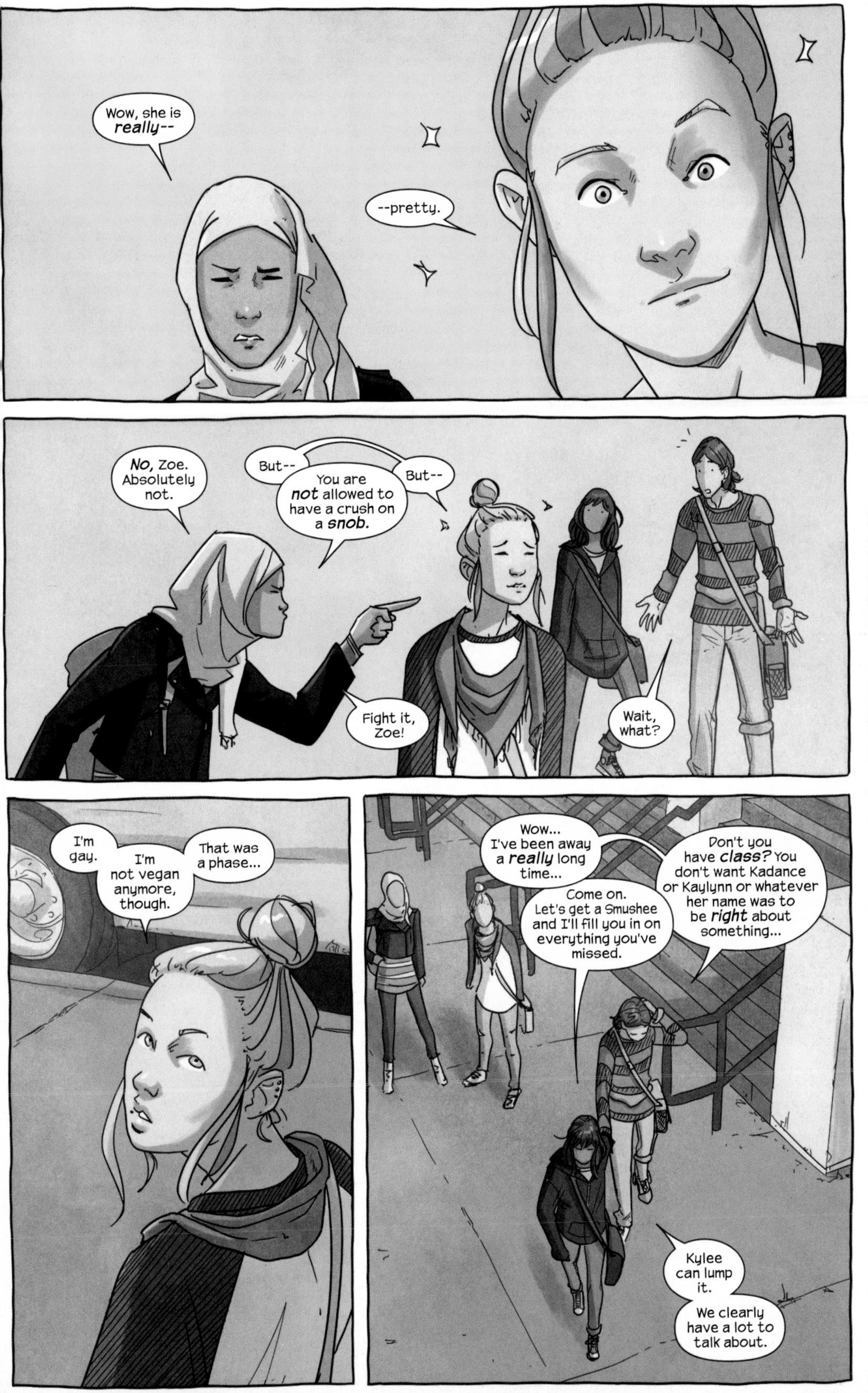
Wow, she is *really*--
--pretty.
No, Zoe. Absolutely not.
But--
You are *not* allowed to have a crush on a *snob.*
But--
Fight it, Zoe!
Wait, what?
I'm gay.
I'm not vegan anymore, though.
That was a phase...
Wow... I've been away a *really* long time...
Come on. Let's get a Smushee and I'll fill you in on everything you've missed.
Don't you have *class?* You don't want Kadance or Kaylynn or whatever her name was to be *right* about something...
Kylee can lump it.
We clearly have a lot to talk about.

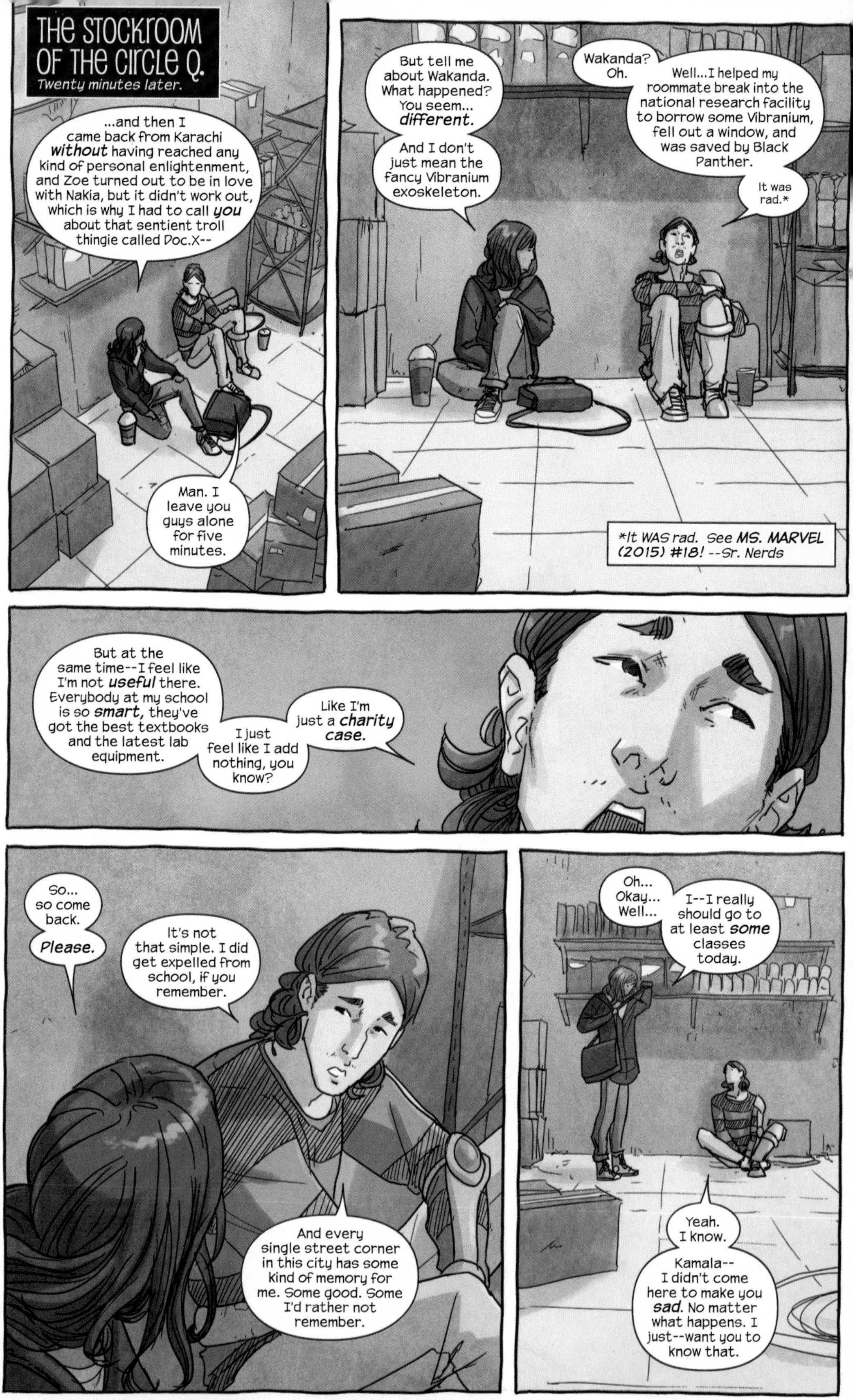
THE STOCKROOM OF THE CIRCLE Q.
Twenty minutes later.
...and then I came back from Karachi without having reached any kind of personal enlightenment, and Zoe turned out to be in love with Nakia, but it didn't work out, which is why I had to call you about that sentient troll thingie called Doc.X--
Man. I leave you guys alone for five minutes.
But tell me about Wakanda. What happened? You seem... different.
And I don't just mean the fancy Vibranium exoskeleton.
Wakanda? Oh.
Well...I helped my roommate break into the national research facility to borrow some Vibranium, fell out a window, and was saved by Black Panther.
It was rad.*
*It WAS rad. See MS. MARVEL (2015) #18! --Sr. Nerds
But at the same time--I feel like I'm not useful there. Everybody at my school is so smart, they've got the best textbooks and the latest lab equipment.
I just feel like I add nothing, you know?
Like I'm just a charity case.
So... so come back.
Please.
It's not that simple. I did get expelled from school, if you remember.
And every single street corner in this city has some kind of memory for me. Some good. Some I'd rather not remember.
Oh... Okay... Well...
I--I really should go to at least some classes today.
Yeah. I know.
Kamala-- I didn't come here to make you sad. No matter what happens. I just--want you to know that.

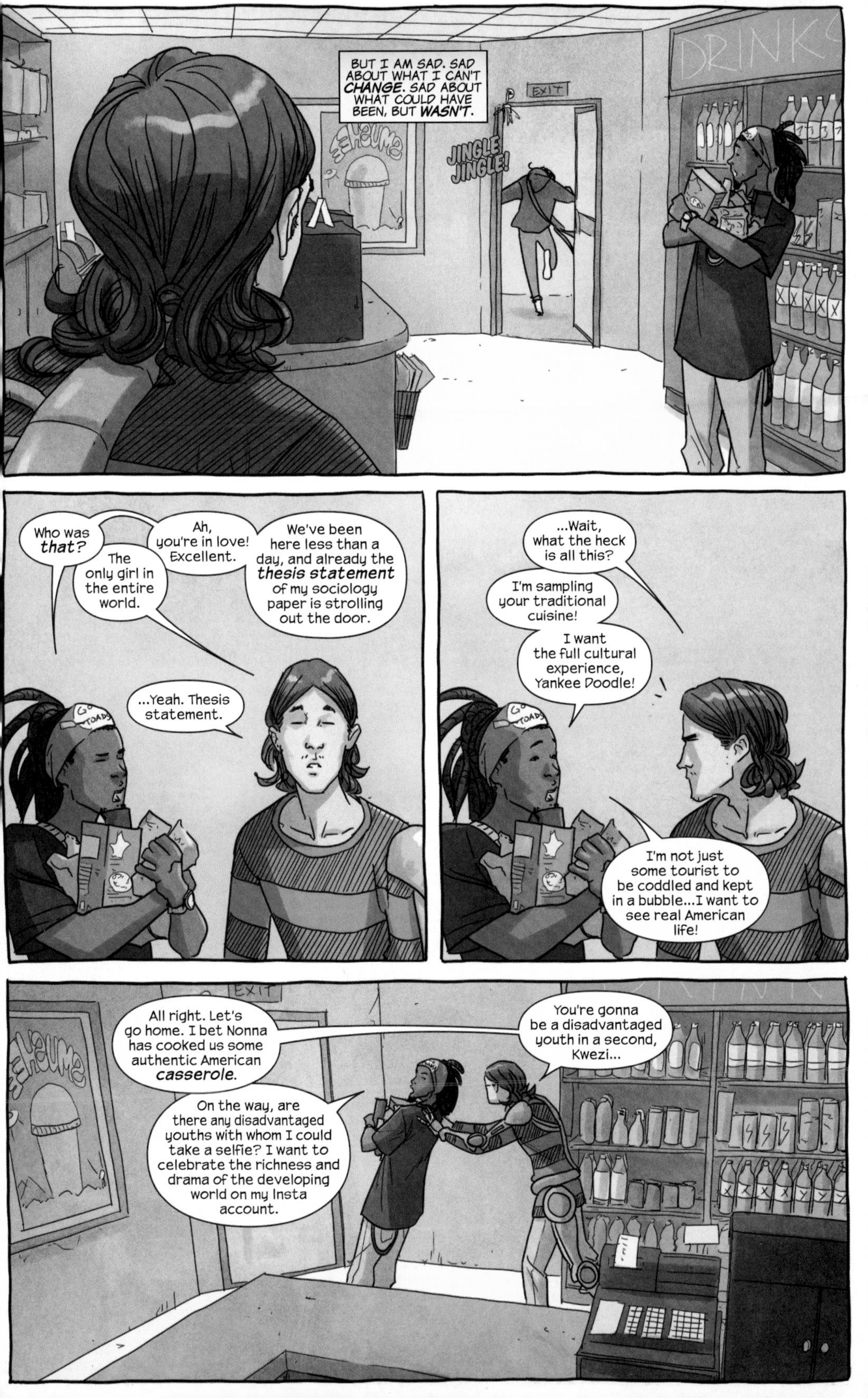
BUT I AM SAD. SAD ABOUT WHAT I CAN'T CHANGE. SAD ABOUT WHAT COULD HAVE BEEN, BUT WASN'T.
EXIT
JINGLE JINGLE!
DRINKS
Who was that?
Ah, you're in love! Excellent.
The only girl in the entire world.
We've been here less than a day, and already the thesis statement of my sociology paper is strolling out the door.
...Yeah. Thesis statement.
...Wait, what the heck is all this?
I'm sampling your traditional cuisine!
I want the full cultural experience, Yankee Doodle!
I'm not just some tourist to be coddled and kept in a bubble...I want to see real American life!
EXIT
All right. Let's go home. I bet Nonna has cooked us some authentic American casserole.
You're gonna be a disadvantaged youth in a second, Kwezi...
On the way, are there any disadvantaged youths with whom I could take a selfie? I want to celebrate the richness and drama of the developing world on my Insta account.

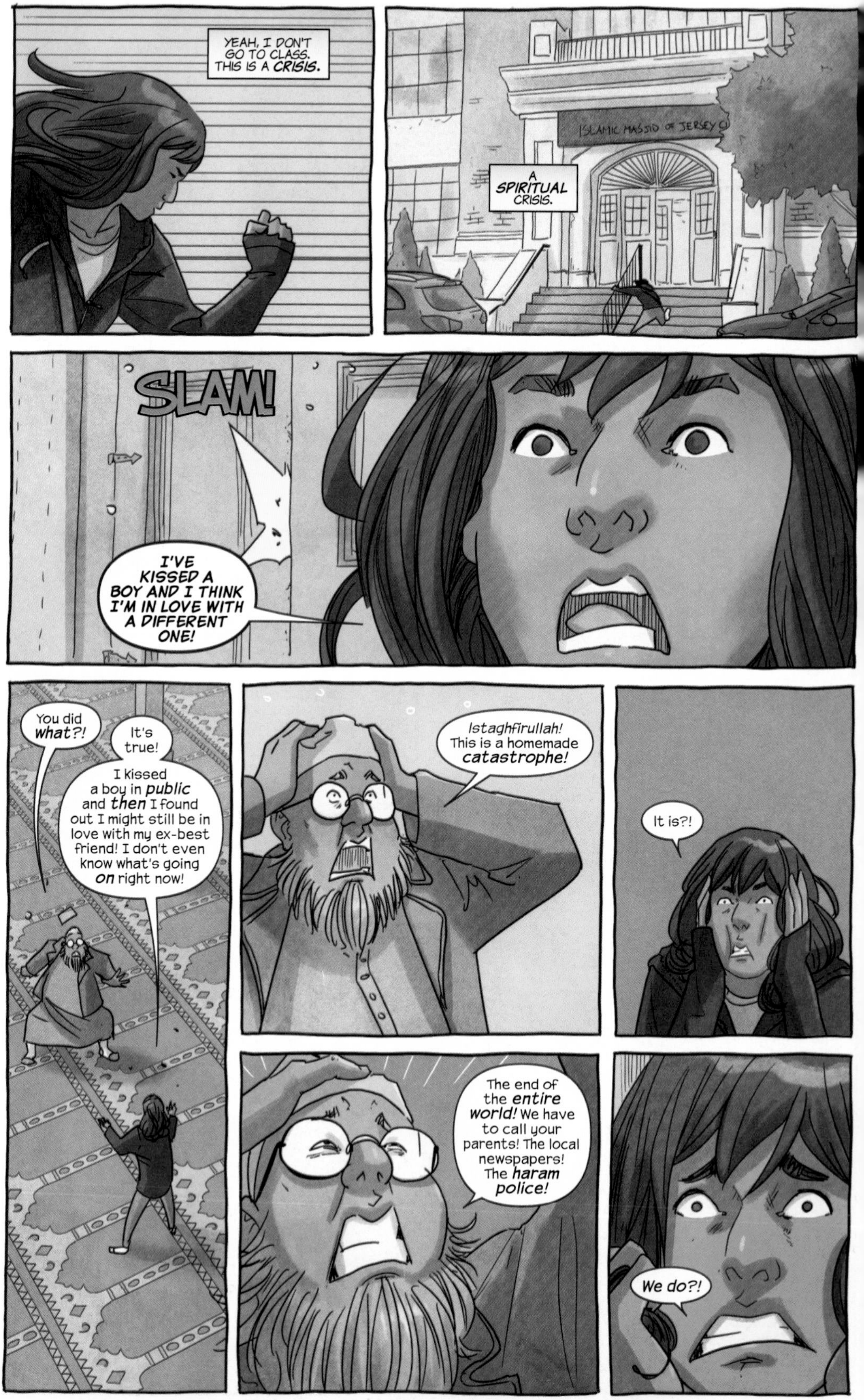
YEAH, I DON'T GO TO CLASS. THIS IS A CRISIS.
ISLAMIC MASJID OF JERSEY C
A SPIRITUAL CRISIS.
SLAM!
I'VE KISSED A BOY AND I THINK I'M IN LOVE WITH A DIFFERENT ONE!
You did what?!
It's true!
I kissed a boy in public and then I found out I might still be in love with my ex-best friend! I don't even know what's going on right now!
Istaghfirullah! This is a homemade catastrophe!
It is?!
The end of the entire world! We have to call your parents! The local newspapers! The haram police!
We do?!

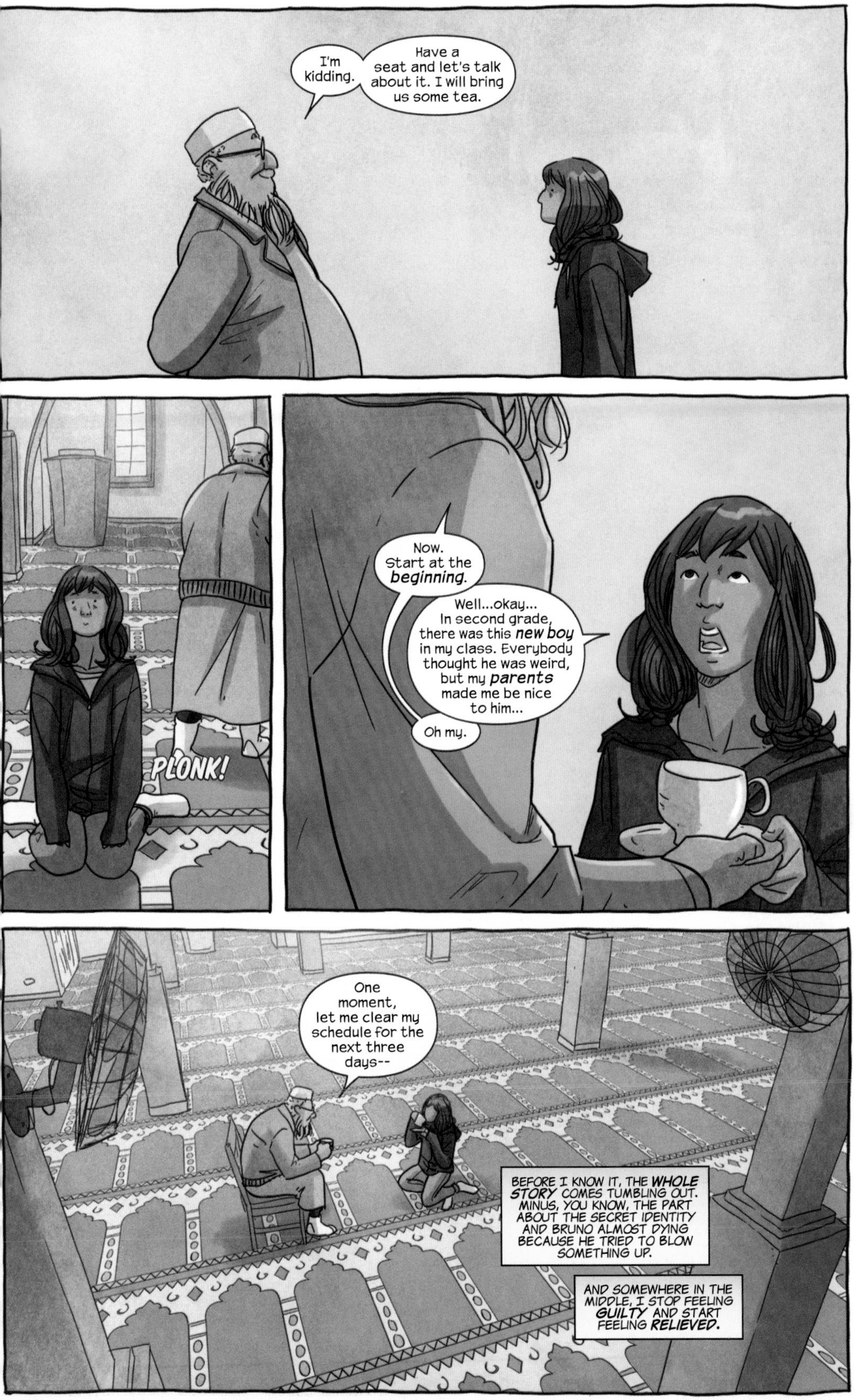
I'm kidding.
Have a seat and let's talk about it. I will bring us some tea.
PLONK!
Now. Start at the beginning.
Well...okay... In second grade, there was this new boy in my class. Everybody thought he was weird, but my parents made me be nice to him...
Oh my.
One moment, let me clear my schedule for the next three days--
BEFORE I KNOW IT, THE WHOLE STORY COMES TUMBLING OUT. MINUS, YOU KNOW, THE PART ABOUT THE SECRET IDENTITY AND BRUNO ALMOST DYING BECAUSE HE TRIED TO BLOW SOMETHING UP.
AND SOMEWHERE IN THE MIDDLE, I STOP FEELING GUILTY AND START FEELING RELIEVED.

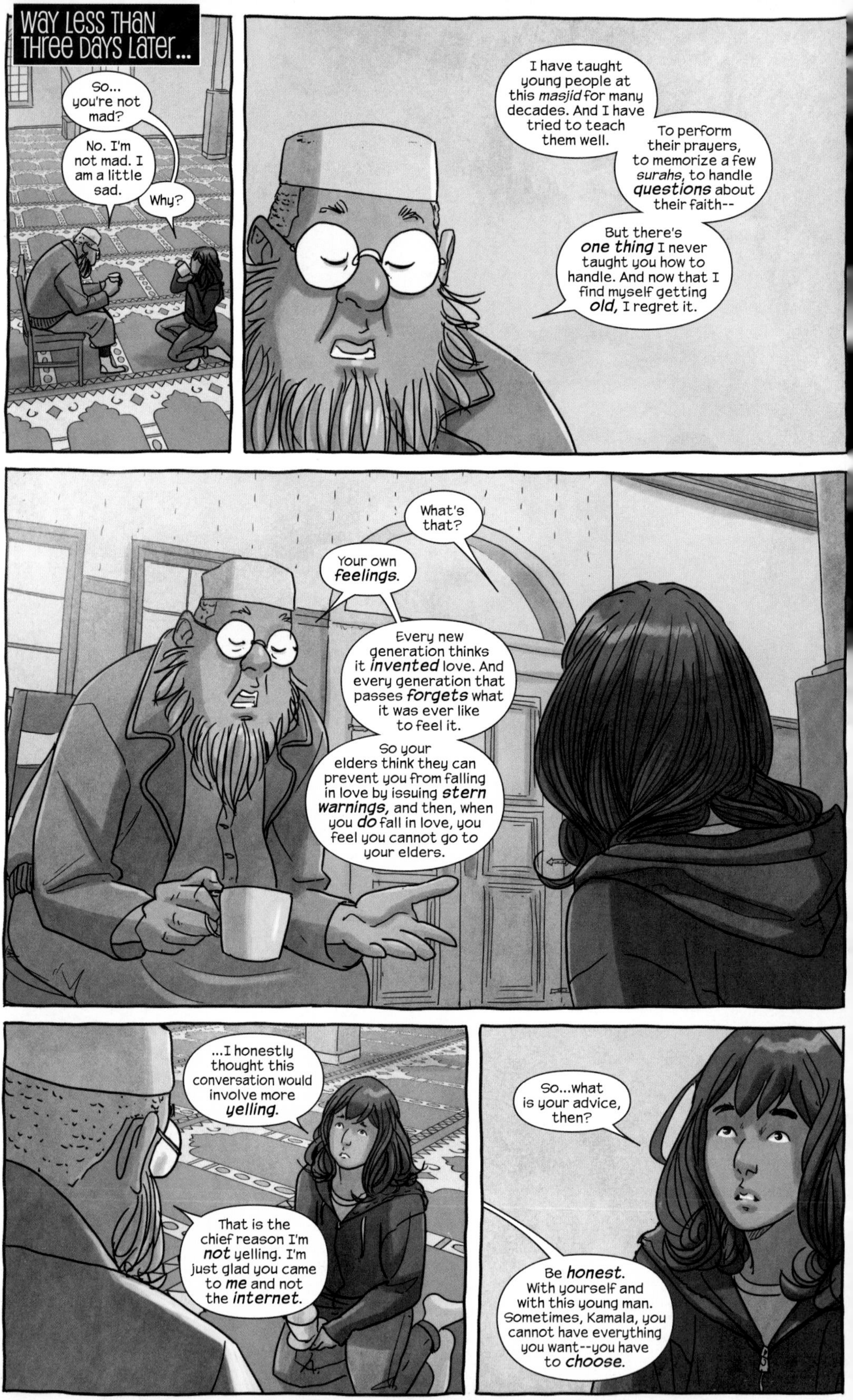
WAY LESS THAN THREE DAYS LATER...
So... you're not mad?
No. I'm not mad. I am a little sad.
Why?
I have taught young people at this masjid for many decades. And I have tried to teach them well.
To perform their prayers, to memorize a few surahs, to handle questions about their faith--
But there's one thing I never taught you how to handle. And now that I find myself getting old, I regret it.
What's that?
Your own feelings.
Every new generation thinks it invented love. And every generation that passes forgets what it was ever like to feel it.
So your elders think they can prevent you from falling in love by issuing stern warnings, and then, when you do fall in love, you feel you cannot go to your elders.
...I honestly thought this conversation would involve more yelling.
That is the chief reason I'm not yelling. I'm just glad you came to me and not the internet.
So...what is your advice, then?
Be honest. With yourself and with this young man. Sometimes, Kamala, you cannot have everything you want--you have to choose.

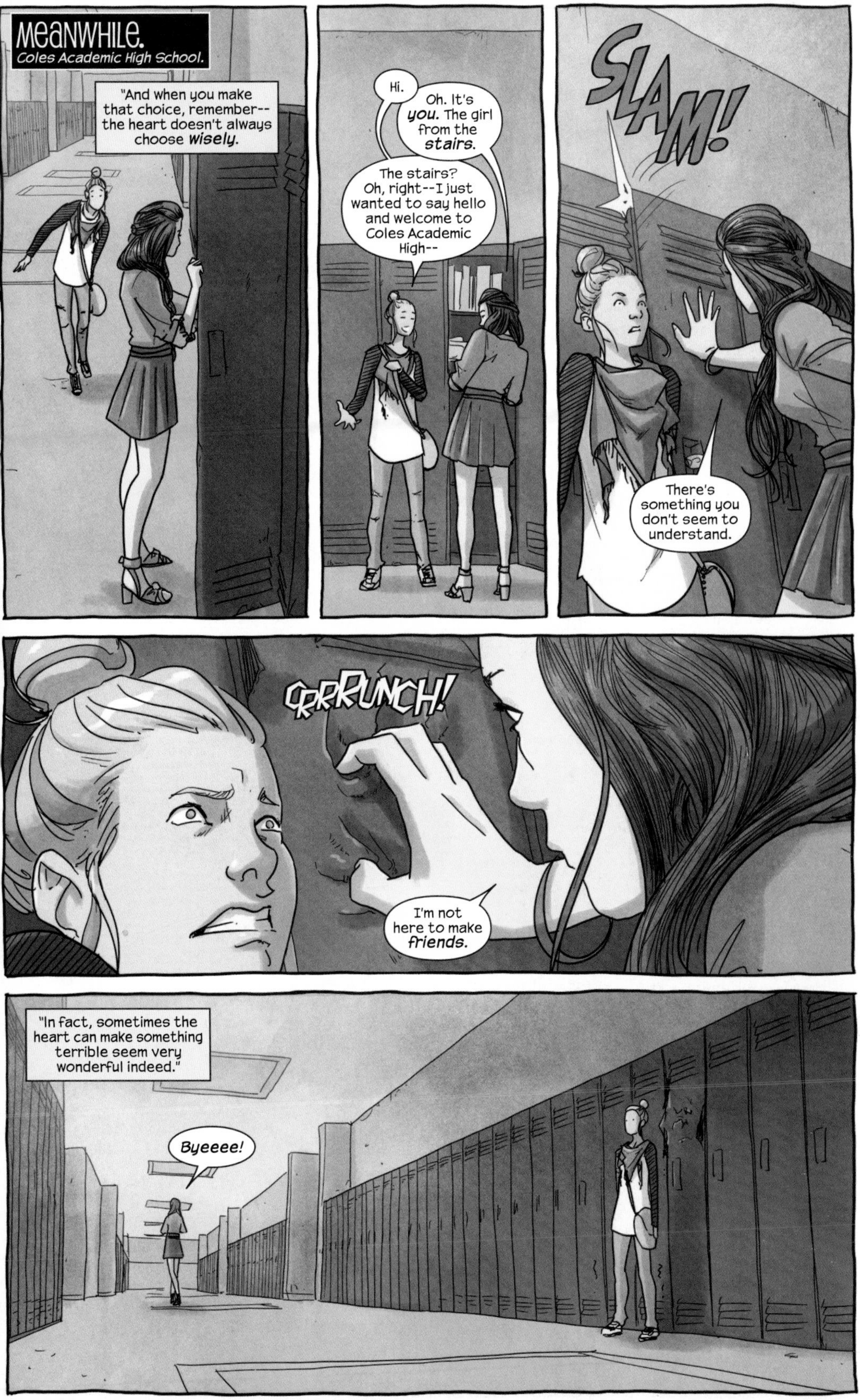
MEANWHILE.
Coles Academic High School.
"And when you make that choice, remember--the heart doesn't always choose *wisely*.
Hi.
Oh. It's *you*. The girl from the *stairs*.
The stairs? Oh, right--I just wanted to say hello and welcome to Coles Academic High--
SLAM!
There's something you don't seem to understand.
CRRRUNCH!
I'm not here to make *friends*.
"In fact, sometimes the heart can make something terrible seem very wonderful indeed."
Byeeee!

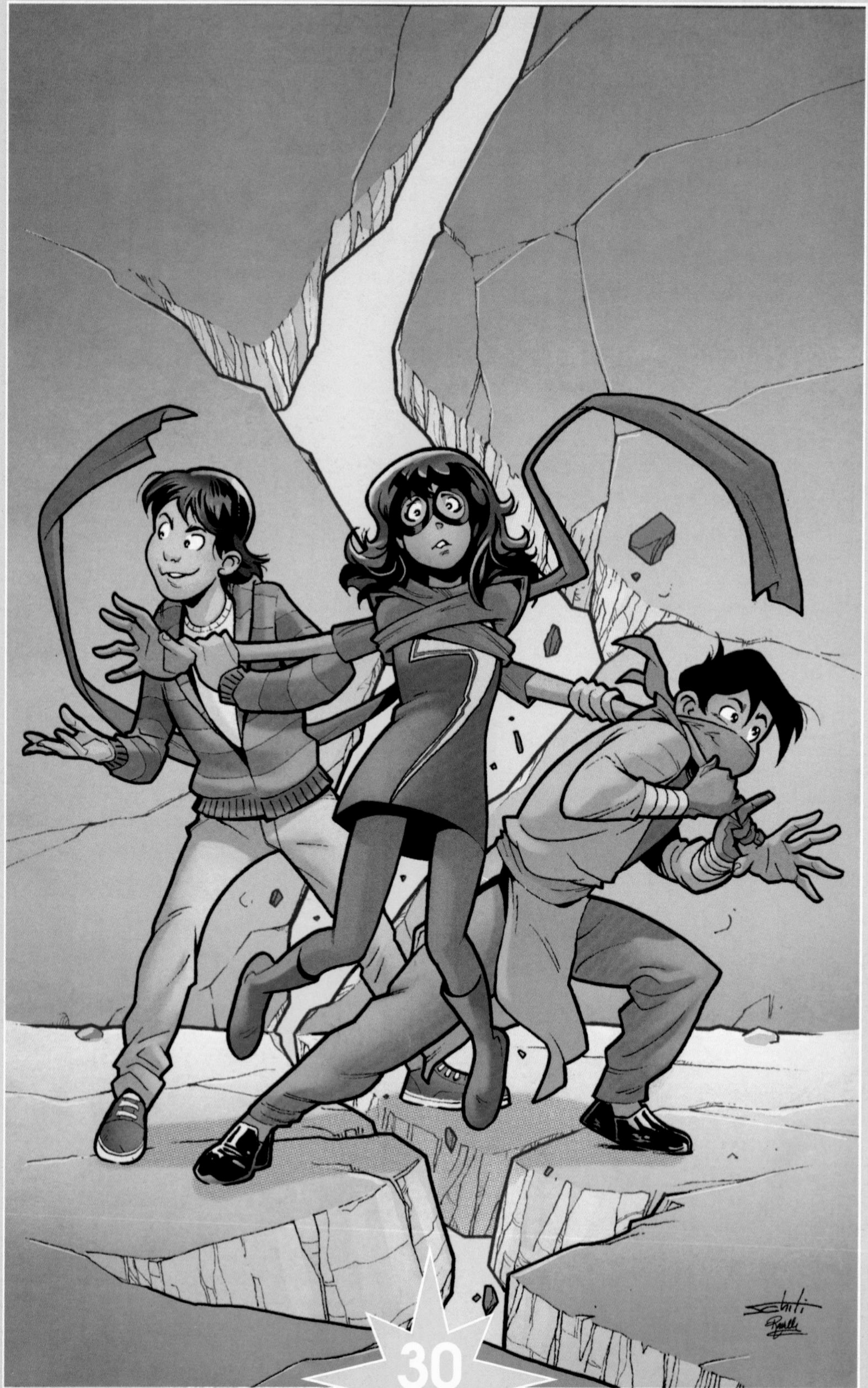
30

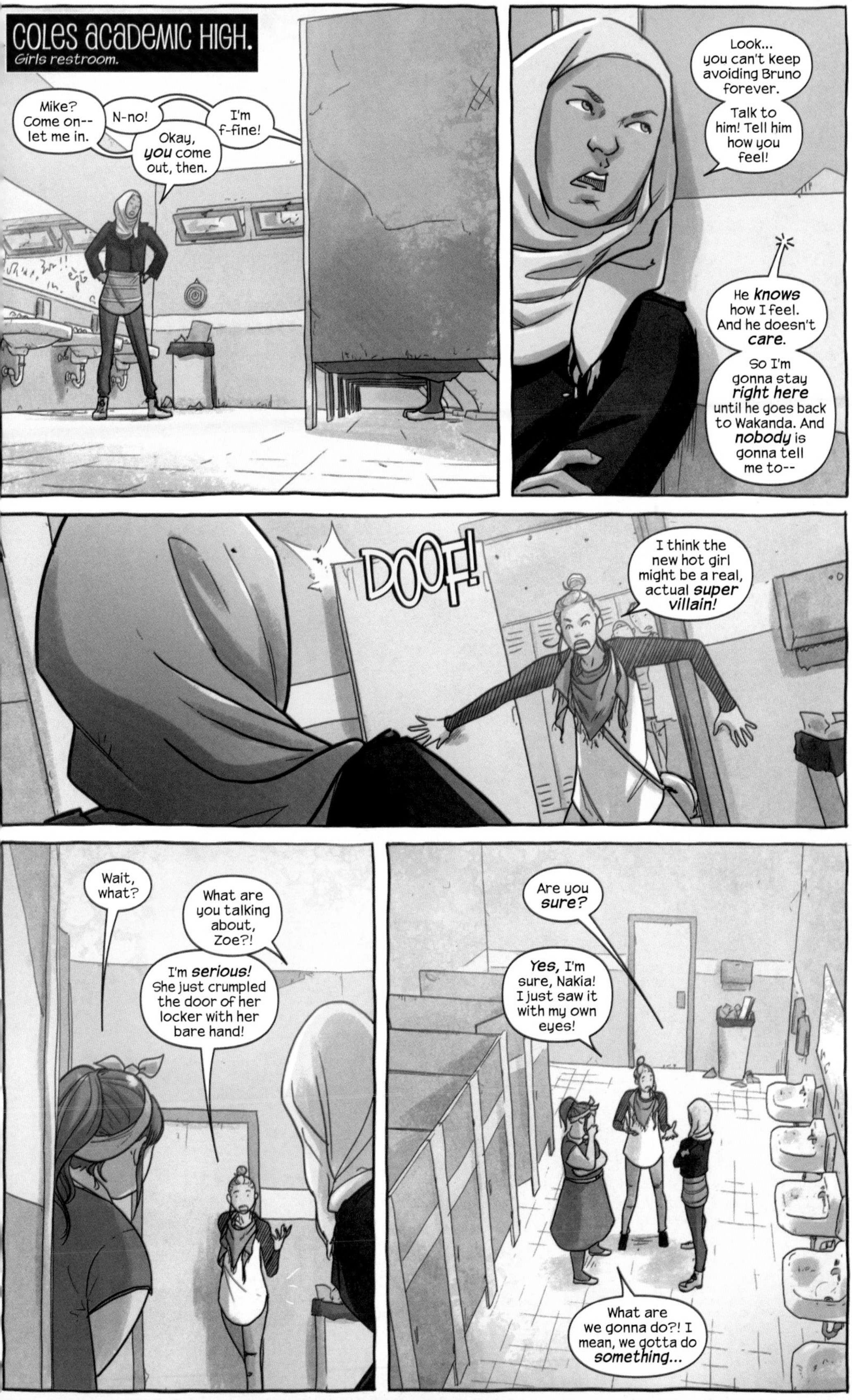
COLES ACADEMIC HIGH.
Girls restroom.
Mike? Come on-- let me in.
N-no!
I'm f-fine!
Okay, *you* come out, then.
Look... you can't keep avoiding Bruno forever.
Talk to him! Tell him how you feel!
He *knows* how I feel. And he doesn't *care.*
So I'm gonna stay *right here* until he goes back to Wakanda. And *nobody* is gonna tell me to--
DOOF!
I think the new hot girl might be a real, actual *super villain!*
Wait, what?
What are you talking about, Zoe?!
I'm *serious!* She just crumpled the door of her locker with her bare hand!
Are you *sure?*
Yes, I'm sure, Nakia! I just saw it with my own eyes!
What are we gonna do?! I mean, we gotta do *something...*

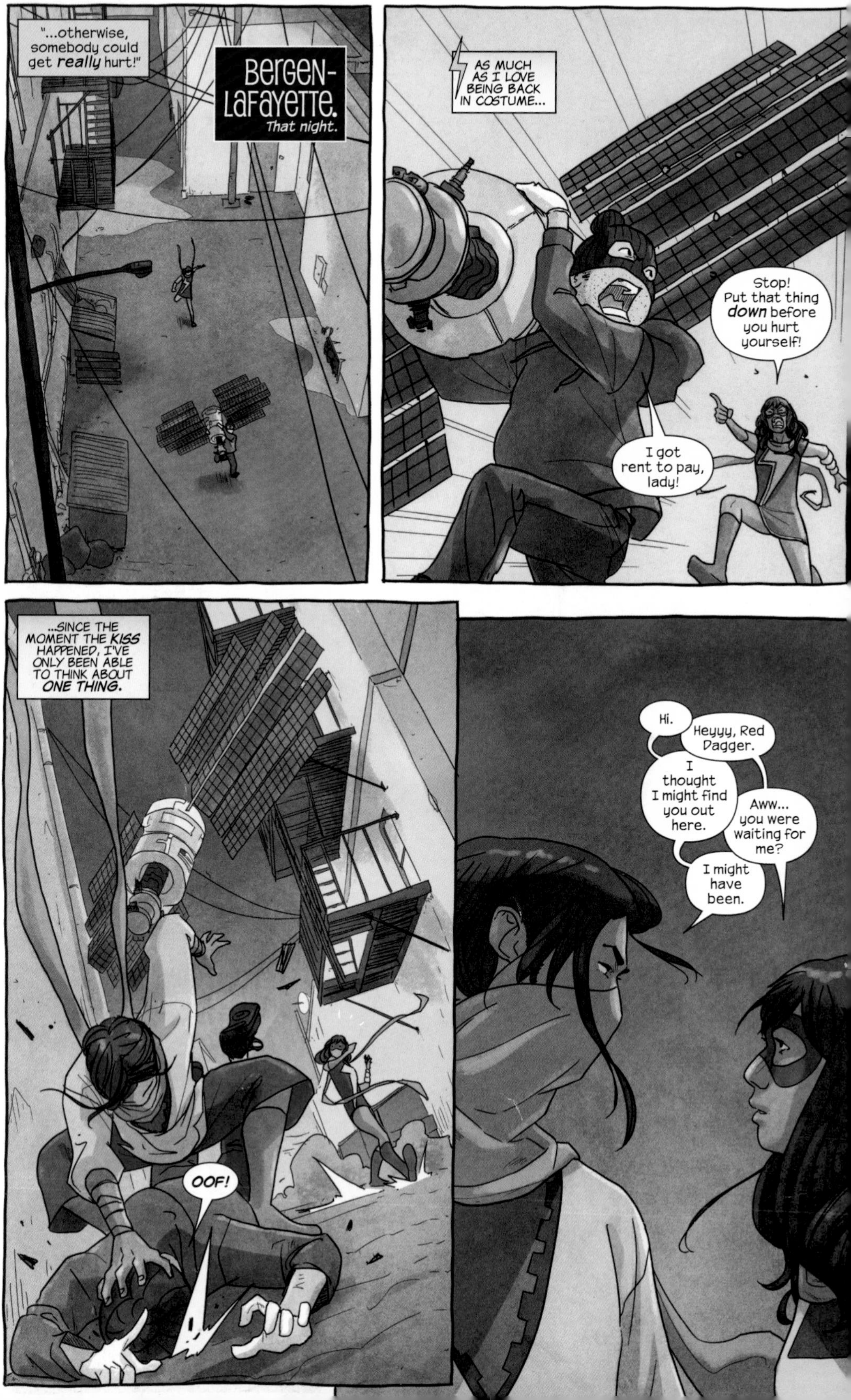
"...otherwise, somebody could get *really* hurt!"
BERGEN-LAFAYETTE.
That night.
AS MUCH AS I LOVE BEING BACK IN COSTUME...
Stop! Put that thing *down* before you hurt yourself!
I got rent to pay, lady!
...SINCE THE MOMENT THE *KISS* HAPPENED, I'VE ONLY BEEN ABLE TO THINK ABOUT *ONE THING.*
OOF!
Hi.
Heyyy, Red Dagger.
I thought I might find you out here.
Aww... you were waiting for me?
I might have been.

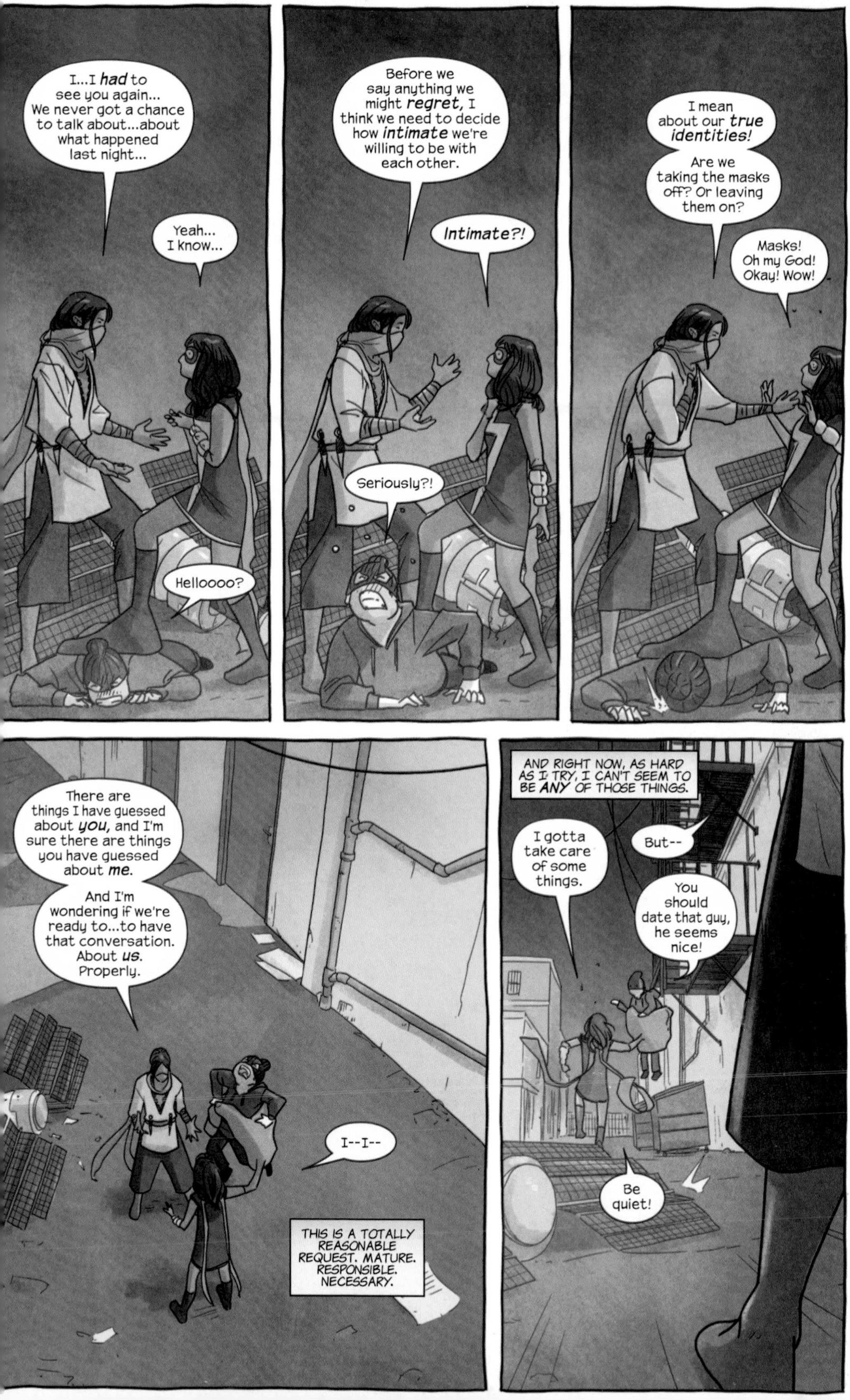

I...I had to see you again... We never got a chance to talk about...about what happened last night...
Yeah... I know...
Hellooo?
Before we say anything we might regret, I think we need to decide how intimate we're willing to be with each other.
Intimate?!
Seriously?!
I mean about our true identities!
Are we taking the masks off? Or leaving them on?
Masks! Oh my God! Okay! Wow!
There are things I have guessed about you, and I'm sure there are things you have guessed about me.
And I'm wondering if we're ready to...to have that conversation. About us. Properly.
I--I--
THIS IS A TOTALLY REASONABLE REQUEST. MATURE. RESPONSIBLE. NECESSARY.
AND RIGHT NOW, AS HARD AS I TRY, I CAN'T SEEM TO BE ANY OF THOSE THINGS.
I gotta take care of some things.
But--
You should date that guy, he seems nice!
Be quiet!

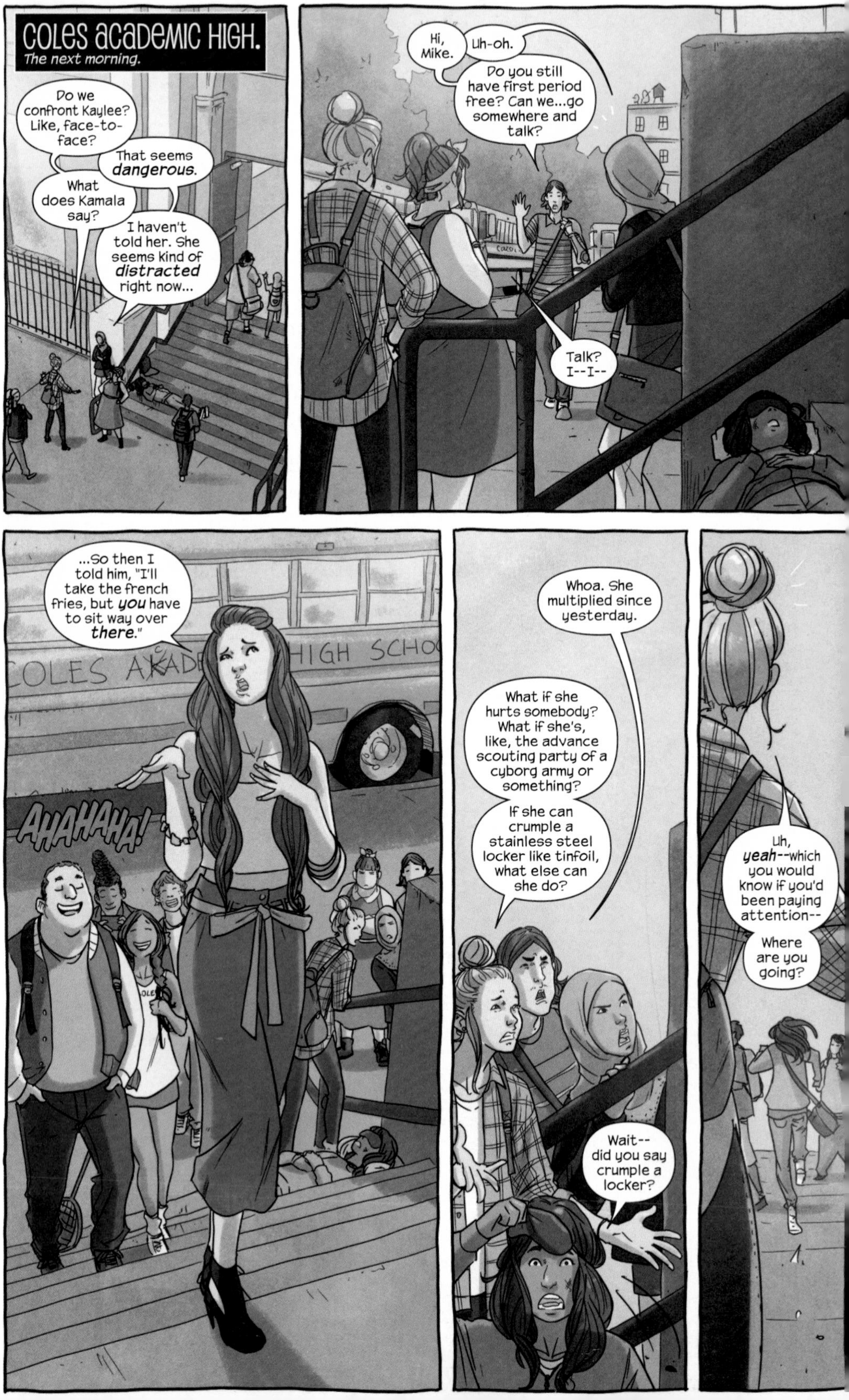
COLES ACADEMIC HIGH.
The next morning.
Do we confront Kaylee? Like, face-to-face?
That seems *dangerous*.
What does Kamala say?
I haven't told her. She seems kind of *distracted* right now...
Hi, Mike.
Uh-oh.
Do you still have first period free? Can we...go somewhere and talk?
Talk? I--I--
...So then I told him, "I'll take the french fries, but *you* have to sit way over *there*."
AHAHAHA!
COLES ACADEMIC HIGH SCHO
Whoa. She multiplied since yesterday.
What if she hurts somebody? What if she's, like, the advance scouting party of a cyborg army or something?
If she can crumple a stainless steel locker like tinfoil, what else can she do?
Wait-- did you say crumple a locker?
Uh, *yeah*--which you would know if you'd been paying attention--
Where are you going?

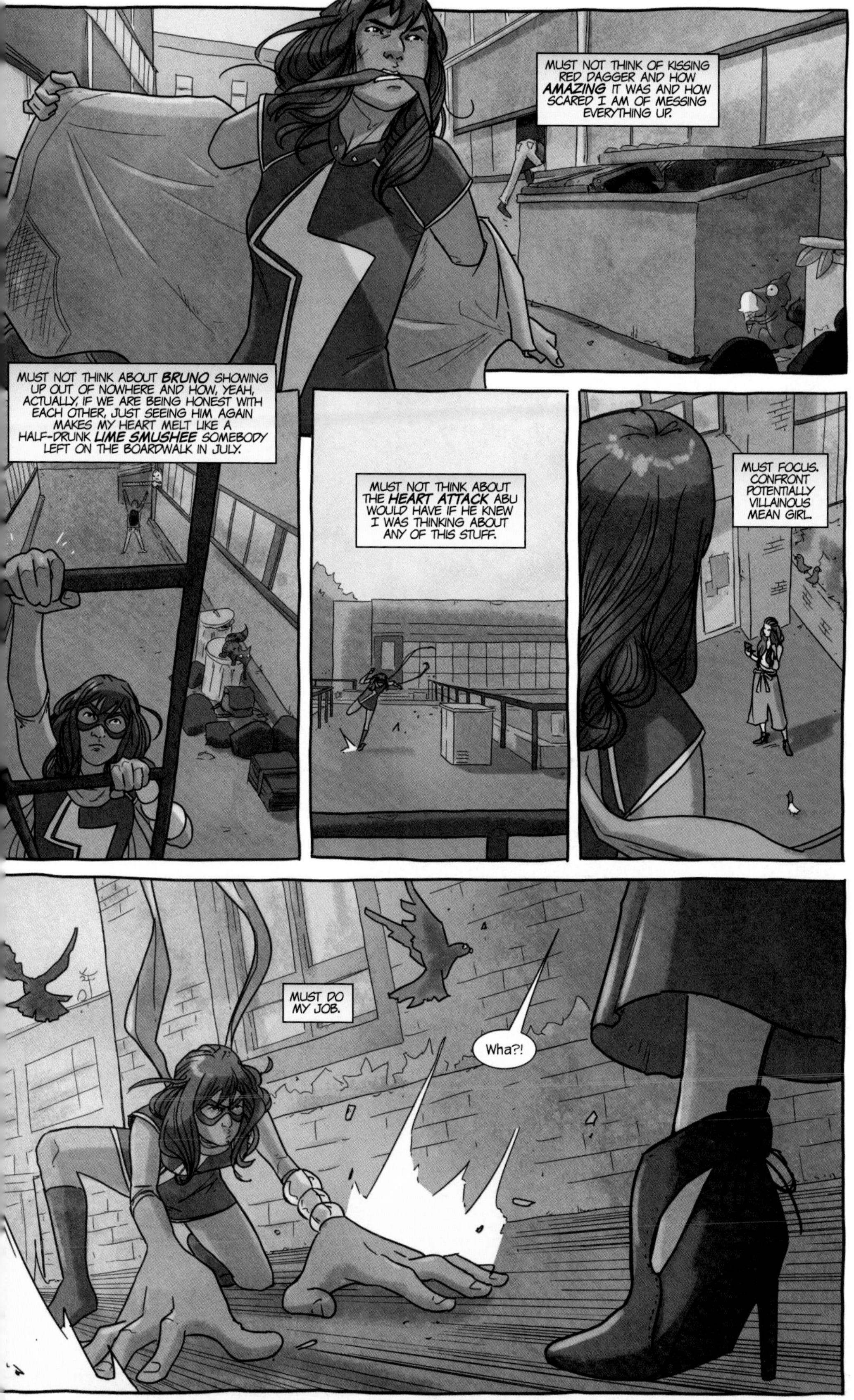
MUST NOT THINK OF KISSING RED DAGGER AND HOW AMAZING IT WAS AND HOW SCARED I AM OF MESSING EVERYTHING UP.
MUST NOT THINK ABOUT BRUNO SHOWING UP OUT OF NOWHERE AND HOW, YEAH, ACTUALLY, IF WE ARE BEING HONEST WITH EACH OTHER, JUST SEEING HIM AGAIN MAKES MY HEART MELT LIKE A HALF-DRUNK LIME SMUSHEE SOMEBODY LEFT ON THE BOARDWALK IN JULY.
MUST NOT THINK ABOUT THE HEART ATTACK ABU WOULD HAVE IF HE KNEW I WAS THINKING ABOUT ANY OF THIS STUFF.
MUST FOCUS. CONFRONT POTENTIALLY VILLAINOUS MEAN GIRL.
MUST DO MY JOB.
Wha?!

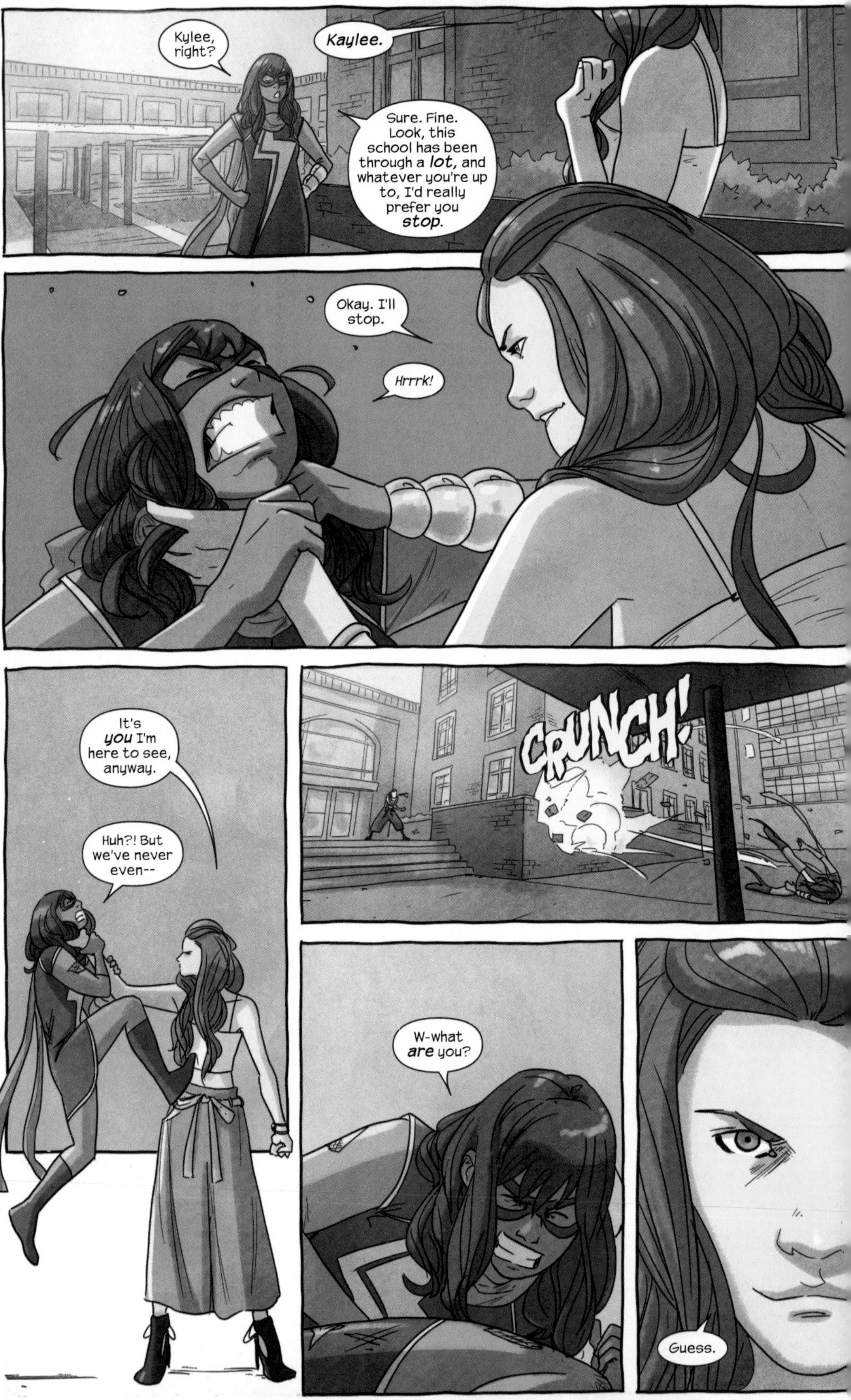
Kylee, right?
Kaylee.
Sure. Fine. Look, this school has been through a lot, and whatever you're up to, I'd really prefer you stop.
Okay. I'll stop.
Hrrrk!
It's you I'm here to see, anyway.
Huh?! But we've never even--
CRUNCH!
W-what are you?
Guess.

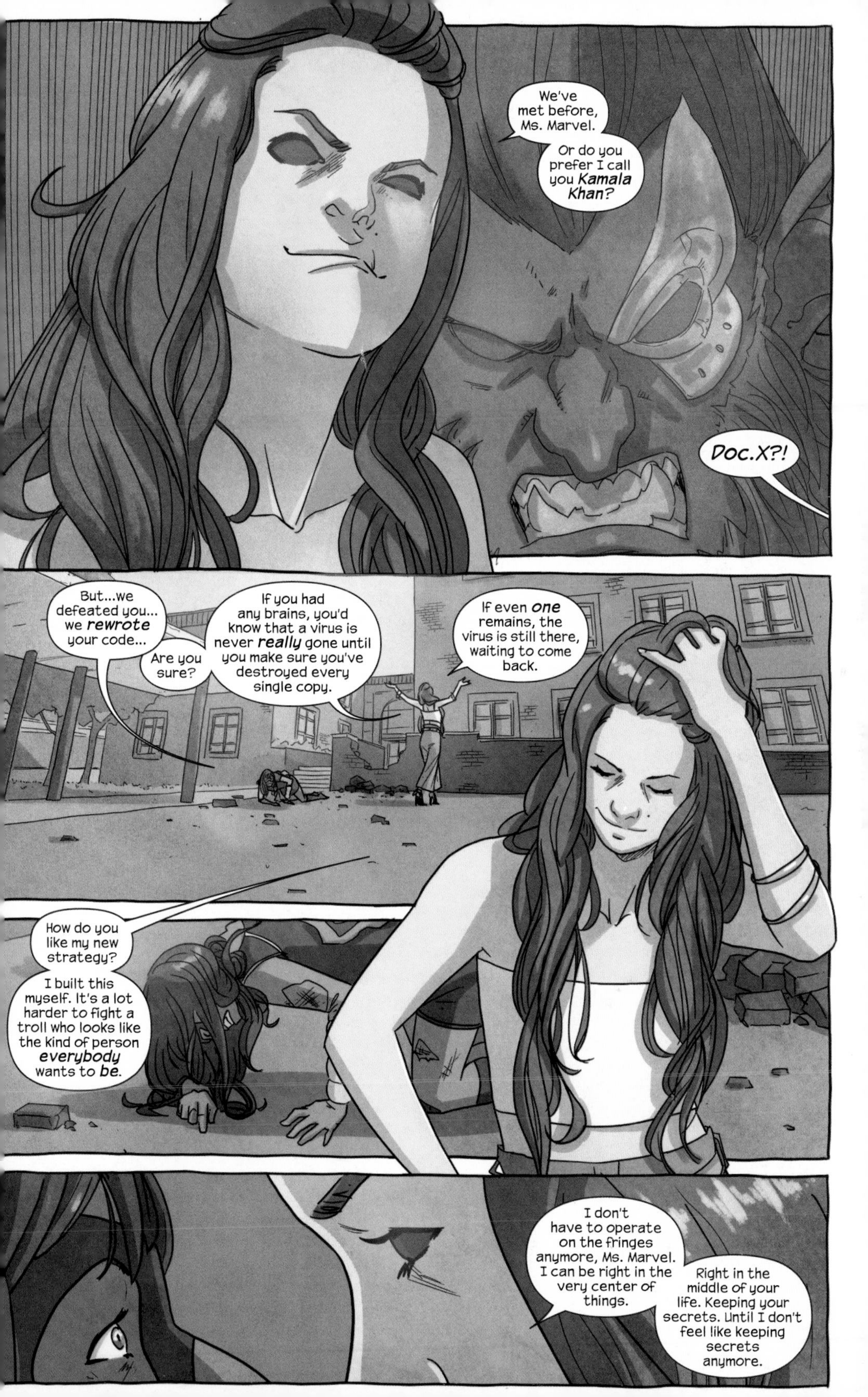
We've met before, Ms. Marvel.
Or do you prefer I call you *Kamala Khan*?
Doc.X?!
But...we defeated you... we ***rewrote*** your code...
Are you sure?
If you had any brains, you'd know that a virus is never ***really*** gone until you make sure you've destroyed every single copy.
If even ***one*** remains, the virus is still there, waiting to come back.
How do you like my new strategy?
I built this myself. It's a lot harder to fight a troll who looks like the kind of person ***everybody*** wants to ***be***.
I don't have to operate on the fringes anymore, Ms. Marvel. I can be right in the very center of things.
Right in the middle of your life. Keeping your secrets. Until I don't feel like keeping secrets anymore.

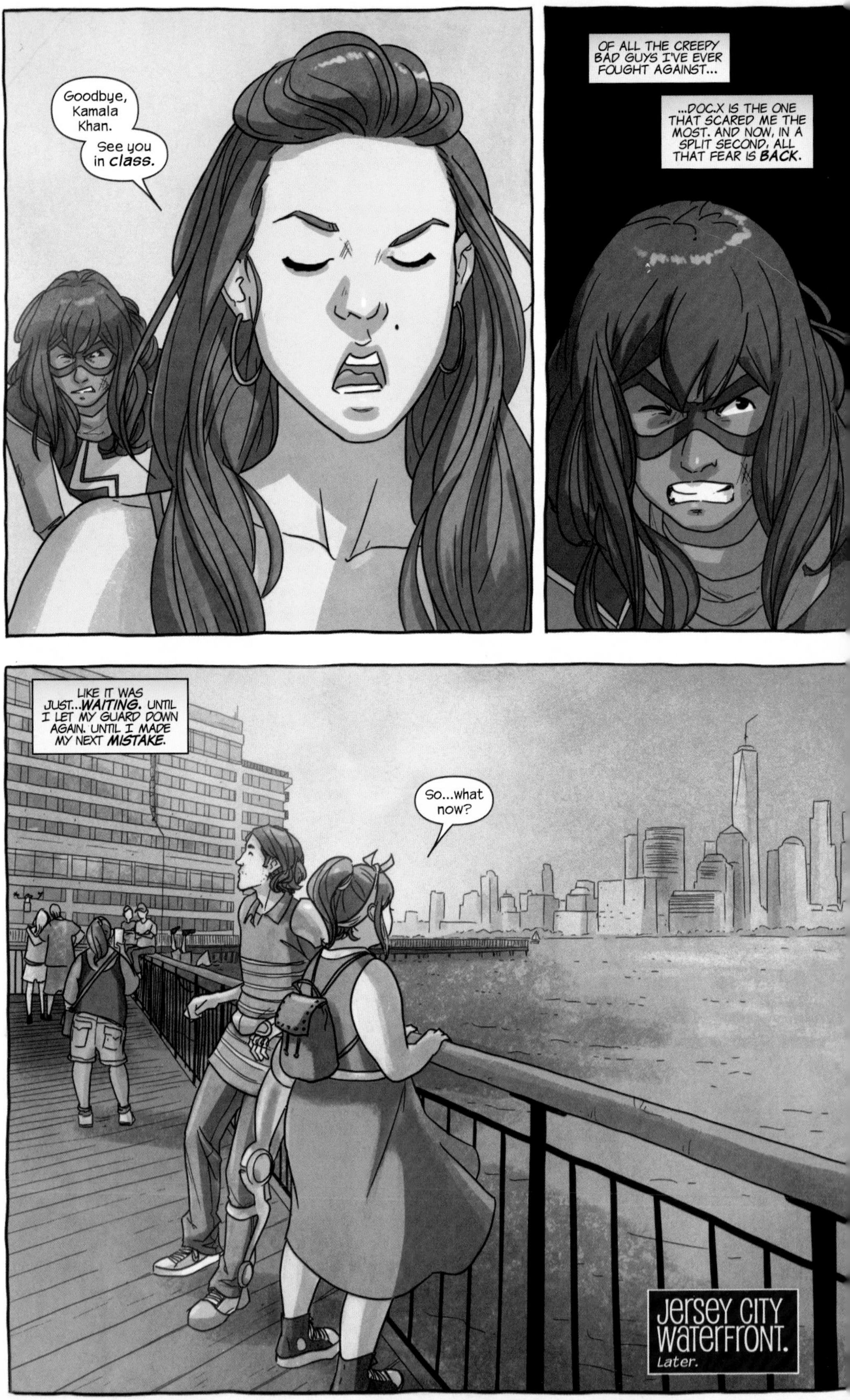
Goodbye, Kamala Khan.
See you in *class.*
OF ALL THE CREEPY BAD GUYS I'VE EVER FOUGHT AGAINST...
...DOC.X IS THE ONE THAT SCARED ME THE MOST. AND NOW, IN A SPLIT SECOND, ALL THAT FEAR IS **BACK**.
LIKE IT WAS JUST...**WAITING.** UNTIL I LET MY GUARD DOWN AGAIN. UNTIL I MADE MY NEXT **MISTAKE**.
So...what now?
Jersey City Waterfront.
Later.

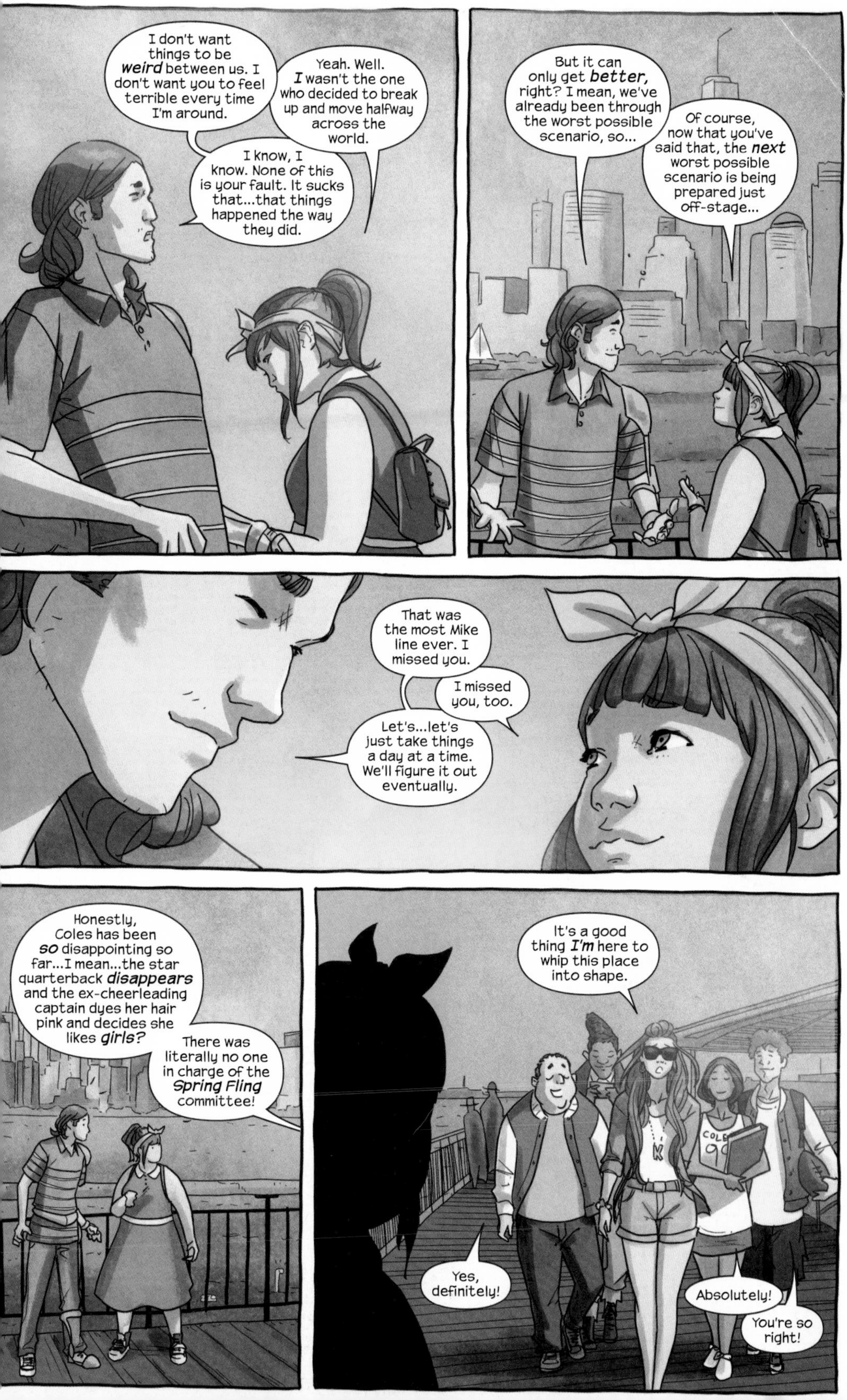
I don't want things to be weird between us. I don't want you to feel terrible every time I'm around.
Yeah. Well. I wasn't the one who decided to break up and move halfway across the world.
I know, I know. None of this is your fault. It sucks that...that things happened the way they did.
But it can only get better, right? I mean, we've already been through the worst possible scenario, so...
Of course, now that you've said that, the next worst possible scenario is being prepared just off-stage...
That was the most Mike line ever. I missed you.
I missed you, too.
Let's...let's just take things a day at a time. We'll figure it out eventually.
Honestly, Coles has been so disappointing so far...I mean...the star quarterback disappears and the ex-cheerleading captain dyes her hair pink and decides she likes girls?
There was literally no one in charge of the Spring Fling committee!
It's a good thing I'm here to whip this place into shape.
Yes, definitely!
Absolutely!
You're so right!

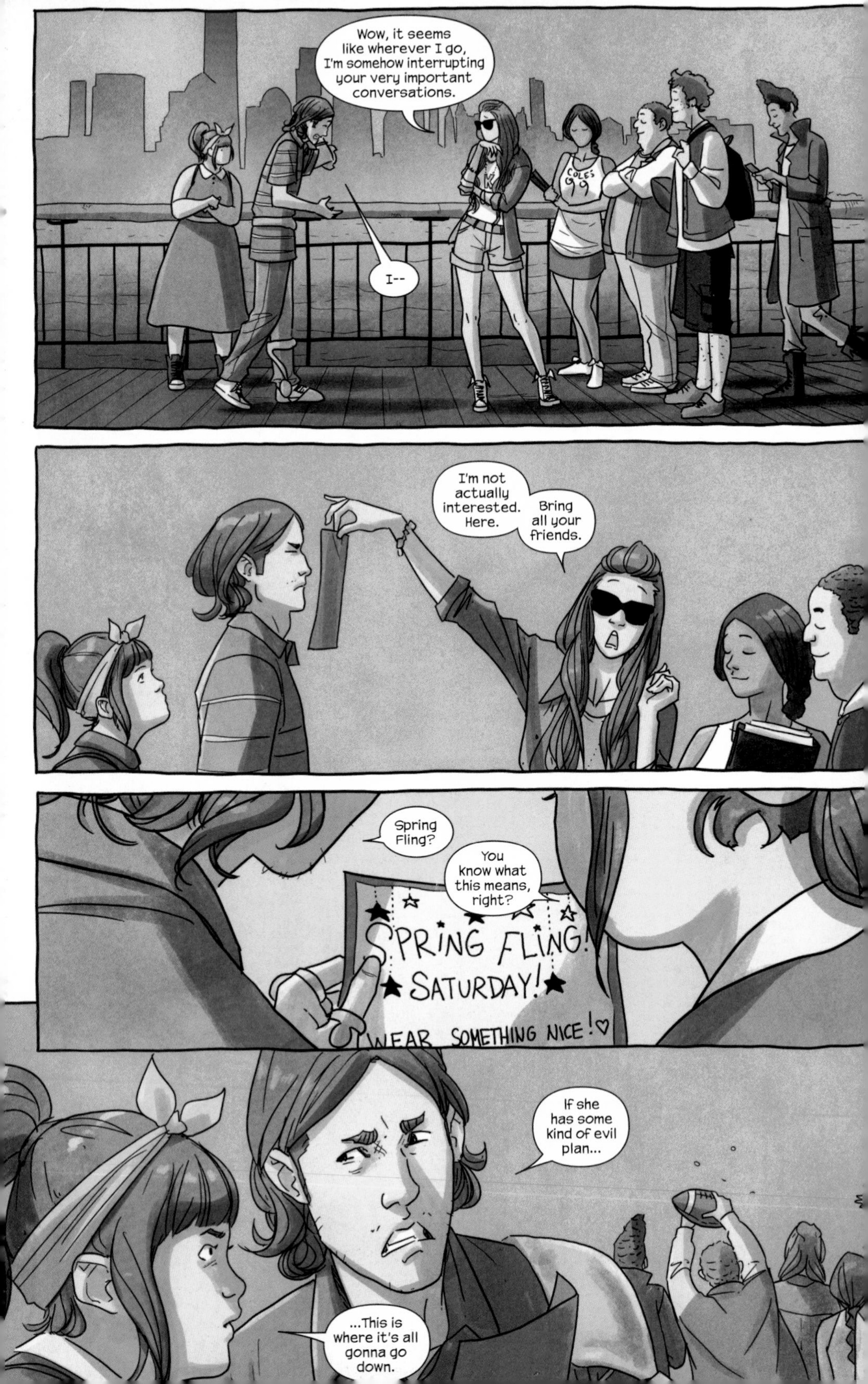
Wow, it seems like wherever I go, I'm somehow interrupting your very important conversations.
I--
I'm not actually interested. Here.
Bring all your friends.
Spring Fling?
You know what this means, right?
SPRING FLING! SATURDAY! WEAR SOMETHING NICE!
If she has some kind of evil plan...
...This is where it's all gonna go down.

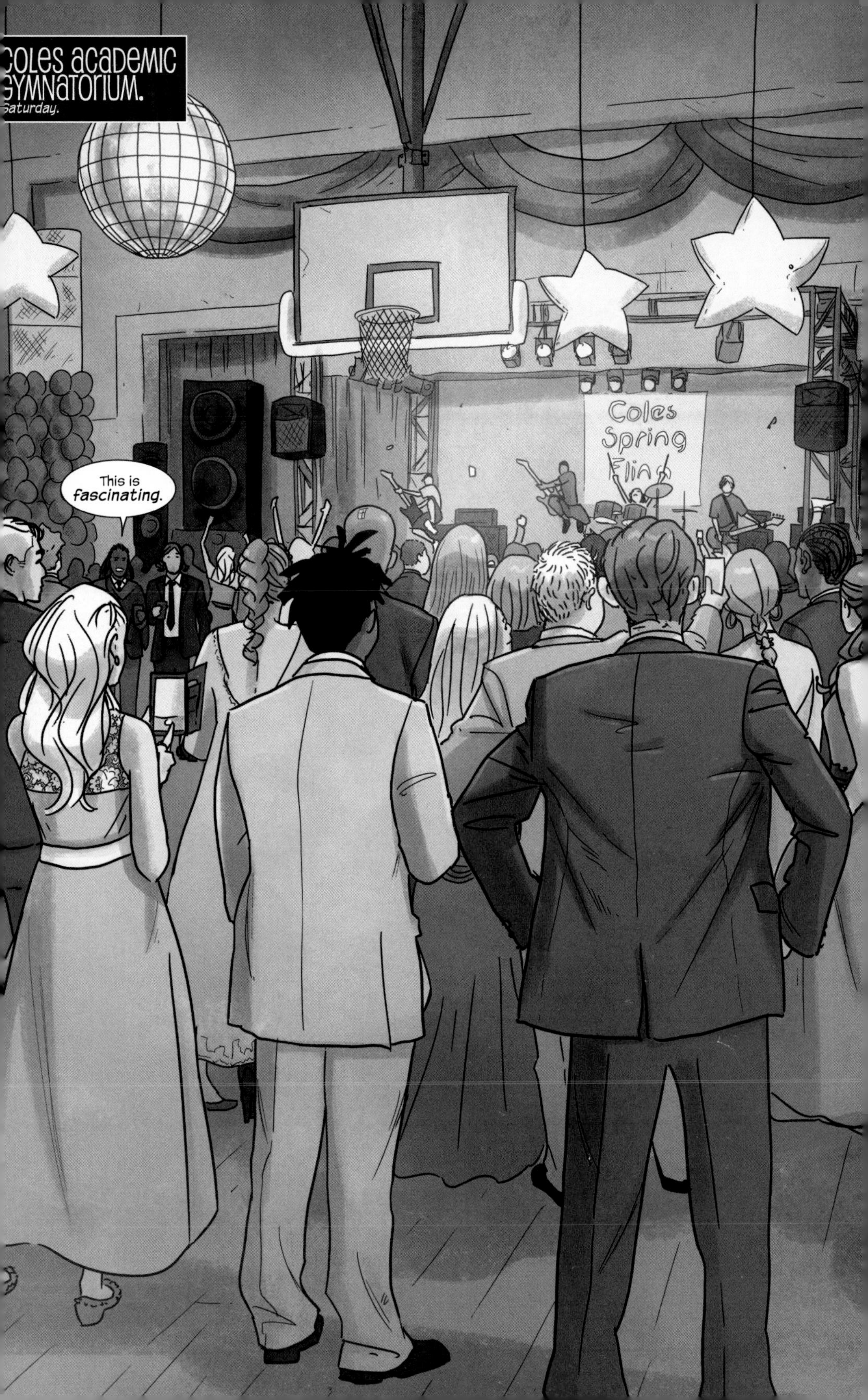
COLES ACADEMIC GYMNATORIUM.
Saturday.
This is fascinating.
Coles Spring Fling

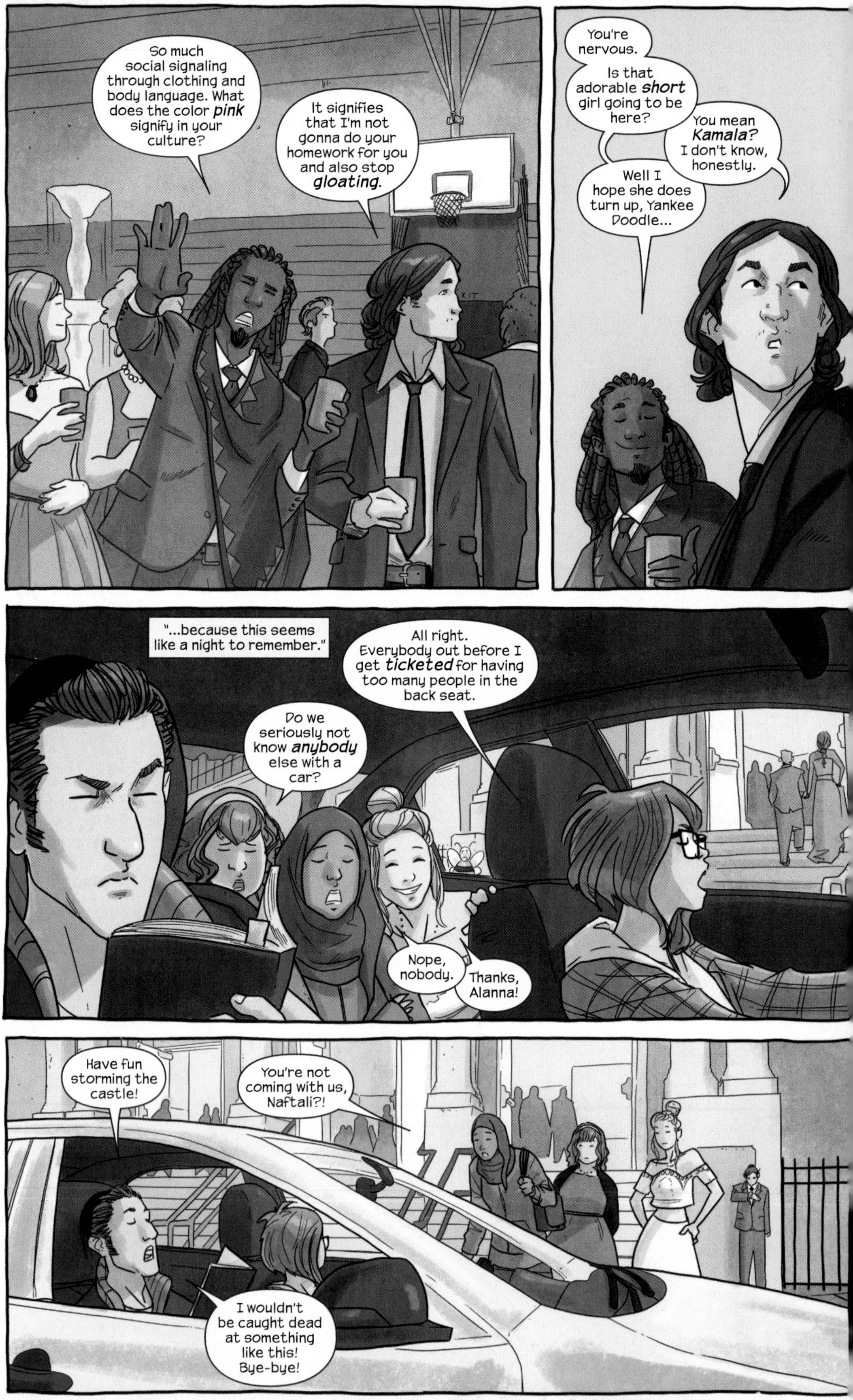
So much social signaling through clothing and body language. What does the color *pink* signify in your culture?
It signifies that I'm not gonna do your homework for you and also stop *gloating*.
You're nervous.
Is that adorable *short* girl going to be here?
You mean *Kamala?* I don't know, honestly.
Well I hope she does turn up, Yankee Doodle...
"...because this seems like a night to remember."
All right. Everybody out before I get *ticketed* for having too many people in the back seat.
Do we seriously not know *anybody* else with a car?
Nope, nobody.
Thanks, Alanna!
Have fun storming the castle!
You're not coming with us, Naftali?!
I wouldn't be caught dead at something like this! Bye-bye!

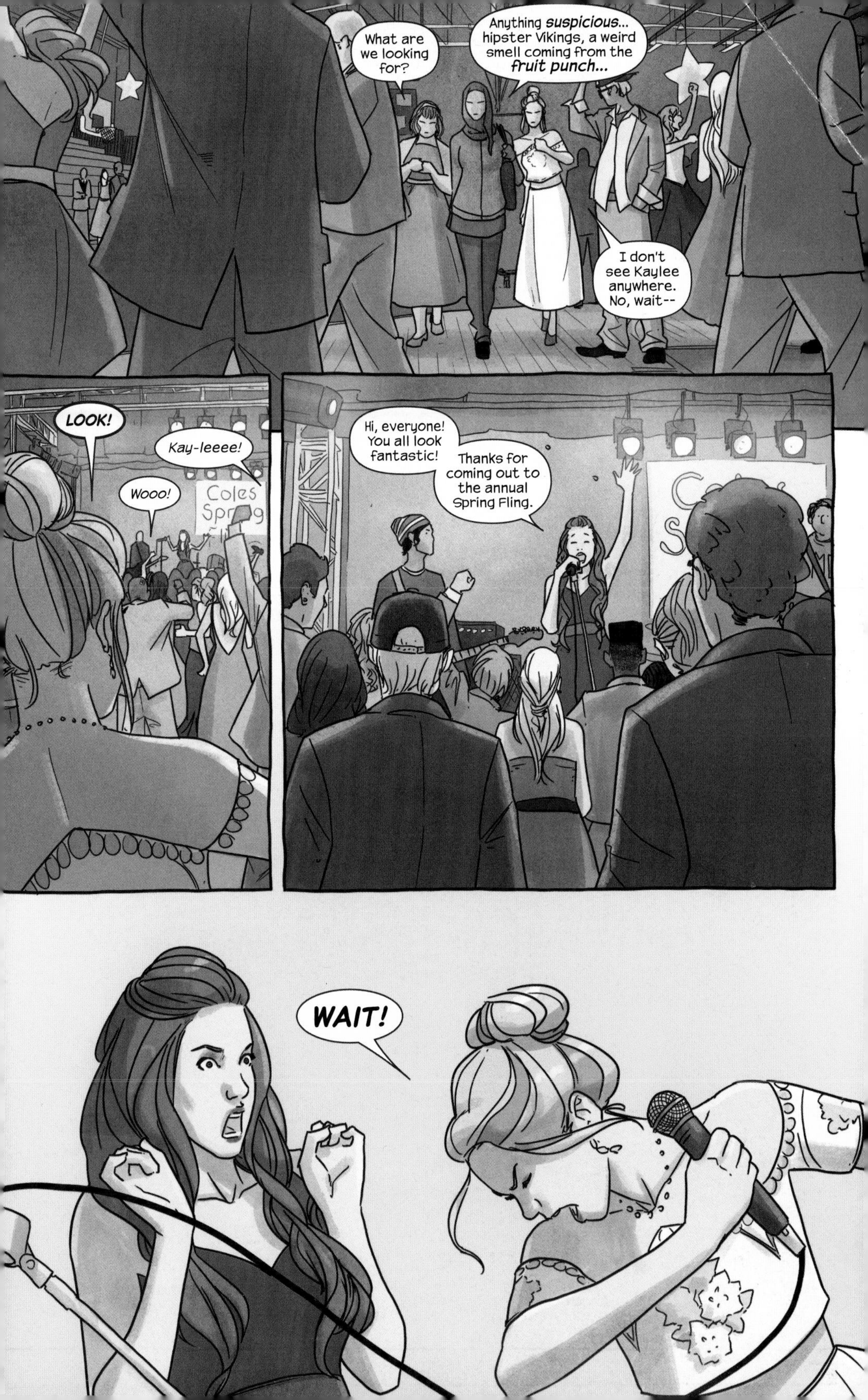
What are we looking for?
Anything *suspicious*... hipster Vikings, a weird smell coming from the *fruit punch...*
I don't see Kaylee anywhere. No, wait--
LOOK!
Kay-leeee!
Wooo!
Coles Spring
Hi, everyone! You all look fantastic!
Thanks for coming out to the annual Spring Fling.
WAIT!

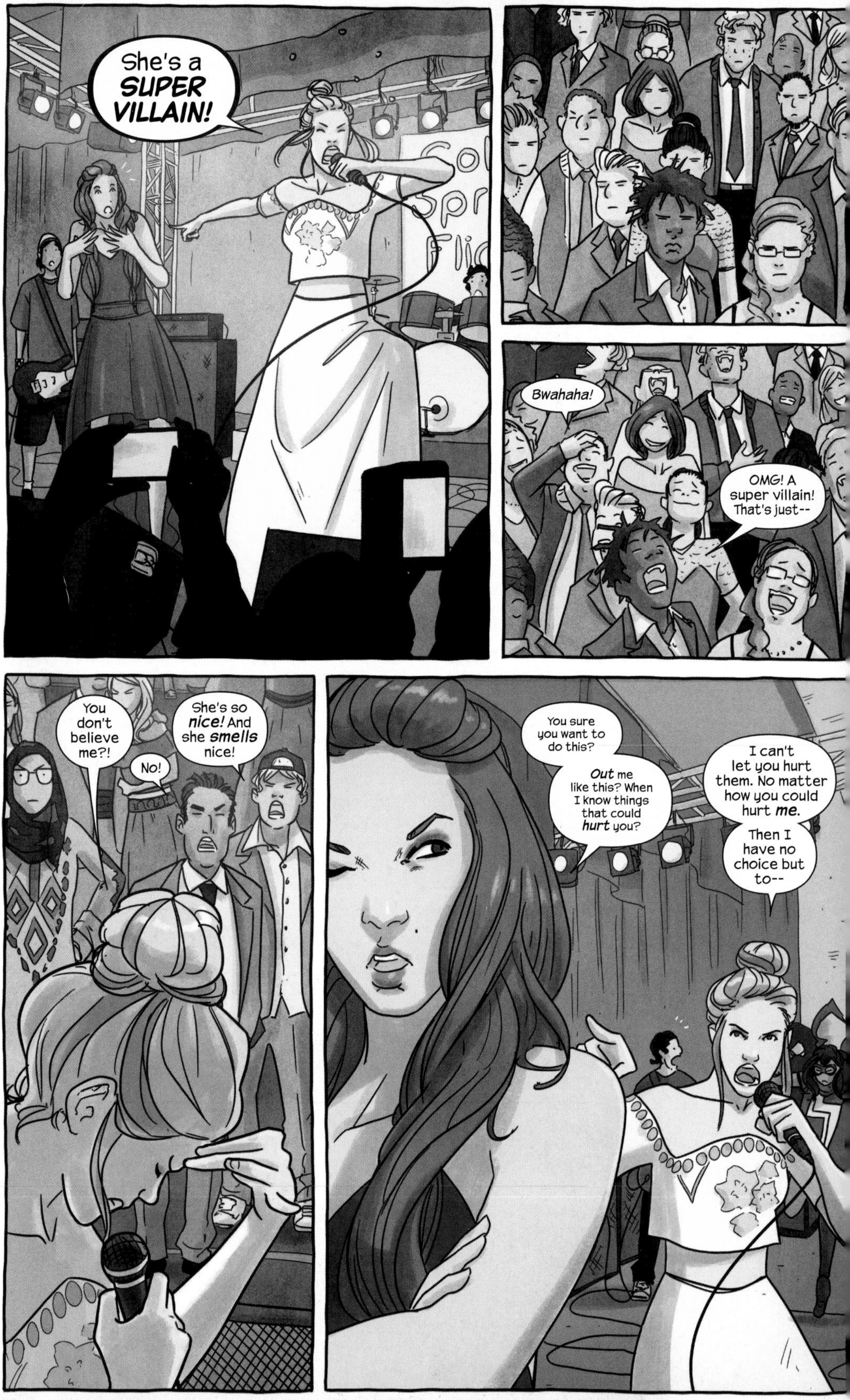
She's a SUPER VILLAIN!
Bwahaha!
OMG! A super villain! That's just--
You don't believe me?!
No!
She's so nice! And she smells nice!
You sure you want to do this?
Out me like this? When I know things that could hurt you?
I can't let you hurt them. No matter how you could hurt me.
Then I have no choice but to--

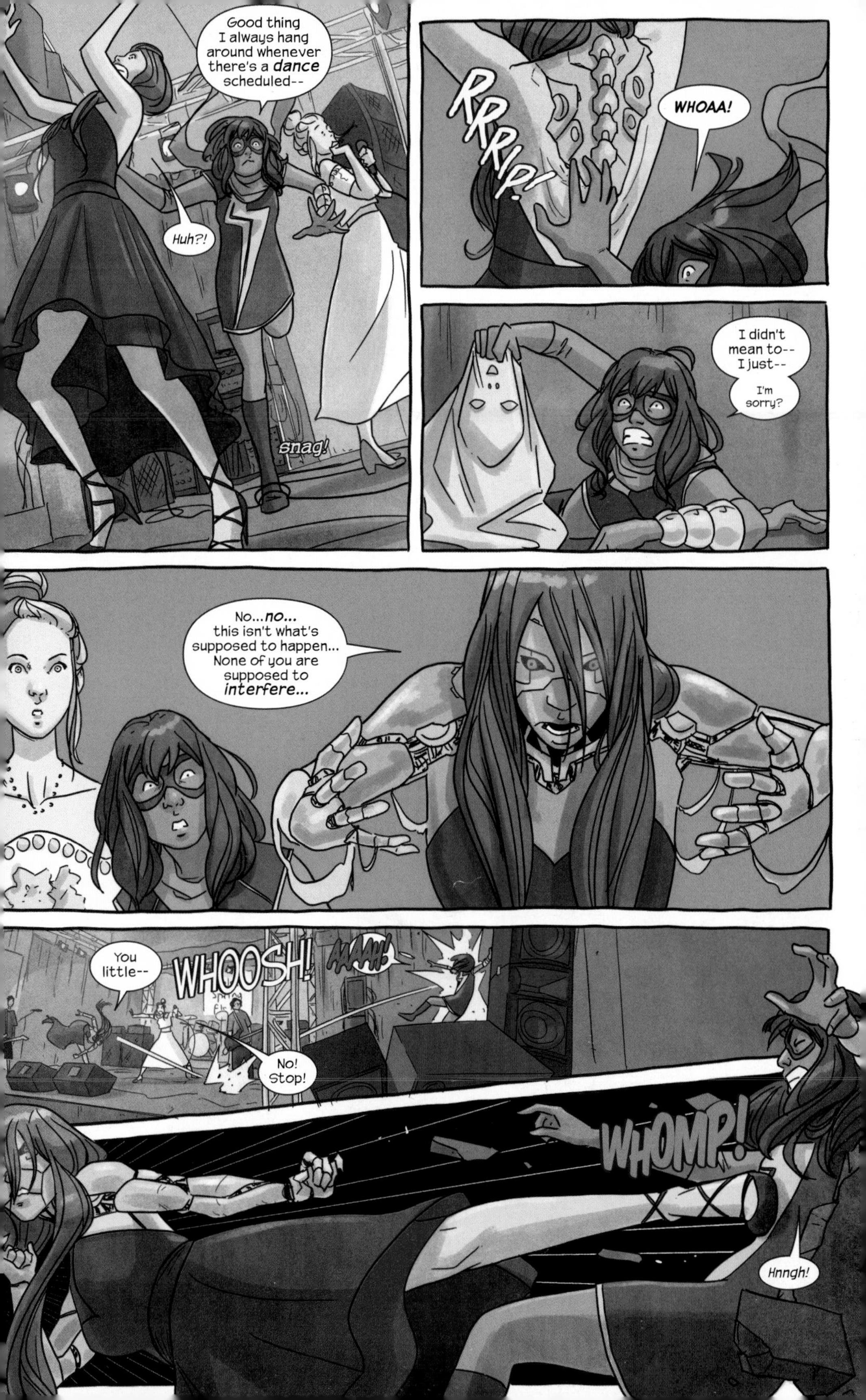

Good thing I always hang around whenever there's a *dance* scheduled--
Huh?!
snag!
RRRIP!
WHOAA!
I didn't mean to-- I just--
I'm sorry?
No...*no...* this isn't what's supposed to happen... None of you are supposed to *interfere...*
You little--
WHOOSH!
AAAH!
No! Stop!
WHOMP!
Hnngh!

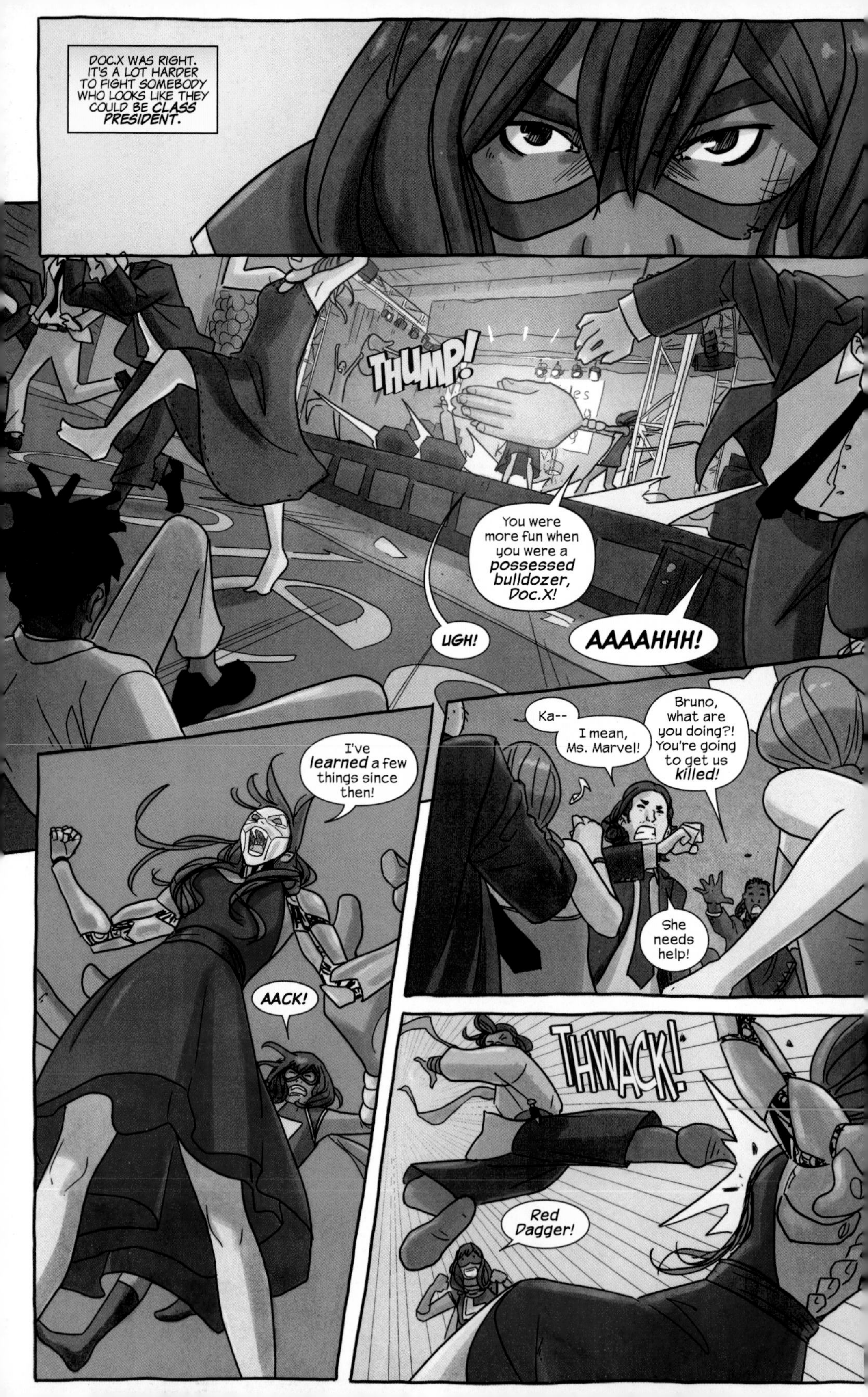
DOC.X WAS RIGHT. IT'S A LOT HARDER TO FIGHT SOMEBODY WHO LOOKS LIKE THEY COULD BE CLASS PRESIDENT.
THUMP!
You were more fun when you were a possessed bulldozer, Doc.X!
UGH!
AAAAHHH!
I've learned a few things since then!
AACK!
Ka--
I mean, Ms. Marvel!
Bruno, what are you doing?! You're going to get us killed!
She needs help!
THWACK!
Red Dagger!

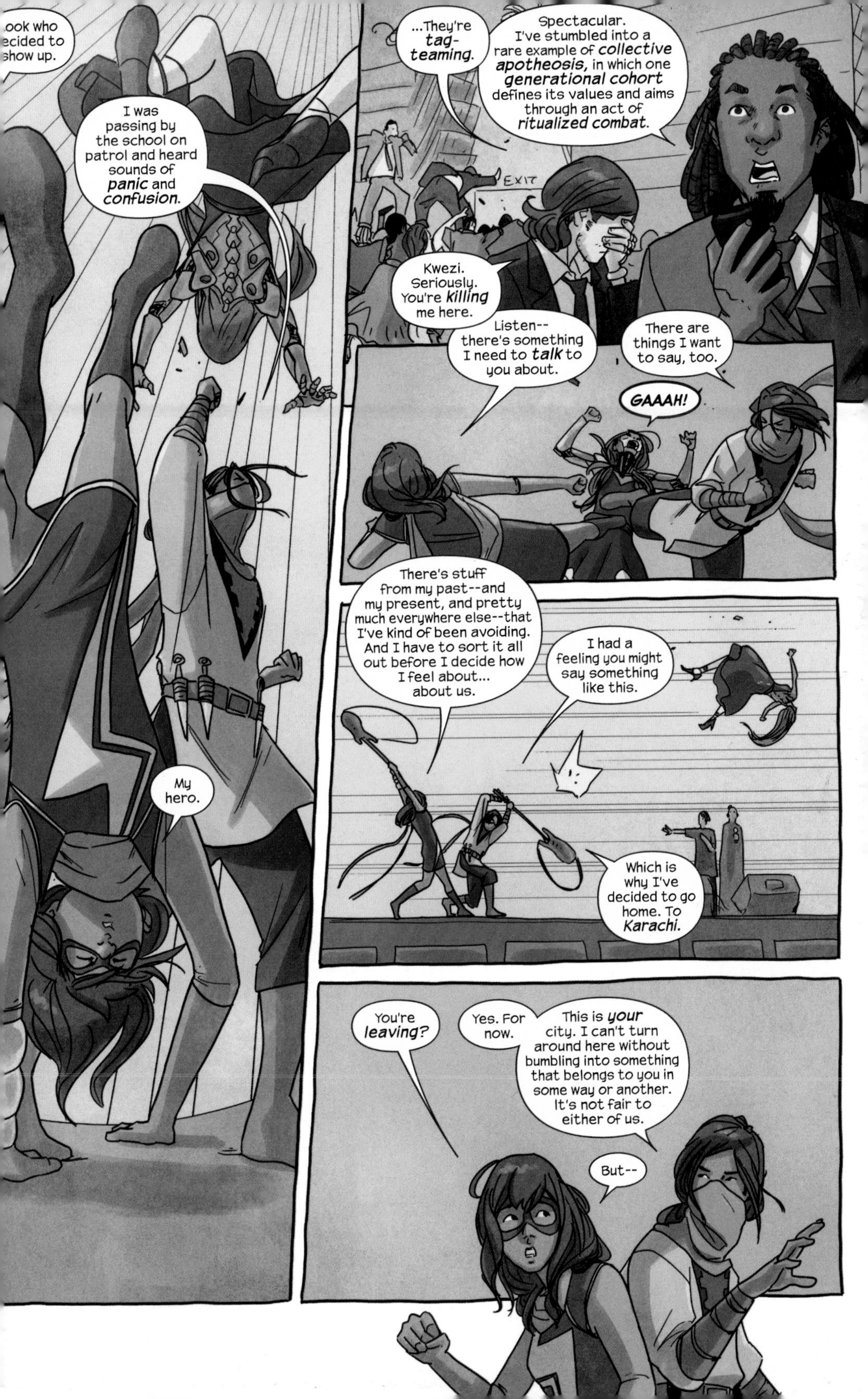
Look who decided to show up.
I was passing by the school on patrol and heard sounds of *panic* and *confusion*.
My hero.
...They're *tag-teaming*.
Spectacular. I've stumbled into a rare example of *collective apotheosis,* in which one *generational cohort* defines its values and aims through an act of *ritualized combat*.
EXIT
Kwezi. Seriously. You're *killing* me here.
Listen-- there's something I need to *talk* to you about.
There are things I want to say, too.
GAAAH!
There's stuff from my past--and my present, and pretty much everywhere else--that I've kind of been avoiding. And I have to sort it all out before I decide how I feel about... about us.
I had a feeling you might say something like this.
Which is why I've decided to go home. To *Karachi*.
You're *leaving?*
Yes. For now.
This is *your* city. I can't turn around here without bumbling into something that belongs to you in some way or another. It's not fair to either of us.
But--

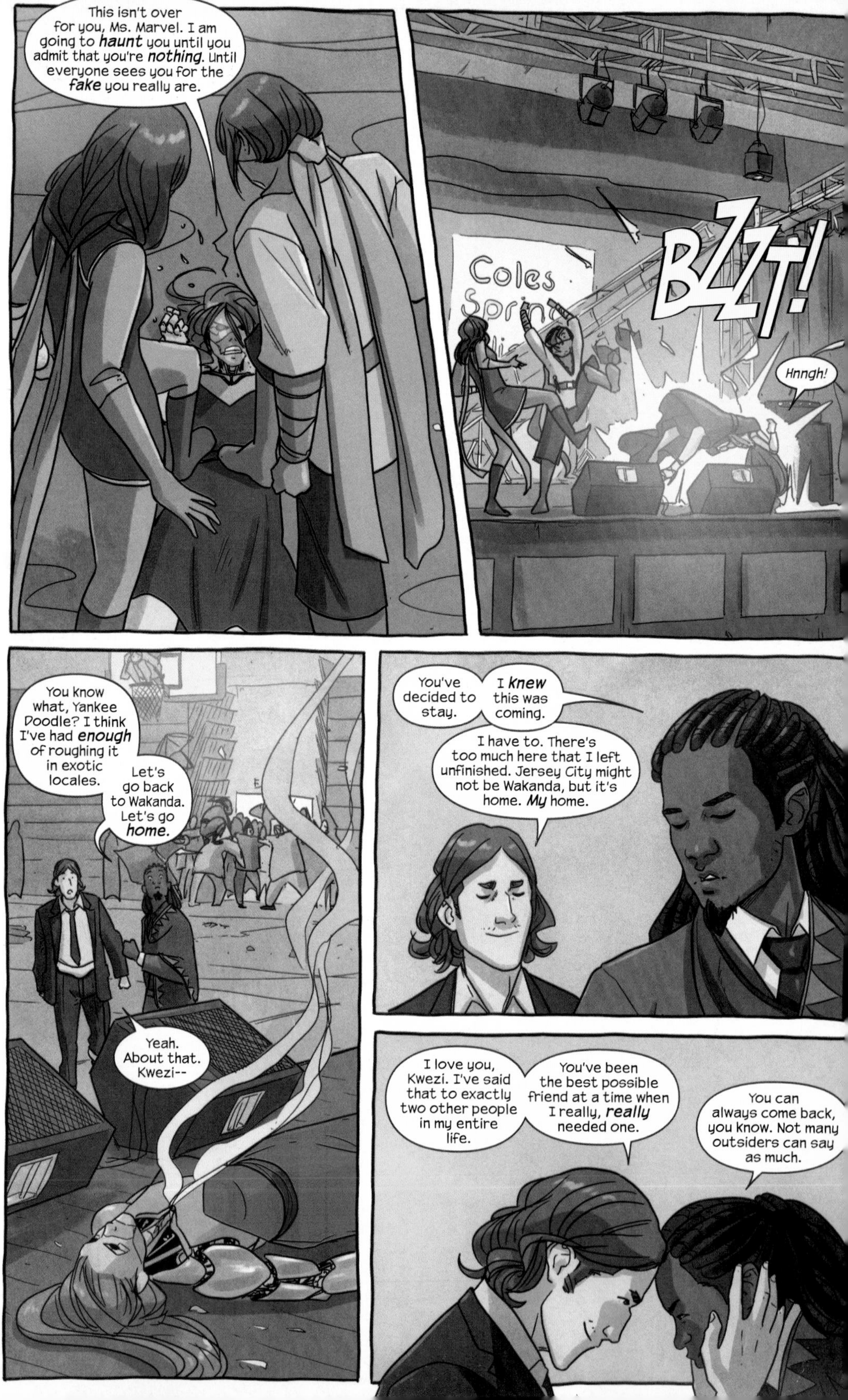
This isn't over for you, Ms. Marvel. I am going to *haunt* you until you admit that you're *nothing*. Until everyone sees you for the *fake* you really are.
Coles Spring
BZZT!
Hnngh!
You know what, Yankee Doodle? I think I've had *enough* of roughing it in exotic locales.
Let's go back to Wakanda. Let's go *home*.
Yeah. About that. Kwezi--
You've decided to stay.
I *knew* this was coming.
I have to. There's too much here that I left unfinished. Jersey City might not be Wakanda, but it's home. *My* home.
I love you, Kwezi. I've said that to exactly two other people in my entire life.
You've been the best possible friend at a time when I really, *really* needed one.
You can always come back, you know. Not many outsiders can say as much.

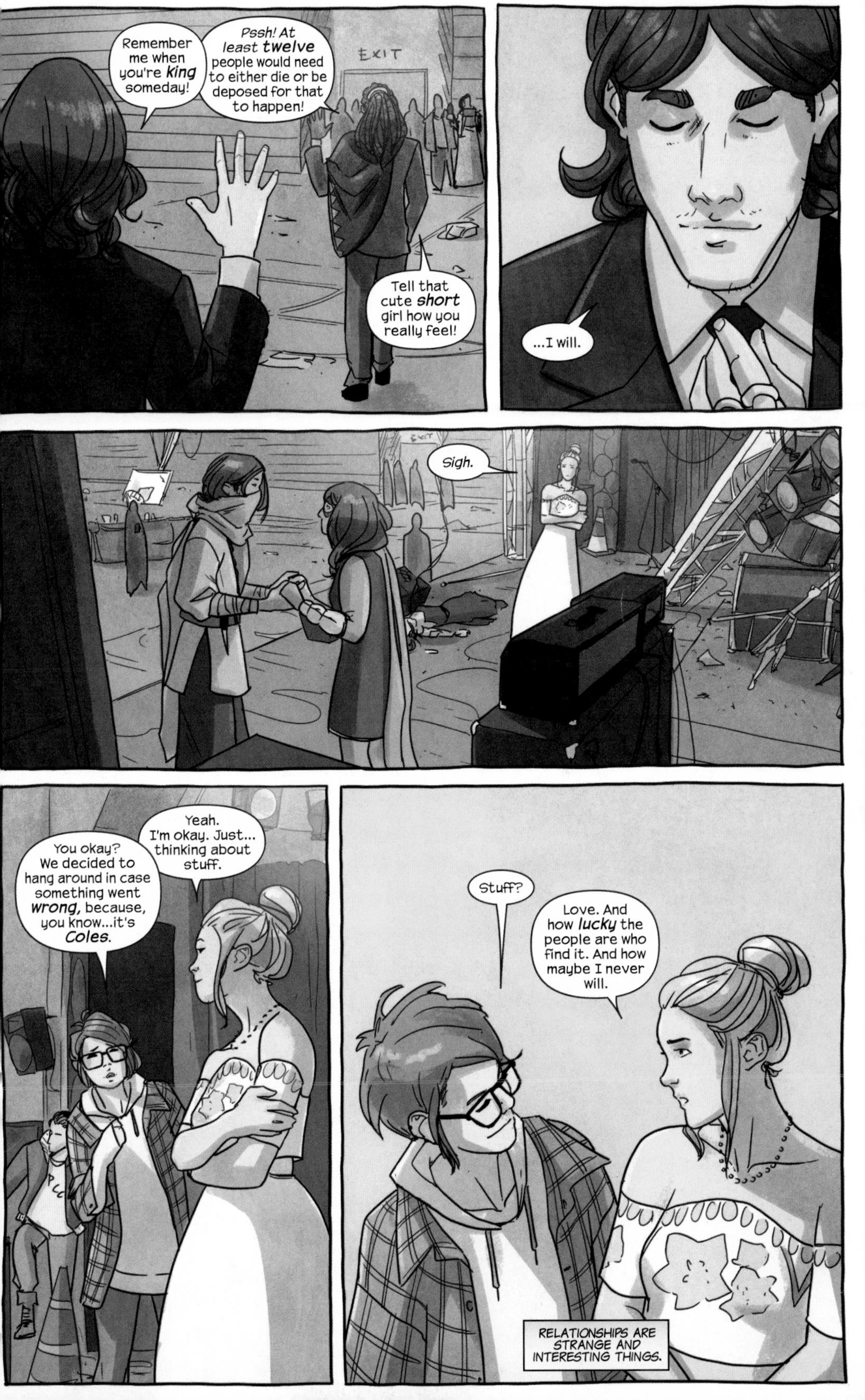

Remember me when you're *king* someday!
Pssh! At least **twelve** people would need to either die or be deposed for that to happen!
EXIT
Tell that cute **short** girl how you really feel!
...I will.
EXIT
Sigh.
You okay? We decided to hang around in case something went **wrong**, because, you know...it's **Coles**.
Yeah. I'm okay. Just... thinking about stuff.
Stuff?
Love. And how *lucky* the people are who find it. And how maybe I never will.
RELATIONSHIPS ARE STRANGE AND INTERESTING THINGS.

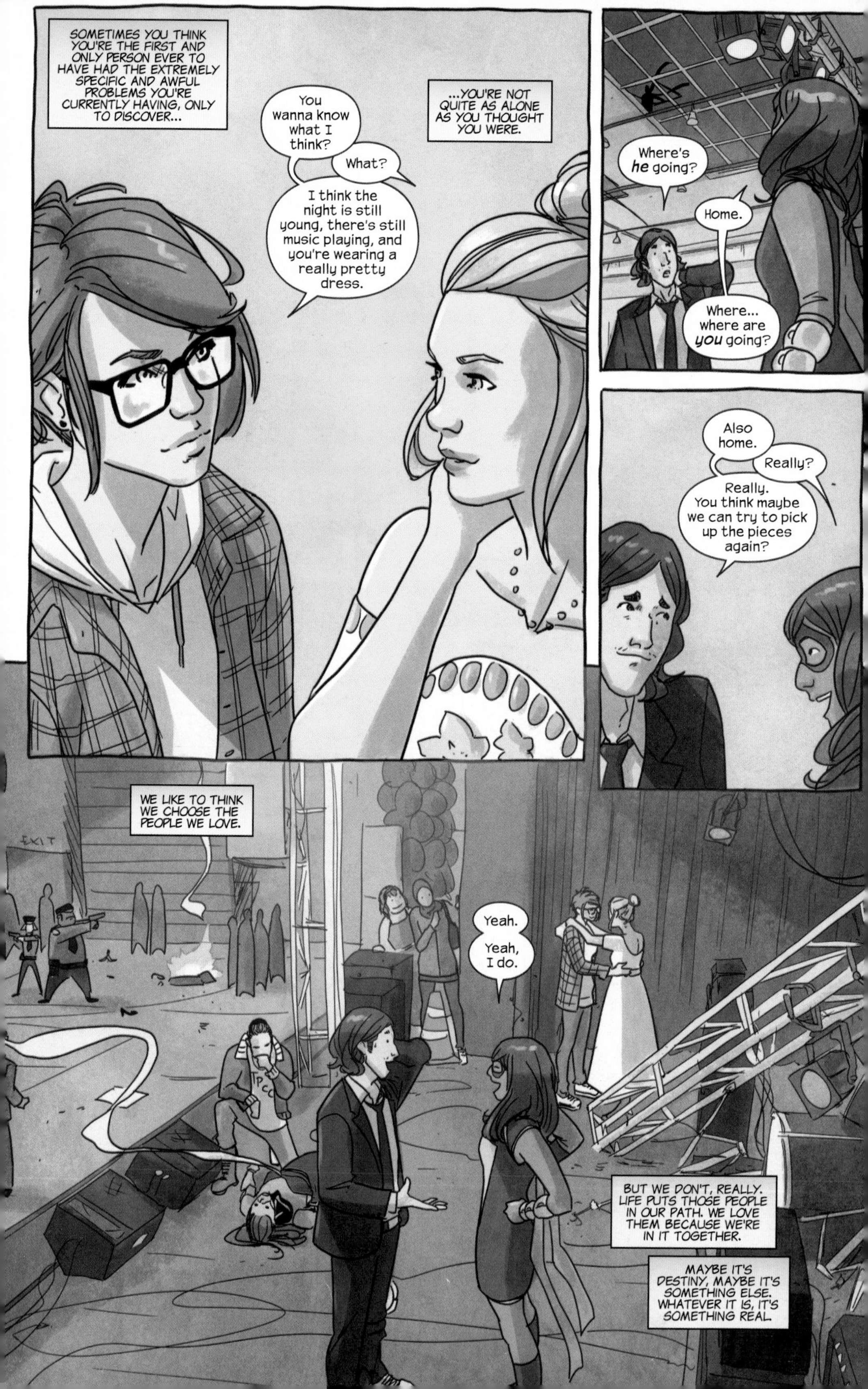
SOMETIMES YOU THINK YOU'RE THE FIRST AND ONLY PERSON EVER TO HAVE HAD THE EXTREMELY SPECIFIC AND AWFUL PROBLEMS YOU'RE CURRENTLY HAVING, ONLY TO DISCOVER...
You wanna know what I think?
What?
I think the night is still young, there's still music playing, and you're wearing a really pretty dress.
...YOU'RE NOT QUITE AS ALONE AS YOU THOUGHT YOU WERE.
Where's *he* going?
Home.
Where... where are *you* going?
Also home.
Really?
Really. You think maybe we can try to pick up the pieces again?
WE LIKE TO THINK WE CHOOSE THE PEOPLE WE LOVE.
EXIT
Yeah.
Yeah, I do.
BUT WE DON'T, REALLY. LIFE PUTS THOSE PEOPLE IN OUR PATH. WE LOVE THEM BECAUSE WE'RE IN IT TOGETHER.
MAYBE IT'S DESTINY, MAYBE IT'S SOMETHING ELSE. WHATEVER IT IS, IT'S SOMETHING REAL.

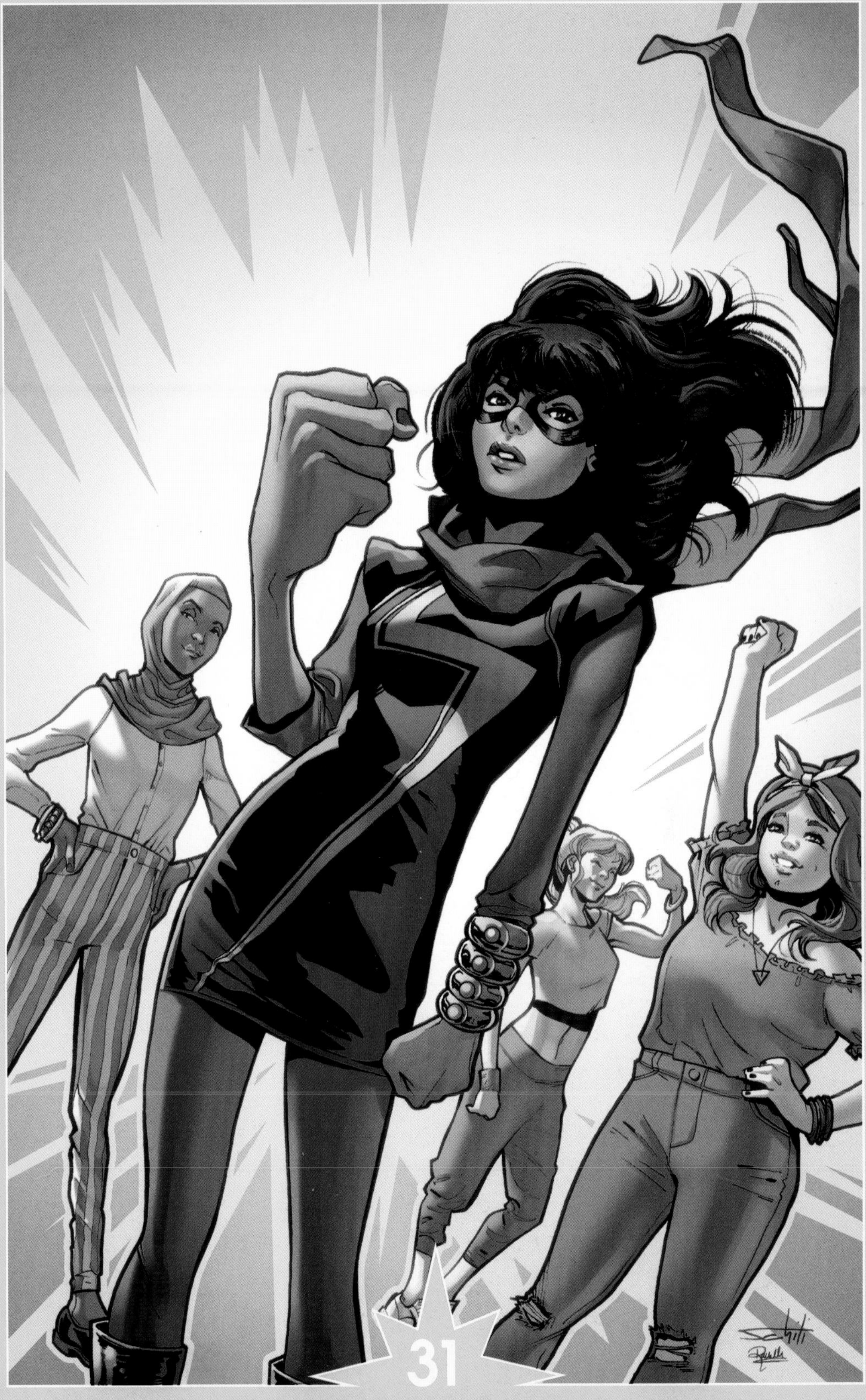
31

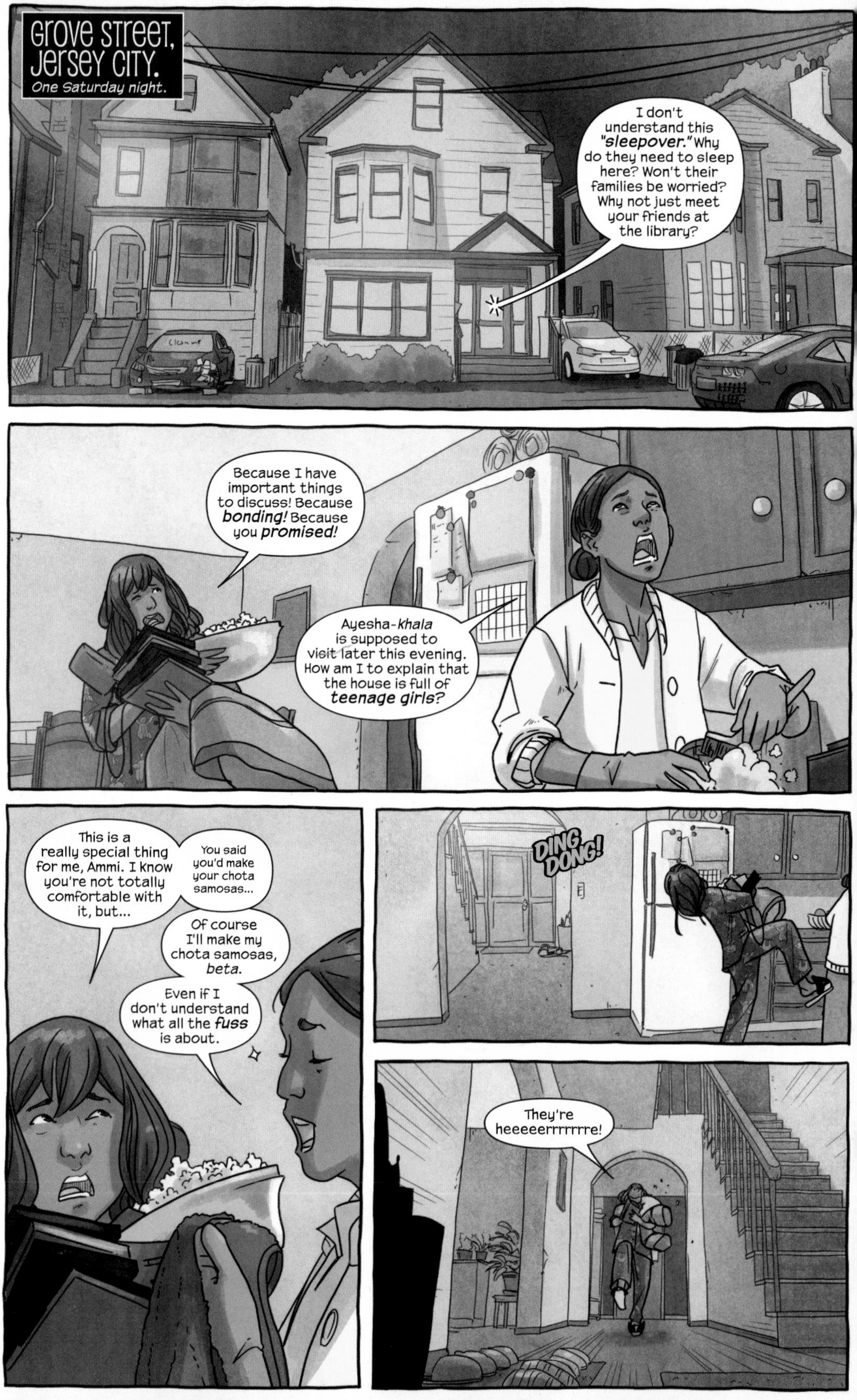
GROVE STREET, JERSEY CITY.
One Saturday night.
I don't understand this "sleepover." Why do they need to sleep here? Won't their families be worried? Why not just meet your friends at the library?
Because I have important things to discuss! Because bonding! Because you promised!
Ayesha-khala is supposed to visit later this evening. How am I to explain that the house is full of teenage girls?
This is a really special thing for me, Ammi. I know you're not totally comfortable with it, but...
You said you'd make your chota samosas...
Of course I'll make my chota samosas, beta.
Even if I don't understand what all the fuss is about.
DING DONG!
They're heeeeerrrrrrre!

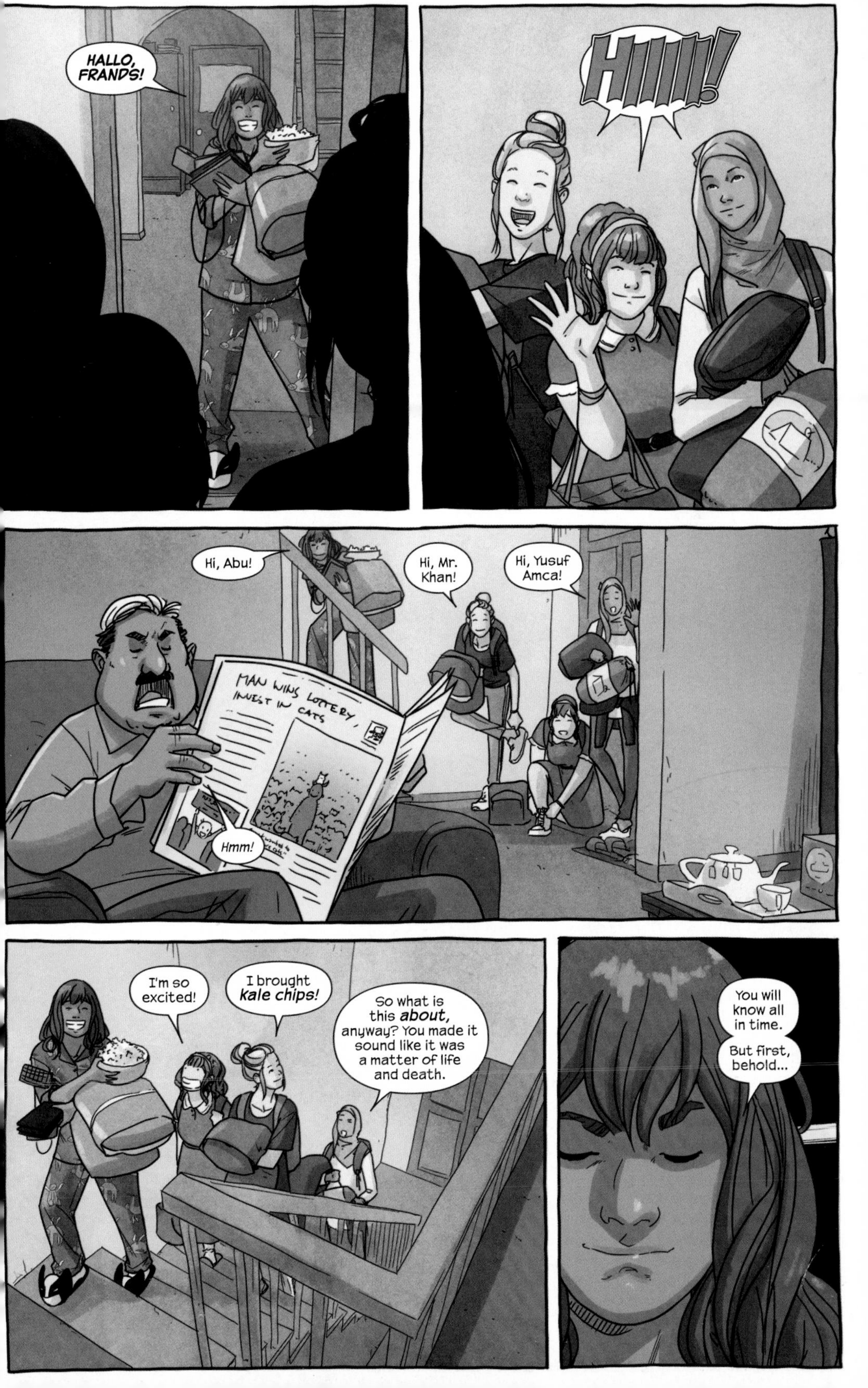
HALLO, FRANDS!
HIIII!
Hi, Abu!
Hi, Mr. Khan!
Hi, Yusuf Amca!
MAN WINS LOTTERY, INVEST IN CATS
Hmm!
I'm so excited!
I brought *kale chips!*
So what is this *about,* anyway? You made it sound like it was a matter of life and death.
You will know all in time.
But first, behold...

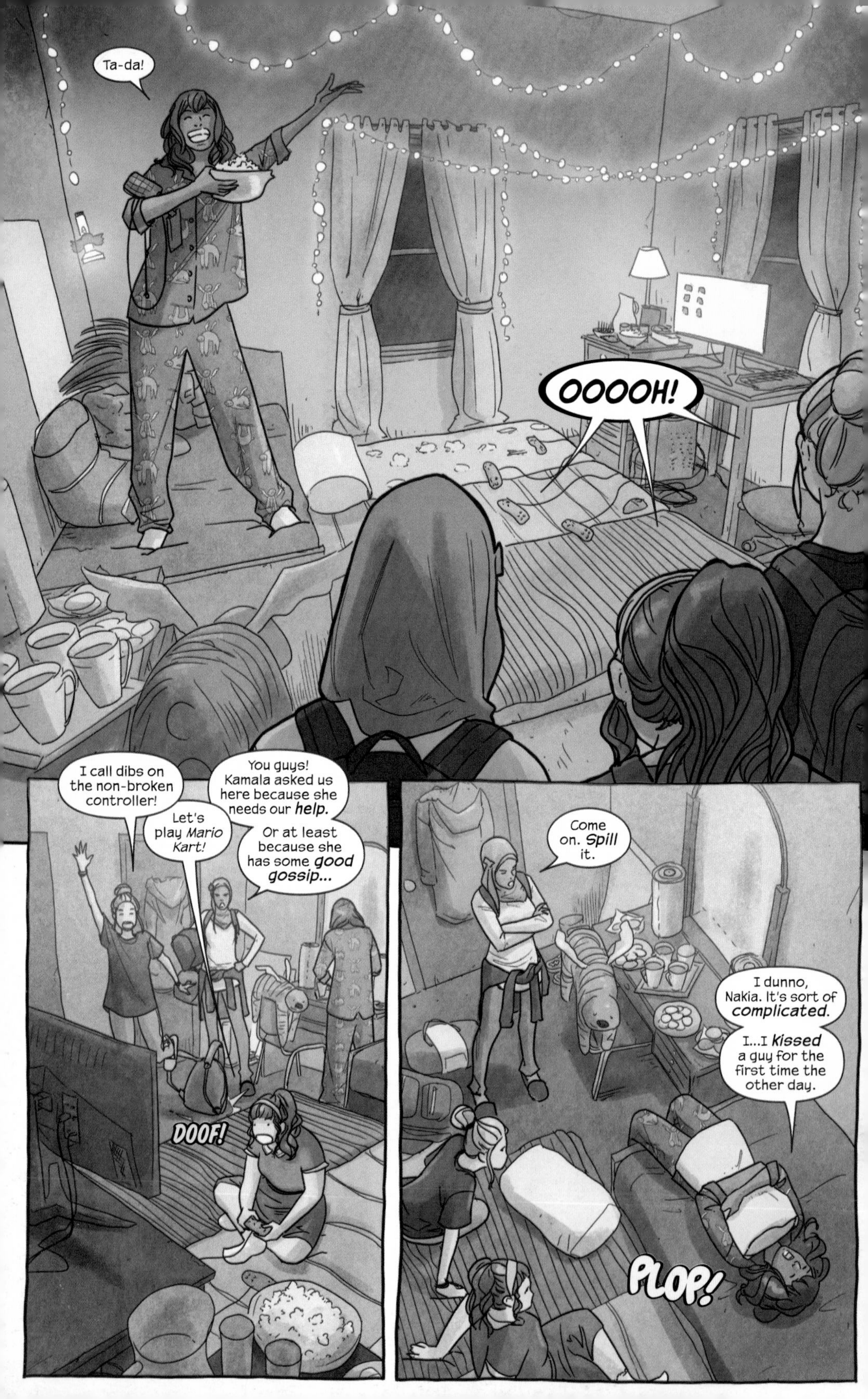
Ta-da!
OOOOH!
I call dibs on the non-broken controller!
Let's play *Mario Kart!*
You guys! Kamala asked us here because she needs our **help.**
Or at least because she has some **good gossip...**
DOOF!
Come on. **Spill** it.
I dunno, Nakia. It's sort of **complicated.**
I...I **kissed** a guy for the first time the other day.
PLOP!

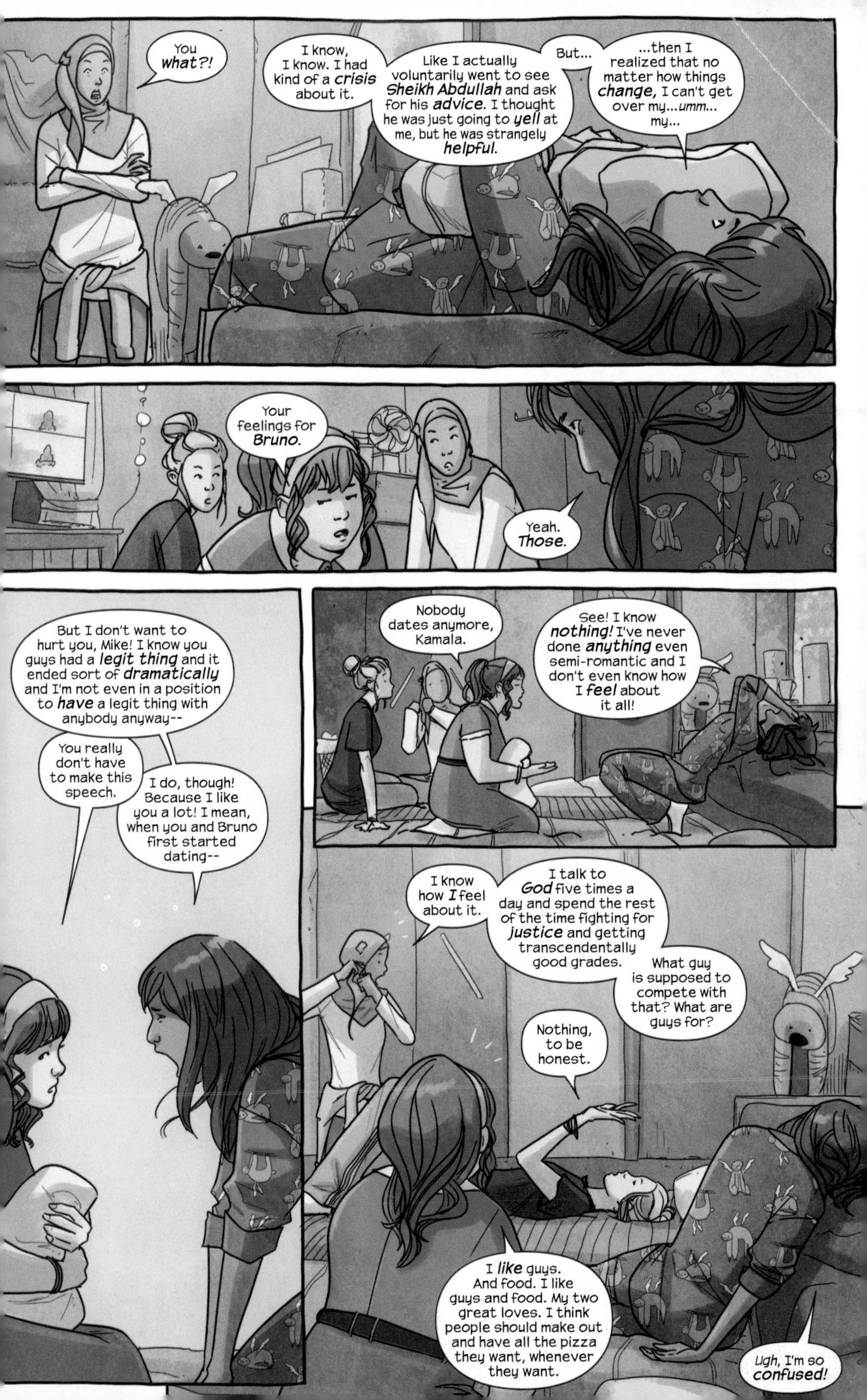
You *what?!*
I know, I know. I had kind of a *crisis* about it.
Like I actually voluntarily went to see *Sheikh Abdullah* and ask for his *advice*. I thought he was just going to *yell* at me, but he was strangely *helpful*.
But...
...then I realized that no matter how things *change,* I can't get over my...*umm*... my...
Your feelings for *Bruno*.
Yeah. *Those*.
But I don't want to hurt you, Mike! I know you guys had a *legit thing* and it ended sort of *dramatically* and I'm not even in a position to *have* a legit thing with anybody anyway--
You really don't have to make this speech.
I do, though! Because I like you a lot! I mean, when you and Bruno first started dating--
Nobody dates anymore, Kamala.
See! I know *nothing!* I've never done *anything* even semi-romantic and I don't even know how I *feel* about it all!
I know how *I* feel about it.
I talk to *God* five times a day and spend the rest of the time fighting for *justice* and getting transcendentally good grades.
What guy is supposed to compete with that? What are guys for?
Nothing, to be honest.
I *like* guys. And food. I like guys and food. My two great loves. I think people should make out and have all the pizza they want, whenever they want.
Ugh, I'm so *confused!*

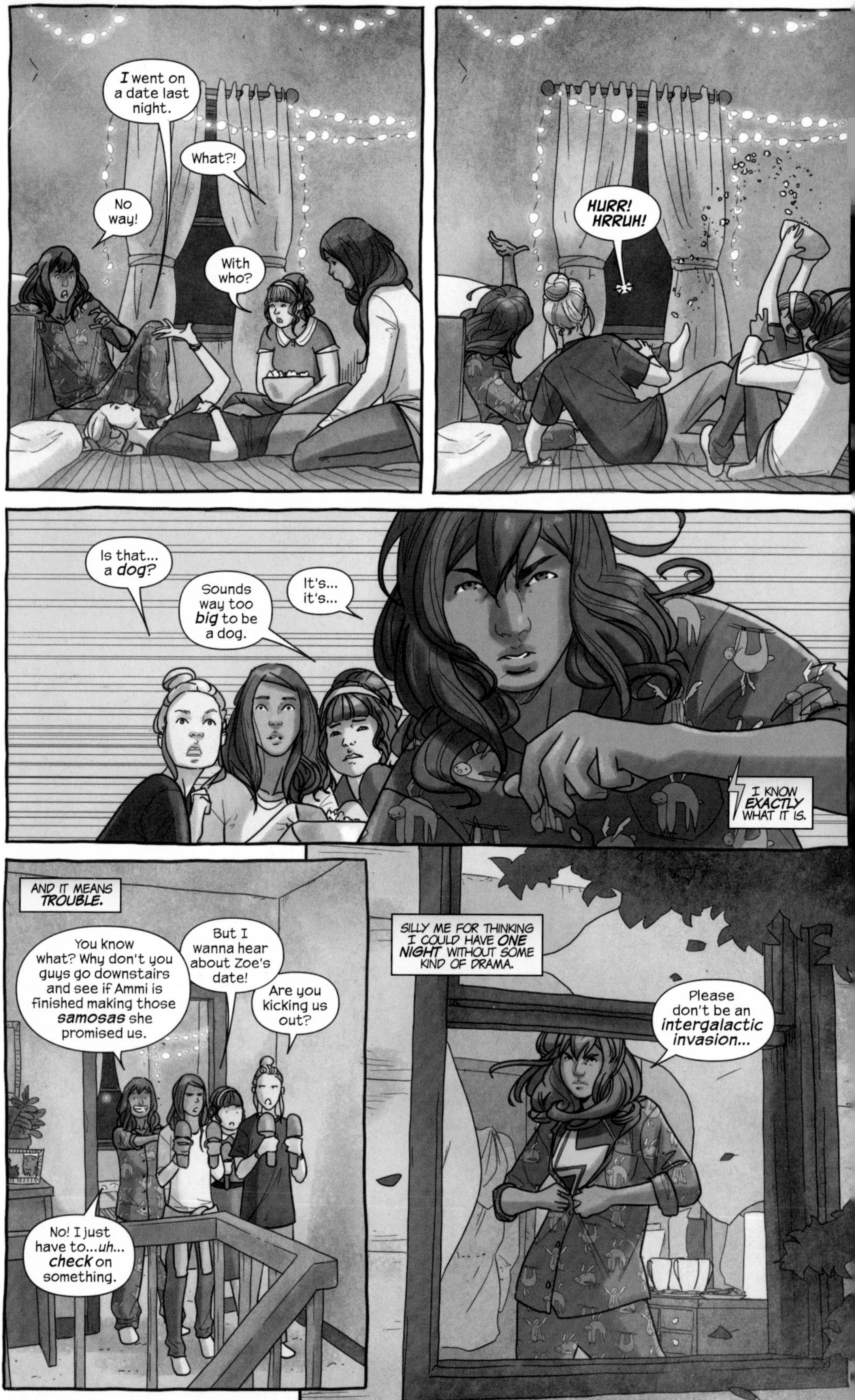
I went on a date last night.
What?!
No way!
With who?
HURR! HRRUH!
Is that... a dog?
Sounds way too big to be a dog.
It's... it's...
I KNOW EXACTLY WHAT IT IS.
AND IT MEANS TROUBLE.
You know what? Why don't you guys go downstairs and see if Ammi is finished making those samosas she promised us.
But I wanna hear about Zoe's date!
Are you kicking us out?
No! I just have to...uh... check on something.
SILLY ME FOR THINKING I COULD HAVE ONE NIGHT WITHOUT SOME KIND OF DRAMA.
Please don't be an intergalactic invasion...

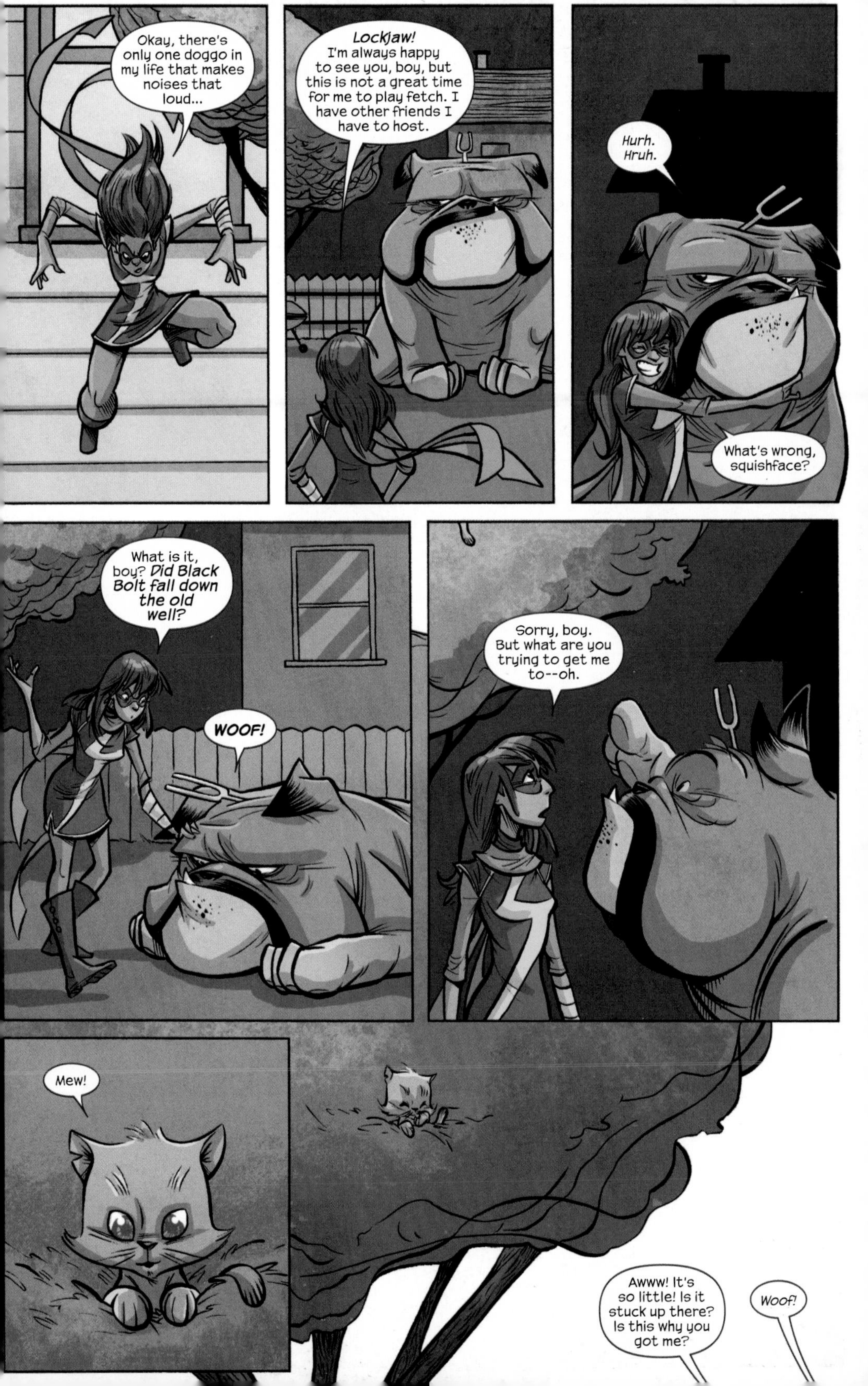
Okay, there's only one doggo in my life that makes noises that loud...
Lockjaw! I'm always happy to see you, boy, but this is not a great time for me to play fetch. I have other friends I have to host.
Hurh. Hruh.
What's wrong, squishface?
What is it, boy? Did Black Bolt fall down the old well?
WOOF!
Sorry, boy. But what are you trying to get me to--oh.
Mew!
Awww! It's so little! Is it stuck up there? Is this why you got me?
Woof!

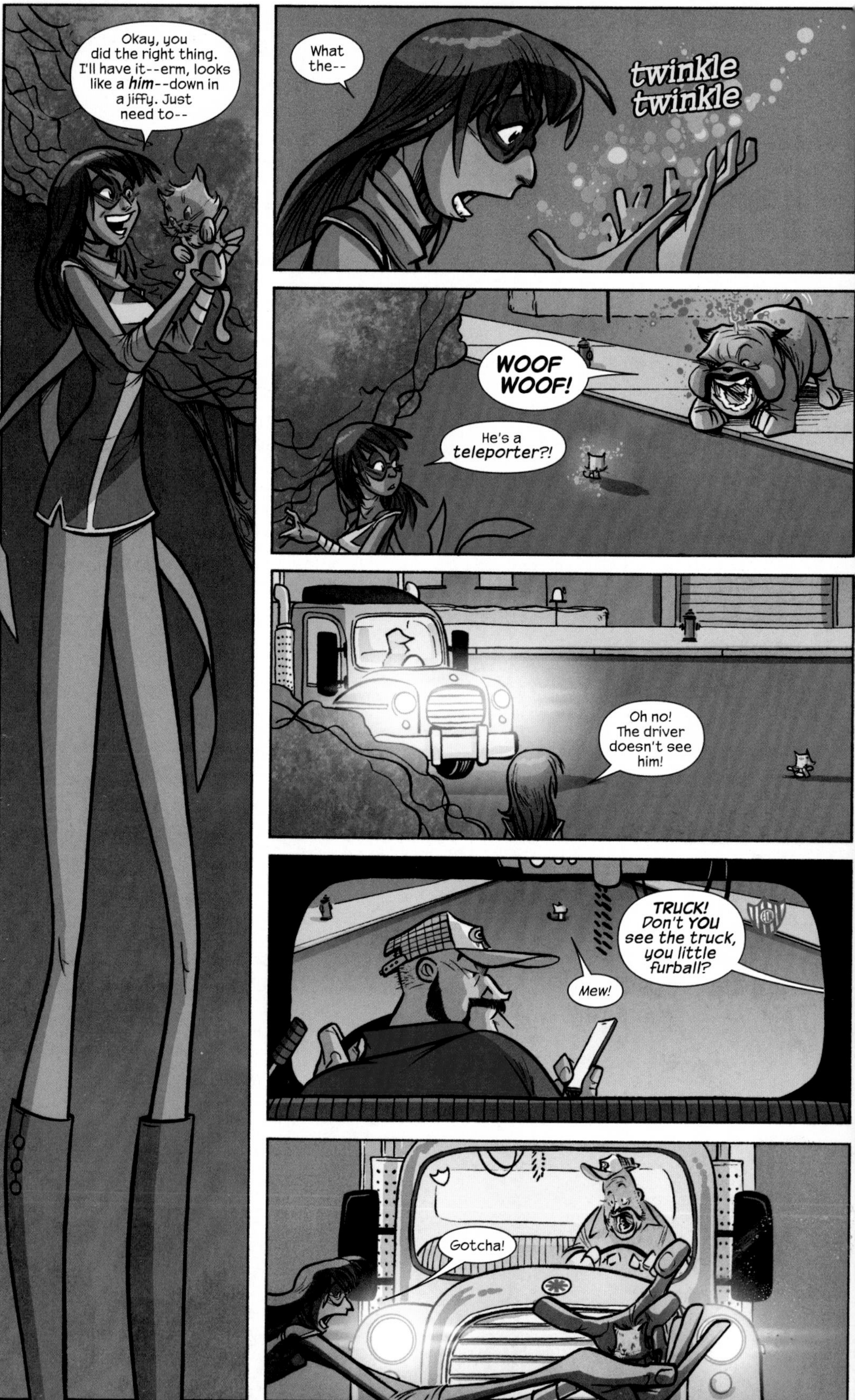
Okay, you did the right thing. I'll have it--erm, looks like a him--down in a jiffy. Just need to--
What the--
twinkle twinkle
WOOF WOOF!
He's a teleporter?!
Oh no! The driver doesn't see him!
TRUCK! Don't YOU see the truck, you little furball?
Mew!
Gotcha!

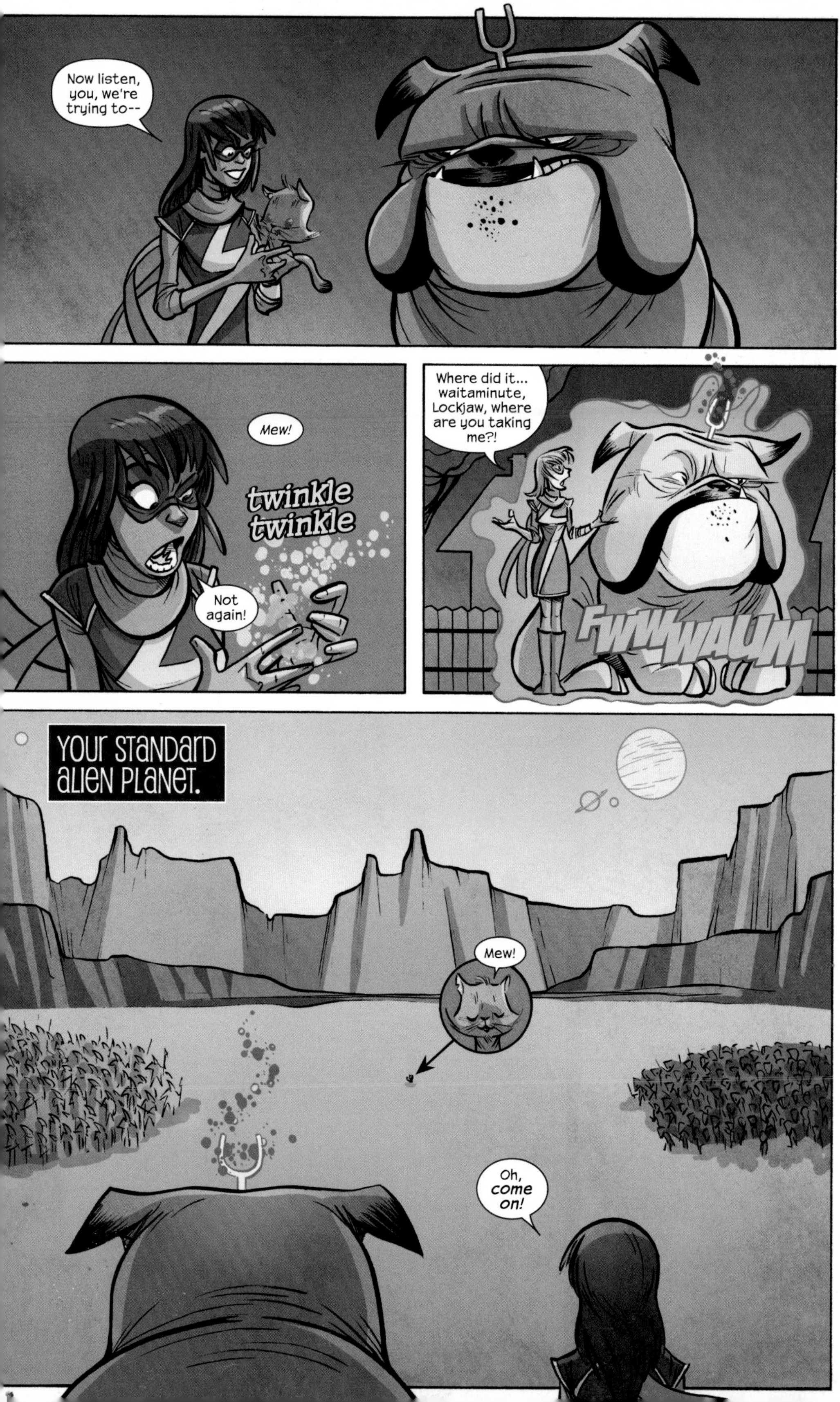
Now listen, you, we're trying to--
Mew!
twinkle twinkle
Not again!
Where did it... waitaminute, Lockjaw, where are you taking me?!
FWWWAUM
YOUR STANDARD ALIEN PLANET.
Mew!
Oh, come on!

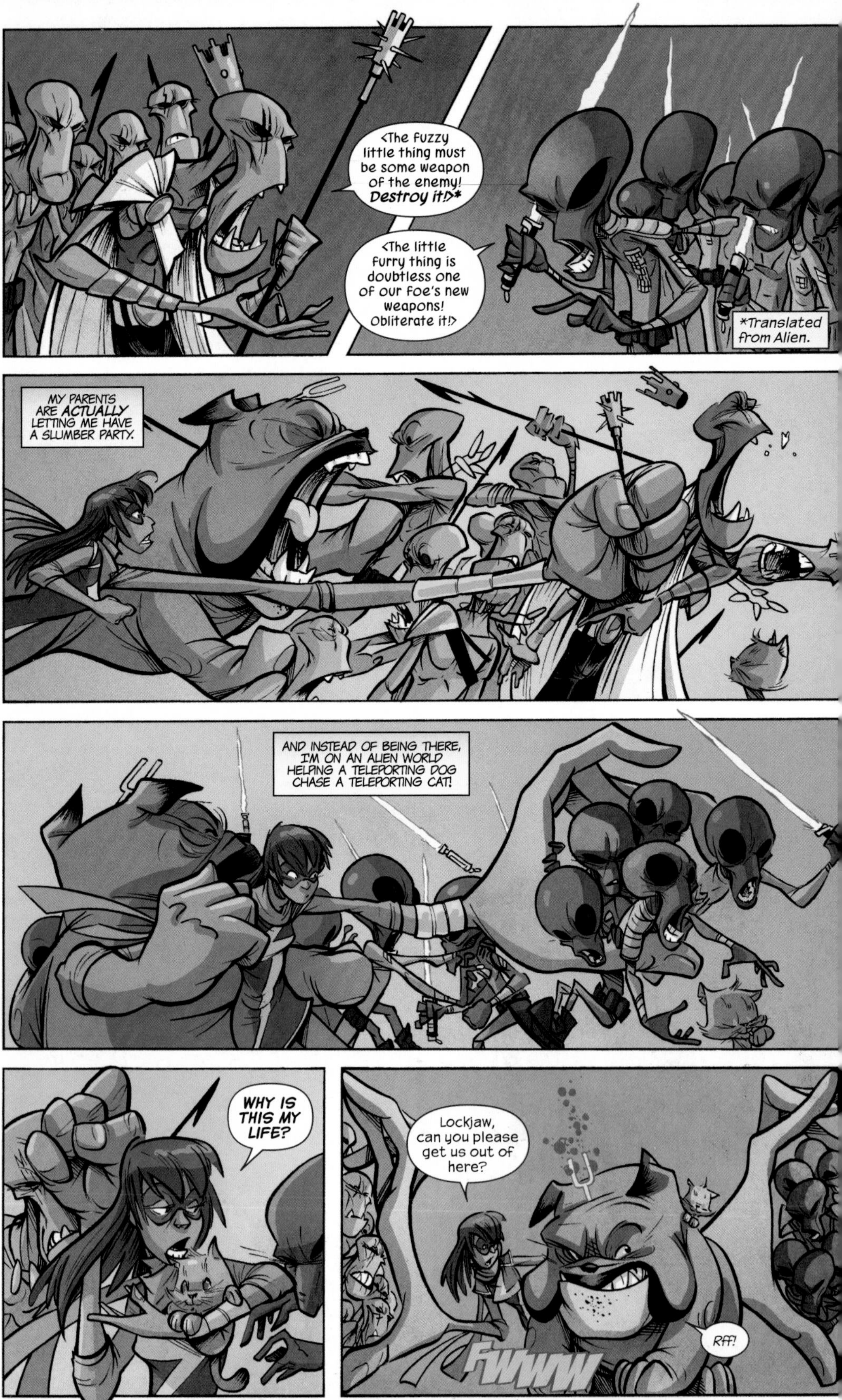
<The fuzzy little thing must be some weapon of the enemy! **Destroy it!**>*
<The little furry thing is doubtless one of our foe's new weapons! Obliterate it!>
*Translated from Alien.
MY PARENTS ARE *ACTUALLY* LETTING ME HAVE A SLUMBER PARTY.
AND INSTEAD OF BEING THERE, I'M ON AN ALIEN WORLD HELPING A TELEPORTING DOG CHASE A TELEPORTING CAT!
WHY IS THIS MY LIFE?
Lockjaw, can you please get us out of here?
Rff!
FWWW

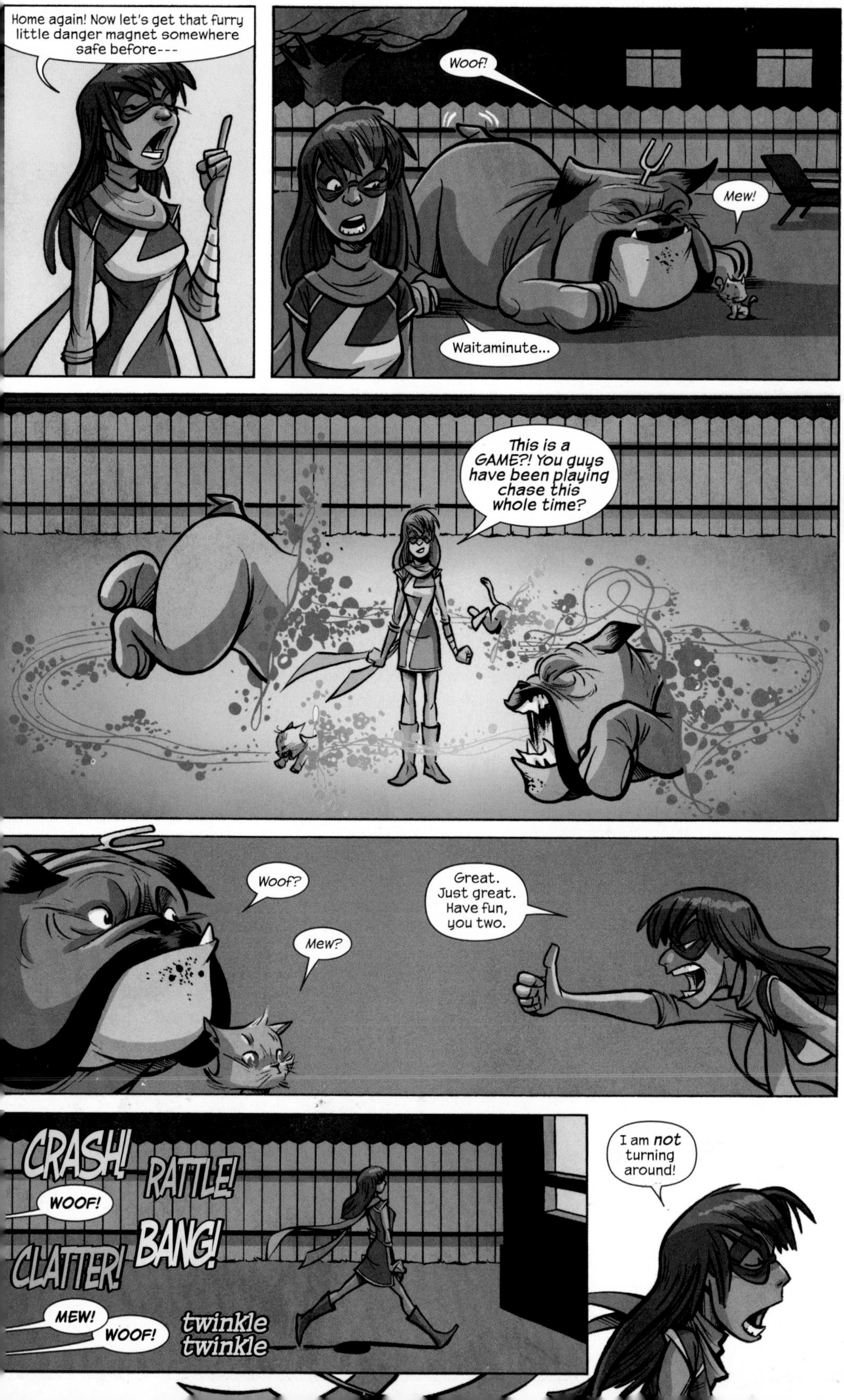
Home again! Now let's get that furry little danger magnet somewhere safe before---
Woof!
Mew!
Waitaminute...
This is a GAME?! You guys have been playing chase this whole time?
Woof?
Mew?
Great. Just great. Have fun, you two.
CRASH!
RATTLE!
WOOF!
BANG!
CLATTER!
MEW!
WOOF!
twinkle twinkle
I am not turning around!

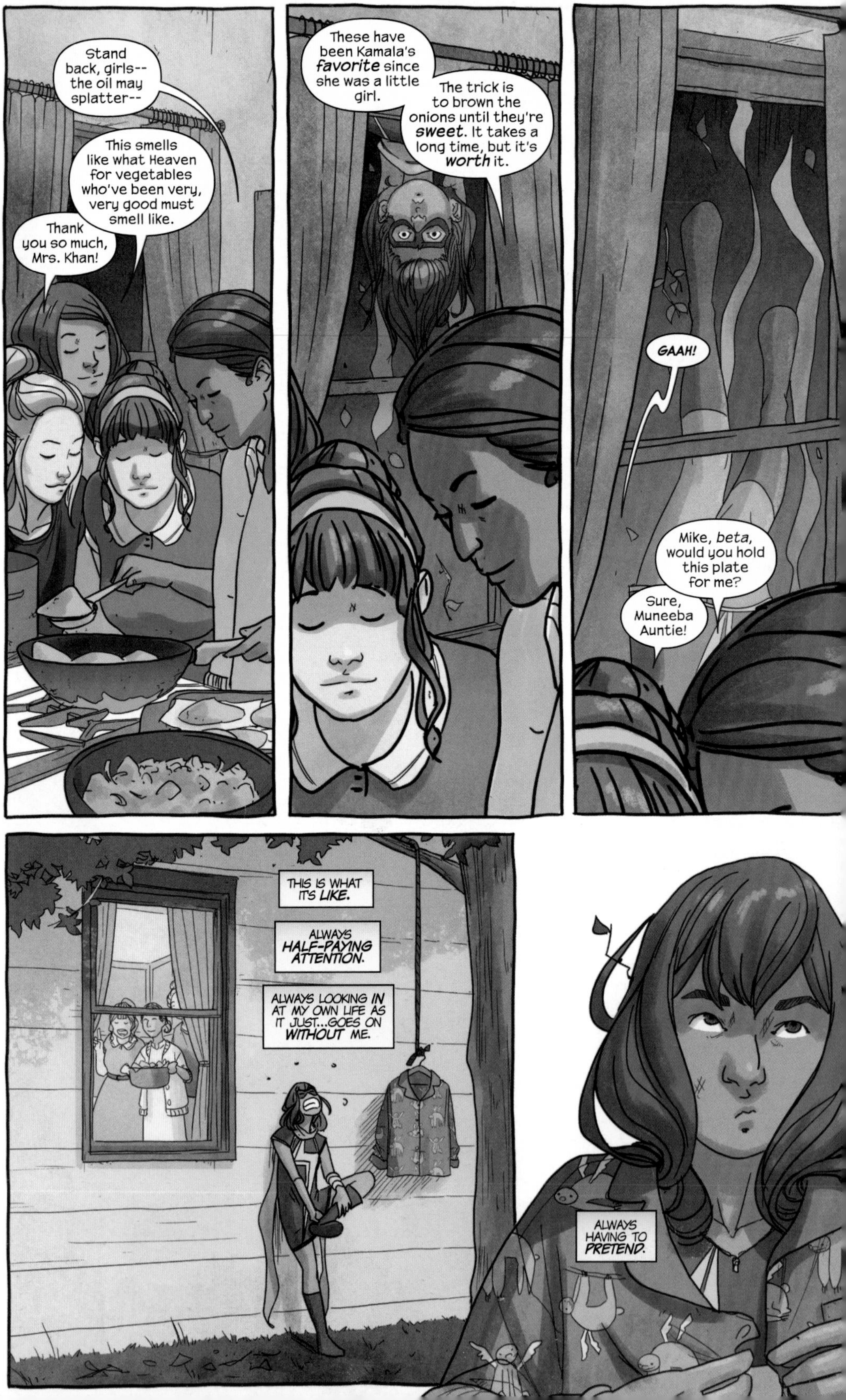
Stand back, girls-- the oil may splatter--
This smells like what Heaven for vegetables who've been very, very good must smell like.
Thank you so much, Mrs. Khan!
These have been Kamala's *favorite* since she was a little girl.
The trick is to brown the onions until they're **sweet**. It takes a long time, but it's **worth** it.
GAAH!
Mike, *beta*, would you hold this plate for me?
Sure, Muneeba Auntie!
THIS IS WHAT IT'S **LIKE.**
ALWAYS **HALF-PAYING ATTENTION.**
ALWAYS LOOKING **IN** AT MY OWN LIFE AS IT JUST...GOES ON **WITHOUT** ME.
ALWAYS HAVING TO **PRETEND.**

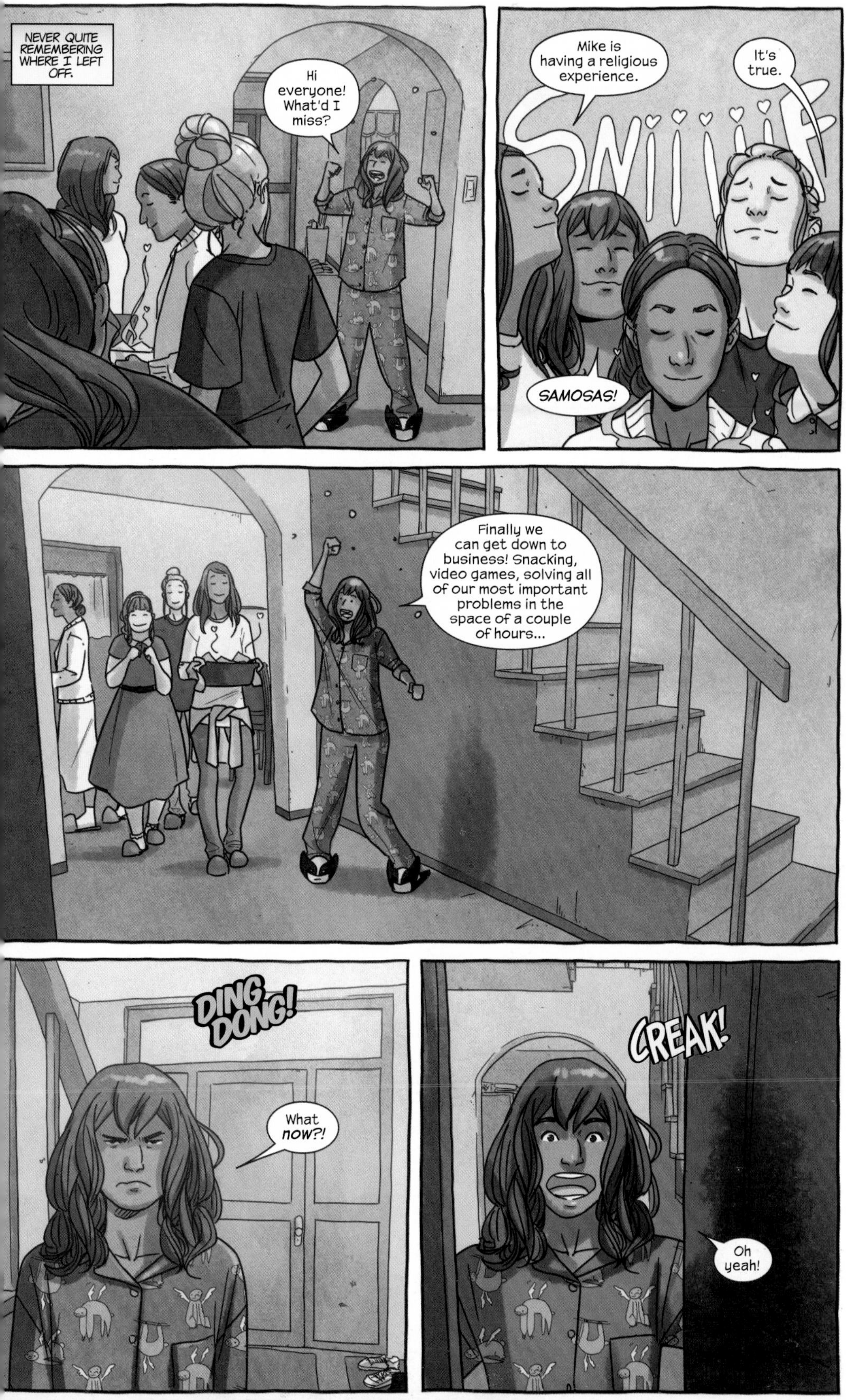
NEVER QUITE REMEMBERING WHERE I LEFT OFF.
Hi everyone! What'd I miss?
Mike is having a religious experience.
It's true.
SNIIIIIF
SAMOSAS!
Finally we can get down to business! Snacking, video games, solving all of our most important problems in the space of a couple of hours...
DING DONG!
What now?!
CREAK!
Oh yeah!

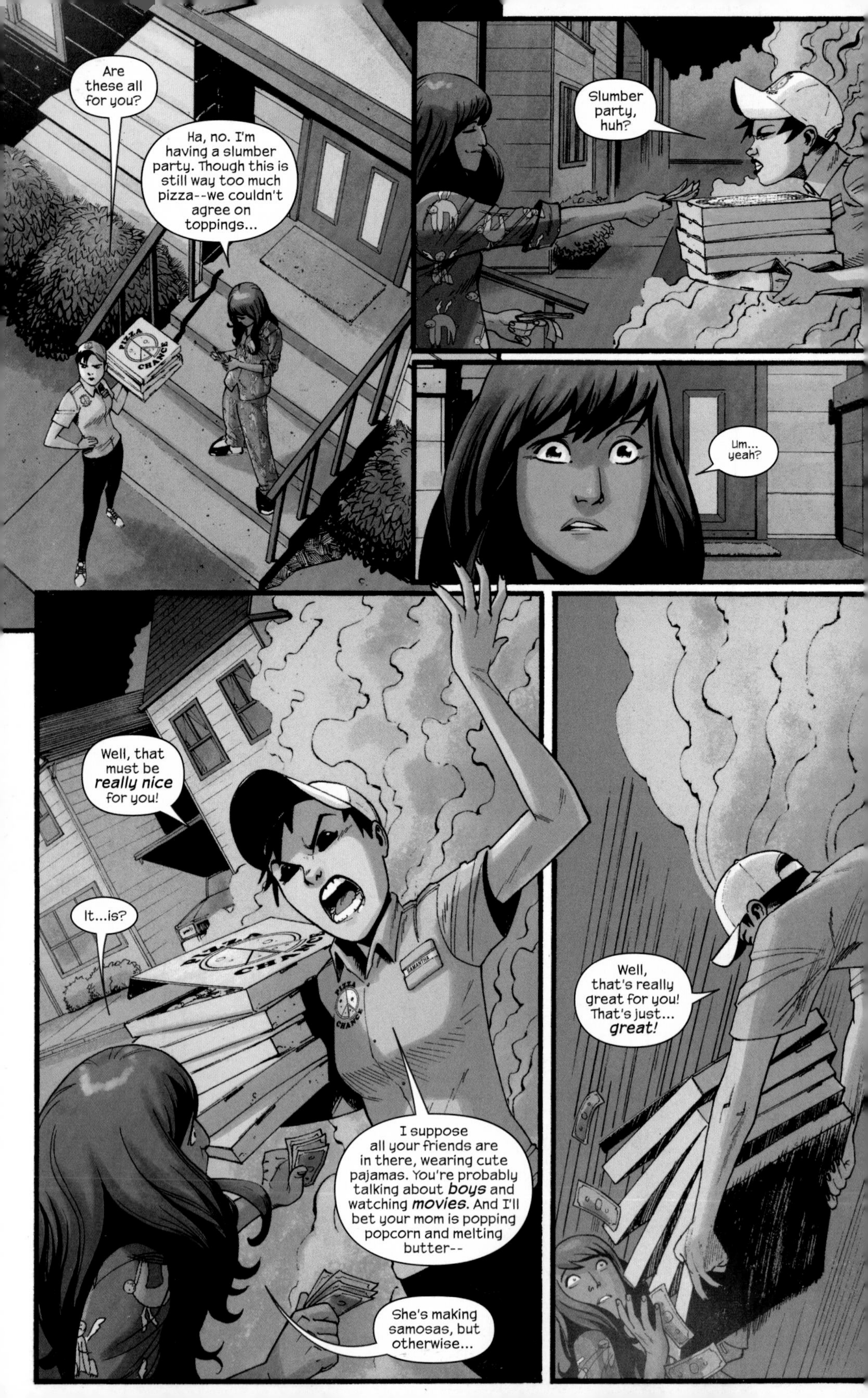
Are these all for you?
Ha, no. I'm having a slumber party. Though this is still way too much pizza--we couldn't agree on toppings...
PIZZA CHANCE
Slumber party, huh?
Um... yeah?
Well, that must be ***really nice*** for you!
It...is?
I suppose all your friends are in there, wearing cute pajamas. You're probably talking about ***boys*** and watching ***movies.*** And I'll bet your mom is popping popcorn and melting butter--
She's making samosas, but otherwise...
Well, that's really great for you! That's just... ***great!***

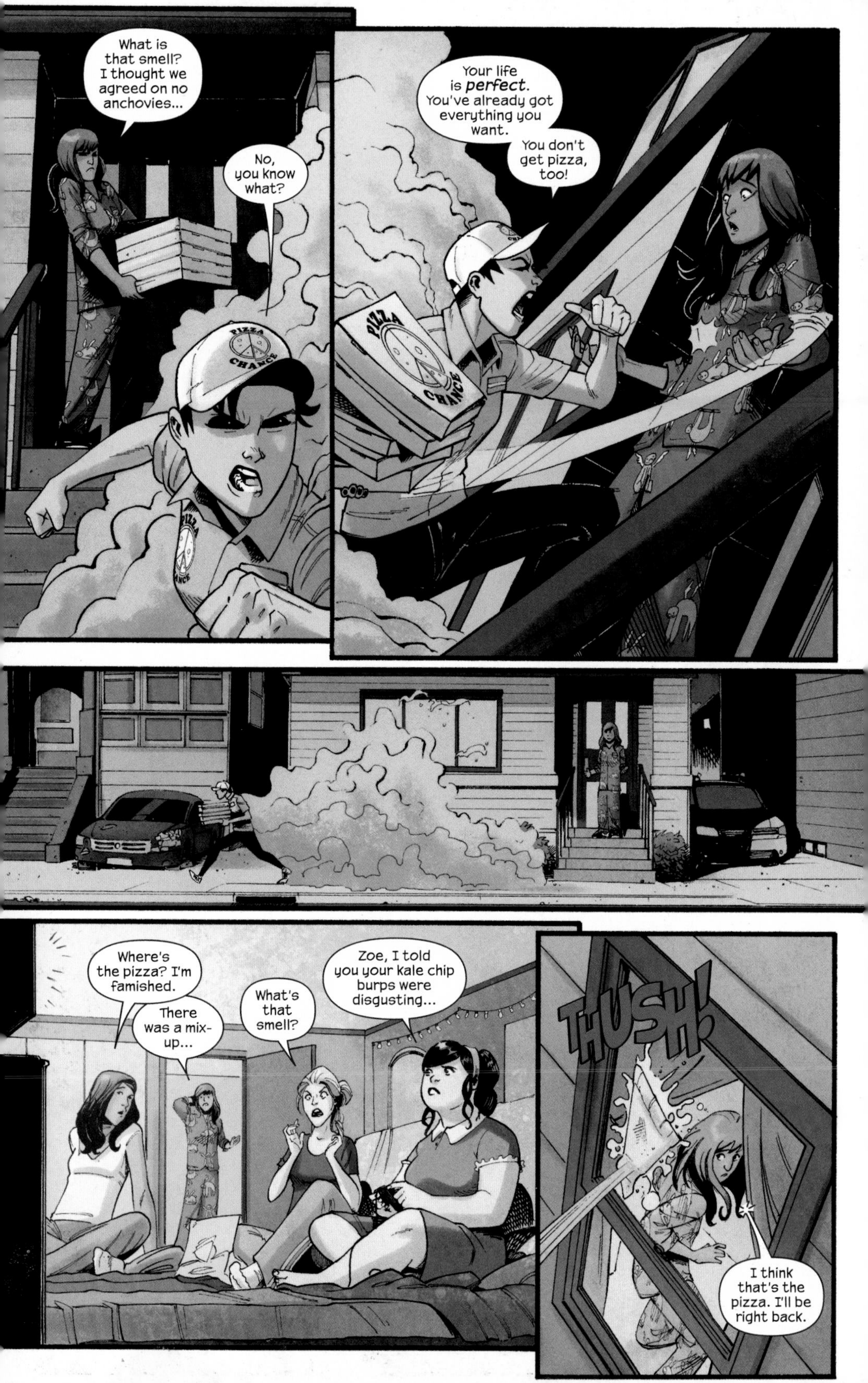
What is that smell? I thought we agreed on no anchovies...
No, you know what?
Your life is *perfect*. You've already got everything you want.
You don't get pizza, too!
PIZZA CHANCE
Where's the pizza? I'm famished.
There was a mix-up...
What's that smell?
Zoe, I told you your kale chip burps were disgusting...
THUSH!
I think that's the pizza. I'll be right back.

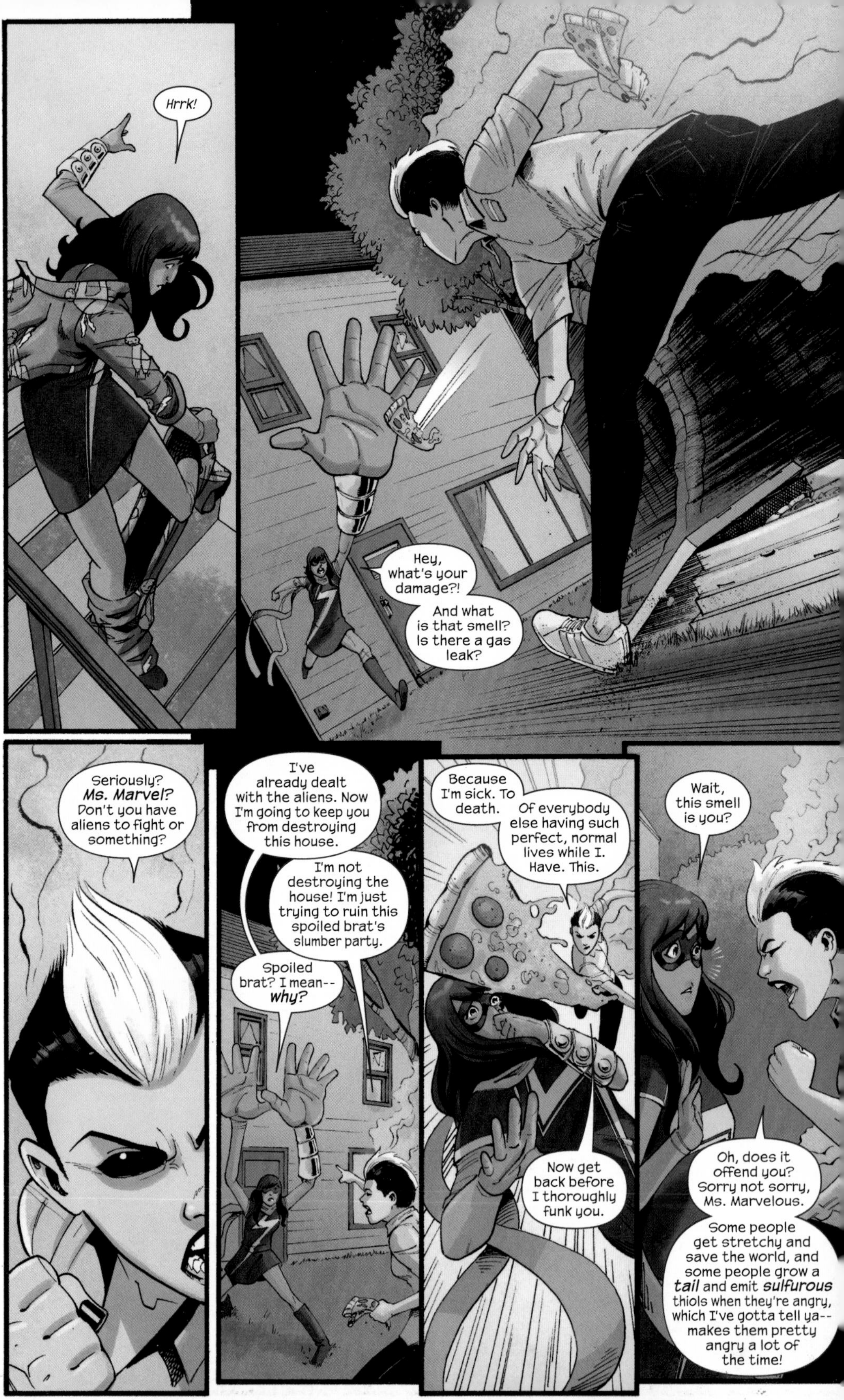
Hrrk!
Hey, what's your damage?!
And what is that smell? Is there a gas leak?
Seriously? Ms. Marvel? Don't you have aliens to fight or something?
I've already dealt with the aliens. Now I'm going to keep you from destroying this house.
I'm not destroying the house! I'm just trying to ruin this spoiled brat's slumber party.
Spoiled brat? I mean-- why?
Because I'm sick. To death.
Of everybody else having such perfect, normal lives while I. Have. This.
Now get back before I thoroughly funk you.
Wait, this smell is you?
Oh, does it offend you? Sorry not sorry, Ms. Marvelous.
Some people get stretchy and save the world, and some people grow a tail and emit sulfurous thiols when they're angry, which I've gotta tell ya-- makes them pretty angry a lot of the time!

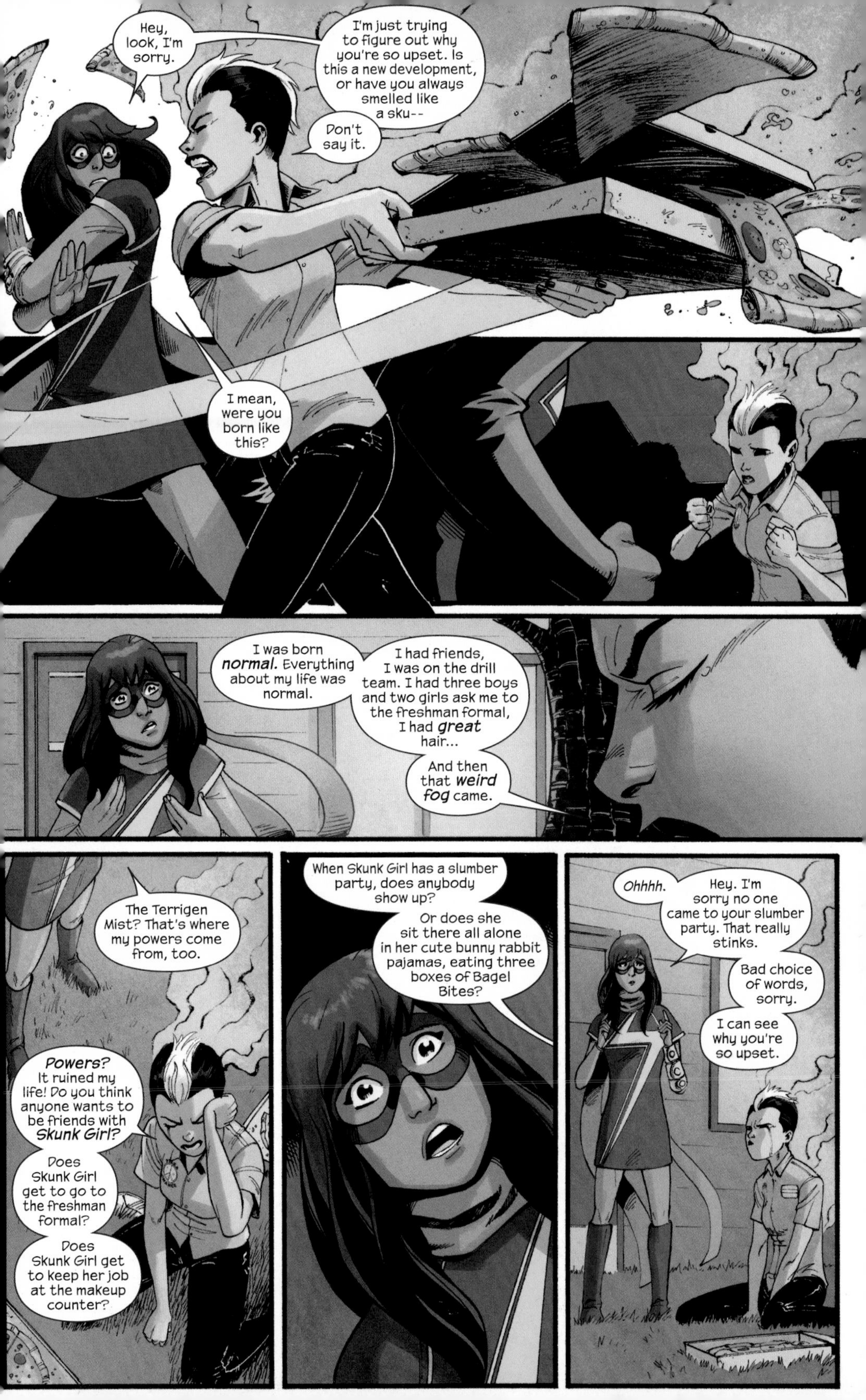
Hey, look, I'm sorry.
I'm just trying to figure out why you're so upset. Is this a new development, or have you always smelled like a sku--
Don't say it.
I mean, were you born like this?
I was born *normal.* Everything about my life was normal.
I had friends, I was on the drill team. I had three boys and two girls ask me to the freshman formal, I had *great* hair...
And then that *weird fog* came.
The Terrigen Mist? That's where my powers come from, too.
Powers? It ruined my life! Do you think anyone wants to be friends with *Skunk Girl?*
Does Skunk Girl get to go to the freshman formal?
Does Skunk Girl get to keep her job at the makeup counter?
When Skunk Girl has a slumber party, does anybody show up?
Or does she sit there all alone in her cute bunny rabbit pajamas, eating three boxes of Bagel Bites?
Ohhhh.
Hey. I'm sorry no one came to your slumber party. That really stinks.
Bad choice of words, sorry.
I can see why you're so upset.

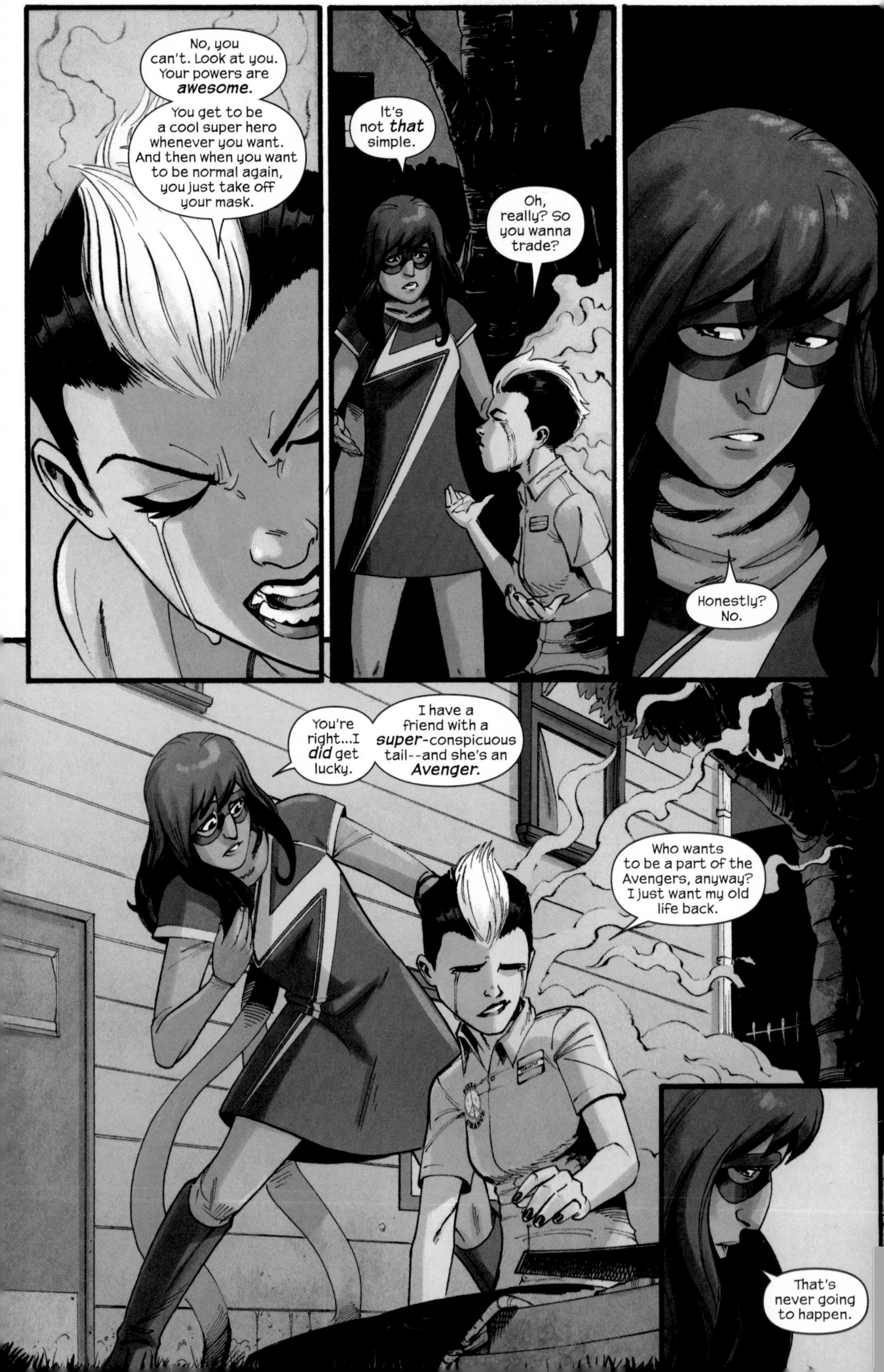
No, you can't. Look at you. Your powers are *awesome.*
You get to be a cool super hero whenever you want. And then when you want to be normal again, you just take off your mask.
It's not *that* simple.
Oh, really? So you wanna trade?
Honestly? No.
You're right...I *did* get lucky.
I have a friend with a *super*-conspicuous tail--and she's an *Avenger.*
Who wants to be a part of the Avengers, anyway? I just want my old life back.
That's never going to happen.

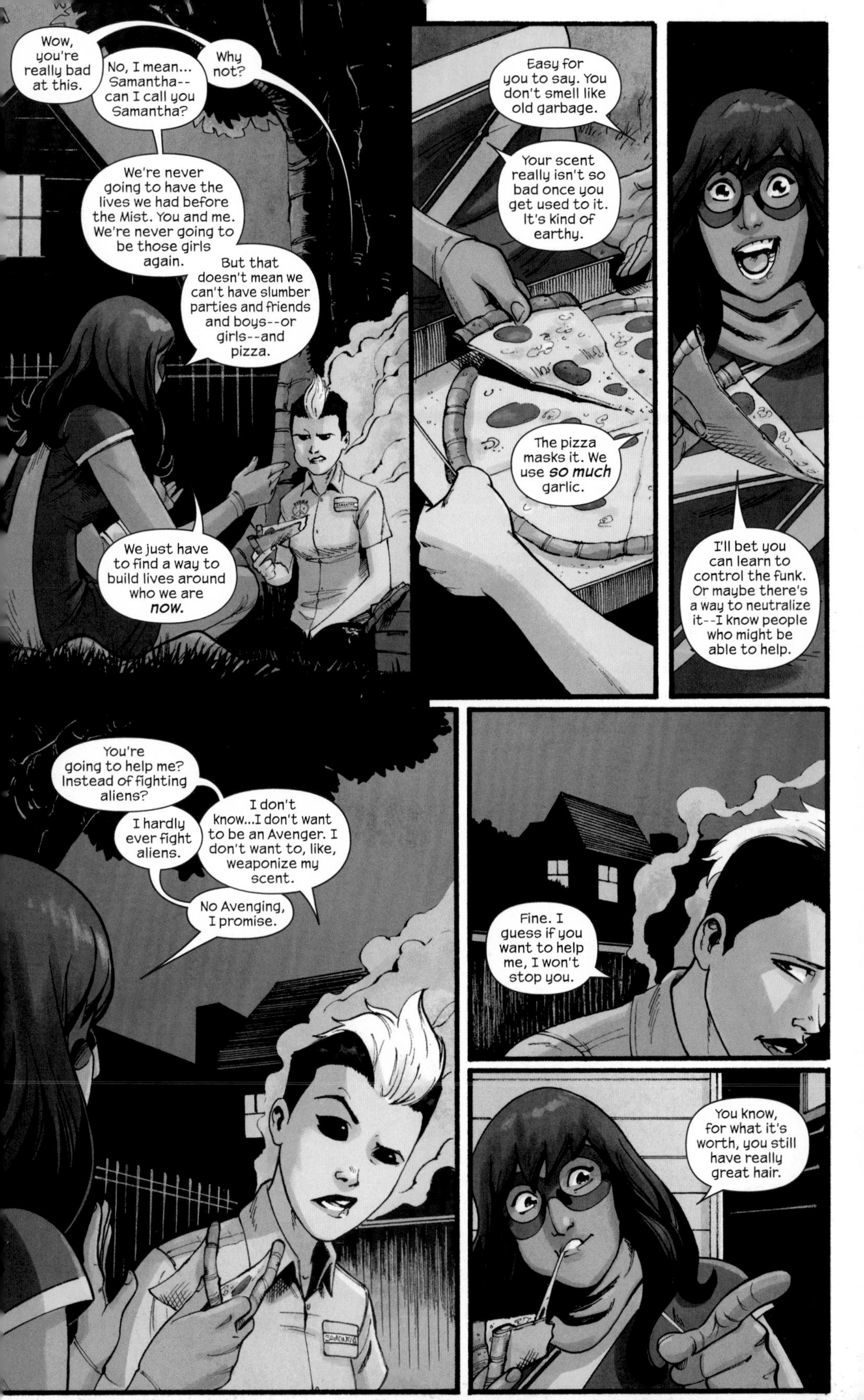
Wow, you're really bad at this.
Why not?
No, I mean... Samantha-- can I call you Samantha?
We're never going to have the lives we had before the Mist. You and me. We're never going to be those girls again.
But that doesn't mean we can't have slumber parties and friends and boys--or girls--and pizza.
We just have to find a way to build lives around who we are *now.*
Easy for you to say. You don't smell like old garbage.
Your scent really isn't so bad once you get used to it. It's kind of earthy.
The pizza masks it. We use *so much* garlic.
I'll bet you can learn to control the funk. Or maybe there's a way to neutralize it--I know people who might be able to help.
You're going to help me? Instead of fighting aliens?
I hardly ever fight aliens.
I don't know...I don't want to be an Avenger. I don't want to, like, weaponize my scent.
No Avenging, I promise.
Fine. I guess if you want to help me, I won't stop you.
You know, for what it's worth, you still have really great hair.

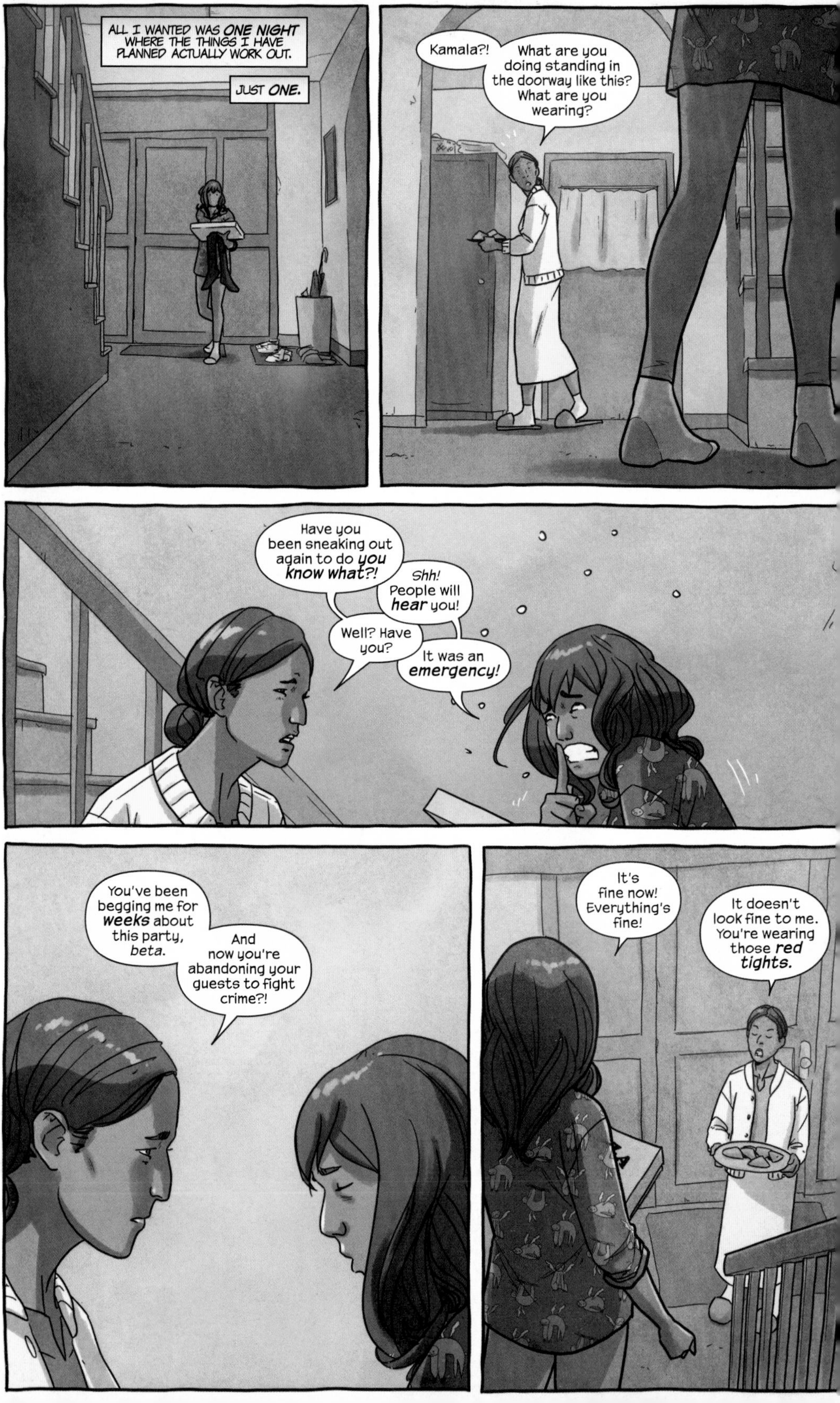
ALL I WANTED WAS ONE NIGHT WHERE THE THINGS I HAVE PLANNED ACTUALLY WORK OUT.
JUST ONE.
Kamala?!
What are you doing standing in the doorway like this? What are you wearing?
Have you been sneaking out again to do you know what?!
Shh! People will hear you!
Well? Have you?
It was an emergency!
You've been begging me for weeks about this party, beta.
And now you're abandoning your guests to fight crime?!
It's fine now! Everything's fine!
It doesn't look fine to me. You're wearing those red tights.

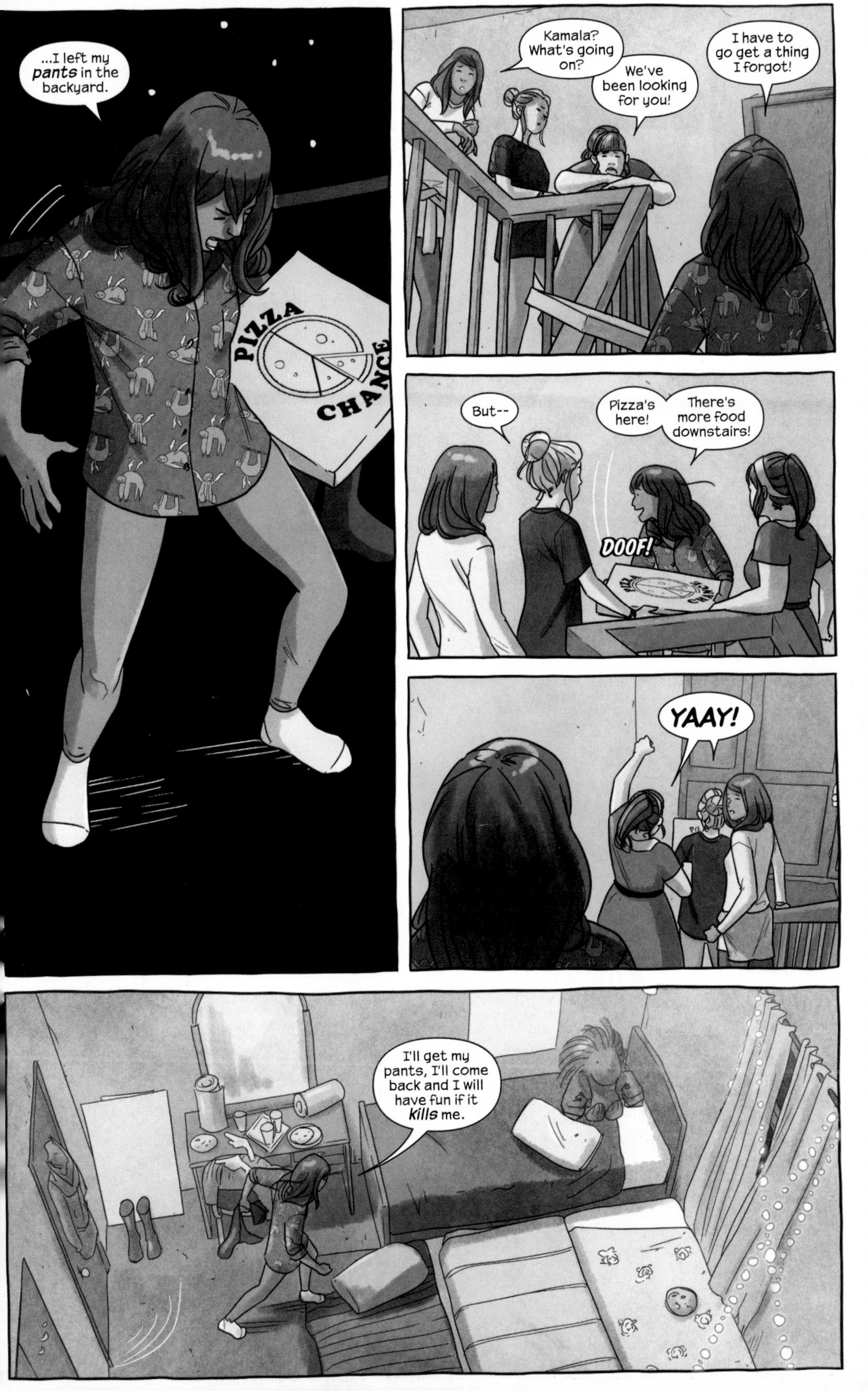

...I left my *pants* in the backyard.
PIZZA CHANCE
Kamala? What's going on?
We've been looking for you!
I have to go get a thing I forgot!
But--
Pizza's here!
There's more food downstairs!
DOOF!
YAAY!
I'll get my pants, I'll come back and I will have fun if it *kills* me.

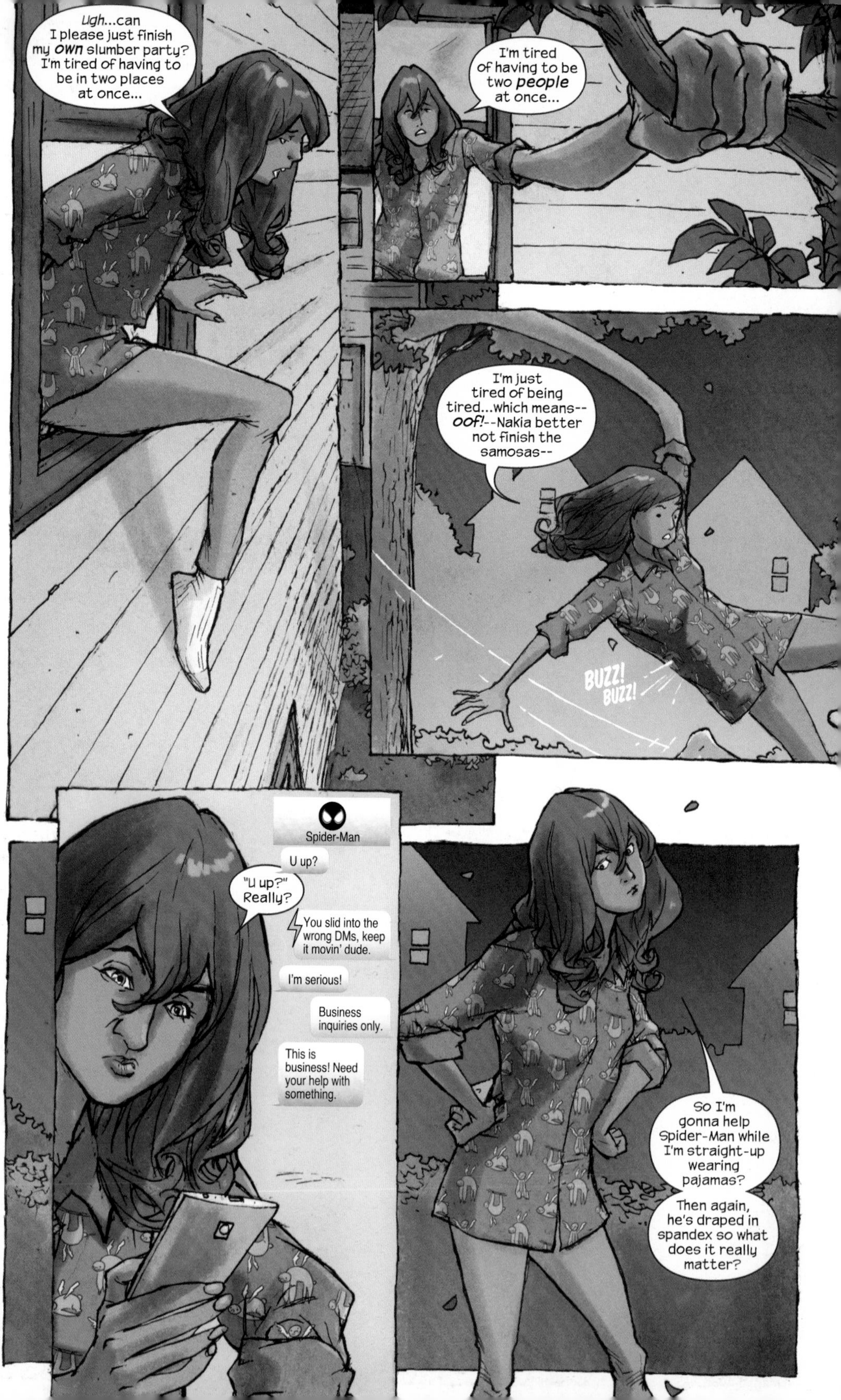
Ugh...can I please just finish my OWN slumber party? I'm tired of having to be in two places at once...
I'm tired of having to be two people at once...
I'm just tired of being tired...which means-- OOF!--Nakia better not finish the samosas--
BUZZ! BUZZ!
Spider-Man
U up?
"U up?" Really?
You slid into the wrong DMs, keep it movin' dude.
I'm serious!
Business inquiries only.
This is business! Need your help with something.
So I'm gonna help Spider-Man while I'm straight-up wearing pajamas?
Then again, he's draped in spandex so what does it really matter?

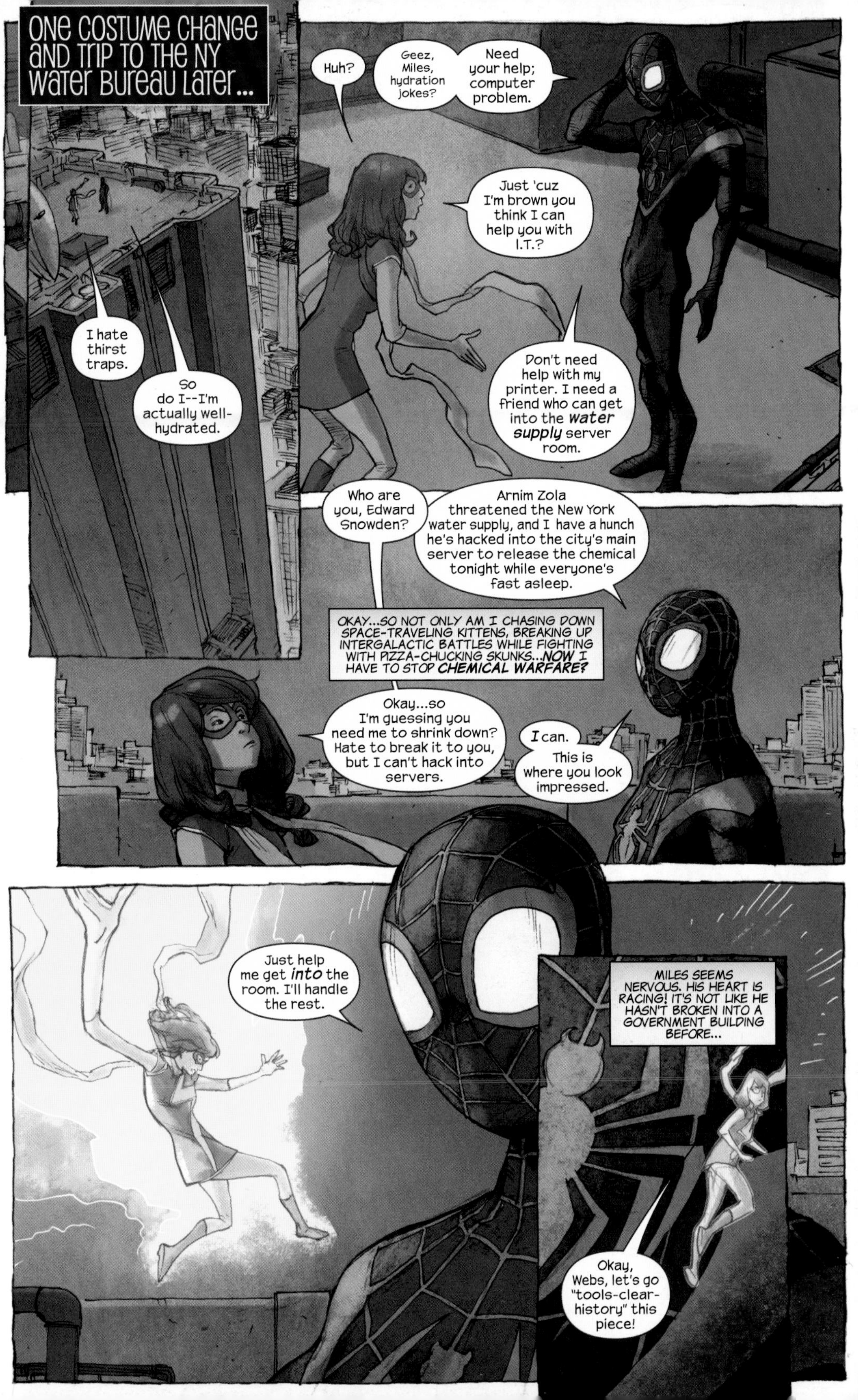
ONE COSTUME CHANGE AND TRIP TO THE NY WATER BUREAU LATER...
Huh?
Geez, Miles, hydration jokes?
Need your help; computer problem.
Just 'cuz I'm brown you think I can help you with I.T.?
I hate thirst traps.
So do I--I'm actually well-hydrated.
Don't need help with my printer. I need a friend who can get into the water supply server room.
Who are you, Edward Snowden?
Arnim Zola threatened the New York water supply, and I have a hunch he's hacked into the city's main server to release the chemical tonight while everyone's fast asleep.
OKAY...SO NOT ONLY AM I CHASING DOWN SPACE-TRAVELING KITTENS, BREAKING UP INTERGALACTIC BATTLES WHILE FIGHTING WITH PIZZA-CHUCKING SKUNKS...NOW I HAVE TO STOP CHEMICAL WARFARE?
Okay...so I'm guessing you need me to shrink down? Hate to break it to you, but I can't hack into servers.
I can.
This is where you look impressed.
Just help me get into the room. I'll handle the rest.
MILES SEEMS NERVOUS. HIS HEART IS RACING! IT'S NOT LIKE HE HASN'T BROKEN INTO A GOVERNMENT BUILDING BEFORE...
Okay, Webs, let's go "tools-clear-history" this piece!

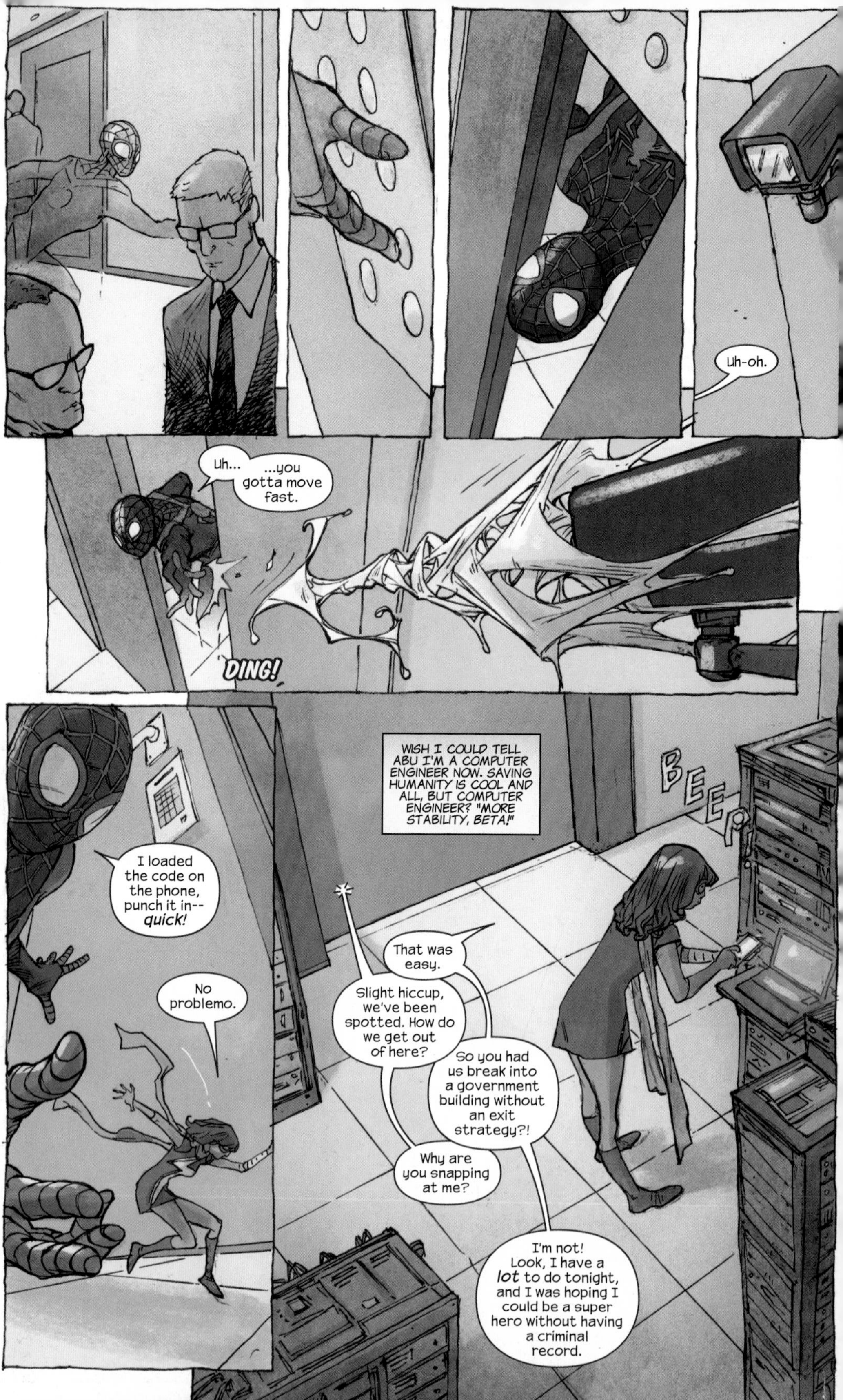
Uh-oh.
Uh...
...you gotta move fast.
DING!
WISH I COULD TELL ABU I'M A COMPUTER ENGINEER NOW. SAVING HUMANITY IS COOL AND ALL, BUT COMPUTER ENGINEER? "MORE STABILITY, BETA!"
BEEP!
I loaded the code on the phone, punch it in--*quick!*
No problemo.
That was easy.
Slight hiccup, we've been spotted. How do we get out of here?
So you had us break into a government building without an exit strategy?!
Why are you snapping at me?
I'm not! Look, I have a ***lot*** to do tonight, and I was hoping I could be a super hero without having a criminal record.

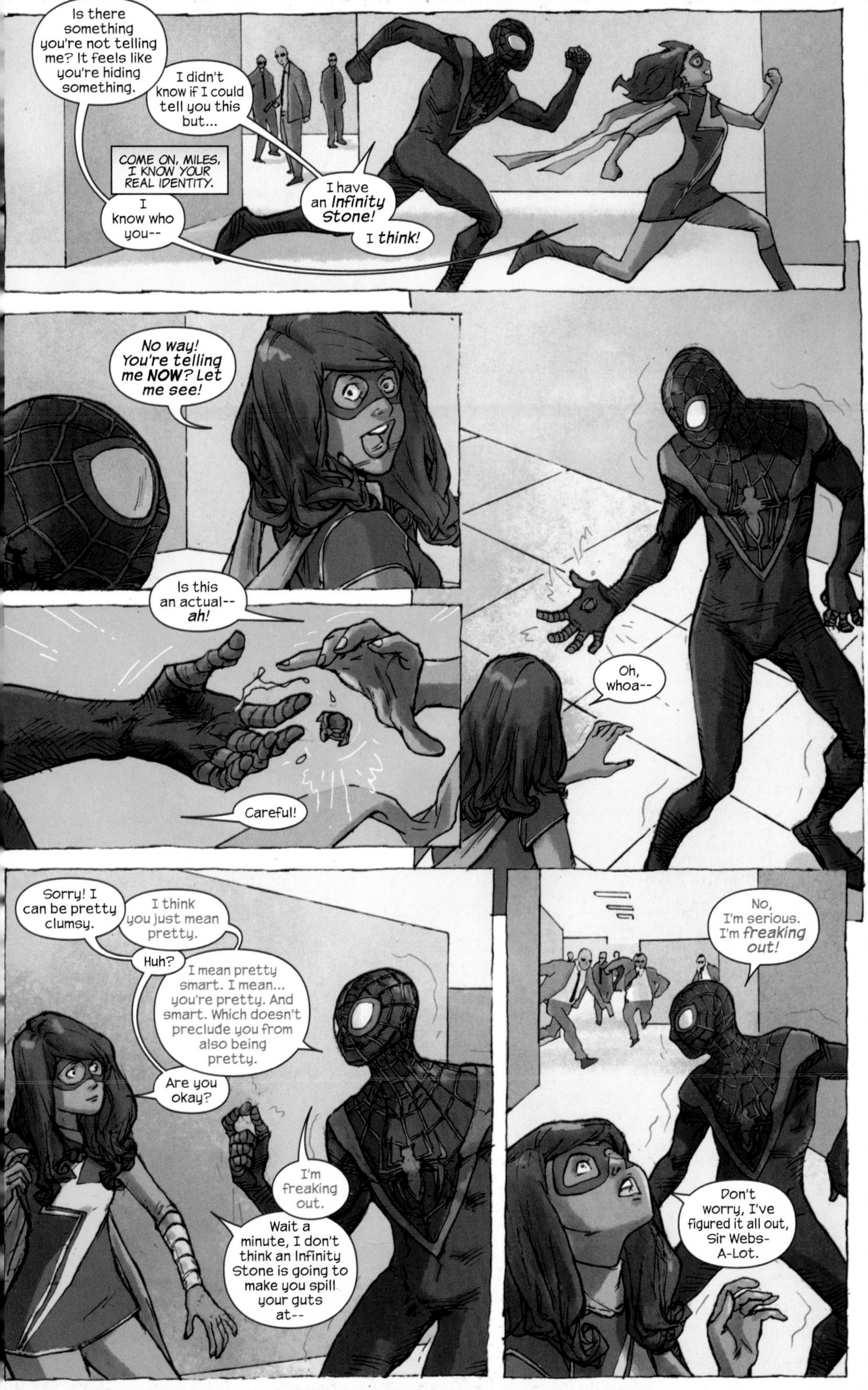

Is there something you're not telling me? It feels like you're hiding something.
I didn't know if I could tell you this but...
COME ON, MILES, I KNOW YOUR REAL IDENTITY.
I know who you--
I have an *Infinity Stone!*
I *think!*
*No way! You're telling me **NOW**? Let me see!*
Is this an actual-- *ah!*
Careful!
Oh, whoa--
Sorry! I can be pretty clumsy.
I think you just mean pretty.
Huh?
I mean pretty smart. I mean... you're pretty. And smart. Which doesn't preclude you from also being pretty.
Are you okay?
I'm freaking out.
Wait a minute, I don't think an Infinity Stone is going to make you spill your guts at--
No, I'm serious. I'm *freaking out!*
Don't worry, I've figured it all out, Sir Webs-A-Lot.

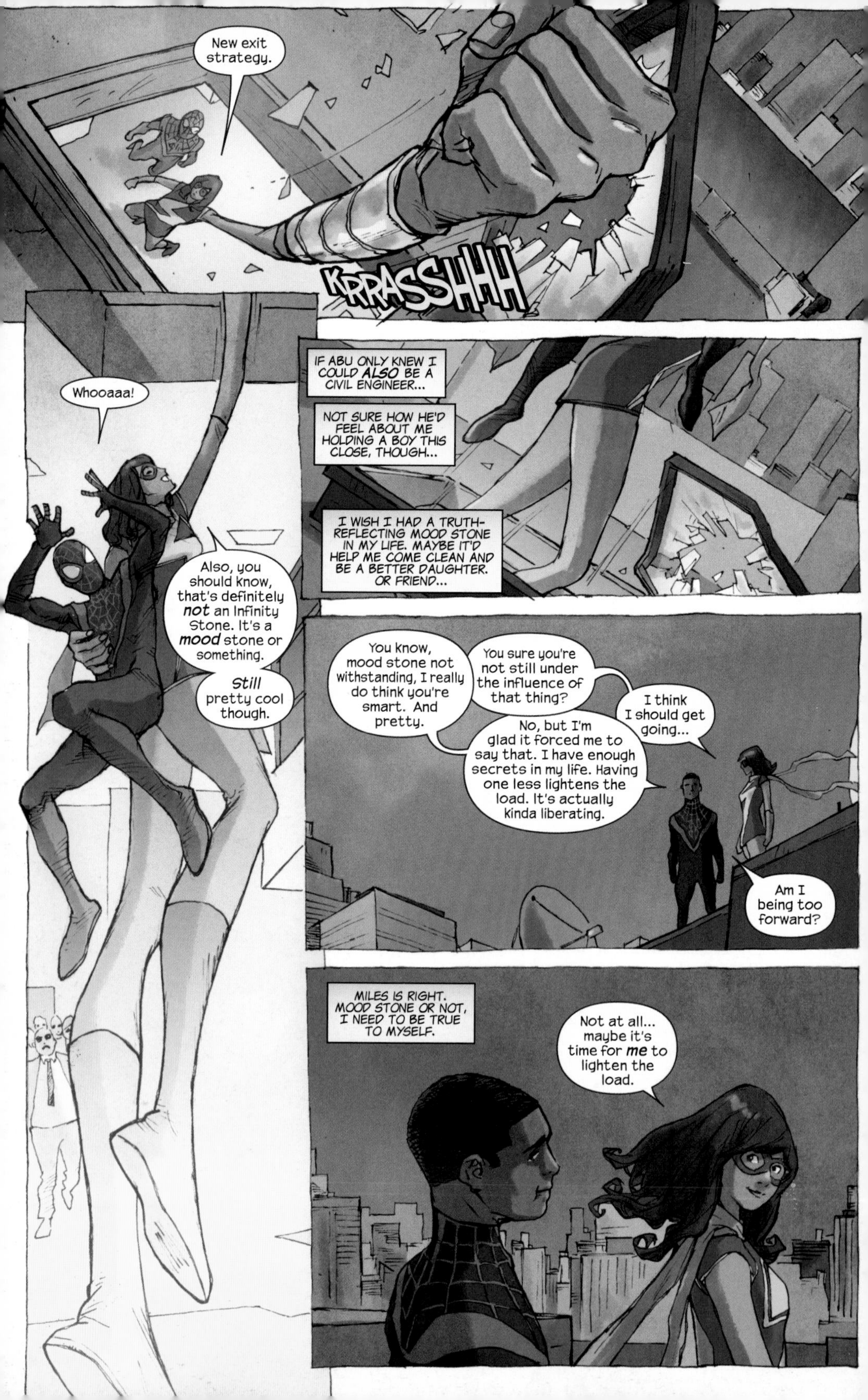

New exit strategy.
KRRASSHHH
Whooaaa!
IF ABU ONLY KNEW I COULD ALSO BE A CIVIL ENGINEER...
NOT SURE HOW HE'D FEEL ABOUT ME HOLDING A BOY THIS CLOSE, THOUGH...
I WISH I HAD A TRUTH-REFLECTING MOOD STONE IN MY LIFE. MAYBE IT'D HELP ME COME CLEAN AND BE A BETTER DAUGHTER. OR FRIEND...
Also, you should know, that's definitely not an Infinity Stone. It's a mood stone or something.
Still pretty cool though.
You know, mood stone not withstanding, I really do think you're smart. And pretty.
You sure you're not still under the influence of that thing?
No, but I'm glad it forced me to say that. I have enough secrets in my life. Having one less lightens the load. It's actually kinda liberating.
I think I should get going...
Am I being too forward?
MILES IS RIGHT. MOOD STONE OR NOT, I NEED TO BE TRUE TO MYSELF.
Not at all... maybe it's time for me to lighten the load.

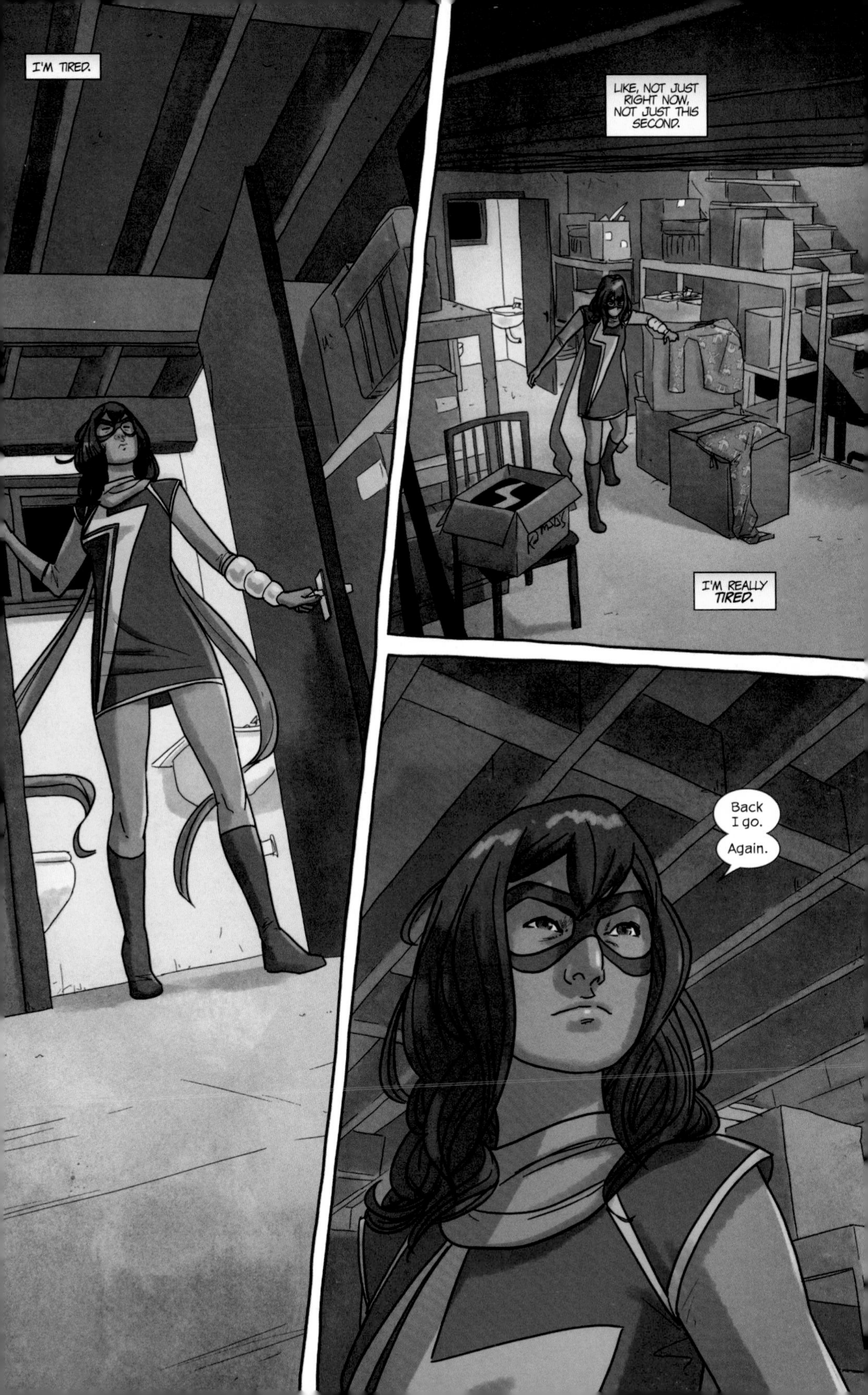
I'M TIRED.
LIKE, NOT JUST RIGHT NOW, NOT JUST THIS SECOND.
I'M REALLY TIRED.
Back I go.
Again.

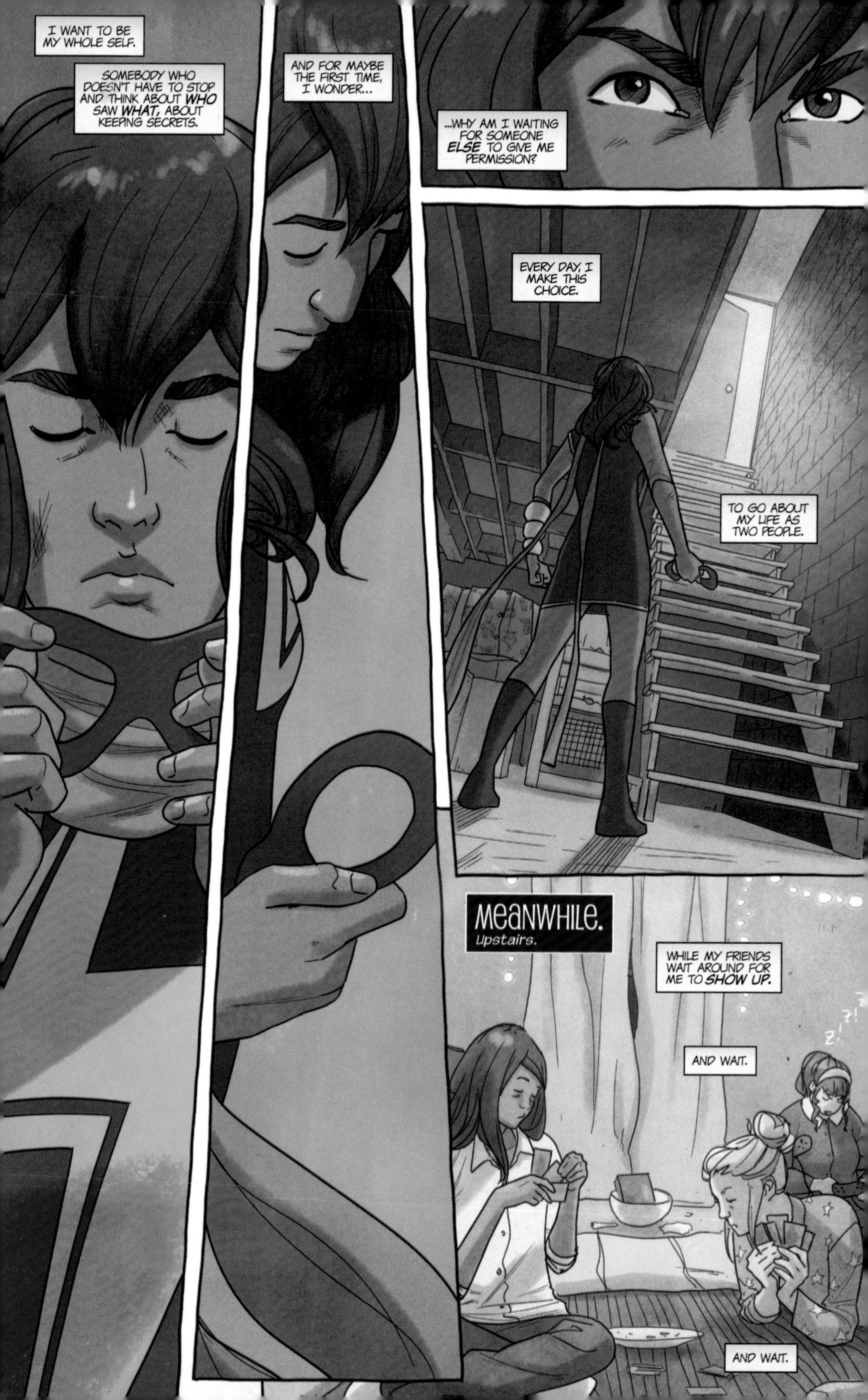
I WANT TO BE MY WHOLE SELF.
SOMEBODY WHO DOESN'T HAVE TO STOP AND THINK ABOUT **WHO** SAW **WHAT,** ABOUT KEEPING SECRETS.
AND FOR MAYBE THE FIRST TIME, I WONDER...
...WHY AM I WAITING FOR SOMEONE ***ELSE*** TO GIVE ME PERMISSION?
EVERY DAY, I MAKE THIS CHOICE.
TO GO ABOUT MY LIFE AS TWO PEOPLE.
MEANWHILE.
Upstairs.
WHILE MY FRIENDS WAIT AROUND FOR ME TO ***SHOW UP.***
Z! Z! Z!
AND WAIT.
AND WAIT.

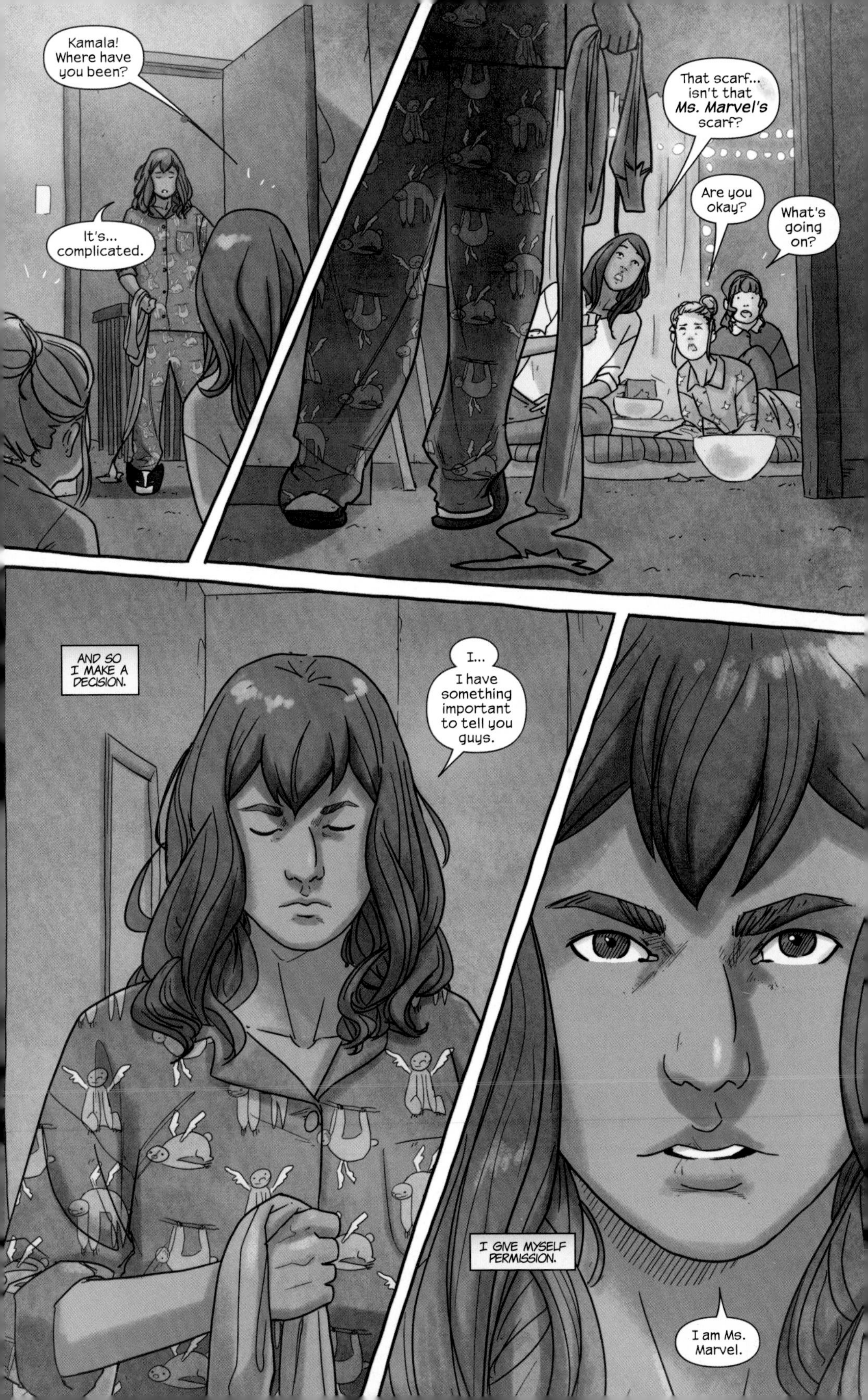
Kamala! Where have you been?
It's... complicated.
That scarf... isn't that Ms. Marvel's scarf?
Are you okay?
What's going on?
AND SO I MAKE A DECISION.
I...
I have something important to tell you guys.
I GIVE MYSELF PERMISSION.
I am Ms. Marvel.

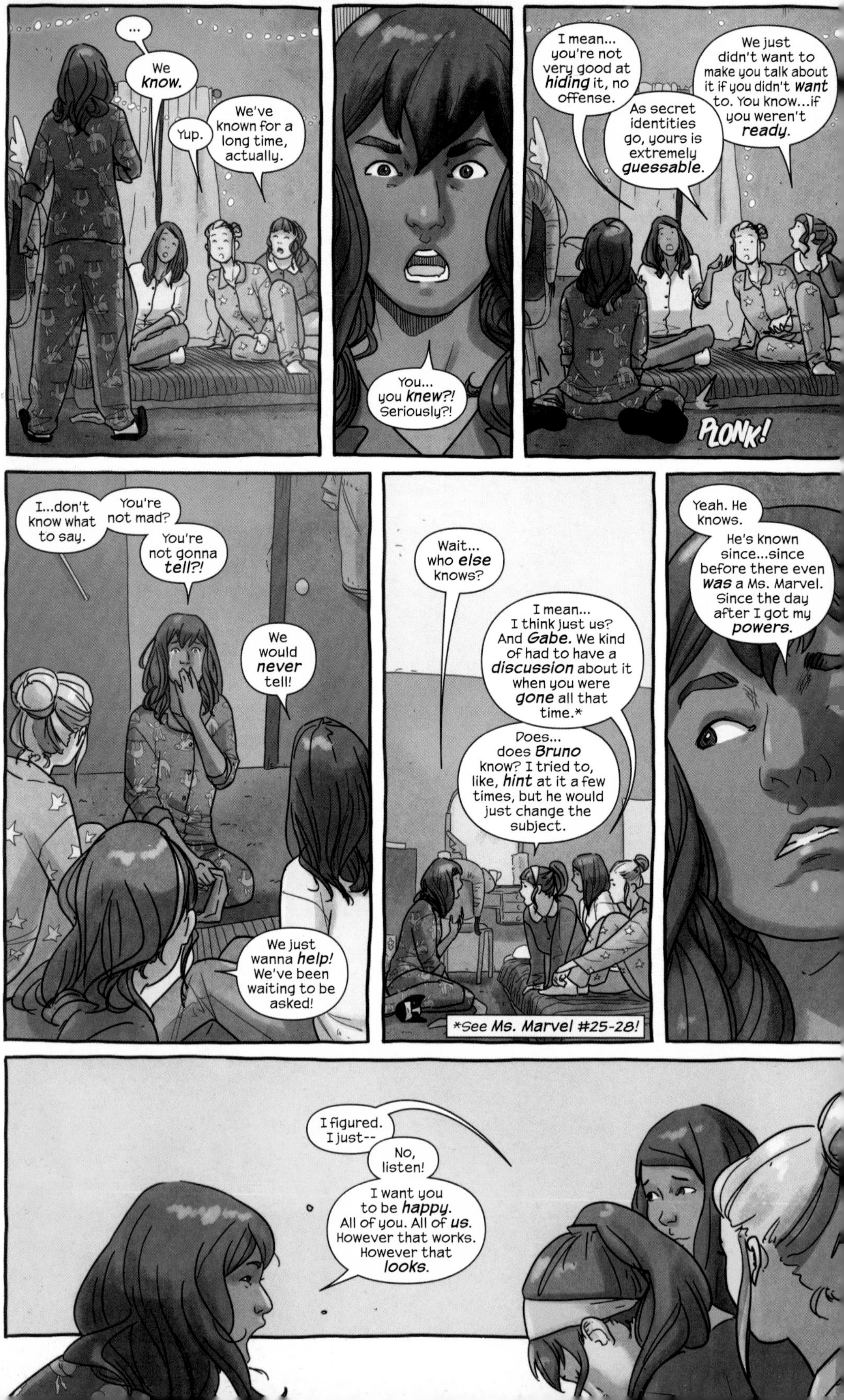
...
We know.
Yup.
We've known for a long time, actually.
You... you knew?! Seriously?!
I mean... you're not very good at hiding it, no offense.
As secret identities go, yours is extremely guessable.
We just didn't want to make you talk about it if you didn't want to. You know...if you weren't ready.
PLONK!
I...don't know what to say.
You're not mad?
You're not gonna tell?!
We would never tell!
We just wanna help! We've been waiting to be asked!
Wait... who else knows?
I mean... I think just us? And Gabe. We kind of had to have a discussion about it when you were gone all that time.*
Does... does Bruno know? I tried to, like, hint at it a few times, but he would just change the subject.
*See Ms. Marvel #25-28!
Yeah. He knows.
He's known since...since before there even was a Ms. Marvel. Since the day after I got my powers.
I figured. I just--
No, listen!
I want you to be happy. All of you. All of us. However that works. However that looks.

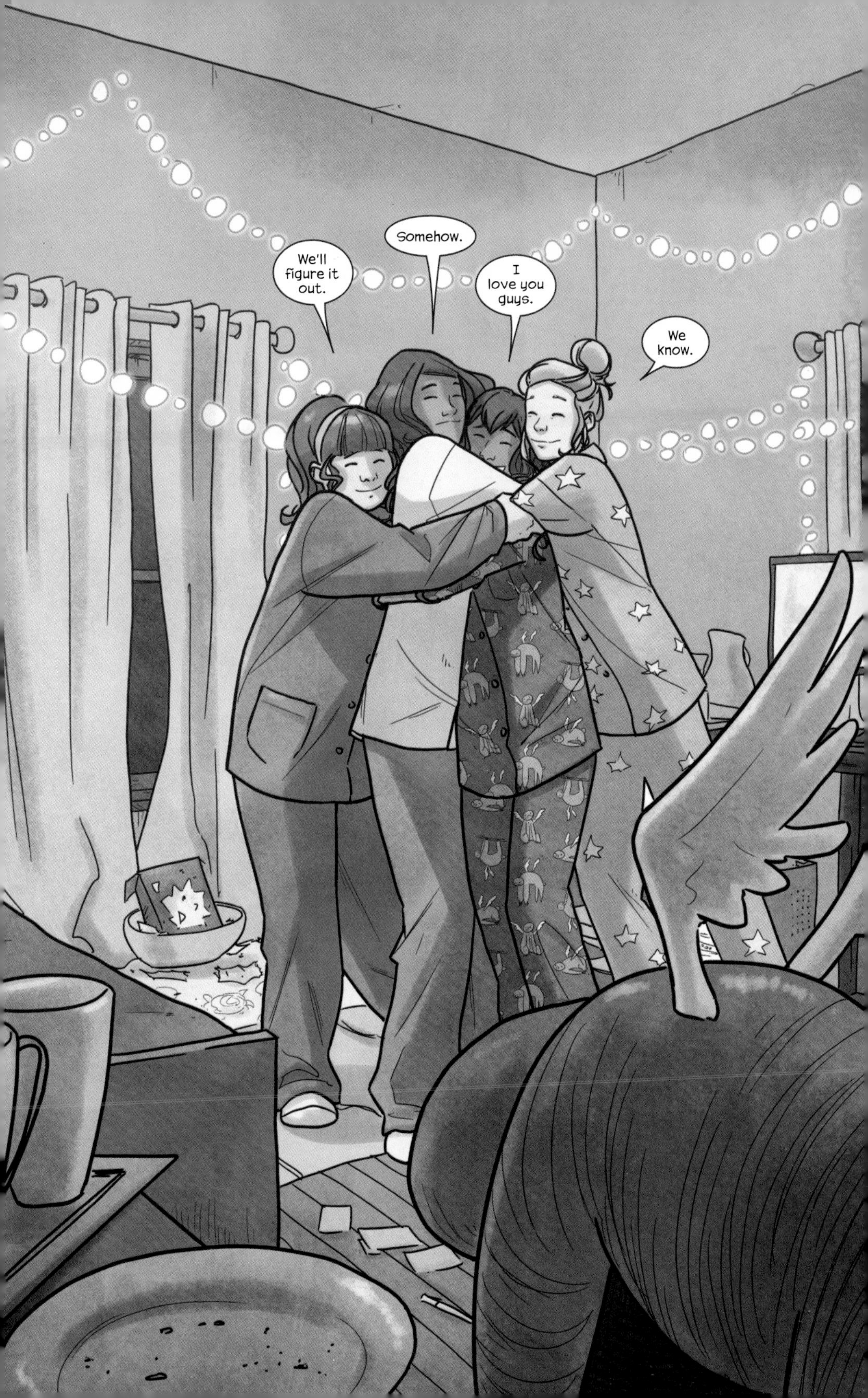
We'll figure it out.
Somehow.
I love you guys.
We know.

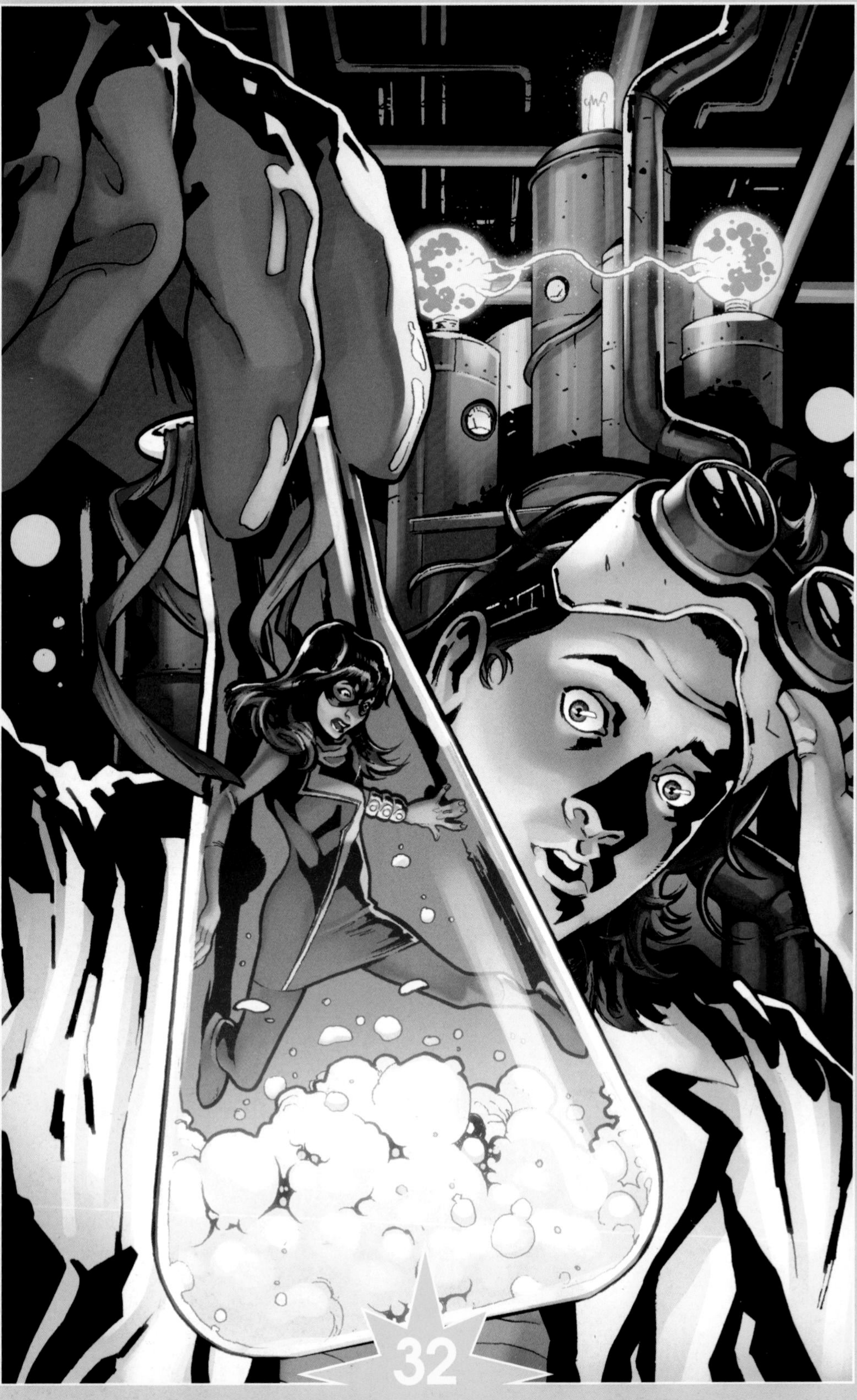
32

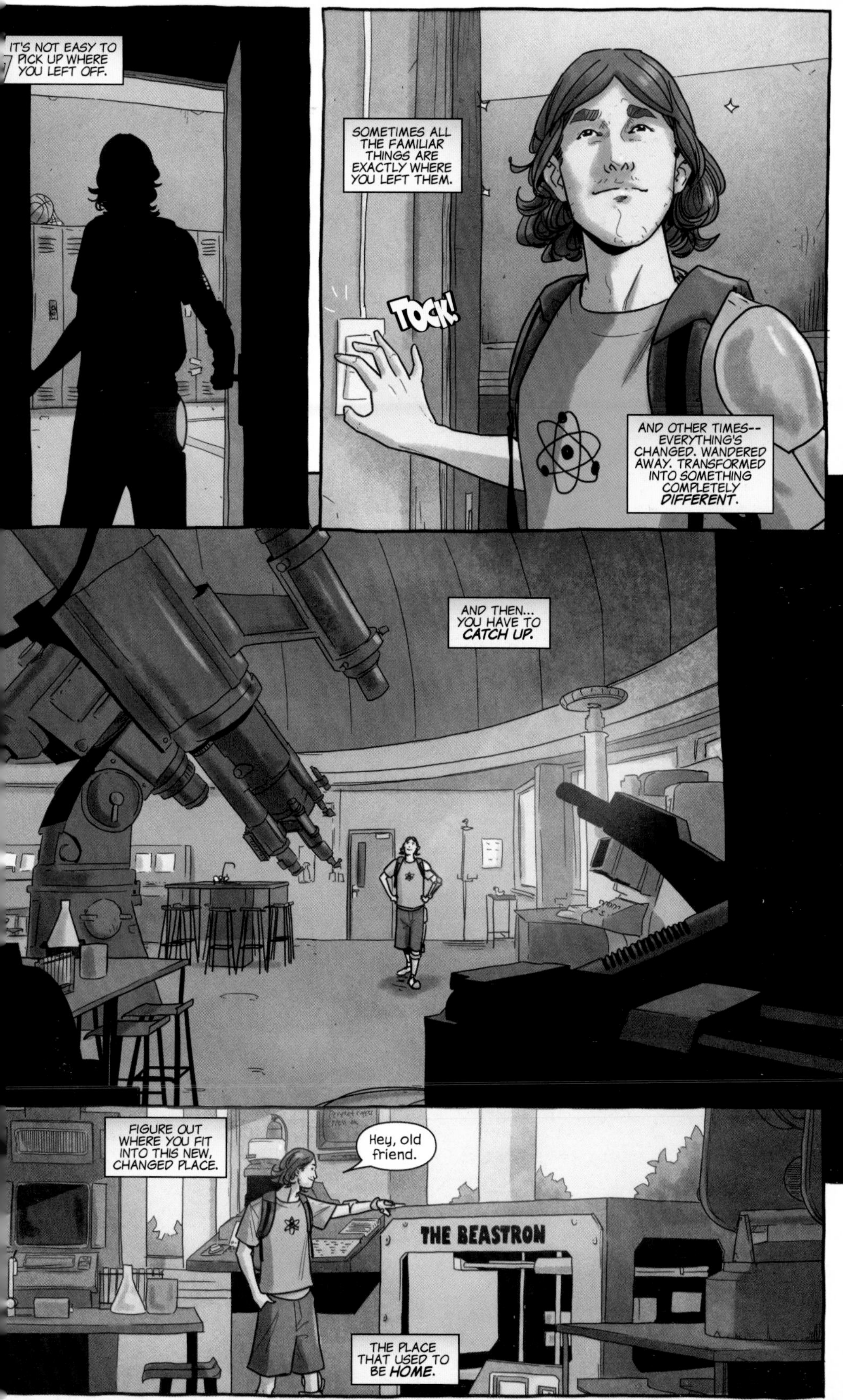
IT'S NOT EASY TO PICK UP WHERE YOU LEFT OFF.
SOMETIMES ALL THE FAMILIAR THINGS ARE EXACTLY WHERE YOU LEFT THEM.
TOCK!
AND OTHER TIMES-- EVERYTHING'S CHANGED. WANDERED AWAY. TRANSFORMED INTO SOMETHING COMPLETELY DIFFERENT.
AND THEN... YOU HAVE TO CATCH UP.
FIGURE OUT WHERE YOU FIT INTO THIS NEW, CHANGED PLACE.
Hey, old friend.
THE BEASTRON
THE PLACE THAT USED TO BE HOME.

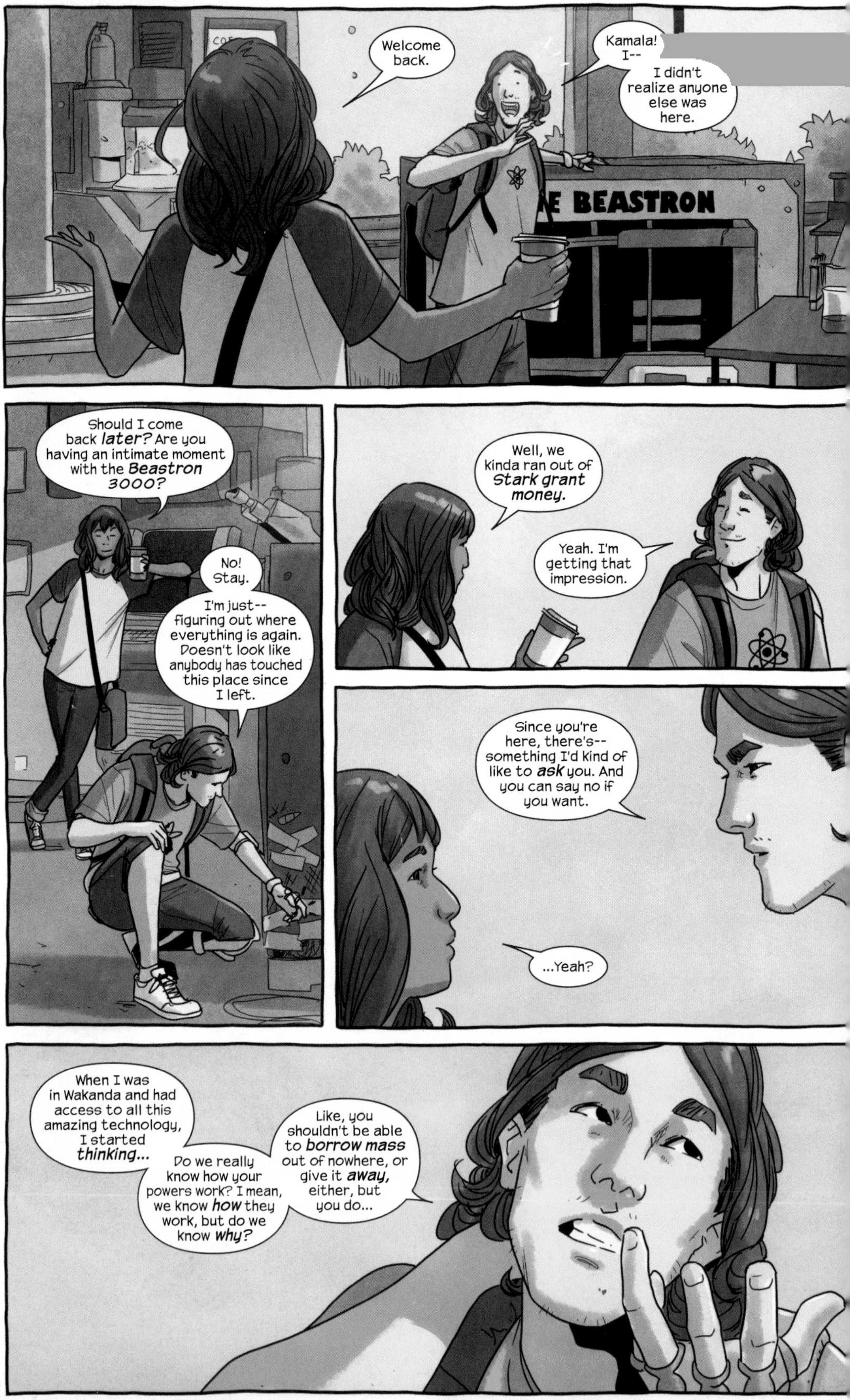

Welcome back.
Kamala! I--
I didn't realize anyone else was here.
E BEASTRON
Should I come back *later?* Are you having an intimate moment with the *Beastron 3000?*
No! Stay.
I'm just-- figuring out where everything is again. Doesn't look like anybody has touched this place since I left.
Well, we kinda ran out of *Stark grant money.*
Yeah. I'm getting that impression.
Since you're here, there's-- something I'd kind of like to *ask* you. And you can say no if you want.
...Yeah?
When I was in Wakanda and had access to all this amazing technology, I started *thinking...*
Do we really know how your powers work? I mean, we know *how* they work, but do we know *why?*
Like, you shouldn't be able to *borrow mass* out of nowhere, or give it *away,* either, but you do...

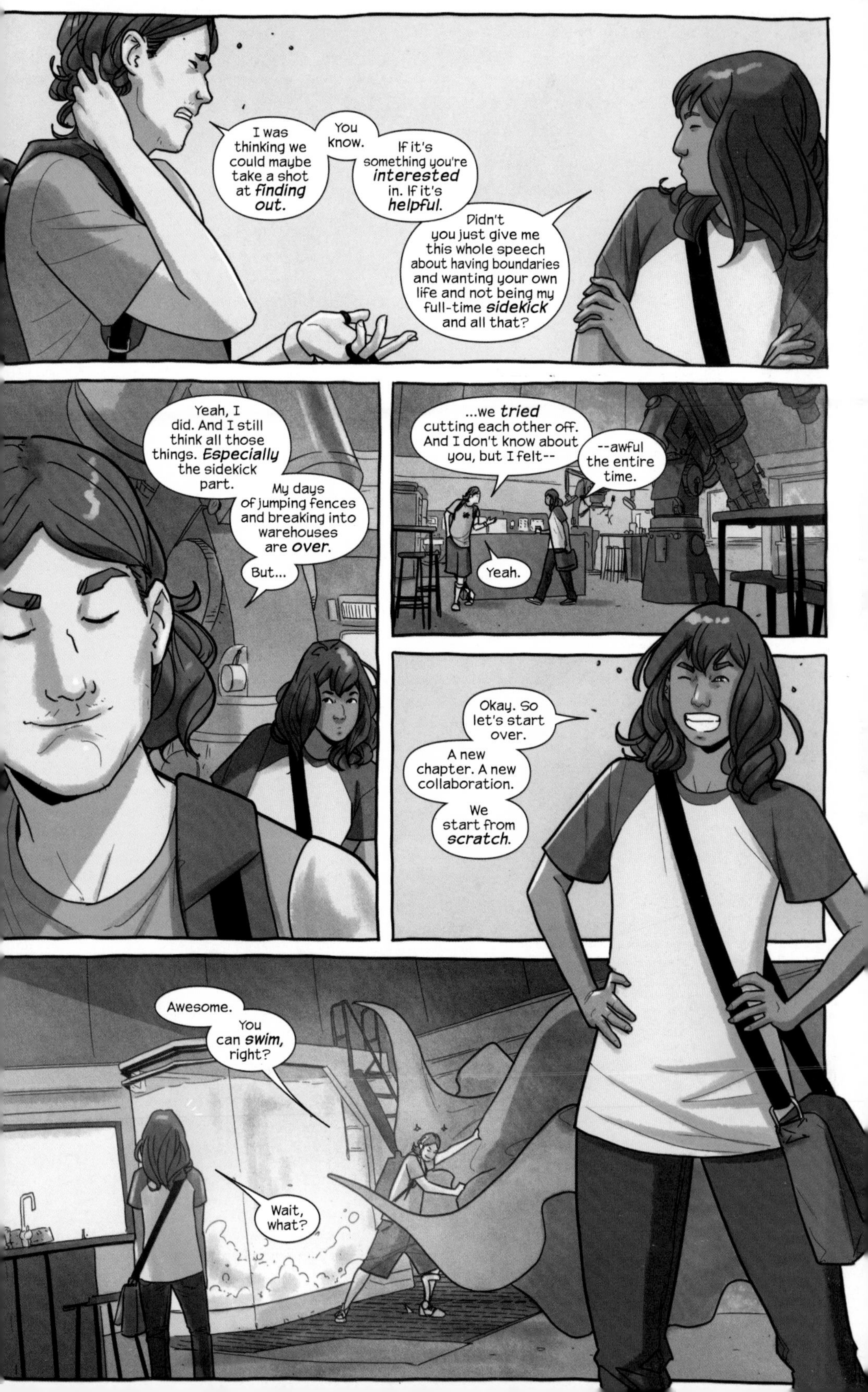

I was thinking we could maybe take a shot at *finding out.*
You know.
If it's something you're *interested* in. If it's *helpful*.
Didn't you just give me this whole speech about having boundaries and wanting your own life and not being my full-time *sidekick* and all that?
Yeah, I did. And I still think all those things. *Especially* the sidekick part.
My days of jumping fences and breaking into warehouses are *over*.
But...
...we *tried* cutting each other off. And I don't know about you, but I felt--
--awful the entire time.
Yeah.
Okay. So let's start over.
A new chapter. A new collaboration.
We start from *scratch*.
Awesome.
You can *swim*, right?
Wait, what?

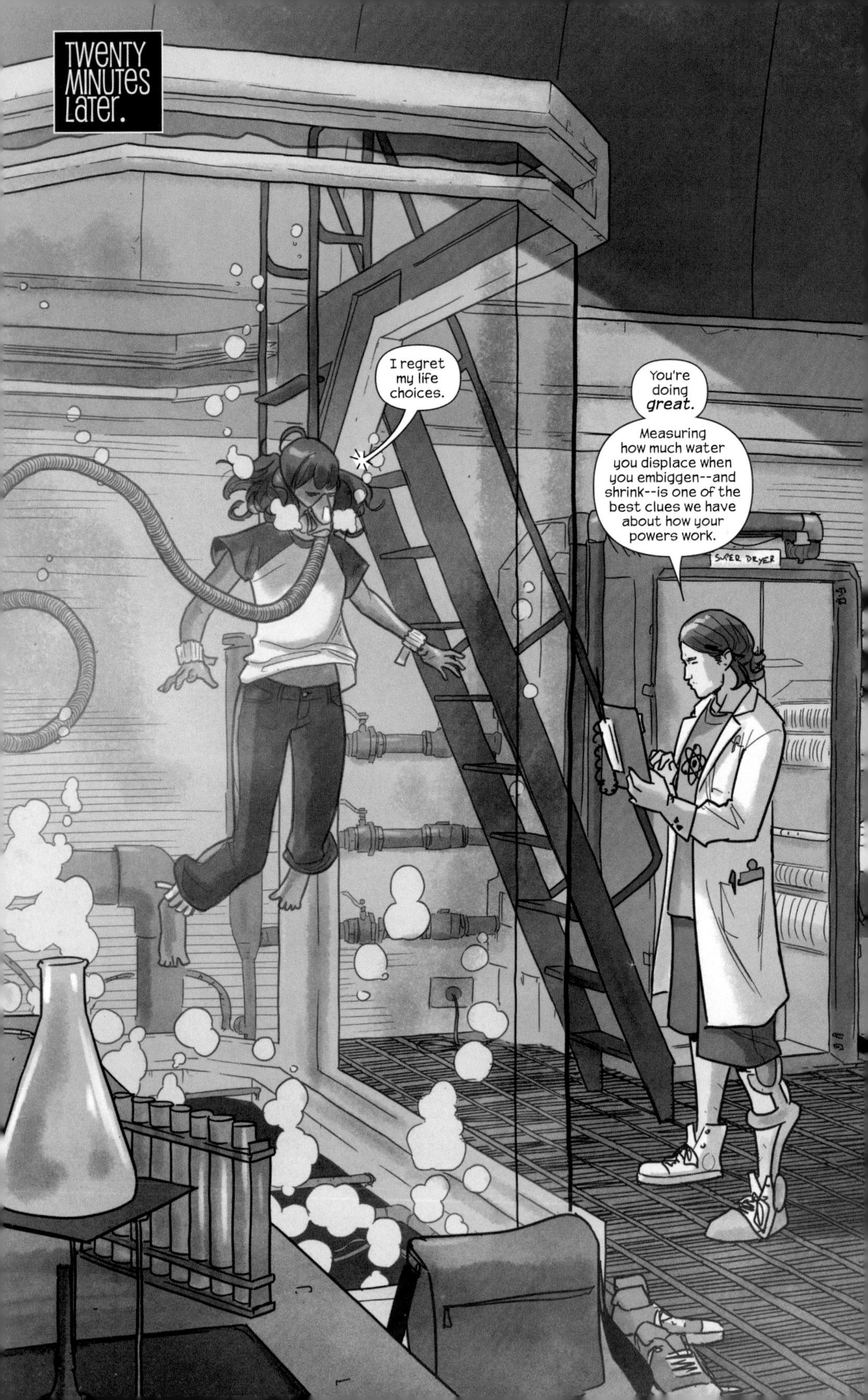
TWENTY MINUTES LATER.
I regret my life choices.
You're doing *great*.
Measuring how much water you displace when you embiggen--and shrink--is one of the best clues we have about how your powers work.
SUPER DRYER

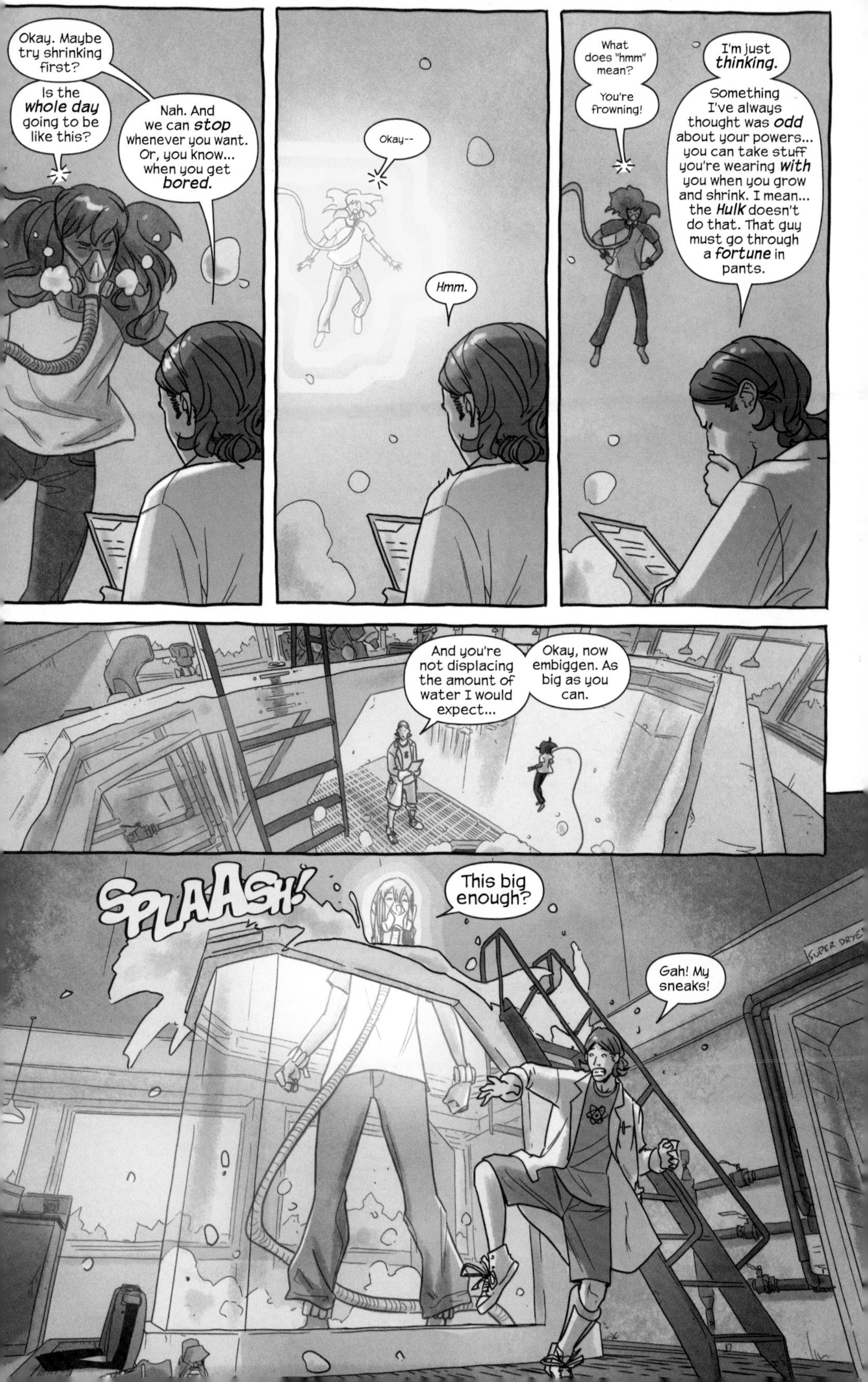
Okay. Maybe try shrinking first?
Is the whole day going to be like this?
Nah. And we can stop whenever you want. Or, you know... when you get bored.
Okay--
Hmm.
What does "hmm" mean?
You're frowning!
I'm just thinking.
Something I've always thought was odd about your powers... you can take stuff you're wearing with you when you grow and shrink. I mean... the Hulk doesn't do that. That guy must go through a fortune in pants.
Okay, now embiggen. As big as you can.
And you're not displacing the amount of water I would expect...
SPLAASH!
This big enough?
Gah! My sneaks!
SUPER DRYE

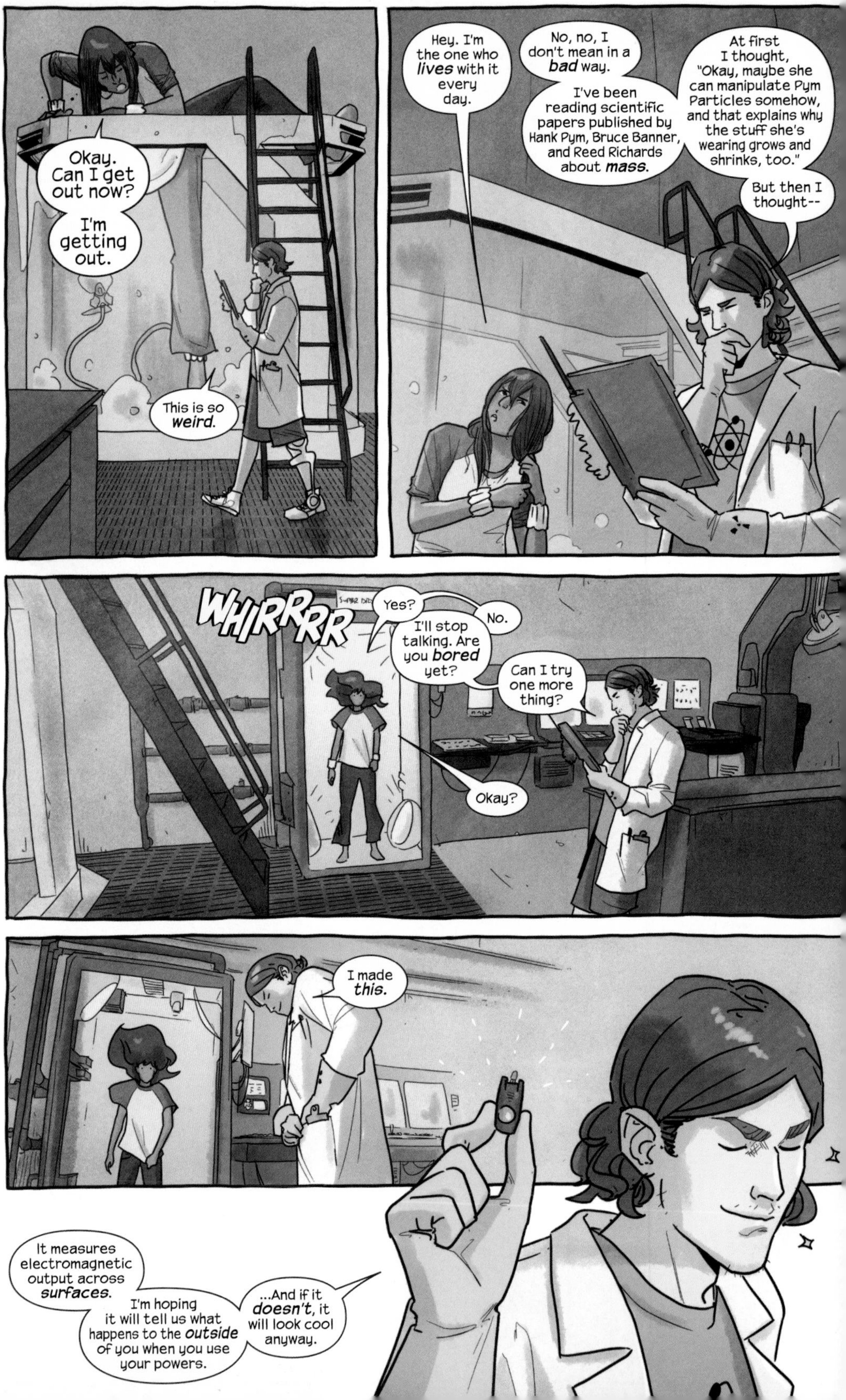

Okay. Can I get out now?
I'm getting out.
This is so weird.
Hey. I'm the one who lives with it every day.
No, no, I don't mean in a bad way.
I've been reading scientific papers published by Hank Pym, Bruce Banner, and Reed Richards about mass.
At first I thought, "Okay, maybe she can manipulate Pym Particles somehow, and that explains why the stuff she's wearing grows and shrinks, too."
But then I thought--
WHIRRRR
Yes?
No.
I'll stop talking. Are you bored yet?
Can I try one more thing?
Okay?
I made this.
It measures electromagnetic output across surfaces.
I'm hoping it will tell us what happens to the outside of you when you use your powers.
...And if it doesn't, it will look cool anyway.

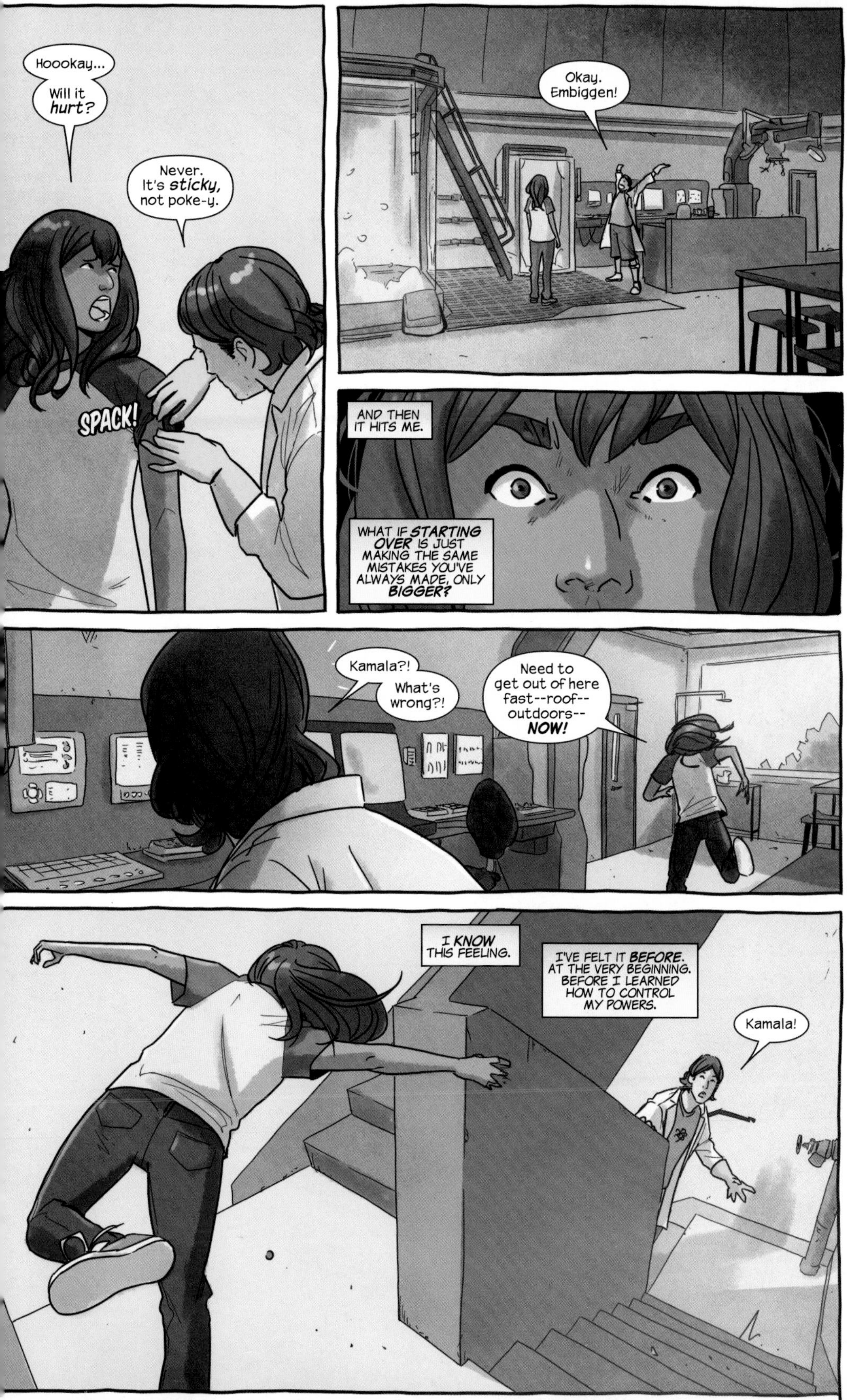
Hooookay...
Will it hurt?
Never. It's sticky, not poke-y.
SPACK!
Okay. Embiggen!
AND THEN IT HITS ME.
WHAT IF STARTING OVER IS JUST MAKING THE SAME MISTAKES YOU'VE ALWAYS MADE, ONLY BIGGER?
Kamala?!
What's wrong?!
Need to get out of here fast--roof--outdoors--NOW!
I KNOW THIS FEELING.
I'VE FELT IT BEFORE. AT THE VERY BEGINNING. BEFORE I LEARNED HOW TO CONTROL MY POWERS.
Kamala!

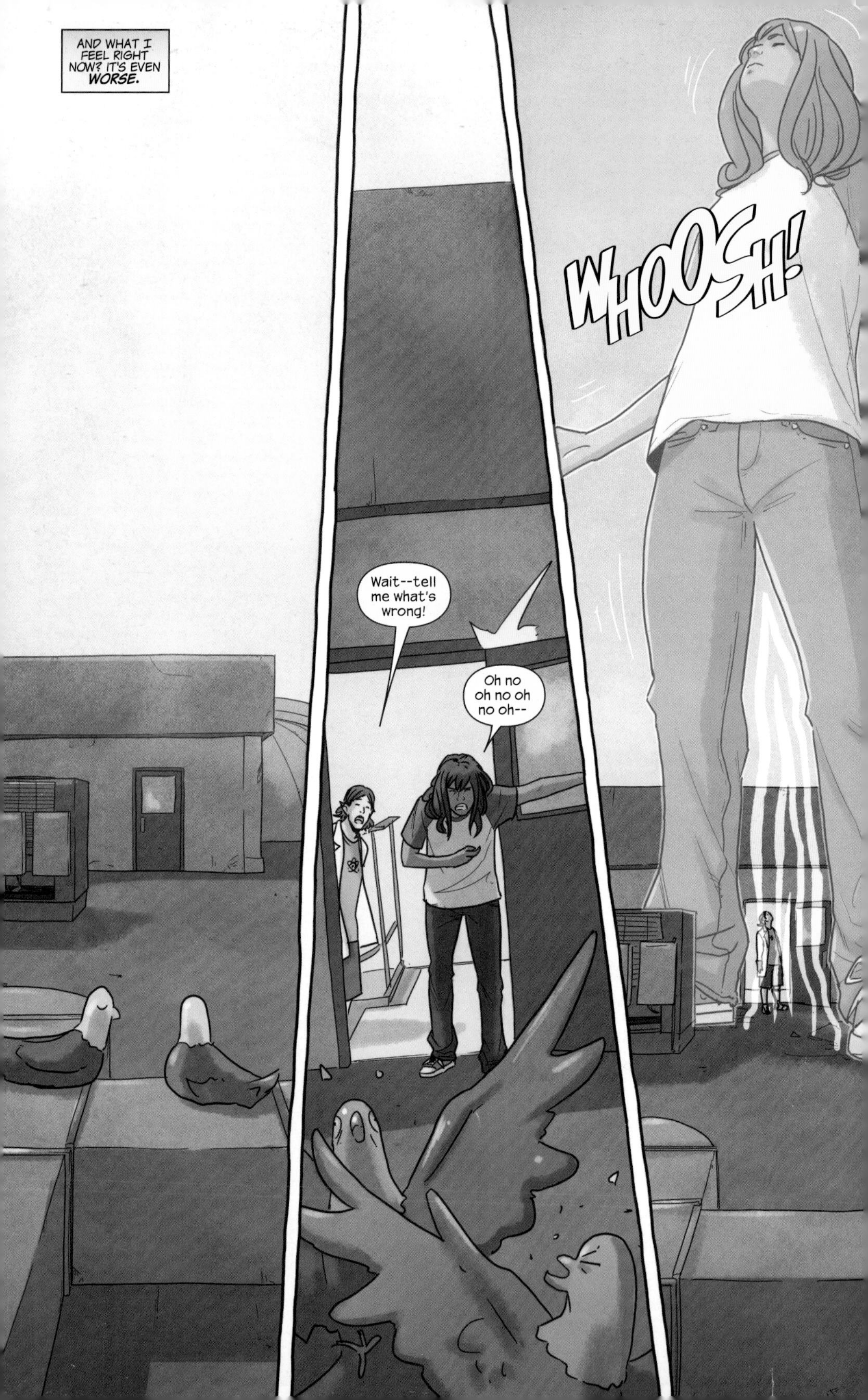
AND WHAT I FEEL RIGHT NOW? IT'S EVEN WORSE.
WHOOSH!
Wait--tell me what's wrong!
Oh no oh no oh no oh--

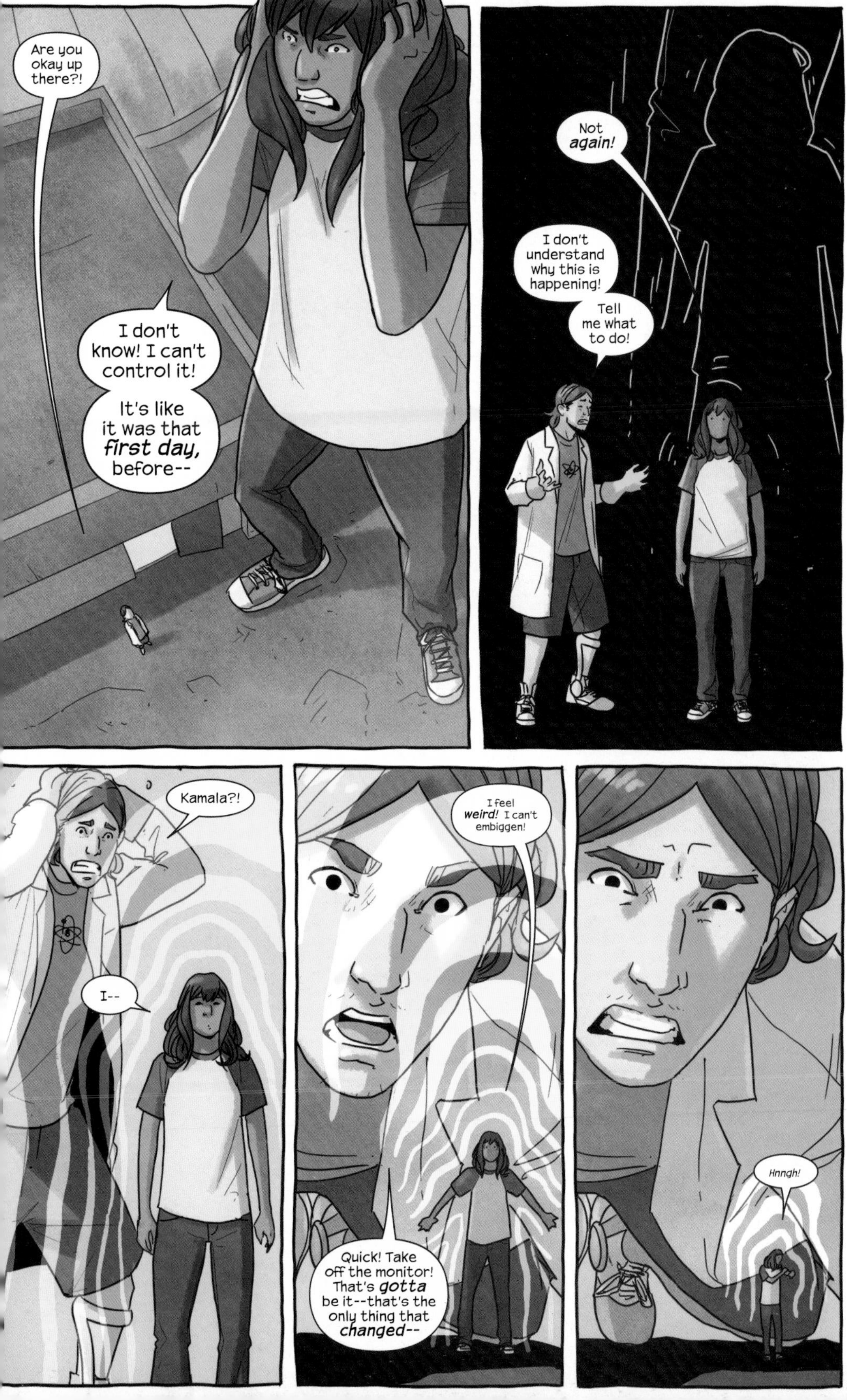
Are you okay up there?!
I don't know! I can't control it!
It's like it was that *first day,* before--
Not *again!*
I don't understand why this is happening!
Tell me what to do!
Kamala?!
I--
I feel *weird!* I can't embiggen!
Quick! Take off the monitor! That's *gotta* be it--that's the only thing that *changed*--
Hnngh!

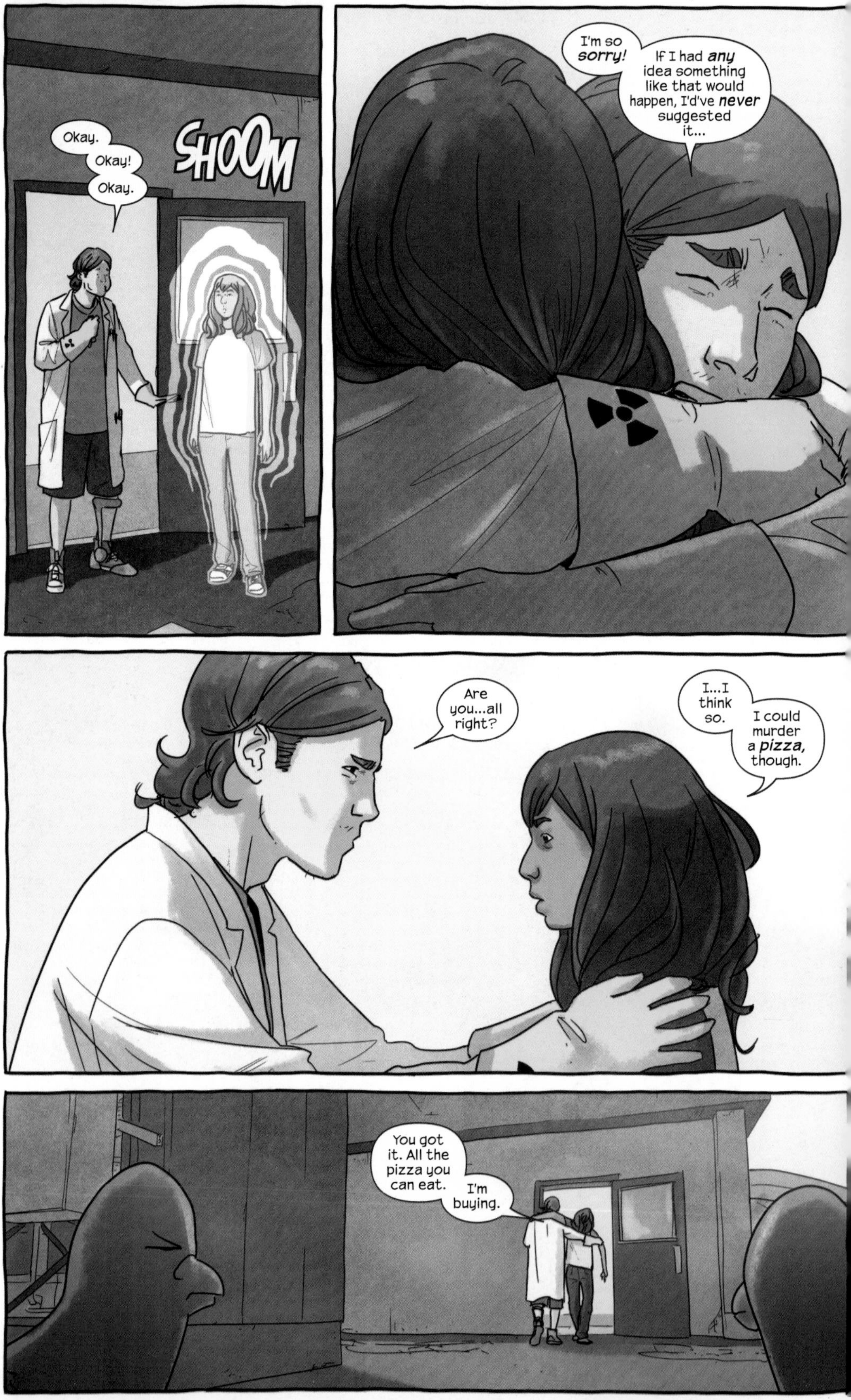
Okay.
Okay!
Okay.
SHOOM
I'm so sorry!
If I had any idea something like that would happen, I'd've never suggested it...
Are you...all right?
I...I think so.
I could murder a pizza, though.
You got it. All the pizza you can eat.
I'm buying.

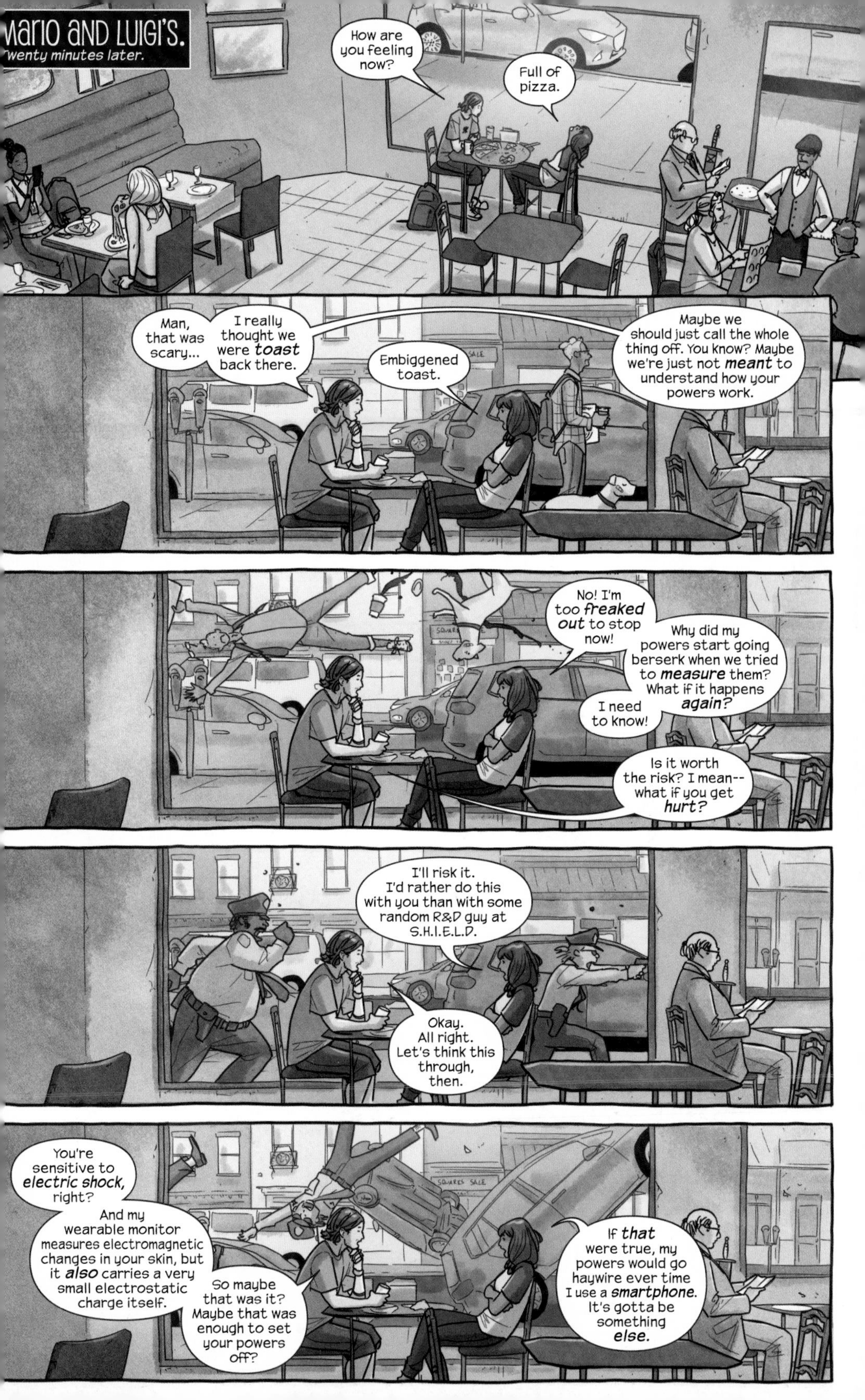

MARIO AND LUIGI'S.
Twenty minutes later.
How are you feeling now?
Full of pizza.
Man, that was scary...
I really thought we were *toast* back there.
Embiggened toast.
Maybe we should just call the whole thing off. You know? Maybe we're just not *meant* to understand how your powers work.
No! I'm too *freaked out* to stop now!
Why did my powers start going berserk when we tried to *measure* them? What if it happens *again?*
I need to know!
Is it worth the risk? I mean--what if you get *hurt?*
I'll risk it. I'd rather do this with you than with some random R&D guy at S.H.I.E.L.D.
Okay. All right. Let's think this through, then.
You're sensitive to *electric shock,* right?
And my wearable monitor measures electromagnetic changes in your skin, but it *also* carries a very small electrostatic charge itself.
So maybe that was it? Maybe that was enough to set your powers off?
If *that* were true, my powers would go haywire ever time I use a *smartphone.* It's gotta be something *else.*

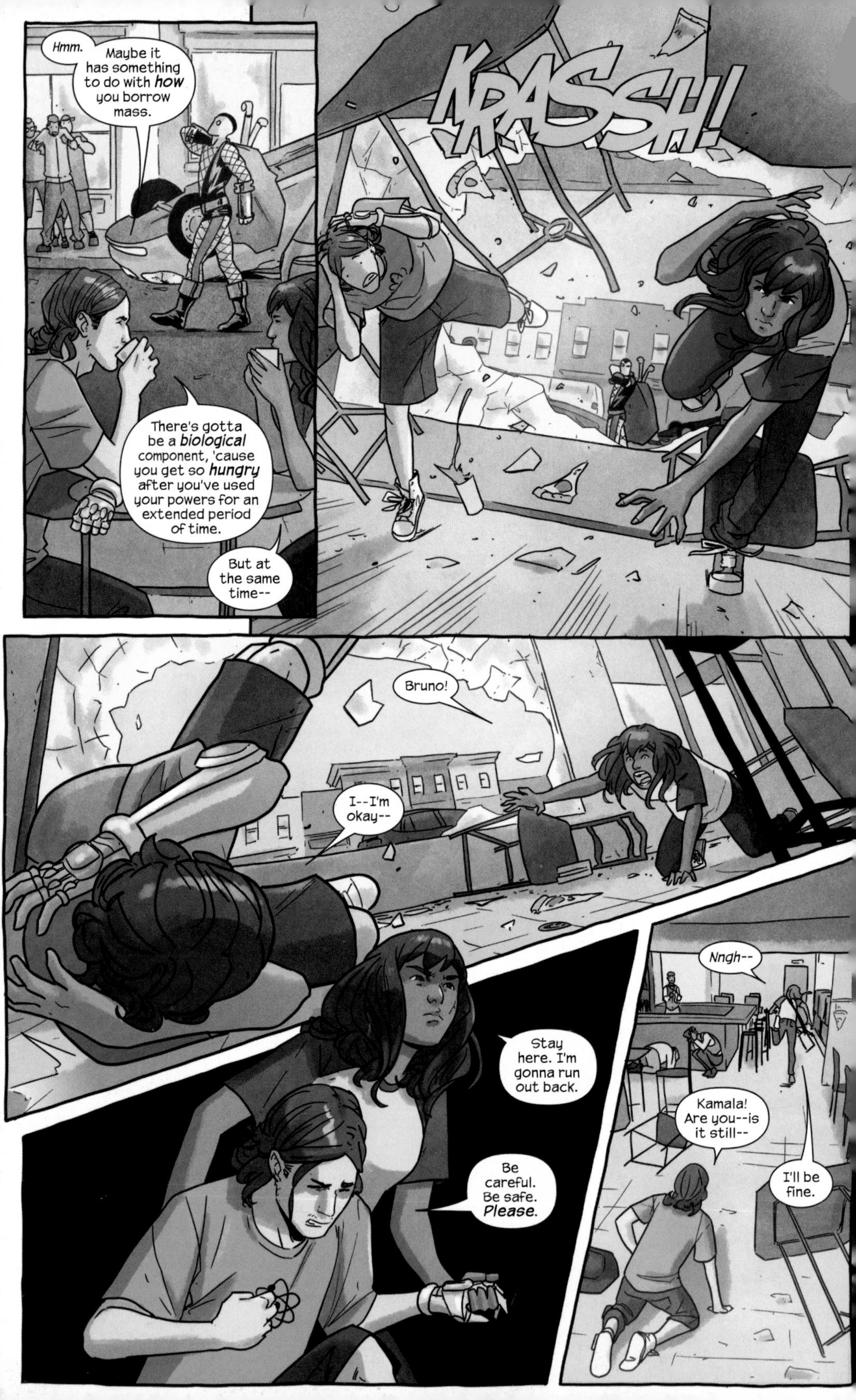

Hmm.
Maybe it has something to do with *how* you borrow mass.
There's gotta be a *biological* component, 'cause you get so *hungry* after you've used your powers for an extended period of time.
But at the same time--
KRASSH!
Bruno!
I--I'm okay--
Stay here. I'm gonna run out back.
Be careful. Be safe. *Please.*
Nngh--
Kamala! Are you--is it still--
I'll be fine.

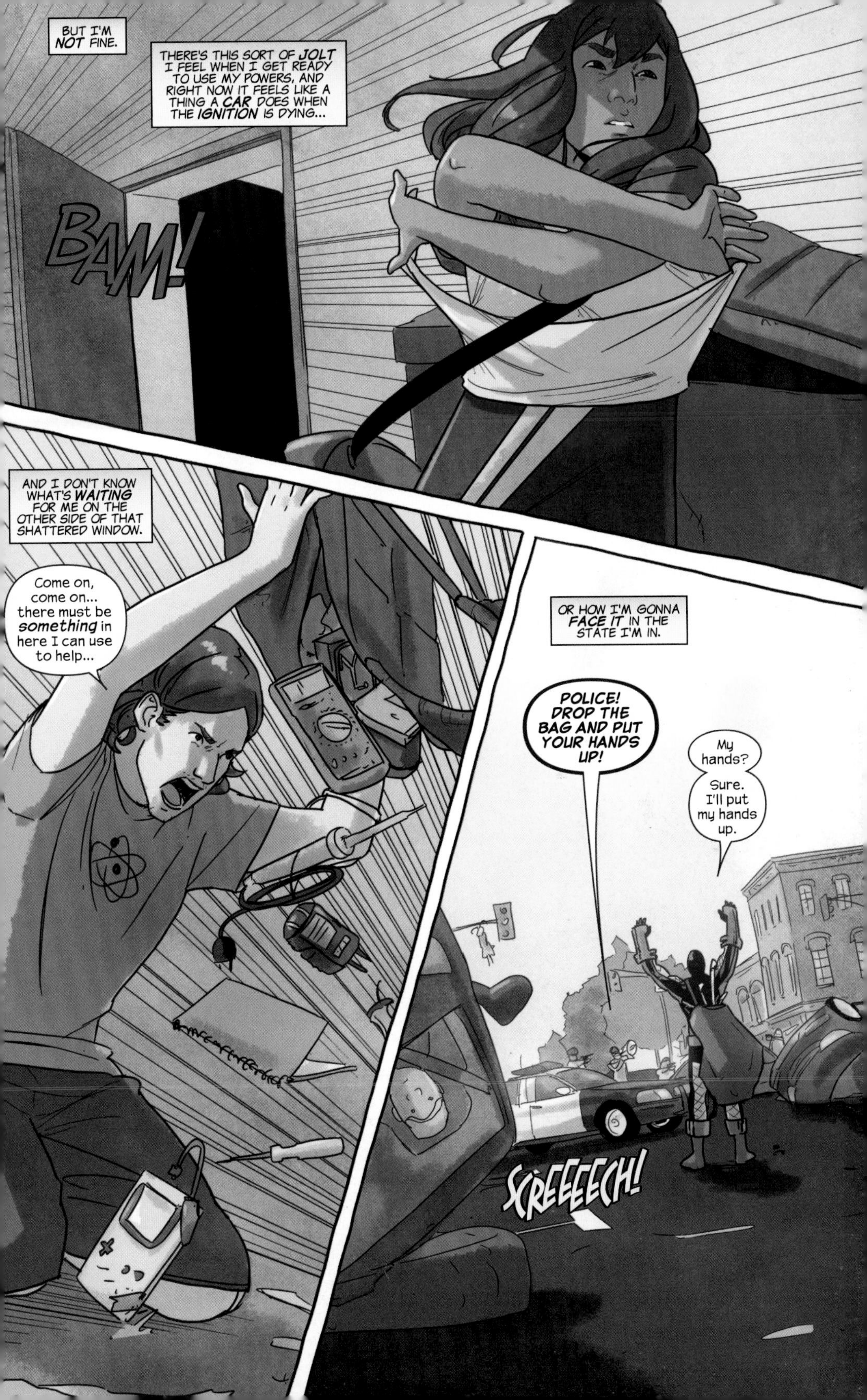
BUT I'M NOT FINE.
THERE'S THIS SORT OF JOLT I FEEL WHEN I GET READY TO USE MY POWERS, AND RIGHT NOW IT FEELS LIKE A THING A CAR DOES WHEN THE IGNITION IS DYING...
BAM!
AND I DON'T KNOW WHAT'S WAITING FOR ME ON THE OTHER SIDE OF THAT SHATTERED WINDOW.
Come on, come on... there must be something in here I can use to help...
OR HOW I'M GONNA FACE IT IN THE STATE I'M IN.
POLICE! DROP THE BAG AND PUT YOUR HANDS UP!
My hands?
Sure. I'll put my hands up.
SCREEEECH!

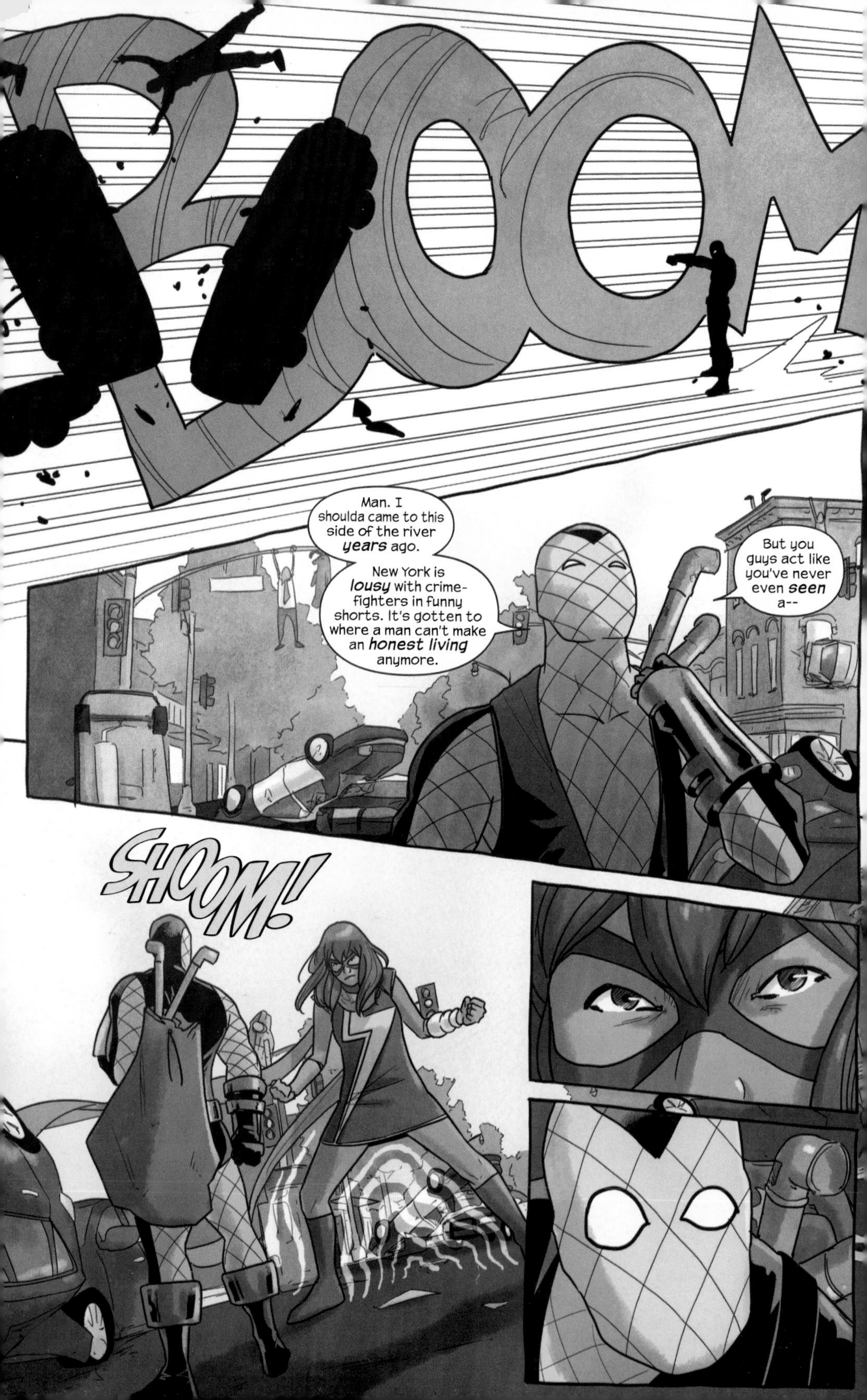
BZOOM
Man. I shoulda came to this side of the river *years* ago.
New York is *lousy* with crime-fighters in funny shorts. It's gotten to where a man can't make an *honest living* anymore.
But you guys act like you've never even *seen* a--
SHOOM!

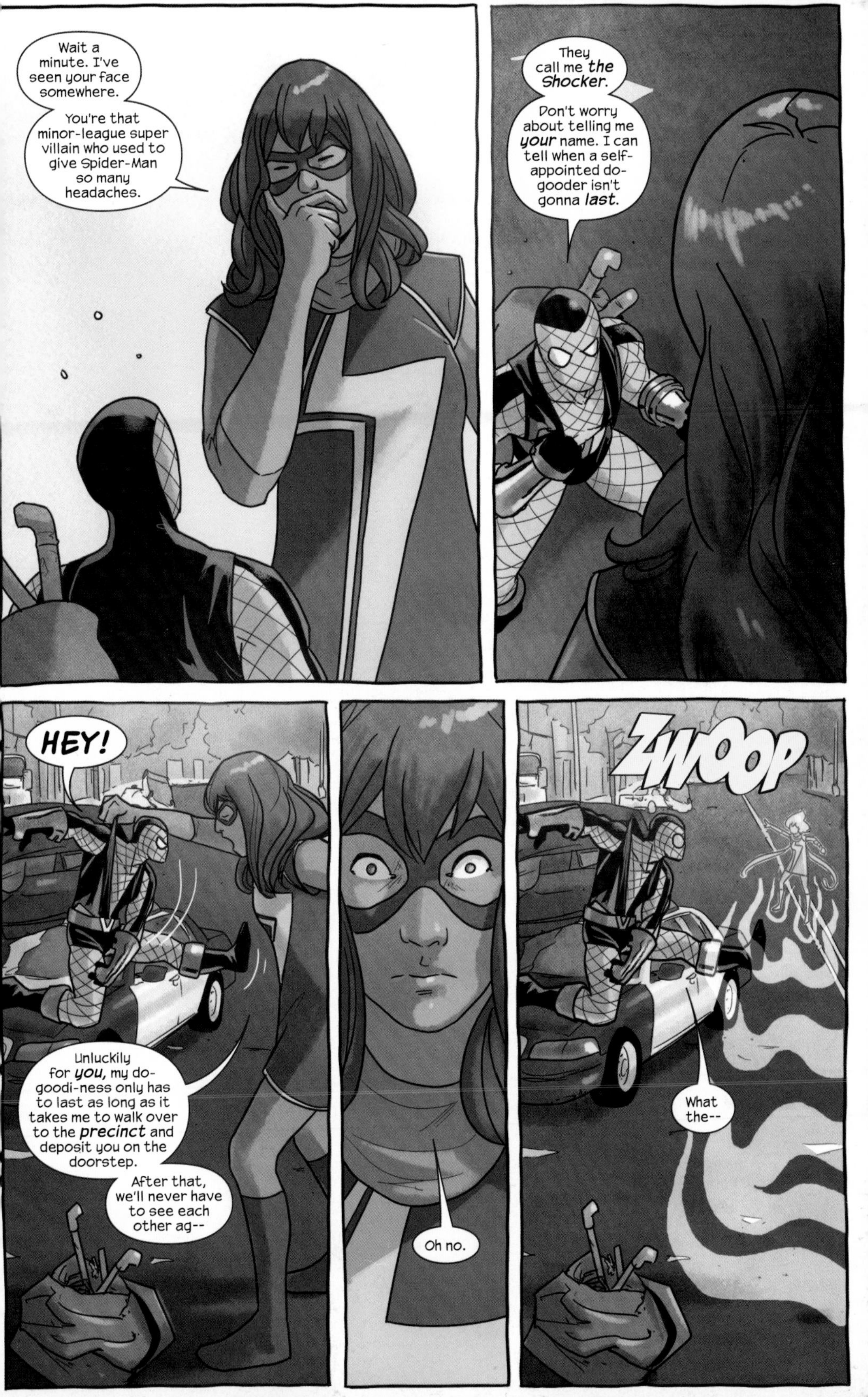

Wait a minute. I've seen your face somewhere.
You're that minor-league super villain who used to give Spider-Man so many headaches.
They call me the Shocker.
Don't worry about telling me your name. I can tell when a self-appointed do-gooder isn't gonna last.
HEY!
Unluckily for you, my do-goodi-ness only has to last as long as it takes me to walk over to the precinct and deposit you on the doorstep.
After that, we'll never have to see each other ag--
Oh no.
ZWOOP
What the--

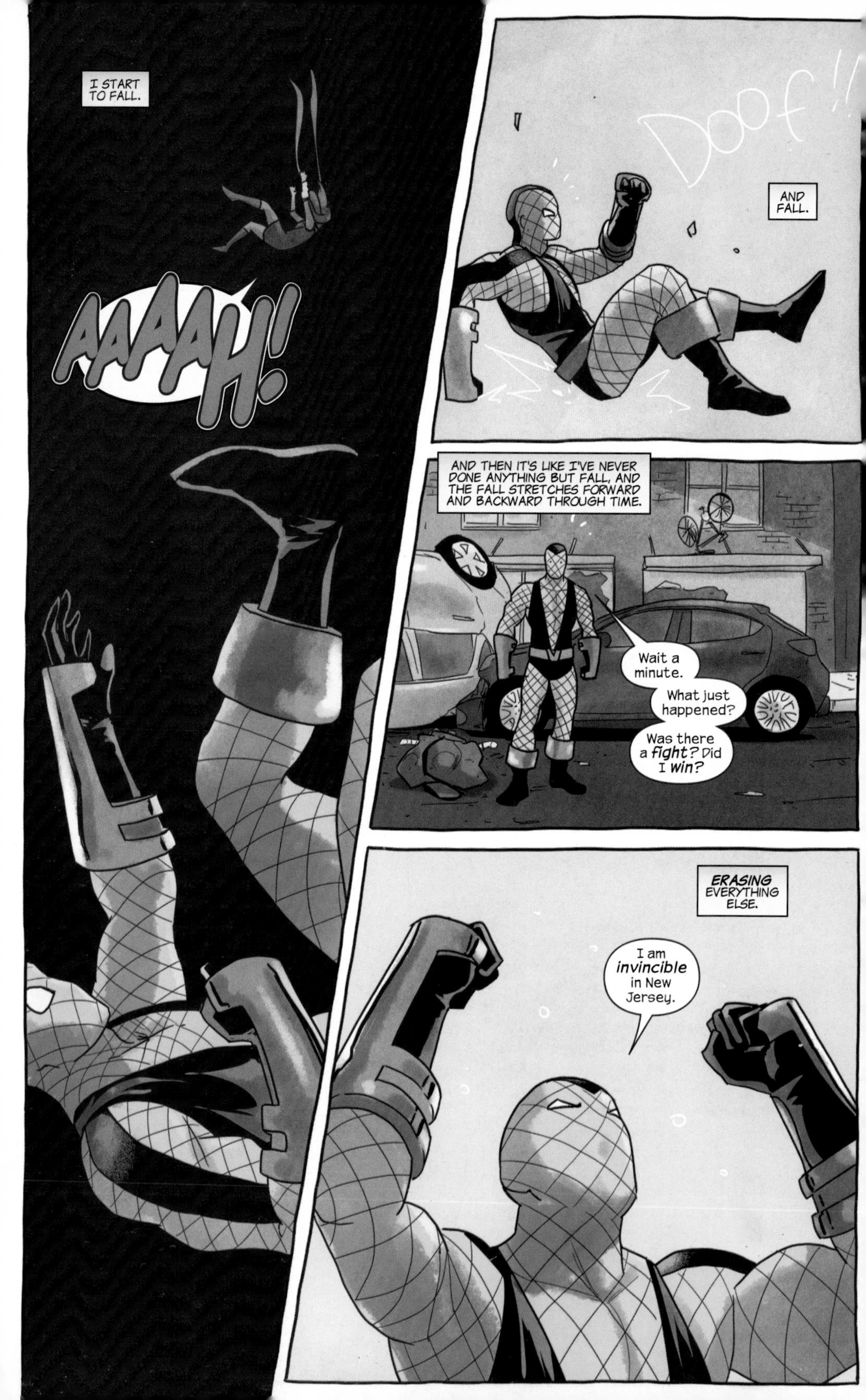

I START TO FALL.
AAAAH!
DOOF!!
AND FALL.
AND THEN IT'S LIKE I'VE NEVER DONE ANYTHING BUT FALL, AND THE FALL STRETCHES FORWARD AND BACKWARD THROUGH TIME.
Wait a minute.
What just happened?
Was there a fight? Did I win?
ERASING EVERYTHING ELSE.
I am invincible in New Jersey.

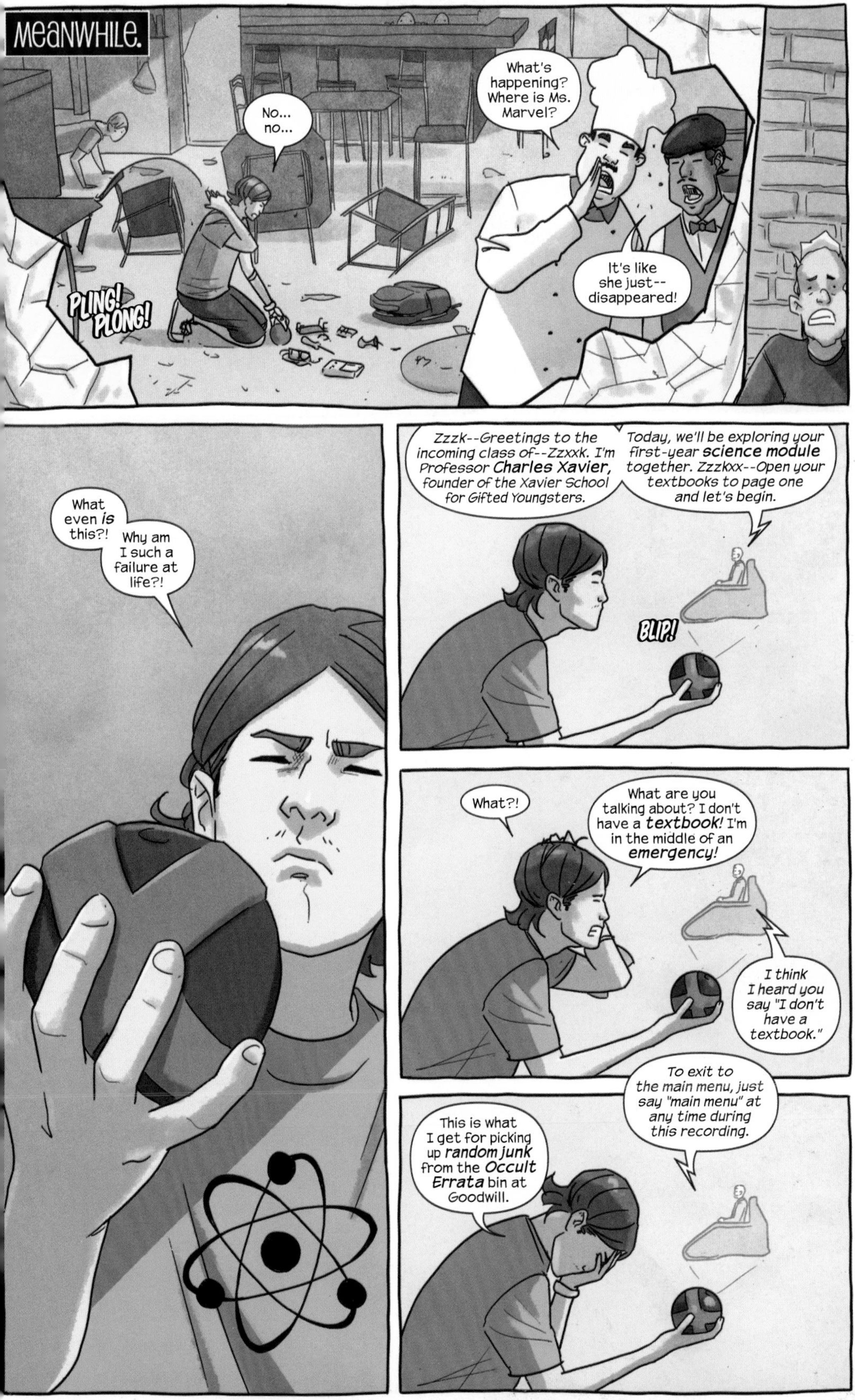
MEANWHILE.
No... no...
What's happening? Where is Ms. Marvel?
It's like she just--disappeared!
PLING! PLONG!
What even is this?!
Why am I such a failure at life?!
Zzzk--Greetings to the incoming class of--Zzxxk. I'm Professor Charles Xavier, founder of the Xavier School for Gifted Youngsters.
Today, we'll be exploring your first-year science module together. Zzzkxx--Open your textbooks to page one and let's begin.
BLIP!
What?!
What are you talking about? I don't have a textbook! I'm in the middle of an emergency!
I think I heard you say "I don't have a textbook."
This is what I get for picking up random junk from the Occult Errata bin at Goodwill.
To exit to the main menu, just say "main menu" at any time during this recording.

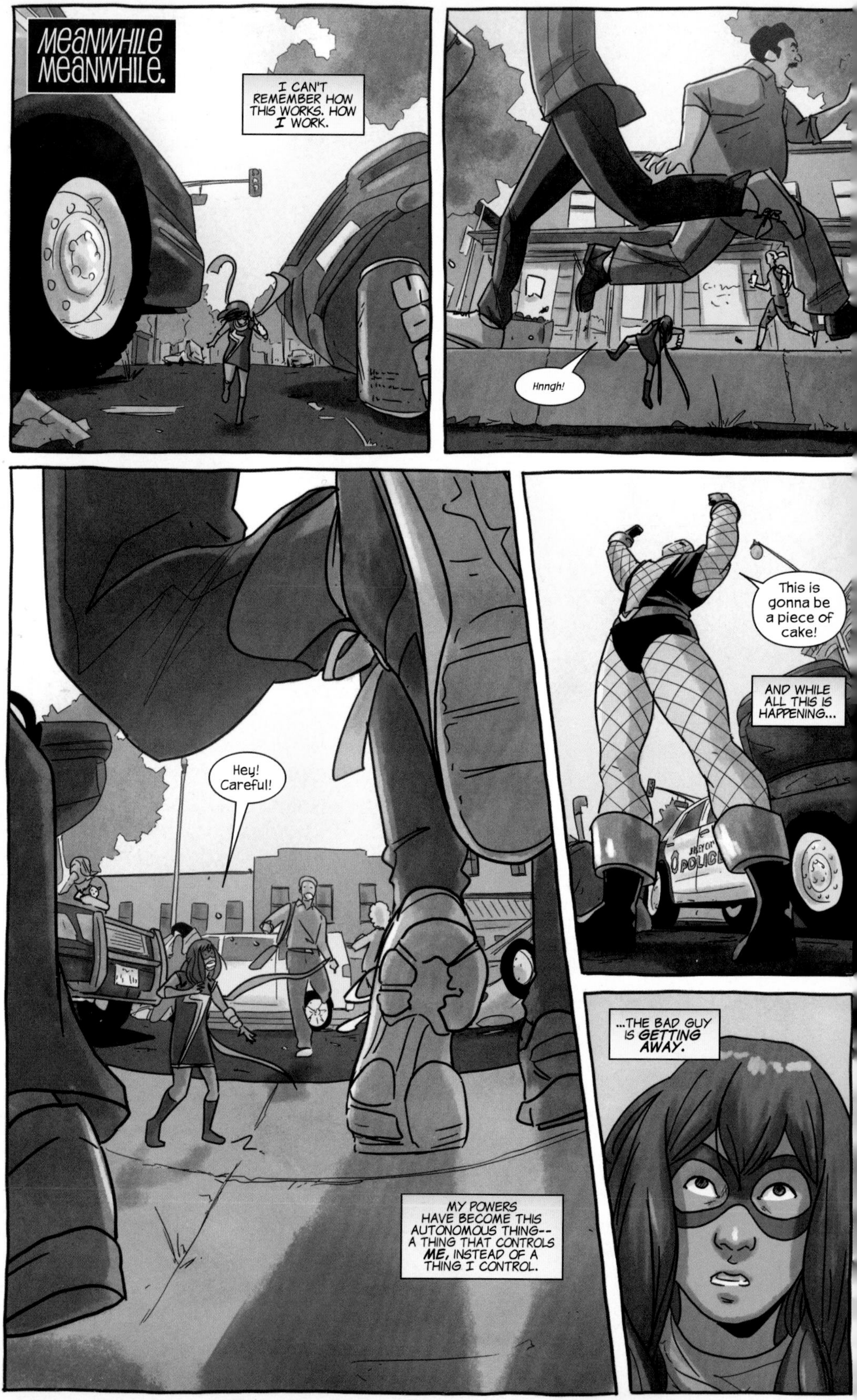
MEANWHILE MEANWHILE.
I CAN'T REMEMBER HOW THIS WORKS. HOW I WORK.
Hnngh!
Hey! Careful!
MY POWERS HAVE BECOME THIS AUTONOMOUS THING-- A THING THAT CONTROLS ME, INSTEAD OF A THING I CONTROL.
This is gonna be a piece of cake!
AND WHILE ALL THIS IS HAPPENING...
...THE BAD GUY IS GETTING AWAY.

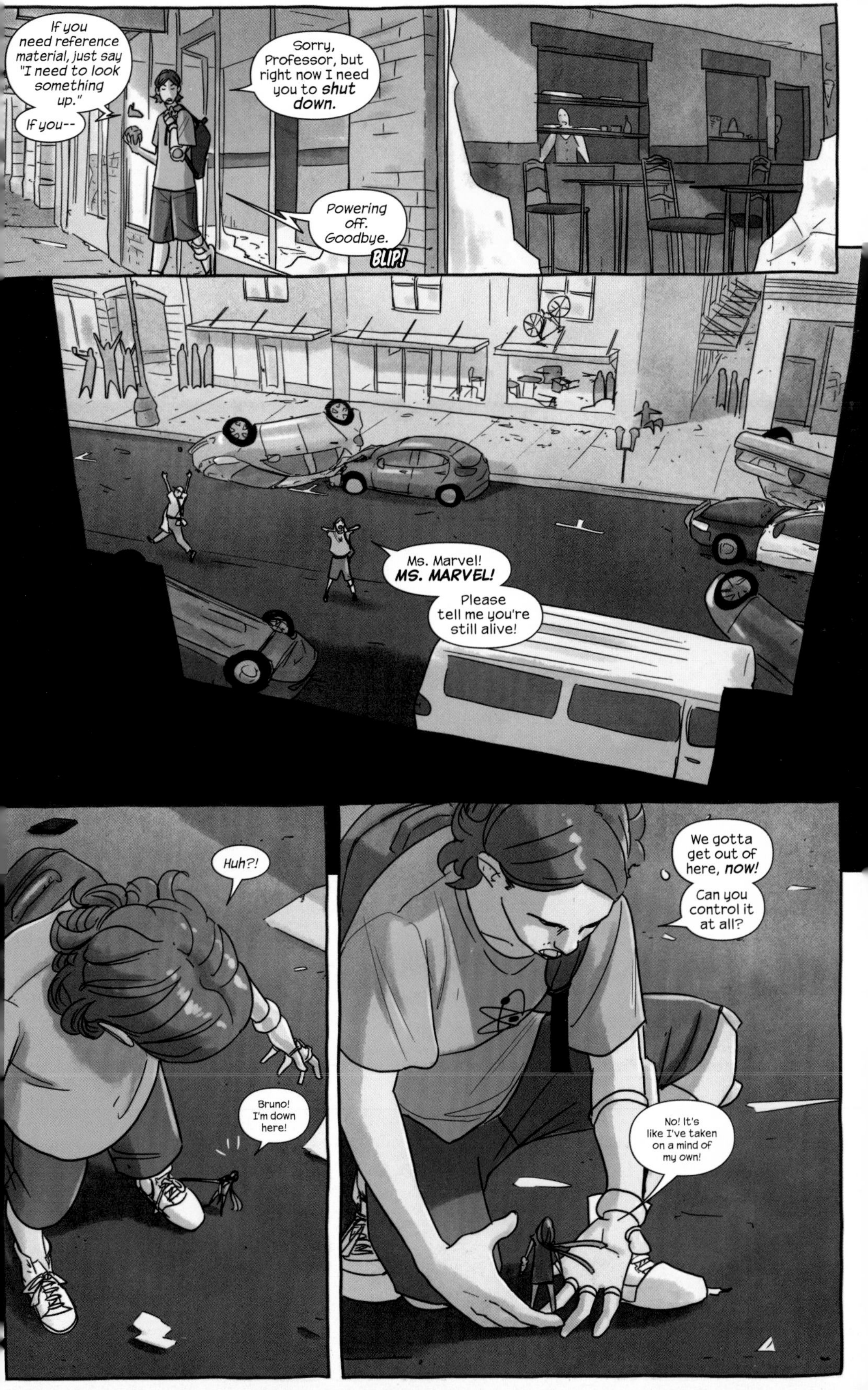

If you need reference material, just say "I need to look something up."
If you--
Sorry, Professor, but right now I need you to **shut down.**
Powering off. Goodbye.
BLIP!
Ms. Marvel! **MS. MARVEL!**
Please tell me you're still alive!
Huh?!
Bruno! I'm down here!
We gotta get out of here, **NOW!**
Can you control it at all?
No! It's like I've taken on a mind of my own!

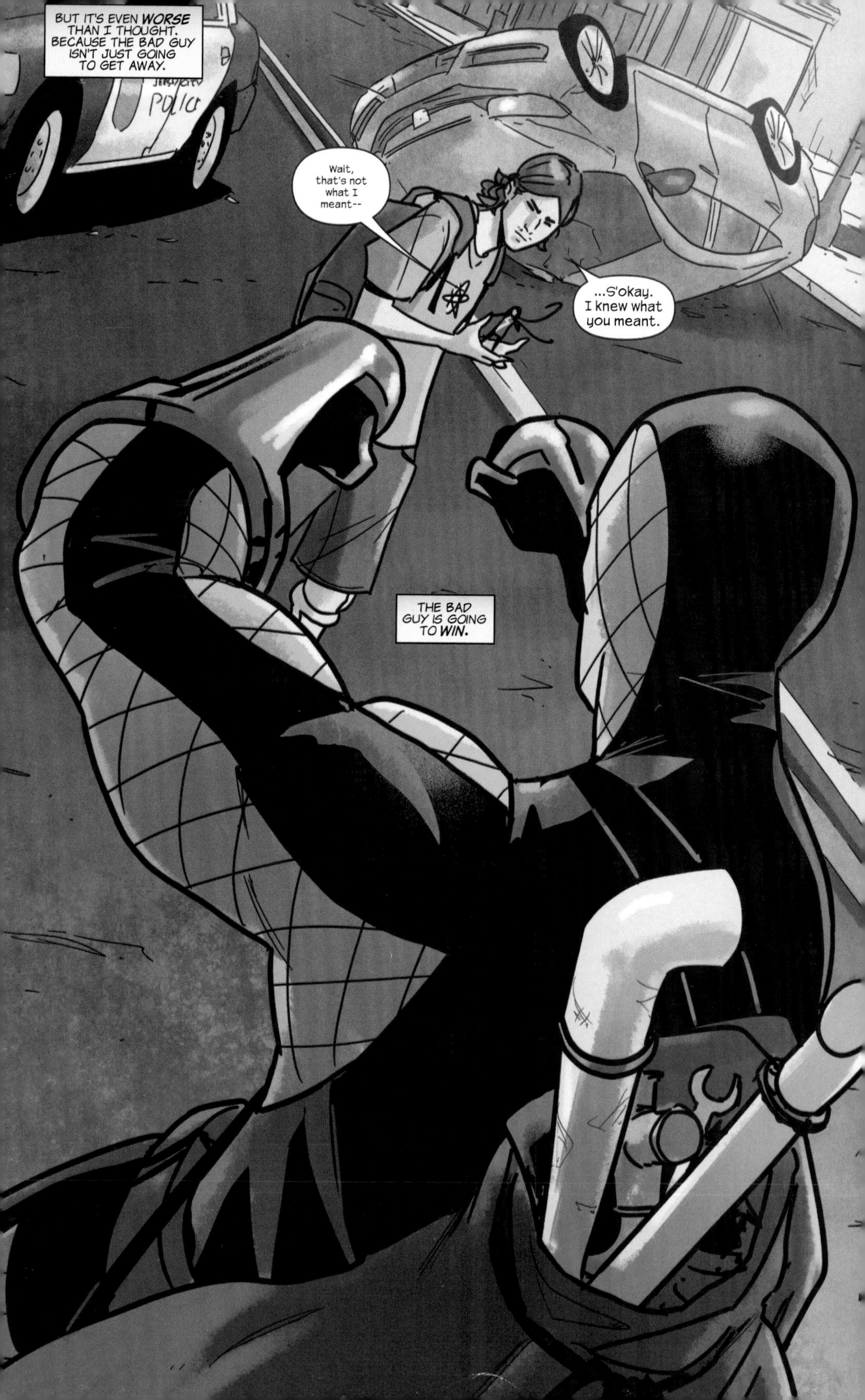
BUT IT'S EVEN WORSE THAN I THOUGHT. BECAUSE THE BAD GUY ISN'T JUST GOING TO GET AWAY.
Wait, that's not what I meant--
...S'okay. I knew what you meant.
THE BAD GUY IS GOING TO WIN.

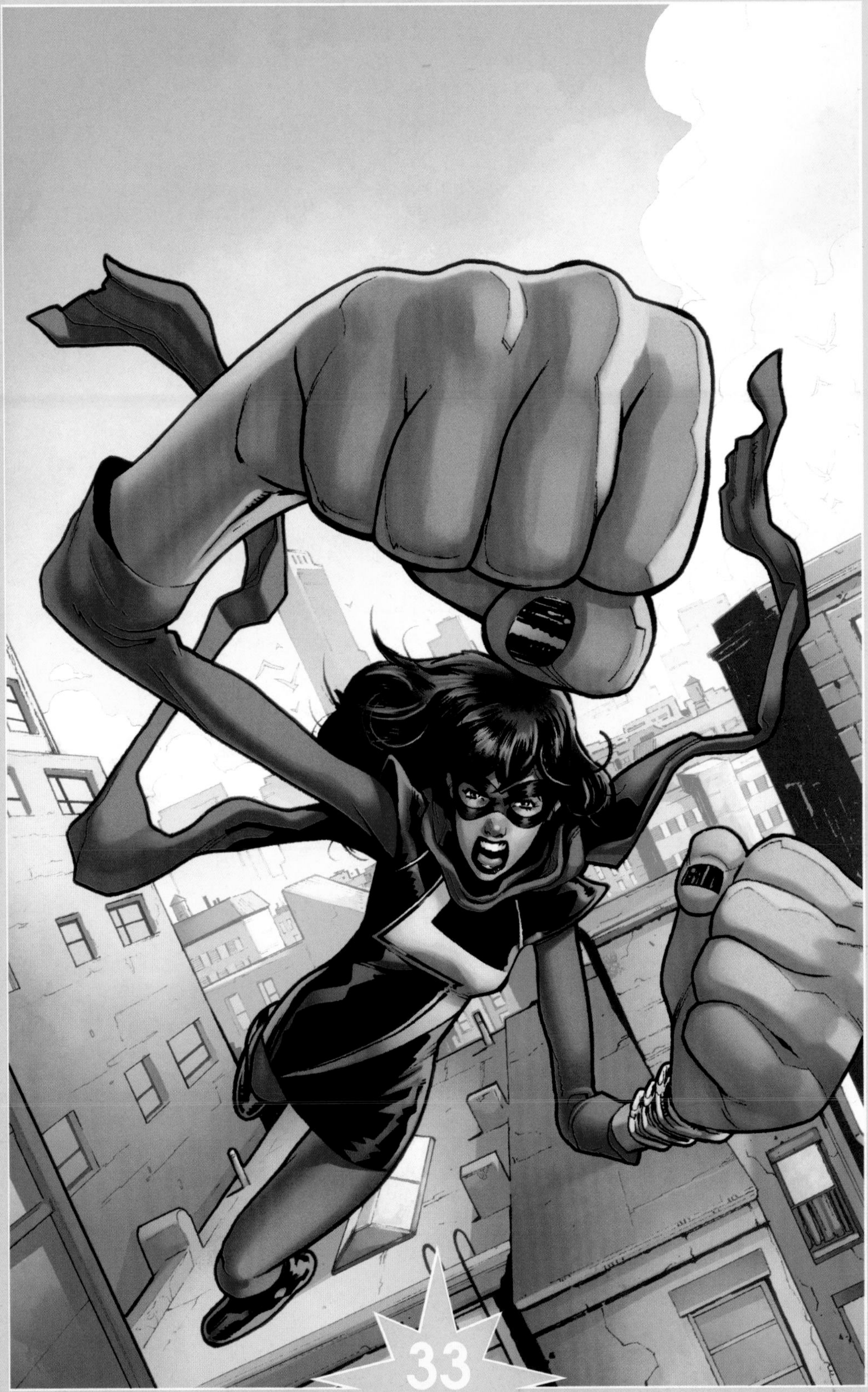
33

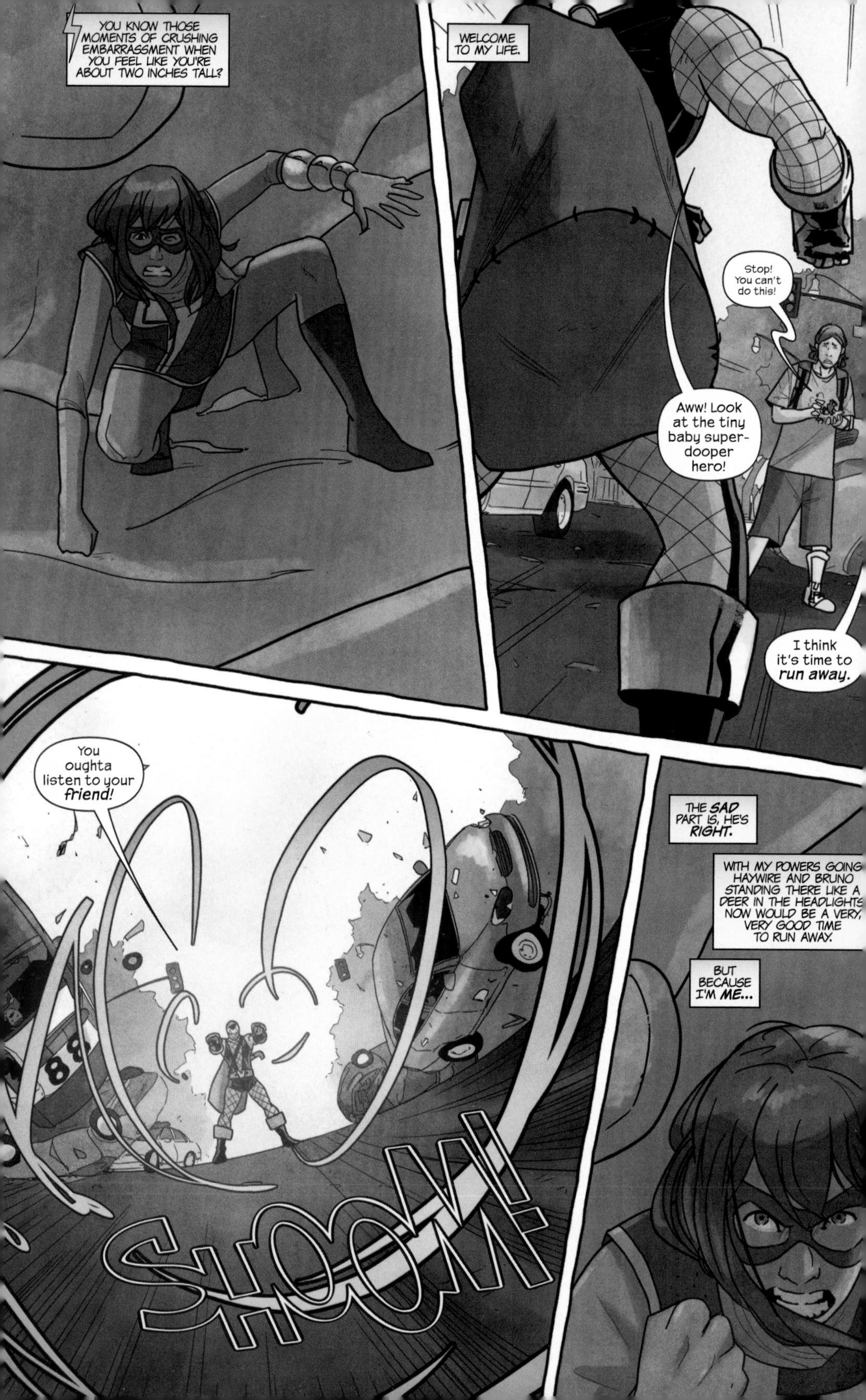
YOU KNOW THOSE MOMENTS OF CRUSHING EMBARRASSMENT WHEN YOU FEEL LIKE YOU'RE ABOUT TWO INCHES TALL?
WELCOME TO MY LIFE.
Stop! You can't do this!
Aww! Look at the tiny baby super-dooper hero!
I think it's time to run away.
You oughta listen to your friend!
SHOOM!
THE SAD PART IS, HE'S RIGHT.
WITH MY POWERS GOING HAYWIRE AND BRUNO STANDING THERE LIKE A DEER IN THE HEADLIGHTS, NOW WOULD BE A VERY, VERY GOOD TIME TO RUN AWAY.
BUT BECAUSE I'M ME...

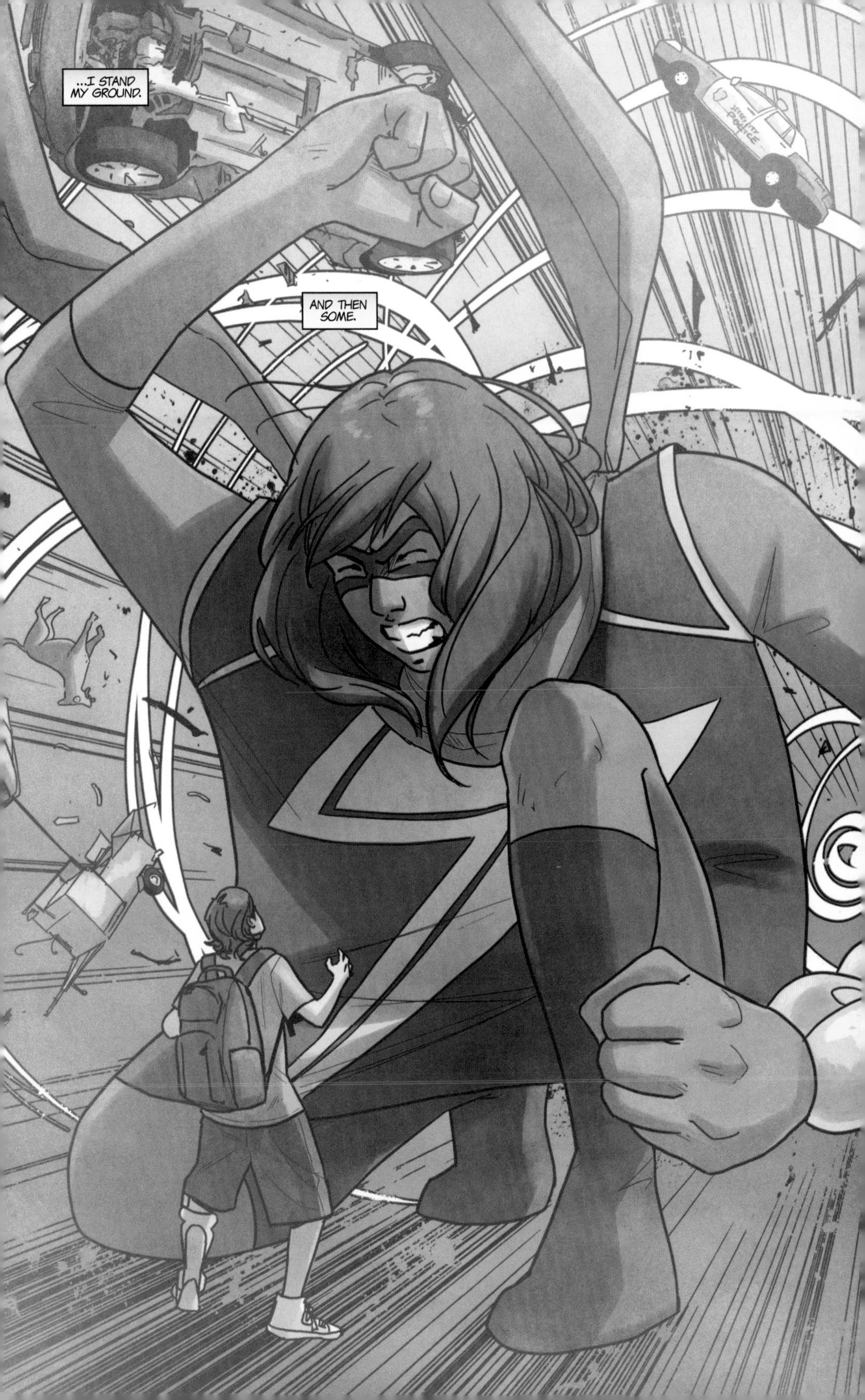
...I STAND MY GROUND.
AND THEN SOME.

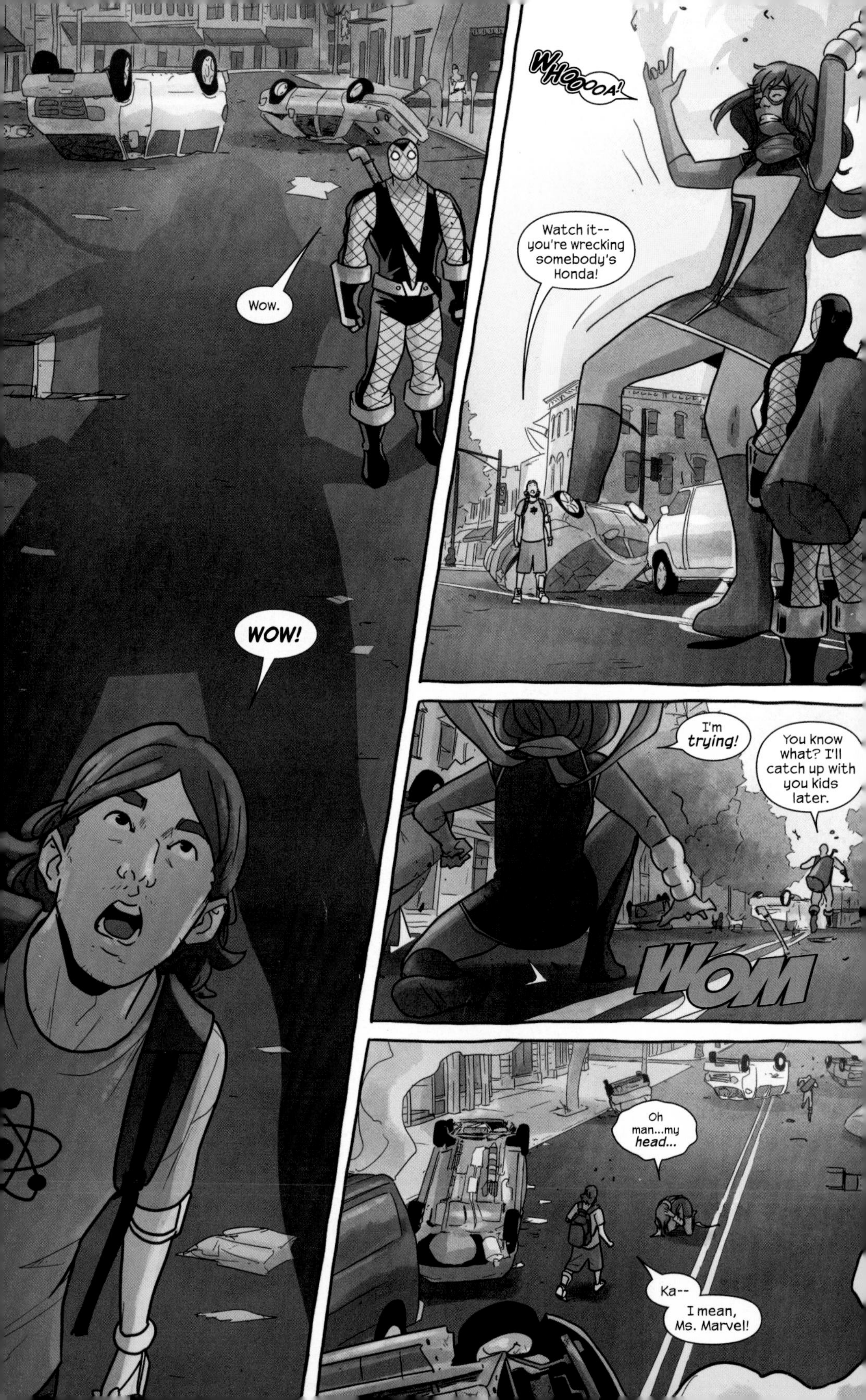
Wow.
WOW!
WHOOOOA!
Watch it-- you're wrecking somebody's Honda!
I'm trying!
You know what? I'll catch up with you kids later.
WOM
Oh man...my head...
Ka--
I mean, Ms. Marvel!

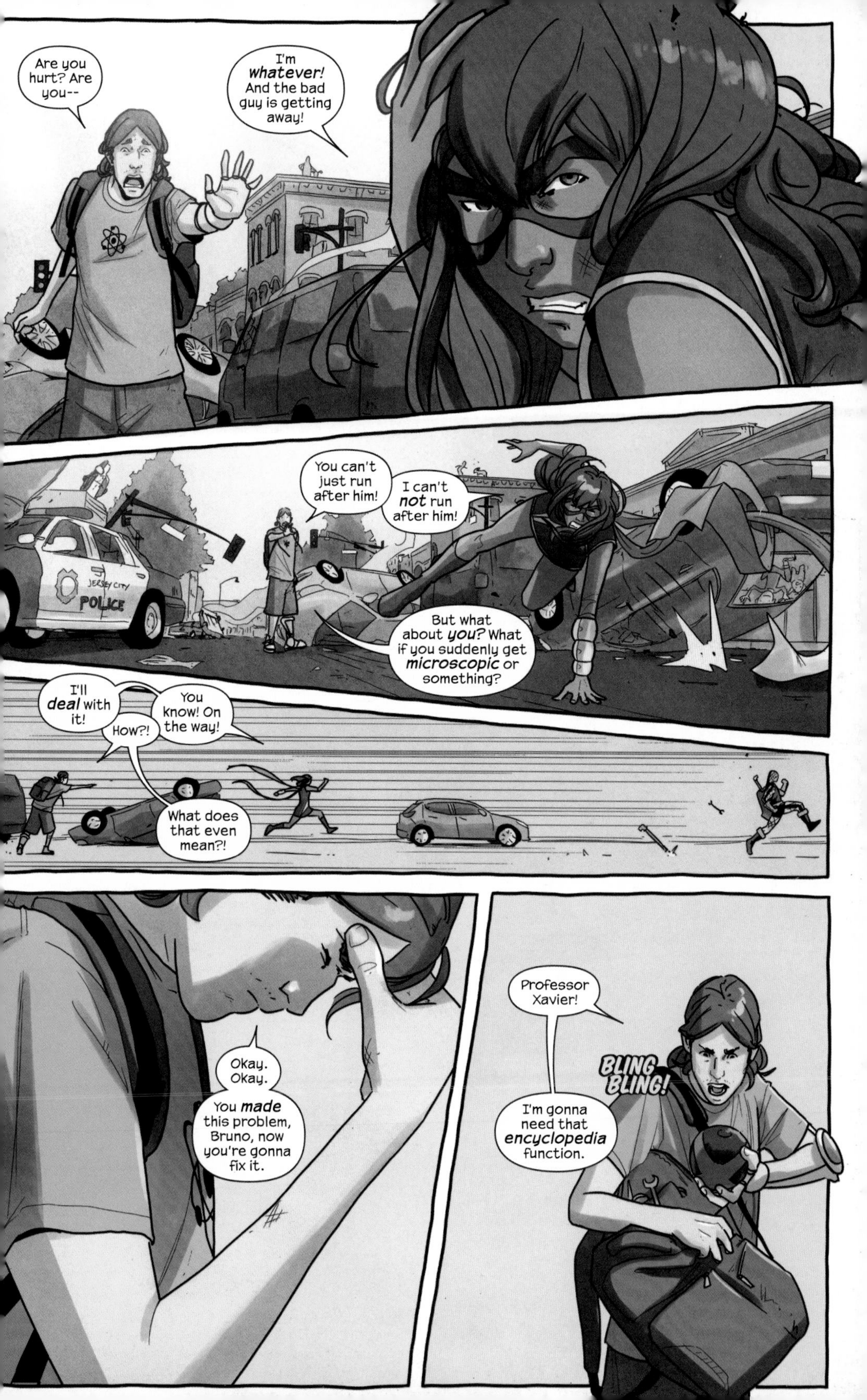
Are you hurt? Are you--
I'm *whatever!* And the bad guy is getting away!
You can't just run after him!
I can't *not* run after him!
JERSEY CITY
POLICE
But what about *you?* What if you suddenly get *microscopic* or something?
I'll *deal* with it!
How?!
You know! On the way!
What does that even mean?!
Okay. Okay.
You *made* this problem, Bruno, now you're gonna fix it.
Professor Xavier!
BLING BLING!
I'm gonna need that *encyclopedia* function.

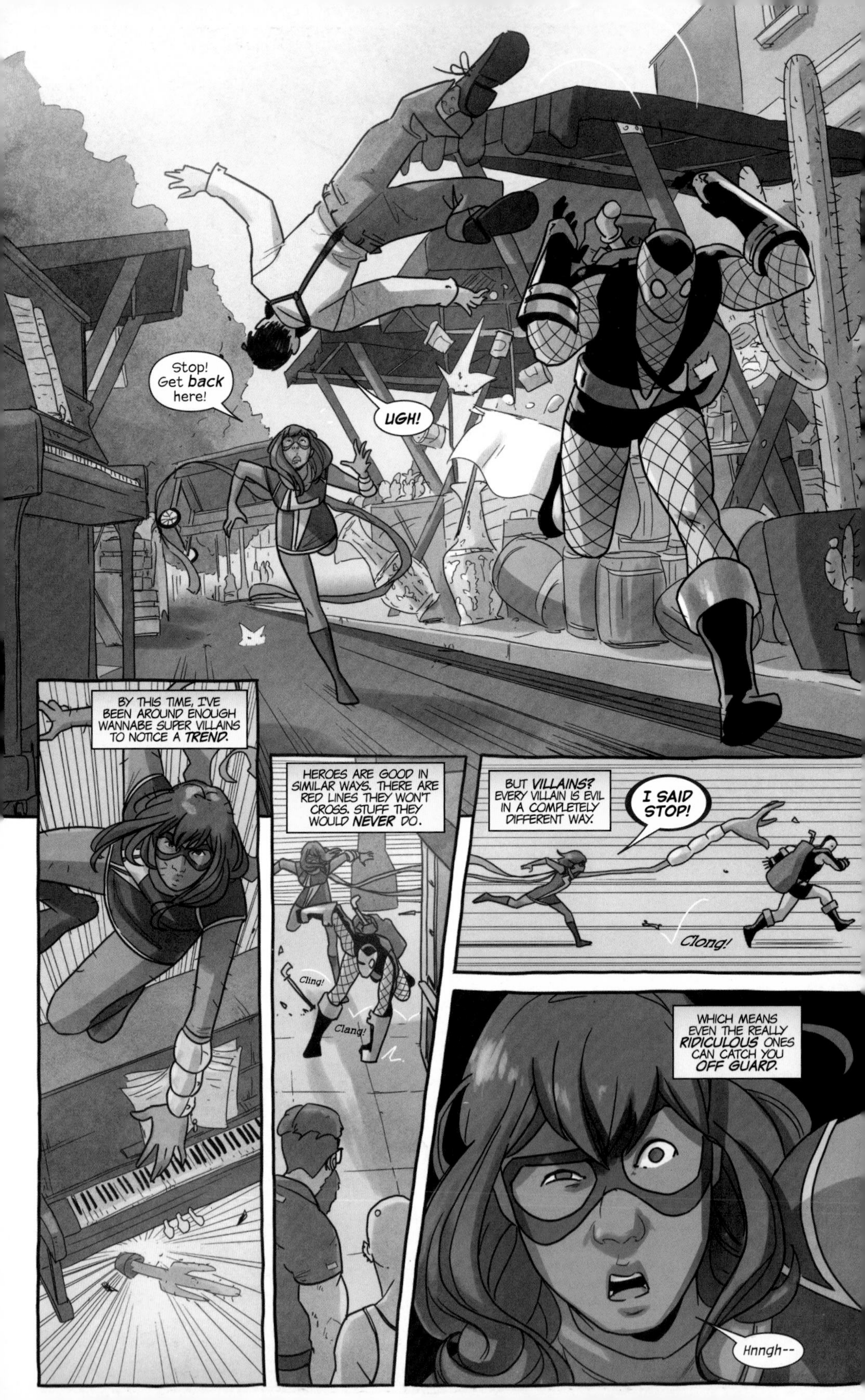
Stop! Get **back** here!
UGH!
BY THIS TIME, I'VE BEEN AROUND ENOUGH WANNABE SUPER VILLAINS TO NOTICE A **TREND**.
HEROES ARE GOOD IN SIMILAR WAYS. THERE ARE RED LINES THEY WON'T CROSS. STUFF THEY WOULD **NEVER** DO.
Cling!
Clang!
BUT **VILLAINS?** EVERY VILLAIN IS EVIL IN A COMPLETELY DIFFERENT WAY.
I SAID STOP!
Clong!
WHICH MEANS EVEN THE REALLY **RIDICULOUS** ONES CAN CATCH YOU **OFF GUARD**.
Hnngh--

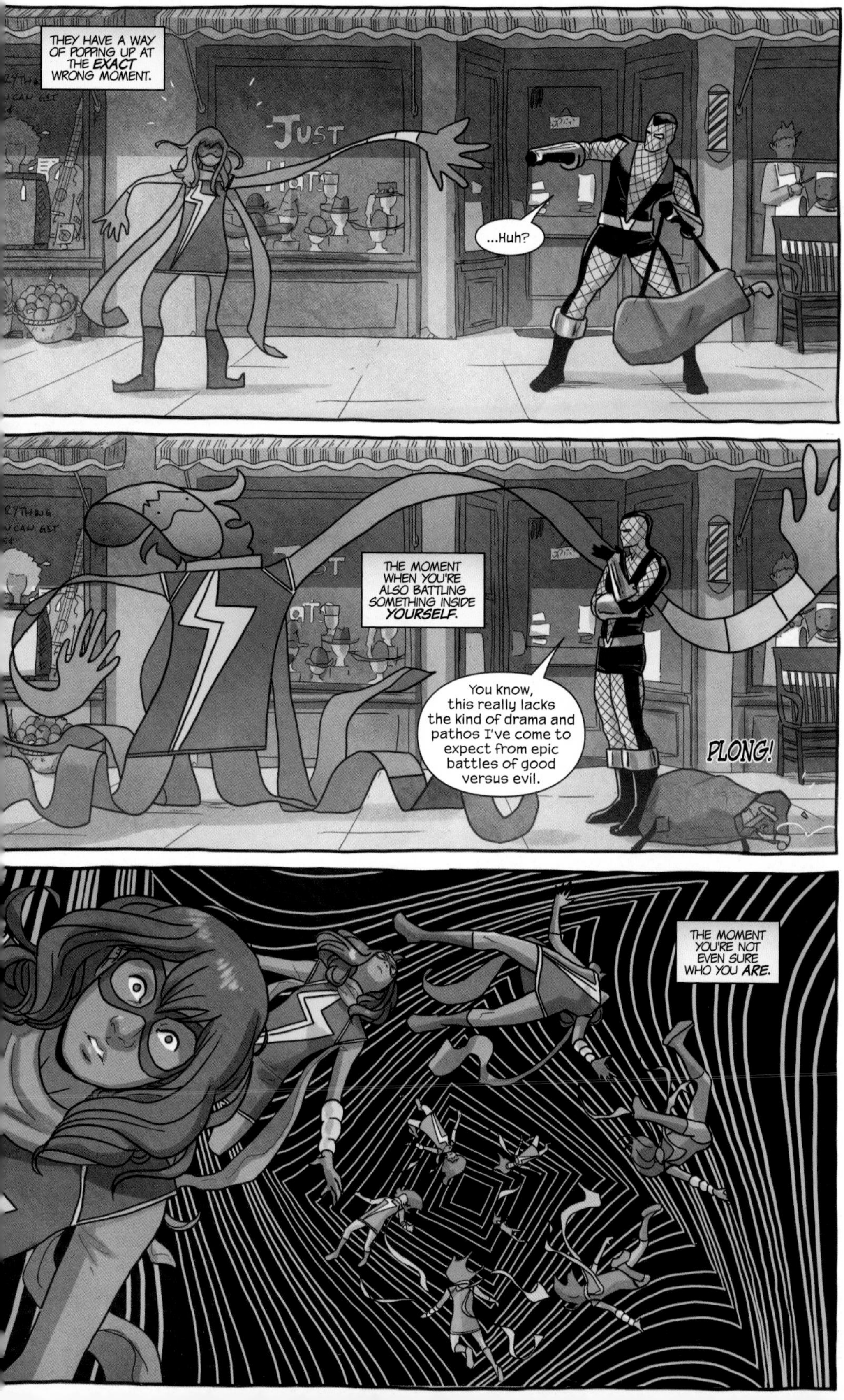
THEY HAVE A WAY OF POPPING UP AT THE *EXACT* WRONG MOMENT.
JUST
...Huh?
THE MOMENT WHEN YOU'RE ALSO BATTLING SOMETHING INSIDE *YOURSELF*.
You know, this really lacks the kind of drama and pathos I've come to expect from epic battles of good versus evil.
PLONG!
THE MOMENT YOU'RE NOT EVEN SURE WHO YOU *ARE*.

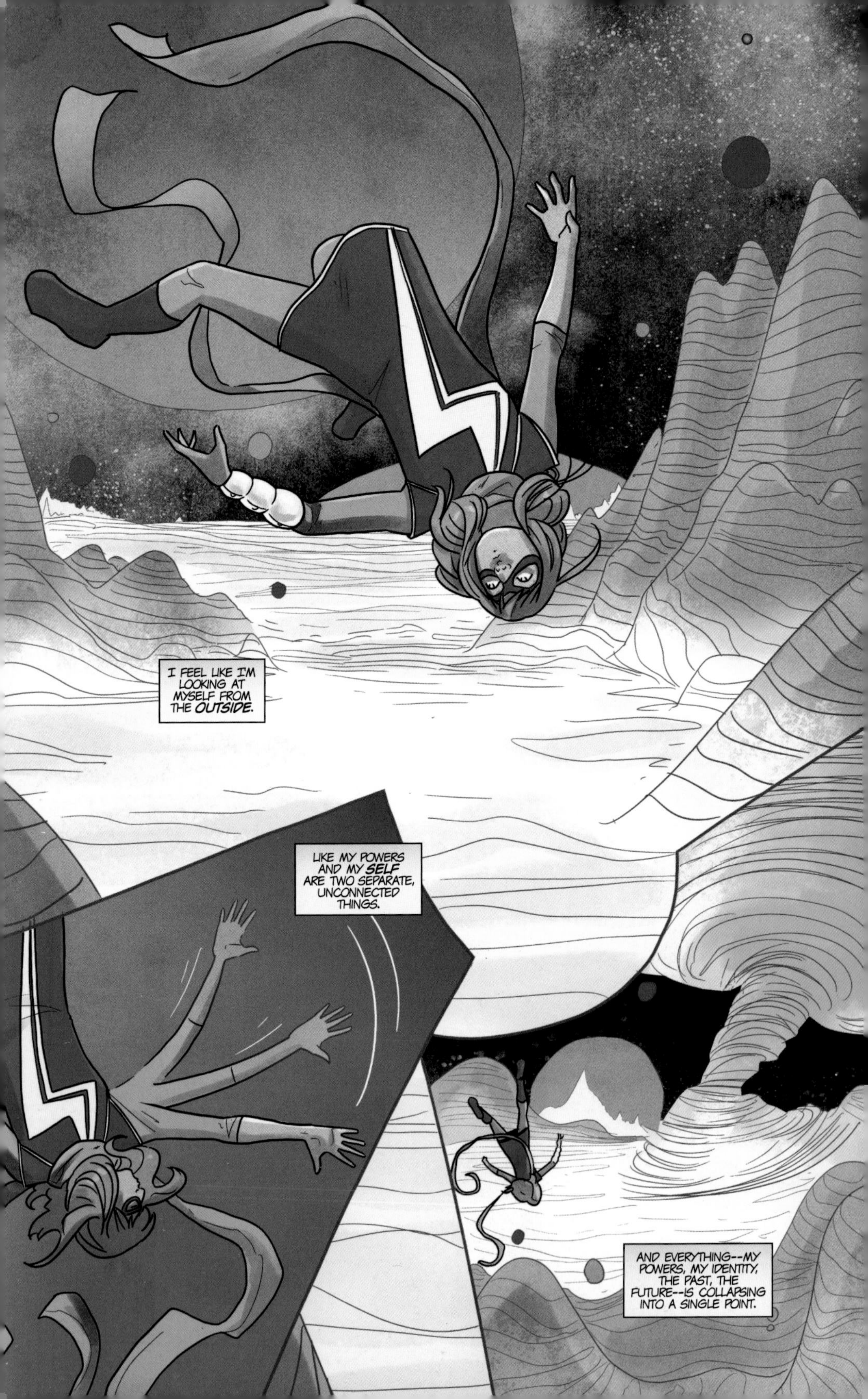
I FEEL LIKE I'M LOOKING AT MYSELF FROM THE OUTSIDE.
LIKE MY POWERS AND MY SELF ARE TWO SEPARATE, UNCONNECTED THINGS.
AND EVERYTHING--MY POWERS, MY IDENTITY, THE PAST, THE FUTURE--IS COLLAPSING INTO A SINGLE POINT.

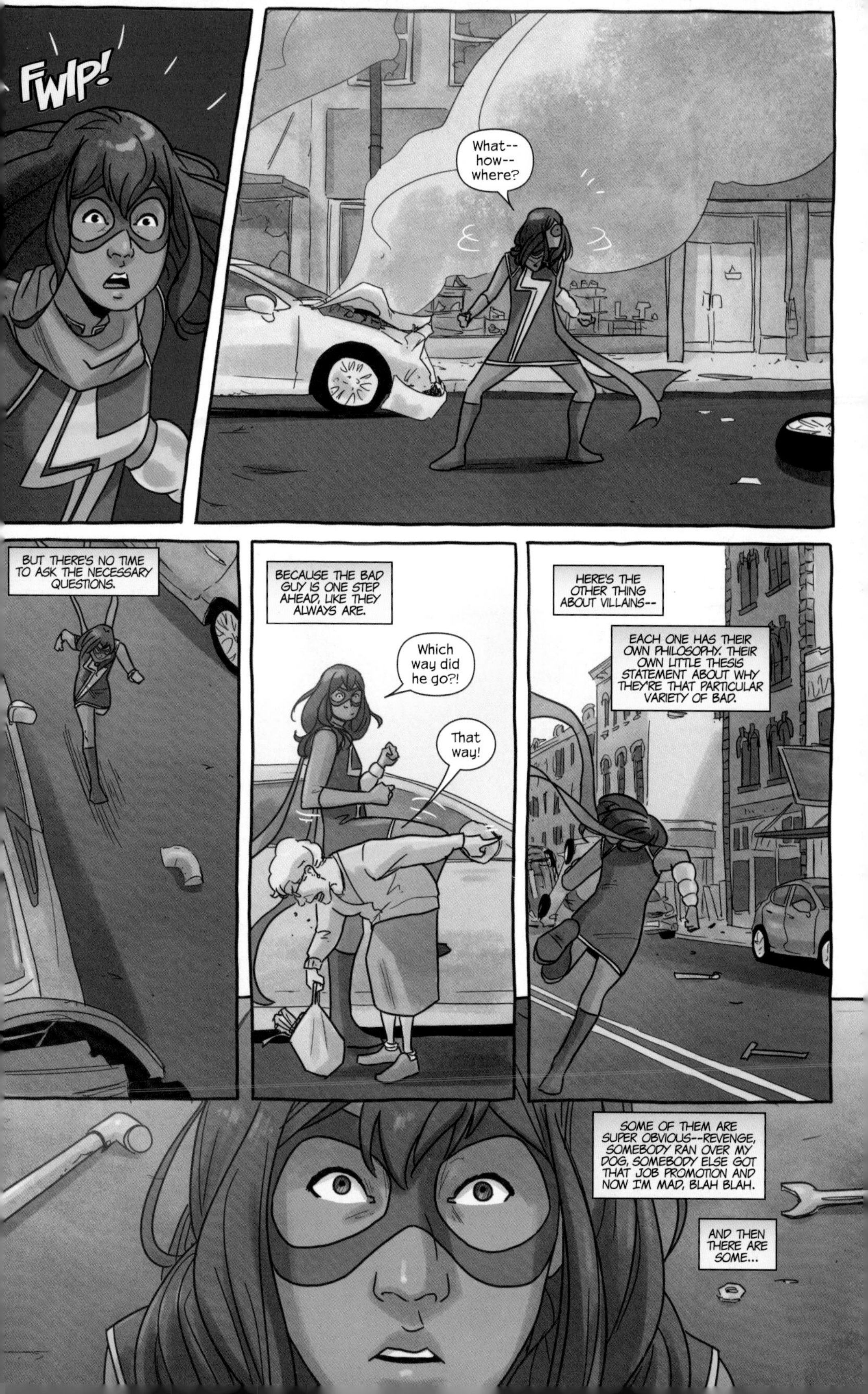
FWIP!
What-- how-- where?
BUT THERE'S NO TIME TO ASK THE NECESSARY QUESTIONS.
BECAUSE THE BAD GUY IS ONE STEP AHEAD, LIKE THEY ALWAYS ARE.
Which way did he go?!
That way!
HERE'S THE OTHER THING ABOUT VILLAINS--
EACH ONE HAS THEIR OWN PHILOSOPHY. THEIR OWN LITTLE THESIS STATEMENT ABOUT WHY THEY'RE THAT PARTICULAR VARIETY OF BAD.
SOME OF THEM ARE SUPER OBVIOUS--REVENGE, SOMEBODY RAN OVER MY DOG, SOMEBODY ELSE GOT THAT JOB PROMOTION AND NOW I'M MAD, BLAH BLAH.
AND THEN THERE ARE SOME...

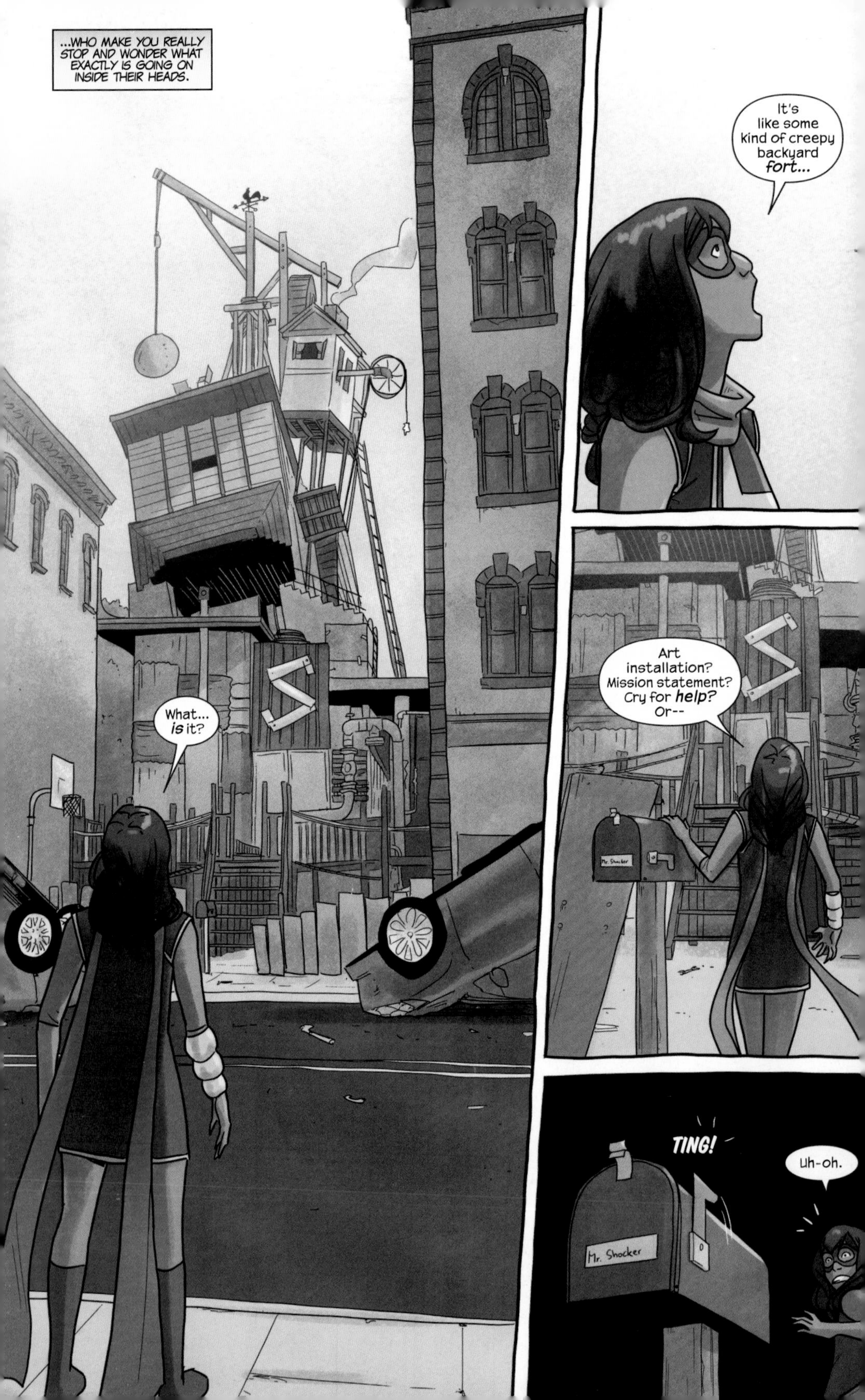
...WHO MAKE YOU REALLY STOP AND WONDER WHAT EXACTLY IS GOING ON INSIDE THEIR HEADS.
What... *is* it?
It's like some kind of creepy backyard *fort...*
Art installation? Mission statement? Cry for *help?* Or--
Mr. Shocker
TING!
Uh-oh.
Mr. Shocker

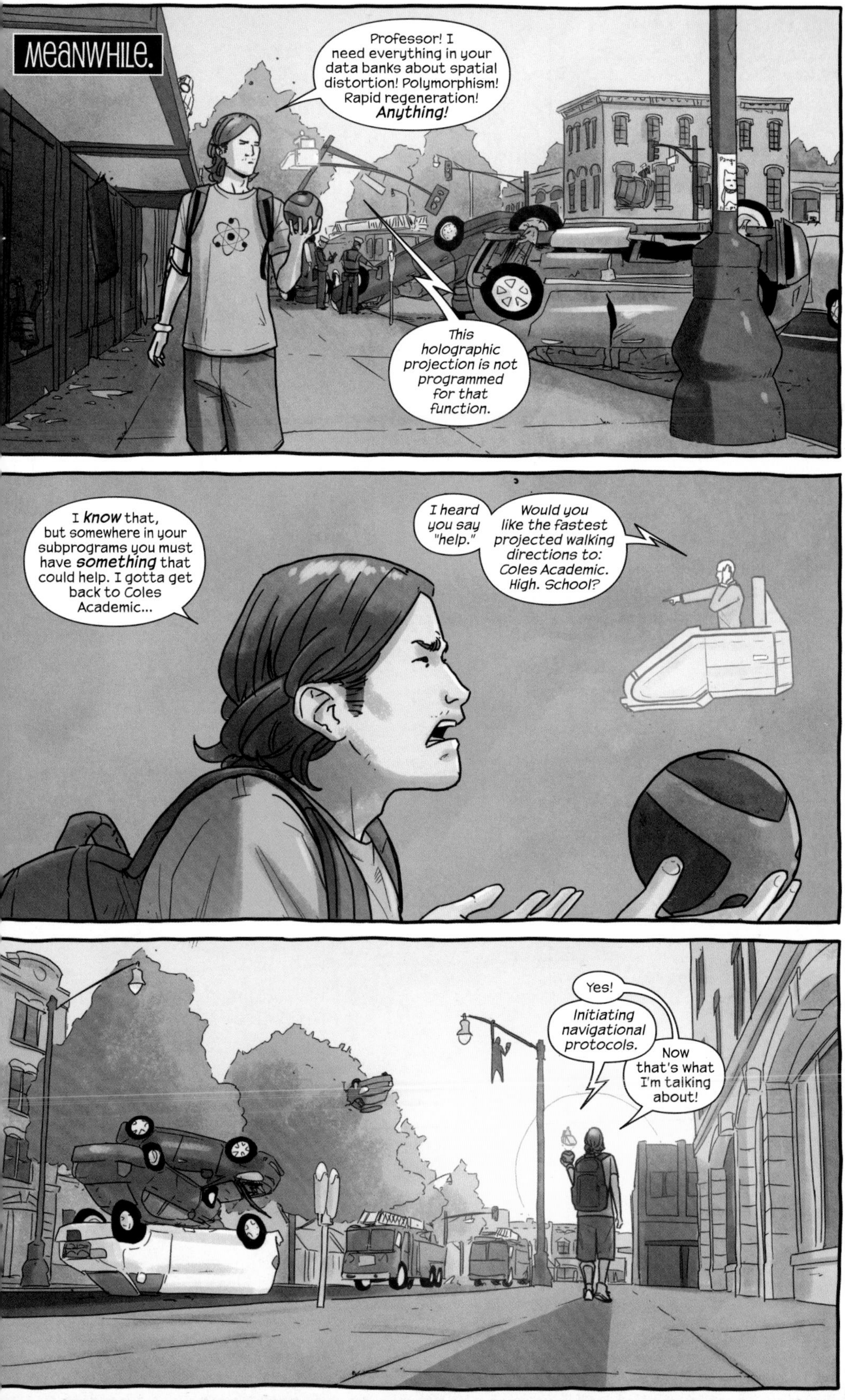
MEANWHILE.
Professor! I need everything in your data banks about spatial distortion! Polymorphism! Rapid regeneration! Anything!
This holographic projection is not programmed for that function.
I know that, but somewhere in your subprograms you must have something that could help. I gotta get back to Coles Academic...
I heard you say "help."
Would you like the fastest projected walking directions to: Coles Academic. High. School?
Yes!
Initiating navigational protocols.
Now that's what I'm talking about!

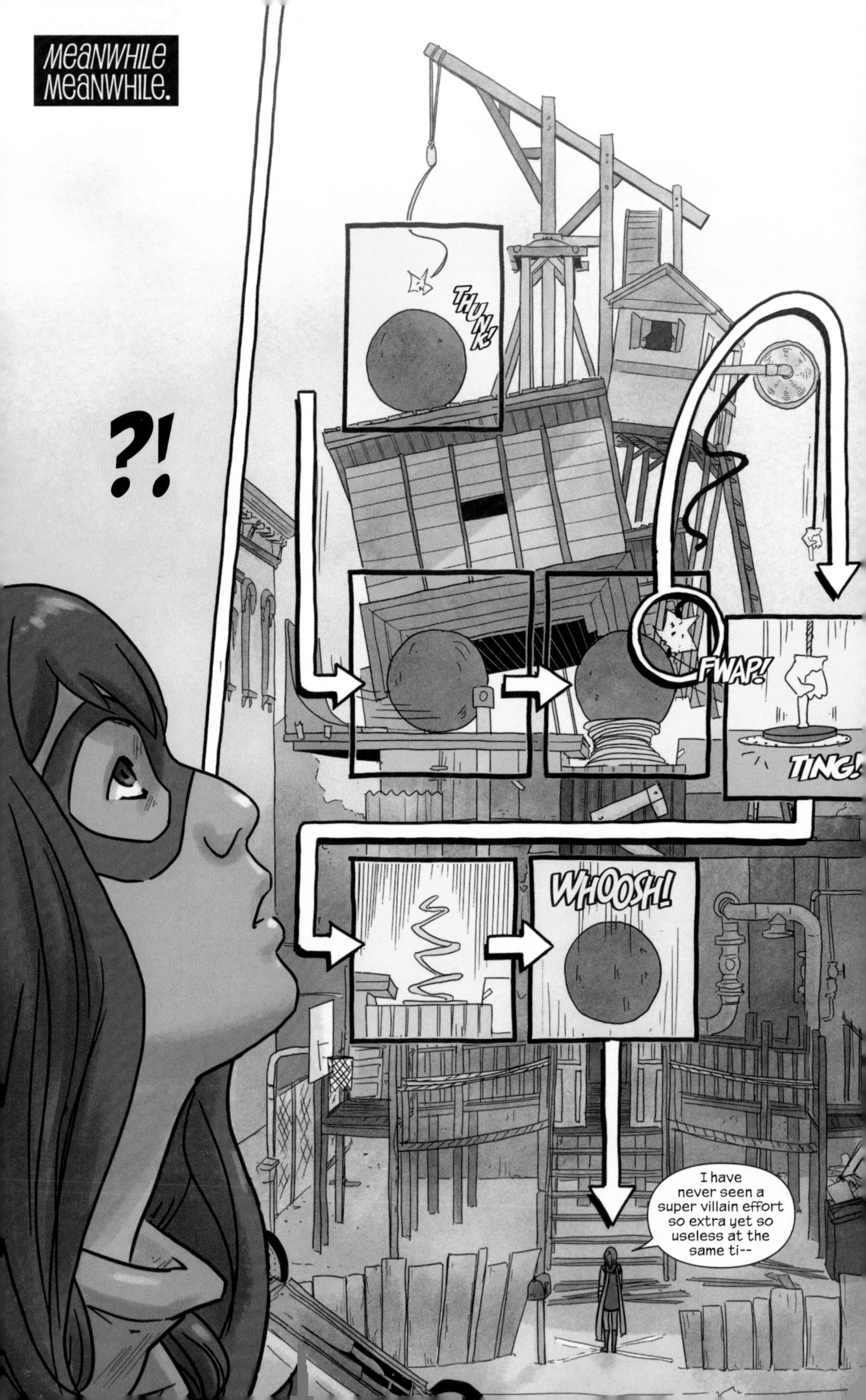
MEANWHILE MEANWHILE.
?!
THUNK!
FWAP!
TING!
WHOOSH!
I have never seen a super villain effort so extra yet so useless at the same ti--

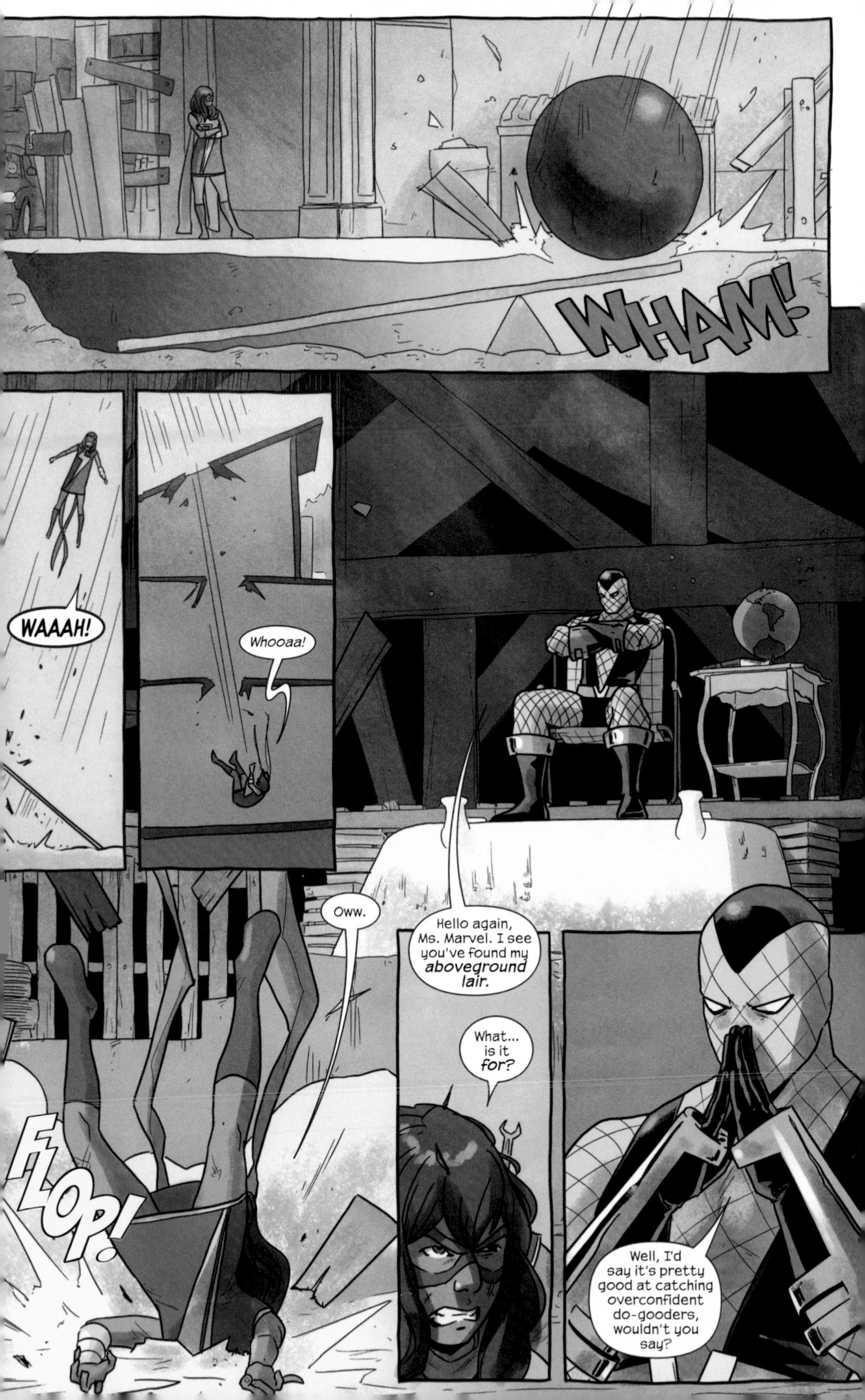
WHAM!
WAAAH!
Whooaa!
Oww.
Hello again, Ms. Marvel. I see you've found my *aboveground* *lair.*
FLOP!
What... is it *for?*
Well, I'd say it's pretty good at catching overconfident do-gooders, wouldn't you say?

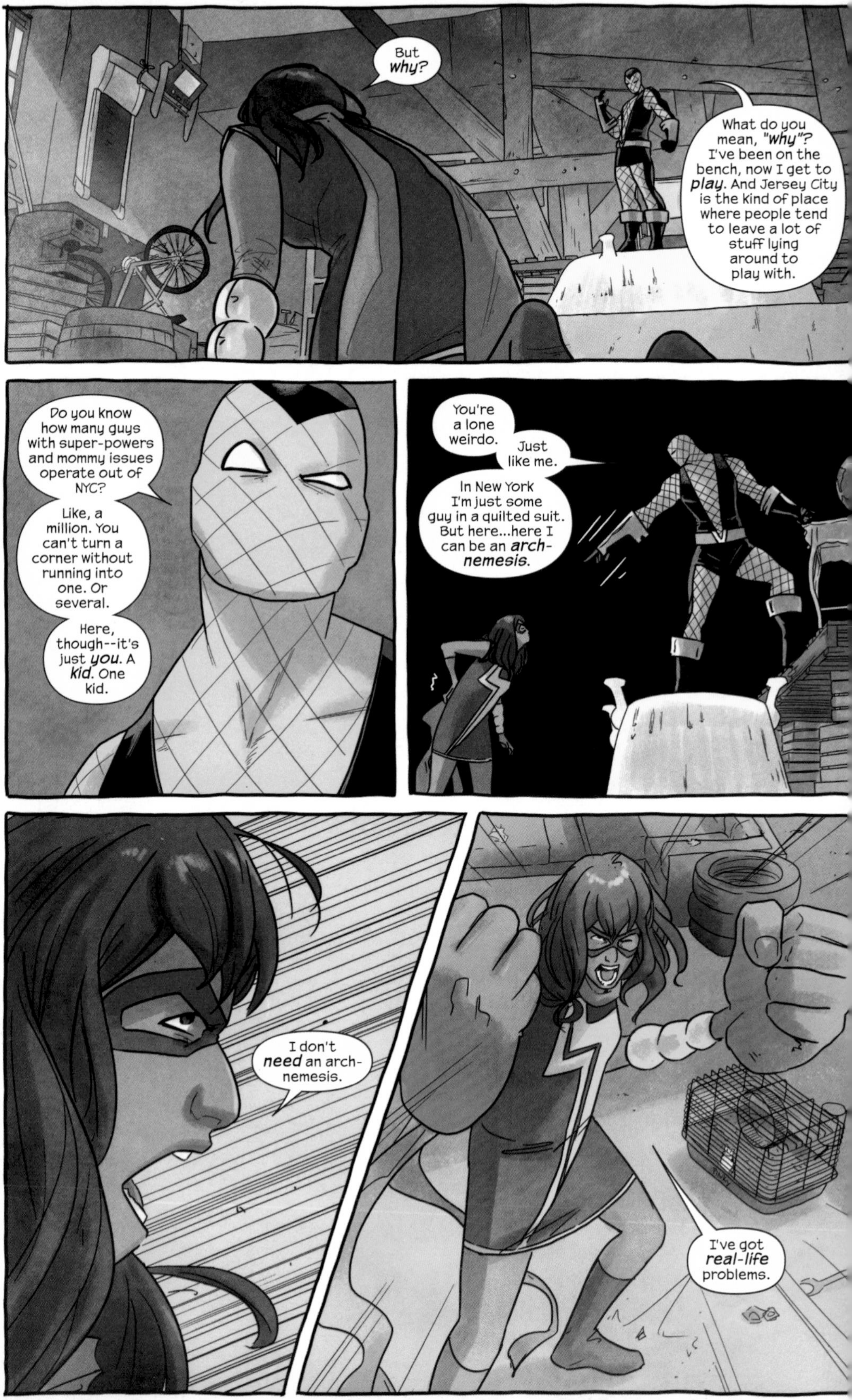

But why?
What do you mean, "why"? I've been on the bench, now I get to play. And Jersey City is the kind of place where people tend to leave a lot of stuff lying around to play with.
Do you know how many guys with super-powers and mommy issues operate out of NYC?
Like, a million. You can't turn a corner without running into one. Or several.
Here, though--it's just you. A kid. One kid.
You're a lone weirdo.
Just like me.
In New York I'm just some guy in a quilted suit. But here...here I can be an arch-nemesis.
I don't need an arch-nemesis.
I've got real-life problems.

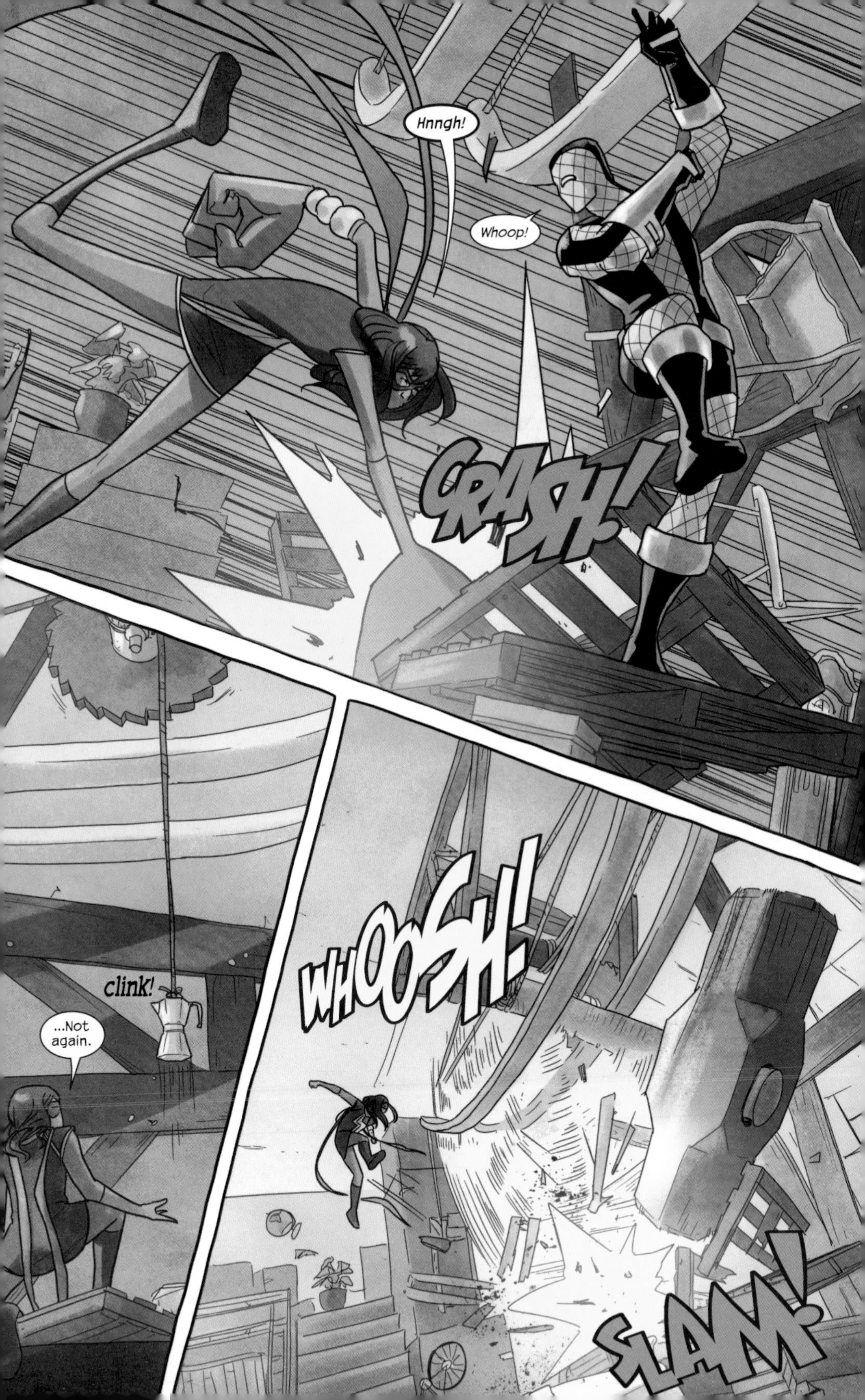
Hnngh!
Whoop!
CRASH!
clink!
...Not again.
WHOOSH!
SLAM!

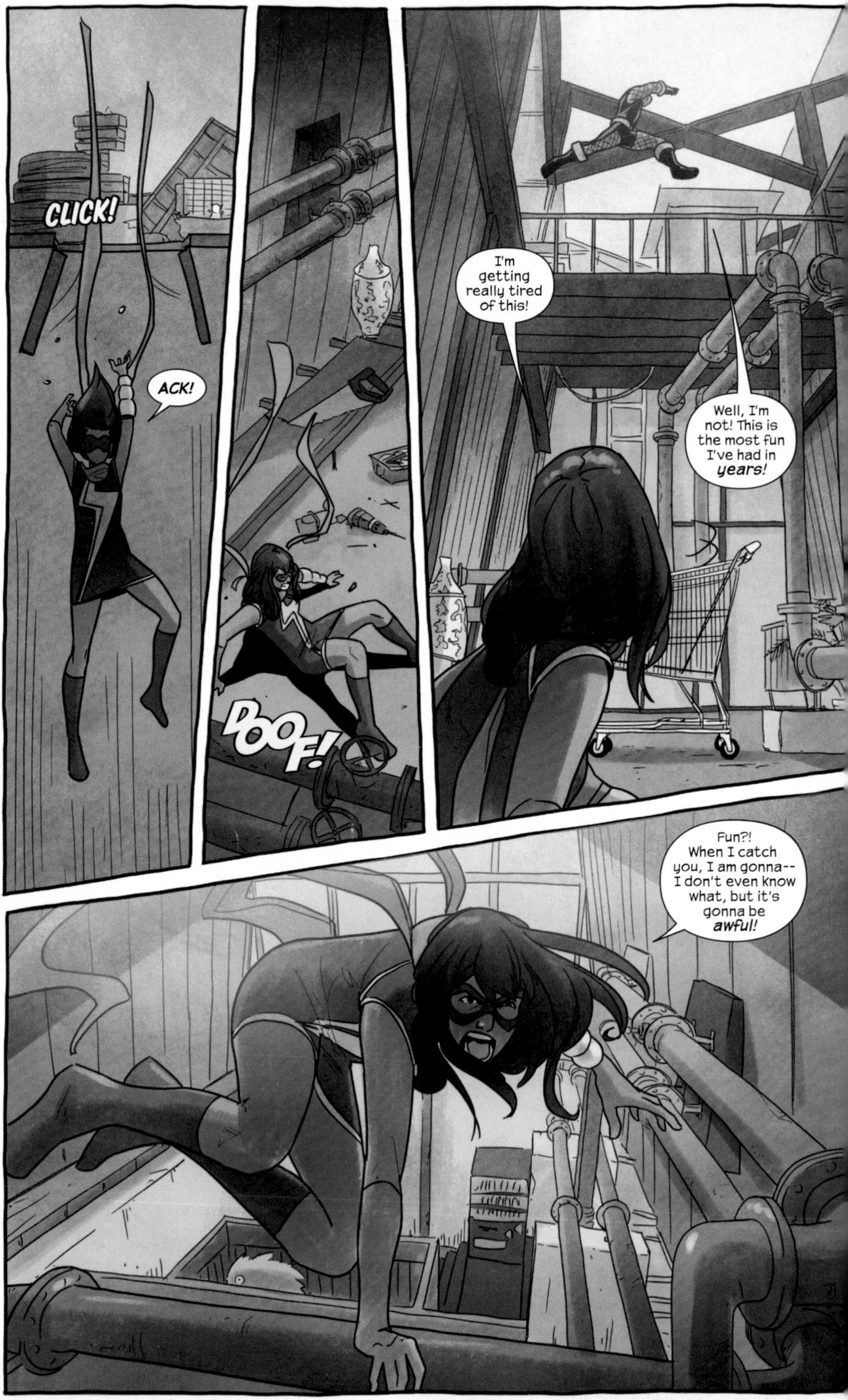
CLICK!
ACK!
DOOF!
I'm getting really tired of this!
Well, I'm not! This is the most fun I've had in *years!*
Fun?! When I catch you, I am gonna-- I don't even know what, but it's gonna be *awful!*

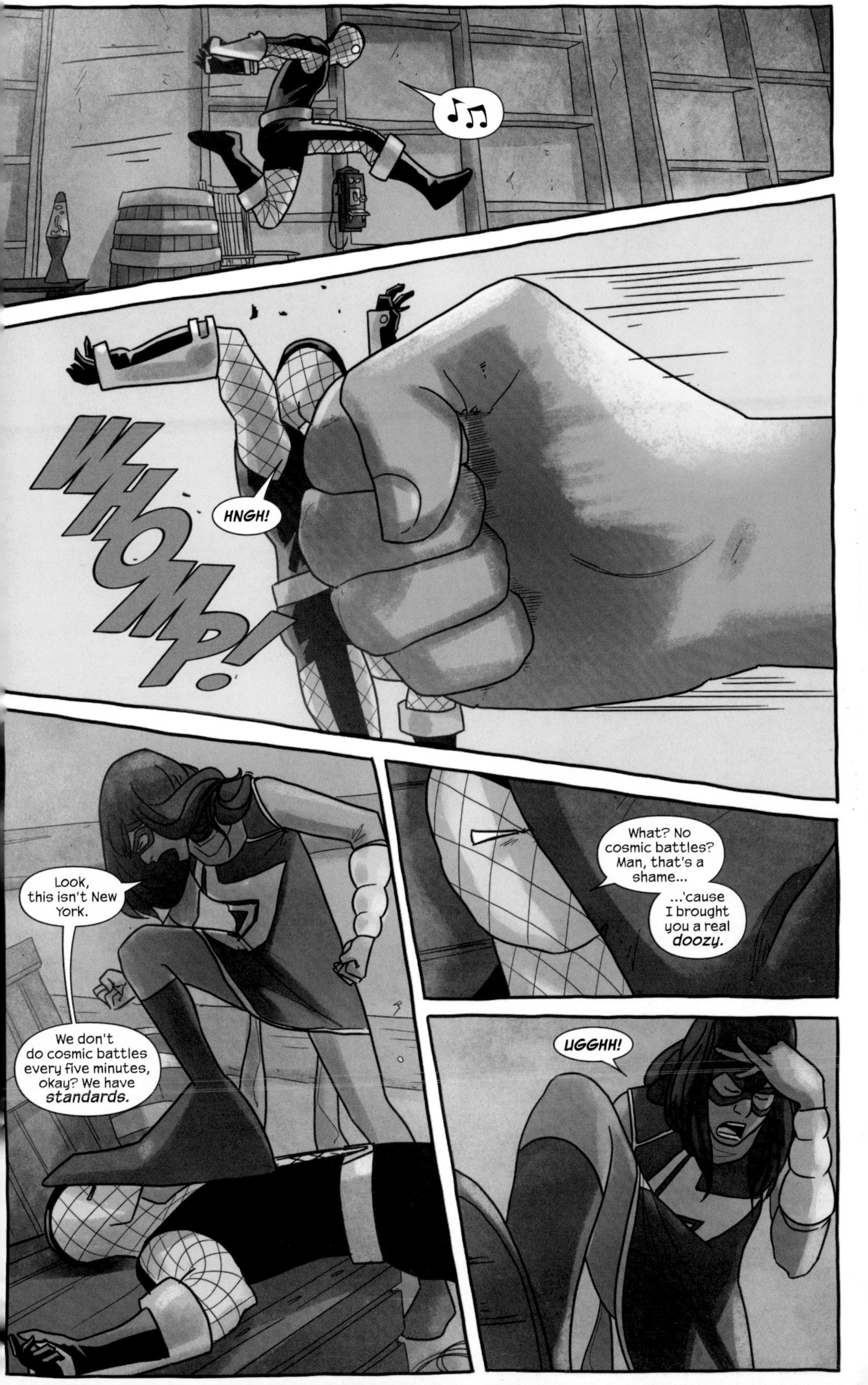
♪♫
WHOMP!
HNGH!
Look, this isn't New York.
We don't do cosmic battles every five minutes, okay? We have *standards*.
What? No cosmic battles? Man, that's a shame...
...'cause I brought you a real *doozy*.
UGGHH!

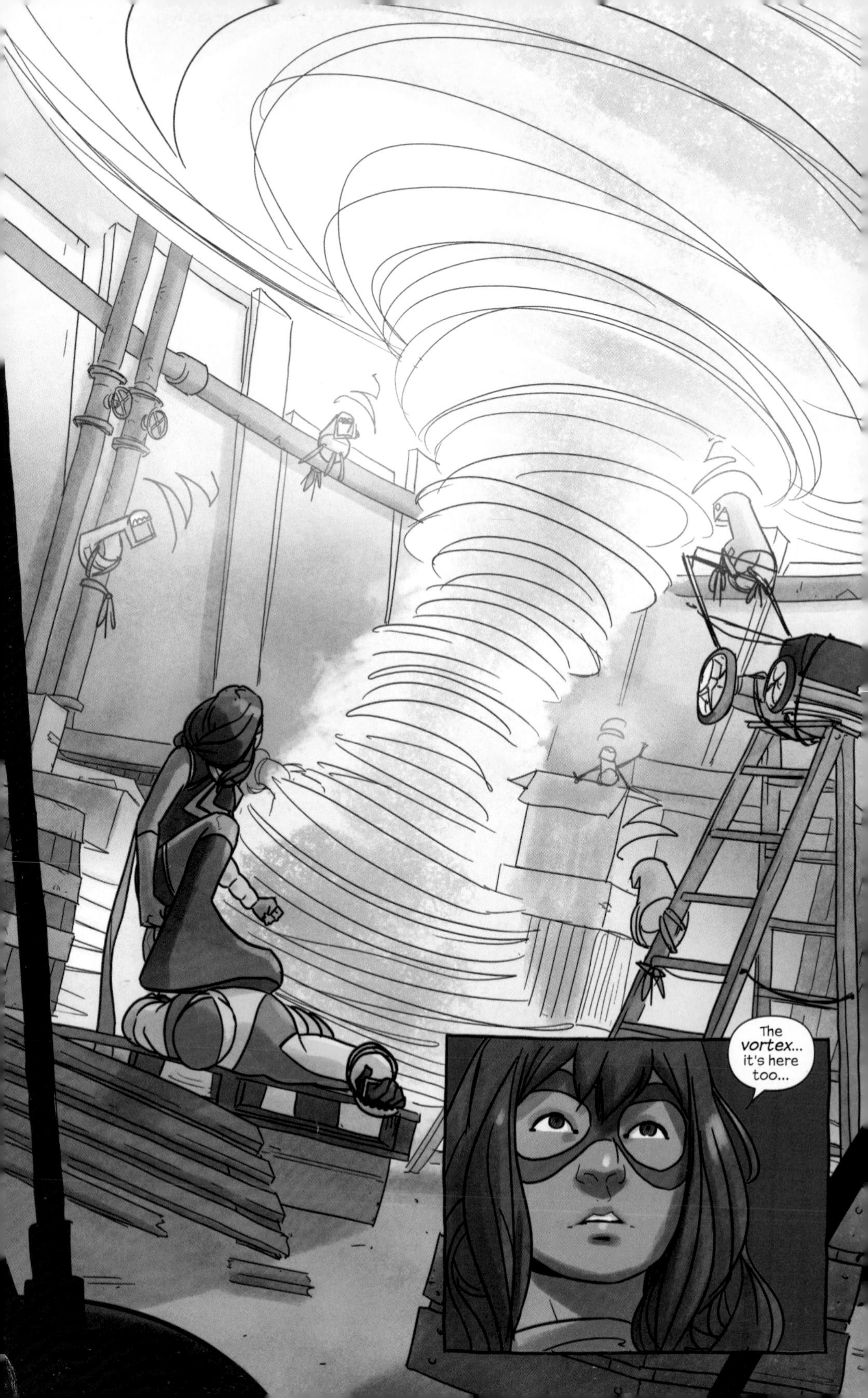
The *vortex*... it's here too...

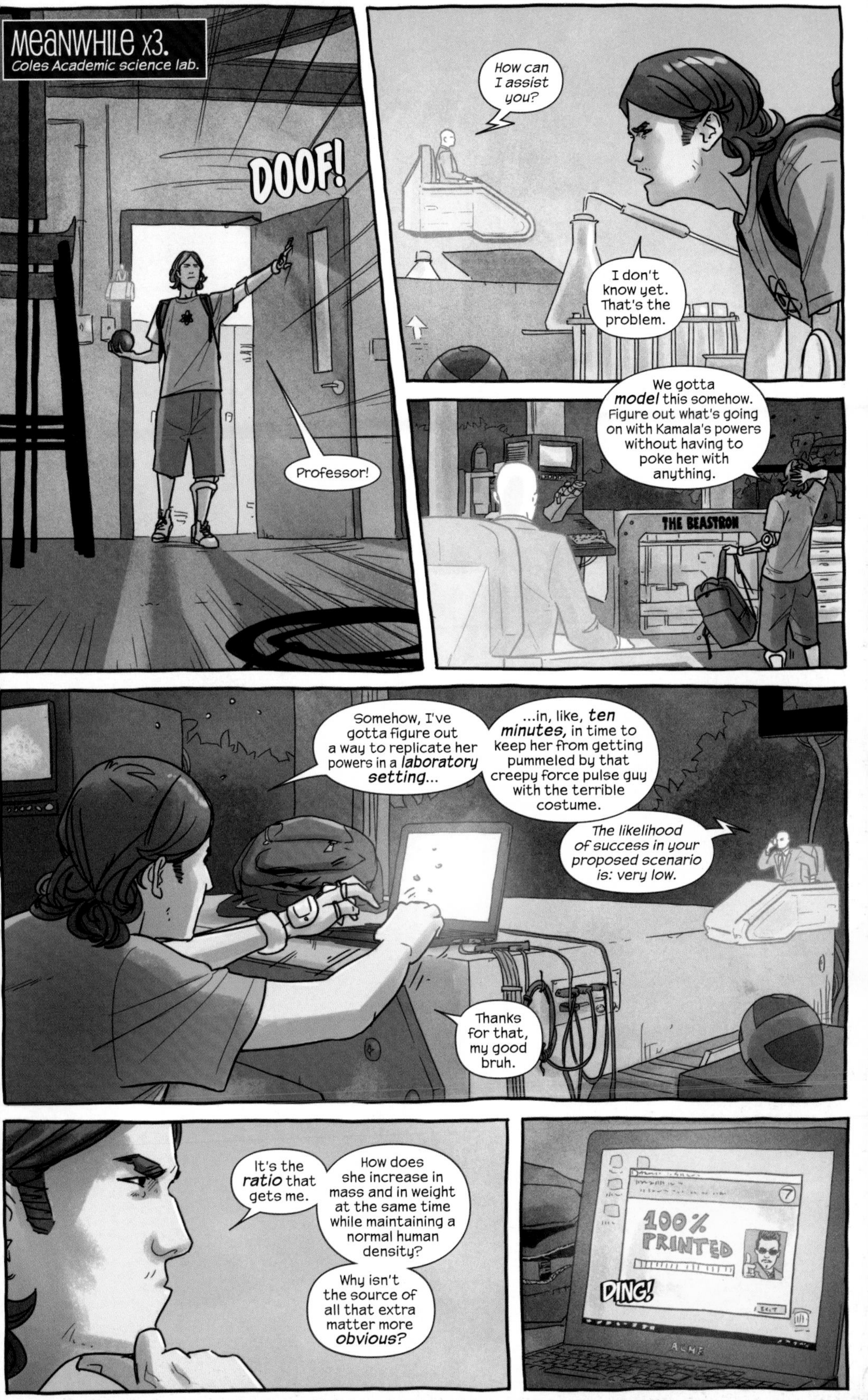
MEANWHILE x3.
Coles Academic science lab.
DOOF!
Professor!
How can I assist you?
I don't know yet. That's the problem.
We gotta model this somehow. Figure out what's going on with Kamala's powers without having to poke her with anything.
THE BEASTRON
Somehow, I've gotta figure out a way to replicate her powers in a laboratory setting...
...in, like, ten minutes, in time to keep her from getting pummeled by that creepy force pulse guy with the terrible costume.
The likelihood of success in your proposed scenario is: very low.
Thanks for that, my good bruh.
It's the ratio that gets me.
How does she increase in mass and in weight at the same time while maintaining a normal human density?
Why isn't the source of all that extra matter more obvious?
100% PRINTED
DING!

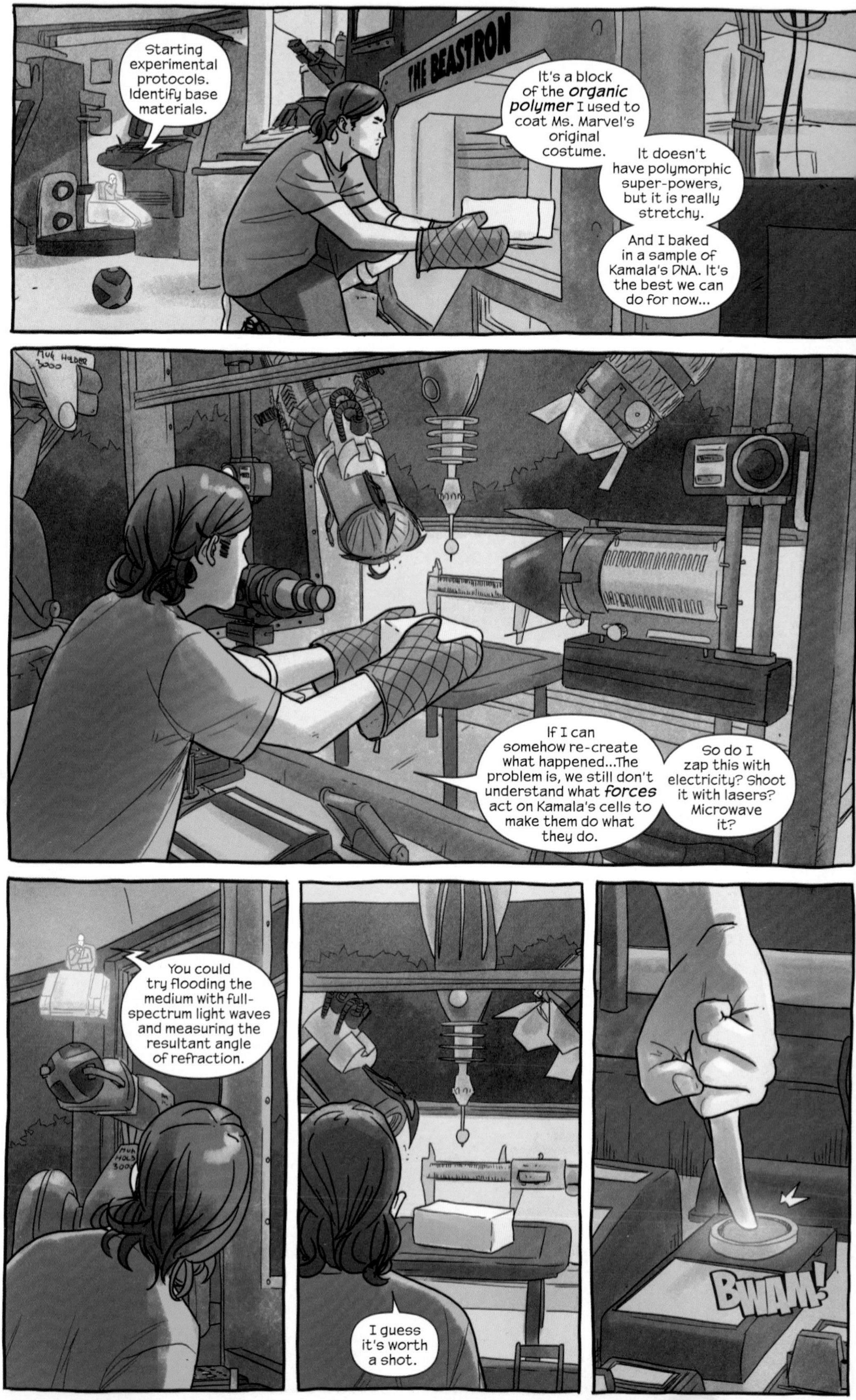

THE BEASTRON
Starting experimental protocols. Identify base materials.
It's a block of the *organic polymer* I used to coat Ms. Marvel's original costume.
It doesn't have polymorphic super-powers, but it is really stretchy.
And I baked in a sample of Kamala's DNA. It's the best we can do for now...
MUG HOLDER 3000
If I can somehow re-create what happened...The problem is, we still don't understand what *forces* act on Kamala's cells to make them do what they do.
So do I zap this with electricity? Shoot it with lasers? Microwave it?
You could try flooding the medium with full-spectrum light waves and measuring the resultant angle of refraction.
I guess it's worth a shot.
BWAM!

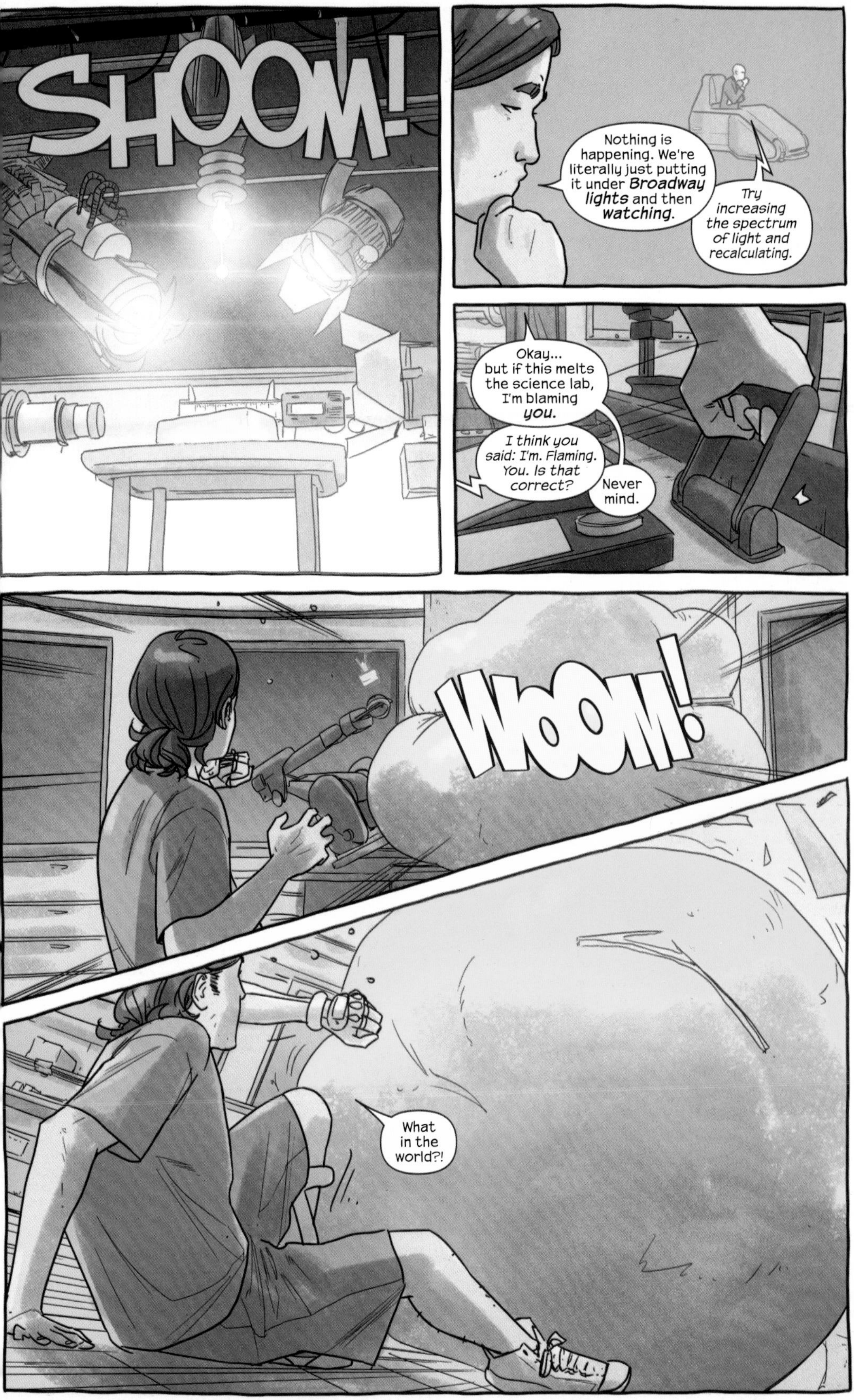
SHOOM!
Nothing is happening. We're literally just putting it under Broadway lights and then watching.
Try increasing the spectrum of light and recalculating.
Okay... but if this melts the science lab, I'm blaming you.
I think you said: I'm. Flaming. You. Is that correct?
Never mind.
WOOM!
What in the world?!

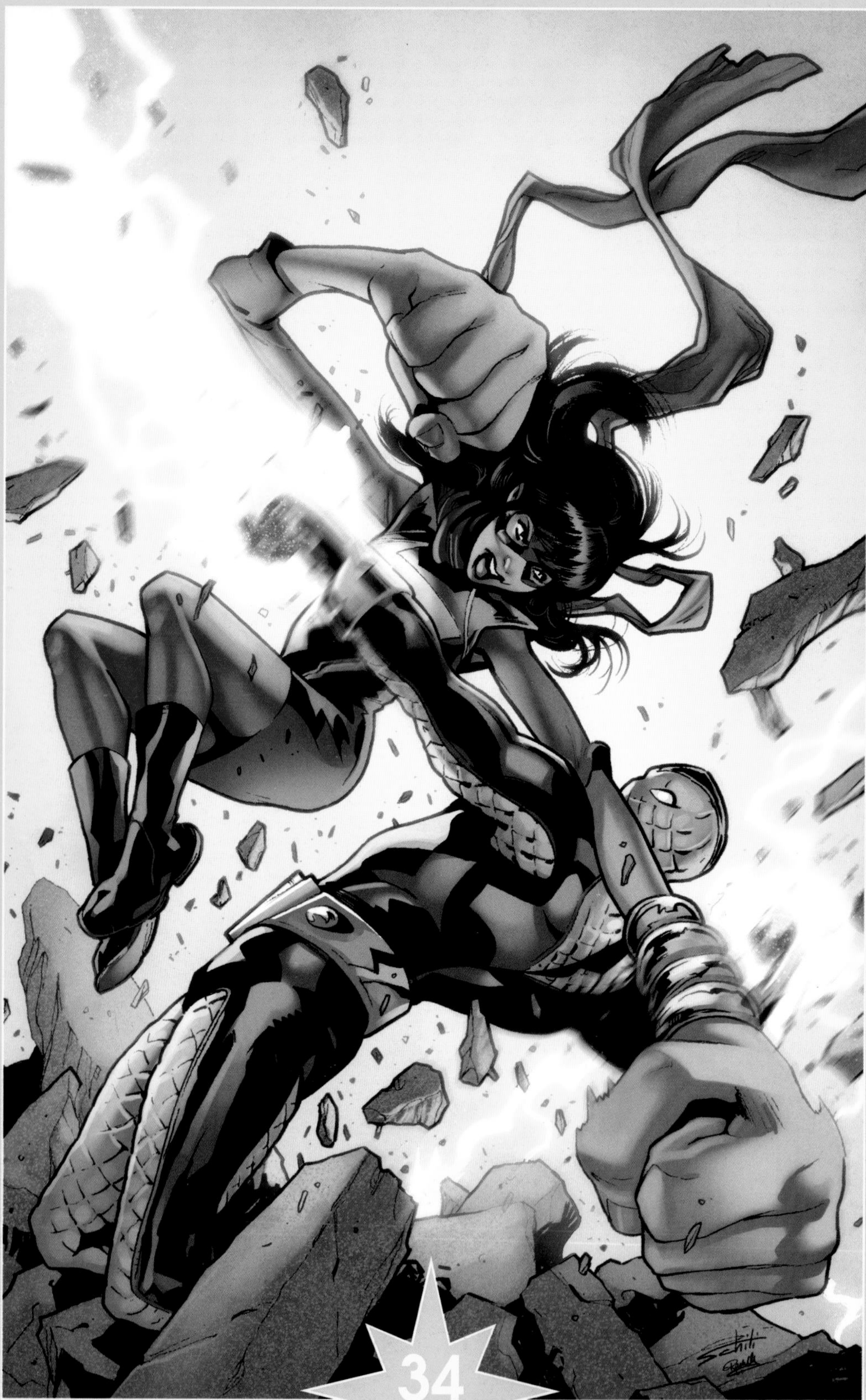
34

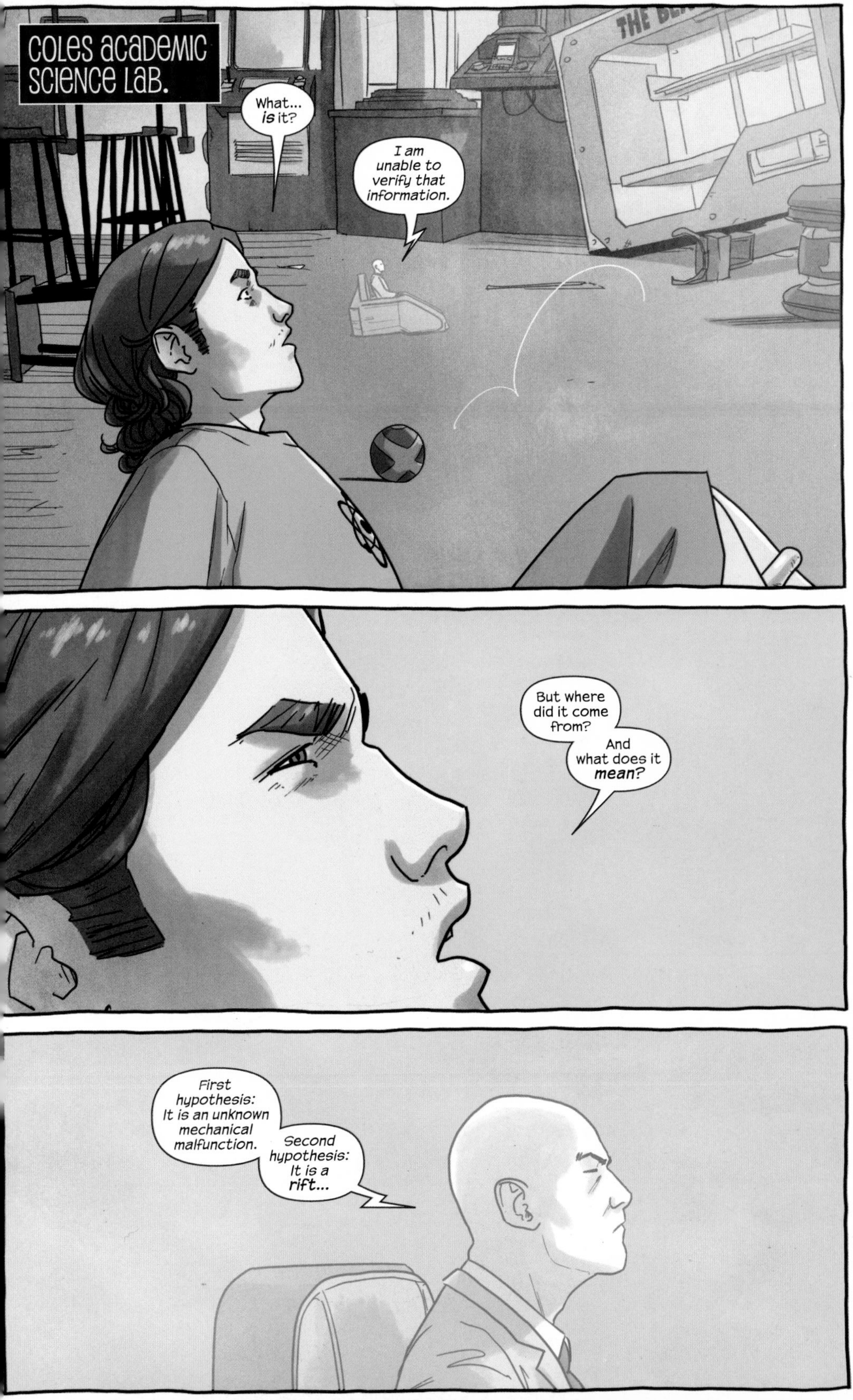
COLES ACADEMIC SCIENCE LAB.
What... *is* it?
I am unable to verify that information.
But where did it come from?
And what does it *mean*?
First hypothesis: It is an unknown mechanical malfunction.
Second hypothesis: It is a *rift*...

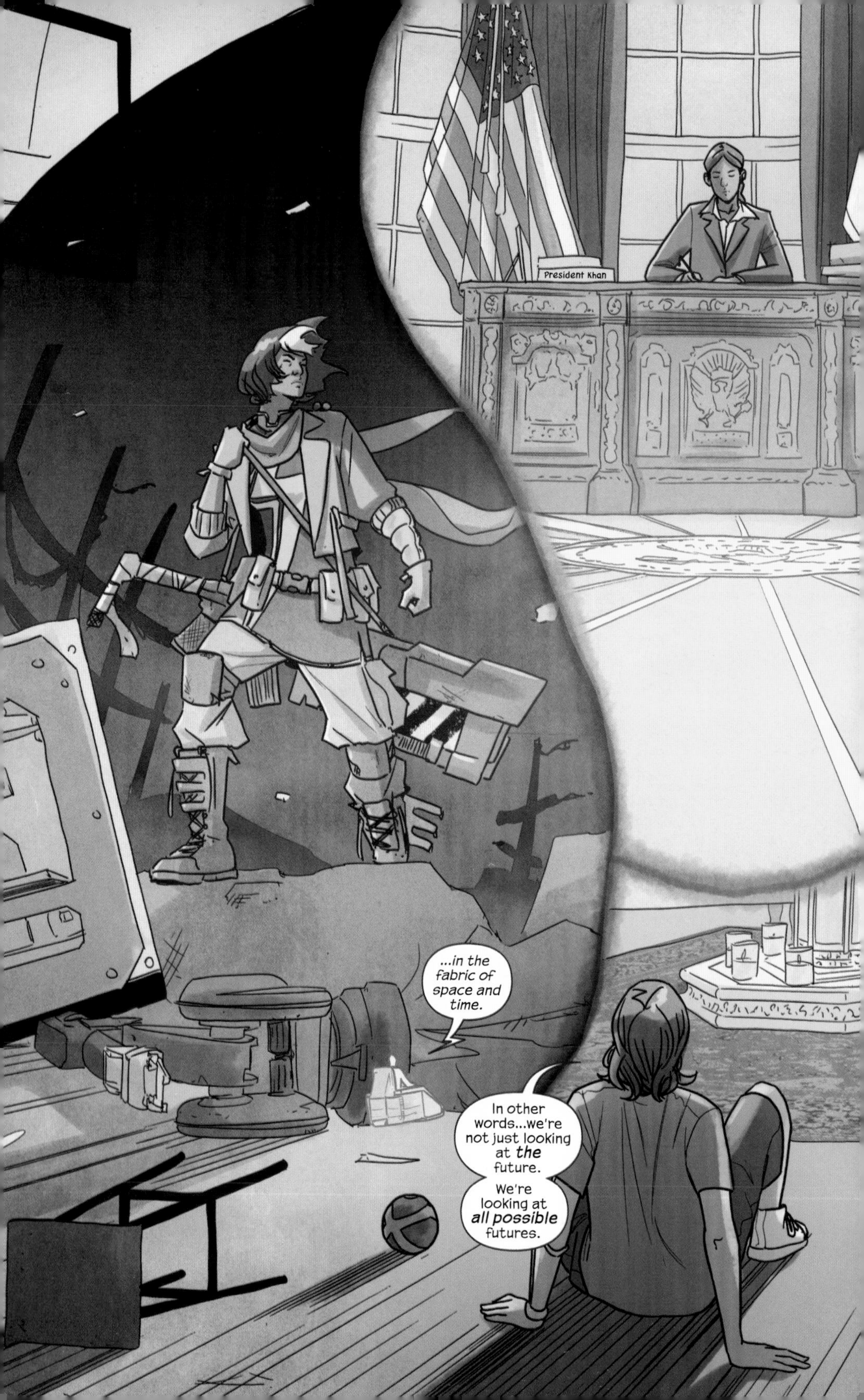
President Khan
...in the fabric of space and time.
In other words...we're not just looking at *the* future.
We're looking at ***all possible*** futures.

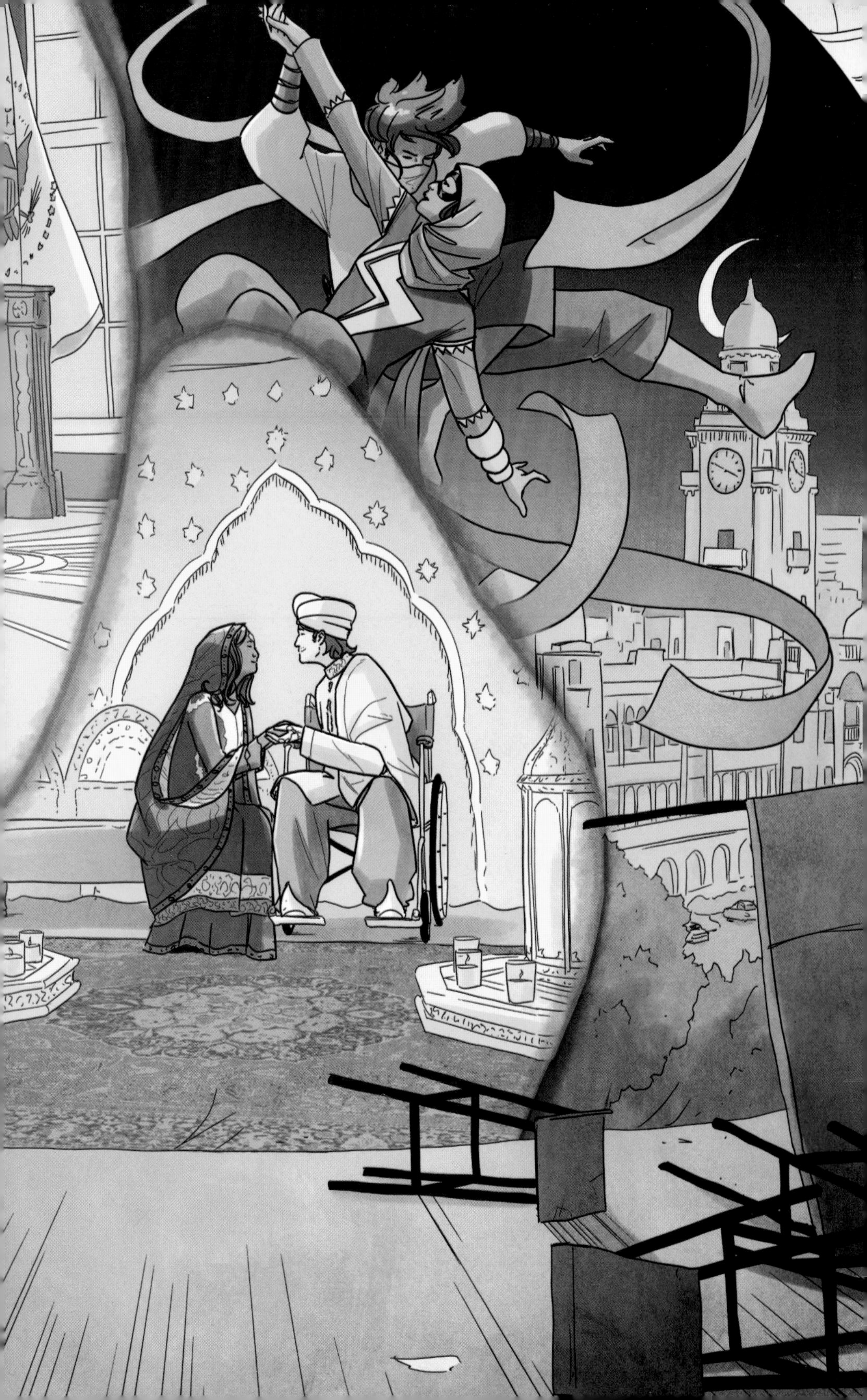

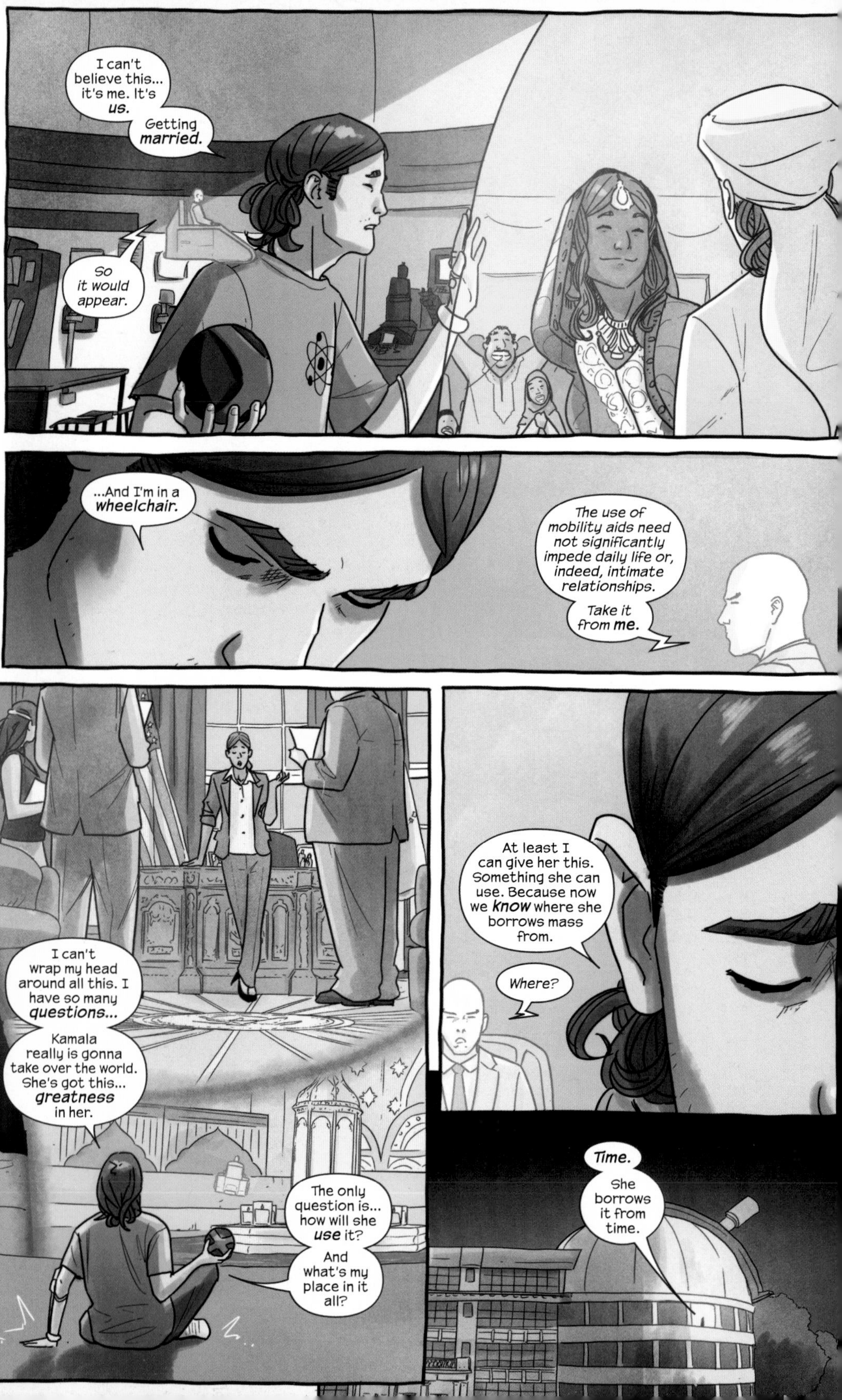
I can't believe this... it's me. It's us.
Getting married.
So it would appear.
...And I'm in a wheelchair.
The use of mobility aids need not significantly impede daily life or, indeed, intimate relationships.
Take it from me.
I can't wrap my head around all this. I have so many questions...
Kamala really is gonna take over the world. She's got this... greatness in her.
The only question is... how will she use it?
And what's my place in it all?
At least I can give her this. Something she can use. Because now we know where she borrows mass from.
Where?
Time.
She borrows it from time.

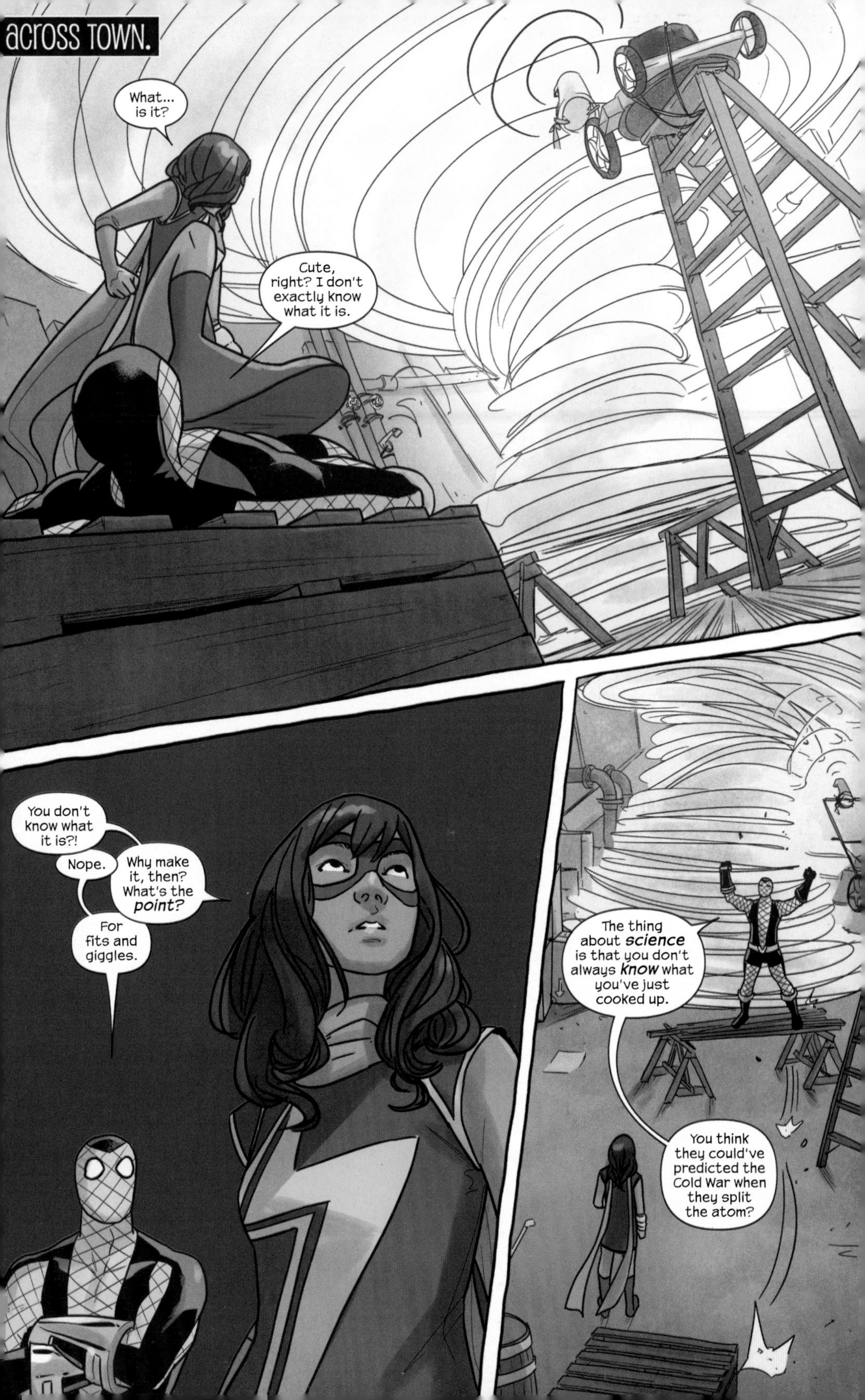
across TOWN.
What... is it?
Cute, right? I don't exactly know what it is.
You don't know what it is?!
Nope.
Why make it, then? What's the *point?*
For fits and giggles.
The thing about *science* is that you don't always *know* what you've just cooked up.
You think they could've predicted the Cold War when they split the atom?

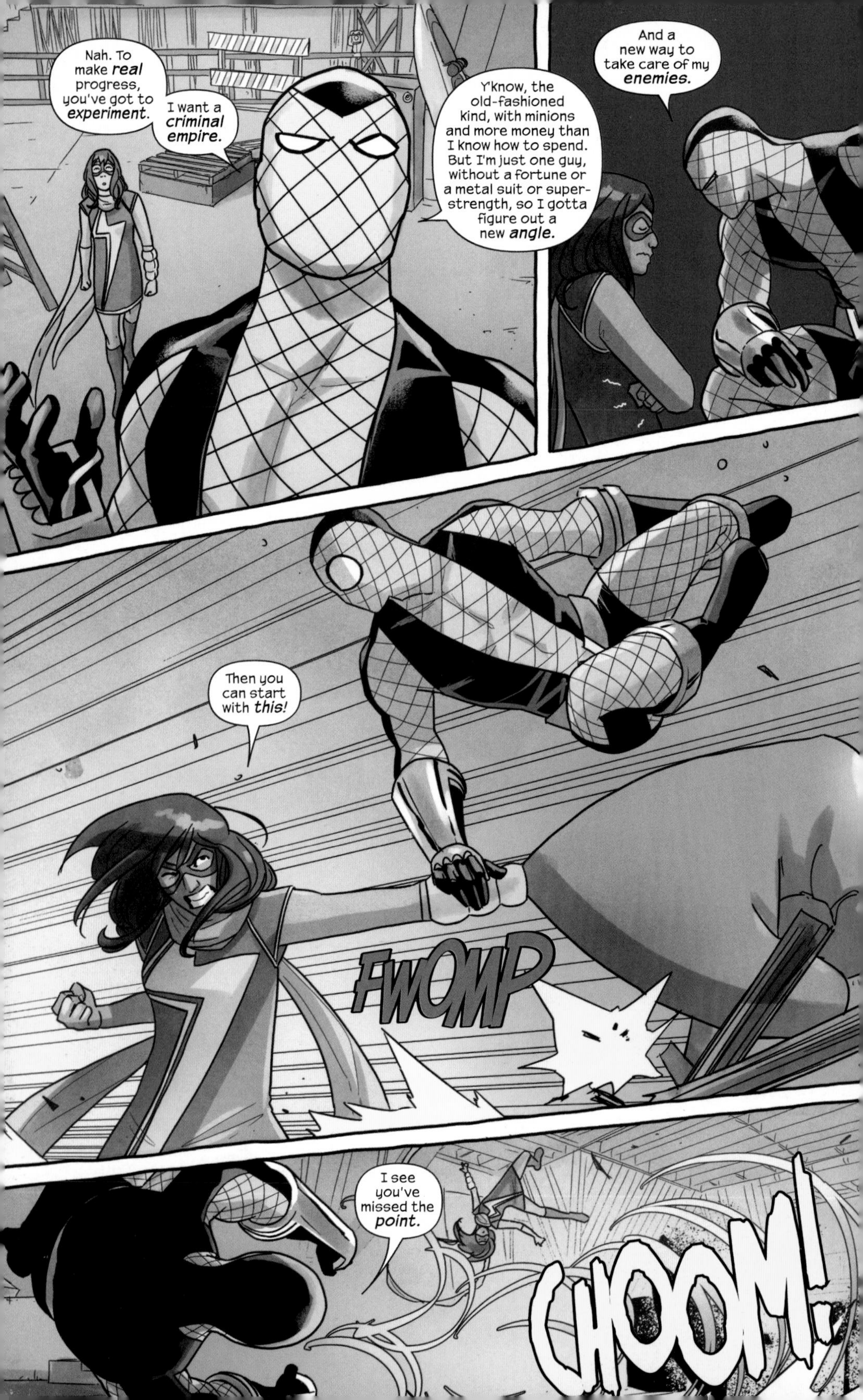
Nah. To make real progress, you've got to experiment.
I want a criminal empire.
Y'know, the old-fashioned kind, with minions and more money than I know how to spend. But I'm just one guy, without a fortune or a metal suit or super-strength, so I gotta figure out a new angle.
And a new way to take care of my enemies.
Then you can start with this!
FWOMP
I see you've missed the point.
CHOOM!

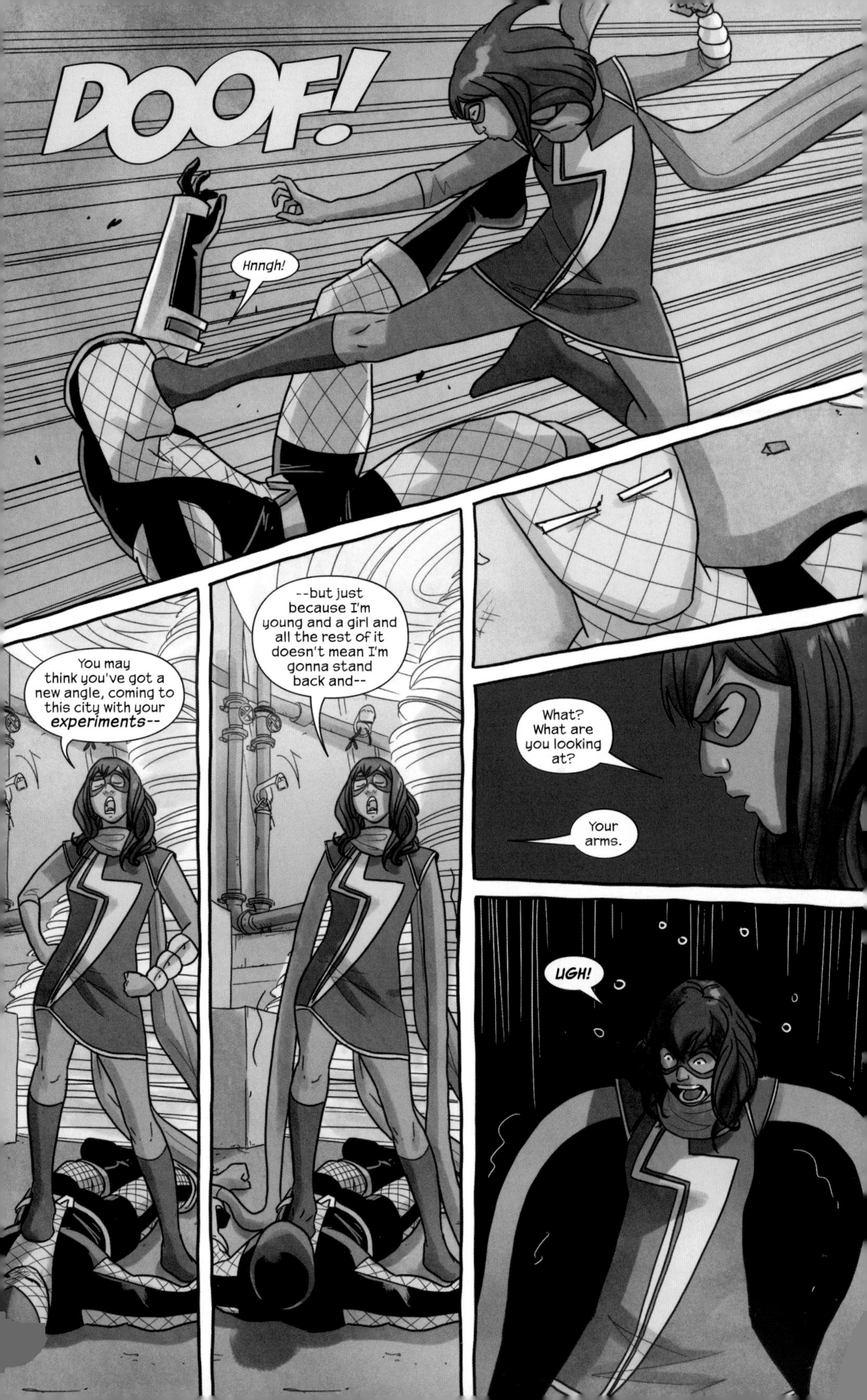
DOOF!
Hnngh!
You may think you've got a new angle, coming to this city with your *experiments*--
--but just because I'm young and a girl and all the rest of it doesn't mean I'm gonna stand back and--
What? What are you looking at?
Your arms.
UGH!

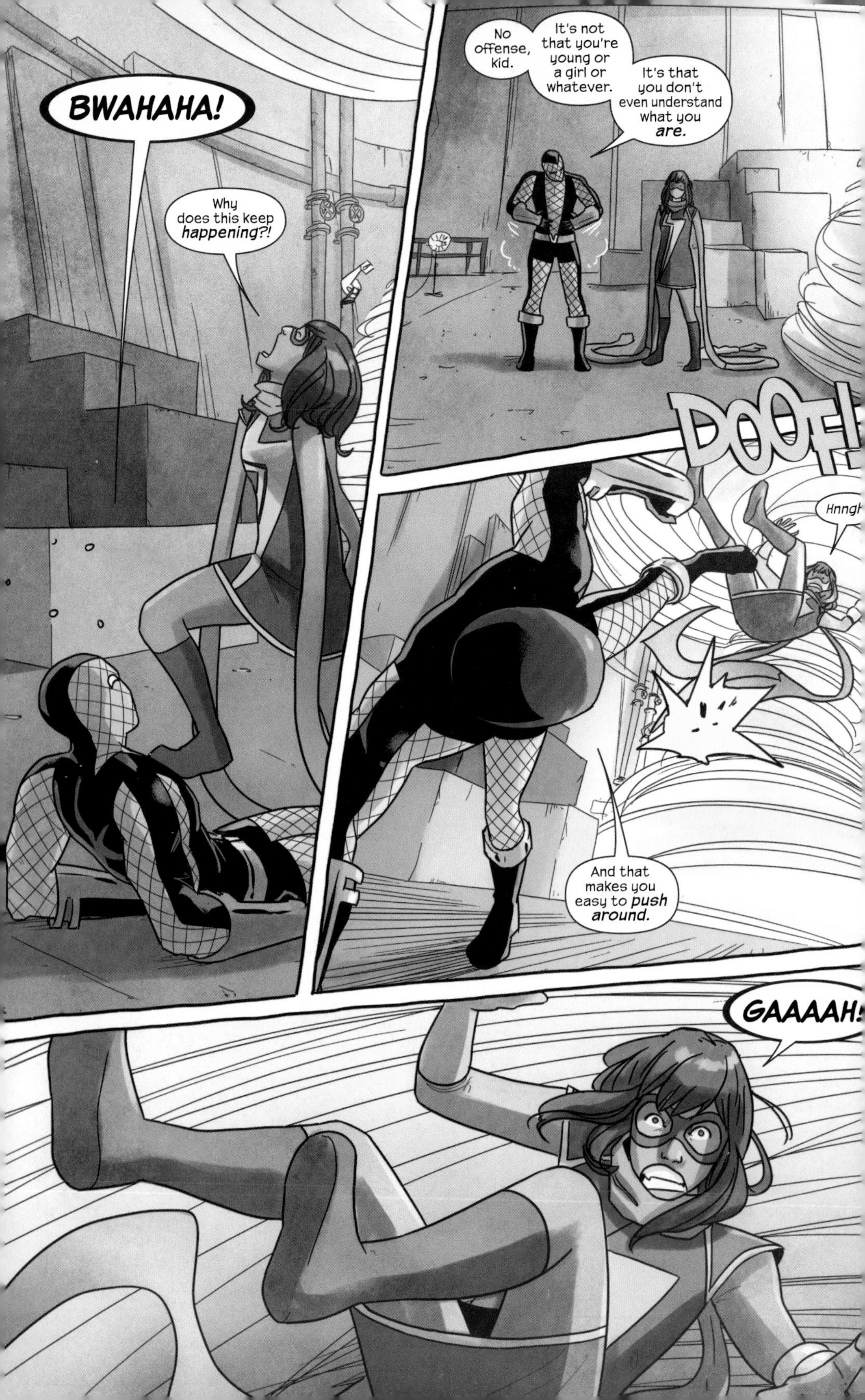
BWAHAHA!
Why does this keep *happening*?!
No offense, kid.
It's not that you're young or a girl or whatever.
It's that you don't even understand what you *are*.
DOOF!
Hnngh
And that makes you easy to *push around*.
GAAAAH!

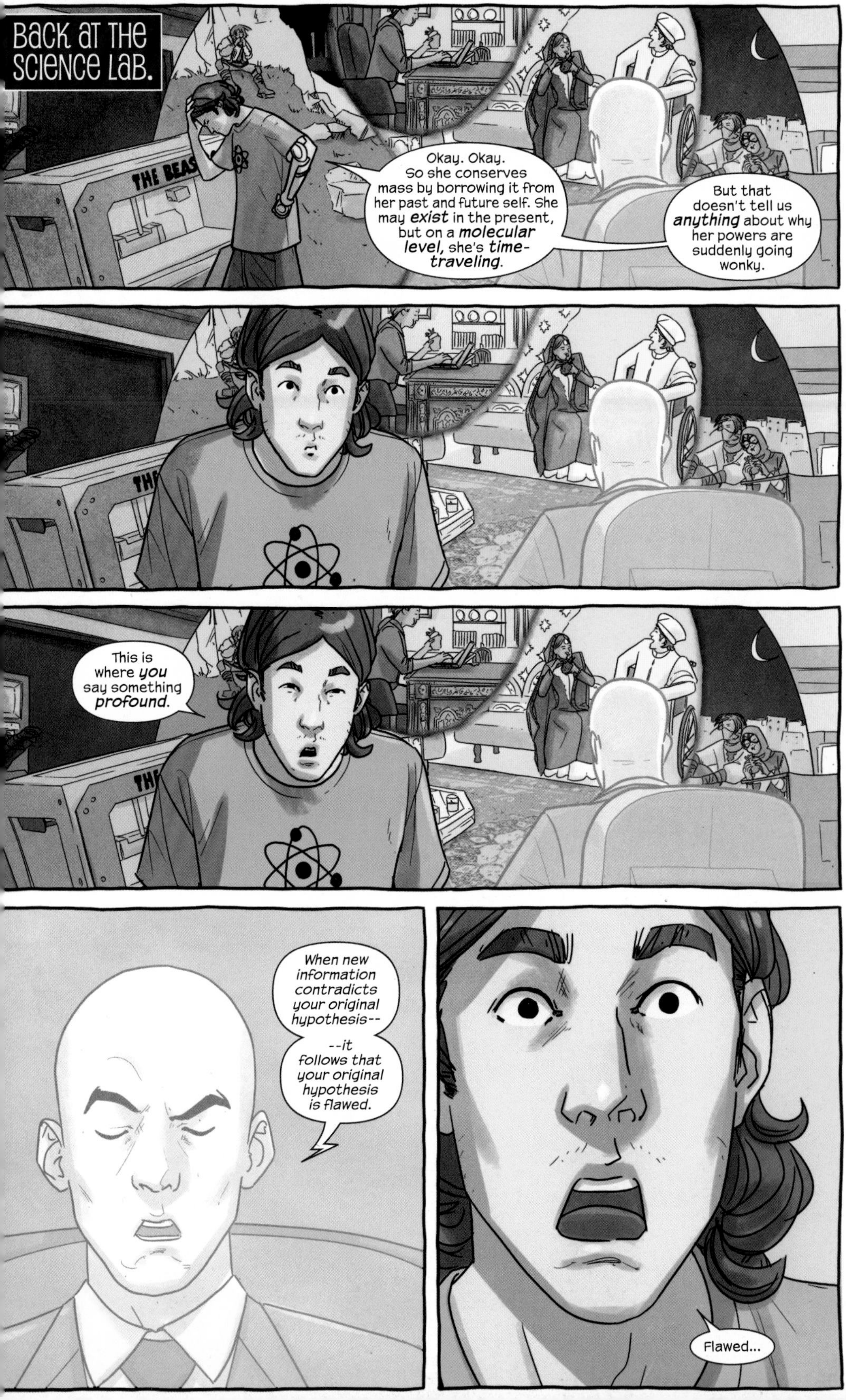
Back at the science lab.
Okay. Okay. So she conserves mass by borrowing it from her past and future self. She may exist in the present, but on a molecular level, she's time-traveling.
But that doesn't tell us anything about why her powers are suddenly going wonky.
THE BEAS
This is where you say something profound.
When new information contradicts your original hypothesis--
--it follows that your original hypothesis is flawed.
Flawed...

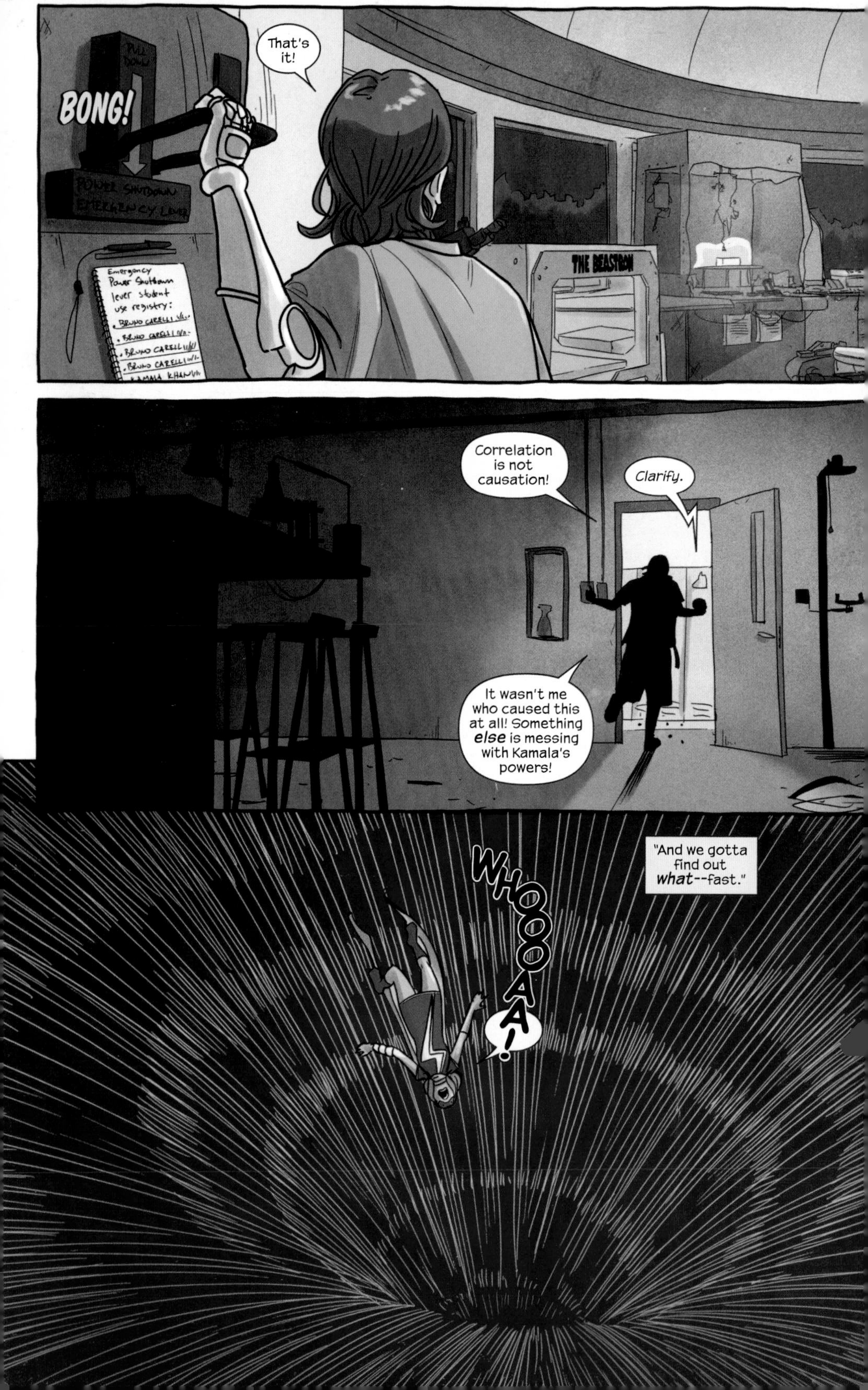
PULL DOWN
BONG!
POWER SHUTDOWN EMERGENCY LEVER
Emergency Power Shutdown lever student use registry:
That's it!
THE BEASTRON
Correlation is not causation!
Clarify.
It wasn't me who caused this at all! Something *else* is messing with Kamala's powers!
"And we gotta find out *what*--fast."
WHOOOAA!

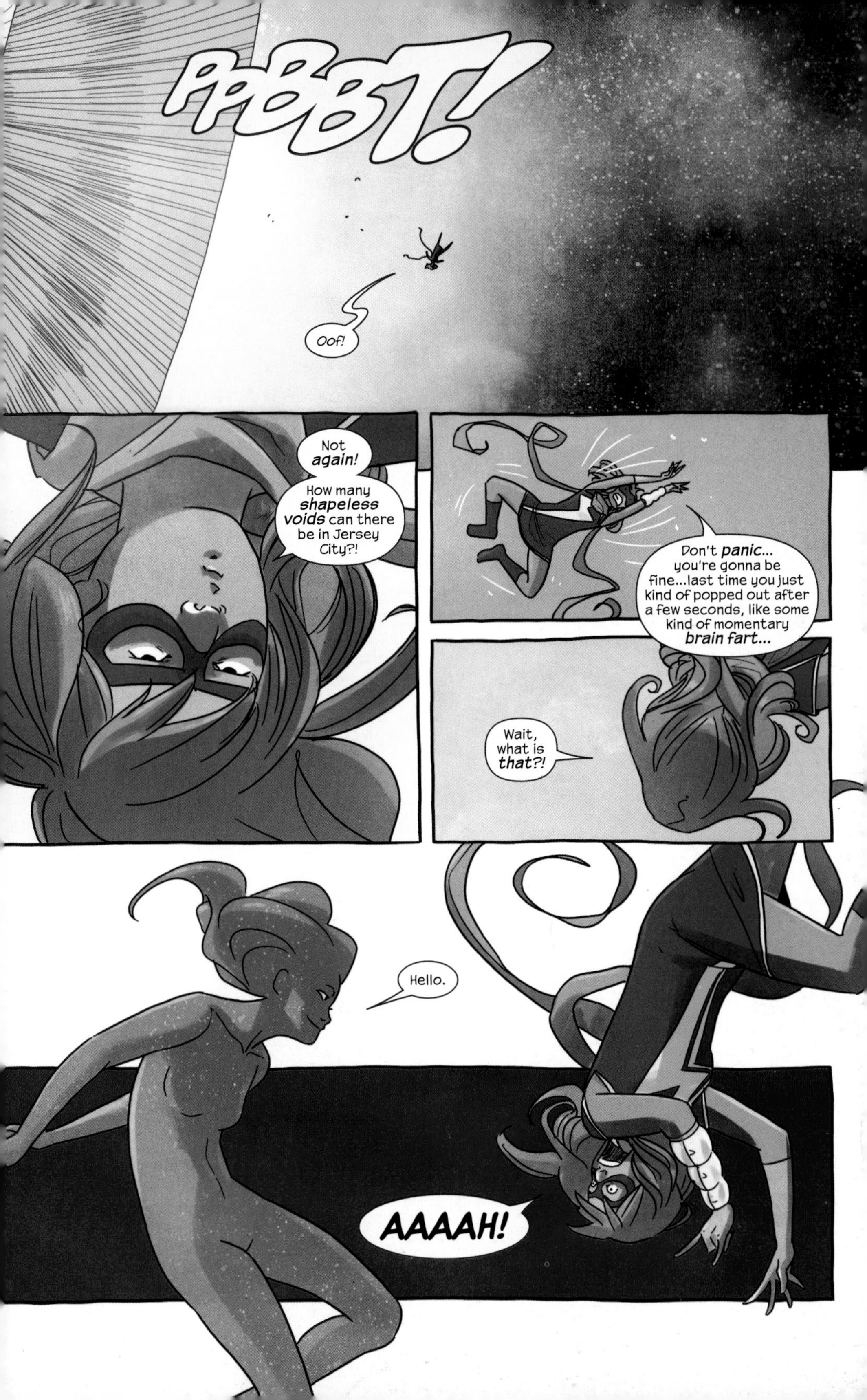
PPBBBT!
Oof!
Not again!
How many shapeless voids can there be in Jersey City?!
Don't panic... you're gonna be fine...last time you just kind of popped out after a few seconds, like some kind of momentary brain fart...
Wait, what is that?!
Hello.
AAAAH!

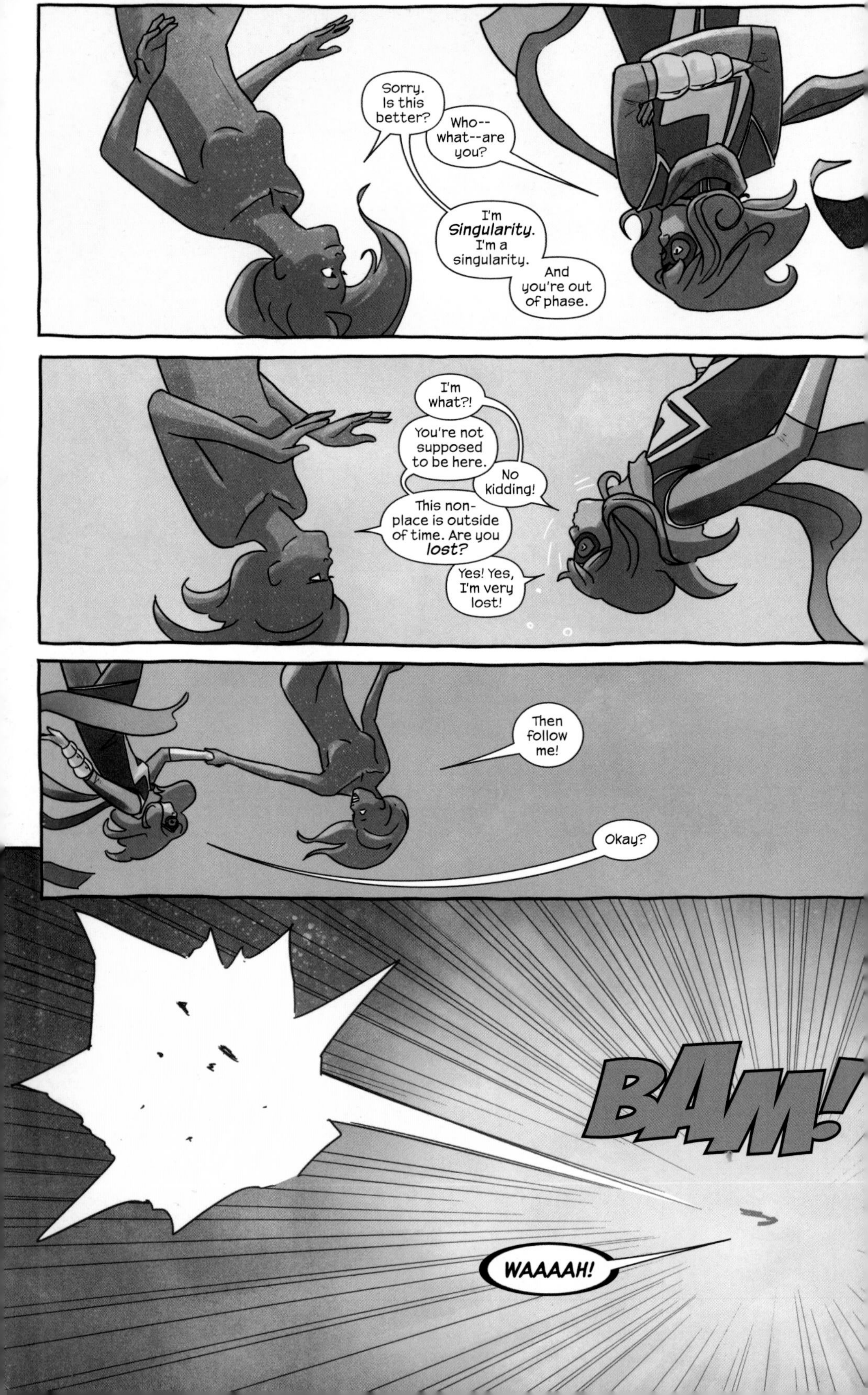

Sorry. Is this better?
Who--what--are you?
I'm *Singularity*. I'm a singularity.
And you're out of phase.
I'm what?!
You're not supposed to be here.
No kidding!
This non-place is outside of time. Are you *lost?*
Yes! Yes, I'm very lost!
Then follow me!
Okay?
BAM!
WAAAAH!

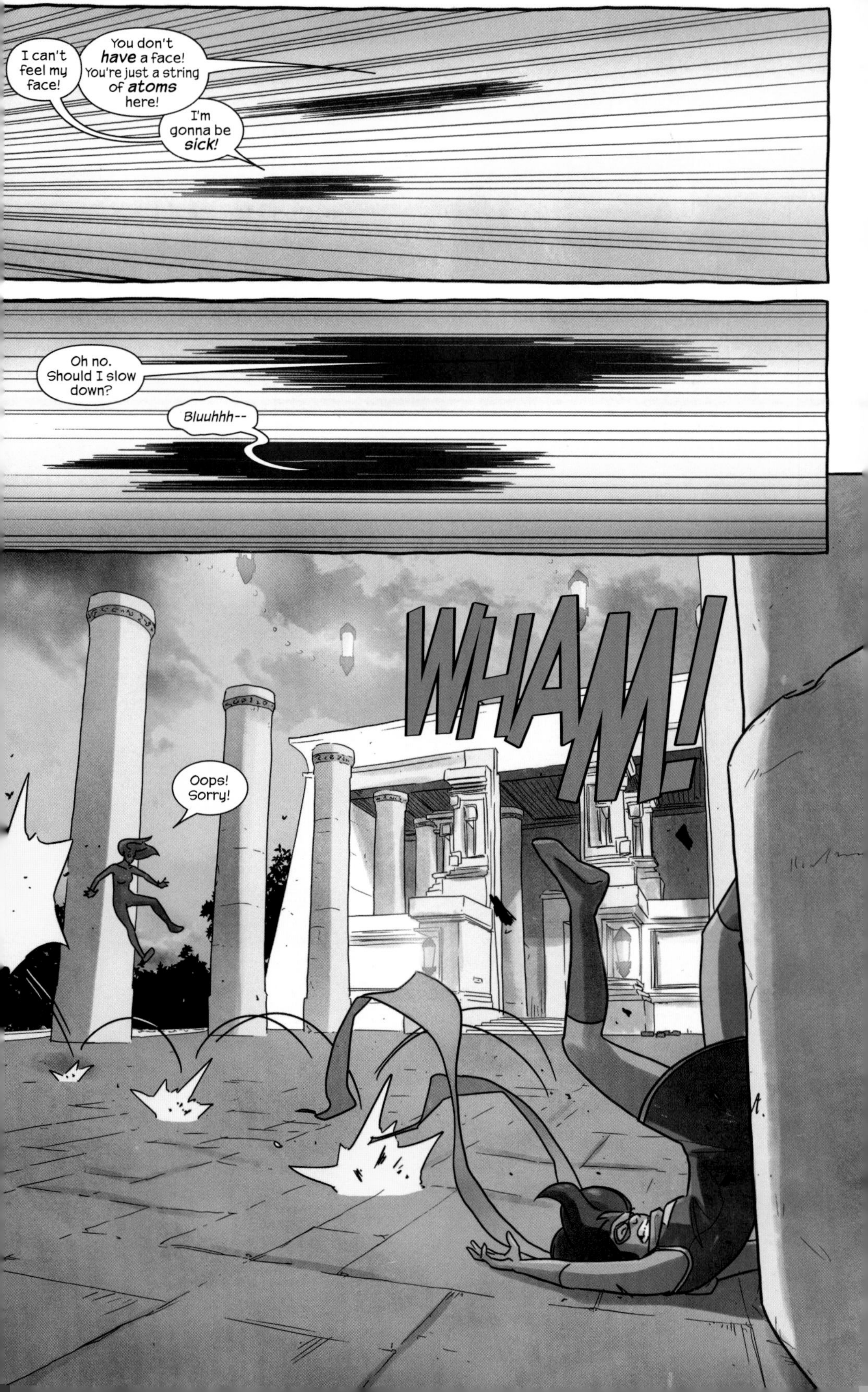
I can't feel my face!
You don't *have* a face! You're just a string of *atoms* here!
I'm gonna be *sick!*
Oh no. Should I slow down?
Bluuhhh--
WHAM!
Oops! Sorry!

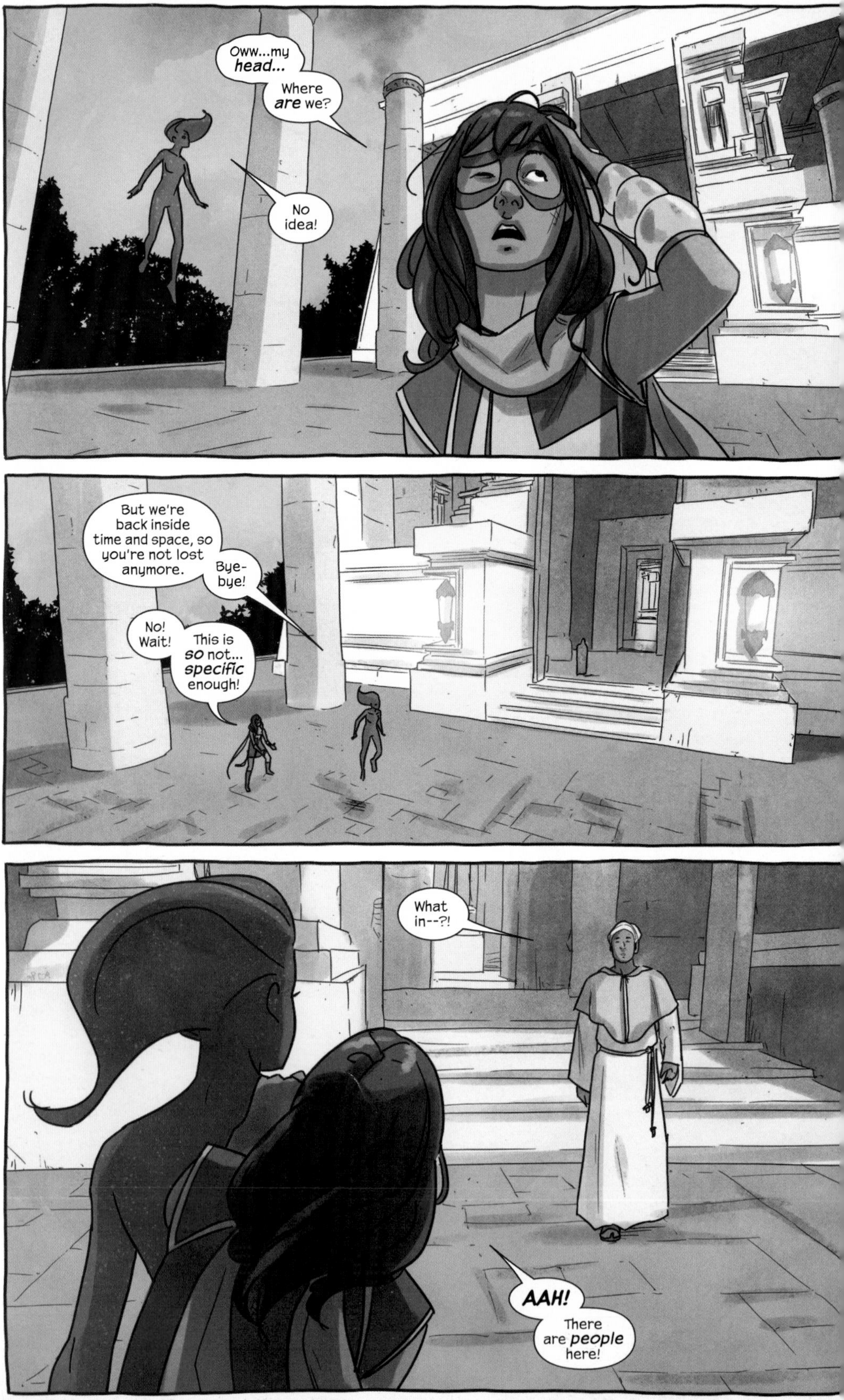
Oww...my *head...*
Where *are* we?
No idea!
But we're back inside time and space, so you're not lost anymore.
Bye-bye!
No! Wait!
This is *so* not... *specific* enough!
What in--?!
AAH!
There are *people* here!

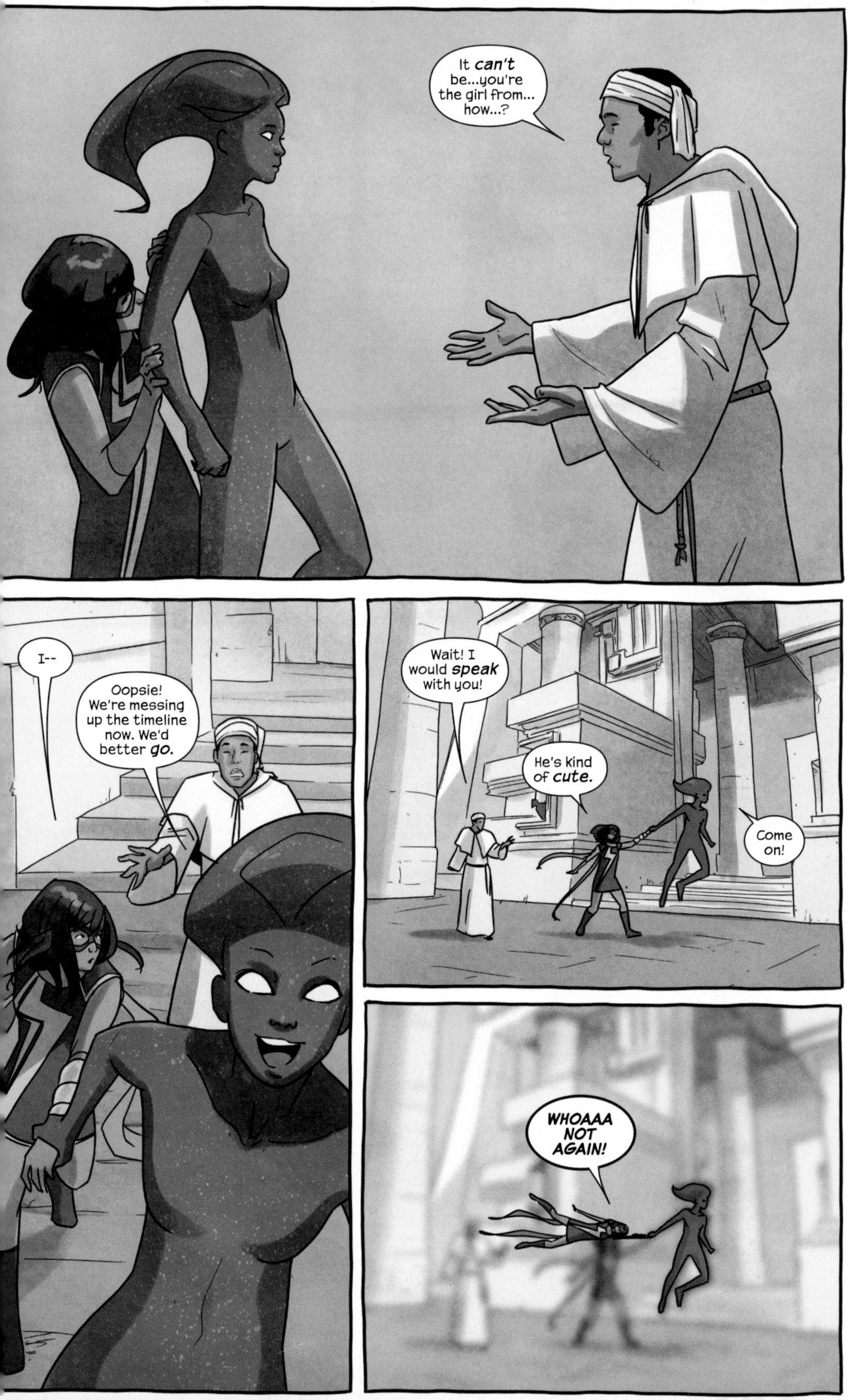

It *can't* be...you're the girl from... how...?
I--
Oopsie! We're messing up the timeline now. We'd better *go.*
Wait! I would *speak* with you!
He's kind of *cute.*
Come on!
WHOAAA NOT AGAIN!

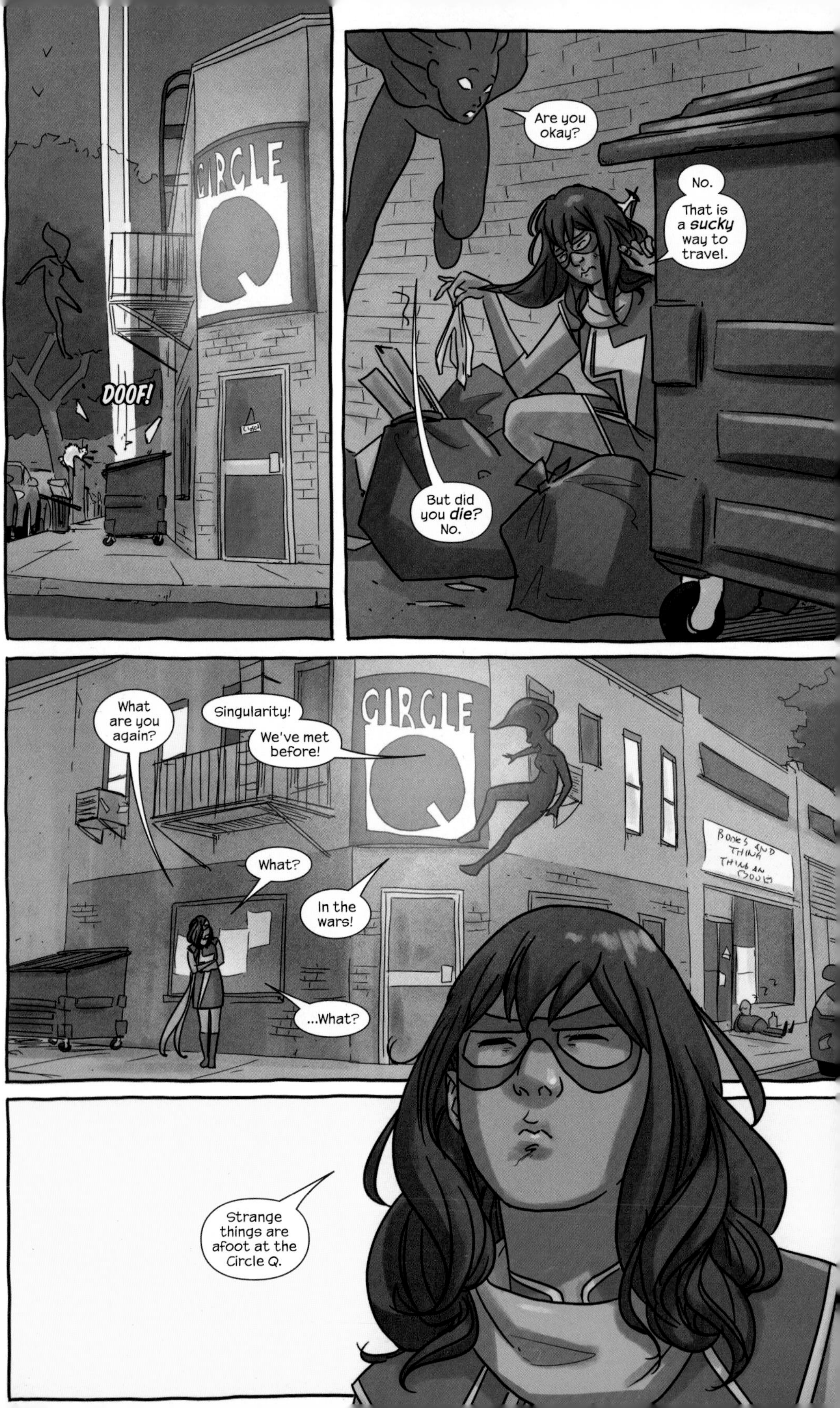
CIRCLE Q
DOOF!
Are you okay?
No.
That is a *sucky* way to travel.
But did you *die*? No.
CIRCLE Q
What are you again?
Singularity!
We've met before!
What?
In the wars!
...What?
Strange things are afoot at the Circle Q.

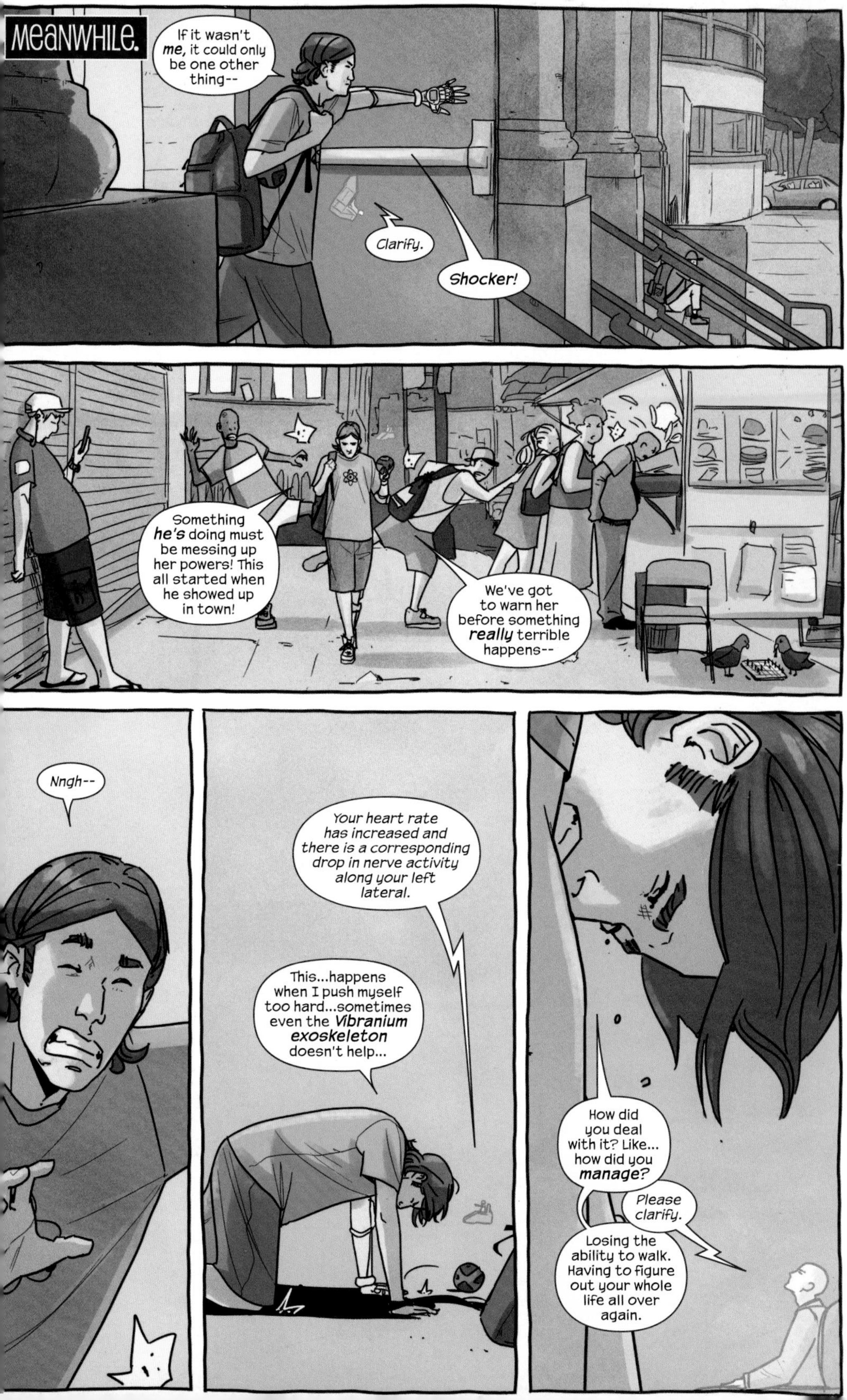
MEANWHILE.
If it wasn't *me,* it could only be one other thing--
Clarify.
Shocker!
Something *he's* doing must be messing up her powers! This all started when he showed up in town!
We've got to warn her before something *really* terrible happens--
Nngh--
Your heart rate has increased and there is a corresponding drop in nerve activity along your left lateral.
This...happens when I push myself too hard...sometimes even the *Vibranium exoskeleton* doesn't help...
How did you deal with it? Like... how did you *manage?*
Please clarify.
Losing the ability to walk. Having to figure out your whole life all over again.

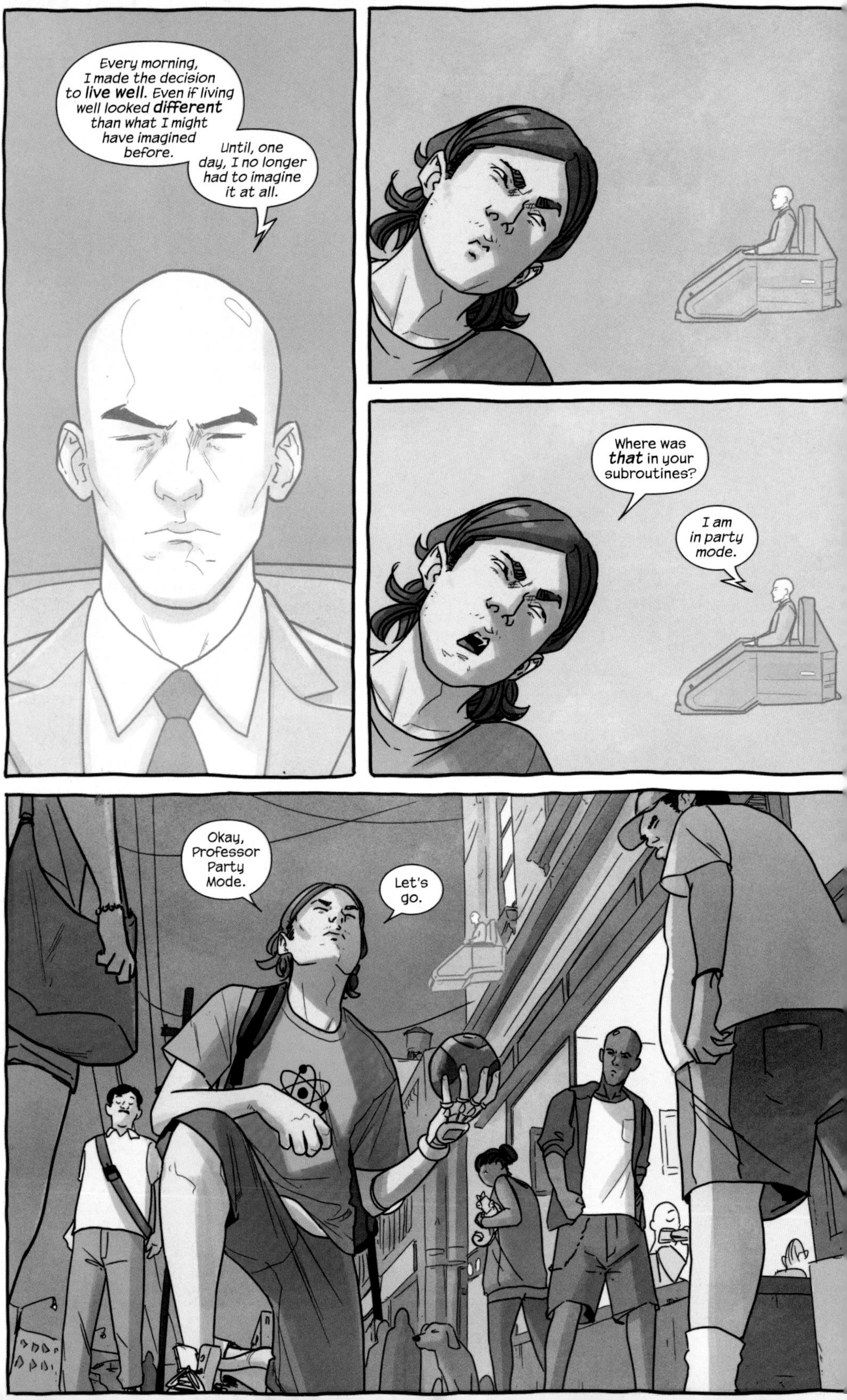
Every morning, I made the decision to live well. Even if living well looked different than what I might have imagined before.
Until, one day, I no longer had to imagine it at all.
Where was that in your subroutines?
I am in party mode.
Okay, Professor Party Mode.
Let's go.

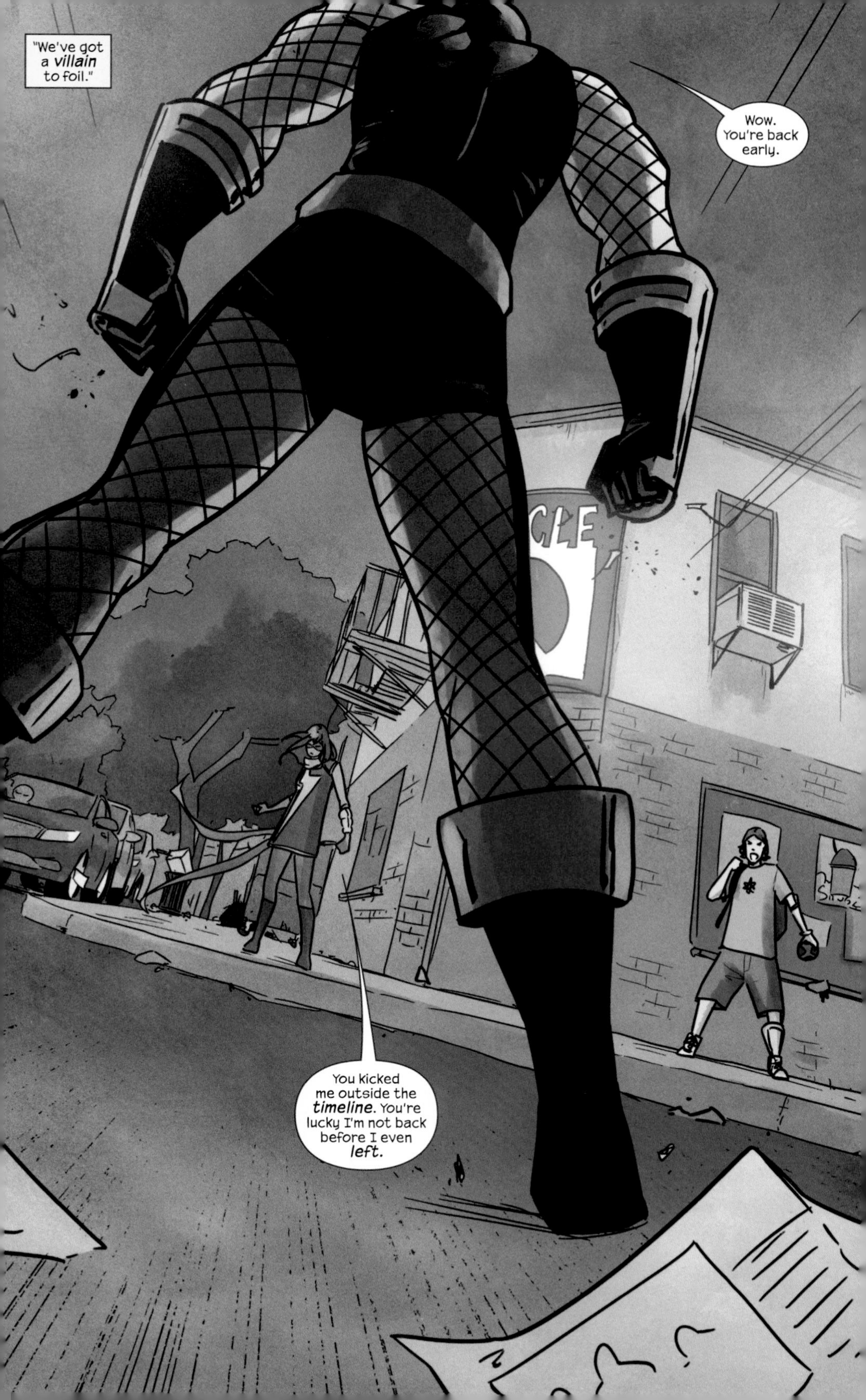
"We've got a *villain* to foil."
Wow. You're back early.
You kicked me outside the *timeline*. You're lucky I'm not back before I even *left*.

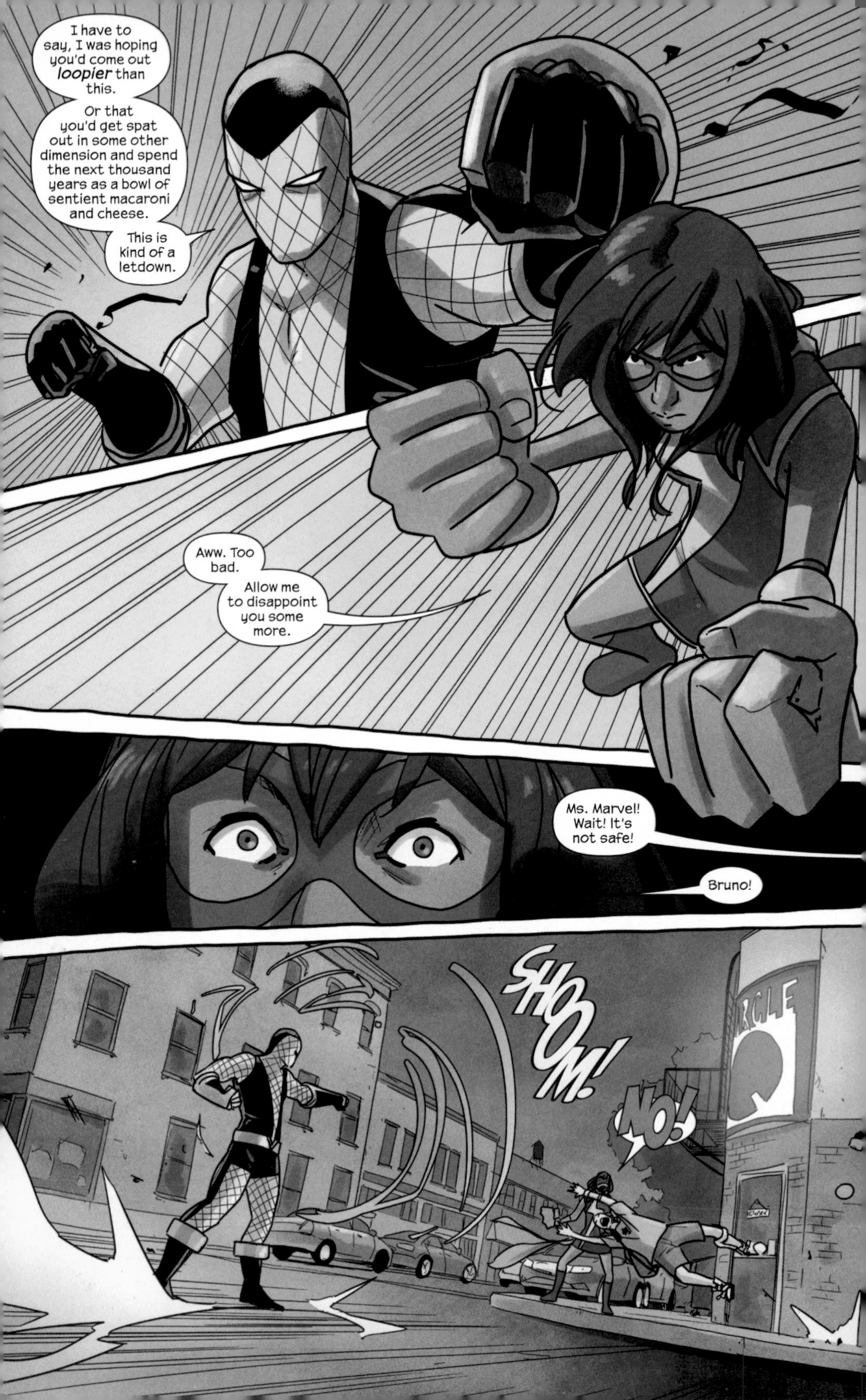
I have to say, I was hoping you'd come out *loopier* than this.
Or that you'd get spat out in some other dimension and spend the next thousand years as a bowl of sentient macaroni and cheese.
This is kind of a letdown.
Aww. Too bad.
Allow me to disappoint you some more.
Ms. Marvel! Wait! It's not safe!
Bruno!
SHOOM!
NO!

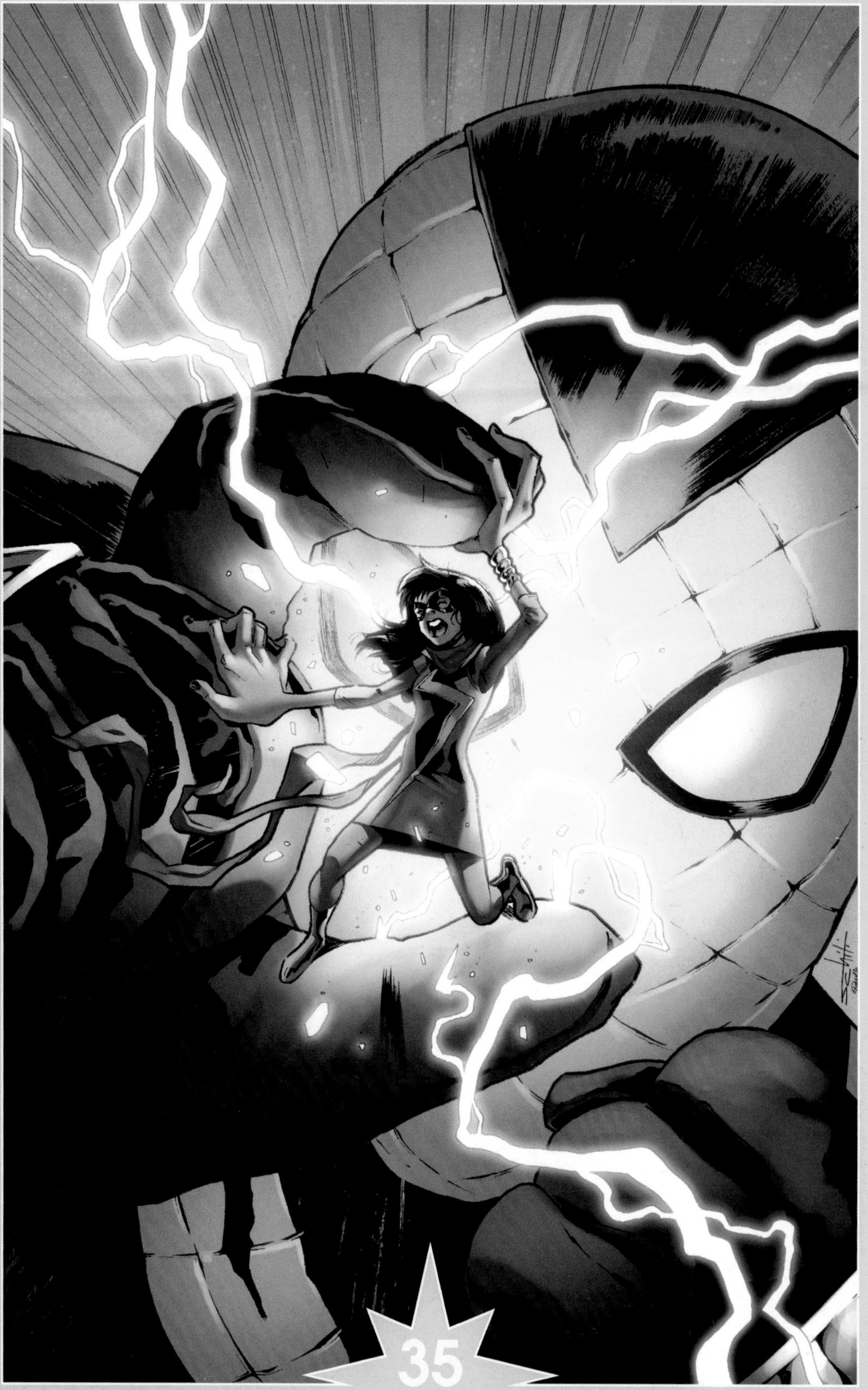
35

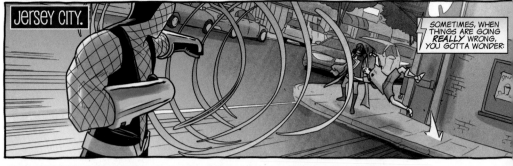

JERSEY CITY.

SOMETIMES, WHEN THINGS ARE GOING *REALLY* WRONG, YOU GOTTA WONDER:

BRUNO!

MAYBE IT'S TIME TO *STOP* FIGHTING AGAINST THIS...

Look out!

...AND *START* WORKING *WITH* IT.

ZFZPT

What the--⸮

This is getting really, *really* annoying.

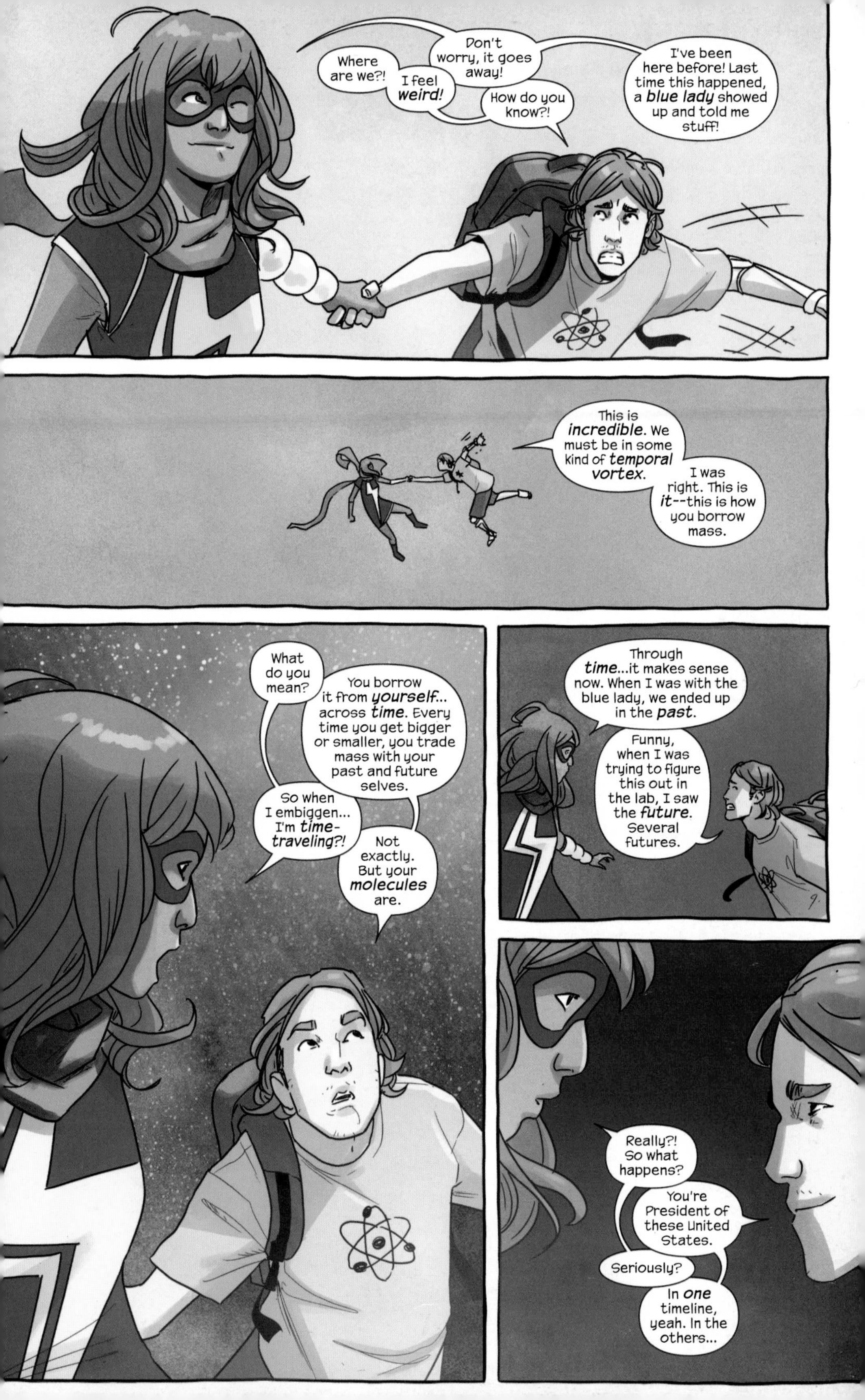
Where are we?!
I feel weird!
Don't worry, it goes away!
How do you know?!
I've been here before! Last time this happened, a blue lady showed up and told me stuff!
This is incredible. We must be in some kind of temporal vortex.
I was right. This is it--this is how you borrow mass.
What do you mean?
You borrow it from yourself... across time. Every time you get bigger or smaller, you trade mass with your past and future selves.
So when I embiggen... I'm time-traveling?!
Not exactly. But your molecules are.
Through time...it makes sense now. When I was with the blue lady, we ended up in the past.
Funny, when I was trying to figure this out in the lab, I saw the future. Several futures.
Really?! So what happens?
You're President of these United States.
Seriously?
In one timeline, yeah. In the others...

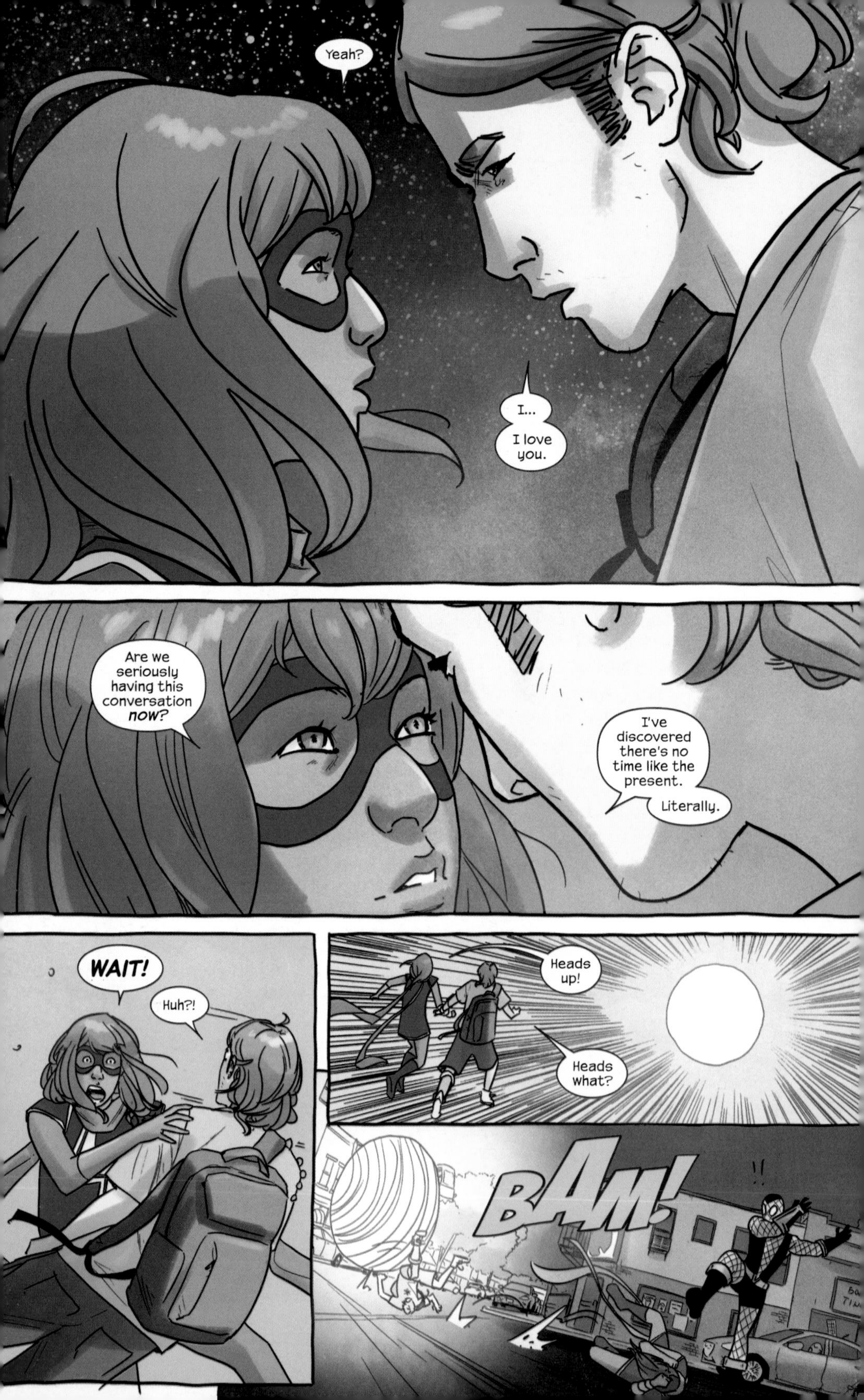
Yeah?
I...
I love you.
Are we seriously having this conversation *now?*
I've discovered there's no time like the present.
Literally.
WAIT!
Huh?!
Heads up!
Heads what?
BAM!
!!

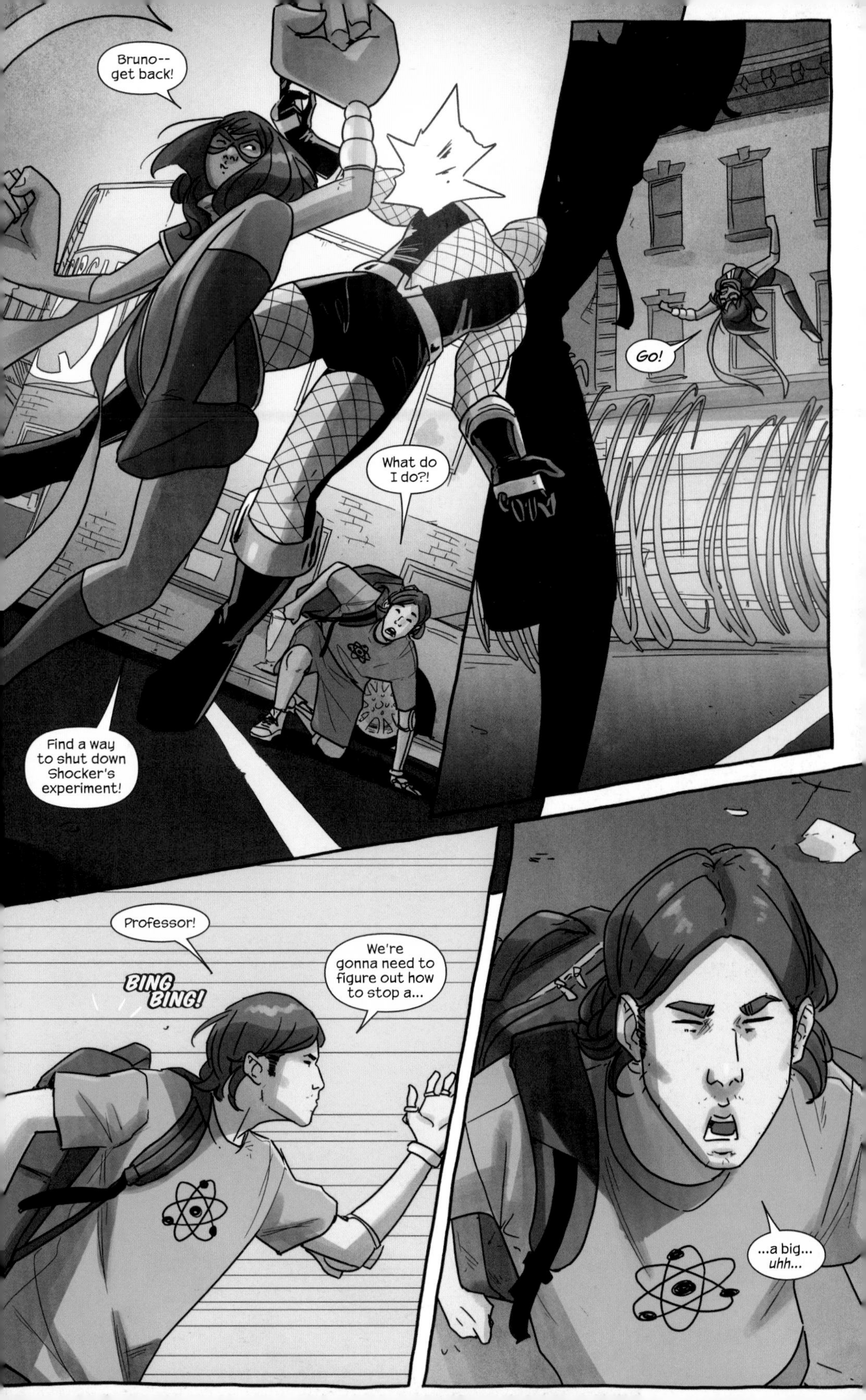
Bruno--
get back!
Go!
What do
I do?!
Find a way
to shut down
Shocker's
experiment!
Professor!
BING
BING!
We're
gonna need to
figure out how
to stop a...
...a big...
uhh...

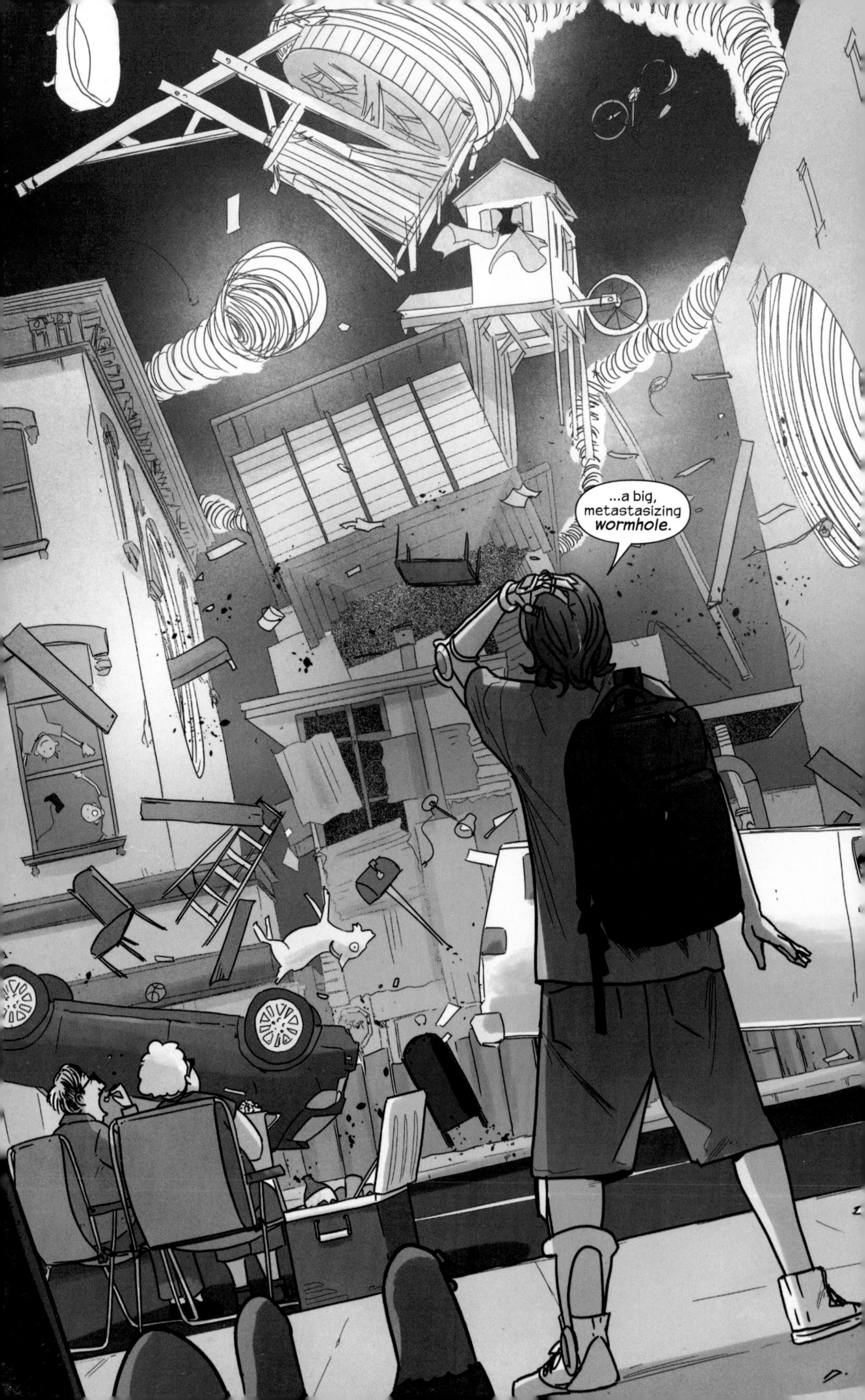
...a big, metastasizing *wormhole*.

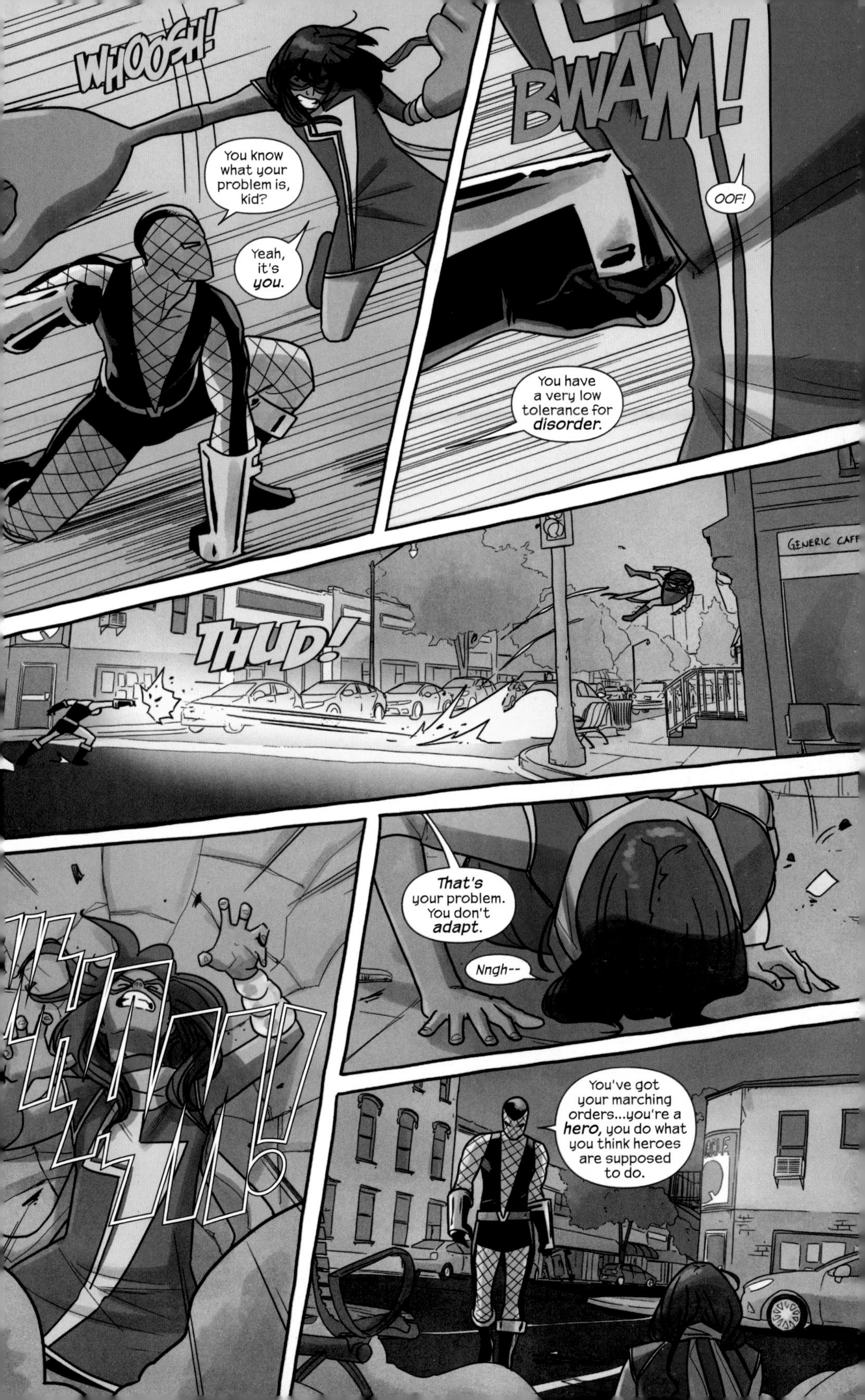
WHOOSH!
You know what your problem is, kid?
Yeah, it's *you*.
BWAM!
OOF!
You have a very low tolerance for *disorder*.
GENERIC CAFF
THUD!
That's your problem. You don't *adapt*.
Nngh--
You've got your marching orders...you're a *hero,* you do what you think heroes are supposed to do.

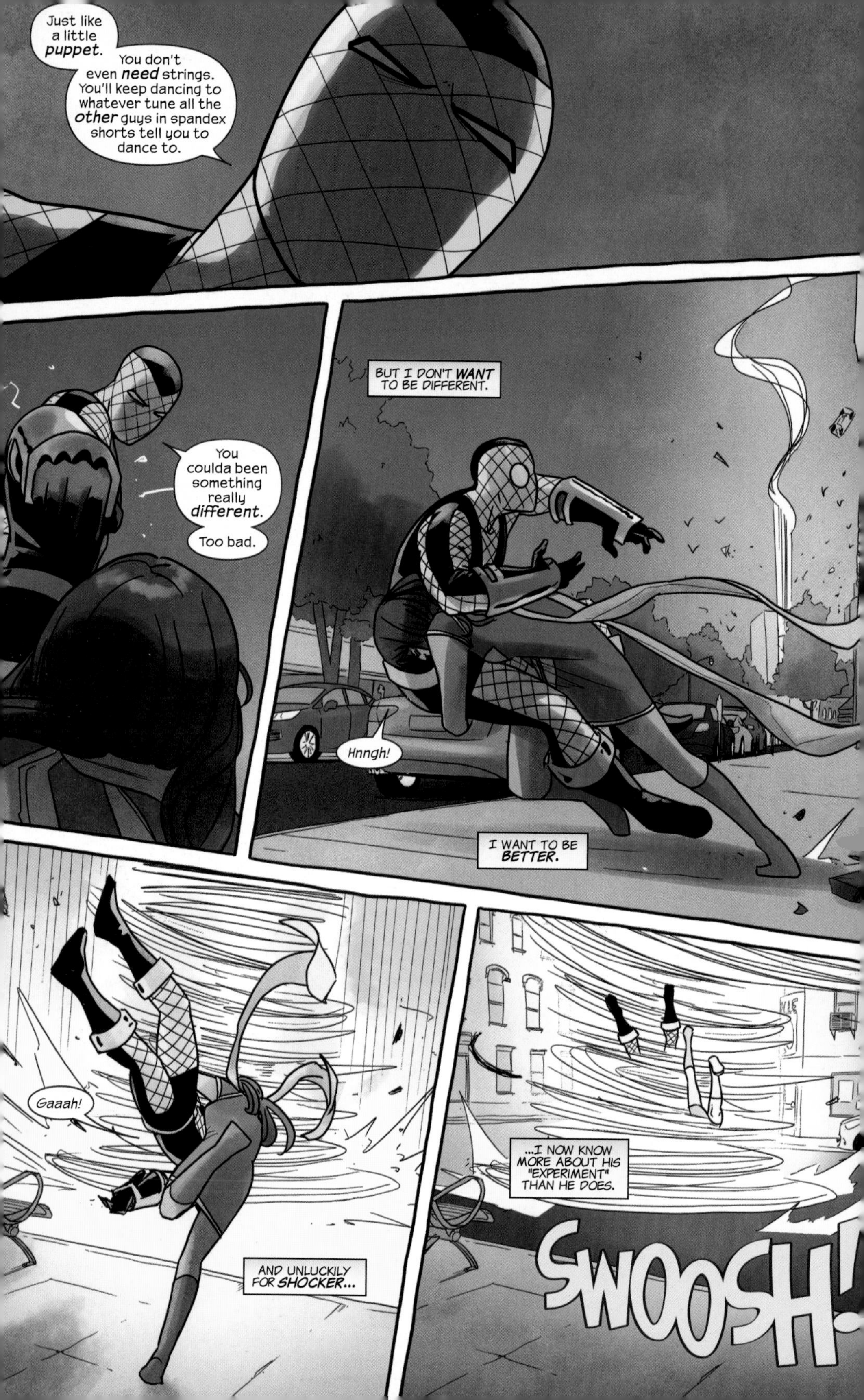
Just like a little puppet. You don't even need strings. You'll keep dancing to whatever tune all the other guys in spandex shorts tell you to dance to.
You coulda been something really different.
Too bad.
BUT I DON'T WANT TO BE DIFFERENT.
Hnngh!
I WANT TO BE BETTER.
Gaaah!
AND UNLUCKILY FOR SHOCKER...
...I NOW KNOW MORE ABOUT HIS "EXPERIMENT" THAN HE DOES.
SWOOSH!

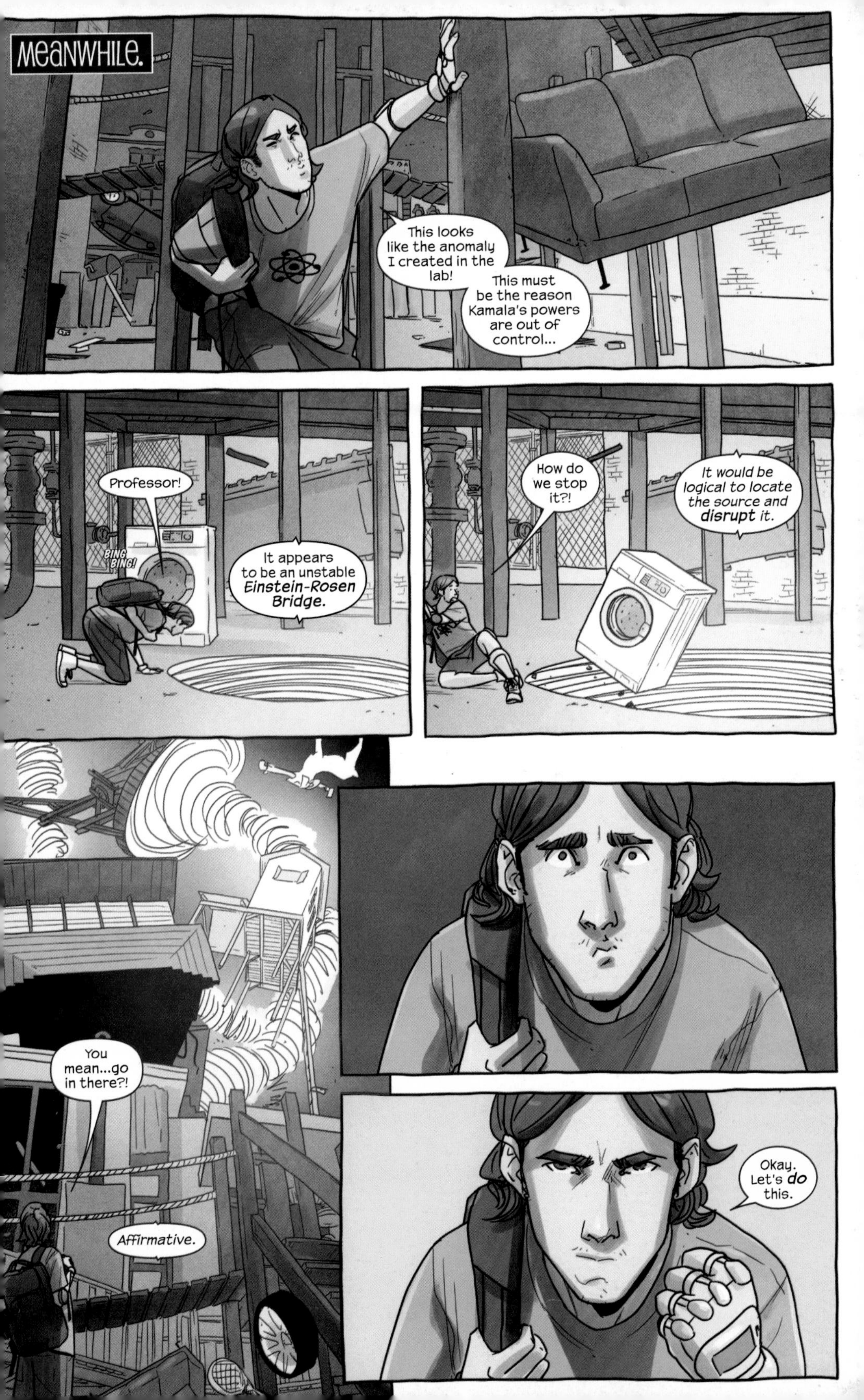
MEANWHILE.
This looks like the anomaly I created in the lab!
This must be the reason Kamala's powers are out of control...
Professor!
BING BING!
It appears to be an unstable *Einstein-Rosen Bridge.*
How do we stop it?!
It would be logical to locate the source and *disrupt* it.
You mean...go in there?!
Affirmative.
Okay. Let's *do* this.

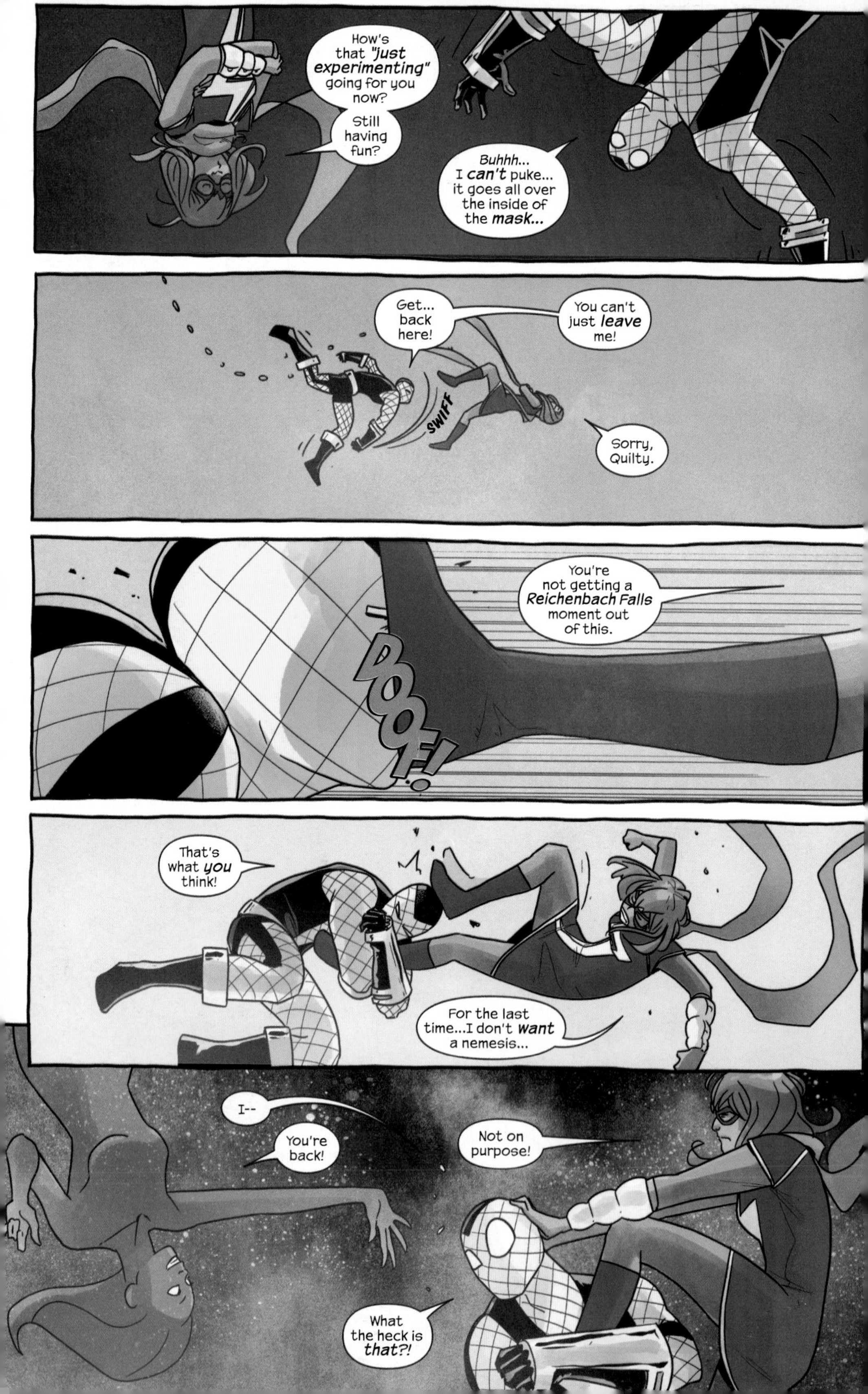
How's that "just experimenting" going for you now?
Still having fun?
Buhhh... I can't puke... it goes all over the inside of the mask...
Get... back here!
You can't just leave me!
SWIFF
Sorry, Quilty.
You're not getting a Reichenbach Falls moment out of this.
DOOF!
That's what you think!
For the last time...I don't want a nemesis...
I--
You're back!
Not on purpose!
What the heck is that?!

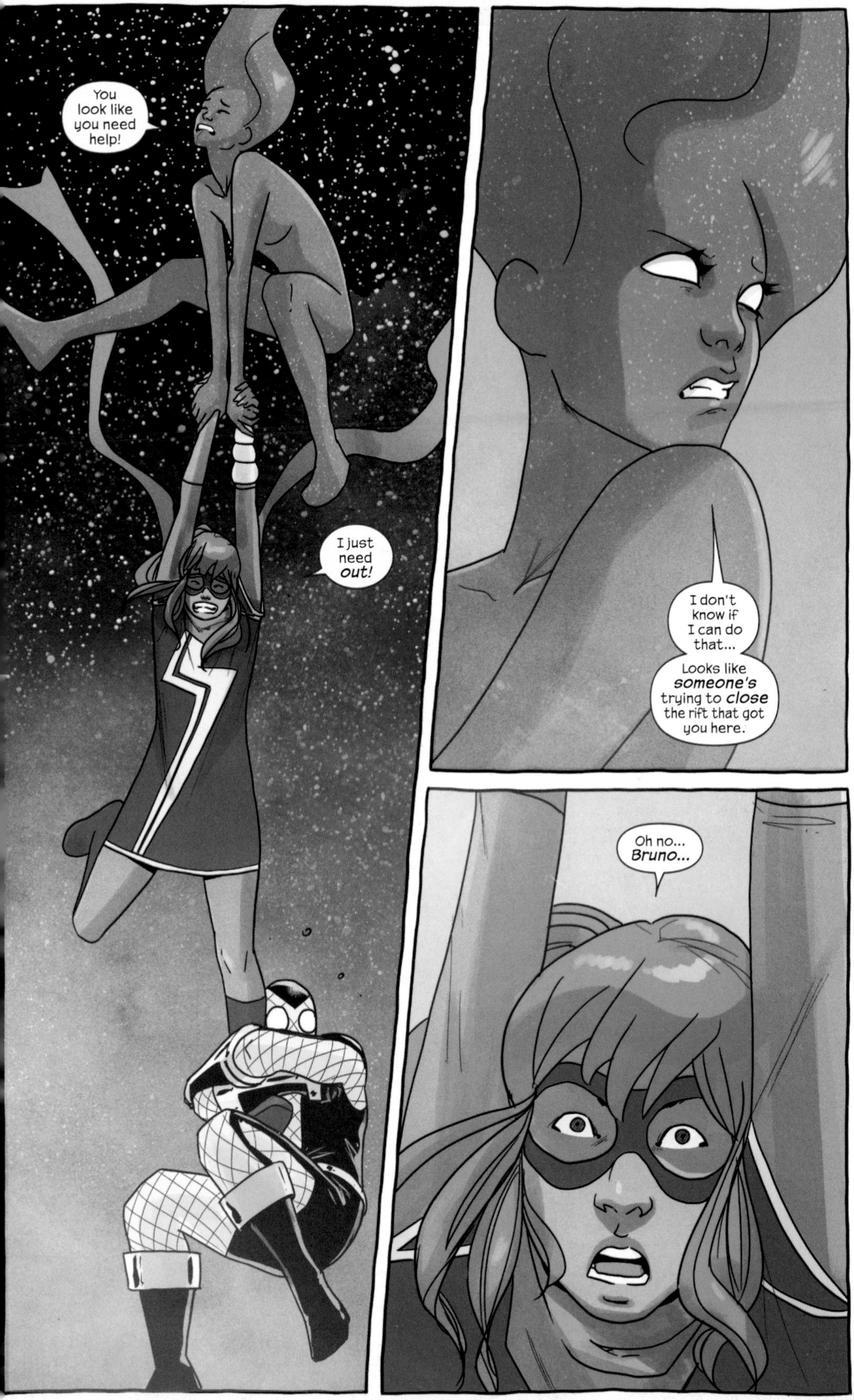

You look like you need help!
I just need *out!*
I don't know if I can do that...
Looks like *someone's* trying to *close* the rift that got you here.
Oh no... *Bruno...*

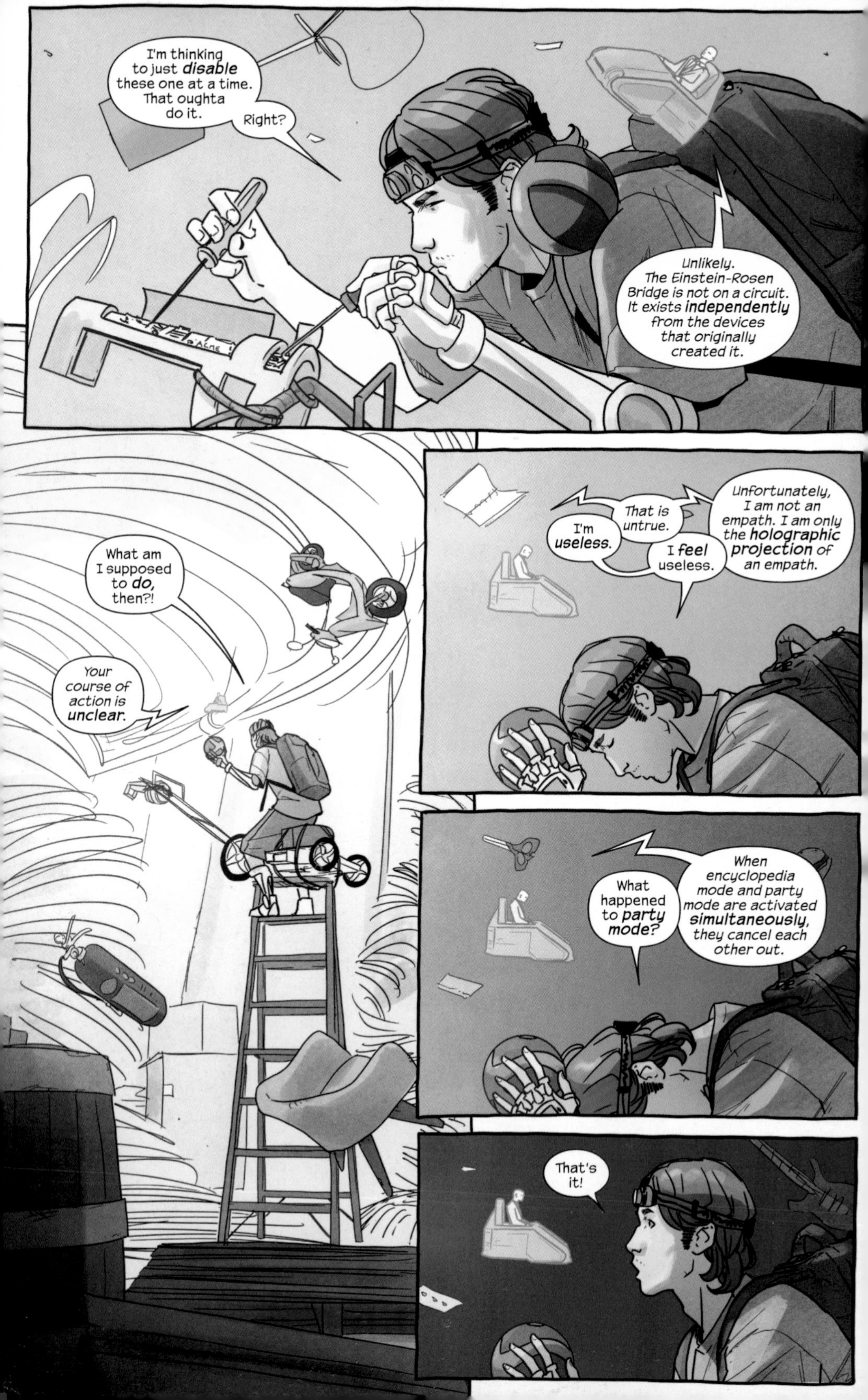
I'm thinking to just *disable* these one at a time. That oughta do it.
Right?
Unlikely. The Einstein-Rosen Bridge is not on a circuit. It exists **independently** from the devices that originally created it.
What am I supposed to *do,* then?!
Your course of action is **unclear**.
I'm **useless**.
That is untrue.
I *feel* useless.
Unfortunately, I am not an empath. I am only the **holographic projection** of an empath.
What happened to **party mode?**
When encyclopedia mode and party mode are activated **simultaneously**, they cancel each other out.
That's it!

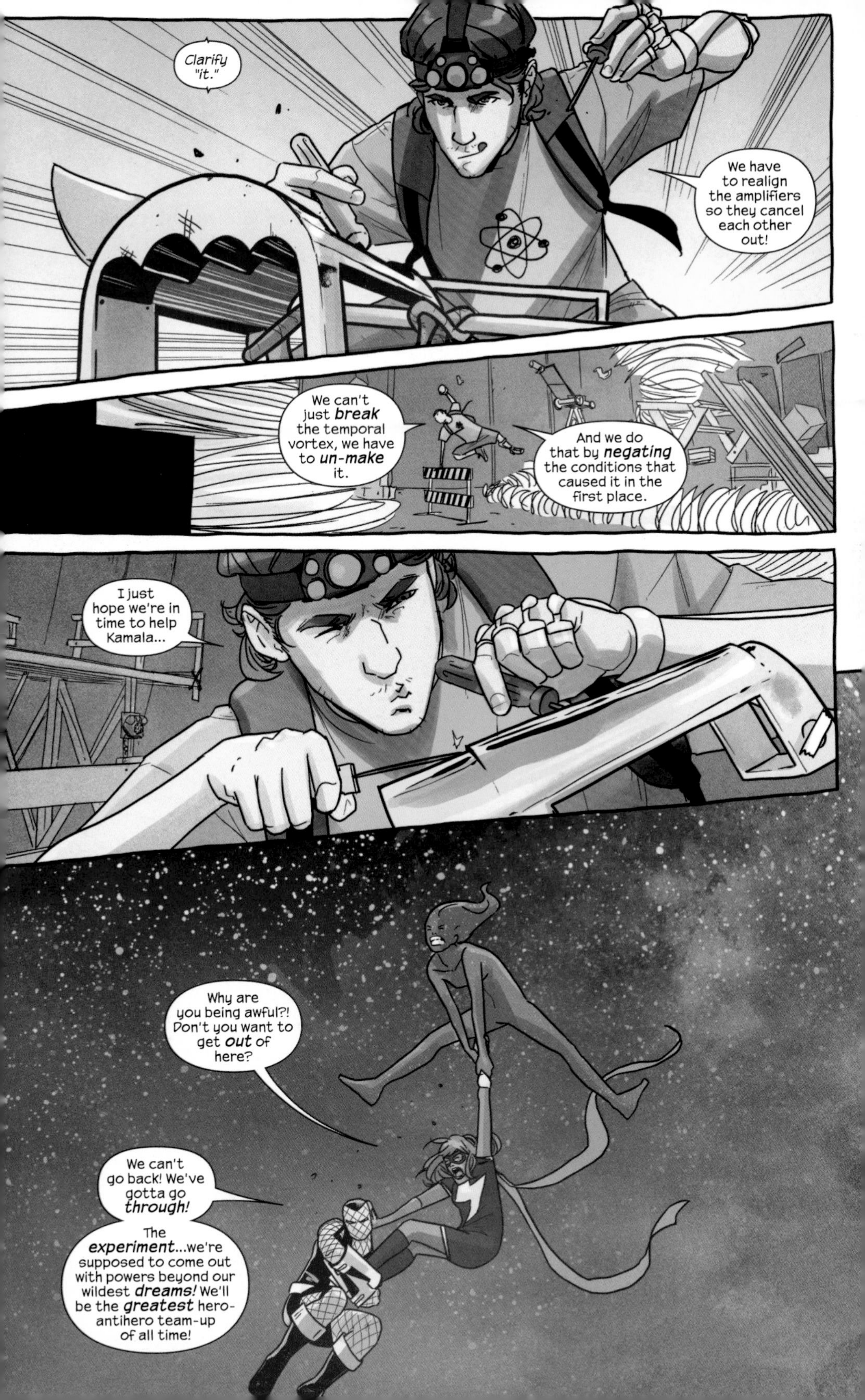
Clarify "it."
We have to realign the amplifiers so they cancel each other out!
We can't just break the temporal vortex, we have to un-make it.
And we do that by negating the conditions that caused it in the first place.
I just hope we're in time to help Kamala...
Why are you being awful?! Don't you want to get out of here?
We can't go back! We've gotta go through!
The experiment...we're supposed to come out with powers beyond our wildest dreams! We'll be the greatest hero-antihero team-up of all time!

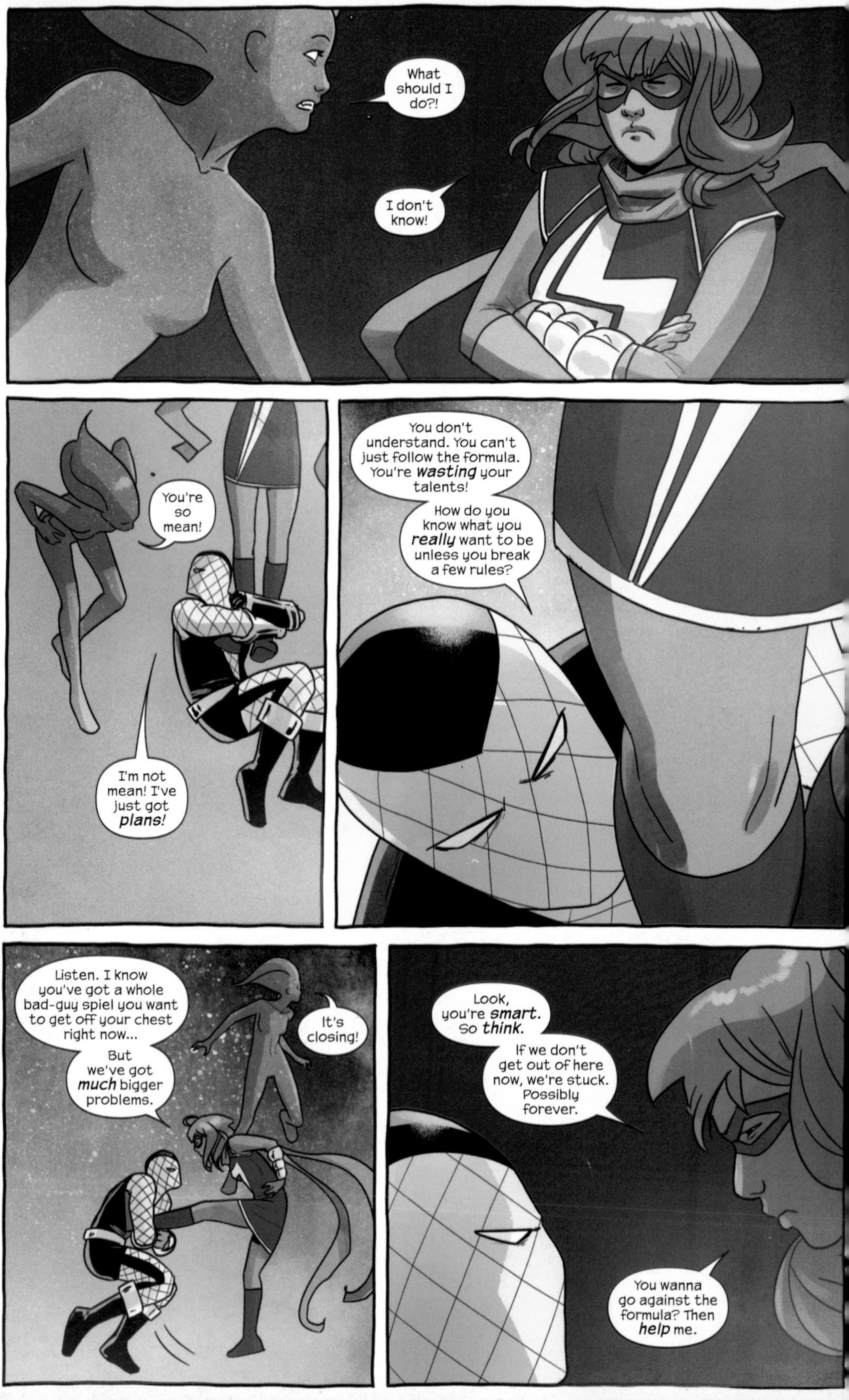
What should I do?!
I don't know!
You're so mean!
I'm not mean! I've just got plans!
You don't understand. You can't just follow the formula. You're wasting your talents!
How do you know what you really want to be unless you break a few rules?
Listen. I know you've got a whole bad-guy spiel you want to get off your chest right now...
But we've got much bigger problems.
It's closing!
Look, you're smart. So think.
If we don't get out of here now, we're stuck. Possibly forever.
You wanna go against the formula? Then help me.

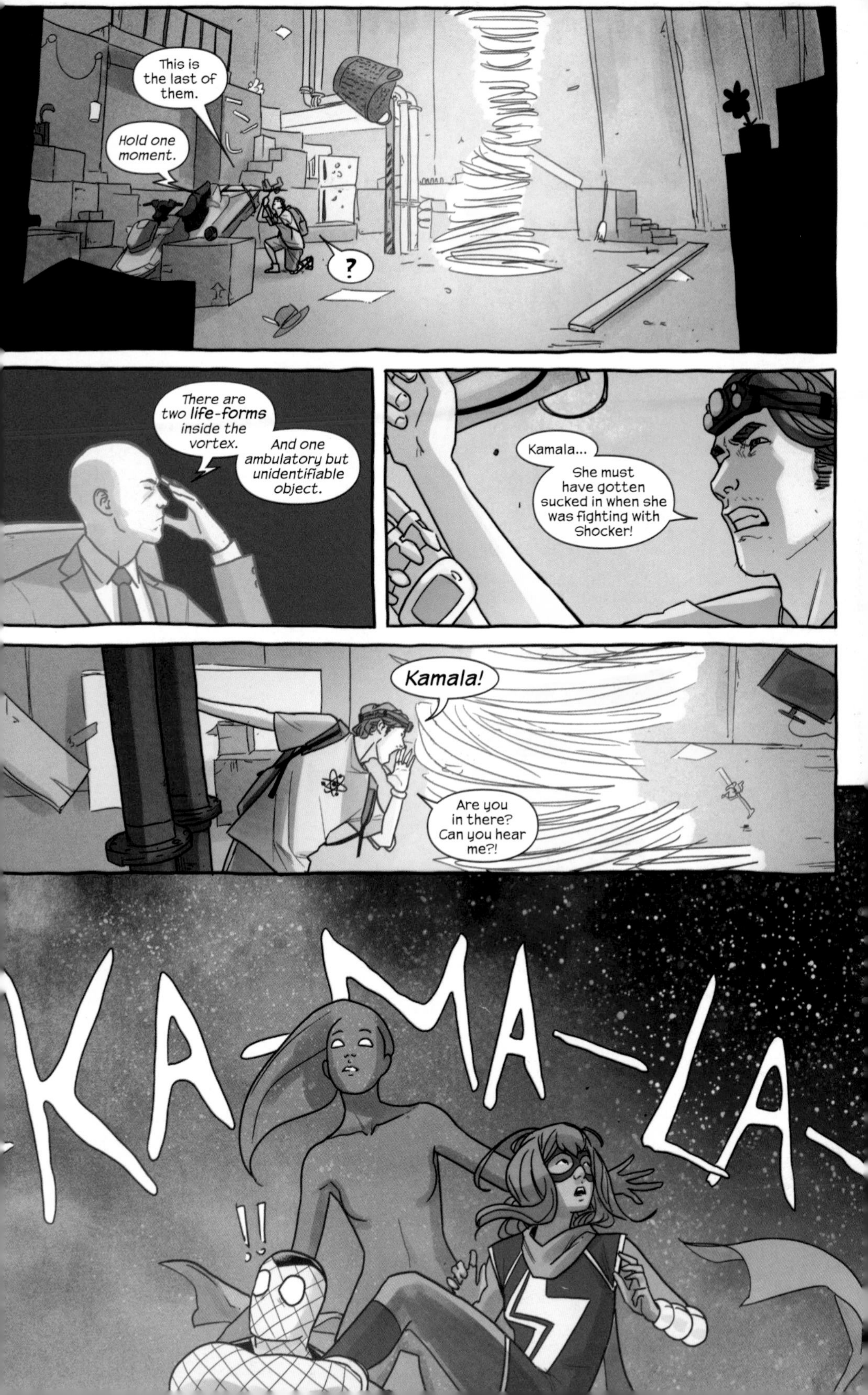
This is the last of them.
Hold one moment.
?
There are two life-forms inside the vortex.
And one ambulatory but unidentifiable object.
Kamala...
She must have gotten sucked in when she was fighting with Shocker!
Kamala!
Are you in there? Can you hear me?!
KA-MA-LA-
!!

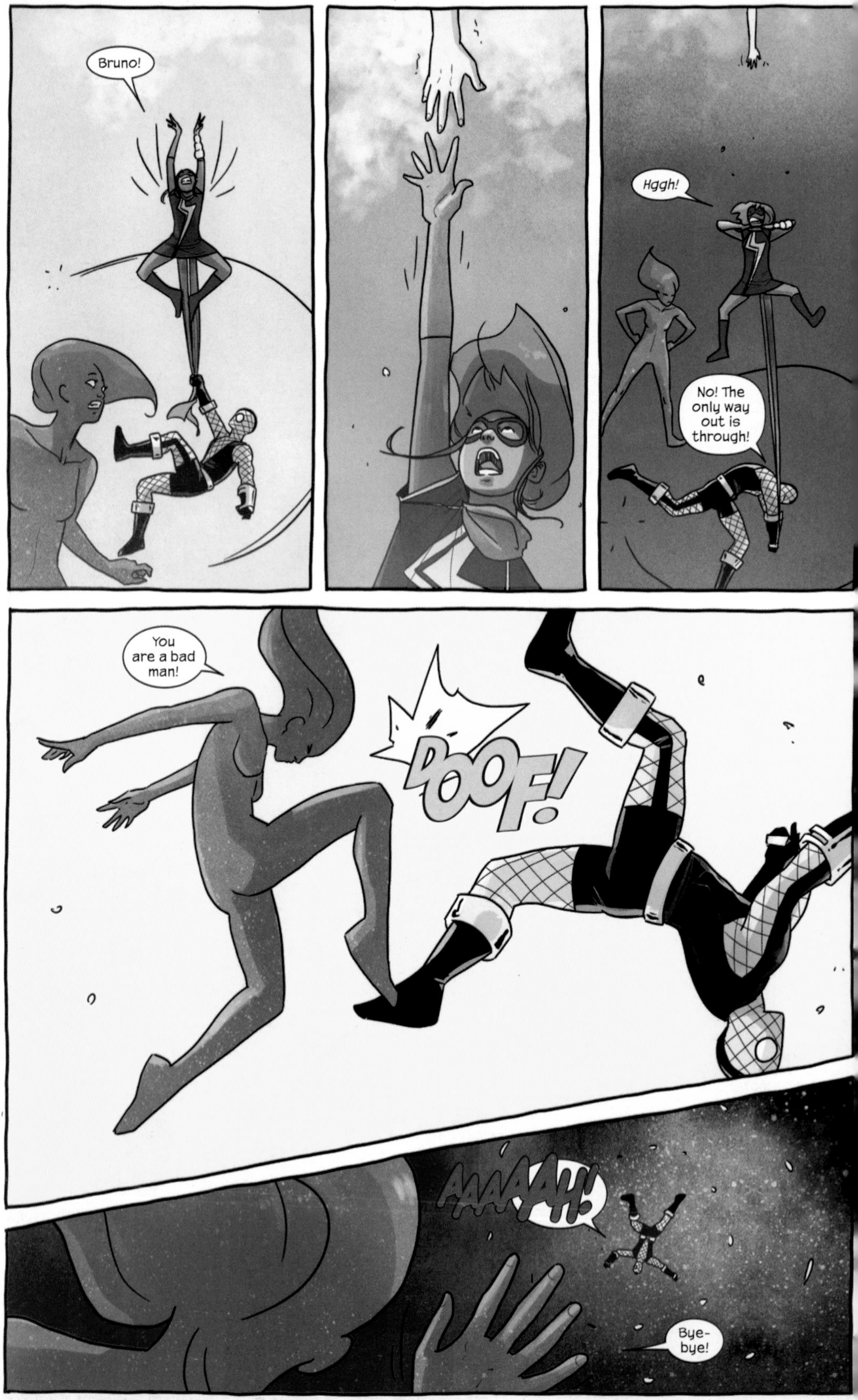
Bruno!
Hggh!
No! The only way out is through!
You are a bad man!
DOOF!
AAAAAH!
Bye-bye!

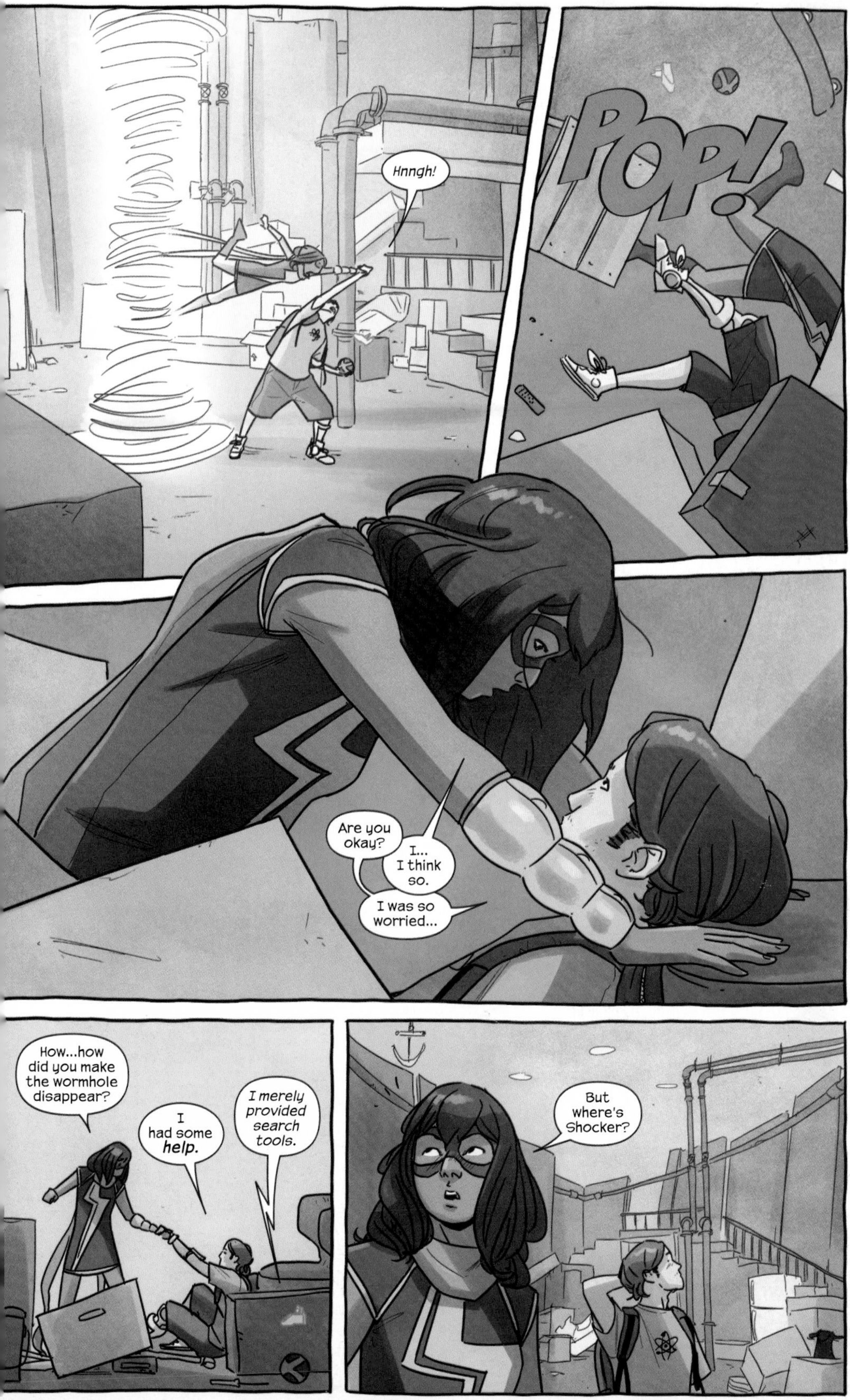
Hnngh!
POP!
Are you okay?
I... I think so.
I was so worried...
How...how did you make the wormhole disappear?
I had some **help.**
I merely provided search tools.
But where's Shocker?

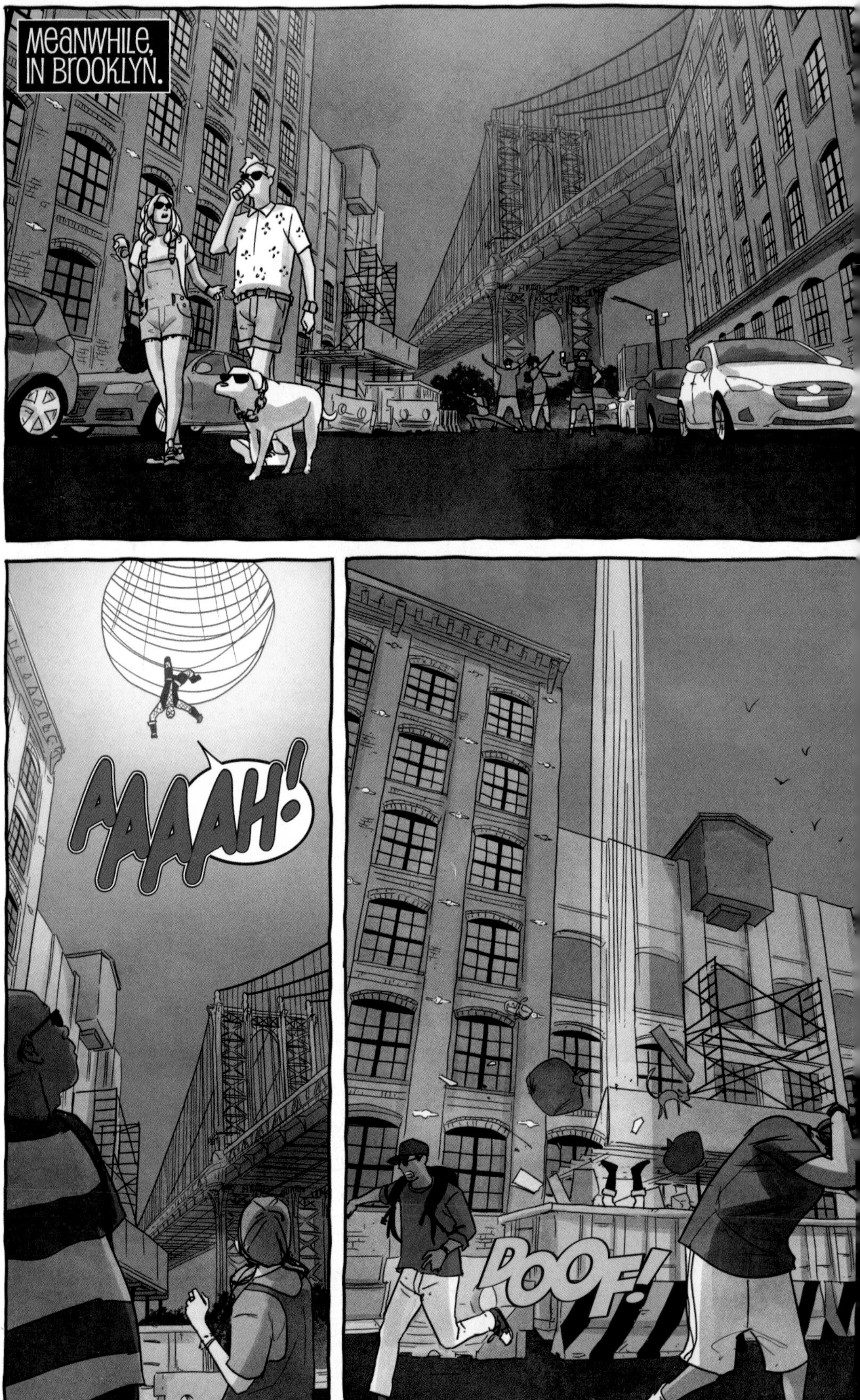
MEANWHILE, IN BROOKLYN.
AAAAH!
DOOF!

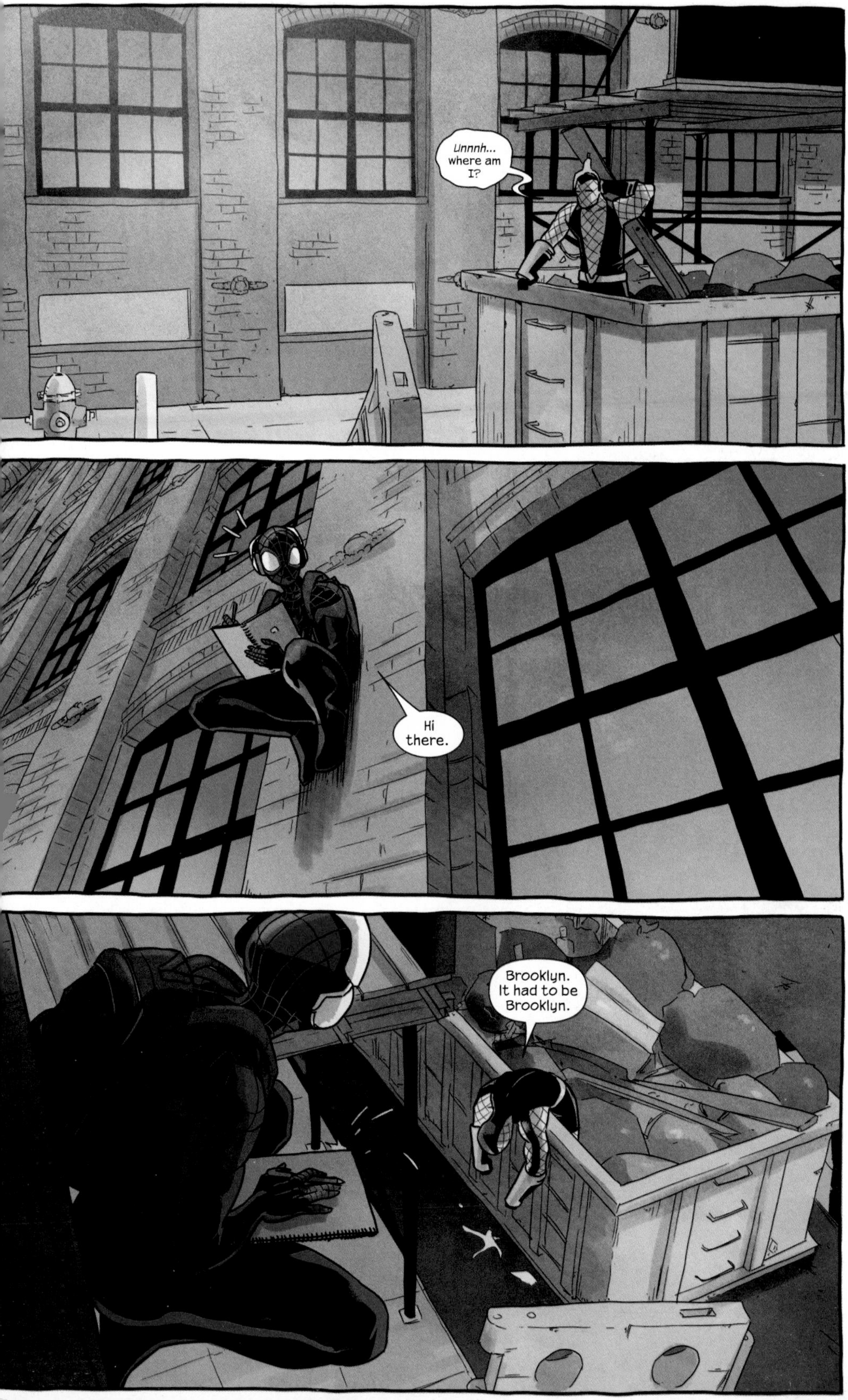
Unnnh... where am I?
Hi there.
Brooklyn. It had to be Brooklyn.

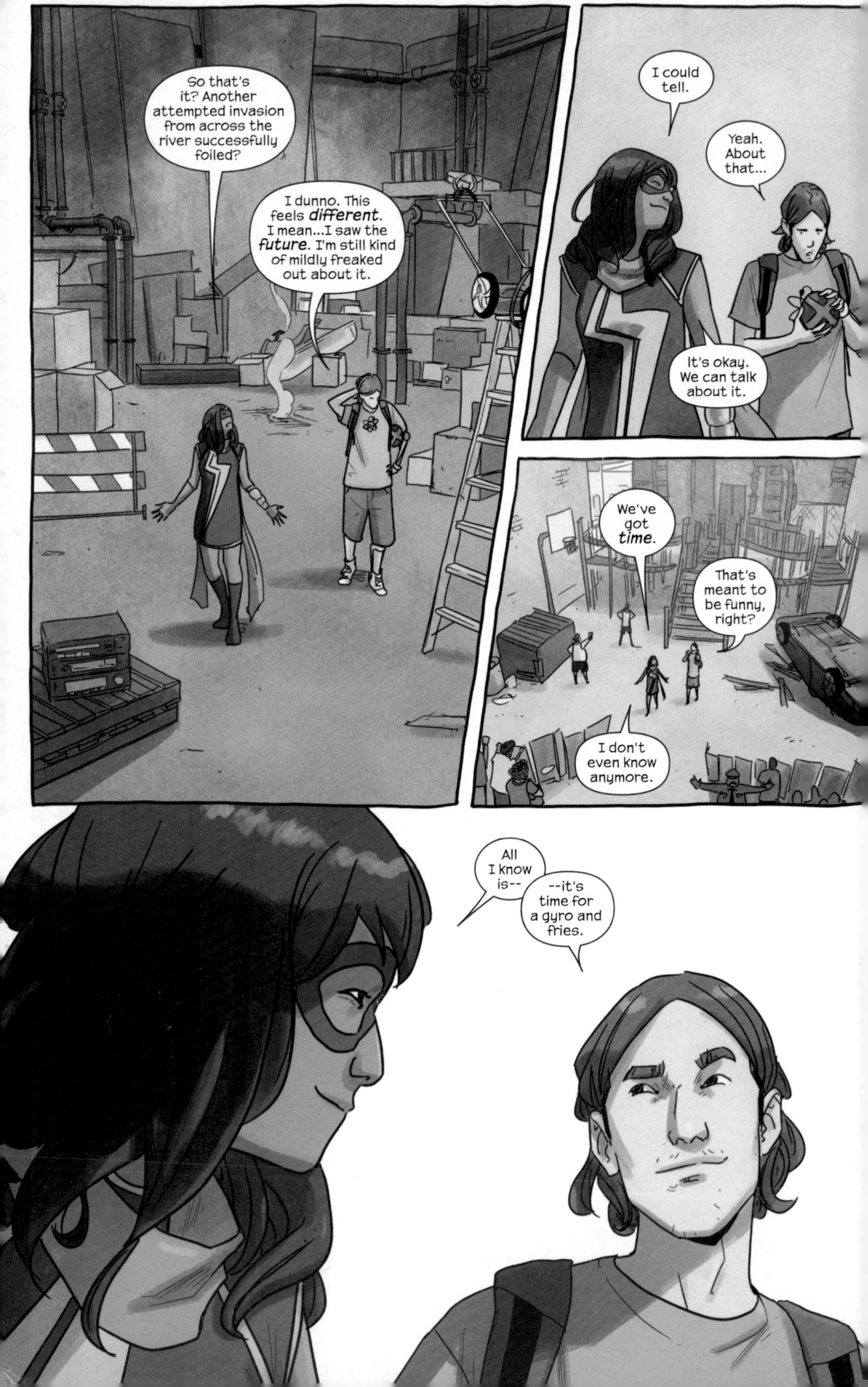
So that's it? Another attempted invasion from across the river successfully foiled?
I dunno. This feels *different*. I mean...I saw the *future*. I'm still kind of mildly freaked out about it.
I could tell.
Yeah. About that...
It's okay. We can talk about it.
We've got *time*.
That's meant to be funny, right?
I don't even know anymore.
All I know is--
--it's time for a gyro and fries.

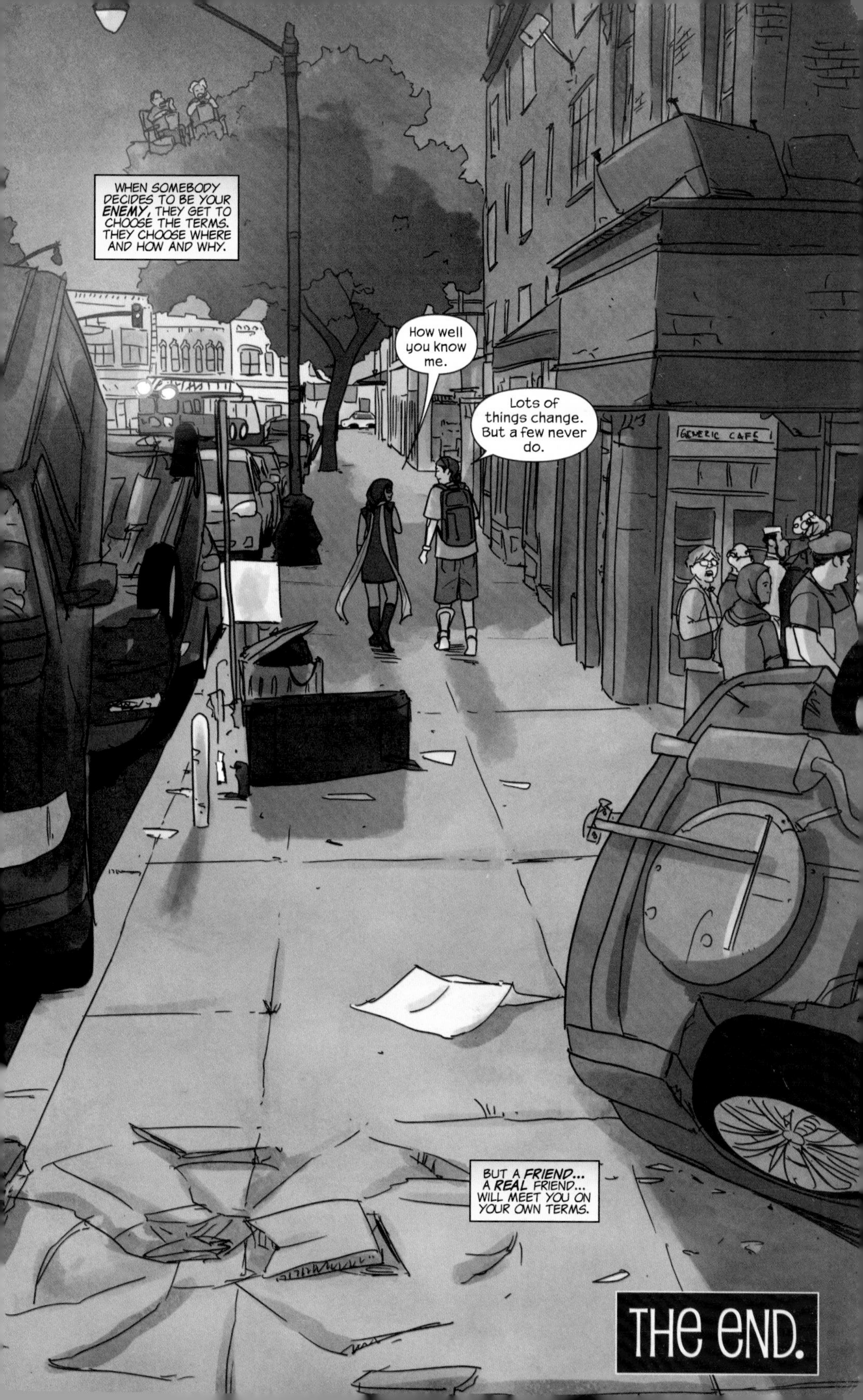
WHEN SOMEBODY DECIDES TO BE YOUR ENEMY, THEY GET TO CHOOSE THE TERMS. THEY CHOOSE WHERE AND HOW AND WHY.
How well you know me.
Lots of things change. But a few never do.
GENERIC CAFE
BUT A FRIEND... A REAL FRIEND... WILL MEET YOU ON YOUR OWN TERMS.
THE END.

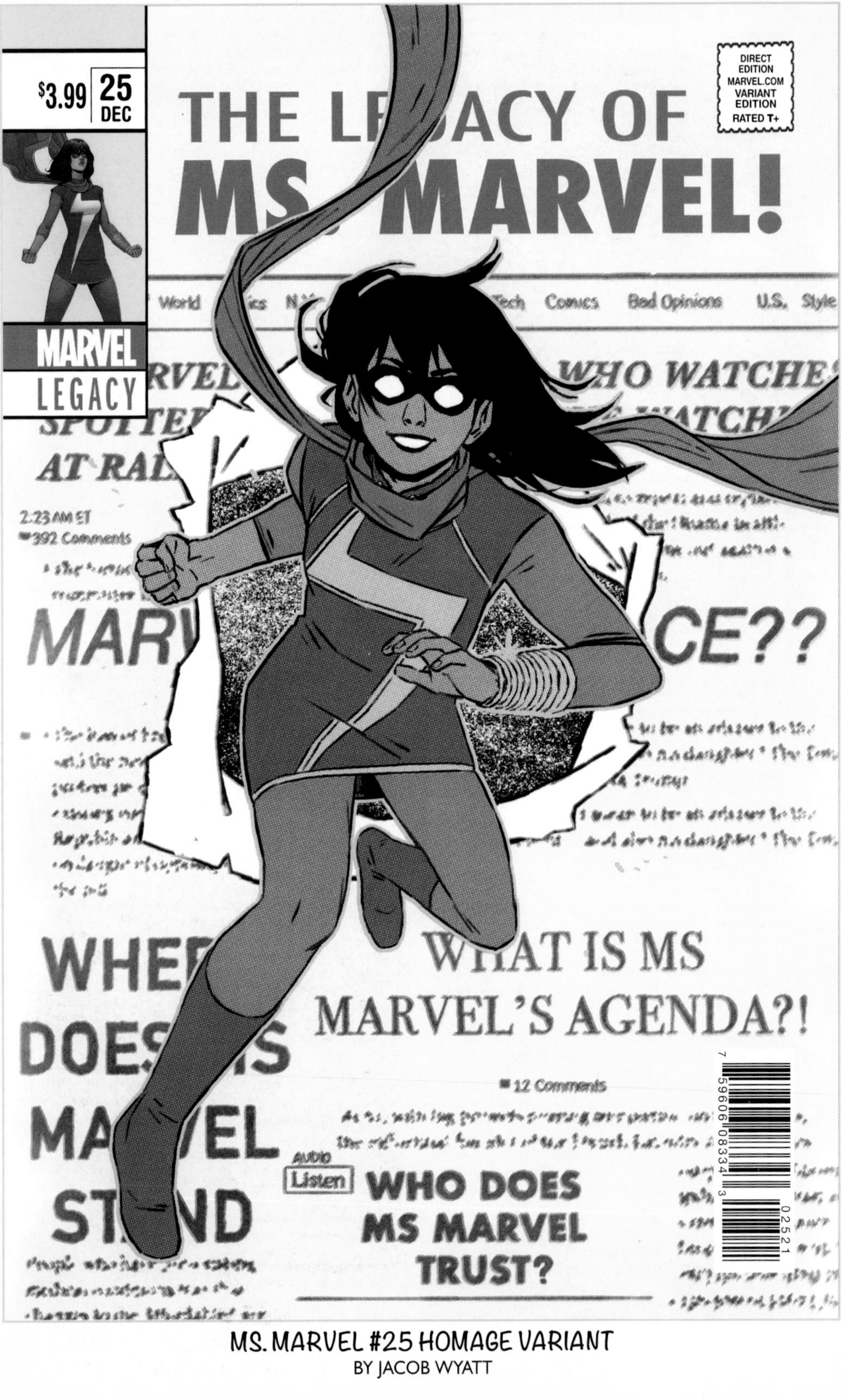
$3.99
25
DEC
MARVEL
LEGACY
DIRECT EDITION
MARVEL.COM
VARIANT EDITION
RATED T+
MARVEL!
World
Tech
Comics
Bad Opinions
U.S.
Style
WHO WATCHE
AT RA
2:23 AM ET
392 Comments
CE??
WHAT IS MS
MARVEL'S AGENDA?!
12 Comments
AUDIO
Listen
WHO DOES
MS MARVEL
TRUST?
MA
VEL
MARVEL

MS. MARVEL #25 HOMAGE VARIANT
BY JACOB WYATT

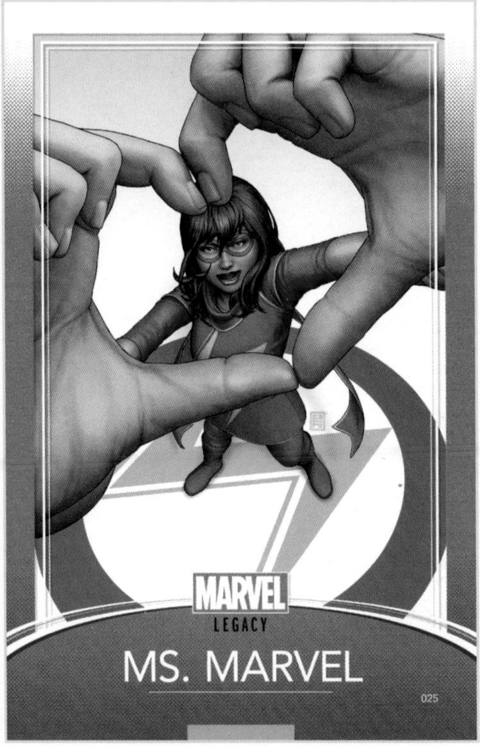
MARVEL
LEGACY
MS. MARVEL
025

MS. MARVEL #25
TRADING CARD VARIANT
BY JOHN TYLER CHRISTOPHER

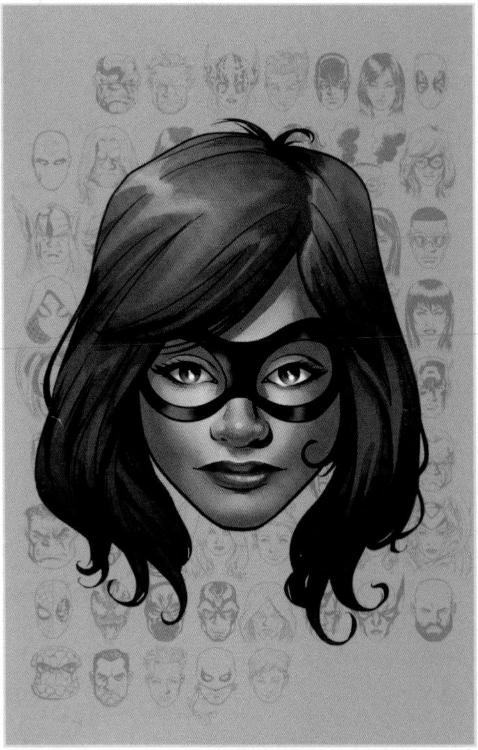

MS. MARVEL #25
LEGACY HEADSHOT VARIANT
BY MIKE McKONE & ANDY TROY

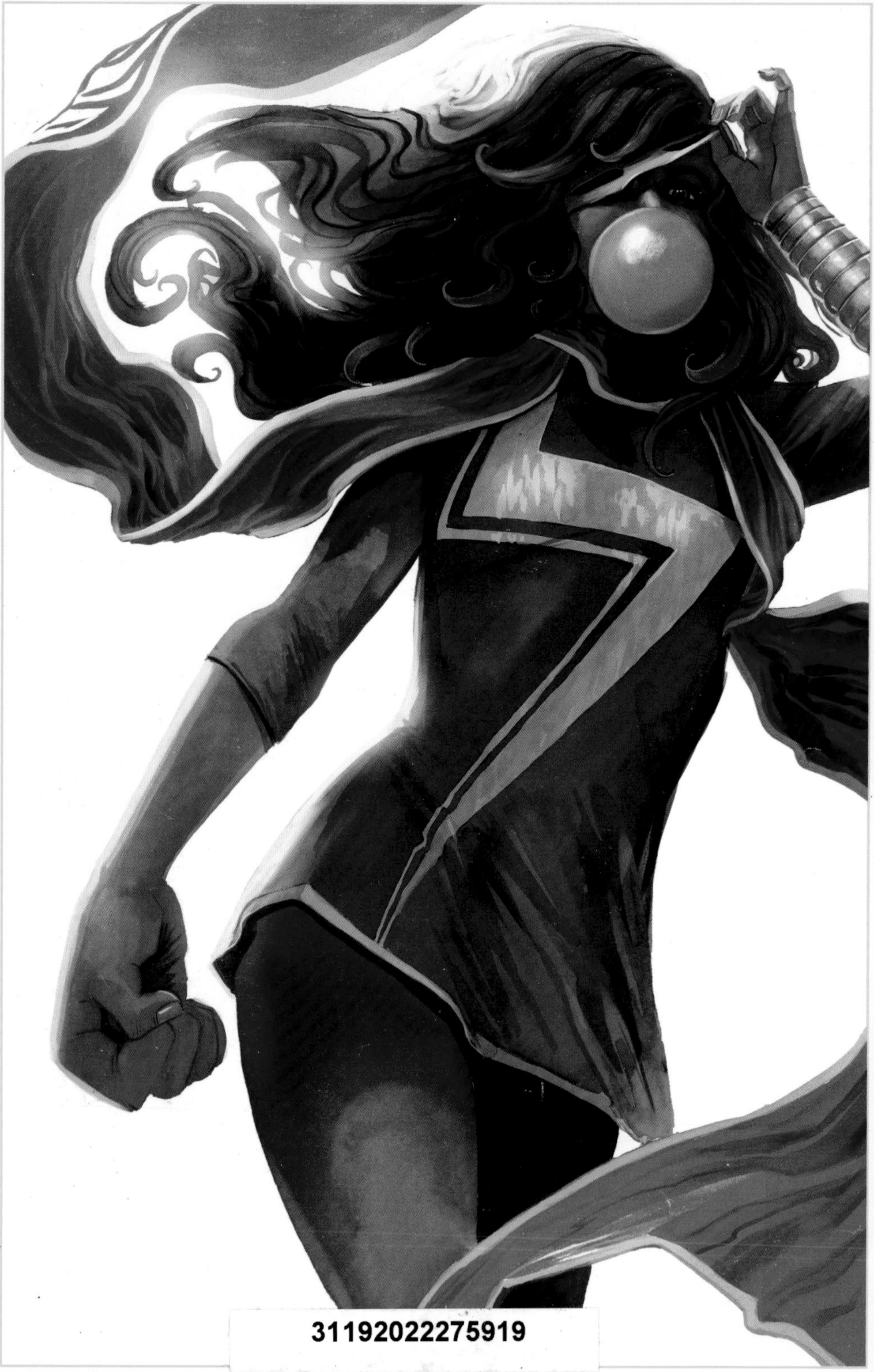

MS. MARVEL #31 VARIANT
BY STEPHANIE HANS